THE LOYAL BLACKS

THE LOYAL BLACKS

by Ellen Gibson Wilson

CAPRICORN BOOKS, New York

G. P. Putnam's Sons, New York

COPYRIGHT © 1976 BY ELLEN GIBSON WILSON

SBN: 399-11683-4

Library of Congress Catalog
Card Number: 75-45762

PRINTED IN THE UNITED STATES OF AMERICA

To Harry

Contents

Illustrations will be found following p. 226

Preface

In March, 1792, a fleet of fifteen sailing ships dropped anchor in the mouth of the Sierra Leone River and disembarked 1,100 men, women and children on a bush-covered shore which had just been named Freetown. They were black, of African ancestry, and they had been slaves in America. This study concerns them and the nearly 400 people of similar heritage and history who preceded them to the West African coast.

The remarkable British philanthropists-capitalists who backed the Sierra Leone Company were interested in developing an "innocent"— but, they hoped, profitable—trade in African products to drive out the slave traffic and also in "civilizing" the inhabitants. They welcomed the black Americans who asked to go there, but the settlers rapidly acquired a reputation for being "perverse and ungovernable." To civilize Africa, in the words of chairman Henry Thornton, it was first necessary to "civilize the Colonists."[1] Most histories of the venture have tended to agree with this judgment.[2]

The last decade of the eighteenth century, in retrospect, was a most unfortunate period in which to launch this great experiment. The sponsors had been given reason to believe that Parliament would soon abolish the British slave trade, and they had been reassured on good authority that no overseas war was likely to break out for many years. But a lively slave trade continued, and the war with France which erupted in 1793 brought the company punishing losses. Furthermore, the verdant African shore was not so fertile as it seemed. The colony "failed" for such important reasons as these. But every postmortem also assigned particular blame to the character of the settlers from America. Who were they? And why did they behave so badly?

This book about them begins in the era of the American Revolution, which inadvertently emancipated them, and ends with their own short-lived rebellion in 1800. It is frankly biased in favor of the settlers. That these 1,500 people managed to get back to Africa, to rebuild their lives after slavery and to create an identity which has lasted to this day seemed remarkable to me. They must have had exceptional motivation, courage and ability.

I have located some new material but chiefly have made a conscious search for the settlers' side of the story in documents and books which were already known to, if not used by, others. In many instances the views of the blacks are put on the record for the first time. Their written record is relatively skimpy, but there was more than I had expected to find. Sometimes, however, it has been necessary to discover their situation or attitudes through the cultural filter of their white associates. It is my hope that the settlers' case is built on evidence substantial enough to be acceptable to most readers and that it will add to the colonial history the *rational* grounds upon which the first Sierra Leone colonists acted.

Trying to keep to the words of the eighteenth-century protagonists, one feels at times the need for a glossary: For "riot" read disturbance, for "turbulent" read questioning, for "indolent" read slow, for "enthusiasm" read fanaticism, for "ignorant" read uneducated, for "respectable" read white and so on. When the blacks denounced their "slavery" or "tyranny" in Sierra Leone, they meant they were not allowed to run things themselves.

Wherever possible, individuals have been identified and quoted. In virtually every case, they have slave names which often include the surname of the American owner with a first name taken by him or her from the Bible, the classics, a place, a nickname, or because it suited a whim. This generation of black Americans did not reject the names they had acquired in North America any more than they rejected the life-styles or political ideas they had absorbed. The idiosyncratic spelling practiced in the eighteenth century, together with the carelessness of record keeping by barely literate clerks, means that one cannot be certain of biographical details. Only the ones that seem trustworthy have been used, however.

At every stage I have benefited from the close supervision and critical advice of my husband, Henry S. Wilson. The book, in fact, was his idea. Descendants of John Clarkson, in particular Lieutenant Commander A. J. Preston, Air Marshal Sir Nigel Maynard, his mother, Mrs. F. H. M. Maynard, Dr. R. G. M. Keeling, Mr. R. W. M. Keeling, and Mrs. Joanna M. Lees, have been especially generous and helpful in allowing me to see and use certain family papers and pictures. Colonel Arthur B. Lloyd-Baker graciously made possible an examination of the Granville

Sharp papers owned by his niece, the late Miss Alice Lloyd-Baker. Mr. and Mrs. C. E. Wrangham allowed me to study the Wilberforce papers under the pleasantest of circumstances. I am grateful to the Henry E. Huntington Library for lending the Macaulay papers on microfilm and to all those institutions, cited in the Notes and Bibliography, which cooperated so generously in making material available.

My longest-running debts are due to the British Library, the Public Record Office and the Royal Commonwealth Society, all in London, and the J. B. Morrell Library of the University of York, with its Inter-Library Loan Service. To Virginia Clark and Margaret I. Gibson go my warmest thanks for research assistance.

ELLEN GIBSON WILSON

NOTES

1. Report to the Proprietors of the Sierra Leone Company, March 26, 1807, Thompson Papers, 1/3, Hull University Library.
2. The first two books published in London on the Sierra Leone settlement, A. M. Falconbridge's *Narrative of Two Voyages to the River Sierra Leone* and C. B. Wadstrom's *An Essay on Colonization*, came out in 1794, and both took a critical look at the relationship between the company and the settlers. Neither seems to have made much impact on British opinion. It was 1813 before a viewpoint somewhat sympathetic to the settlers began to appear in William Allen's magazine *The Philanthropist*. Recent historians, led by Christopher Fyfe with *A History of Sierra Leone* in 1962 and Philip D. Curtin with *The Image of Africa* in 1964, have helped redress the balance. Yet inaccurate and oversimplified accounts continue to appear.

THE LOYAL BLACKS

Chapter 1

AN AIR OF LIBERTY

> I can now read the Bible, so that what I have in my heart, I
> can see again in the Scriptures.
>
> —DAVID GEORGE[1]

The American Revolution was the work of a slave-owning society. It
had the unintended effect of liberating several thousand slaves. For some
1,500 of these, the war years were the start of an adventure which was to
guarantee them a place in the annals of the British empire as the "turbulent" black settlers of Sierra Leone. In the America they rejected, they
are only shadowy figures.

As the first blacks to return to Africa from North America and,
moreover, as men and women inoculated with the revolutionary virus,
they were the natural agents of another revolt involving typically American notions of free land, political rights and religious liberty. This
attempt to reconstruct their lives and times begins in the "great debate"
over freedom which agitated sections of colonial society on the eve of the
Revolution.

The prewar social climate kindled hopes among the half million
blacks—one-fifth of the population and overwhelmingly slave in status—as well as within the white majority (a good number of whom were
bonded servants)[2] for an improvement in their condition. The cry was for
"liberty." With ideas of individual rights, social justice and democratic
government being everywhere explored, it was a liberating atmosphere
in which unthinkable things could happen.

It is unlikely that the black population was simple enough to believe
that the slavery of which white colonists complained subsumed their
own. But the effect of a language of protest which had such an obsessive
preoccupation with slavery as a metaphor for a political condition must

1

nevertheless have been profound on black bondsmen. That slavery was an eighteenth-century word for "absolute political evil"[3] was an unconscious admission of guilt for the traffic in African men and women and the institutionalization of slave labor in Southern agriculture. Antislavery voices were not numerous, but they also were not new, and the fruitless prewar attempts of colonial legislatures and the Continental Congress to prohibit imports of slaves reflected not only irritation with British commercial domination but uneasiness about the business itself. The central contradiction was that almost everyone now believed in liberty and everyone knew that slavery was its denial, but almost everyone also thought that abolition would be ruinous, economically or socially.

Before 1750 there had been at least fifteen published attacks in America on black slavery. Nearly all came from Quakers and appeared in the North. But they were known and discussed in Southern circles and were part of a transatlantic dialogue among Americans, British and French.[4] The argument quickened in the later eighteenth century, as the freedom of white colonists was associated in some minds with the emancipation of blacks. The Massachusetts attorney James Otis predicted in 1763 that "those who every day barter away other mens liberty, will soon care little for their own."[5] Samuel Cooke in 1770 asserted that in tolerating Negro slavery, "we the patrons of liberty, have dishonored the Christian name." Richard Wells in 1774 demanded to know how Americans could "reconcile the exercise of SLAVERY with our *professions of freedom.*" And the Baptist preacher John Allen cried: "Blush ye pretended votaries for freedom! ye trifling patriots! who are . . . making a mockery of your profession by trampling on the sacred natural rights and privileges of Africans." Dr. Benjamin Rush was convinced: "The plant of liberty is of so tender a nature that it cannot thrive long in the neighborhood of slavery."[6]

"Honesty" addressed the Sons of Liberty through a Connecticut newspaper in 1774: "We that declare, and that with much warmth and zeal, it is unjust, cruel, barbarous, unconstitutional, and without law to enslave, *do we enslave?* Yes, verily we do! . . . Can we expect to be free, so long as we are determined to enslave?"[7]

The irony was not lost on the British "oppressors." Granville Sharp, a friendly critic, recognized that "toleration of domestic Slavery in the Colonies greatly weakens the claim or *natural Right* of our American Brethren to Liberty. Let them put away *the accursed thing* . . . before they presume to implore the interposition of *divine* Justice."[8] Less kindly, Samuel Johnson wondered, "How is it that we hear the loudest *yelps* from liberty among the drivers of negros?"[9] Thomas Day was unsparing in his condemnation of American hypocrisy:

> If there be an object truly ridiculous in nature, it is an American patriot, signing resolutions of independency with the one hand, and with the other brandishing a whip over his affrighted slaves. . . . If there be certain natural and universal rights, as the declarations of your Congress so repeatedly affirm, I wonder how the unfortunate Africans have incurred their forfeiture.—Is it the antiquity, or the virtues, or the great qualities of the English Americans, which . . . entitle them to rights from which they totally exclude more than a fourth part of the species?—Or do you choose to make use of that argument, which the great Montesquieu has thrown out as the severest ridicule, that they are black, and you white; that you have lank long hair, while their's is short and woolly?

As a new immigrant Thomas Paine begged Americans to consider "with what consistency, or decency they complain so loudly of attempts to enslave them, while they hold so many hundred thousands in slavery; and annually enslave many thousands more."[10]

The famous test case in England in 1772 of James Somerset (sometimes Somersett) had important repercussions among the American slaves. Brought by Granville Sharp, it resulted in a decision of Lord Mansfield that Somerset's master could not forcibly return him to the West Indies.[11] The judgment was reported in colonial newspapers and widely and erroneously taken to have emancipated the slaves then in England and to assure that any slave who set foot on English soil would become free.[12] It tempted some in America to try to reach Britain, "where they imagine they will be free (a Notion now too prevalent among the Negroes)," according to an advertisement in the *Virginia Gazette*.[13] Running away was the most common form of black protest, but there were many other expressions of it: thieving, resistance to work ("laziness," pretended sickness, self-mutilation, sabotage), suicide, or, more rarely, assault on owners or overseers. Slave conspiracies were a continual source of alarm to owners of laborers fresh from Africa.

In the North, slaves tried legal methods such as petitions and lawsuits. Despite pitifully small resources, slaves, often encouraged by sympathetic whites, had initiated twelve legal actions before 1750 in Massachusetts alone.[14] The trend was disturbing enough to inspire the Reverend Cotton Mather, on the occasion of the hanging of a freed slave for the murder of his wife, to caution the slaves in his audience, "There is a *Fondness for Freedom* in many of you, who live Comfortably in a very easy Servitude; wherein you are not so *Well-advised* as you should be."[15]

One of the most celebrated as well as earliest suits was brought by Adam, a slave rented in 1694 by John Saffin to another man with the promise that after seven years Adam would be freed. Adam proved unsatisfactory and was returned a year early. But when the seven years were up, he successfully sued his now reluctant master for the promised manumission. The episode prompted Samuel Sewall to write *The Selling of Joseph* in 1700, one of the earliest American denunciations of slavery.[16]

The tempo of black as well as white protest picked up on the eve of the Revolution, and in a series of cases in the 1760s and 1770s, slaves sued in New England courts for freedom and won. In an echo of the reputed Mansfield decision, they claimed that under the royal charter, those residing in Massachusetts were as free as subjects in Britain.[17] Their individual victories did not abolish slavery itself until the Quok Walker decision in 1783. Walker had cited the new Massachusetts Constitution which copied the assertion in the Declaration of Independence that "all men are born free and equal." According to Dr. Jeremy Belknap, a contemporary observer, this clause was inserted "with a particular view to establish the liberation of the negroes . . . and so it was understood by the people at large." Although it is still argued whether the Massachusetts Supreme Court did in fact abolish slavery at that time, there can be no quarrel with Dr. Belknap's verdict that the Walker case dealt Slavery a "mortal wound" in Massachusetts.[18] Indeed Dr. Belknap saw a public acceptance of "the inconsistency of pleading for our own rights and liberties whilst we encouraged the subjugation of others . . . the success of the negroes in these suits operated to the liberation of all."[19]

The petitions handed in by blacks were couched in courteous, Christian but outraged terms. They make clear that the seething political climate was understood in the slave sector of the population. Peter Bestes, Sambo Freeman, Felix Holbrook and Chester Joie, representing slaves in the town of Thompson, appealed in 1773 to the Massachusetts legislature, making pointed reference to the current propaganda war: "We expect great things from men who have made such a noble stand against the designs of their *fellow-men* to enslave them. . . . The divine spirit of *freedom*, seems to fire every humane breast."[20] In the same year James Swan published a revised edition of *A Dissuasion to Great-Britain and the Colonies from the Slave-Trade to Africa* under the sponsorship of Boston blacks. Swan commented on their anguish, living as they did among "people who boast of their liberties yet keep blacks in slavery."[21]

Abigail Adams was in Boston in 1774 when what she described as "a conspiracy of the negroes" took place. "They . . . got an Irishman to draw up a petition to the Governor, telling him they would fight for him, provided he would arm them and engage to liberate them if he conquered." She added, "I wish most sincerely there was not a slave in the province. It always appeared a most iniquitous scheme to me—to fight ourselves for what we are daily robbing and plundering from those who have as good a right to freedom as we have."[22]

The eloquent appeal of "a Grate Number of Blackes of this Province who by divine permission are held in a state of Slavery within the bowels of a free and christian Country" contended that blacks in common with all men had a natural right to freedom, for they were a "freeborn Pepel and have never forfeited this Blessing by aney compact or agreement whatever." Massachusetts law, furthermore, did not authorize slavery of themselves or, even more particularly, of their American-born children.

In 1777 Boston slaves followed the laudable example of the Declaration of Independence to point out "that Every Principle from which America has Acted in the Cours of their unhappy Dificultes with Great Briton Pleads Stronger than A thousand arguments in favours of your petioners."

Slaves in Fairfield County in 1779 requested the state assemblymen, who were so "nobly contending in the Cause of Liberty," to spare some thought for creatures of another color who were unjustly bound. Boldly they said, "we perceive by our own Reflection, that we are endowed with the same Faculties with our masters, and there is nothing that leads us to a Belief or Suspicion, that we are any more obliged to serve them, than they us, and the more we Consider of this matter, the more we are Convinced of our Right . . . to be free."[23]

The cry of taxation without representation was raised during the war by blacks. In 1780 John and Paul Cuffe, free African-Indian brothers of Westport, Massachusetts, joined a petition against taxes on their land because they were denied the vote.[24]

With so much evidence of opposition to slavery, it is not surprising that the first antislavery society in any country was formed at Philadelphia by a mainly Quaker group just five days before the Battle of Lexington. It was called the Society for the Relief of Free Negroes Unlawfully Held in Bondage.[25]

One must not, however, understate the absolute helplessness of nearly all the 500,000 blacks. Most white Americans actively believed in slavery, or condoned it, or rarely thought about it, being "long accustomed to the practice and convenience of having slaves."[26] Many blamed Great Britain for the system and felt no more responsible than they would have done for a hereditary disease.[27] The powerful Henry Laurens of South Carolina, who made a fortune importing slaves as a merchant and working them on his plantations, told his son in 1776 that he looked forward to abolition but happened to have been born in a country where slavery was established by British law. Speaking of his own slaves, valued at £20,000, Laurens insisted, "I am not the man who enslaved them; they are indebted to Englishmen for that favour."[28]

No man prominent in Virginia politics publicly advocated an end to slavery. Jefferson disliked it but was so convinced of the inherent inferiority of blacks that he could not envisage a multiracial society. In his first draft of the Declaration of Independence he harshly indicted George III for the cruel slave trade and for vetoing colonial efforts to restrain it, but the adopted document, although it speaks of tyranny, says nothing at all about slavery in deference to the feelings of Georgia, Rhode Island and South Carolina. A clause in the Virginia Bill of Rights declaring men by nature free was allowed through on the understanding that slaves were not members of society and could not benefit from it.[29]

There seemed truly little danger to the status quo in uttering calls for liberty or natural rights. "The master passion of the age was not with extending liberty to blacks but with erecting republics for whites."[30] Private property was a keystone of the new, as of the old, society, and if property in slaves were questioned, the whole structure might be at risk. The challenges in the courts to slavery had been confined to the North, where fewer than 60,000 slaves were kept. Such actions were useful as tokens of a relatively open society which many well-meaning people could applaud, while not striking at the vitals of a system endorsed in the populous, planter-ruled South.[31]

Yet the potentially dangerous doctrine of individual worth was being spread more widely than contemporary observers realized. The carrier was the new Protestant evangelist who delivered the word of God in towns and hamlets, on farms, plantations or in clearings in the wilderness, from pulpits, kitchen tables or tree stumps. Several future Sierra

Leone settlers experienced this religious revival, their first step to freedom. For example, David George, destined to begin Baptist churches in Nova Scotia and Sierra Leone, found his faith in slave prayer meetings in South Carolina. Boston King, a Methodist missionary-to-be, also from South Carolina, and Mary Perth from Virginia were introduced to lifelong Christianity at this time. For each one such case that can be documented, there must have been thousands unremarked.

The American experience determined both the sects and the style of worship which were carried to Africa, so it is worth a look at the denominations of the revolutionary era as the blacks knew them. Their oldest friends were the Quakers, who individually and in meetings condemned slaveholding, freed their own slaves, admitted blacks to their services and sponsored schools. One of the first great abolitionists, Anthony Benezet, the Philadelphia teacher, was almost alone in his time in believing in the equal ability of blacks, possibly because he was one of the few who actually knew any in something other than a master-slave relationship. In both North Carolina and Virginia, Quakers contested for the right to manumit slaves and to protect their free status afterward. But as a small minority the Quakers were more a nuisance than a menace and in contact with comparatively few blacks.[32] Of the two officially connected churches, the Congregational in New England also had small direct effect, but the Anglican was well known to Southern blacks. It was served by missionaries from the Society for the Propagation of the Gospel in Foreign Parts, an appellation that greatly annoyed many Tory colonials. The Church of England was weakened by the rising anti-British sentiment and the demand for religious freedom. More important to blacks, it was the planters' church. The SPG, nonetheless, was the earliest body to seek out blacks and Indians, and "great multitudes" underwent a conversion which was "sold" to slave owners on the grounds that Christianity helped create obedient workers. Southern legislatures made sure that baptism was no ticket to freedom. Some slaves were required to take an oath that they were not asking for baptism in an effort to emancipate themselves. The fact that local vestries, dominated by slave-owning men of property, virtually ran the Southern church accounts as much for the lack of zeal in teaching blacks as any institutional intention to slight them.[33]

Anglicans believed in an orderly society where people were born to certain stations. The Reverend Jonathan Boucher found "the negroes in general in Virginia and Maryland in my time were not . . . worse off nor less happy than the labouring poor in Great Britain. . . . Slavery is not

one of the most intolerable evils incident to humanity, even to slaves."
The clergy themselves, of course, including Boucher, owned slaves. He
also, in the 1760s, busily taught and baptized slaves, a duty shirked by his
predecessors in Virginia, and trained a few black men to teach others to
read.[34]

The first serious penetration of the Southern slave population came
from the Great Awakening. The revivalist preachers did not attack
slavery, but they believed salvation must be offered to everyone. The
dynamic younger sects were socially democratic and racially mixed at
this time. A discriminatory tendency set in at the turn of the century.
Black preachers were heard as early as 1743.[35] The itinerant white
Methodists and Baptists were often common men themselves, frequently
gifted with fiery eloquence and well grounded in Scripture. Ordinary
men and women responded to religion as they expounded it in a fashion
that no formal rituals had evoked. By the end of the war such sects had
incorporated the natural rights doctrine and were coming out for the
abolition of slavery.[36] Slaves had a limited freedom to observe or share in
religious exercises. They could hear the Gospel preached, sing the
hymns and see men of their race listened to by whites, even in places
where for fear of conspiracy they were forbidden to form churches of
their own. Some whites as well as blacks saw the Anglican faith as too
pallid. During the Revolution the influential Virginia planter Robert
Carter joined the Baptists and encouraged his slaves to attend meetings.
Many were converted.[37]

The Reverend Francis Asbury, probably the greatest circuit rider of
them all, who arrived in the colonies in 1771, was deeply impressed by
the religious response of blacks. "To see the poor Negroes so affected is
pleasing, to see their sable countenances in our solemn assemblies, and
to hear them sing with cheerful melody their dear Redeemer's praise,
affected me much." Once, preaching to a crowd that overflowed the
meetinghouse, "I was obliged to stop again and again, and beg of the
people to compose themselves. But they could not: some on their knees,
and some on their faces, were crying mightily to God. . . . Hundreds of
Negroes were among them, with the tears streaming down their faces."
Asbury sometimes traveled with Harry Hosier, a superb black preacher.[38]

The Reverend George Whitefield's impact on the black John Marrant,
later a missionary in Nova Scotia, illustrates the appeal of such men.
Whitefield, at twenty-four, was the first traveling preacher in the colonies. His strong, musical voice and electrifying style set a fashion. "It
was usually with tears and even sobs that his hearers would part company

with him. . . . Sometimes his feelings seemed almost to overcome him, as with broken voice and streaming eyes he pleaded with the souls of men." Sometimes he stamped his feet while his throngs exulted, wept and trembled with him. "I love those who thunder out the word," Whitefield said. A black witness saw the revivalist "sweating, as much as I ever did while in slavery.[39] On his seventh and final American tour, beginning in late 1769, Whitefield visited Charleston, where John Marrant was living.[40] Marrant was born in New York in 1755 and taken as a child to Georgia, where he attended school until he was eleven. The family then moved to Charleston, where the boy learned to play the violin and French horn and was in flattering demand for balls and assemblies. At thirteen he was "a slave to every vice suited to my nature and to my years." The roster of vices is not specified beyond fishing and hunting on the Sabbath.

One day this frivolous boy heard "hallooing" and stepped into a meetinghouse with some mischief in mind. The great Whitefield pointed a finger and intoned his text: "Prepare to meet thy God, O Israel." Marrant, convinced that the finger was aimed at him, fell to the ground and remained senseless for twenty-four minutes. Afterward Whitefield told him, "Jesus Christ has got thee at last." Marrant became so obsessed with the Bible that people thought him mad. Saintlike, he went off into the woods for long trials of strength. Once, threatened with death in a Cherokee town, he converted his potential executioner, the chief's daughter and finally the chief himself. He began a career of preaching in the backwoods settlements.

Marrant appears to have been born free. The impact of religion on the colonial slave population is more vividly seen in the lives of David George, Boston King and Mary Perth. George was one of the founders of the African-American church,[41] and it was he who introduced the Baptist faith to Africa. His memoir, a valuable slave narrative, was related to fellow Baptists on a visit to England in 1793, when George was about fifty. Not the least of its importance lies in his view "from the bottom up" of life on a Virginia plantation. Since all other parts of his story stand up to scrutiny and comparison with contemporary documents, his description of the barbaric treatment of slaves at his birthplace may also be taken as true.[42]

He was born about 1743 on a Nottoway River plantation in Essex County, Virginia, owned by a Mr. Chapel. His parents, John and Judith, both transported from Africa, had nine children. As a boy David fetched water, carded cotton and labored in the corn and tobacco fields. His owner was a "very bad man to the Negroes." His sister, Patty, was whipped until her back was "all corruption, as though it would rot." His brother, Dick, ran away, was captured and escaped again. This time Dick was hunted with dogs and horses. Found and brought back, he was dangled from a cherry tree with his legs tied tightly together. A pole was thrust between his legs, and Chapel's two sons sat on either end of it "to keep him down." After "500 lashes, or more, they washed his back with salt water, and whipped it in." Then Dick was sent back to work in the field.

David George himself was flogged "sometimes till the blood has run down over my waistband; but the greatest grief I then had was to see them whip my mother, and to hear her, on her knees, begging for mercy. She was master's cook, and if they only thought she might do anything better than she did, instead of speaking to her as to a servant, they would strip her directly, and cut away." The horror of watching, helplessly, a parent or a child punished "without delicacy or mercy" was a great trauma of slavery.[43]

Occasionally, the young David George had attended "the English church" eight miles away, but he was not a Christian. "I used to drink," he admitted, "but not steal; did not fear hell, and was without knowledge."

Despite the exemplary punishment of his brother, David ran away one midnight. He was about nineteen and his mother was dying. For almost five years he was a fugitive, relentlessly pursued by his former master. He crossed the Roanoke River into North Carolina and made his way to the Pee Dee. There he found work, but in three weeks came the hue and cry, with an offer of 30 guineas' reward. His new master advised George to make for the Savannah River. Slowly George crossed South Carolina, working about two years for a John Green before "they came after me again." This time he escaped deep into Creek Indian territory in central Georgia. One day his tracks were spotted near the Ocmulgee River. He was trailed to the spot where he was building a raft and captured. Black feet, the Indians later told him, were flatter than their own.

Many runaway slaves took refuge with the Creek and were encouraged to do so. Other slaves were captured in raids conducted to harass the white settlers. These captives were then slaves of the Indians, as George was, but the servitude usually was milder, and there were possibilities of assimilation through marriage. Some free blacks lived among the Indians as sharecroppers. It was a highly organized, mixed society which would have been instructive to young George. Chiefs were elected and functioned with an advisory council. William Bartram, roaming the South for botanical specimens to send Dr. John Fothergill in London, visited the Creek around this time and described them as a contented and well-off people, whose principal worry was the gradual encroachment of the whites.[44]

George may have been with the Lower Creek Oktchunalgi (Salt) clan, for he spoke of a king named Blue Salt: "I was his prize." At Blue Salt's winter camp in the woods George ate bear and deer meat, turkey and wild marsh potatoes. The quantity of meat impressed the slave from Virginia, where the staple of diet was corn. With the spring, Blue Salt moved into the Creek capital of Augusta, where George was kept busy making fences, plowing and planting corn. Though the people were kind to him, he was not safe. "S.C. my master's son, came there for me, from Virginia, I suppose 800 miles, and paid king Blue Salt for me in rum, linnen, and a gun; but before he could take me out of the Creek nation, I escaped." Luckily he found a comfortable sanctuary with the Natchez chief, Jack, while young Chapel hung around Augusta, hoping to go home with the runaway after all.[45]

George saw a solution to his predicament in John Miller, an agent of the Indian trader George Galphin of Silver Bluff, on the Savannah River south of Augusta. Through Miller, Galphin was persuaded to pay Chapel an agreed price for the slave, and George began to work for Miller, mending deerskins and taking care of the horses. Once a year he brought a load of skins to Silver Bluff from the Indian country. It was about 1766, according to his narrative, when George asked to remain with Galphin. "He told me I should: so he took me to wait upon him, and was very kind to me."

In George Galphin, David George had made a brilliant choice of master. Galphin was an Ulsterman who had emigrated in the 1730s and built a lively frontier town on the ruins of an Indian village. Galphin was to become the American Indian agent during the Revolution and keep the Indians neutral, though they were pro-British. The frontier trading post had an open multiracial society. Galphin was married and had two children but fathered others with both mulatto and Indian mistresses and remembered all his progeny generously in his will, distributing freedom to the slave offspring and land, livestock and slaves to all the children. Bartram admired Galphin as "a gentleman of very distinguished talents and great liberality, who possessed the most extensive trade, connections and influence, amongst the South and South-West Indian tribes, particularly with the Creeks and Chactaws."[46]

As a house servant, David George's horizons widened. About 1770 he married Phillis, possibly half Indian. After the birth of his first child, he began to attend slave prayer meetings addressed by a black named Cyrus from Charleston. Cyrus predicted that unless George took his soul more seriously, he would "never see the face of God in glory." Anxiously, George tried to save himself with endless repetition of the Lord's Prayer but only felt the worse for it:

> I saw myself as a mass of sin. . . . I did not think of Adam and Eve's sin, but *I* was sin. I felt my *own* plague; and I was so overcome that I could not wait upon my master. I told him *I was ill.* . . . I saw that I could not be saved by any of my own doings, but that it must be by God's mercy—that my sins had crucified Christ; and now the Lord took away my distress. I was sure that the Lord took it away, because I had such pleasure and joy in my soul, that no man could give me.

The slaves at Galphin's trading post and farm were allowed the rare privilege of a meeting place, the mill. There one day George was reunited with a figure from his boyhood, George Liele. He was now owned by Henry Sharp of Burke County, Georgia, a Baptist deacon. Liele had been converted and baptized by the local minister, and "called by grace," he had begun to preach to other slaves along the Savannah River. Tactfully, he addressed only those with permission to hear him and never dwelled on the wrongs the slaves suffered. He was regarded as a "wholesome influence." Like David George, Liele was to be evacuated with the British after the coming war, and as George carried the Southern Gospel to Canada and Africa, Liele was to establish the first Baptist church in Kingston, Jamaica.

At Galphin's mill, Liele preached on "Come unto me all ye that labour, and are heavy laden, and I will give you rest," and George's conversion was complete. Eight slaves, including George's wife, had now been converted. The little band was baptized in the millstream by an exhorter, the Reverend Wait Palmer. This event, marking the birth of the Silver Bluff Baptist Church, the first black church in America, was sometime prior to December, 1777.[47]

Liele was preaching to a gathering of slaves in a cornfield one day when George experienced his first compulsion to preach himself. Liele encouraged him to begin by praying with his friends, and from that George went on to exhort and sing. The first hymn he recalled mastering began "Thus saith the wisdom of the Lord" and was from Isaac Watts' *Psalms and Hymns,* which next to the Bible was the favorite book among Southern slaves.[48] Under Palmer's instructions, George became an elder. When the war broke out and traveling preachers were denied access to the slaves, "lest they should furnish us with too much knowledge," George began to preach to the blacks. He was still shackled by illiteracy. Galphin employed a schoolmaster, however, and George obtained a spelling book. It was illegal to teach a slave to read, but the thirty-year-old slave turned "to the little children to teach me a, b, c." They set him a lesson and he would go back to see if he had learned it right. Like Christian conversion, reading was liberation. "The reading so ran in my mind, that I think I learned in my sleep . . . and I can now read the Bible, so that what I have in my heart, I can see again in the Scriptures."

Another future Sierra Leone settler, Mary Perth, was born about 1740. She belonged to John Willoughby of Norfolk, Virginia, and somehow learned to read the New Testament. She, too, was driven to help others. At night, after her master and mistress were in bed, she would tie her baby on her back and walk ten miles into the country where slaves would assemble to be taught. Then she would walk the ten miles home to be there when her owners awoke. She continued this until the group was large enough to have its own preacher, then carried on with her mission elsewhere.[49]

English Methodists preserved a larger history of Boston King, who likewise returned to Africa.[50] He was born about 1760 and found his religious vocation only in early manhood in Canada. Again his recollections help fill in the outline of colonial slavery. He was much better off than David George. His father, kidnapped in Africa when a boy, had become a driver on Richard Waring's plantation, twenty-eight miles from Charleston, where Boston was born. His mother was a seamstress and a nurse, who had learned herbal lore from the Indians. The father was loved by his master and the mother indulged over other slaves. The father was a Christian, no doubt a convert of the Anglican SPG missionaries who served St. George's Parish. The Reverend Francis Varnod had between 20 and 50 black communicants there and the Reverend Stephen Roe, who followed him in 1741, reported 100 slaves had been baptized and 15, along with 48 whites, had become communicants of the church. In the decade before Boston King was born this work came to a halt, however. There had been several cases of slaves poisoning their masters, and because the victims were said to be noted for leniency (perhaps intending to manumit slaves on their deaths), an outcry rose against further pampering. The incumbent was told to stop missionary work until "passions abated."[51]

Thus, Boston King refers to his Christian father resorting secretly to the woods on Sundays to pray:

> [He] lived in the fear and love of GOD. He attended to that true Light which lighteth every man. He lost no opportunity of hearing the Gospel, and never omitted praying with his family every night. He likewise read to them, and to as many as were inclined to hear. On the Lord's Day he rose very early, and met his family: After which he worked in the field till about three in the afternoon, and then went into the woods and read till sun-set. . . . Those who knew him, say, that they never heard him swear an oath, but on the contrary, he reproved all who spoke improper words in his hearing. To the utmost of his power he endeavoured to make his family happy, and his death was a very great loss to us all.

The child began work at six as a house servant and at nine was tending cattle and learning from his comrades "the horrible sin of Swearing and Cursing" out of earshot of his father. He was twelve when he dreamed of the Last Judgment:

> At mid-day, when the cattle went under the shade of the trees, I dreamt that the world was on fire, and that I saw the supreme Judge descend on his great white Throne! I saw millions of millions of souls; some of whom ascended up to heaven; while others were rejected, and fell into the greatest confusion and despair. This dream made such an impression upon my mind, that I refrained from swearing and bad company, and from that time acknowledged that there was a GOD; but how to serve GOD I knew not.

At sixteen King was apprenticed to a carpenter in Charleston and put in charge of the master's tools. During one holiday when the carpenter's house was left in his care, a robbery occurred. Boston was whipped severely, and later, when some nails were taken, he was "beat and tortured most cruelly, and was laid up three weeks." Waring, however, reprimanded the carpenter, and the ragging ceased. King became a skilled craftsman, better prepared than many slaves for the opportunities that the unsettling war would bring.

There was another idea stirring in minds troubled by slavery in the eighteenth century: African colonization. It occurred to blacks as well as whites. The earliest proposal for an African colony of freed blacks from America was published in 1713 by, it is thought, the Quaker antislavery spokesman William Southeby,[52] who recommended that subscriptions be collected to carry the freed men and women to their "own country." Slavery would continue for those "as had rather serve their Masters, than go home." The ones who chose Africa should be instructed in Christianity to enable them to convert their countrymen. "I know of no other way to make them Restitution for the wrong done them," the argument concluded.[53]

As the quarrel with Britain became more heated and thoughts more concentrated on liberty, more emigration schemes were bruited, and 1773 was a bumper year for them. The first known proposal from blacks was contained in the petition to the Massachusetts legislature from Bestes, Freeman, Holbrook and Joie, who wanted slaves to be able to earn wages so that they could buy their freedom. They said:

> We are willing to submit to such regulations and laws, as may
> be made relative to us, until we leave the province, which we
> determine to do as soon as we can, from our joynt labours
> procure money to transport ourselves to some part of the Coast
> of *Africa,* where we propose a settlement.[54]

Dr. Fothergill, the eminent English Quaker doctor, wrote Anthony Benezet in 1773 about an African colony scheme. He may have got the idea from the French Abbé Roubaud, who in 1762 had proposed to cultivate the tropical produce Europe required (especially sugar) on the African coast.[55] Such a colony could employ free labor, and it would no longer be "necessary" to enslave Africans to grow these crops in the West Indies or Southern colonies of North America. Colonization to this end—and as a means of making restitution to slaves—was within the antislavery movement and not, as it seemed to some in the nineteenth century, a racist device to purge American society of its black members. Dr. Fothergill was willing to put £10,000 into an African colony, but Benezet had reservations. His concern was that Africa was too strange by now to most American slaves. It would take "a conductor from heaven, as in the case of the Israelites," to settle a million blacks peacefully overseas. They would confront even greater difficulties than they now faced in America. He favored their gradual emancipation and settlement among whites in the new communities which would spring up between the Alleghenies and the Mississippi River.[56]

When, in 1773, the Reverend Samuel Hopkins produced the first concrete colonization plan, he had mixed motives. He believed slavery a sin, and therefore the slaves must be freed. He believed Americans had become deeply prejudiced against blacks, particularly freed slaves. Therefore, they must return to Africa for their own welfare and to persuade whites to accept emancipation. He furthermore wanted to spread Christianity (and very likely his own eccentric doctrines), so he would train black Christians to serve as missionaries. Their colony would strike a blow at the slave trade.

Hopkins was a brave man. He had once owned a slave (and is supposed to have contributed the proceeds of his sale to the plan for Africa), but after he moved to the slave trade center of Newport, Rhode Island, he became a fierce critic of both the trade and slavery. Newport then had thirty rum distilleries and 150 ships directly engaged in the traffic, and cargoes of slaves were landed at the wharf near his church and home. Thanks to Hopkins' crusade, his First Congregational Church became the first in the world to forbid members to own slaves. He welcomed blacks (in the gallery) at his church and at their invitation addressed them on Sunday evenings at services which whites also could attend. Seventeen faithful blacks even subscribed for his esoteric *System of Divinity*. Together with his black parishioners, Hopkins developed a scheme to educate blacks for African missions.[57]

The plan was approved by the Reverend Ezra Stiles of the Second Congregational Church, and in 1773 they made a public appeal for funds. The first two candidates were Bristol Yamma and John Quamine, both of whom spoke African languages. Yamma, a domestic servant, was in the process of buying his freedom. Quamine, born at Anomabu, had been sent at ten by his father to be educated in the American colonies, but he was sold by the ship's captain. Later he bought his freedom. A third prospect was Salmar Nubia, who wanted to be a schoolteacher. In 1774 Yamma and Quamine were sent to President John Witherspoon at Princeton for training, and by 1776 they were ready to go. The war, in which Quamine was killed on an American privateer, frustrated the plan.[58] Hopkins and his black church members never gave it up, however, and were to become deeply interested spectators of the Sierra Leone experiment launched in Britain in the 1780s.

NOTES

1. "An Account of the Life of Mr. DAVID GEORGE, from Sierra Leone in Africa," *The Baptist Annual Register for . . . 1793*, p. 476. Hereafter referred to as David George Narrative.

2. Morris, *The American Revolution Reconsidered*, pp. 35, 36, 71.

3. Bailyn, *The Ideological Origins of the American Revolution*, pp. 232-46.

4. Jordan, *White over Black*, pp. 195, 37.

5. Fishel and Quarles, eds., *The Black American, a Documentary History*, p. 44.

6. Bailyn, pp. 236-241.

7. Logan, "The Slave in Connecticut During the American Revolution," p. 73, quoting the Norwich *Packet*, July 7, 1774.

8. Sharp, *A Declaration of the People's Natural Right to a Share in the Legislature*, p. 28 n.

9. David Brion Davis, *The Problem of Slavery in Western Culture*, p. 3.

10. Day, "A Fragment of a Letter on the Slavery of the Negroes," pp. 76-77; *The Writings of Thomas Paine*, vol. 1, p. 7.

11. Walvin, *Black and White*, p. 117 ff. See also the important study by Shyllon, *Black Slaves in Britain*, esp. pp. ix-xi and Chapter 10, pp. 165 ff.

12. Nadelhaft, "The Somersett Case and Slavery: Myth, Reality, and Repercussions," pp. 194, 195.

13. Mullin, *Flight and Rebellion*, p. 131, quoting the *Virginia Gazette*, September 30, 1773. The *Gazette* carried an accurate account of the Mansfield decision on August 12, 1772.

14. Towner, " 'A Fondness for Freedom': Servant Protest in Puritan Society," p. 213.

15. *Ibid.*, pp. 201-2.

16. *Ibid.*, p. 218; Towner, "The Sewall-Saffin Dialogue on Slavery," p. 47.

17. [Tucker and Belknap], "Queries Respecting the Slavery and Emancipation of Negroes in Massachusetts," p. 202; Lorenzo J. Greene, *The Negro in Colonial New England*, pp. 183-84.

18. Tucker and Belknap, pp. 203, 198, 201; Meier and Rudwick, *From Plantation to Ghetto*, p. 42; Commager, ed., *Documents of American History*, p. 110; George Bancroft, *History of the United States of America*, vol. 5, pp. 418-20; MacEacheren, "Emancipation of Slavery in Massachusetts: A Re-examination 1770-1790," pp. 289-306; O'Brien, "Did the Jennison Case Outlaw Slavery in Massachusetts?" pp. 219-41; Zilversmit, "Quok Walker, Mumbet and the Abolition of Slavery in Massachusetts," pp. 614-24.

19. Dexter to Belknap, February 23, 1795, in "Letters and Documents Relating to Slavery in Massachusetts," p. 386.

20. Fishel and Quarles, p. 45; Aptheker, ed., *A Documentary History of the Negro People in the United States*, pp. 7-8; Kaplan, *The Black Presence in the Era of the American Revolution*, pp. 11, 12.

21. Swan, *A Dissuasion to Great-Britain and the Colonies from the Slave-Trade to Africa*, pp. ix, 12.
22. Charles Francis Adams, *Familiar Letters of John Adams and His Wife Abigail Adams*, pp. 41-42.
23. Aptheker, pp. 8-9, 10, 11; Logan, p. 77; "Letters and Documents Relating to Slavery in Massachusetts," pp. 432-37; Kaplan, pp. 11-14.
24. Sheldon H. Harris, *Paul Cuffe*, pp. 33-36, 159-61. The Cuffes refused to pay taxes from 1778 to 1780.
25. Jameson, *The American Revolution Considered as a Social Movement*, p. 34.
26. [Jay], *The Correspondence and Public Papers of John Jay*, vol. 3, p. 342.
27. Tucker and Belknap, p. 191.
28. Wallace, *The Life of Henry Laurens*, p. 446.
29. McColley, *Slavery and Jeffersonian Virginia*, p. 116; *The Writings of Thomas Jefferson*, vol. 2, draft facsimile opposite p. 50; Locke, *Anti-Slavery in America from the Introduction of African Slaves to the Prohibition of the Slave Trade*, pp. 1-2. See Morgan, "Slavery and Freedom: The American Paradox" on how slavery enabled Virginians to talk of freedom.
30. Freehling, "The Founding Fathers and Slavery," p. 83.
31. Jameson, p. 31; Greene, pp. 101-3.
32. McColley, p. 154; Aptheker, "The Quakers and Negro Slavery," 25: pp. 331-62; Joseph R. Washington, Jr., *Black Religion*, p. 184.
33. Washington, pp. 166-69, 181; Pascoe, *Two Hundred Years of the S.P.G.*, vol. 1, pp. 8, 15; Klingberg, *An Appraisal of the Negro in Colonial South Carolina*, pp. 9, 29, 13; Jordan, pp. 206-9.
34. [Boucher], *Reminiscences of an American Loyalist*, pp. 97-98, 57, 59.
35. Jordan, p. 214.
36. Washington, Jr., p. 187; Carol V. R. George, *Segregated Sabbaths*, p. 14.
37. Mays and Nicholson, *The Negro's Church*, p. 3; Morton, *Robert Carter of Nomini Hall*, pp. 237, 240.
38. [Asbury], *The Journal and Letters of Francis Asbury*, vol. 1, pp. 9-10, 222, 403; vol. 3, p. 15.
39. *George Whitefield's Journals*, pp. 6, 11, 8; *Countess of Huntingdon's New Magazine 1851*, p. 209; Stephen, *Essays in Ecclesiastical Biography*, vol. 2, pp. 70-99; Sweet, *Revivalism in America*, p. 107; [Equiano], *The Interesting Narrative of the Life of Olaudah Equiano or Gustavus Vassa, the African*, vol. 2, pp. 4-5.
40. [Marrant], *A Narrative of the Lord's Wonderful Dealings with John Marrant; The Monthly Review*, vol. 73 (1785) p. 399; Kaplan, pp. 95-99.
41. *Ibid.*, p. 95.
42. David George Narrative, pp. 473-83. George's account of his life was the basis for Kirk-Greene, "David George: The Nova Scotia Experience", *Bill,*

Fifty Years with the Baptist Ministers and Churches of the Maritime Provinces of Canada, pp. 19-26; and Kaplan, pp. 75-76.

43. See Othello, "Essay on Negro Slavery No. 2," pp. 509-12.

44. Corkran, *The Creek Frontier*, pp. 68, 71; Swanton, "Social Organization and Social Usages of the Indians of the Creek Confederacy"; Hallowell, "American Indians, White and Black: the Phenomenon of Transculturalization," p. 522; Webb Hodge, *Handbook of American Indians*, vol. 1, p. 1364; Bartram, *Travels Through North & South Carolina, Georgia, East & West Florida*, p. 212.

45. Hodge, pp. 363-64; Mullin, p. 50.

46. For Galphin references I am indebted to Terry W. Lipscomb, South Carolina Department of Archives and History. The will, dated 1776, is in *Abstracts of Old Ninety-Six and Abbeville District Wills and Bonds*, compiled by Willie Pauline Young. MacDowell, "George Galphin, Nabob of the Backwoods," pp. 51-56. His name often is spelled Gaulfin.

47. *Baptist Annual Register 1790-1793*, pp. 332-37; Woodson, *The History of the Negro Church*, pp. 43-47; Holmes, "George Liele: Negro Slavery's Prophet of Deliverance," pp. 333-45. Covenant of these "Anabaptists" printed in *General Baptist Repository*, pp. 229-40.

48. Gewehr, *The Great Awakening in Virginia*, p. 236.

49. Book of Negroes, PRO 30/55/100, ff. 70-71; *The Missionary Magazine for 1796*, vol. 1, pp. 177-78; Philip, *The Life, Times and Missionary Enterprises of the Rev. John Campbell*, pp. 175-76.

50. [King], "Memoirs of the Life of BOSTON KING, a Black Preacher," pp. 105-10, 157-61, 209-13, hereafter Boston King Narrative, the basis for Blakeley, "Boston King: a Negro Loyalist Who Sought Refuge in Nova Scotia." King is said to have written this memoir when at Kingswood School.

51. Klingberg, pp. 58, 87, 89, 99.

52. Davis, p. 317.

53. Native of America, "Arguments Against Making Slaves of Men," in Hepburn, *The American Defence of the Christian Golden Rule*.

54. Fishel and Quarles, p. 45.

55. Davis, p. 431.

56. Richard Hingston Fox, *Dr. John Fothergill and His Friends*, pp. 222-23; Brookes, *Friend Anthony Benezet*, p. 303; Benezet, *Some Historical Account of Guinea*, p. 116; Benezet to Fothergill, April 28, 1773, vol. 1, Gibson Manuscripts, Friends Library.

57. [Hopkins], *The Works of Samuel Hopkins*, vol. 2, p. 607; [Stiles], *The Literary Diary of Ezra Stiles*, vol. 1, p. 363; Sweet, p. 155; DuBois, *The Suppression of the African Slave-Trade to the United States of America*, p. 34; *Hopkins Works*, vol. 1, p. 115; Hopkins to Sharp, January 15, 1789, Granville Sharp Papers, Hardwicke Court, and in Hoare, *Memoirs of Granville Sharp*,

Esq., vol. 2, pp. 125-28; *Hopkins Works,* vol. 2, p. 574; Hopkins: *A Discourse Upon the Slave-Trade,* Appendix, p. 23; *Hopkins Works,* vol. 1, pp. 157, 166.
58. Sherwood, "Early Negro Deportation Projects," pp. 498-99; *Hopkins Works,* vol. 1, pp. 130, 135; James Edward Alexander, *Narrative of a Voyage of Observation Among the Colonies of Western Africa,* vol. 1, p. 56. No missionary went from Newport, but two of Hopkins' students made it to Liberia in their old age.

Chapter 2
CHOOSING SIDES

> I began to feel the happiness of liberty, of which I knew
> nothing before.
> —BOSTON KING on reaching the British lines[1]

If the Revolutionary War had been photographed, the participation of blacks would have been appreciated generations ago. Now, thanks to recent scholarship, their contributions, especially as patriots, are realized.[2] But there has been some reluctance to face the implications of the fact that the overwhelming majority of blacks who acted from choice were pro-British. An estimated 5,000 blacks served the patriot cause. "Tens of thousands" poured into the British lines, a few—perhaps 1,000—to bear arms and the rest to form a great and vital pool of noncombatant labor.[3]

We need reminding that the Revolution was a civil war and "a much more ugly and unpleasant affair than most of us imagine."[4] Callousness was the hallmark of the policy toward the black population on both sides and throughout the war. First of all, blacks were property and only secondly a human resource. But slaves would be accustomed to sorting out degrees of exploitation. If their goal was freedom, the British offered the quickest route to it, almost the only route, in fact, in the South. They had no other stake in the war; it was about liberty, but not about slavery.[5]

The majority of the blacks did not or could not choose. Virtually all were thought to hope, however, that "the British army might win, for then all Negro slaves will gain their freedom."[6] They were categorized by Crèvecoeur as "Toryfied."[7] "The negroes in general followed the British army," a contemporary British historian wrote.[8] There is no way of knowing how many slaves were lost to the colonies by the Revolution, but it could be as many as 80,000 to 100,000.[9]

The British were the first to appeal to blacks to join them, but only to those with rebel masters. White men's military services traditionally were rewarded with land and money. The blacks' prize was freedom. It soon was general knowledge that any child born behind British lines would be born free. British policy was made pragmatically by commanders on the scene, whose decisions, long afterward, were approved by Whitehall. In contrast, the American army's decisions affecting blacks were controlled by the Continental Congress, where the South's implacable opposition to arming or releasing slaves from plantation chores weighed heavily. It was folklore that Lord Mansfield's decision in the Somerset case had banned slavery on British soil and by extension within the British lines in America. "The idea that slavery was a sin against humanity was unknown to parliament . . . and would have been hooted at by the army."[10] By guarding their loyalist supporters against loss, British commanders recognized the institution of slavery. Their efforts to lure away the slaves of rebels were solely to undercut the economy and keep the South immobilized in fear of slave uprisings and thus constituted good military tactics.

There had always been dread of what the blacks would do in times of strife. They had sided with Creek Indians in border raids and in the Seven Years' War thought the French might free them.[11] To join the oppressor's enemy was a dramatic expression of hatred for American slavery. Blacks may not have understood the British cynicism, but they knew American society with its institutionalization of racism and ambivalence toward natural rights doctrines. The armed colonials the Southern blacks saw were slave catchers' patrols. It was not irrational to choose the devil you did not know. This would explain why many free as well as slave blacks sided with the British. About 14 percent of the black loyalists who survived the war and were evacuated from New York in 1783 said that they were born free, had been freed before they joined the British or, in a handful of cases, had bought their freedom earlier.[12]

British field officers dutifully tried to screen out and return (grudgingly sometimes) slaves who ran away from the king's supporters or who were inadvertently seized along with other booty. Any owner not in arms against the Crown or holding a rebel office was permitted to search the British camp for his slaves and "to take them if they are willing to go with him," as Cornwallis blandly assured the Virginia governor. The royal army's ad hoc rule was to "give up those that are willing to return & can be conveniently spared from the publick service."[13]

Blacks who had successfully emancipated themselves explained later that it was unknown for a slave to desert a loyalist owner, but if such a master were captured by the patriots, the slave would remain with the rebel unit until the first opportunity of running away.[14]

It seemed to matter little whether an owner was a "good" or a "bad" master. Of the slaves' reputation for stealing, a visiting Scotswoman had observed, "They are indeed the constant plague of their tyrants, whose severity or mildness is equally regarded by them in these Matters."[15] She could as well have been speaking of desertion. History records Robert Pleasants, the Quaker planter on the James River, as a solicitous master who liberated eighty or more slaves.[16] But twenty-two slaves, belonging to him and relatives for whom he acted as trustee, deserted to the British side. Though Virginia laws made it difficult, the various Pleasants, by their wills, had provided that each slave with his or her children would be free at age eighteen, in the case of women, or twenty-one or thirty in the case of men. Before manumission, they would be properly instructed for their new condition. When some of these slaves joined the British, Pleasants assumed that they went off "with an expectation . . . more fully to enjoy the liberty intended them," and in his correspondence with a British officer he was chiefly worried that in the wartime chaos they might fall into the hands of designing men who would sell them, unaware of their special status and future rights. He feared that one, Charles White, who was already freed but who had departed with his wife and two daughters, had been taken by force because White had left some property behind. A boy of fifteen, named London, had joined General Benedict Arnold as a trumpeter in the American Legion six years before his manumission was due. At the same time Arnold's troops carried off a horse much valued by the aging Pleasants for its gentleness. Pleasants asked for the return of the horse but not "the Negro man," unless by the latter's own choice. He signed as "a friend to Peace, to Liberty, & to mankind in General." London and at least one other Pleasants slave were evacuated from New York in 1783, still with the British.[17]

Yet cruelty must have played its part in motivating escapes. We do not know where Warwick Francis lived, but the savage treatment of slaves which he saw could have caused him to flee to the British lines. He described a series of atrocities to Paul Cuffe in 1812 in Sierra Leone. His statement follows:

> Sufferings and usage . . . Seen among Slaves in America by
> Aron Jelot a Doctor a slave Boy tied on a wooden spit so near
> the fire that it Scorch him well and basted with Salt and Water,

the same as you would a pigg. I have seen this same Aron Jelot took a pinchers and clap it to a mans tooth the Soundest in his head about one hour and a half and then draw it out the two persons was his own Slaves. I have seen the same A Jelot shoot a man Down the same as You would a Buck. This was about Nine or ten o'clock at night.

I have also seen Joseph Belseford in the same County chain two of his slaves and make them Walk on a plank at a mill pond and those 2 got drownd and the said Joseph Belseford gave a man 360 lashes and then wash him down with Salt and Water and after that took brand that he branded his Cattel with & make the Brand red hot and put it on his buttocks the same as you would brand a creater.

I have seen John Crimshire oversear on Barnet Elicot [or Elliot] estate a man whose name is Tom had 300 Lashes and put on the pickit with his Left Hand tied to his left toe behind him and his Right hand to post and his Right foot on the pickets till it worked through his foot.

John Draten I have Seen him take his Slave and put them in a tierce and nailed spikes in the tierce and Roale down a Steep hill.

The crueltity and punishment of the Slave which I have seen would not permitt me to make mention but for Lashes 300 or 400 a [nd] to be Washed Down with Salt and Water is but Slite punishment.

Many poor Women which I have Seen likely to be Deliver the child and oblige to wear a mouth peace and Lock out the Back part of it the keys the Driver keeps and are obliged to Worke all Day and at Night put in Clos Houses.

I have Seen them with a thim Screw Screwed till the Blood gushed out of their Nails. This I have Seen at Isaac Macpersons. . . . this is what I have said I am an Eye Witness to it it is not what I have heard. Time will not permit me to go further.[18]

Three British proclamations were cited specifically by blacks leaving New York as having inspired their defection. They named those of Lord Dunmore, Sir William Howe and Sir Henry Clinton. Of these, that of Lord Dunmore was the earliest, the most famous and the most effective.

No colony depended more on slaves than Virginia, where the Scots peer was the last royal governor. They filled every conceivable skilled and unskilled job. Travelers were often shocked at the laziness of the whites; one described the horror of seeing a grown man being fanned by a female slave. The visitors often reported indolence among blacks, it is true, but what work was done in Virginia was largely their doing. There were 200,000 blacks, 40 percent of the population.[19] Dunmore, a tactless and provocative governor, regarded the Virginia planters as ambitious and selfish, and he knew their weak spot. When he seized the gunpowder in the Williamsburg magazine and moved it on board the *Fowey* in the James River, his public excuse was fear of a slave uprising, but officially he suspected his "undutifull" subjects would take it themselves. When they demanded its return, he retorted that unless all rebel activities stopped, he would reduce Williamsburg to ashes, arm his own slaves and "receive all others that will come to me whom I shall declare free."[20]

Dunmore had hardly 300 troops he could call his own, and as anger mounted against him, he retreated from the governor's palace to the *Fowey,* reporting with marked understatement, "My declaration that I would arm and set free such Slaves as should assist me if I was attacked has stirred up fears in them which cannot easily subside."[21] Dunmore had seriously underestimated the extent of rebel support, and now his threat to arm the slaves united Virginians almost solidly against him. He added slaves to his small force and to keep up loyalist spirits conducted raids for supplies (and slaves, it was charged). In November, hearing that a force of North Carolina rebels was coming to join the Virginians at Great Bridge, Dunmore intercepted and routed them at Kemp's Landing with a band of his regulars and loyalists, both black and white. This "trifling success" brought the moment to risk a declaration of martial law and offer of freedom to all slaves and indentured servants of rebels who joined the king's standard. He had heard nothing from London since May. "God only knows," he recounted later, "what I have suffered . . . not knowing how to act . . . not having one living Soul to advise with, & . . . fearing if I remained a tame Spectator . . . they would delude many . . . well disposed Subjects." He drafted his proclamation, "the most disagreeable, but now absolutely necessary step," on board the *William* off Norfolk on November 7, 1775, and published it a week later. In part this emancipation proclamation read:

> . . . to the end that peace and good order may the sooner be restored, I do require every person capable of bearing arms to resort to His Majesty's standard . . . and I do hereby further declare all indented servants, Negroes, or others (appertaining

to Rebels,) free, that are able and willing to bear arms, they
joining His Majesty's Troops, as soon as may be, for the more
speedily reducing this Colony to a proper sense of their duty to
His Majesty's crown and dignity.[22]

To us, Dunmore is important not only as the first to call for slave
participation, but also as the only British commander committed to using
blacks in combat. Most British officers wanted blacks as manual laborers, spies, guides, messengers, wagon drivers, smiths, sailors, carpenters, nurses, laundresses, personal servants or cooks or working on
captured estates to supply food and timber. One historian has estimated
that 800 black people flocked to Dunmore. But slave owners believed the
number was twice as high.[23] There also was a powerful delayed reaction,
so that from the end of 1775 to the last months of the war Southern slaves
still were escaping to the British forces of Tarleton, Prevost, Cornwallis
or others. John Adams was told by two Southerners that 20,000 slaves in
South Carolina and Georgia alone would answer any British offer of
freedom. "The negroes have a wonderful art of communicating intelligence among themselves; it will run several hundreds of miles in a week
or fortnight," they said.[24]

The fact that Dunmore had no land base made it hard to reach him, and
many who tried failed. Roads and shores were patrolled to stop them.
Those who were captured might be banished to the backcountry, sold to
the West Indies or hung. A rumor that Dunmore retained only the fit and
sent the rest to the West Indies did not deflect others. Impassioned letters
in the local newspapers told the blacks that their best interests lay not with
the British who ran the slave trade but with their humanitarian masters
who pitied them and would, if circumstances and law allowed, restore
their freedom. Blandishments, arguments and threats were unavailing in
stemming the rush.[25]

At least fifteen of Landon Carter's male slaves "ran off to Dunmore."
All attempts to retrieve them failed. No doubt like many another exasper-
ated owner, Carter ruminated about his past good treatment of them and
their penchant for the liberty they were not born to. He dreamed of seeing
the runaways "meager and wan," hiding in a cave, living on roots,
willing to come home if he could see they were not hanged. His nephew
Robert, the Baptist, had met the challenge head on. He owned about 350
slaves, and when Dunmore's fleet moved into the Potomac, he called
them together to tell them about the proclamation, the war and the patriot
cause. He doubted that if the king won, Dunmore would keep his pledge

to the slaves. He asked whether any wanted to join Dunmore and risk the consequences. According to Carter, they said, "We all fully intend to serve you our master and we do now promise to use our whole might & force to execute your Commands." He bade them collect their belongings and families and hide in the woods to escape Dunmore's foraging parties. None deserted him, but thirty were stolen by a British privateer several years later.[26]

Dunmore's plan was to raise two regiments, one white and the other black, to be named Lord Dunmore's Ethiopian Regiment. By December he had 300 in uniforms on which was stitched the explosive slogan "Liberty to Slaves." Even a defeat at Great Bridge—the first real battle of the South—where Dunmore's force of about 600 was almost half black, did not check the volunteers. He was sure he would have got 2,000 under arms, "with whom I should have had no doubt of penetrating into the heart of this Colony," except for the fever and smallpox which broke out on the overcrowded ships and carried off far more blacks than whites. The shores were reported "full of Dead Bodies chiefly negroes."[27]

It is thought that most of Dunmore's black troops did not survive their adventure. Five hundred are believed to have died of typhus or smallpox. But about 300 survivors sailed with Dunmore to New York and there were attached to other units and departments. A famous Dunmore recruit, Colonel Tye, conducted guerrilla raids in New Jersey as late as 1780. Among 1,800 blacks evacuated from New York at the end of the war whose place of origin is known, more than 750 had come from Virginia, the largest number from a single state.[28] Even in the spring of 1782, with the war all but over, Dunmore continued to press for greater use of black troops, preferring them by far to Russian mercenaries whose coming had been rumored. Dunmore argued for a force of 10,000 blacks as "the most efficatious, expeditious, cheapest, and certain means of reducing this Country to a proper sense of their Duty." They were "not only fitter for service in this Warm Climate than White Men, but they are also better guides, may be got on much easier terms, and are perfectly attached to our Sovereign, and by employing them you cannot desire a means more effectual to distress your Foes . . . for without their labour they cannot subsist; and from my own knowledge of them, I am sure they are as soon disciplined as any set of raw Men that I know of." To each black who enlisted, he would give one guinea, one crown and freedom at the war's end. At least some of the British also gave a rare courtesy. An American prisoner on a British ship was shocked to see them receiving and shaking hands with three blacks.[29]

Among those who answered Dunmore's 1775 proclamation, several are known who later colonized Sierra Leone. One, Ralph Henry, about twenty-six, belonged to fiery Patrick Henry. He served with the royal artillery and after the British defeat was evacuated to Nova Scotia with his wife and two freeborn children. The most notable in Sierra Leone history was James Reid, twenty-six, who belonged to a Norfolk doctor in 1776, when he joined Lord Dunmore. His wife, Sally, was only sixteen when she left her owner on the James River for Dunmore's side. They were also attached to the royal artillery. Others were Bristol Garnet, John Steward, James Tucker, Michael Wallace and James Jackson, a river pilot in his forties.[30]

At the time Dunmore was becoming the "African hero," the American army was closed to all blacks, slave or free, excluded along with vagabonds, small boys and old men. Clearly influenced by Dunmore's action, General Washington modified the policy to allow the reenlistment of blacks who had served in local militia units. Like virtually everyone else of his class, Washington was outraged by Dunmore, the "arch-traitor to the rights of humanity." A few like the Reverend Samuel Hopkins suggested that the Americans could thwart the British more easily if they would themselves give the blacks "proper encouragement to labour, or take arms in the defence of the American cause, as they shall choose." Thomas Jefferson, like Washington a substantial slaveholder, added in his first draft of the Declaration of Independence another charge against George III of "exciting those very people to rise in arms among us, and to purchase that liberty of which *he* has deprived them, by murdering the people upon whom *he* also obtruded them; thus paying off former crimes committed against the *liberties* of one people, with crimes which he urges them to commit against the *lives* of another."[31]

Actually, not all the British approved of Dunmore's daring, though official assent came. London gentlemen, merchants and traders (many with West Indian interests) indignantly petitioned the king that slaves were being incited against "our American brethren." The action was condemned as "tending to loosen the bonds of society, to destroy domestic security, and encourage the most barbarous of mankind, to the most horrible crimes." Unwillingly Britain became identified with thoughts of race war, black supremacy and other notions which it never for a moment entertained. Virginians when setting up their independent government stripped the refugee royal governor of his property, leased out his farms and sold his eleven remaining slaves and other property at public auction.[32]

In a strange way, the warring sides competed for the blacks. After the American army was opened to free blacks, General Sir William Howe, following his recapture of New York in 1776, offered protection to all who came within his lines. After Congress in 1779 adopted Colonel John Laurens' plan to arm slaves in Georgia and South Carolina (which the respective states' legislatures at once recoiled from), General Sir Henry Clinton announced that since the Americans were recruiting blacks, he would guarantee freedom to any rebel's slave who took refuge within the lines and a choice of occupation to any black who deserted from the American forces. According to Major John André a year later, "Their property we need not seek, it flys to us and famine follows." A disproportionate number of blacks from New York, New Jersey and Pennsylvania appear among the black evacuees. Clinton recruits turned up as far away as Savannah.[33]

In their reminiscences, David George and Boston King shed little direct light on their reasons for joining the British. Both their masters were prominent rebels, and they lived in the only two states, Georgia and South Carolina, which never legalized black enlistments. By the time the war came David George's little congregation had grown from eight to thirty members. The trading post at Silver Bluff was stockaded and renamed Fort Galphin. The British launched a Southern offensive in 1778, captured Savannah and began to push into the interior the following year. As George put it, "being afraid, he [Galphin] now retired from home and left the Slaves behind." The small band of black Baptists had its own contingency plan. George, his wife, their two children and more than fifty others immediately set out for Savannah, where their old leader, George Liele, was preaching. The party encountered the British forces at Ebenezer. There was an interval while George was jailed on a trumped-up charge of white loyalists that he was misleading the slaves, but at last the group reached the Savannah suburb of Yamacraw, an old Creek settlement. Meanwhile, the British captured and garrisoned Fort Galphin and renamed it Fort Dreadnought. They held it until May, 1781, when it was taken after a brief skirmish by an American force under Colonel "Light Horse" Harry Lee. Galphin had died. The George family never saw the place again.[34]

The Baptists flourished at Yamacraw and Savannah during the British occupation of 1779 to 1782. The lively community included such leaders as Andrew Bryan, who carried on the work after George and Liele left in the British evacuation.[35] The runaway slaves lived as free blacks and supported themselves in odd jobs. Phillis George worked as a laundress, taking in General Clinton's wash during his short stay there in 1780. The family's worst days came during the French-American siege in the autumn of 1779, when a cannonball wrecked a stable in which they had sheltered and George came down with the smallpox. He sent his wife and children into Savannah, remaining behind, as he thought, to die, either from the pox or the Americans. Years later he remembered that he had two quarts of cornmeal to sustain him. This he boiled. He had eaten only a little of it when a stray dog devoured the rest. Some kind person gave him rice. For two years George supported his family by running a butcher's stall with livestock supplied by his brother-in-law in the country. He rented a house with a garden and field. He carried a pass signed by the town adjutant certifying that he was "a good Subject to King George" and a "Free Negro Man."[36] Certificates of this kind were issued by several British officers and looked on as emancipation papers.

Wartime Savannah was a scatter of wooden houses built on a sandy bluff overlooking rice fields. Its population included under 2,000 whites (British regulars and provincial troops plus loyalist refugees), some 5,000 blacks and a few hundred Indians. The British had good reason to appreciate the blacks. The town had been taken from the Americans after a surprise attack guided by an aged slave, Quamino Dolly, and in the 1779 siege, Major General Augustine Prevost armed 250 blacks and "found them very usefull most of them were run aways or had followed the Army from Carolina they certainly did wonders in the working way and in the fighting they really shewed no bad countenence." Hundreds more toiled on the fortifications under the brilliant engineer Captain (soon Major) James Moncrief. The French fleet and American land forces considerably outnumbered the defenders, but the deficiency was offset by the "extraordinary zeal and ardour which animated the besieged, from the commander in chief down to the humble African, whose incessant and cheerful labours, in rearing those numerous defences which were completed with so much expedition as to astonish the besiegers, ought not to be forgotten." After they were safe, Savannah residents complained of the insolence of the blacks and insisted that they be disarmed.[37]

After Yorktown, when the British decided to abandon the Southern seaports, Savannah, the most vulnerable, was the first to be evacuated. Rebels had established a government at Augusta. They were raising troops by promising to pay in slaves captured from loyalists and threatening to "come down like a torrent against Savannah." British forces and friends, pinned in the town, faced famine. The order to evacuate was sent in May, 1782, and 7,000 people went into exile in July. They included most of the 5,000 blacks, the majority of whom were sent to East Florida and Jamaica into continued slavery.[38] But David George had made his own escape plan. He and Phillis with their three children sailed to Charleston, where Boston King had gone before him.

King's war proved considerably more adventurous than that of George, the pious family man.[39] When the British captured Charleston in May, 1780, he was working as a carpenter some miles away. Among the 6,000 Americans taken prisoner was King's master, Richard Waring. King "determined to go to Charles-Town, and throw myself into the hands of the English," as scores of his fellow slaves were doing. Lieutenant Colonel Banastre Tarleton, one British officer who thought them a great nuisance, declared that "all the negroes, men, women and children, upon the approach of any detachment of the King's troops, thought themselves absolved from all respect to their American masters, and entirely released from servitude . . . quitted the plantations, and followed the army." A patriot historian wrote, "The hapless Africans, allured with hopes of freedom, forsook their owners, and repaired in great numbers to the royal army," where to win favor, they tipped off the British to hidden property, helped carry it off and generally became "insolent and rapacious." Far too many inundated the British forces, and Clinton instructed Lord Cornwallis, who was taking over the Southern command, to discourage them somehow. Clinton also insisted that slaves belonging to loyalists should be hired by the army (the money going to their masters) or returned so that agriculture was not neglected, but only after the master or mistress "shall have promised in the presence of the Negro not to punish him for past Offences." Slaves of rebels were Crown property "and after serving it faithfully during the War are entitled to their Freedom." In a curious postscript, Clinton made a suggestion which was to get nowhere: "Why not settle the Negroes on Forfeited Lands after the War? Perhaps they would be a check upon the others—and 'tis possible just the contrary."[40]

Luckily, Boston King could offer his youth and his skilled hands, and he recalled that the British "received me readily."

"I began to feel the happiness of liberty, of which I knew nothing before," he recalled, "altho' I was much grieved at first, to be obliged to leave my friends, and reside among strangers."

Unfortunately, he soon came down with smallpox, which swept away so many blacks crowding into Charleston, where the disease had been unknown for seventeen years. It ravaged the blacks and probably would have done similar damage to white troops if not for the practice of quartering them separately.[41] Boston King suffered greatly at the place a mile from camp where the sick blacks were collected. "We lay sometimes a whole day without any thing to eat or drink; but Providence sent a man, who belonged to the York volunteers whom I was acquainted with, to my relief. He brought me such things as I stood in need of; and by the blessing of the Lord I began to recover."

When his regiment moved out, King with other convalescents feared capture, but the Americans, finding the stragglers had smallpox, "precipitately left us." Wagons collected the twenty-five invalids and moved them to a cottage near a hospital at what may have been Monk's Corner. When he recovered, King marched with the army to Cornwallis' headquarters at Camden. His original regiment was thirty-five miles off. King probably was still at headquarters when Cornwallis defeated General Horatio Gates on August 16, 1780. Among the wounded was his benefactor from the York Volunteers. "As soon as I heard of his misfortune, I went to see him, and tarried with him in the hospital six weeks, till he recovered; rejoicing that it was in my power to return him the kindness he had showed me."

King next served as an orderly to a British regular, one Captain Grey. He was off fishing when word came to break camp in fifteen minutes, and he returned to find the place occupied by a few Southern loyalist militiamen, to his astonishment and alarm, for the provincial troops reflected Southern attitudes to slaves. As King told it:

> Captain Lewes, who commanded the militia, said, "You need not be uneasy, for you will see your regiment before 7 o'clock to-night." This satisfied me for the present, and in two hours we set off. As we were on the march, the Captain asked, "How will you like me to be your master?" I answered, that I was Captain Grey's servant. "Yes," said he; "but I expect they are all taken prisoners before now; and I have been long enough in the English service, and am determined to leave them." These words roused my indignation, and I spoke some sharp things to him. But he calmly replied, "If you do not behave well, I will put you in irons, and give you a dozen stripes every morning." I now perceived that my cause was desperate, and that I had nothing to trust to, but to wait the first opportunity for making my escape. The next morning, I was sent with a little boy . . .

to an island to fetch the Captain some horses. . . . we found
about fifty of the English horses, that Captain Lewes had stolen
from them at different times. . . . Upon our return . . . he
immediately set off by himself.

Such loyalist militiamen were probably in Brigadier General Alexander Leslie's mind when he reported to General Clinton, as British
fortunes declined, that "a great part of our Militia are with the Enemy,
after getting all they could from us." The militia "were in general
faithless, and altogether dissatisfied in the British service," a contemporary British military historian reported.[42]

King, resolving to make his own way to the British army, walked
twenty-four miles, stayed at a farmer's house overnight "and was well
used," and completed the journey to Captain Grey the following day. He
reported Captain Lewes' defection. Three weeks later the British went to
the island, burned Lewes' house and recovered forty horses. Lewes
escaped. Eventually, King became a servant to the commanding officer
at Nelson's Ferry. The situation "was very precarious, and we expected
to be made prisoners every day; for the Americans had 1600 men, not far
off; whereas our whole number amounted to only 250: but there were
1200 English about 30 miles off; only we knew not how to inform them of
our danger, as the Americans were in possession of the country."[43] The
commanding officer decided to send King with dispatches to the British,
promising him a large reward if he made it through the American lines.
Six miles from his destination, he heard approaching troops, ducked off
the road and "fell flat upon my face till they were gone by. I then arose,
and praised the Name of the Lord for his great mercy," and continued to
Monk's Corner. A frightened tavernkeeper there told him that 100
Americans had left only an hour before.

I desired him to saddle his horse for me, which he did, and
went with me himself. When we had gone about two miles, we
were stopped by a picket-guard, till the Captain came out with
30 men: As soon as he knew that I had brought an express from
Nelson's-ferry, he received me with great kindness, and expressed his approbation of my courage and conduct in this
dangerous business. Next morning, Colonel Small gave me
three shillings, and many fine promises, which were all that I
ever received for this service from him. However he sent 600
men to relieve the troops at Nelson's-ferry.

King later got to Charleston and joined the crew of a man-of-war headed for New York. It captured a rich prize in Chesapeake Bay en route, but there is no record that he shared the prize money.

Among the first blacks to apply for Sierra Leone in London in 1786 were two others who saw war service. Benjamin Whitecuff, a free small farmer on Long Island, was a British spy. He was credited with saving 2,000 troops under General Clinton in one engagement in New Jersey. Captured by the Americans, he was hanged, only to be rescued in three minutes by a British cavalry unit. John Twine, slave of a Virginia tavernkeeper, served as a wagon driver for a rebel regiment at first but deserted to the British because his captain kept him "very bare in Cloaths" and he had heard there was "more money & better Usage in the British army." In 1781, according to his story, he was wounded in the thigh at Camden.[44]

Thomas Peters became the leader of the black exodus from Nova Scotia to Sierra Leone. He and several followers served in the Black Pioneers, a company of the British regiment of Guides and Pioneers. Although many British units were referred to as black pioneers or black brigades, this was the only one mustered under that name. It was formed in 1776 and operated in many campaigns until the surrender at Yorktown. Peters remembered being sworn in on November 14, 1776, at New York by Alderman William Waddell. His captain was George Martin. The men were promised after the war to be "at our own Liberty to do & provide for our selves." All the officers were white, but there were three black sergeants and one to three black corporals. The unit varied in strength from sixty to seventy men. Peters, Mingo Leslie and Murphy Steele were sergeants, and George Kendle was a corporal. The unit drew the same pay as other provincial infantrymen, a shilling a day for a sergeant, eightpence for a corporal and sixpence for a private.[45]

Sergeant Peters had been a slave of William Campbell, Wilmington, North Carolina, and was about thirty-eight when he joined the British unit. Steele was also from Wilmington and had been owned by Stephen Daniel. He ran off in 1776, in his early twenties. Mingo Leslie was about thirty-one when he left his owner, John Leslie of Charleston. Corporal Kendle had been a slave of John Kendle on the eastern shore of Virginia until he left in 1777 when about twenty-nine. An undated list of "Capt. Martin's Company" supplies the names of three other future settlers of Sierra Leone, Abram Leslie, Abraham Croy, African-born, and John Bird, all from the Carolinas.[46]

At the end of the war, sixty-seven of the blacks evacuated to Nova

Scotia were identified as Black Pioneers, including twenty-one men, twenty-eight women and eighteen children. A total of eighty-two others (forty-three of whom were men) went as members of a Black Brigade, which appears to have been the remnant of units raised at Savannah and Charleston. One-third had run away from masters in Virginia, and two specifically cited Lord Dunmore's proclamation, while among the group was one, Sarrah, forty-two and "stone blind," who had been a slave of Dunmore's, and Phillister, thirty, a mute, who belonged to Benjamin Harrison.[47]

Of Mary Perth's war experiences we know nothing. She abandoned her master at Norfolk in 1776, taking with her three girls of ten, fifteen and eighteen, who might have been pupils or her own though the names differ. She was about thirty-six at the time. Whether her husband was then, as later, Caesar Perth is not clear, for he, although also from Norfolk, had belonged to another man, Hardy Weller, whom he said he did not desert until about 1779.[48]

Not all the blacks aided the British out of choice. Robert Stafford, who later settled in Sierra Leone, was only sixteen when seized on a Virginia plantation by a Royal Navy party. John Marrant, the fanatical young convert of Whitefield's, was taken by a press gang on the sloop *Scorpion* as a musician. He served nearly seven years. In his autobiography he described the scene in Charleston when the British marched in. The Cherokee chief whom Marrant had so impressed in the wilderness was riding alongside the victorious General Clinton when he saw Marrant, "alighted off his horse, and came to me; said he was glad to see me." Marrant served on the *Princess Amelia* in one naval engagement off the Dogger Bank when the toll was terrible and he himself was covered with the blood and brains of the slain. He was wounded in the war and after his discharge in England, thanks to the charitable zeal of George Whitefield's patron the Countess of Huntingdon, he resumed his religious training and was ordained at Bath in 1785.[49]

Perhaps these sparse accounts of a few blacks who left a record help show what the American Revolution was like for their people. Any possibility that the Revolution might have brought the abolition of slavery foundered on the South's steadfast resistance. The North probably was not ready either. Staughton Lynd believes that the decisive act came in 1779, when the Continental Congress approved Colonel John Laurens' plan to arm slaves in Georgia and South Carolina and "give them their freedom with their swords." This, along with military service in other provinces, might have become the start of an emancipation program. His plan was defeated, Laurens said, by the "triple-headed monster that shed the baneful influence of Avarice, prejudice, and pusillanimity." The Deep South would rather lose the war than win by these means.[50]

There is no evidence that Britain had any postwar plan for the thousands of blacks who had sought its protection and were now called free, except for Clinton's idle remark. Had British commanders made abolition a war aim, as was suggested by some, they would have been overruled undoubtedly by pressure of the slave-trading and West Indian planter lobbies.[51]

For white Americans, however, the failure to deal with slavery in the process of liberating themselves determined the unhappy future course of domestic affairs. Despite unease, slavery was sanctioned in the Constitution and the slave trade continued to 1808. The Marquis de Lafayette told Thomas Clarkson, "I would never have drawn my sword in the cause of America if I could have conceived that thereby I was founding a land of slavery."[52]

"The whole of our war . . . was a contest for *Liberty*," Samuel Hopkins said, "but if . . . we have taken or withheld these same rights from the Africans . . . we have justified the [British] in all they have done against us, and all the blood which has been shed . . . is chargeable on us." Begging General Nathanael Greene, the Rhode Island Quaker war hero who had been given a confiscated plantation by a grateful South Carolina, to help stop the slave trade, Benjamin Rush declared, "For God's sake, do not exhibit a spectacle to the world, of men just emerging from a war in favor of liberty, with their clothes not yet washed from the blood which was shed in copious and willing streams in its defense, fitting out vessels to import their fellow creatures from Africa to reduce them afterwards to slavery."

But Rush, no more than his benighted compatriots, was ready for emancipation. All he could suggest was to make the slaves comfortable until "time may unfold" some way to make amends for the injustice of slavery.[53]

NOTES

1. Boston King Narrative, p. 107.
2. Benjamin Quarles, *The Negro in the American Revolution* is essential, particularly for the participation of blacks on the American side. Kaplan, *The*

Black Presence in the Era of the American Revolution is an important recent work linked to an exhibition in Washington, D.C., in 1973. Tribute also should be paid the pioneer studies of George H. Moore, *Historical Notes on the Employment of Negroes in the American Army of the Revolution* (1862), William C. Nell, *Services of Colored Americans, in the Wars of 1776 and 1812* (1851), and Joseph T. Wilson, *The Black Phalanx: A History of the Negro Soldiers of the United States in the Wars of 1775-1812, 1861-1865* (1888).

3. Quarles, pp. 40, 119; Quarles, *The Negro in the Making of America*, p. 55; Wallace Brown, "Negroes and the American Revolution," p. 558. Wilson, p. 22, says 15,000 joined the British army, but all figures are informed guesses for lack of sufficient records stating race.

4. Fisher, *The True History of the American Revolution*, p. 9.

5. Norton, "The Fate of Some Black Loyalists of the American Revolution," pp. 402-3. Calhoon, "Loyalist Studies at the Advent of the Loyalist Papers Project," pp. 284-93, analyzes the explosion in loyalist studies.

6. Tappert and Doberstein, *The Notebook of a Colonial Clergyman*, p. 180.

7. Crèvecoeur, *Sketches of Eighteenth Century America*, p. 301.

8. Stedman, *The History of the Origin, Progress, and Termination of the American War*, vol. 2, p. 217.

9. Quarles, "The Negro Response. Evacuation with the British," p. 133, estimates the South alone lost 65,000 slaves. Morris, *The American Revolution Reconsidered*, p. 76, reckons that as many blacks as white Tories were evacuated—possibly 80,000 to 100,000. Norton, *The British-Americans: the Loyalist Exiles in England*, p. 9, puts the white evacuees at 60,000 to 80,000. See also Wallace Brown, *The Good Americans: The Loyalists in the American Revolution*, p. 192.

10. Lindsay, "Diplomatic Relations Between the United States and Great Britain Bearing on the Return of Negro Slaves, 1788-1828," pp. 392-93, credits the British military with disseminating the Mansfield judgment in American, an idea which had been scoffed at by George Bancroft, *History of the United States of America*, vol. 5, p. 374.

11. Quarles, *Negro in the Revolution*, p. vii; Aptheker, *American Negro Slave Revolts*, pp. 19, 20; DuBois, *The Gift of Black Folk: The Negroes in the Making of America*, p. 82. DuBois makes the point that whatever others fought for in America's wars, blacks always fought for their personal freedom and self-respect.

12. Boorstin, *The Americans: The Colonial Experience*, pp. 355, 356; Book of Negroes, PRO 30/55/100, my analysis of data on the 1783 embarkation. Fitchett, "The Traditions of the Free Negro in Charleston, South Carolina," pp. 139-52 illuminates the marginal position of free blacks. The effect of slavery on free blacks and the whites' resentment of them are discussed in Morris, *Government and Labor in Early America.*

13. Cornwallis to Nelson, August 6, 1781, PRO 30/11/90; Ross to Paterson, June 20, 1781, PRO 30/11/87; claim of John Murray, AO 12/73, f. 87 ff.

14. Clarkson Papers, BL Add. MSS. 41,262B, Notebook, f. 17.

15. Schaw, *Journal of a Lady of Quality*, p. 177.

16. Drake, *Quakers and Slavery in America*, p. 83.

17. Pleasants to Philips, May 14, 1781, PRO 30/11/90; cases of Robert Pleasant, 30, and London, 17, Book of Negroes, PRO 30/55/100, ff. 62-63, 104-5.

18. Frances, "Sufferings Seen Among Slaves in America," February 18, 1812, Paul Cuffe Papers, New Bedford Public Library.

19. McColley, *Slavery and Jeffersonian Virginia*, pp. 19-20, 21; Burnaby, *Travels Through the Middle Settlements in North-America*, p. 111; Brissot de Warville, *New Travels in the United States of America*, vol. 1, p. 237; Jameson, *The American Revolution Considered as a Social Movement*, p. 31; Mullin, *Flight and Rebellion*, p. 6; CO 5/1352, ff. 21-22.

20. Berkeley, *Dunmore's Proclamation of Emancipation*, pp. 3, 5, 6; Eckenrode, *The Revolution in Virginia*, pp. 49-50; Dunmore to Secretary of State, May 1, 1775, CO 5/1353; "Williamsburg—the Old Colonial Capital," pp. 43-45, and Quarles, "Lord Dunmore as Liberator," pp. 494-507, which is the source, unless otherwise noted, on Dunmore's activities.

21. Dunmore to Secretary of State, June 25, 1775, CO 5/1353.

22. Smith, *Loyalists and Redcoats*, pp. 15-16; Morris, *American Revolution Reconsidered*, p. 74; Fishel and Quarles, *The Black American*, p. 56; Moore, *Diary of the Revolution*, vol. 1, pp. 160-65; Kaplan reproduces Dunmore's proclamation, p. 62.

23. Mullin, p. 196 n.

24. [Adams], *The Works of John Adams*, vol. 3, p. 428.

25. Livermore, *An Historical Research Respecting the Opinions of the Founders of the Republic on Negroes as Slaves, as Citizens, and as Soldiers*, pp. 136-38; *Archives of Maryland*, vol. 11, pp. 191, 511, 517; [Carter], *The Diary of Col. Landon Carter of Sabine Hall*, vol. 2, pp. 1056, 1057.

26. *Ibid.*, pp. 1049, 1052, 1055, 1056, 1075, 1084, 1085, 1064, 1110; Morton, *Robert Carter of Nomini Hall*, pp. 55-56, 99.

27. Dunmore to Secretary of State, December 6, 1775; March 30, 1776, and June 26, 1776, CO 5/1353; Price to Maryland Council of Safety, July 23, 1776, *Archives of Maryland*, vol. 12, p. 98; Kaplan, pp. 20-21, 60.

28. George Bancroft, vol. 5, p. 5; Book of Negroes, PRO 30/55/100, my analysis of data; Quarles, *Negro in the Revolution*, pp. 147-48; Kaplan, pp. 66-67.

29. MS Memoirs of William Smith, vol. 7, April 22, 1782, New York Public Library; Dunmore to Secretary of State, February 5, 1782, enclosing copy of recommendations to Clinton and plan for 10,000 black troops; Nelson, *The American Tory*, p. 112.

30. Book of Negroes, PRO 30/55/100, ff. 144-45, 58-59, 146-47, 27-28; List of Pilots in Constant Pay, November 21, 1782, PRO 30/55/55, f. 6230.

31. [Washington], *The Writings of George Washington*, vol. 4, pp. 8 n., 86, and Washington to Reed, December 15, 1775, p. 167; Frank Moore, pp. 3-4; [Jefferson], *Writings of Thomas Jefferson*, vol. 2, draft opposite p. 50.

32. Secretary of State to Dunmore, July 5, 1775, CO 5/1535; Quarles, *Negro in the Revolution*, pp. 111-12; *Annual Register*, vol. 19 (1776), p. 19; John Chester Miller, *Origins of the American Revolution*, p. 479; Harrell, *Loyalism in Virginia*, p. 44.

33. General Howe's Proclamations, August 23, 1776, and November 30, 1776, PRO 30/55/37, ff. 254 and 334; General Clinton's Proclamation, June 30, 1779, PRO 30/55/17, f. 2094; Book of Negroes, PRO 30/55/100, my analysis of data; Clarke to Cornwallis, July 10, 1780, PRO 30/11/2.

34. David George Narrative, except as indicated; Corkran, *The Creek Frontier*, pp. 83, 323; McCrady, *The History of South Carolina in the Revolution*, pp. 266, 552; Lee, *Memoirs of the War in the Southern Department of the United States*, pp. 236-37.

35. *Baptist Annual Register 1790-1793*, pp. 339-44; Benedict, *A General History of the Baptist Denomination in America*, vol. 2, p. 190.

36. Pass signed Edward Cooper, December 11, 1779, PANS 170/332.

37. [Russell], "The Siege of Charleston; Journal of Captain Peter Russell," p. 482; Siebert, *Loyalists in East Florida*, vol. 1, pp. 105, 106; Siebert, *The Legacy of the American Revolution to the British West Indies and Bahamas*, p. 7; Quarles, *Negro in the Revolution*, pp. 144, 148; Campbell to Clinton, January 16, 1779, PRO 30/55/14; Prevost to Clinton, November 2, 1779, PRO 30/55/20; Coleman, *The American Revolution in Georgia*, p. 128; Uhlendorf, *The Siege of Charleston*, p. 167; Stedman, vol. 2, pp. 127-28.

38. Wright to Balfour, August 16, 1781, PRO 30/55/32; Wright to Clinton, October 16, 1781, PRO 30/55/33; Carleton to Leslie, May 23, 1782, PRO 30/55/41. The British also used blacks for bounties or for currency, as when Cornwallis instructed an officer to "sell a Negro to help provide yourself," Cornwallis to Grey, October 2, 1780, PRO 30/11/81.

39. Boston King Narrative and Phyllis Blakeley, "Boston King," are the sources unless noted, of his story.

40. McCrady, p. 359; Tarleton, *A History of the Campaigns of 1780 and 1781*, pp. 89-90; Ramsay, *The History of the Revolution of South-Carolina*, vol. 2, pp. 31-32. Gordon, *The History of the Rise, Progress, and Establishment, of the Independence of the United States*, p. 259, repeated the point about slaves exposing hidden property, for he had access to Ramsay's manuscript. Siebert, *Loyalists in East Florida*, vol. 1, p. 77; Clinton to Cornwallis, May 20, 1780, PRO 30/11/2; Clinton Memorandum, n.d. [June, 1780], PRO 30/55/23, f. 2800.

41. Simpson to Clinton, July 16, 1780, PRO 30/55/24; Ramsay, vol. 2, p. 67.

42. Leslie to Clinton, December 27, 1781, CO 5/104; Stedman, p. 206 n. and pp. 205-10, describes actions in which Boston King may have been involved. King's narrative is imprecise on places and names.

43. The commanding officer may have been Cornwallis.

44. Whitecuff case, AO 12/99, f. 345; AO 13/56, f. 638; AO 12/19, f. 148, 150; Twine case, AO 13/54, f. 142; Wallace Brown, *The King's Friends*, p. 275.

45. Petition of Thomas Peters with certificate of Captain Martin, November 4, 1790, FO 4/1, f. 421; Waddell case, AO 12/100, f. 283; Peters and Still to Parr, August 24, 1784, PANS 359/65; Memorial of Major John Aldington, n.d., PRO 30/55/84; f. 9712; Return of the Company of Black Pioneers, September 13, 1783, PRO 30/55/82; photograph in Kaplan, p. 70; Raymond, "Loyalists in Arms 1775-1783," pp. 189-223, with Table of Provincial Troops, pp. 220-21; Abstracts of pay for Black Pioneers in PRO 30/55/47, 52, 57, 58, 63, 69, 70, 73, 78.

46. Book of Negroes, PRO 30/55/100, ff. 130-31, 154-55. Peters' name is spelled Petters. His enlistment date was certified, so the date of 1780 here for his escape from his master must be incorrect. MS Captain Martin's Company, Clinton Papers, Box 8, Clements Library, University of Michigan.

47. Book of Negroes, PRO 30/55/100, my analysis of roster; Sarrah and Phillister, ff. 125-26.

48. *Ibid.*, ff. 70-71, 94-95.

49. *Ibid.*, pp. 17-18; [Marrant], *A Narrative of the Lord's Wonderful Dealings with John Marrant.*

50. Lynd, *Class Conflict, Slavery, and the United States Constitution*, p. 179; [Hamilton], *The Works of Alexander Hamilton*, vol. 1, p. 77, Hamilton to Jay, March 14, 1779; vol. 3, p. 121, Laurens to Hamilton, July, 1782. Lorenzo J. Greene, "Some Observations on the Black Regiment of Rhode Island in the American Revolution," p. 155.

51. Morris, *American Revolution Reconsidered*, p. 76. The Reverend Thomas Vivian, writing to Lord Dartmouth, January 16, 1777, hoped a new Constitution could be brought in by British arms in which slavery would be abolished. See Royal Commission on Historical Manuscripts, 14th Report, Part X, vol. 2, p. 433.

52. Clarkson to Chapman, October 3, 1845, Gerrit Smith Papers, Syracuse University.

53. [Hopkins], *The Works of Samuel Hopkins*, vol. 2, p. 617; [Rush], *Letters of Benjamin Rush*, ed., vol. 1, pp. 285-86, Rush to Greene, September 16, 1782.

Chapter 3

PAWNS OF THE PEACEMAKERS

> . . . peace was restored between America and Great
> Britain, which diffused universal joy among all parties,
> except us, who had escaped from slavery, and taken refuge
> in the English army. . . .
>
> —BOSTON KING.[1]

The British withdrawal was complicated by an unprecedented problem: what to do with the thousands of loyalists who either believed that they dared not stay among the triumphant rebels or preferred to live elsewhere under King George. Bitterly disappointed, often impoverished, this "crust of . . . aristocratic pretensions"[2] crowded into the British-held seaports clamoring for passage.[3]

Few patriots were sorry to see the white loyalists depart, but the disappearing blacks became a hotly contested issue. Protests began well before the war ended that the British were transporting to East Florida and the West Indies uncounted slaves who had escaped to their lines or who had been taken as plunder. There are reasonable estimates that 4,000 blacks embarked at Savannah, another 6,000 left Charleston, and 3,000 to 4,000 sailed from New York before that last British garrison was handed over on November 25, 1783.[4]

No one had foreseen that the war would generate so many refugees, certainly not the British, who had expected to win, leaving the Americans, black or white, where they had found them, but more compliant.

In the general disorder of the closing months of the conflict, the blacks everywhere were in extreme peril. Slaves were being snatched as last-minute booty by British, Hessian, American and French troops alike. Loyalists were trying desperately to hold onto their slaves and get them out of the country with the rest of their goods. American slave owners were doggedly tracking down their fugitives behind the British lines.

41

Most of them were not successful, and the quarrel over compensation for this "lost property" plagued British-American relations for many years.

The majority of blacks who left the United States, as it now was, sailed without reference to their wishes. They were still slaves; only the scene and sometimes the master had changed. There were others, however, who, having earned their freedom in the British campaigns and having been labeled "obnoxious" for it, chose their destinations. A considerable number selected Britain or Nova Scotia. That a choice was theirs is confirmed by surviving certificates issued in Charleston and New York. The Charleston commissioner of claims on October 12, 1782, gave Phillis Thomas, "a free Black woman," permission to go "to the Island of Jamaica or elsewhere *at her own option.*" Two days later he authorized Ned and Jemimah Elliott and their children, Castle, Ned and Dublin, to go "to Halifax, or elsewhere *at their Option.*" The commanding officer in New York in April, 1783, gave John Williams and William O'Neal leave to "go to Nova Scotia, *or wherever else he may think proper.*" All of these people in the end chose Nova Scotia, and the Elliotts and O'Neal and two John Williams, perhaps this one, eventually opted for Africa.[5]

Our story now concentrates on those loyal blacks who went to Nova Scotia, mainly from Charleston and New York. That they effected their escape is due to the actions of several British officers, but above all to General Sir Guy Carleton and his stern sense of honor. A career soldier now in his late fifties, Carleton had been governor of Quebec for ten years up to 1778. A dispute over his conduct of a military expedition against the Northern colonies led him to ask for a recall. After a restless retirement, he was appointed to succeed Clinton as commander in chief and joint commissioner with Admiral Digby "for restoring peace and granting pardon to the Revolted Provinces," or as the press put it, "commissioner for peace or war." He reached New York on May 5, 1782, and General Clinton had the happy release which he said he had prayed for. Carleton was welcomed joyously by the loyalists who thronged New York, and Clinton departed, a lonely figure, "laughed at by the rebels, despised by the British, and cursed by the loyalists." The key to the loyalists' anger was the tenth article of the Yorktown capitulation which seemed to make a devastating distinction between them and British regular troops. In the event, few civilian refugees and almost none of the 2,000 blacks in Cornwallis' camp succeeded in boarding the single ship allowed out with dispatches. Clinton had assured the loyalists elsewhere that they would be on an equal footing in future, and Carleton conveyed the king's word to the same effect. He promised that the military would be the last to leave any post, and his pledge was kept at Charleston and New York.[6]

Carleton's public character was very similar to that of the revered George Washington. The two men were said even to look alike. Carleton's appointment had followed a call from the House of Commons to end offensive operations and mend relations with the thirteen colonies, and he was specifically instructed to remove all British forces and salvageable property from New York, Charleston and Savannah and divert them to the West Indies for use against France and Spain. The operation was supposed to take place in one swift movement. Almost at once Carleton discovered this was impossible for lack of shipping, and the plan he improvised called for evacuation of the weakest spots first, Savannah and then Charleston.[7] He also was charged to give refugees his "tenderest and most honorable care." But the instruction which must have struck him as all-important was to behave so generously to the Americans as to "captivate their Hearts" and revive their old affection for a Britain now exhibiting more liberal sentiments toward their grievances. Like George III, who was responsible for his appointment, Carleton truly believed that North America's best interests lay with Britain. Thus his shock was great when in August, 1782, with his work scarcely begun, he was informed that Britain was granting unconditional independence at the start of the peace negotiations. Carleton promptly resigned. He wanted no part in the breakup of the empire, and although he shared the loyalists' grief and sense of betrayal, he did not wish to remain in New York a mere "caretaker of refugees." Months went by, however, before he learned that the government agreed to his return and had appointed Lieutenant General Charles Grey in his stead. By then the final treaty was so close that it was decided not to send Grey after all. To Carleton fell the unhappy task of presiding over the final break with as much dignity as could be mustered.[8]

Carleton became a father figure to the loyalists, their "Primo, Media, Ultima," and his conception of Britain's obligation to them included the debt to the blacks among them. Their wartime presence in the military camps and campaigns had created a bond with regular troops and officers from Britain, a relationship of English master and servant. Among loyalist provincial forces, it was often still one of owner and slave. The obligations and privileges of each ruling class were similar, but different. The British indeed recognized slavery, for whatever the Mansfield decision had meant, it was never applied to Britain's overseas possessions, and the nation waxed rich on the slave trade and slave labor of the West Indian colonies. But slavery was practiced at home only by returning West Indian planters with their entourages. Most of the slaves who allied themselves to military units and survived to go to Nova Scotia were connected with British regulars such as the royal artillery or engineers. They were transported in groups and settled together as free men. Those who went to Nova Scotia with such disbanded provincial corps as the New Jersey or New York Volunteers or the King's American Dragoons usually traveled as slaves (sometimes euphemistically labeled servants).[9]

Americans first and last were conditioned to think of slaves as property, and valuable property at that. A skilled craftsman would cost £150, a domestic servant £50 to £100, field hands £60 to £75 and children around £15 to £20 each.[10] Slaves, like "four footed animals," must be restored if they strayed or were stolen.[11]

Carleton's sense of *noblesse oblige* had its first important test at Charleston. How to cope in evacuation plans with the thousands of blacks attached to the British garrison in that beautiful little capital had been debated for some time. General Leslie had proposed that at least some be armed and put under Lieutenant Colonel Moncrief, promoted again after the engineers' masterful work on the siege of Charleston, who was "well acquainted with their disposition and in the highest estimation among them." Moncrief believed a brigade of armed blacks would maintain their confidence in the British. He had praised their services in dispatches.[12]

Besides those blacks who had come on their own volition, there were the captured slaves. In 1780 Cornwallis had ordered the seizure of estates of persistent rebels and put John Cruden in charge of them. Cruden claimed that the slaves he received were "almost wholly without clothing, many of them without food" and although he had inoculated them and supplied what he described as wholesome food, good clothing, comfortable quarters and hospital care, many fell sick and died. It had been intended to keep the estates going with slave labor to furnish rice, wood and other supplies for the troops, but the countryside was lost. Those who survived within British lines worked in army departments in and around a Charleston choked with refugees and increasingly difficult to feed.[13] Troubled over the status of the sequestered blacks, Leslie pelted headquarters with questions. Could Cruden sell some to pay the loyalists for their property losses, as they were demanding? What if an officer captured an enemy's horse and a slave was with the beast? "Is that negro looked on to be the property of the officer?" Leslie, like other commanders, treated those who had joined the British "under the faith of our protection" as a separate category. These blacks, he said, "have been very usefull both at the Siege of Savannah and here. [and] have been promised their freedom." Carleton replied that Leslie must use his own judgment on the disposal of captured slaves, but "such as have been promised their freedom, to have it."[14]

Their official correspondence presents the British as behaving scrupulously, but the Americans saw things differently. To Southerners, Moncrief, especially, was a rapacious rogue, and they accused him later of taking and selling for personal profit 800 of his hardworking blacks. Mrs. Mary Butler, appealing for the return of her 200 slaves, charged that Moncrief had boasted he would remove all of them, her "absolute property (if you will allow me to make use of the expression with respect to a fellow creature)," to his East Florida plantations.[15]

Leslie labored under enormous pressure not only from South Carolina rebels, but also from the distraught Charleston loyalists. Most of them were merchants and businessmen, loyalist in name only, and wretched at the thought of losing about £1,000,000 in debts, plus their stocks and slaves. The new governor, John Mathews, threatened to cancel all debts owed them if any slaves belonging to American patriots were taken. When Leslie proposed that confiscated rebel property be sold to compensate the loyalists for their losses, Mathews protested that the latter had not lost a tenth as much as they meant to take in "Negroes and other effects." Leslie suggested each side appoint commissioners to consider the touchy issue. His instructions to his commissioners again drew the distinction that the Americans could not recognize—slaves of American owners who were designated obnoxious because of their service to Britain or who had come over under specific promises of freedom could not be given up. Certificates would be issued for them, however, and a market value set in case of future compensation agreements.[16]

An arrangement was reached on October 10 that the prices for the black refugees were to be paid in six months or deducted from loyalist property left behind. No slave who was returned to his master was to be punished for desertion. The loyalists got only an assurance that the state would not prevent the payment of their just debts or interfere in their attempts to recover other property. This, to them, smacked of victory for the "Carolina Revolters."[17] The frustration among the loyalists going into exile contributed to the difficulty of policing the embarkation. British regular officers were also troublesome. After their long stays in America, Leslie complained, they were attached to their black servants, and "the Slaves are exceeding unwilling to return to hard labour, and severe punishment from their former masters." They wanted to go with the British, taking their wives and children at what looked like becoming a "monstrous Expence." He requested Carleton to set some ceiling on the number of blacks who would be permitted to go.

"Every department, and Every Officer, wishes to include his Slave into the Number to be brought off—They pretend them Spys, or Guides, and of course obnoxious, or under promises of freedom." By another account, "Scarcely an Officer or his wife or mistress was without one or more of the planters' slaves, to whom no doubt they would all have promised freedom," and there were "a great number of amorous connections both sides may have been loath to break."[18]

A joint inspection of departing vessels was arranged, and a place and time were appointed to hand over to the Americans any blacks not entitled to sail. On a search of merchant ships bound for St. Augustine, 136 were judged returnable. But several events then nullified the agreement and prevented the delivery of these or any others. First, British naval commanders refused to allow a search aboard the king's ships. Then in a minor brush between the British and Americans three British soldiers were taken prisoner. The British refused to release any slaves until the soldiers were freed. Mathews would not, or could not, interfere in General Greene's military operations and abruptly withdrew his commissioners. Thereafter General Leslie used an all-British board to screen the embarkees. He blamed Mathews for the collapse of the plan, comparing his own forbearance with the insolence of the victory-flushed Americans. Mathews did have a reputation for a hasty temper, and Americans watching their slaves disappear into the ships bound for the West Indies, Canada, Europe or New York under the blanket label of obnoxious might have wished he had been more mollifying. The governor observed sourly that a "very extraordinary advantage was taken of this discretionary power," so that "almost every negroe, Man, Woman & Child, that were worth the carrying away, were reported as obnoxious, & put on board the transports."[19]

The military clash which had occurred, insignificant in itself, had resulted from Leslie's struggle to keep the unhappy Charleston garrison decently fed during the long wait for ships. He had failed to get a cease-fire agreement from General Greene to allow him to buy provisions in the neighborhood. The Americans were afraid sufficient provisions would simply prolong the evacuation. Leslie therefore sent out armed parties to forage for rice, corn and cattle. In one such expedition the British were attacked by an American contingent led by the impetuous Colonel John Laurens. The young officer, former aide to General Washington, "idol of his country—the glory of the army," and author of the plan to raise and command Southern slave troops, was killed in this "paltry little skirmish."[20]

The evacuation which began slowly in August was completed by December 14, 1782. During the loyalists' last days at Charleston, David George had been befriended by Major General James Paterson. In August, 1782, Paterson was ordered to take over the Halifax military district, and George and his family were among the black refugees who sailed there with him on November 19. He had been gone nearly a month when General Leslie marched his troops through the excited town to the wharf, where they slowly filed onto the ships. General Greene escorted Governor Mathews to the statehouse amid the cheers, and tears, of the inhabitants. Gone were, by Greene's exaggerated estimate, 5,000 to 6,000 blacks "the greater part of which they had once promised to deliver up."[21] These were the lucky ones, it would seem from the contemporary account of David Ramsay. Many blacks were left behind:

> They had been so thoroughly impressed by the British with the expectations of the severest treatment . . . that in order to get off with the retreating army, they would sometimes fasten themselves to the sides of the boats. To prevent this dangerous practice the fingers of some of them were chopped off, and soldiers were posted with cutlasses and bayonets to oblige them to keep at proper distances. Many of them, labouring under diseases, forsaken by their new masters, and destitute of the necessaries of life, perished in the woods. Those who got off with the army were collected on Otter island, where the camp-fever continued to rage . . . some hundreds of them expired. Their dead bodies . . . were devoured by beasts and birds, and to this day [1785] the island is strewed with their bones.[22]

The events at Charleston were well known to Colonel Laurens' grief-stricken father, Henry, when he joined the American negotiators at the Paris peace talks in late November. He became the author of the only clause in the treaty that dealt with black Americans. It put those still awaiting evacuation at New York in deeper jeopardy, for by Article 7, as amended by Laurens, Britain agreed to withdraw its land and naval forces "with all convenient speed, and without causing any destruction, or carrying away any negroes or other property of the American inhabitants." To appreciate this portentous action, we must linger a little over the negotiators. Laurens had built his fortune on slavery, while claiming to abhor it. His slaves were "strongly attached" to him, and none had deserted or been captured. He denounced the British for pretending to set the blacks free while selling them to worse slavery in the West Indies. "What meanness! What complicated wickedness appears in this scene!" he had written his son.

On a diplomatic mission, Laurens was captured at sea and held prisoner for nearly two years in the Tower of London. After he was exchanged for Lord Cornwallis, the Congress directed him to join the Paris talks, but he procrastinated until November 29, 1782. The chief British negotiator was his "particular friend" Richard Oswald, who had furnished bail for his release. Oswald was a wealthy merchant and army contractor who had for years owned the British slave factory, or trading post, on Bance (now Bunce) Island in the Sierra Leone River. His cargoes of slaves had been handled at Charleston for a 10 percent commission by Laurens. Before Laurens reached Paris, the negotiations had covered boundaries, fisheries, compensation for war damages and the collection of debts. Laurens introduced the subject of "the plunders in Carolina, of negroes, plate, &c.," John Adams reported. The next day, November 30, two meetings were held. According to Adams:

> Mr. Laurens said there ought to be a stipulation that the British troops should carry off no negroes or other American property. We all agreed. Mr. Oswald consented. Then the treaties were signed, sealed, and delivered, and we all went out to Passy to dine with Dr. Franklin. . . . I was happy that Mr. Laurens came in, although it was the last day of the conference, and wish he could have been sooner; his apprehension, notwithstanding his deplorable affliction under the recent loss of so excellent a son, is as quick, his judgment as sound, and his heart as firm as ever. He had an opportunity of examining the whole . . . and the article which he caused to be inserted at the very last . . . which would most probably in the multiplicity and hurry of affairs have escaped us, was worth a longer journey, if that had been all.[23]

When he wrote to Secretary of State Robert Livingston, Laurens said modestly that he had reached Paris "in time to offer suggestions which my colleagues were pleased to accept and adopt as necessary." Oswald, sending the signed and sealed treaty to Secretary of State Townshend, pointed to the alteration in Article 7 along with other changes "we have been under the necessity of admitting" without further explanation. "It was easy enough for two old slave merchants like Oswald and Laurens to agree on this," comments diplomatic historian Samuel Flagg Bemis.[24]

This provisional treaty (the final treaty signed on September 3, 1783, did not alter Article 7) reached America the following March, and an armistice followed. In New York, the last British post and packed with refugees, including at least 3,000 blacks, the terms were published in the *Royal Gazette* on March 26, 1783. Boston King recollected that the restoration of peace "diffused universal joy among all parties, except us, who had escaped from slavery, and taken refuge in the English army," for a rumor, prompted by Article 7, swept the black community that all the escaped slaves would be handed back to their owners. White loyalists—despite King's assessment—were equally gloomy. When the proclamation of the end of war was read to a large crowd at the city hall on April 8, it was greeted with groans and hisses. White loyalists were scathing in their denunciations of the British negotiators who, they said, had been routed by the artful Americans. In most states the loyalists were proscribed as traitors, their property was seized, and local committees were trying and even executing them. As at Charleston, they had only promises; by the treaty the United States had agreed to recommend that states modify their confiscation laws and not prevent the collection of debts. Everyone knew that Congress had no power to make them.[25]

General Carleton on April 14 requested Congress to appoint observers to supervise the embarkation under Article 7. The next day he issued a proclamation quoting the article in full and ordering that it be "STRICTLY attended to and COMPLIED with." Overseers were named for both sides.[26]

Carleton must have seen at once that the Paris negotiators, with the government's subsequent approval, had committed his country to a policy radically different from the one he had inherited. The treaty recognized slavery in speaking of "negroes and other property," and by forbidding the removal of "any negroes" of American owners, the negotiators had overturned the pledge of freedom made by successive commanders to those who had deserted to the British side. John Jay, an American negotiator, later summed up the British dilemma neatly: "By this agreement, Britain bound herself to do great wrong to these Slaves;

and yet by not executing it she would do great wrong to their Masters.''

Without hesitation, General Carleton acted to keep his country's promises to the blacks, who indeed, ''refused to be delivered in so unwarrantable a manner,'' insisting on their rights under the proclamations. Their claim far outweighed that of their rebel masters, who had shattered his dream of a stronger and better British America. And he never believed for a moment that his government had intended to break its word to the fugitives. The treaty in his eyes did not deal with them since they were no longer ''property.'' He had found them free, and they would remain so. As he punctiliously advertised the treaty provisions and invited the Americans to help see that they were carried out, he simultaneously performed his obligation to the loyal blacks. He did stop further desertions by specifying that only refugees who had spent a year within the British lines would qualify for transport. All those embarking would require a certificate from Brigadier General Samuel Birch, the New York commandant, that they met the eligibility requirements. In all this, General Carleton acted off his own bat, for he had received no instructions from home.

The certification procedure permitted nearly all black refugees to leave. Boston King exulted, ''Each of us received a certificate . . . which dispelled all our fears, and filled us with joy and gratitude.'' When the onetime slaves duly presented themselves to the embarkation inspectors the magic initials G.B.C. for General Birch's certificate appeared beside their names.[27]

A typical ''passport to freedom'' read:

> This is to certify to all Concerned that the bearer hereof, a Negro, named Joseph Clayton, Aged forty Years, and formerly the property of John Clayton in the Province of Virginia, appears to have come within the British Lines, under the Sanction, and Claims the Privilege of the Proclamation respecting Negroes, heretofore issued for their Protection. Given at New York this fifth Day of May 1783. By order of the Commandant. E. Williams. Major of Brigade.[28]

As Boston King remembered the demoralizing days immediately following publication of the treaty, the blacks had been filled ''with inexpressible anguish and terror'' at the sight of slave owners from Virginia, North Carolina· and elsewhere, now permitted to enter New York, seizing their slaves in the streets ''or even dragging them out of their beds. . . . Many of the slaves had very cruel masters, so that the thoughts of returning home with them embittered life to us. For some days we lost our appetite for food, and sleep departed from our eyes." A Hessian officer heard that returning slaves were treated "so cruelly that it is beyond description."

The parties of slave catchers were often unsuccessful and denounced Carleton's "obstructionist" tactics. One group of thirteen owners from Norfolk and Princess Anne counties in Virginia, trying to recover at least 300 blacks, protested to their state's delegation in Congress when Carleton's aide told them "that no slaves were to be given up, who claimed the benefit of their former proclamations for liberating such slaves as threw themselves under the protection of the British government." They urged the Congress to do something about this glaring violation of the treaty, for hundreds of slaves had already sailed to Nova Scotia. To attempt to recover them from there would cost as much as the slaves were worth. Among these men was John Willoughby, loser of ninety slaves, including Mary Perth and the three girls she had taken with her. Among other blacks who were targets of this search party were Lewis Moore, fifty, now with the engineers department; African-born Robert Keeling, twenty-six, with his wife and small child; and a Godfrey family also attached to the engineers, consisting of Abigail, seventy-five and "nearly worn out," Ned, forty-two, his wife, Elizabeth, thirty, and two children. All these escapees reached Nova Scotia and years later moved on to Sierra Leone.[29]

Theodorick Bland, whose Virginia plantation had been plundered by the British in April, 1781, sent Jacob Morris to New York to look for slaves still at large. Some already had returned, and one at least had been whipped. Another had been outlawed, and Bland had put a price on his head. Morris wrote that he had found Isaac [White], but Kit was at sea. Morris doubted that either would "be prevailed upon to return to their duty, as [Isaac] tells me that by intelligence from Virginia he finds the negroes have been treated with very great severity by their former masters after they returned." Morris also warned that they were "vastly altered for the worse. The blacks at present in this town are, I think, the most worthless, profligate set of scoundrels in the world. I would for my own part scarcely accept of them as a gift."[30]

Virginia Governor Benjamin Harrison was tracing slaves taken in 1781 from his James River plantation. He wanted back, among others, two Black Pioneers, Bobb Harrison, twenty-one, and Phillister, the mute, and William Cheese, forty-five. However, the latter, with his wife, Anney, thirty, went first to Nova Scotia and finally to Sierra Leone. Harrison's emissary in New York was a Richmond merchant, Hugh Walker, who was told by Carleton's secretary he could take none back "without their own concent." Both Bland and Harrison appealed to General Washington to bring pressure on the British commander. Washington had reason to sympathize, having lost slaves, too, but he seemed resigned. He told Harrison, "several of my own are with the Enemy but I scarce ever bestowed a thought on them; they have so many doors through which they can escape from New York, that scarce any thing but an inclination to return . . . will restore many." Washington had told his commissioner in New York, "I am unable to give you their Descriptions; their Names being so easily changed, will be fruitless to give you. If by Chance you should come at the knowledge of any of them, I will be much obliged by your securing them, so that I may obtain them again."[31]

Washington had been considerably embarrassed by an earlier effort to get some of his slaves back. In his long absence from Mount Vernon, a cousin, Lund Washington, was in charge. In 1781 Lund sent gifts of poultry, sheep, hogs and other foodstuffs to a prowling British frigate, the *Savage,* hoping to prevent the sack of Mount Vernon and obtain the return of slaves belonging to both him and the general who had fled to or been seized by the British. Washington reprimanded him: "It would have been a less painful circumstance to me, to have heard . . . they had burnt my House, and laid the plantation in ruins . . . to . . . commune with a parcel of plundering Scoundrels, and request a favor by asking the surrender of my Negroes, was exceedingly ill-judged."

The *Savage* was alleged to have taken a boat and seventeen blacks, in all. Seven were recovered, two of them at Yorktown. But in New York Deborah, now the wife of Harvey Squash, embarked for Nova Scotia. She was described as twenty, stout and pockmarked and had been taken and sold by an artillery captain. Daniel Payne, twenty-two, who said he had abandoned Washington in 1779, also sailed to Nova Scotia, as did Henry Washington, forty-three, who said he had left the general in 1776. Henry Washington was to make the historic move to Sierra Leone.[32]

Advertisements also pursued the escaped slaves. Patrick Wall offered a two-guinea reward for Hannah, who was married to a man leaving with the wagonmaster general's department. Eight dollars were offered for Dianna, about twenty-six, a "mulatto wench" who had run off with a ten-month-old child who was "very black, and had her fore teeth out."

The mother "talks remarkable good English." There was a two-dollar reward for a boy of seven, Ben. "It is supposed he is taken away by some of the people going to Nova-Scotia."[33]

The clamor for the return of slaves intensified as soon as the treaty terms were known. Oddly, Washington did not seem to have noticed Article 7 until Bland pointed it out to him. He was exceptional in his almost fatalistic attitude toward the blacks in British hands. Yet as a fourth-generation slave owner, as one of Virginia's wealthiest planters, and as a conscientious commander in chief he shared the view of his Virginia friends and the members of Congress that the British attitude was totally unacceptable.[34] The "spring fleet" had sailed on April 27 for Nova Scotia with about 7,000 loyalist civilians and troops on board and, among the passengers, 660 black men, women and children. Two ships had left without inspection, contrary to orders, and there was a continuous trickle of refugees making private sailing arrangements. A confrontation with Carleton was inevitable.

The meeting took place on May 6, 1783, at Washington's headquarters, then at the DeWint house at Tappan, New York.[35] The small, snug stone building with steep brick gables has two rooms divided by a passage on ground level, and in the square beamed parlor the two strong-minded generals argued the fate of the 3,000 or so blacks who had yet to make good their escape.

General Carleton sailed up the Hudson River to the rendezvous on board the frigate *Perseverance*. He spent the night at Dobbs Ferry and crossed the river in the morning to be met by the Americans. The generals proceeded the mile or so inland to headquarters in a "chariot," while the rest of the assemblage walked. At the DeWint house an hour was spent in small talk before the conference began. William Smith, in Carleton's party, said Washington opened the meeting by listing the three points for discussion. The first was "The Preservation of Property from being carried off and especially the Negroes." The others related to the timetable for evacuating New York and release of prisoners. Washington spoke, said Smith, "without animation & in a low tone." The evacuation would take time, said Carleton, because of the refugees, some thousands of whom, including blacks, had already departed.

"Mr. Washington appeared to be startled—already imbarked says he," Smith's diary recounts. Even the official American version had him "express his Surprize that after what appeared to him an express Stipulation to the Contrary in the Treaty Negroes . . . should be sent off."

According to Smith: "Sir Guy then observed, that no Interpretation could be put upon the Articles inconsistent with prior Engagemts. binding the National Honor which must be kept with all Colours, and he added that the only Mode was to pay for the Negroes in which case Justice was done to all Parties the Slave and his Owner.'' His government could not have intended to violate ''their Faith to the Negroes who came into the British lines under the Proclamation of his Predecessors.'' Delivering up the blacks would be sending them to possible execution or severe punishment. The very suggestion that a king's minister would deliberately agree to a ''notorious breach of the public faith towards people of any complection'' was an unfriendly act.

The American general argued that Carleton's conduct violated the letter and spirit of the treaty. If this were proved true, Carleton responded, the owners would be compensated. He described the register[36] being kept during the embarkations which listed names, ages, distinguishing marks, names and addresses of former masters. Washington denied that the value of a slave could be determined by such information; the value lay in the slave's industry and sobriety. Slaves might easily change their names or lie about their former masters. They would have no need to lie, Carleton insisted, since they were free and safe. Furthermore, even should Washington's reading of the treaty prove correct, Carleton's method was most likely to produce something for the owners, since without such care or control, the blacks ''would very probably go off and not return to the parts of the Country they came from, or clandestinely get on board the Transports.''

The generals quit the meeting as they entered it. Washington showed no grasp of the ''point of honor'' that seemed so crystal clear to Carleton. In a marquee on the lawn, the party drank wine and bitters, then tucked into a ''plentiful Repast.'' The British returned to their ships.[37]

The plan for a second session on May 7, after each side had put its position in writing, went awry. Carleton took to his bed with an attack of his recurring fever and ague. It could have been a diplomatic illness since it came on just after Carleton received from Washington not the expected memorandum, but a series of questions. William Smith advised him to reply in writing from New York after deliberation. The captain of the frigate was host to Washington and his suite at dinner, and when the American left, with a seventeen-gun salute, ''Sir G left his Bed a few minutes before to take Leave of him.''[38] Washington had not got much for the £500 he reputedly spent on entertaining the recent enemy.[39]

He knew it was hopeless. He wrote Governor Harrison the same day that ''the Slaves which have absconded from their Masters will never be restored to them." And to Lund Washington he said, "the owners of Slaves have very little chance to recover . . . the Negroes, if they do the value of them. . . ."[40]

The Congress was furious. Madison called it a "shameful evasion" and charged Carleton with "a palpable & scandalous misconstruction of the Treaty." Bland proposed that British prisoners of war be held until the slave issue was satisfactorily resolved, but the exchange was too far advanced. Others saw a chance for refusing to conform to the treaty obligation regarding debts owed to loyalists. After all, it was said, Laurens' motive for inserting the provision on slaves was to make sure that they were returned so that their owners would be able to pay these debts. A majority of the Congress opposed an outright declaration that the treaty was broken, but remonstrances were sent to Carleton, and the American delegation in Paris was instructed to protest to Great Britain. The British persistence in "sending away the negroes . . . has irritated the citizens of America to an alarming degree," it was said.[41] Among the Tory refugees, however, Carleton's steadfast conduct was another proof of his dependability.[42]

Washington was instructed on July 16 to withdraw the apparently impotent American embarkation commissioners, but the general decided to maintain the connection for buying beef for the army.[43]

General Washington and the Congressional delegates alike found it hard to believe that Carleton's position was his personal choice and not a trick of the home government. Speculation was rife then over the British (*i.e.,* Carleton's) motives, and they have been the subject of some historical interest since. Greed? Vengeance? Humanity? Honor would seem the correct answer. The New York judge and loyalist exile Thomas Jones, though often an outspoken critic of Britain, grasped this point. The honor of Britain had been pledged, by proclamation, to these "blackamoors," as Jones chose to call them.

> What the Ministry thought when they entered into the provisional articles is another thing. But a set of men who could dismember the Empire . . . for the sake of a peace purposely designed to keep themselves in power, thought the sacrifice of 2,000 negroes, though attended with a breach of national honour . . . a mere bagatelle, when put in a competition with a peace they were humbly begging from American rebels. Sir Guy, however, thought differently of national honour and public faith. He possessed the honour of a soldier, the religion

of a Christian, and the virtues of humanity. He loved his country, he loved his King, and was determined to see neither disgraced. He shuddered at the article that gave up the blacks, and at once resolved to apply a substitute. He was lucky in the thought.[44]

If the British government, as Jones suspected, had been willing to abandon the last enclave of black refugees in New York, it was never put in writing. Indeed, Lord North told Carleton, "The Removal of the Negroes whom you found in the possession of their freedom upon your arrival at New York . . . is certainly an Act of Justice due to them from Us, nor do I see, that the removal of those Negroes, who had been made free before the Execution of the Preliminaries of Peace, can be deemed any Infraction of the Treaty." He praised Carleton's precaution of keeping a record. The king expressed, "in the fullest and most ample Manner, His Royal Approbation."[45]

For forty-three years the rancorous argument over compensation for war-liberated slaves rumbled on, snarling the fulfillment of other treaty provisions and contributing to the bad feeling which brought about the War of 1812. One of Britain's most irritating arguments must have been its insistence that Carleton's policy had been in the best interests of the United States. To have executed Article 7 in the American sense, "as by Mr. Washington, in personal Conference, and with all the Grossness and Ferocity of a Captain of Banditti, was demanded of Him," would have meant the virtual loss of all the slaves. Many would have run away (and been secretly aided to do so); a great number would have "laid Violent Hands on Themselves and, in all likelihood, have destroyed their Wives and Children rather than have been thrown upon a Fate probably not less severe," all with no advantage to anyone. The fact was the American government wanted an excuse for not meeting its treaty obligations to the loyalists. Congress lacked not the will, but the power over the states, in which case it was hardly qualified to negotiate a treaty.[46]

In 1790 Washington's administration stopped asking for the return of the slaves in person; monetary compensation would do. Some agreement on claims was made and paid in 1798, but no account of the settlement appears to survive.[47] In the 1812 War, Britain again made an offer to the slaves of the seaboard to desert. Again many responded and were taken away at the end of the war, 2,000 of them to Nova Scotia. Article I of the Treaty of Ghent in 1814 again spoke of "Slaves or other private property" which must not be carried away. Again the dispute raged over the meaning, the Americans contending that having accepted the slaves as property in the language of the treaty as they did in 1782, Britain could not properly destroy such property by setting it free. The czar was called upon to arbitrate, and in 1822 he decided in favor of the United States. In 1826 Britain agreed to pay a lump sum of $1,204,960 for 3,601 slaves, half of the value claimed.[48]

Even at the time there were those who were uneasy about America's grim pursuit of its freed slaves. In his 1786 address to Congress, Secretary of State John Jay, soon to become president of the Society for the Promotion of the Manumission of Slaves, upheld the legality of the owners' titles to the fugitives but agreed, with Carleton, that it would have been "cruelly perfidious" to have returned them. The acceptance of a money payment as a compromise would be fair to both sides, for "although no price can compensate a Man for bondage for life, yet every Master may be compensated for a runaway Slave."[49]

NOTES

1. Boston King Narrative, p. 157.
2. Wallace Brown, "The Loyalists and the American Revolution," p. 157.
3. Norton, *The British-Americans*, p. 9, estimates 60,000 to 80,000 fled. Some say more—perhaps 100,000. See Note 9, Chapter 2.
4. *Ibid.*
5. Certificates, PANS 170/338, 336, 341, 347. Italics added.
6. Bradley, *Lord Dorchester*, pp. 39, 59, 163; Paul H. Smith, "Sir Guy Carleton, Peace Negotiations, and the Evacuation of New York," p. 252; Willcox, *The American Rebellion, Sir Henry Clinton's Narrative of His Campaigns*, p. 362; Mayor's Address of Welcome, May 24, 1782, PRO 30/55/41; Jones, *History of New York During the Revolutionary War*, vol. 2, pp. 222, 223; MS William Smith Memoirs, vol. 7, May 8 and 13, 1782; Articles of Capitulation at Yorktown, PRO 30/11/58, ff. 12-21; Franklin to Germain, November 6, 1781, CO 5/175; Franklin to Clinton, November 14, 1781, PRO 30/55/33; Franklin to Clinton, December 19, 1781, PRO 30/55/34; Germain to Clinton, January 2, 1782, and Clinton to Clark, January 6, 1782, PRO 30/55/35; Shelburne to Carleton, June 5, 1782, PRO 30/55/42; Carleton to Townshend, November 1, 1782, CO 5/107.
7. Abbott, *New York in the American Revolution*, p. 265; Wrong, *Canada and the American Revolution*, p. 397; Syrett, *Shipping and the American War*, pp. 232-34, 237.
8. Shelburne to Carleton, April 4, 1782, CO 5/106; Wrong, pp. 369-70; Paul Smith, p. 247; Carleton to Haldimand, August 3, 1782, PRO 30/55/45;

Carleton to Haldimand, August 2, 1782, and Carleton to Shelburne, August 14, 1782, CO 5/106; Townshend to Carleton January 1, 1783, PRO 30/55/59; North to Carleton, April 19, 1783, CO 5/108.

9. Associated Loyalists to Carleton, February 13, 1783, PRO 30/55/62; Book of Negroes, PRO 30/55/100, my analysis of data. Those who served with regular units furnished many candidates for Sierra Leone. The notion that the Mansfield decision had ended slavery on British soil appears, however, in the unsigned "Précis relative to Negroes in America," n.d., CO 5/8, Part 1, ff. 112-14.

10. Just one "price list," this from the claim of John Murray of Georgia, AO 12/73, f. 87.

11. Mathews to Leslie, April 12, 1782, enclosed in Carleton to Townshend, May 31, 1783, CO 5/109.

12. Leslie to Clinton, March 12, 1782, PRO 30/55/36; Leslie to Clinton, March 30, 1782, and Moncrief to Clinton, March 13, 1782, PRO 30/55/90; Mathews to White, July 2, 1782, PRO 30/55/44; Carleton to Leslie, September 10, 1782, PRO 30/55/49.

13. Cruden's report, May 22, 1783, in Carleton to Townshend, May 31, 1783, CO 5/109; Leslie to Clinton, December 4, 1781, PRO 30/55/55.

14. Leslie to Carleton, June 27, 1782, PRO 30/55/43; Leslie to Carleton, August 10, 1782, PRO 30/55/46; Leslie to Carleton, October, n.d., 1782, PRO 30/55/53; Carleton to Leslie, n.d., f. 5180, PRO 30/55/45.

15. Ramsay, *History of the Revolution of South-Carlina*, vol. 2, p. 384; McCrady, *History of South Carolina in the Revolution*, p. 661; Butler to Carleton, September 16, 1782, PRO 30/55/49; Siebert, *Loyalists in East Florida*, vol. 1, pp. 115, 341-42.

16. Carleton to Ogilvie and Dupont, n.d., f. 5579, PRO 30/55/49; Loyalists to Carleton, July 23, 1782, PRO 30/55/91; Mathews to Leslie, August 17, 1782, PRO 30/55/46; Mathews to Leslie, October 1, 1782, PRO 30/55/51; Leslie to Wright and Johnson, October 9, 1782, PRO 30/55/90.

17. Agreement of October 10, 1782, PRO 30/55/51; Observations on Charleston Agreement, October 10, 1782, PRO 30/55/54.

18. Leslie to Carleton, October 18, 1782, PRO 30/55/52; McCrady, pp. 661, 662.

19. Blake to Mathews, October 14, 1782, PRO 30/55/51; Mathews to Leslie, October 19, 1782, PRO 30/55/52; McCrady, pp. 658-60; Leslie to Carleton, November 18, 1782, dispatch and private letter, PRO 30/55/54; McCrady, p. 661; Mathews to South Carolina delegates, February 1, 1783, PRO 30/55/61.

20. McCrady, pp. 637, 640-45. Greene's army was worse off, a third of the men "naket" and their beef "perfect carrion." Lee, *Memoirs of the War in the Southern Department*, p. 420; Leslie to Carleton, September 8, 1782, PRO 30/55/48; Ramsay, vol. 2, p. 374.

21. *The Siege of Charleston by the British Fleet and Army*, p. 8; Leslie to

Carleton, November 18, 1782, PRO 30/55/54; Sparks, *The Diplomatic Correspondence of the American Revolution*, vol. 2, p. 287; Siebert, *Legacy of the American Revolution*, p. 8, says 2,211 slaves left Charleston.

22. Ramsay, vol. 2, pp. 32-33.
23. Commager, *Documents of American History*, p. 119; Commager and Morris, *The Spirit of Seventy-Six*, p. 405; Stedman, *History of the Origin, Progress, and Termination of the American War*, vol. 2, p. 443; Wharton, *The Revolutionary Diplomatic Correspondence of the United States*, vol. 5, p. 731; Bemis, *The Diplomacy of the American Revolution*, pp. 194, 195; Hildreth, *The History of the United States of America*, vol. 3, p. 420; John Adams, *Works*, vol. 3, pp. 335, 336-37. A Foreign Office copy of the treaty (FO 93/8/1) shows the "Negro clause" inserted with a caret.
24. Sparks, vol. 2, p. 481; CO 5/8, Part 3, f. 377; Bemis, p. 238.
25. Boston King Narrative; Van Tyne, *The Loyalists in the American Revolution*, pp. 267, 286; Barck, *New York City During the War for Independence*, p. 211; Jones, vol. 2, p. 238; Channing, *A History of the United States*, vol. 3, pp. 367-68.
26. Carleton to Livingston, April 14, 1783, and printed announcement signed Ol. de Lancey, April 15, 1783, PRO 30/55/66; Washington's instructions to commissioners, May 8, 1783, PRO 30/55/68; Carleton Order Book, April 7, 15, 18, 1782, WO 28/9; *Manual of the Corporation of the City of New York*, pp. 774-79.
27. *Journals of Congress*, 1786, vol. 31, p. 866; Uhlendorf, *Revolution in America*, p. 569; Carleton to Townshend, May 28, 1783, CO 5/109; Book of Negroes, PRO 30/55/100, accompanying document on embarkation procedures; "Précis Relative to Negroes in America," n.d., CO 5/8, which may be Carleton's work. Also see Quarles, *Negro in the Revolution*, pp. 167-72. Birch was replaced by Musgrave in August, 1783.
28. PANS 170/344; Book of Negroes, PRO 30/55/100, f. 27; a John Clayton, possibly the same, sailed to St. Johns and had escaped in 1775, *ibid.*, f. 43.
29. Uhlendorf, p. 556; Petition of Inhabitants of Norfolk and Princess Anne Counties, April 28, 1783, PRO 30/55/92; [Madison], *The Papers of James Madison*, vol. 7, pp. 5-6, 6 n.; Book of Negroes, PRO 30/55/100, ff. 70-71, 29-30, 86-87; *Manual of New York*, p. 809.
30. [Bland], *The Bland Papers*, vol. 1, p. xxx; vol. 2, pp. 18, 55, 111; Book of Negroes, PRO 30/55/100, ff. 74-75.
31. *Madison Papers*, vol. 7, p. 7 n.; Book of Negroes, PRO 30/55/100, ff. 70-71; 124-25; Harrison to Carleton, April 18, 1786, PRO 30/55/66; *Writings of Washington*, vol. 26, Washington to Harrison, April 30, 1783, p. 370, and Washington to Parker, April 28, 1783, p. 364.
32. Chastellux, *Travels in North America*, vol. 2, p. 597; *Writings of Washington*, vol. 22, pp. 14-15, 14 n., Washington to Lund Washington, April 30, 1781; Book of Negroes, PRO 30/55/100, ff. 90-91, 150-51. A Daniel, about

nineteen, is on the list of those taken by the *Savage* in 1781, as is a hostler named Harry, about forty. The dates in the text are those the men gave on embarkation.

33. *Royal American Gazette*, July 15, June 17, June 12, 1783.

34. Sparks, vol. 21, pp. 306, 331; *Writings of Washington*, vol. 26, Washington to Bland, March 31, 1783; Mellon, *Early American Views on Negro Slavery*, p. 40; Main, "The One Hundred," pp. 364, 368-83.

35. Some documents relating to the meeting are dated from Orange Town (now Orangeburg) and others from Tappan. MS William Smith Memoirs, vol. 7, May 9, 1786 ff.; *Writings of Washington*, vol. 26, Substance of a Conference, May 6, 1786, pp. 402-6; Washington to Congress, May 8, 1783, p. 411. Carleton to Washington, May 12, 1783, PRO 30/55/69; Washington to Carleton, May 6, 1783, PRO 30/55/68.

36. Carleton's register is, of course, the Book of Negroes, PRO 30/55/100, to which frequent reference has been made.

37. MS William Smith Memoirs.

38. *Ibid.*

39. Abbott, p. 277.

40. *Writings of Washington*, vol. 26, Washington to Harrison, May 6, 1783, and Washington to Lund Washington, May 6, 1783, pp. 401, 406.

41. *Madison Papers*, vol. 7, p. 42, Madison to Randolph, May 13, 1783; p. 7, Madison to Jefferson, same date; p. 28; p. 77, Jones to Madison, May 25, 1783; p. 150, Pendleton to Madison, June 16, 1783. Burnett, *Letters of Members of the Continental Congress*, Izard to Middleton, May 30, 1783, p. 176; *Annals of the Congress of the United States*, vol. 5, col. 1006; Burt, *The United States, Great Britain and British North America*, p. 108; *Journals of Congress*, vol. 4, p. 224; *Manual of New York*, p. 792, Bourdinot to Franklin, June 18, 1783.

42. "Extract of a Letter from an American at New York," Hardwicke Papers, Add. MSS. 35,621 ff. 364-66, printed in Crary, *The Price of Loyalty*, pp. 360-62.

43. *Madison Papers*, vol. 7, p. 165 n., 5; *Writings of Washington*, vol. 26, Washington to Commissioners, June 10, 1783; Commissioners to Carleton, June 17, 1783, copy to North, June 21, 1783, CO 5/8; Smith to Washington, July 15, 1783, in *New York City During the Revolution*, p. 142.

44. Jones, vol. 2, pp. 256-57.

45. North to Carleton, August 8, 1783, and North to Carleton, December 4, 1783, CO 5/8.

46. "Memorandum on the Right of Englishmen Under the 7th Article of the Treaty to Withdraw Negroes from the United States," 1784, Shelburne Papers, Clements Library, vol. 87, p. 389; "Précis relative to Negroes," n.d., CO 5/8.

47. Lindsay, "Diplomatic Relations Between the United States and Great Britain bearing on the Return of Negro Slaves, 1788-1828," pp. 400-18.

48. Hunter Miller, *Treaties and Other International Acts of the United States of*

America, vol. 3, pp. 112, 115, 117, 118-19, 140; Riddell, "Slavery in the Maritime Provinces," pp. 374-75; Lindsay, pp. 417-18; Clairmont and Magill, *Nova Scotian Blacks*, p. 13; John N. Grant, "Black Immigrants into Nova Scotia, 1776-1815," pp. 261-70.

49. *Journals of Congress*, vol. 31, pp. 863-66.

Chapter 4

"OFF AT LAST!"

Now, farewell, my Massa, my Missy, adieu,
More blows and more stripes will I ne'er take from you, . . .
And if I return to the Life that I had,
You can put me in chains, 'cause I surely be mad.[1]

In 1776, not long after the British had reoccupied it, New York was swept by a raging fire. It began about midnight on September 21, in a pile of shavings in a dockside lumberyard—or in a house of ill fame on the wharf near White Hall. It was started by rebel infiltrators or sympathizers—or by accident. In ten hours 493 houses—or perhaps it was 1,000—were consumed. At all events, a fourth of the city was lost. The fire ate its way up the treelined Broad Way, noted for its elegant houses and fine churches. It fanned out toward the North River. The 140-foot steeple of Trinity Church was a flaming beacon. Troops toiled at pulling down buildings to stop the fire's advance. The place was alive with rumors of people found with bundles of matches dipped in rosin and brimstone and of leather water buckets slashed as they sped from hand to hand to be emptied on the flames.[2]

Much of the devastated area was never rebuilt. Sailcloth was stretched between skeletal walls and chimney stacks, and temporary huts, roofed in canvas, were hastily erected. In this "Canvas Town" were crowded many of the black refugees, camp followers, roustabouts and sundry "very lewd and dissolute persons" up to the British departure in 1783. Officers and loyalist gentry commandeered the principal houses, and many others were taken over for troops and public use. With a prewar population of 20,000, New York was second only to Philadelphia among North American cities. About 5,000 inhabitants remained behind when Sir William Howe took it. Badly situated though it was for defense or for provisioning itself from the countryside, New York became the chief base and last stronghold of British operations and the final haven for loyalist refugees. By the end of the war more than 40,000 soldiers and civilians were packed into the southern tip of Manhattan Island.[3]

To speak for them, refugee whites organized the Associated Loyalists, headed by Benjamin Franklin's only son, William, on a salary of £200 a year. In the tedium of confined living, they gathered in the taverns to read gazettes, exchange rumors or draw up petitions. They attended the lively theater, organized charity functions and celebrated the king's birthday each June 4 with a splendid "Feu de Joy." As first Philadelphia, then Savannah and Charleston fell into patriot hands, many lost hope of returning home and arranged passages to Canada, the West Indies or Britain. The massive outflow did not get under way until the peace terms became known. A French aristocrat, the Chevalier de Lavalette, in charge of French troops at Baltimore, indelicately asked General Carleton if he might visit New York before he sailed for France. Carleton, who was anyhow unalterably opposed to the French substituting for America's old British tie, drew a touching cameo in his reply:

Sir,
People in grief shun the inspection of strangers, more particularly of such as have contributed to their misfortune: This City I am persuaded can afford no entertainment to you; multitudes embarking & on the point of leaving the place of their activity, their habitations & their friends for ever; under the agitations of mind inseparable from these distresses tis to be feared even civilities might be mistaken for insult. On a different occasion I should be happy in shewing you every attention in my power, & of convincing you Sir that I am
with much consideration
Your most obedient humble servant[4]

Many inhabitants lived on the king's bounty. For white loyalists there were pensions, housing, free fuel and candles. Orphans, the aged and other indigents received subsistence from the overseers of the poor who collected the rents on houses which rebels had abandoned as well as license fees, fines, contributions and the proceeds of lotteries. By the autumn of 1783 the bill for refugees alone was running above £40,000 a year. Work was exceedingly hard to find, and food, much of it imported, was dear. The winters, given the poor shelter available to so many, were cruel. The 1779-80 season was the worst of the occupation. Snow began to fall in November, and by mid-March it was four feet deep in some places. The harbor was frozen over for thirty-six days, hard enough to pull a cannon across and exposing the city to possible attack.[5]

The blacks formed their own community. The evacuation of 3,000 of them is documented, and since many earlier departures went unrecorded and many remained behind, the total must have been well over that. It was a community in which friendships and marriages were begun and families founded among people from widely separated colonies. Some hundreds continued to work for military departments, while unattached individuals competed for employment as domestic servants, laundresses or artisans. Those best off held steady jobs with the British forces. Many worked in racially mixed company. Most of them were described as laborers or delivered wood and coal, but in one quartermaster general's roll at least two future Sierra Leoneans worked at skilled trades. Charles Dixon, forty-seven, a carpenter when a slave of Willis Wilkinson of Nansemond County, Virginia, continued joinery work in New York, and Peter Young, twenty-one, who had run off from Charles Conner of Crane Island, Virginia, became a blacksmith.[6]

The blacks tended to have the lowest-paid jobs or to be paid less than whites for the same work in the army. The barrackmaster general's department, for example, paid whites more than £4 a month and blacks just under £2.10.0, although all fell in the category of laborer. Another Sierra Leone settler, Toby Castenton (Castleton), and three companions were paid less than £2 each a month in laboring jobs for this department. It may have been economic exploitation, but at least it was not slavery. Castleton had joined Lord Dunmore in 1776.[7]

Some blacks were housed in barracks. At least four were established in New York, at 18 Great George Street, 8 Skinner Street, 36 St. James Street and 10 Church Street, and in Brooklyn near the wagon yard. They were crowded: Sixty-four laborers shared one set of five and a half rooms, seventy-eight others had six and a half rooms, and thirty-seven Black Pioneers lived in three and a half rooms. The ration was one lamp and pint of oil or one pound of candles per room per week.[8]

Attentions to the blacks rankled the Tory historian Judge Thomas Jones. "There were . . . a number of houses . . . which would have rented for at least £1,000 a year . . . which were occupied by a pack of dirty, idle, thieving negroes, invited into the lines by a proclamation of General Clinton," he fumed. "These wretches were supplied with rations of all kinds, equally with the King's troops."[9]

Even more did he resent the punishments meted out to whites who injured blacks under military protection. Jones recounted the case of one Micah Williams, a young loyalist, who kicked a black driver named Quamino who came in a foraging party to pull down a fence for fuel. On Quamino's say-so, Williams was arrested and threatened with a court-martial. He was freed only after apologizing to all, including the black. "Such cruelties did his majesty's loyal subjects suffer," wrote Jones. [10]

A worse penalty was ordered for Thomas Willis, an employee of the police court, who faced a court-martial for trying to force a black man named Caesar onto a ship. Willis had received "a Piece of Gold Coin" for this unsuccessful attempt to return a runaway to New Jersey, but Caesar had come to the British under a proclamation. Willis was found guilty of beating Caesar with a stick, tying his hands behind his back and forcing him to walk through the public streets in that condition. The sentence was 500 lashes. However, in consideration of long service, General Carleton simply ordered him out of New York to Europe or the West Indies as he chose. [11]

The most noticed case involved Jacob Duryee of Westchester County and his escaped slave Francis Griffin. It is not clear just when Griffin escaped and claimed British protection, but Duryee was court-martialed for tying him up and forcing him on board a sloop. Duryee was expelled from British lines and fined 50 guineas, the sum to be appropriated for the "Use Comfort, and Relief of the Poor and Sick Negroes." Later Carleton suspended sentence. The incident provoked an emotional public report that Duryee's sloop was boarded by an insolent "negro colonel and a company of Hessian soldiers" who seized him and his accomplices and held them for trial. The writer called attention to the treaty's directive to the British to "return our slaves, and harbour or conceal no more of them," and to the rising American resentment of the continuing loyalist presence in New York. Griffin soon sailed to Nova Scotia. [12]

Begging and thievery were commonplace in occupied New York, and the jails were full. But Jones' blanket indictment of the blacks reflects a current stereotype of slaves, not fact. The military provost's returns show relatively few black offenders among the many men and women accused of theft, including two large white gangs. The most common offense charged to members of either race was robbery, and the usual sentence for a black was deportation to the West Indies. One black's sentence for attempted arson was six months in jail and 100 lashes each month. [13]

Boston King's New York experiences, if not typical, illustrate the life many of his fellows led. He had arrived on a warship from Charleston, probably in 1781. He could find no work as a carpenter because he did not own his own tools. He became a house servant, but at such low wages that he could not clothe himself. After four months with a second employer he got no pay at all. He quit and worked at odd jobs until he married. His bride, Violet, was twelve years his senior and a former slave of a Colonel Young at Wilmington, North Carolina. King found a paying job on a pilot boat but again was unlucky. On its ninth day at sea the boat was captured by an American whaleboat. Both sides in the war used these small, fast and nearly silent craft for raiding. King was a slave again. "I went on board . . . with a chearful countenance, and asked for bread and water, and made very free with them," he said. "They carried me to Brunswick and used me well."[14]

It was a difficult place to escape from. [New] Brunswick, New Jersey, was an American headquarters, and to get to New York, he would have to cross a mile-wide river mouth from Perth Amboy and walk the length of Staten Island. While thinking and praying, he visited in jail a boy who had been caught while trying to escape. The lad had been tied to a horse's tail and dragged twelve miles to the headquarters. He was kept fastened in stocks. It was "a terrifying sight." King's own experience was teaching him that slavery could be less harsh in the North. Slaves around Baltimore, Philadelphia and New York "have as good victuals as many of the English; for they have meat once a day, and milk for breakfast and supper; and what is better than all, many of the masters send their slaves to school at night, that they may learn to read the Scriptures. This is a privilege indeed. But alas, all these enjoyments could not satisfy me without liberty!"

King observed that at low tide people waded the river at a ferry crossing, guarded to stop slaves. One Sunday night he crept to the riverside. The guards were asleep or in a nearby tavern. He had waded some distance from the shore when he heard them disputing whether a man had entered the water. They were afraid to fire for fear of punishment for negligence. King walked until dawn. He hid through the day and continued to the harbor, stole a boat and rowed to safety.

The New York churches, except for the proloyalist Anglican and related Methodist, were used by the British for hospitals, jails, stores and barracks. Fences and pews became fuel, and the buildings were left in "loathesome" condition.[15] It is possible that some of the blacks in "Canvas Town" kept up their prayer meetings. Some attended the Anglican Trinity Church, where they were catechized by the Reverend

Amos Bull, director of the Charity School, and sometimes given a lecture or sermon. Many became communicants, according to the Reverend Charles Inglis, the rector and future Bishop of Nova Scotia. "This attention to the Negroes is become the more necessary as some thousands of them have escaped into New York from the revolted Colonies," he wrote in 1780. The whole congregation of Trinity went into exile in Nova Scotia.[16]

The Carleton policy of protecting the escaped blacks from seizure and arranging their evacuation became the pretext for harsher acts by patriot committees in the surrounding area. They stripped loyalists of their property, refused to pay compensation and abused them physically if they ventured home after the armistice. A Newark, New Jersey, association alleged violation of Article 7, and as Carleton predicted, this charge "in the same narrow spirit" was taken up by other "elated and intoxicated" Americans. Angry resolutions were passed against allowing those who "wrap our Citizens in flames & cover'd our land with blood" to "pollute a land with their presence (now sacred to liberty)." The persecution did nothing to change Carleton's mind, but it drove increasing numbers of loyalists to New York to seek passage, and with ships in critically short supply, the crush greatly slowed the British evacuation. Carleton told Lord North that it was "utterly impossible to leave exposed to the rage and violence of these people, men of character, whose only offence has been their attachment to the King's Government." He observed to Elias Boudinot, president of the Congress, a body which reflected a nearly universal American suspicion that the British were inexcusably slow to go, that the "violence in the Americans" was making it very hard to carry out his evacuation orders. Humanity and the honor of Britain required him to stay until transport was found for all.[17]

Well over 29,000 loyalists dispersed to Nova Scotia alone. On a single day in August, 5,339 persons applied at the adjutant general's office for passage. There was not room in the transports for many possessions, and New York became a bargain hunter's paradise. Auctions of houses, horses, furniture, books, pictures, clothes and army commissions were advertised daily. Charles Loosley, a tavernkeeper, sold his "superb" royal arms, a profile on copper of the king and his "capital" organ to fellow émigrés going to Nova Scotia, where all would be installed in a new church at St. John. The first tune played on the organ there, he assured readers, would be "God Save the King." Surplus people were disposed of as well. One evacuee offered for sale a "Negro wench," a good plain cook and excellent washer, and her two-year-old child. The

mother was unwilling to go with the family. Another emigrant wished to
sell a boy chimney sweep who would return his new owner a clear
£150-a-year profit.[18]

However it looked to white patriots, the blacks knew that leaving was
not easy. Under the system Carleton had devised, the embarkation
inspectors referred cases in which blacks were claimed to their meetings
as a joint board on Wednesdays at Fraunces Tavern. Surviving records of
their sessions run to August 10, 1783. The disputed blacks were taken off
the ships and held—sometimes in prison—until their hearings. If the case
went to the board (and only ten are recorded), the blacks rarely won. If
the owner was a loyalist, there just was no chance. No British subject
could be divested of his property without his own consent; rebels could,
of course, because their slaves were either freed by proclamation or taken
as war prizes. Judith Jackson had been the slave of a John McLean of
Norfolk, Virginia, a loyalist who, before fleeing to Britain, sold her to a
Jonathan Eilbeck. She, however, had regarded herself as released when
her owner left the country, and she had gone into the British army, where
she washed and ironed for Lord Dunmore, among others. She was
evacuated from Charleston to New York with General Leslie. She
obtained a certificate from General Birch's office and was about to go to
Nova Scotia when Eilbeck arrived in New York, "to Steal me Back to
Virginia & he took all my Cloaths which his Majesty gave me," and
threatened to hang the aide who had signed her certificate. He took her
money and "Stole my Child from me & Sent it to Virginia." The board's
conclusion that she had been rightfully sold to Eilbeck was upheld by
Carleton's adjutant.

Peggy Gwynn's appeal to go with her husband to Nova Scotia was
denied. As her petition explained, a "certain Mr. Crammon . . . wants to
detain me & deprive me of my Liberty that I have had & enjoyed."
Although she claimed protection under Howe's proclamation, "As she is
not a free woman, she must be delivered up to her owner."

Mercy, mother of three, lost her case because she had never actually
been outside the British lines. The property of Gabriel Legget of
Westchester County, who claimed British protection to save his farm,
Mercy deserted him in 1779, the year of Clinton's proclamation, but she
went only to Long Island, and after the Legget farm was commandeered
by the military, she went back, coming into New York only in the
summer of 1783. She was taken off a ship for Nova Scotia and held with
her children in jail for more than a month, while it was decided she did
not qualify.[19]

The great majority of blacks sailed from April through November, 1783, when Carleton's register was kept. It listed 3,000 individuals— 1,336 men, 914 women and 750 children—of whom 2,775 were headed for Nova Scotia. The other 225 went to the West Indies, where some had an option of military service, Quebec, England or Germany (in the case of 50, including a drum corps, attached to a Hessian regiment).[20] The destinations for most of them were Port Roseway (Shelburne-to-be), Annapolis Royal and Port Mouton.

Among the emigrating blacks were many who had been born in Africa and who had reached America in the holds of slave ships. Most of the others were only a generation removed from that agonizing Middle Passage from Africa to America. This time they voyaged as passengers on eighty-one vessels, operating on a veritable shuttle service between New York and the Nova Scotian ports.

Most ships carried racially mixed passenger lists, but in the autumn, as military units began to move out, some ships were almost all black. A total of 1,423 sailed as "Black Companies." A number went still as slaves or as hired or indentured servants to disbanded officers or civilians. Some went as apprentices. A goodly number were recorded under the endearing tag "on his (or her) own Bottom."

The register was the last hurdle in the obstacle course they had run during the war. The inspectors met them on deck to examine their papers and, in the case of claims which could not be settled on the spot, to refer them to the board. Their capsule biographies were then noted solely to establish their market value in case the United States was ever awarded compensation. It was a harrowing interview, but at least it was the last time that they were to be sized up as merchandise.

This Book of Negroes was written by several hands and by people with an erratic, not to say whimsical, approach to spelling and scant knowledge of American geography, so it is probably unreliable on some points. But it tells a good deal about colonial slavery. It shows that the blacks had escaped from every state but New Hampshire and from the West Indies. Two-thirds came from the South (Virginia, South Carolina, Georgia and North Carolina providing recruits in that descending order), while the remainder came from the Middle States of New York, New Jersey and Pennsylvania. They had rejected the "mild" slavery of the North, as well as the "harsher" plantation system. Tom Cain, thirty, had even abandoned a black master, one John Thomas, described as a freeman of Charleston.

Isaac James, twenty-two, a Virginia slave blind in the left eye, and

Samuel Dickison (Dickerson), twenty-four, a slave in New York, were captured by the British, James when his master was killed and Dickison when "taken in arms" in 1776. Both ended their days in Sierra Leone.[21]

About 14 percent told the inspectors they had been born free, had been freed before or during the war or had purchased their own freedom. Among them were a couple freed by Lord Dunmore and a young man whom Maryland's Lord Baltimore had manumitted. A remarkable free family, soon to be outstanding in the Nova Scotia settlement, included Stephen Blucke. He was recorded as thirty-one, physically "stout" and born free at Barbados. With him was his wife, Margaret, forty, who had purchased her freedom from the New York family into which she was born. They were accompanied by twenty-year-old Isabel Gibbins, possibly a daughter. Margaret Blucke had bought Isabel from her own former mistress and then given Isabel her freedom.

There were others of mixed race. Robin Willett at fifty-three was described as "Worn out half Indian. Perfectly Free." Fanny Lacey, thirty-three, was "Born free her Mother being a White Woman." Another Fanny, bearing tribal marks—three scars on each cheek—was liberated when her mistress died in England six years before. Dinah, twenty-three-year-old wife of Bill Browne, a runaway New Jersey slave, was "Born free her Mother an Indian, served her time with Edmd. Palmer who lived & was hang'd at Peeks Kill for being a Tory." Lucinda, twenty-five, presumably was free by marriage, for she, a "stout mulatto wench," went to the St. John River as the wife of a white refugee, Manual Housterman.[22]

In view of American charges that the British evacuated only the fit, leaving the aged, disabled or ill to American charity, it is worth calling attention to the number already seen to be elderly (for that day) or handicapped. Many others, described as crippled, worn out or useless, appear on the rolls. It might have been to the British interest to underrate their money value, of course. Peter French, at ninety-three, was the senior black refugee. He was attached to the wagonmaster general's department and considered "remarkably stout of his age." In the annals of Sierra Leone, the most important of the handicapped evacuees was Moses Wilkinson, blind and lame, who was listed as thirty-six years old at the time of leaving New York for Port Roseway. The former property of Miles Wilkinson of Nansemond County, Virginia, he had escaped in 1776.[23]

Charles Dixon, a carpenter who ended up in Sierra Leone, headed one of the largest family units when he boarded ship in New York. He had run away in 1779 and was now on his way to Port Roseway with a family consisting of his wife, Dolly, forty-one, a "Sizable wench Molo. [mulatto]," and five children. The youngest children on the rolls throughout were usually born free within the British lines.[24]

Nova Scotia became a major sanctuary not because it was ideal, but because it was nearby and thinly settled. The tip of its elongated peninsula was only 100 miles off the Maine coast, and the naval base at Halifax was barely 600 miles from New York. Since the 1760s, most of its settlers had come from New England, and had it not been for a strong British mercantile and military presence and the isolation of its scattered rural residents, Nova Scotia might well have been a fourteenth participant in the rebellion. The sparse population, in addition to the Americans who made up three-fourths of the number, included minorities of French Acadians, Germans and Swiss, English, Ulstermen and Scots. The Micmac, the major Indian tribe, were neither numerous nor troublesome. Although Nova Scotia had a bleak image in many minds, reports that reached General Carleton spoke of "amazing great crops" grown on the drained marshes along the Bay of Fundy, of fine fruits and vegetables "in the greatest perfection," of splendid forests, abundant game and fish as plentiful as anywhere in the world. It was convenient for the West Indian trade, and the climate, if cold, was healthy. Rude Americans, impatient for the Tories to get out, jeered about "Nova Scarcity, where they say is nine months winter, and three months cold weather."[25]

The first loyalists to explore the prospects tended to be lyrical. Edward Winslow, Jr., praised the "magnificent and romantic scene" to friends still in New York and offered to exchange Nova Scotian fish and cranberries for brown sugar and molasses. "We are monstrous poor," he said. But his correspondent, Ward Chipman, assured him that among the loyalists "Nova Scotia is all the rage." Another earlybird, General Timothy Ruggles, raved about delicious apples and scallops as big as saucers and declared Nova Scotia to be "as fine a country as I ever saw in my life."[26]

(At this time Nova Scotia included the largely wilderness area across the Bay of Fundy which, in 1784, would become the separate loyalist-dominated province of New Brunswick.)

In Nova Scotia the refugees would be the responsibility of a new governor, Lieutenant Colonel John Parr. He was sworn in at Halifax on October 9, 1782. Almost the first dispatches he must have studied were from General Carleton. Introducing General Paterson, Carleton warned that many refugees could be expected and land should be reserved for them. A month later Carleton was sending the first loyalist agents to look for sites. Carleton passed along the loyalists' rosy hopes for 500 to 600 acres per family and recommended these outcasts as "real efficient Settlers, already acquainted with all the necessary Arts of Culture, and habituated to Situations of the like Kind, and who, independent of their just claims, will bring a great Accession of Strength as well as Population into the Province."[27] Parr replied, on his inauguration day, on a dismal note. Land was about all he could promise, for "there is not any Houses or Cover to put them under Shelter; this Town is already so crouded" that army recruits had to be "Hutted in the Woods. . . . And when I add the Scarcity and difficulty of providing fuel, and lumber for building which is still greater, the many inconveniences and great distress these people must suffer, if any of them come into this Province this Winter, will sufficiently appear."[28]

The man upon whom the loyalists were being dumped was a dapper figure, nicknamed Cock Robin for his small erect frame, "withered" face, bright eyes and "quick jerky walk." Like Carleton, he was from an English family transplanted to Northern Ireland and a career soldier. He had spent the Revolution as major of the Tower of London. He was extremely sensitive about his rank and dignity.[29] In the next months Carleton regularly recommended that impending arrivals be treated generously, and Parr repeatedly declared that he had reserved land and would provide as many other necessities as he could. Parr worried incessantly about the cost of all this and hoped, even before the trickle of 1782 turned into the flood of 1783, that the treasury was prepared for the expense of the resettlement. As he got to know them, Parr was not quite so pleased with the loyalists as Carleton professed to be. The governor found it impossible to satisfy some, especially the "damned rascally Lawyers and Attorneys," and a few were positively ungrateful.[30]

At no time does Carleton appear to have notified Parr that the newcomers would include a sizable black contingent, about 10 percent of the whole, nor did he propose any special consideration or help to the free blacks because of their former slavery. Leading civilian white loyalists commissioned agents to explore Nova Scotia for the best places to settle, but blacks, along with the majority of whites, were relocated under blanket arrangements for the disbanded military. Without mentioning blacks, Carleton pointed out that certain categories, such as artificers, laborers and armed boatmen, could not be spared until the final evacuation but that land should be held for them. He approved a suggestion that 140 blacks at Port Roseway and Halifax work for the army engineers on a voluntary basis for a year on the same pay and terms as the Black Pioneers to speed up the necessary new building. The suggestion had been made because of the "very extravagant" cost of local labor.[31]

Carleton pushed hard for one measure affecting all the settlers, the abolition of the quitrent. This tax is so insignificant today that it requires definition. As levied in fifteenth-century England, it allowed peasants to discharge their duty to the lord of the manor in a single annual monetary payment instead of in traditional labor or produce. By implication it was low, and the revenues were applied in some way to the general welfare. In England it had come as a welcome substitute for services which were inefficient to collect and onerous to perform. In the North American colonies the quitrent had been levied by the land proprietors or the Crown. In an atmosphere of expanding freedom and on a continent with cheap and plentiful land, the quitrent came to seem an arbitrary and distasteful symbol of feudalism. It was never successfully imposed in New England. Even in Maryland, where it was tactfully administered, it was treated as a burden galling to the settlers' pride. It might be as high as 5 or 10 shillings per 100 acres in Georgia or as low as a shilling or a red rose in South Carolina or Pennsylvania. This "seemingly trivial detail" of the colonial land system "involved a principle quite as fundamental as that of no taxation without representation, and one that probably had more actual influence in bringing about independence than had some of the widely heralded political and constitutional doctrines."[32] The British acknowledged the importance of the tax when they tried to win over rebels by remitting quitrent arrears and offering exemption from the tax for twenty years on postwar land grants. Five hundred tenants of Livingston Manor, New York, required to pay rents in winter wheat, labor or fat hens, took up arms on the Tory side in 1777, believing that if Britain won, they would get freehold titles. They were put down. But during and after the Revolution the quitrent was abolished in the United States, and free tenure became the rule.[33]

In Nova Scotia the quitrent had been introduced early in the eighteenth century, but it yielded little, and nothing at all had been collected since 1772. As a former royal governor General Carleton understood the deep antagonism the levy aroused. In every recommendation he sent to Halifax or London, he argued powerfully for loyalist grants without fees or quitrents:

> Every source of jealousy or suspicion, shou'd be done away for ever. . . . Not only quit rents and fees of office of every sort

should be dispensed with, but no taxes should be imposed in future by Great Britain, nor should any be permitted but for their own benefit and for their provincial defence and security, till their strength becomes respectable, and their wealth will really enable them to contribute to the general support of the Empire.[34]

But London's only concession was to suspend the quitrents for ten years on the grants to loyalists. Carleton made a final appeal to Lord North: Nova Scotia would soon be so important as to repay the public expense. A liberal policy would ensure the colonists' attachment to Britain. (Carleton feared the "republican" sentiment rumored to exist in Nova Scotia, even in high places.) He went on:

Quit Rents will, in all cases, sooner or later become a source of popular disquiet in this Country: They will never, for any considerable length of time, or to any great amount, be either willingly paid or faithfully collected: They will be considered by the people, not like taxes levied from time to time with the free consent of their own representatives, but as a perpetual tribute exacted by the Crown, and at least as a proof that they are Tenants only and not Proprietors of the lands they possess. At the same time it will furnish topics of declamation, which may contribute to propagate the spirit of revolt; and when the minds of the people are once inflamed, they who join the cry of tyranny & oppression, tho' for the sole purpose of evading the payment of their debts to the British merchants, will find a popular pretence for alarm in these Rents. . . . The question is not how far this may be reasonable, but how far it is likely to have weight with the people. . . . Upon accurate enquiry this claim will be found to have yielded, in America, nothing worth notice to the revenues of the Crown.[35]

The general lost his fight in 1783, but as Lord Dorchester and governor general he won it for Upper Canada in the Constitution Act of 1791. For the black loyalists, the issue arose next in Africa. When the proprietors of the Sierra Leone colony sought to impose a quitrent on the settlers from America, they reacted like typical Americans. Carleton had predicted it.

The land grants to the American loyalists were smaller than generally asked for, 100 acres for each civilian household head and 50 acres for each "White or Black person the Family shall consist of." Officers and men of the disbanded forces were entitled to more. The land was to be surveyed without cost to the settlers, and the quitrent (two shillings per 100 acres annually) was suspended for ten years. Certain conditions on improvements and cultivation were imposed, and every grantee had to take an oath of allegiance.[36]

In addition to free passage, most of the refugees leaving New York were promised a year's provisions and tools. It is not clear if the blacks were included—as they ought to have been—among the "realy Poor," who were issued at New York a spade and ax, two yards of woolen cloth, seven yards of linen, two pairs of shoes, two pairs of stockings and one pair of mitts (in the case of men) and for women, three yards wool, six yards linen, two pairs stockings, one pair mitts and one pair of shoes.[37] Boston and Violet King sailed from New York aboard *L'Abondance* on July 31, 1783. Their destination was the rapidly rising settlement of Port Roseway. King was registered as twenty-three and a "stout fellow." She was thirty-five and, in the inspectors' limited vocabulary, a "stout wench." King reported nothing in his memoir of the voyage except to say the ship was "furnished with every necessary." Mary Perth, now listed as forty-three and another "stout wench," boarded the same ship with her three protégées. With her was her husband, Caesar, thirty-seven, a "stout fellow," whom she may have met in New York. On this voyage, *L'Abondance* carried more blacks than any other single ship making the crossing, and they were together to form at Birchtown, near Port Roseway, the most important black community in Nova Scotia.[38]

Thomas Peters, forty-five, described with gross inaccuracy as an "ordinary fellow," sailed in November on the *Joseph James* with the Black Pioneers and others attached to military units. Peters carried a passport "to all Commanders" from Lieutenant Colonel Allan Stewart attesting to faithful, honest service which had "gained the good wishes of his officers and Comrades." With him as the ship weighed anchor on November 3 were his wife, Sally, thirty, and two children, Clairy, twelve, a "likely child," and John, eighteen months. The ship was blown off course by gales and spent the winter in Bermuda. The Peters family did not reach Annapolis Royal until May 25, 1784.[39]

The last blacks sailed on November 30, 1783, from Staten Island, but New York itself was evacuated on November 25, a cold, bright day. The remaining British troops, in smart red coats, marched through the war-worn streets from the Bowery to the river and boarded their boats. General Washington and his "ill-clad and weather beaten" men assembled at the Bowery and Third Avenue to listen for the cannon signal that the British had gone. At the Bull's Head Tavern, where he waited to start the victory parade, Washington learned from an angry aide that there was a delay in raising the American flag at Fort George. Some British bad loser or practical joker had cut the halyards, knocked off the cleats and greased the pole. British sailors were leaning on their oars offshore enjoying the Americans' futile attempts to scramble up. Finally, new cleats were found, and the flag was hauled up to thirteen rounds and three cheers, signaling the end of British rule in the United States. The greatest display of fireworks ever seen in America lit up the sky that night. It began with a dove descending with an olive branch. Carleton composed a dispatch to Lord North on board the frigate *Ceres* off Staten Island, reporting that the British had embarked "without the smallest circumstance of irregularity or misbehavior of any kind."[40]

On General Washington's day of triumph he did not meet Carleton, who, according to a loyalist straggler, appeared "unusually dejected." This partisan observer thought the Americans seemed a shabby lot. All the "respectable people" had left.[41]

The white refugees left their old home with sorely mixed feelings of sorrow, relief and resentment at the British for losing the war. For the freed blacks, however, it was a time of unalloyed thanksgiving. Although once more they faced an uncertain future, they were taking on a new identity as a body of self-selected, self-emancipated, highly motivated men and women who were willing, as they had proved, to take chances with their lives.

The voyage to Nova Scotia took from a week to a fortnight, depending on the destination and the weather. Many of the passages were preceded by at least as long a period aboard a stuffy ship while it was loaded. The experiences written down by Sarah Frost were probably commonplace.[42] With others of the Lloyd's Neck, Long Island, refugee settlement she and her family boarded the *Two Sisters* on May 25, 1783, but it was June 16 before she could write "Off at last!" in her diary. The 250 passengers included 7 blacks who may have been servants or slaves. Before the voyage they had whiled away the days visiting, shopping or picking gooseberries onshore. At night, unable to sleep in the stifling cabin, Mrs. Frost would remain on deck as long as possible. ". . . as it grows towards night, one child cries in one place and one in another. . . . I think sometimes I shall be crazy. There are so many of them." They were still waiting on June 4, when the king's birthday was celebrated with salutes and fireworks from the ships in the harbor, crowded with warships, transports and the somber hulks that held American war prisoners. After a week at sea the convoy was dispersed by the fogs in which Nova Scotia was wreathed so frequently. Three days of calm followed before land was sighted, and on June 26 the Frosts and their fellow passengers were in the St. John River, anchored off Fort Howe.

A Connecticut refugee group, sailing in the *Union* on April 26, spent fifteen days on the same voyage, according to the young teacher, Walter Bates. These people were from a refugee colony at Eaton's Neck, Long Island, and included two blacks, a runaway slave from Connecticut and a nine-year-old indentured girl.

Mrs. Frost and her children stepped onshore to "the roughest land I ever saw" with "not a shelter to go under." Bates reported, as his party reached the site of the future Kingston, thirty miles from the river's mouth, "Nothing but wilderness before our eyes; the women and children *did not refrain from tears!*"

Contemporary Britain felt that it had done well by the loyalists. Many Britons were proud that in the process of finishing a disagreeable war they had freed a good many slaves. When the board of agents for the loyalists in 1788 presented an address of thanks to George III, an allegorical picture was produced by Benjamin West, the American expatriate and court painter. It showed Britannia, attended by Religion and Justice, with outstretched arms receiving the American loyalists. Among such representative figures as Law, Church, Government and an Indian chief were, in the artist's words, "a Negro and Children looking up to Britannia in grateful remembrance of their emancipation from Slavery."[43]

NOTES

1. Chapter title, Sarah Frost's Diary, June 16, 1783, see Note 42; verse, Brand, *Songs of '76: A Folksinger's History of the Revolution*, p. 165, from a broadside printed in England soon after the Revolution.
2. Watson, "Olden Time Researches & Reminiscences of New York City," in *Annals of Philadelphia*, p. 57; "Old New York and Trinity Church," *Collections of the New York Historical Society*, 1871, pp. 270-73; Crary, *The Price of Loyalty*, pp. 166-71.
3. Watson, pp. 17-18; Mayor David Mathews' report, August 25, 1783, PRO 30/55/79; Barck, *New York City During the War for Independence,* pp. 74-96;

Syrett, *Shipping and the American War*, p. 238; Mohl, *Poverty in New York 1783-1825*, pp. 6, 46, 52; Mathews, *The Mark of Honour*, pp. 93 ff.; Jones, *History of New York*, vol. 1, pp. 300-1; Schlesinger, *The Birth of the Nation: a Portrait of the American on the Eve of Independence*, p. 244; Van Tyne, *Loyalists in the Revolution*, pp. 245 ff.; Carleton's Order Book, June 4, 1782, and June 4, 1783, WO 28/9.

4. De Lavalette to Carleton, April 11, 1782, PRO 30/55/55; Carleton to De Lavalette, April 16, 1783, PRO 30/55/66.

5. Van Tyne, p. 255; Barck, pp. 90, 96, 108-9, 111; Mohl, pp. 46-47; Mathews, p. 100.

6. Quartermaster General's Return of Clerks etc., July 1, 1781, PRO 30/55/31; Book of Negroes, PRO 30/55/100, ff. 33-34, 144-45.

7. Expences Barrackmaster General's Department, May 5-26, 1782, PRO 30/55/41; Abstracts of Pay, August 25-October 24, and October 25-November 24, 1783, PRO 30/55/85 and 86; Book of Negroes, PRO 30/55/100, ff. 156-57.

8. List of Barrack Houses, PRO 30/55/97, f. 10349; Coroner's inquest, October 20, 1783, PRO 30/55/84; Returns of Regiments . . . receiving fuel (May, 1782), PRO 30/55/40; Carleton's Order Book, January 9, 1783, WO 28/9.

9. Jones, vol. 2, p. 76.

10. *Ibid.*, pp. 84-85.

11. Carleton's Order Book, May 11, 1783, WO 28/9.

12. Court-martial proceedings, July 11 and 18, 1783, CO 5/110; Carleton's Order Book, July 8 and 22, 1783, WO 28/9; *Manual of the Corporation of New York*, p. 794; Quarles, *The Negro in the American Revolution*, p. 147, says that Hessians sometimes filled vacancies in their ranks with blacks; also Uhlendorf, *Revolution in America*, p. 89. Book of Negroes, PRO 30/55/100, ff. 80-81.

13. Abbott, *New York in the American Revolution*, p. 263; State of the Provost Returns, PRO 30/55/99, including case of James, March 17, 1783; Carleton's Order Book, February 25, 1783, WO 28/9.

14. Boston King Narrative; Book of Negroes, PRO 30/55/100, ff. 70-71; Barck, p. 201.

15. Watson, p. 62; *Manual of the Corporation of New York*, p. 787.

16. Lydekker, *The Life and Letters of Charles Inglis*, pp. 193, 203; Wallace Brown, "The Loyalists and the American Revolution," p. 152.

17. Carleton to Townshend, May 27, 1783, and Carleton to North, June 2, 1783, CO 5/109; Carleton to Boudinot, August 17, 1783, PRO 30/55/78; Carleton to Townshend, November 1, 1782, CO 5/107.

18. Return of Loyalists Gone from New York, November 24, 1783, CO 5/111; Syrett, p. 240; *Manual of the Corporation of New York*, p. 806; Abbott, pp. 273-74; *Royal American Gazette*, June 12, July 2, April 16, 1783.

19. Minutes of the Board of Commissioners, May 30 etc., 1783, PRO

30/55/100; Board of Commissioners on Debt, September 1, 1783, PRO 30/55/93; Jackson to Carleton, September 18, 1783, PRO 30/55/81, printed in Crary, p. 374; Board to Mackenzie, September 20, 1783, PRO 30/55/82; Gwynn to Carleton, n.d., PRO 30/55/82; (a Henry Gwin sailed on July 30, 1783); State of the Provost, August 4, 18, 25, 1783, PRO 30/55/99.

20. Book of Negroes, PRO 30/55/100, f. 157; Return of Loyalists, November 24, 1783, CO 5/111.

21. Book of Negroes, PRO 30/55/100, ff. 90-91, 35-36, 23-24.

22. *Ibid.*, ff. 127-28, 129-30, 22-23, 72-73, 31-32, 23-24, 37-38, 66-67, 19-20.

23. Yoshpe, *The Disposition of the Loyalist Estates in the Southern District of the State of New York*, pp. 91-93; Book of Negroes, PRO 30/55/100, ff. 137-38, 63-64, 127-28, 90-91. The data for Cato Perkins and Moses Wilkinson should be exchanged on f. 90.

24. *Ibid.*, ff. 135-36. It is notable how many escaped as family units.

25. Campbell to Carleton, June 20, 1782, PRO 30/55/42; *Manual of the Corporation of New York*, p. 791.

26. Raymond, *The Winslow Papers*, pp. 189, 106-8.

27. Carleton to Hammond, August 25, 1782, PRO 30/55/48; Carleton to Hammond, September 22, 1782, PRO 30/55/49.

28. Parr to Carleton, October 9, 1782, PRO 30/55/51.

29. Macdonald, "Memoir of Governor John Parr," pp. 47-48. In this eulogy of Parr's services to the loyalists, the author's only reference to blacks is to incoming slaves who "proved a curse to the province for generations," p. 54.

30. Parr to Nepean, October 1, 1783, and Parr to Shelburne, December 16, 1783, CO 217/59.

31. Carleton to Parr, August 22, 1783, and Proposals of Morse to Fox, August 23, 1783, PRO 30/55/78; Fox to Carleton, August 26, 1783, PRO 30/55/79; Carleton to Fox, September 15, 1783, PRO 30/55/81.

32. The basic source for the quitrent in colonial America is Bond, *The Quit-Rent System in the American Colonies*, here specifically pp. 25, 33, 30, 61-62, 38-39, 191-92, 214, 128, 17, 459. Quotation from Professor Charles M. Andrews' "Introduction," p. 11.

33. Dartmouth to Campbell, November 7, 1775, PRO 30/55/68; Morris, *The American Revolution Reconsidered*, p. 61; Lynd, *Class Conflict, Slavery, and the United States Constitution*, pp. 63-77.

34. Carleton to Hammond, September 22, 1782, PRO 30/55/49; Carleton to Townshend, March 15, 1783, CO 5/108.

35. Carleton to Fox, September 5, 1783, and Carleton to North, October 5, 1783, CO 5/111.

36. Bond, p. 380; Abstract of Instructions on Land Grants, n.d., with additions June 10 and August 7, 1783, CO 217/56.

37. Necessaries and Provisions given to Loyalists, June 14, 1783, FO 4/1.

38. Book of Negroes, PRO 30/55/100, ff. 70-71, 94-95.

39. *Ibid.*, ff. 131-32; Certificate of Steward, October 26, 1783, FO 4/1; Report of Enquiry into Complaint of Thomas Peters, March 19, 1792, CO 217/63.

40. *Manual of the Corporation of New York*, pp. 826, 843; Carleton to North, November 28, 1783, CO 5/111; Flexner, *George Washington in the American Revolution, 1775-1783*, pp. 533-34; Abbott, pp. 279-81; Freeman, *George Washington*, vol. 5, pp. 459-62; Ramsay, *The History of the American Revolution*, vol. 2, p. 329.

41. *Winslow Papers*, pp. 152-53.

42. Raymond, *Kingston and the Loyalists of the "Spring Fleet" of A.D. 1783, with Reminiscences of Early Days in Connecticut: a Narrative by Walter Bates, to which is appended a diary written by Sarah Frost on the voyage to St. John, N.B., with the Loyalists of 1783*. Another first-hand account, by Hannah Ingraham, is in Crary, pp. 401-3.

43. Einstein, *Divided Loyalties: Americans in England During the War of Independence*, pp. 241-42; Wilmot, *Historical View of the Commission for Enquiring into the Losses, Services, and Claims of the American Loyalists*, p. vii. I too am convinced that the British were admirable in safeguarding the freedom of escaped slaves, but a moral judgment on British policy should consider this: To serve the New York garrison, 3,000 women—whites from England and blacks from the West Indies—were imported by contract with a Jackson and kept in a huge brothel camp. They are not mentioned in the headquarters papers. Abandoned at the evacuation, they were hounded by rebels and fled into the New Jersey hills, where they became known as Jackson's Whites. See Ottley, *Black Odyssey, the Story of the Negro in America*, p. 64.

Chapter 5

BLACK SATELLITES

> The little town they have built is, I suppose, the only town
> of negroes . . . in America—nay, perhaps in any part of the
> world, except only in Africa.
>
> —JOHN WESLEY[1]

Birchtown, named for the New York commanding officer whose
signature confirmed the free status of the refugee blacks and their largest
community in Nova Scotia, was a satellite of Shelburne, where another
black community existed, made up of the loyalists' slaves and servants.
Thus, free and slave black groups lived nearly side by side for many
years. Birchtown alone contributed half of all the men and women who in
1792 chose to go to Sierra Leone. For such reasons, it merits special
notice.

It lay on the northwest arm of a deep, heart-shaped bay on the Atlantic.
Shelburne was built on the northeast arm, a short ferry ride or walk of
over three miles away. On the little tongue of land between them, an
army barracks for 300 men was put up, and a road was cleared to enable
the troops to march to church. This also improved communications with
Birchtown.[2] The Associated Loyalists were attracted to this area by
reports that it was almost uninhabited and had a beautiful broad harbor,
with a luxuriant growth of spruce, pine, red oak, birch and maple along
the shore. The opportunities for cod fishing, shipbuilding and trade
seemed limitless. What was not so readily discernible was how agricul-
turally poor the sandy soil was and how impenetrable the forest and
swamps would be. Nor was it realized that the harbor could freeze over in
winter.

The vanguard of the refugee influx sailed from New York in a fleet of
almost 300 ships, convoyed by two men-of-war, and dropped anchor in
Port Roseway Harbor on May 4, 1783. The civilians numbered more

than 3,000 and included more than 1,000 who were politely listed by British officials as servants. Among other early arrivals were nearly 800 disbanded troops with 40 more "servants."[3] On board the *Esther* were 36 free blacks, including 18 pioneers attached to the royal engineers department who were to start work on the barracks, storehouses and wharves. Most of the pioneers came from the South and probably had worked with Moncrief at Savannah and Charleston.[4]

Until rough shelters of log, sod and bark could be erected, many newcomers lived on board ships or under tents onshore. A surveying party headed by Benjamin Marston had arrived before them. Marston was an impoverished merchant from Massachusetts, a Harvard College graduate with no known experience in laying out land when appointed deputy surveyor for Shelburne on the recommendation of his influential cousin Edward Winslow. Marston's diary records Shelburne's rise and furnishes many clues to its almost equally rapid decline.[5] Marston had brought a plan for a town on a grid pattern with streets a grand fifty feet wide. He was soon dealing with an anxious and fretful population, notable for a "cursed republican, town-meeting spirit," which insisted in participating in his every decision. In New York the civilian loyalists had been organized into sixteen companies with captains. With one representative of each company, Marston had settled on a town site. But the choice was denounced by others as rough and uneven, so three men from each company chose a different location, and the settlers began "very cheerfully" to fell the trees. The weather was fine and dry, but it was hot in the woods, where the black flies became at times insupportable. Within a week, Marston found his workers becoming indolent, waiting until 11 A.M. to begin and flouting the orders of the "captains." A poor sort for pioneering, Marston decided, being mostly "of the lower class of great towns," barbers, tailors, shoemakers, mechanics, led by a sort of committee of captains as "illiterate" as themselves. Complaints and sounds of mutiny began with the first drawing for town lots. On May 26 a fire, caused by arson or stupidity in the dry brush piled in the streets, destroyed all the belongings of one or two families. On June 4, the king's birthday, no one came to work. They celebrated with a ball to which Marston pointedly refused to go. For several days after, hardly any work was done.

This was the week the Reverend William Black, a twenty three-year-old Methodist evangelist from a Yorkshire immigrant family, chose to make his first visit. After a dancing, cardplaying youth, Black had been converted in 1779 and soon began his tireless travels throughout the province, exhorting with "lips . . . touched with holy fire."[6] When he reached Shelburne, not a house had been completed. He and a companion were given the only bed in the tent of James Barry, who slept in a chair. "The rain beat in upon us during the greater part of the night."[7] Among citizenry of the sort Marston had described, who, if they were anything, probably were Anglicans, and in the general hangover from the king's birthday, Black had no easy time. He preached outdoors to small but attentive groups once on arrival and three times on Sunday. On Monday, June 9, while he was praying, a settler "in the habit of a gentleman" but obviously antagonistic to Dissenters, cursed him, demanding to know by what authority he preached. Black replied that he had as much authority to preach as his critic had to swear. "He went away, uttering dreadful menaces; but presently returned, with two of his companions. . . . They came on like mad bulls of Bashan, with mouths full of blasphemy, oaths, and dreadful imprecations, declaring they would tear me down." A man on the outskirts of the crowd threw a stone, which Black managed to duck. Another leaped upon a stump to compete with the evangelist, but when Black said he was to be pitied, the pretender "belched out a few more oaths" and left. It was good for attendance: "This disturbance brought many more to hear." At the next day's worship most of the congregation was caught up in his oratory and reduced to tears.[8]

This was the rough-and-ready scene when David George reached Shelburne on June 25 with Major General Paterson. George had debarked at Halifax the preceding December with 500 Charleston refugees. Theirs had been a twenty-two-day passage, and he felt "used very ill" on it. No preparation had been made for them in Halifax, but with General Paterson's help, George had looked after his family through the winter.[9] By now George was completely devoted to his ministry. Finding no opportunity to preach "to my own color," he decided to move on to the burgeoning settlement at Shelburne. General Paterson's visit there was connected with the laying out of a grant of land in his name. The arrival was recorded in an irritated note in Marston's diary to the effect that little work was done, that the general's party had dined in his tent, that the "D---l is among these people" and that a boxing match had been staged.[10] It was left to George to record the launching that day of the second Baptist church in Nova Scotia. (The first began at Horton in 1778.) As in far-off Georgia, he began "to sing in the words":

The Black people came far and near, it was so new to them: I

kept on so every night in the week, and appointed a meeting for
the first Lord's-day in a valley between two hills, close by the
river; and a great number of White and Black people came, and
I was so overjoyed with having an opportunity once more of
preaching the word of God, that after I had given out the hymn,
I could not speak for tears.

George's success provoked an uproar among the same element that
had tried to silence William Black. They wanted to drive him out of
town. A white settler, whom he had known in Savannah, however,
offered him a lot with permission to build a house. George quickly put
together a "smart hut" of poles and bark where he carried on his nightly
preaching, the people flocking to him "as though they had come for their
supper." Within a month, his wife and children reached Shelburne on *La
Sophie,* the armed sloop carrying Governor Parr on an official tour of the
loyalist settlements. By now the population had grown to 5,000, the
streets had been named, the town lots numbered and distributed by
lottery, and many of the 50-acre farms were also assigned. Parr stepped
ashore on July 22 and was greeted by cheering residents lined up and
presenting arms on either side of King Street, which divided the town
into halves. From the porch of the brand-new Frith House, he read a
proclamation officially changing the name from Port Roseway to Shelburne, in honor of the Secretary of State who had presided over the peace
negotiations. It was not altogether a happy choice; a good many of the
exiles blamed Shelburne for the "peace without honor." Or, in the
words of a poem composed by the Reverend Jacob Bailey, Shelburne
commemorated:

> A peace that makes men stare and wonder
> And laugh at all the British thunder.[11]

Nonetheless, the crowd raised three cheers and cannon were discharged.
The flag was hoisted upside down, a bad omen. The governor appointed
several magistrates, including Benjamin Marston, and entertained them
on shipboard at an elegant dinner. The next night the leading citizens
gave a public supper and ball which went on "with the greatest festivity
and decorum" until five in the morning.[12] Parr advised General Carleton
that Shelburne would shortly be the most flourishing town in that part of
the world, even though, since the better loyalists had gone elsewhere, he
had to make magistrates of "men whom God Almighty never intended

for the office." Parr directed 500 acres to be laid out for himself a mile and a half below the town and planned a summer holiday house there. He even forecast that Shelburne might one day replace Halifax as the capital.[13]

With the arrival of his family, George received a quarter-acre town lot for a garden and provisions for six months. By his account, this was Governor Parr's doing, but he should have had them anyway. Possibly he had been discriminated against because of his missionary activities. He was delighted that a creek ran through his plot, as it would be convenient for baptisms. The surveyor, Marston, suspected that much land speculation was going on and that the first comers were trying to grab all they could so that late arrivals would have to buy from them.[14]

Although a few additional black families trickled into Shelburne during June, the real start of a separate black community dates from the arrival of *L'Abondance* in August with 409 men, women and children, among them the Boston Kings and Mary and Caesar Perth. The passenger list was studded with other names of people who would become important here or in Sierra Leone, such as the Blucke family, Moses Wilkinson, the blind preacher and Henry Washington, the general's ex-slave. Others were Joseph Brown, thirty, and Luke Jordan, thirty-six, both from Virginia, Hector Peters, twenty, a free man from Charleston, and Nathaniel Snowball, thirty-nine, also an escaped slave from Virginia with his wife, Violet, a son and namesake and baby daughter.[15]

L'Abondance, a military transport, was escorted by the frigate *Cyclops,* on which on August 27, 1783, Marston held a breakfast conference with Captain Christian about the blacks "who by the Governor's orders are to be placed up the N.W. harbor." The next day he showed the site to Stephen Blucke. Blucke is always referred to as "colonel," but there is no record of any wartime service. He was, however, commissioned a lieutenant colonel of the black militia in the Shelburne district on September 7, 1784.[16]

Blucke and his associates approved the site. The work of "laying out lands for Colonel Blucke's black gentry" began on August 30, and Marston was there again running lines on September 1. On September 7, a Sunday, he sent two assistants to what by now had been called Birchtown to continue the job. But there the work was stalled. The Birchtown site was near an area designated for 50-acre farm lots, and on September 19, Marston learned that loyalists, among them Andrew Barclay, had ordered the area laid out for them. The new survey affected 100 acres of Birchtown, "which will utterly ruin it," Marston noted, because it would "shift the niggers at least two lots . . . it seems he has laid out that many on the Black men's grounds." Although the whites were determined to have the land, Marston persuaded the ringleaders to "overhaul that business."[17] It is not clear when the Birchtown survey finished or even how much each black was apportioned. It is clear that their accommodation was slower than for the whites, the first of whom were given house lots seventeen days after arrival. Blacks do not seem to have got any of the eighty-one farms varying from 50 to 550 acres in size which were granted in their vicinity later.[18] Boston King's narrative is not helpful on such points: "We arrived at Burch Town in the month of August, where we all safely landed. Every family had a lot of land, and we exerted all our strength in order to build comfortable huts before the cold weather set in."

A new invasion of 5,000 white settlers in September was neither expected nor welcomed. Common ground at Shelburne had to be sub-divided into lots, and new streets run.[19] It was a mild winter, luckily since many settlers still lived in tents or on ships. The first homes were simple log structures which were later covered in clapboard or replaced with frame dwellings. Usually there was only one room, with a garret above for children's pallets and stores.[20]

David George remained at Shelburne even after Birchtown was established, and when the snow made outdoor meetings uncomfortable, he began to erect a meetinghouse. His first four converts were baptized just before Christmas in his creek. Of all the new settlements, Governor Parr boasted at the end of 1783:

> the most considerable, most flourishing and the most expedi-
> tious, that ever was built in so short a space of time is Shel-
> burne, 800 Houses are already finished, 600 more in great
> forwardness, and several Hundred lately begun upon, with
> Wharfs and other Erections, upwards of 12,000 Inhabitants,
> about 100 sail of Vessels, a most beautiful situation, the Land
> good, and the finest and best Harbour in the World.—I have
> not a doubt of it's being, one day or other, the first Port in this
> part of America.[21]

A more exact population count may be the 8,645 who were "victual-led" at Shelburne in January, 1784, of whom 1,485 were described as "Free Blacks" and as disbanded soldiers. The provincial census later showed Birchtown to have 1,522 persons in 686 households. The original body of settlers there had been increased by more than 40 from London and others from Port Mouton, where the first settlement had burned to the ground.[22] The Shelburne-Birchtown area had the highest concentration of blacks in the province, forming about 40 percent of the population. As with white loyalists, the blacks were organized into companies for convenience in issuing the free government food. In Birchtown there were twenty-one companies run by Colonel Blucke and twenty captains, including John Cuthbert, Robert Nicholson, William O'Neil (O'Neal), Caesar Perth, James Read (Reid) and Nathaniel Snowball, who were to go to Sierra Leone.

The 1784 census showed Birchtown's potential as a nearly self-sufficient village, with thirty-eight occupations listed.[23] The major gap, reflecting the lack of capital, was commerce. There was no storekeeper, but there was one peddler. Unsurprisingly, the largest number of workers, 209, were laborers. There were also 46 carpenters, 37 sawyers and 11 coopers. Fifteen were sailors and 20 involved in boatbuilding as ship's carpenters, calkers, a ropemaker, anchorsmith and sailmaker. There were six blacksmiths, five barbers, four cooks, four bakers, four shoemakers, three tailors and two chimney sweeps. There were one each in such categories as bricklayer, painter, mason, butcher, skinner, miller, tanner, gardener, seamstress, hatter, clothier, weaver, doctor, carman, gentleman's servant, coachman and chairmaker.

Only 31 were listed as farmers. Each household had yard space for growing fruits and vegetables and should also in time receive a tract for farming. As we shall see, many did not, and for those who did there were insuperable problems. Lack of capital and credit were chief among them, but in addition, as whites, too, would learn, it was hard to scratch out a living in that terrain. Most of the whites had to engage in fishing, lumbering, trade or boatbuilding rather than agriculture. Blacks sought paid work in all these fields, on monthly wages or by indenturing themselves, usually for a year at an agreed price of up to $60 or less if food and clothing were furnished. Some employers did meet these obligations, but the muster roll offers numerous examples of serious hardship and discrimination. Some blacks got no money at all, only provisions. All loyalist refugees were entitled to free pork and flour, but if a black worker left the family he had first registered with, he lost his government issue food. Where provisions alone were expected to compensate him, the family got the work virtually free. So many cases occur where, on one or another pretext, the employer withheld the free food that it almost seems to have been a racket.

Some cases hold particular interest, since many of those figuring in them later migrated to Sierra Leone.

Phillis Kizell, eighteen-year-old wife of John, worked for George Patton in return for clothes and provisions, but the muster list says "(never gave her any)." Her husband, then twenty-four, was hired out for three years at $60. African-born and kidnapped by a slave trader as a child, he had joined the British at the Charleston surrender and was with Major Patrick Ferguson, the best British practitioner of guerrilla warfare, when Ferguson was killed at the Battle of King's Mountain on October 7, 1780.[24]

John Gray was hired by Richard Brezels for eight months at 12 guineas. "Never paid him," says the muster list. Jacob Wickfall (Wigfall), a carpenter, was indentured to Joe Wheaton for two years at £40 a year.[25] He fell ill, and Wheaton "turned him away August 1st, 1783 and never gave him any provisions neither has he received any." Betsey Rogers was listed in the Robert Turnbull family, probably as a servant, and Turnbull drew her provisions for a year but gave her none since she did not live on the premises but in Birchtown with her husband, John, and a child of fourteen.

One of the most exploitative employers was Alphea Palmer. Henry McGregor, a laborer, indentured himself to Palmer for a year at £50 but only stayed eight months since they "could not agree." He was unceremoniously "turned off without pay." Thomas London, a cooper, also worked for Palmer, who collected London's food ration from December, 1783, to August, 1784, but gave London only two and a half months' provisions during the whole period. In a third case, Cyrus Williams, married with a small son, also had indentured himself to Palmer for a year for £50. He served the year, according to the muster, "& instead of receiving any Wages [was] obliged to pay 12/-[shillings] a week for drawing his provision."

Thomas Plumm came to Nova Scotia in the Andrew Ross family but left them in July, 1783. Ross still owed Plumm for four months' rations which he withheld from Plumm "at a time he met with an Accident of a piece of Timber falling on his head & fractured his Skull." Samuel Wiley, a single man, was bound for three years at £40 a year, plus victuals and clothing, to Daniel McLeod, but he was "turned off at the end of One Year as he was troubled with the Rheumatism.'' John Primus, was hired by Dr. Kendrick at £4 a month: ''never paid him, lived with him a year.'' His wife, engaged by the doctor at £2 a month, also never received any wages.

Henry Gray, a married laborer, worked for the John Holes family, ''lived with him a Year & Eat in the Family, never paid him anything.'' Stephen Fickland received provisions with loyalist Captain Murray up to February 14, 1784, but ''provisions drawn since he imagines by Captain Murray.'' Cato Perkins, a carpenter, lived with another loyalist family the first six months ''& his provision has been rec'd for a Year by McDonald without his receiving the 6 mo. after he left him.'' John Demps, indentured for a year at £50 to Charles Hart, was not paid, and his wife, Abbey, working in the William Patton family, ''did not get anything but her provisions.'' Patty Thomas ''has always lived by herself & not rec'd. any provisions.''

The free blacks were, in fact, a reservoir of cheap labor.[26] Frequently unable to get work on the surrounding farms, they traveled considerable distances to find jobs. Most white settlers preferred casual labor to regular servants, and they did not always want to maintain the slaves they had brought. The small-scale farms, trades and industries did not make efficient use of large numbers of workers.[27] Some of the slaves were sold to the United States or West Indies, and some were hired out. Others were simply turned out when the free provisions ran out.

Simeon Perkins, the Liverpool merchant, shipowner and farmer, was one of the ''old inhabitants'' of Nova Scotia who took advantage of the influx of workingmen and women. His assiduously kept journal tells a good deal about the labor market. In December, 1783, he purchased from Daniel Grandine, a Shelburne loyalist, the services of two indentured blacks, Anthony and Hagar Loyal. Perkins paid Grandine £50 for the period of December 1 to May 1, 1784. The couple returned to Grandine on schedule and were promptly hired out again to a carpenter. In 1785 they were back with Perkins. Hagar was still with him on February 13, 1788, when Perkins noted approvingly that she knew how to turn the thin skin of a hog's kidney fat into ''exceedingly fine white Leather'' by soaking it for three weeks in soft soap. A few days later he caught ''my Negro hired man Anthony'' drawing rum in his store. It was the first time such a thing had happened, and Loyal pleaded sickness. Perkins promised to think about it, and apparently the outcome of his pondering was favorable, for Loyal was still there in December.[28]

On May 4, 1789, Perkins bought the time of Mary Fowler, fifteen, who had been indentured for nine years from 1785 to Benjamin Arnold. Perkins paid £10 for the remainder of her bond. A year after she joined Perkins, Mary was sent packing. "She does not Suite in our Family, being Saucy, & used to bad Language and going out a Nights." On August 11, 1790, Perkins wrote to Dr. Kendrick at Shelburne for "a Black woman to work in our House." On January 9, 1792, possibly in response to this or a later request, it was noted that "Black Betty, a Negro woman, comes to live at my House on Tryal."[29]

Perkins had his own black servants, or slaves, before the loyalists came, and he also employed free black workers for limited periods in his manifold enterprises. Shelburne or Birchtown men who worked for him included Ned Thomas, a seaman on the schooner *Betsey*; Moses Mount, hired for logging; and Benjamin Field, recruited to build a stone wall. All worked alongside whites. Perkins also took responsibility for some blacks who were stranded by employers or owners. Usually his black workmen were paid lower rates than the whites, but since white wages also fluctuated, it is not easy to discern racial discrimination.

On December 4, 1787, Perkins described the crew of the *Good Fortune* as consisting of three whites paid 40 shillings ($8) a month each and one black paid 30 shillings ($6) for unspecified duties. In May, 1788, Perkins employed Charles Bailey (a former Virginia slave, about twenty-four), whom he described as "part of a carpenter," at 40 shillings a month in shipbuilding. Perkins was to pay $1 in cash and the other $7 in goods. Just a week earlier Perkins had hired a white man, Samuel Fraser, "a good ship carpenter," at 115 shillings, or $23 a month, to be paid in mackerel. Fraser was discharged in June, when he wanted more money. Bailey was then raised to 45 shillings ($9) a month, but in August, after cutting his foot badly, he was fired. At this time his job was helping the calker, and a white man, James Canon, was taken on in his place for the higher pay of $10 a month.[30]

Stephen Blucke, appointed to run a charity school in Birchtown by the Society for the Propagation of the Gospel, augmented his income of 12 shillings per scholar per year by operating a small fishing smack. But most of his fellow inhabitants were not able to do as well as he, and at Christmas, 1787, he appealed to the SPG for clothes for the thirty-eight pupils. He said:

The innumerable hardships, that this new country abounds with, and the very few Opportunitys that the poor blacks enjoy bereaves them of the means for Obtaining more than a scanty pittance of food, and in some families hardly that, which Occasions the poor little objects to be in the pityfull situation, they now endure, and must experience still more, if some relief be not handed them; . . . I apply for this relief humbly beseeching that your charity, may cover them, with a a suit of clothes, a pair of Shoes and a Blanket. . . . Pardon my presumption, worthy Gentlemen . . . my intrusion takes its springs from the anxiety, I am under, for these poor little ones. . . .[31]

Boston King's autobiography adds further details. He lived in Birchtown working as a carpenter (there is no record of his ever receiving a farm) until the harsh winter of 1789, a season of famine.[32] The weather was bitterly cold, bread was scarce, and destitution spread throughout the province. "Many of the poor people," King recalled, "were compelled to sell their best gowns for five pounds of flour, in order to support life. When they had parted with all their clothes, even to their blankets, several of them fell down dead in the streets through hunger. Some killed and eat their dogs and cats; and poverty and distress prevailed on every side."

King was hired by a Shelburne man to make a chest. He worked through the night and early in the morning carried it to the man's house through three-foot drifts of snow. The chest did not suit, and the man ordered another. "On my way home, being pinched with hunger and cold, I fell down several times, thro' weakness, and expected to die upon the spot," said King. He struggled back to Shelburne with the second chest and his saw, which he had decided to sell. This time the chest was accepted and paid for in cornmeal. King managed to sell the other chest for about 25 cents, and he sold the saw as well. It had cost him a guinea, but he took a quarter the price, thankful for a "reprieve from the dreadful anguish of perishing by famine." At least he did not have to "sell" or bind himself as so many other blacks.

Later King was commissioned to build several flat-bottomed boats at £1 each for the salmon fishing, and the same employer persuaded him to go on a fishing voyage. King worked on the salmon and herring catches from June to October. Paid off in Halifax, he and his shipmates each received £15 and two barrels of fish. He returned to Birchtown, bought clothes for Violet and himself, a barrel of flour, three bushels of corn and nine gallons of treacle. His wife had grown twenty bushels of potatoes. "This was the best Winter I ever saw in Burchtown," King declared.

As King was aware, many whites also suffered during these early years. Some at Shelburne had imprudently built showy houses rather than the fishing vessels which, in his opinion and that of many observers, would have made the town prosper. The number of whites on relief became so great that in February, 1789, the overseers of the poor reported that there was no money left over to help the distressed blacks. The legend that most of the loyalist whites were educated, cultured and well-off has given way to an understanding that they were in fact a cross section of America. Uprooting meant drastically reduced circumstances for virtually all of them, and though their hardship in general was relatively milder than the blacks', in many cases they suffered alike. There were few Edward Winslows and Philip Marchintons.[33] The Reverend Jacob Bailey witnessed the trials of Annapolis, where 3,000 loyalists debarked. The church, courthouse and every store and private building were used to shelter them. House rents shot up, and nearly 400 of the "miserable exiles" perished in a violent storm. Bailey feared that "disease, disappointment, poverty, and chagrin, will finish the course of many more." Even five years later, some lived in single-room sod huts, where "men, women, children, pigs, fowls, fleas, bugs, mosquitos, and other domestic insects, mingle in society."[34]

Grinding poverty doubtless contributed to the tensions which exploded at Shelburne in the summer of 1784 in race rioting. The disturbance was a microcosm of the ills of the day, of which poverty was one and exclusivity, greed and rivalry over land grants, distrust of new religious sects and disillusion were others. The blacks became the target for all kinds of pent-up venom.

Not many details are known about the violent events of 1784. We do know that white settlers had tried to grab land meant for the blacks at Birchtown. David George had encountered hostility in finding a place to preach. And Birchtowners had been instrumental in "reducing very considerably the price of work, and various materials."[35] On July 26, 1784, Marston wrote in his diary: "Great Riot today. The disbanded soldiers have risen against the Free negroes to drive them out of Town, because they labour cheaper than they—the soldiers." The rioting went on the following day. Marston reported, "The soldiers force the free negroes to quit the Town—pulled down about 20 of their houses."

The news reached Liverpool on July 29 by way of a fishing schooner. Simeon Perkins recorded it: "They Report that an Extraordinary mob or Riot has happened at Shelburn. Some thousands of People Assembled with Clubbs & Drove the Negroes out of the Town, & threatened Some People."

Marston's diary indicated that he was employing some of disbanded soldiers in surveying operations. It is more than likely that he also employed blacks, possibly for less money. It is reasonable to speculate that Marston at times had more sympathy for the blacks than the "lower order" of whites he treated so scornfully in his diary. Early in his forced exile from Massachusetts he had made several trading voyages to the Caribbean, and at Santa Cruz he had been the horrified spectator of a slave auction. At some stage, the anger of the Shelburne mob turned on him. He was advised to get out. He crossed to the barracks and boarded a ship for Halifax. On August 4 two friends arrived there with the news that the riot was still going on, and Marston might have been hanged had he stayed. The name of one black driven out of Shelburne, Jerry Peiro, appears in the Birchtown muster list.

David George was also persecuted. He had become a huge success as a preacher, with about fifty members in his Baptist church. Nevertheless, like other blacks, he was extremely poor and grateful to Mr. and Mrs. William Taylor, Baptists from London, who gave him a bushel of seed potatoes that first spring. Another white couple, William and Deborah Holmes, lived at Jones Harbor, about twenty miles away. They had been converted by reading the Bible, and hearing of David George, they sailed to Birchtown to meet him. Afterward they took him back to Jones Harbor and then to Liverpool to preach on May 23. They returned to Shelburne with George and testified at his church on a Thursday. On the Sunday he baptized them in his creek. This angered their Shelburne relatives, who, according to George, "raised a mob, and endeavoured to hinder their being baptized. Mrs. Holme's sister especially laid hold of her hair to keep her from going down into the water; but the justices commanded peace, and said that she should be baptized, as she herself desired it."

He continued to be hounded, however, and was finally forced to flee with his family to Birchtown. His Shelburne home probably was in Parr's division, where most of the old soldiers also had been put. "Several of the Black people had houses upon my lot," he recounted, "but forty or fifty disbanded soldiers were employed, who came with the tackle of ships, and turned my dwelling house, and everyone of their houses, quite over; and the Meeting house they would have burned down, had not the ringleader of the mob himself prevented it.'' One night these rioters threatened George while he was preaching. He refused to stop, and ''the next day they came and beat me with sticks, and drove me into a swamp.'' This was when he retreated to Birchtown.

The uprising was so serious that Governor Parr sailed for Shelburne. To placate his ''dear Shelburnites,'' he made Marston a scapegoat. No charges were laid and no investigation was held, despite Marston's demand, and the surveyor was fired. Parr's version of events—that the chief cause of troubles was the surveyor's ''ill-conduct''—was accepted in London. Parr attributed the unrest basically to delays in land allocations.[36]

Where some blacks were slaves, others of their race could never be completely free. The black settlers of Birchtown and Shelburne did not acquire the vote even in those cases where they received land, and their exclusion from elections was a grievance among those who later sought a new home in Africa. They could, however, be taxed.[37] For crimes or misdemeanors they seemed to suffer the same penalties as whites. Prince Frederick, who had served in the wagonmaster general's department, was sentenced at Shelburne to 39 lashes for stealing a pair of shoes, and a white man, Daniel Anderson, suffered an identical penalty for taking a shilling's worth of towels. Britain Murray was hanged for breaking into a house and stealing a large sum of cash. It is interesting, however, that the first person publicly whipped in Shelburne was a black named Diana, sentenced to 200 lashes at the cart's tail one Saturday and 150 more a week later. The last public whipping there also, a sentence of 21 strokes at the whipping post, was administered in 1826 to another black woman.[38]

Even the free blacks in Birchtown were not secure from slavery. Pretending to send one man from there to the town of Barrington, a certain William Castels ''sent him to the West Indies & Sold him,'' leaving the man's wife, Mary Randon, twenty, destitute. Binah Frost's husband had been taken to Jamaica and sold.[39] Slaves were also sold on the open market. The *Royal American Gazette* at Shelburne carried such advertisements as: ''TO BE SOLD. A Healthy, stout, NEGRO BOY, about fourteen years of age.—He has been brought up in a Gentleman's Family, is very handy at Farming, House-work, or attending table, is strictly honest, and has an exceedingly good Temper.'' A $5 reward was offered for Dinah, about twenty-five, who, dressed in a ''blue and white Ticking Petticoat, a purple and white Callico short Gown, and an old blue cloak,'' ran away from Robert Wilkins.[40] One black refugee, Richard, was tracked by his former American master, David Hurd, to Shelburne. Richard was then working as a servant for a William Hill, who did not object to giving him up. But the Shelburne magistrates before whom the case was heard ruled that Richard had been freed by General Carleton's evacuation policy. Hurd appealed, unsuccessfully so far as is known, to Carleton, contending that Richard had lied to the British.[41] In 1786 the Presbyterian minister at Shelburne paid £50 for the freedom of a girl owned by one of his congregation. In 1787, also in Shelburne, Jesse Gray was tried for selling Mary Postill to William Mangham for 100 bushels of potatoes. It was said that Gray did not own her, but when he produced evidence that he had once owned her in the South, he was acquitted.[42]

In a recorded New Brunswick case, a future Sierra Leonean, Zimrie Armstrong, was betrayed in the bargain he had struck with a refugee white loyalist, Samuel Jarvis. Armstrong had agreed to a two-year indenture in return for a promise that Jarvis would buy the freedom of his family, who were slaves. Jarvis was also to set Armstrong up in a trade later. Instead, Jarvis returned to the United States (where he sold Armstrong's wife and children) and left Armstrong working as a servant to his brother, John.[43]

One limitation on the freedom of the blacks, on quite another plane, probably made Birchtown a social center. An early ordinance passed in Shelburne ordered "that fifty handbills be printed immediately, forbidding negro dances and frolicks in this town."[44]

Although Birchtown never rated any encomiums on its physical attractions, its fame spread widely. The novelty of a community of free blacks who had endured such wartime adventures was bound to attract notice. In New York the "Black Town" which had sprung up as part of the "almost incredible" emigration of loyalists was written about. In London the press touted the marvels of Shelburne and "Birch-town, peopled by the negroes from New York . . . whose labours have been found extremely useful . . . in reducing very considerably the price of work." Curiosity prompted a visit by a trio of aides and drinking companions of Prince William Henry (later William IV), who was cruising in Nova Scotian waters in 1788. The men left the barracks to walk two miles to the "negro town called Birch Town," and it was an eye-opener to at least one of them:

> The place is beyond description wretched, situated on the coast
> in the middle of barren rocks, and partly surrounded by a thick
> impenetrable wood. Their huts miserable to guard against

the inclemency of a Nova Scotia winter, and their existence almost depending on what they could lay up in summer. I think I never saw such wretchedness and poverty so strongly perceptible in the garb and countenance of the human species as in these miserable outcasts. I cannot say I was sorry to quit so melancholy a dwelling [thought to be Stephen Blucke's]. We returned by the barracks and dined again with his Royal Highness.[45]

The word that the itinerant preachers spread about Birchtown was of its throbbing religious life, and therefore, a different image was impressed upon John Wesley in England.
He wrote of it affectionately to James Barry in Shelburne:

The little town they have built is, I suppose, the only town of negroes which has been built in America—nay, perhaps in any part of the world, except only in Africa. I doubt not but some of them can read. When, therefore, we send a preacher or two to Nova Scotia, we will send some books to be distributed among them; and they never need want books while I live.[46]

NOTES

1. See Note 46.
2. T. Watson Smith, "The Loyalists at Shelburne," p. 74. Raymond, "The Founding of Shelburne: Benjamin Marston at Halifax, Shelburne and Miramachi," p. 245.
3. Return of Associated Loyalists Embarked for Port Roseway, April 18, 1783, and Embarkation Return of Troops, April 23, 1783, CO 5/109; T. Watson Smith, "The Slave in Canada," pp. 23-24; Mathews, *The Mark of Honour*, p. 95.
4. Edwards, "The Shelburne That Was and Is Not," pp. 194-95; Raymond, pp. 217-18; Book of Negroes, PRO 30/55/100, ff. 29-30.
5. Raymond, pp. 204, 216, 205. Marston's wartime experiences are told in his Memorial, May 1, 1786, AO 12/10. Among his losses were three slaves. *Winslow Papers*, p. 85.
6. Thomas Jackson, *The Lives of Early Methodist Preachers*, vol. 3, p. 146; Fingard, *The Anglican Design in Loyalist Nova Scotia, 1783-1816*, p. 119;

MacLean, *William Black, the Apostle of Methodism in the Maritime Provinces of Canada*, pp. 14, 25.

7. [Wesley], *The Letters of the Rev. John Wesley*, vol. 7, p. 224; Thomas Jackson, p. 152.

8. Jackson, pp. 152-53; T. Watson Smith, "Loyalists at Shelburne," pp. 71-72.

9. David George's Narrative; Parr to Townshend, December 7, 1782, CO 217/56.

10. Raymond, p. 220.

11. Eaton, *The Church of England in Nova Scotia and the Tory Clergy of the Revolution*, p. 136; T. Watson Smith, "Loyalists at Shelburne," p. 64; *Winslow Papers*, p. 142; Edwards, p. 186. As late as 1787 the customs collector was still calling it Port Roseway, Parr to Nepean, May 25, 1787, CO 217/60; Raymond, p. 225.

12. T. Watson Smith, "Loyalists at Shelburne," p. 71; Murdoch, *A History of Nova-Scotia, or Acadie*, vol. 3, pp. 18-19.

13. Parr to Carleton, July 25, 1783, PRO 30/55/75; Raymond, pp. 229, 260, 262; Parr to Nepean, August 13, 1784, CO 217/59.

14. Raymond, pp. 221, 262; Mathews, p. 112. Complaints of bribery and favoritism were reaching Carleton in New York, Carleton to Parr, October 23, 1783, PRO 30/55/84.

15. Book of Negroes, PRO 30/55/100, ff. 92-93, 94-95, 70-71.

16. Raymond, p. 227; [Clarkson], *Clarkson's Mission to America*, p. 191, note 41. Blucke also is often described as an "educated mulatto." He did teach school, but the Book of Negroes, which is very color-conscious, does not list him as part white.

17. Raymond, pp. 228, 232, 233, 235.

18. Gilroy, *Loyalists and Land Settlement in Nova Scotia*, pp. 76 ff., grants at Birchtown, 1787.

19. Dole to Carleton, September 19, 1783, PRO 30/55/93.

20. G. G. Campbell, *History of Nova Scotia*, pp. 152-59.

21. Parr to Shelburne, December 16, 1783, CO 217/59.

22. Persons Victualled at Shelburne January 8, 1784, with Muster Book of the Free Black Settlement of Birch Town, Port Roseway, PAC, MG 9, B 9-14, vol. 1, pp. 107-208.

23. *Ibid.*, occupations are not shown for all adults.

24. Armistead, *A Tribute for the Negro*, pp. 348-50; African Institution 1812 Report, p. 145; Egerton, *The Royal Commission on the Losses and Services of American Loyalists 1783 to 1785*, pp. 46 n., 50 n.; Frank Moore, *Diary of the American Revolution*, vol. 2, pp. 338, 340.

25. It can generally be calculated that the Spanish silver dollar in circulation was worth five shillings ($1) or $4 equal to £1 sterling. A guinea was £1 pound and 1

shilling. Metal English coins also were in use, and accounts were kept in pounds, shillings and pence. See Flemming, "Halifax Currency," pp. 111-37; also helpful is Reverend Kennedy B. Wainwright, "A Comparative Study in Nova Scotian Rural Economy 1788-1872," pp. 78-119.

26. [Hollingsworth], *The Present State of Nova Scotia: With a Brief Account of Canada, and the British Islands on the Coast of North America*, p. 130.

27. Greaves, *The Negro in Canada*, p. 18.

28. [Simeon Perkins], *The Diary of Simeon Perkins*, vol. 36, December 20, 1783; May 27, 1785; February 28 and December 1, 1788; Book of Negroes, PRO 30/55/100, ff. 30-40; Muster Book of Birch Town, 1784.

29. Book of Negroes, PRO 30/55/100, ff. 29-30, 43-44; *Diary of Simeon Perkins*, vol. 36, May 4, 1789; vol. 39, May 5 and August 11, 1790.

30. *Diary of Simeon Perkins*, vol. 36, September 3 and March 1, 1786; scattered entries May-August, 1786, and April 30, 1787; Book of Negroes, PRO 30/55/100, ff. 104-5, 135-36, 86-87.

31. Blucke to Lyttleton, August 1, 1788 and Blucke to Society, December 22, 1787, Dr. Bray's Associates, Canadian Papers, USPG.

32. Boston King Narrative; Akins, "The History of Halifax City," p. 95.

33. Overseers of the Poor to the Honourable Magistrates of Shelburne, February 3, 1789, PAC, MG 9, B 9-14, vol. 1, ff. 209-11. There have been many accounts of the sufferings of white loyalists, for example, Wallace Brown, *The Good Americans*, pp. 197-213. Winslow quickly acquired large holdings; his father received a £300-a-year pension and a 1,000-acre grant. Marchinton, an army supplier at Philadelphia, retired to Halifax with £35,000. *Winslow Papers*, pp. 98, 135, 150-52, 300-1; Wainwright, pp. 102-3.

34. Bartlet, *The Frontier Missionary: A Memoir of the Life of the Rev. Jacob Bailey*, pp. 195, 196, 200, 216.

35. Hollingsworth, p. 130.

36. *Diary of Simeon Perkins*, vol. 36, July 29, 1784; Raymond, "Benjamin Marston of Marblehead, Loyalist, His Trials and Tribulations During the American Revolution," p. 90; Muster Book of Birch Town, 1784, f. 49. Perkins' diary dates George's appearance at Liverpool. Raymond, "Founding of Shelburne," pp. 245, 265-66, 209; Parr to Nepean, August 13, 1784, CO 217/39; Parr to Sydney, September 6, 1784, Parr to Nepean, September 8, 1784, and Parr to Sydney, April 29, 1785, CO 217/57; Sydney to Parr, March 8, 1785, PANS 33. Marston later went to England to press his claim for losses in the Revolution, but received only £105. Poor, without prospects, he joined a 1792 expedition to colonize Bulama, off the West African coast. Philip Beaver, a leader of the disastrous venture, recorded the death of "that truly good and valuable man" on August 12, 1792; Beaver, *African Memoranda*, p. 116. See also John L. Watson, "The Marston Family of Salem, Mass.," pp. 390-403.

37. Raymond, "The Negro in New Brunswick," p. 34; Sharp to Clarkson, July 24, 1792, Clarkson Papers, BL Add. MSS. 41,262A; Thomas Peters' petition,

November, 1790, FO 4/1, f. 419. For slavery in Canada before and after the Revolution, see Winks, *The Blacks in Canada*, Chapters I and II. Also, Riddell, "Slavery in the Maritime Provinces."

38. Book of Negroes, PRO 30/55/100, ff. 144-45; Edwards, p. 318; Smith, "Loyalists at Shelburne," pp. 69, 76-77; *Royal American Gazette*, June 26, 1786; Callahan, *Flight from the Republic*, p. 16.

39. Muster Book of Birch Town, 1784.

40. *Royal American Gazette*, June 19 and July 24, 1786.

41. Memorial of David Hurd, n.d., PRO 30/55/87, f. 9687.

42. Smith, "Loyalists at Shelburne," p. 76; Book of Negroes, PRO 30/55/100, ff. 62-63, lists John Postell, twenty-two, with Robin, twelve, embarked for Shelburne. They had left Andrew Postell in South Carolina five years earlier.

43. Spray, *The Blacks in New Brunswick*, pp. 18-19.

44. Smith, "Loyalists at Shelburne," p. 77.

45. *Manual of the Corporation of New York*, p. 814; *General Evening Post*, August 31-September 2, 1786; [Dyott], *Dyott's Diary, 1781-1845*, p. 57; Smith, "Loyalists at Shelburne," p. 76.

46. Wesley to Barry, July 3, 1784, in *Letters of Wesley*, vol. 7, p. 225.

Chapter 6

THE SCRAMBLE FOR LAND

> . . . of course the black people, unequal to solicit and
> manage as the white people did, and habitually less
> considered . . . were late located, and without proper
> method.
> —LIEUTENANT GOVERNOR SIR JOHN WENTWORTH[1]

The first important test of "British freedom" came in the distribution
of land. This was the focus of swirling local controversies, one cause of
the Shelburne race riot and Governor Parr's greatest administrative
headache. The prospect of free land had enticed men to enlist as soldiers
and had strengthened civilians in their resolve to remain true to the king.
It was understood by those blacks who enlisted in or served with the
British forces that they would fare much the same as the whites of their
rank where future allocations of lands and provisions were concerned.

Thomas Peters and Murphy Steele, the Black Pioneer sergeants, for
example, referred directly to promises made at their enlistment that
Pioneers would receive "land & provitions the same as the rest of the
Disbanded Soldiers" when they petitioned Governor Parr on behalf of
their unit at Annapolis Royal in 1784. Thomas Richardson, William
Goding and the nonagenarian Peter French appealed to the governor in
1786 on behalf of their fellow "Free Negroes" at Manchester for "such
things as we are entitled to." Similarly, Pompey Younge petitioned
individually for "his proportion of Land." And in New Brunswick,
William Fisher, sick and starving during the winter of 1785, applied to
Governor Carleton for the land and provisions "the same as is granted to
all other loyalists." At least some of the blacks believed they were to get
50 acres of land running from the water's edge.[2]

There is no doubt that provincial officials failed to meet the blacks'
expectations and, what was worse for the community as a whole, failed
to provide them, as the white settlers were provided, with the essential

basis for self-support. The majority received no land. This guaranteed that most newly freed blacks would become a rootless servant class. Some land was allotted to a minority of blacks, and in doing that much, Nova Scotia could be said to be progressive for the day. It was crucial, however, to the continuing development of the black loyalists as a group that in the main their hopes to become independent yeomen were dashed.

The division of land in Nova Scotia and that part of it which became New Brunswick was based on 1764 instructions for new settlers which allowed 100 acres for the head of the family and 50 acres more for each member of the household. Since households tended to be large and the count included servants or slaves, as well as children, holdings averaged about 500 acres per family. Certain special favors were given the loyalists: No purchase price was required, not even a token one; surveys and grants were to be free, and quitrents would not be exacted for ten years. Large additional grants were available to former field officers.[3] Keenly interested as he was in every detail of the loyalists' relocation, General Carleton offered Governor Parr a plan giving each family a town lot and 20 acres on the outskirts on which to grow vegetables and pasture cows. For those who wanted to be "real Farmers," up to 200 acres more would be granted beyond a nine-mile radius of the town, although these people could also have a town lot if they built a house on it.[4]

The only reference to land distribution for blacks which I have found is also General Carleton's, and it gives them smaller farms. In notifying Halifax of the impending departure of the Black Pioneers for Annapolis Royal, Carleton recommended that each family be given a town lot and "about twenty acres in the vicinage . . . and if as farmers at a distance, their Grant may be extended to one hundred acres."[5] The absence of any special government instructions for the black settlers could have been an oversight or a sign that they were to be on the same footing with all comers.

With the single exception of Stephen Blucke, who in 1787 was granted 200 acres on Port Roseway Harbor,[6] no black immigrant acquired holdings that compare with those given whites. Everywhere in this empty land, no matter who did the surveying or supervised the lotteries, they got markedly less. It was either official policy or unstated assumption. It bred bitterness in the black settlers and in numerous cases dissipated the purposiveness with which they had thrown in their lot with the British.

Less than half the blacks obtained any land at all. Those who fell into this category received substantially smaller tracts and often at a considerably later date than whites. An examination of loyalist land papers by Marion Gilroy revealed 167 grants of land to identified blacks and 327 warrants (that is, orders to survey in preparation for granting) issued to black settlers between 1784 and 1789. Thus, 494 of the blacks— including 26 women—received or were in the process of receiving property within six years of their arrival.[7] There may have been a few others in this fortunate group. For example, 39 persons on land lists for Preston probably were black. A 1784 report on land grants shows 10 names awarded 50 acres each, compared with 100- to 1,000-acre allotments to the other 114 recipients. At least 6 of the 10 went to Sierra Leone, and so were black; probably all 10 were. Several of these persons also received town lots in 1784 or 1787, usually 1 1/2 acres in size. Then, in a 1786 list of grants where 57 names are down for 100 to 250 acres each, there are 29 other names with 50-acre allotments. At least 14 of the 29 went to Sierra Leone, and again it is probable that all the group were black. Two of them, Squire Courtland and Scott Murray (with different spellings on different lists), several months later received another 50 acres or exchanged their grants. Christopher Edmunson of Preston received 100 acres in 1787, the only black with a farm so large there.[8]

If one then adds the 39, the total with land allotments becomes 533, or 40 percent of the adult male blacks who left New York in 1783.

As for the size of holdings, the Preston grants are one example of the way the blacks show up at the bottom. There are others. Warrants for surveying land at Clements in Annapolis County were issued in 1789 to 148 blacks and were for 50 acres each with one exception, 100 acres to Joseph Leonard, teacher and spokesman. Whites at the same time were allotted 100 to 600 acres. In Shelburne township, there were warrants to 179 blacks for farms of 20 to 40 acres. Most of the whites on the same list received more than 100 acres. In sum, the available information points to such unequal treatment that only one black, Stephen Blucke, received the allotment due a three-member household, and only four were given 100 acres, the entitlement of an unmarried adult, while, to repeat, 60 percent are not recorded as having got any land at all.[9]

Black refugees found new homes in many parts of the province, but rarely where the land was good. Most of them found themselves on the Atlantic shore, on the edge of the undulating, forested upland region, where the soil was shallow and marginally fertile. Birchtown was the largest black community in this region, and another sizable settlement

was made at Preston, east of Halifax. A third grew up around Guysborough and Tracadie in the northeast, "the worst land in Nova Scotia."
Fewer blacks were located on the best land—the lowlands on the north,
including the Annapolis and Minas Basins and the marshlands where
high tides of the Bay of Fundy deposited rich silt. Here there were black
communities only at Digby and Clements. Across the bay, a few hundred
blacks reached the St. John River and spread farther afield.[10]

One notes that the great majority of blacks settled in segregated
communities, but this is not necessarily a sign of racial prejudice. It was a
characteristic of Nova Scotian settlement through several waves of
migration that groups tended to settle as groups. Yorkshiremen, Germans, Scots-Irish and New Englanders in turn had founded communities. In the case of loyalists, some congregations moved bodily to
Nova Scotia, troops were disbanded with their units, and there were
separate settlements for Hessians.

Even if all the black settlers had received their quantity of land, and
even if it had been of a quality to support them, special hardship would
have attended them for they came virtually empty-handed. They had no
tools, no capital, no livestock and no credit. They had no servants to
share the backbreaking work of clearing and planting. They had fewer
children than the white families. The 1784 muster roll of blacks in
Annapolis County showed that of the fifty-nine married couples, twenty-
six had no children, and in the other households the children per family
averaged 1.5. The Birchtown muster the same year disclosed the same
ratio. A typical black household averaged 2.3 persons compared to a
white family average of 5.[11]

Furthermore, for virtually all the blacks, this was the first experience
of landowning and management. To these handicaps should be added the
special burden of habits and attitudes implanted by a lifetime of slavery,
but it must be said that these black loyalists had proved remarkably
adaptable thus far on their journey to independence. Yet few white
settlers were quite as destitute as they, and no special allowance was
made or attention provided for them by the admittedly hard-pressed
government. Blessed only with their freedom and the indomitable will
which had brought them to Nova Scotia, the blacks scrambled to live,
working on their own or other men's lands for part of the crop, hiring out
as laborers and artisans or indenturing themselves as servants in a marginally, but significantly different, form of slavery. Again, British wartime policy was seen to be not so much a humanitarian one, to help black

people, as a practical method of hurting their masters by removing their labor, and that objective had been achieved. Freed, the blacks were cut adrift. General Carleton said that the Black Pioneers were considered disbanded when they embarked. They could make no further demands for pay and clothing. Disbanded British regulars at least got two pairs of stockings, two pairs of mitts, a pair of shoes, extra clothing, an ax and a spade.[12]

White settlers had their own complaints about the way the land was apportioned, but virtually all white loyalists who sought an allotment got it. Each refugee had to apply, and the procedure thereafter involved six pieces of paper and the collaboration of the governor and council, surveyor general of the king's woods, surveyor general and attorney general. Few newcomers had completed the process within a year. A 1784 report, showing the presence of 28,347 loyalists or New Inhabitants including "about 3,000 Negroes" in a population of 42,747, regretted that only a "very small proportion were yet on their lands." The author, Colonel Morse, concluded, "if these poor people who, from want of land to cultivate and raise a subsistence . . . are not fed by Government for a considerable time longer, they must perish."[13]

The royal bounty of food was repeatedly extended after the first year. It had been hoped (devoutly by the cost-conscious government) that the new population would be able to support itself fully in three years' time, but as much as fifteen years after the influx, supplicants were still asking for assistance. As he forwarded to London one appeal of nearly 600 loyalists in Annapolis County in 1786, Governor Parr confirmed that the signers were actually eating their next year's seed. These were all white settlers. A starving slave was hanged in Halifax in 1785 for stealing a bag of potatoes. Cornmeal and molasses constituted the diet of most blacks, and whites supplemented these basic foodstuffs with codfish and biscuit.[14] The periodical musters, or censuses, were ordered to weed out from the relief list the venal, wealthy or lazy and to force people to work on their farms, on roads to open up new territory or at the fishing, logging and shipbuilding which it was hoped would in time bring prosperity. Whites, as well as blacks, were berated for idleness, dissipation and irresponsibility while the free provisions held out. But judgments often were harsher on the blacks. One New Brunswick historian, for example, declared that "it was quickly discovered that they had no aptitude or temper for work in the freshly turned fields" and "only in the domestic routine of households were they really useful." Ignoring the fact that they seldom had a chance to become farmers, he concluded that they "showed no disposition" to farm and "drifted into honourable servitude on the estates of landed proprietors who were pleased to take them at high wages." But in another work, the same author reaches a markedly different conclusion: ". . . the blacks had shown themselves, *like most whites,* to be incapable of farming *inferior and stony soil.*"[15] White refugees, when single and the government bounty ran out, also left their farms to become servants, get other work or, an option not open to blacks, go back to the United States.[16]

Bishop Inglis was a fairly evenhanded critic of both races of settlers. Replying to a query from the Archbishop of Canterbury, he said of the blacks, "In general, they are very indolent and improvident (the natural consequence of their former state, and sudden emancipation,) and hereby reduced to distress and want. Latterly they seem to manage better. . . . It is probable that the descendants of those Blacks who are now free, will in general be as industrious and useful as white people of the same rank." To another correspondent he spoke of the "indolence & expensive living" characterizing the white settlers, and his pleasure at seeing how necessity, in a very few years, had produced industry and frugality among them.[17]

In the surviving records of men of affairs such as Edward Winslow, the presence or the plight of the blacks is almost never noticed. But when, in August, 1784, the *Sally* sailed into Halifax Harbor from London with nearly 300 more destitute loyalist pensioners, disbanded soldiers and blacks formerly in the land or sea services, Winslow was provoked. He wrote his wife:

> It is not possible for any pen or tongue to describe the variety of wretchedness that is at this time exhibited in the streets of this place. This is what we call a board day, & the yard in front of my House has been crowded since eight o'clock with the most miserable objects that ever were beheld. . . . The good people of England have collected a whole ship load of . . . vagrants . . . and sent them out to Nova Scotia. . . . Such as are able to crawl are begging for a proportion of provisions at my door. . . . As soon as we get rid of such a sett as these, another little multitude appears of old crippled Refugees. . . . Next to them perhaps comes an unfortunate set of Blackies begging for Christ's sake that Masser would give 'em a little provi-

sion if it's only for one week. "He wife sick; He children sick; and He will die if He have not some." I long to retreat from such scenes.[18]

Sir John Wentworth, former royal governor of New Hampshire and in 1783 made surveyor general of the king's woods, wrote of the black settlers only thirteen years later, when as lieutenant governor he had to deal with the newly arrived Jamaican Maroons, the second black immigrant group in Nova Scotian history. Although given to sweeping generalization, Wentworth shows an awareness of the special problems the blacks faced. They were "slaves, suddenly emancipated from Masters, whose essential Interest it was to suppress and extinguish every idea of providing for themselves, or having any property. With these habits, they joined the army . . . where obedience and provided subsistence were still united; here they gathered more dissoluteness than economical discretion." After their arrival with thousands of others in need, he noted:

> The approaching winter excited apprehensions, and universal competition to provide places and lodgments. The government here . . . were embarrassed in the midst of their endeavours and exertions to accommodate the people; of course the black people unequal to solicit and manage as the white people did, and habitually less considered, they had not as much attention as otherwise they might have had, and which was more necessary for them. . . . It therefore resulted, that they were late located, and without proper method.[19]

Another observer, Alexander Howe, a loyalist and Annapolis County judge, also with hindsight concluded that the black loyalists had been victims of "An injudicious and unjust mode of assigning them their lands." When they left Nova Scotia, he believed, it was chiefly because they had not been treated properly in this particular.[20]

It is instructive to compare the treatment of the Maroons in 1796. The 500 Maroons were deported from Jamaica and arrived unheralded in Halifax. From the first, they were handled as a special case, lodged together two miles from the capital, supplied with teachers, doctors and a chaplain, amply fed and furnished with heavy linen, flannel, stout blue greatcoats lined with red baize, yarn hose, woolen caps, blankets, shoes and household utensils. They even had their own laws; small offenses could be tried before their own supervisors from Jamaica. Attempts were made to draw them into various kinds of employment, notably in Governor Wentworth's personal service, while plans were developed to settle them on a tract affording about six acres per person. Unlike the Nova Scotians, few of the Jamaican Maroons were at all interested in farming, alien to their tradition.[21]

By contrast, the petition of Richardson, French and Goding told a story of neglect. The signers (with marks) pointed out that in the two years they had been in (old) Sydney County they had received neither town nor farm lots. Now they had been ordered off the town common on which they squatted. They begged the governor to locate them on lands "without which we most inevitable perish." They received no farm tools and had no money to purchase them. Nor had they been given clothing, ammunition for hunting or boards for building.[22]

A year later, and four years after their arrival, French and Richardson joined Thomas Brownspriggs and others in a petition for land, and this time they were successful in getting a tract along Tracadie Harbor. The history of this group is again the story of struggle. They were the survivors of nearly 150 veterans of service with the wagonmaster general's department who had moved in 1784 to Chedabucto Bay near Guysborough, a small town of French origin renamed to honor General Carleton. During the winter of 1785-86 both blacks and whites suffered severely when a supply ship was hijacked. The blacks lived in the woods but had no guns or ammunition to hunt game. Their white neighbors were slightly better off but did not help them; prejudice tended to be most intense in the most isolated places. A story is told of Tom Thompson,[23] a South Carolina slave who had defected to the British and who now lived on what was locally known as Niggertown Hill. Although he was not yet thirty, Thompson was weak from the lack of food. Trying to get home one day, he felt faint and decided to ask for help. As he approached Captain Ralph Cunningham's house, he heard a voice calling a dog. Believing that the dog would be set upon him, Thompson went away. By the time he reached home his feet were frozen. Both were amputated.

After Brownspriggs and other survivors of this dreadful winter turned to Governor Parr for land, 3,000 acres were laid out at Tracadie Harbor in 40-acre farms for seventy-four people, at some distance from the white settlement. The land was too poor and the grants too small to make them independent. Nevertheless, the grantees cleared it, built huts and planted potatoes. In 1788, Bishop Inglis appointed Brownspriggs a teacher for the Society for the Propagation of the Gospel. He was given 100 books and tracts, and the school soon had twenty-three pupils.[24] None of the Tracadie settlers went to Sierra Leone. In their remote community, none of them heard the news of it.[25]

The muddles that land distribution could involve are illustrated at Preston, almost a suburb of Halifax, where there grew up an important free black community that in due course sent a strong contingent to Sierra Leone. According to the surveyor Theophilus Chamberlain, very few blacks were included in the original grant of land in 1784 because of "not being here." The list shows only ten names which are or could be blacks. The next large grant in the spring of 1786 included 29 identifiable names. Eleven more were assigned lands later that year. All but one of the Preston grants to blacks were for 50 acres each, though no white got less than 100. A general survey was made of the tract, but nothing was done to divide it into individual lots, for about this time the government stopped the pay of Chamberlain and other surveyors. Chamberlain, no longer on a government salary, believed the grantees should pay the costs of running lines, despite the promise made all loyalists that the lands would be free of expense. On the whole, the whites made their own arrangements. Two or three blacks also paid the fees, but the rest made "continual murmurs and complaints." To those who grumbled that they had not even seen their allotted lands, Chamberlain declared himself willing to show them, "but for this they have been too negligent, and every one knows that Acres of Land are not like a Flock of Sheep that may be drove by Thousands before Peoples Door for them to look on." About 150 blacks continued to live amid four times as many whites in the Preston area, but not all on the farms intended for them.[26]

Only one inquiry was held on a complaint by a black settler, and that in 1791. It was precipitated by the doughty Thomas Peters, who disembarked at Annapolis Royal with other Black Pioneers belatedly on May 25, 1784. The town was a French, then a British, military post. The county of Annapolis also included Granville, Wilmot and Digby at the opposite end of the basin. As he once passed Digby, Benjamin Marston dismissed it as a "sad grog drinking place." Near Digby, the county's largest black community had sprung up by the time of Peters' arrival. About 500 white families, nearly all disbanded officers and soldiers, lived at Digby. True to the pattern elsewhere, their families averaged almost 5 persons, while the black population of some 109 families, on average, had 2 to the household.[27]

Peters and his fellow sergeant, Murphy Steele, became the spokesmen for the little band of latecomers. On August 21 they petitioned Governor

Parr to intercede. The Pioneers would be much obliged if they could have the articles allowed by government. They pointed out: "When We first Inlisted & swore we was promised that we should have land & provitions the same as the Rest of the Disbanded Soldiers, Which We have not Received."[28]

Under the land grant procedure, a local board of loyalist agents assigned lands and heard disputes. Grants were issued when the board furnished the surveyor general in Halifax with an allotment plan. Peters' effort to reach the governor directly had passed through the hands of Charles Morris, the surveyor general, who had sent the petition to Parr with a note to the effect that if Parr would indicate what quantity of land should be given the Pioneers, Morris would see that it was laid out. Parr set the figure at 20 acres, including a one-acre town lot, for each of the twenty-one men for whom Peters and Steele spoke. The three sergeants (the other was Abram Leslie) were to have 30 acres each.[29] The one-acre town lots were laid out in George Brinley township and granted in 1785 by Major Thomas Millidge, a deputy surveyor.

Millidge, a New Jersey loyalist, took a serious interest in the welfare of the black people. In March, 1785, after laying out the town lots and while waiting for the snow to melt in the woods so that he could plot the little farms, he recommended to Governor Parr that the blacks remain undisturbed, although there were "some in the place that wished to remove these People." The blacks were living a mile above Digby, on Little Joggin, a convenient mooring place for small fishing craft. They had built huts, some of them quite comfortable, and had planted gardens. Millidge believed that "if suffered to enjoy the Lands they are now in possession of may be in a likely way with industry to make themselves a comfortable liveing." If forced to move, they would have to "begin anew, with much Cost and expence which they are not able to undergo. I do not believe they have Five Pounds to move with; if they are obliged to remove nothing but the utmost distress will be the consequence."

He concluded: "As the Negroes are now in this Country the principles of Humanity dictate that to make them useful to themselves as well as Society is to give them a good chance to Live, and not to distress them."[30]

Whatever white loyalists might think of Governor Parr's performance, he had a reputation among blacks for responding to such appeals as reached him. Peters was to testify that the governor earned "the highest Gratitude and affection" because of his "constant attention to their welfare and happiness."[31] Peters became convinced, however, that the governor's intentions were not carried out by his bureaucrats. Parr thanked Millidge for the "friendship you have expressed for these poor people" and directed that they be given farms "in the most advantageous Situation" possible. The survey for the Pioneers was completed in July, 1785, but when Surveyor General Morris saw the maps, he warned Millidge, "you have laid out for those Negroes the Lands reserved for the Glebe, School and other Publick uses, therefore the Grant to those People cannot pass." Glebe and school lands had been authorized in every township to support the Church of England. In the end, Peters and his brethren received nothing but their one-acre town lots. As late as 1791 the land denied them was still an unused reserve.[32]

Peters himself never applied for alternative farmland there, but at least 130 of the blacks did, including Joseph Leonard, who initiated a petition from 31 black settlers to Governor Parr for lots "in and near George Brindley Town—as they never have received no Lands Hitherto." It took several years. Soon after the survey work began, the government ceased paying surveyors, and as at Preston, the blacks had to pay for the work if it was to proceed. The governor suggested they could reduce the costs by helping as axmen or chainmen. Matters drifted until 1787, then were impeded by Millidge's illness and questions of whether the lists of waiting settlers were up to date. A new year came, and they were still landless. In late October, 1788, John Greben, a deputy surveyor in Clements township, was asked to lay out suitable land along Bear River where white loyalists had given up holdings to return to the United States. He quickly produced a survey assigning a 50-acre tract to each family and 100 acres to Leonard. Millidge wrote the surveyor general: "I have had Joseph Leonard the Head and Supreme Representative of his Ethiopian Brethren from Digby at my House," he said, and Leonard had confirmed that he was "infinitely satisfied." The survey warrants were issued in mid-1789, six years after the blacks had left New York.[33]

The second complaint of Thomas Peters and Murphy Steele had related to the free flour and pork which made the difference between life and death to most of the refugees until they found full employment or harvested a good crop. The food was issued periodically to captains of the refugee companies. Peters, for example, had 160 adults and 26 children for whom he drew rations. Peters and Steele complained that the food had been wrongly withheld by the Reverend Dr. Edward Brudenell, an ex-army chaplain and Digby agent for the commissary at Annapolis Royal. The reason appeared to be the refusal of some recipients to work on the roads. In Nova Scotia, as in all the American pioneer communities, inhabitants were expected to provide some labor on public works. The response was never enthusiastic. Parr at one point sought Carleton's help in getting an order for the disbanded troops, at least, to work on the roads.[34] However desirable or necessary to the loyalists' own interests the work was, and however illogical their recalcitrance may have seemed, the fact remained that initially there had been no strings attached to the British pledge of free provisions. To the blacks, in addition, such "forced labor" must have smacked of a return to slavery.

How many people were affected by Brudenell's stoppage is not clear, but the Peters family was one which was left destitute. It was later contended that Peters would have got his provisions if he had not left Digby. Shortly after the word came that the 20-acre farms could not be granted to the Pioneers, Peters had traveled to St. John, New Brunswick, to see what the new province could offer his people. Lieutenant Governor Thomas Carleton, brother of the general, replied that they would be treated like all other arrivals. Only Peters, of the Pioneers, applied for a lot, however, and the place he chose in Fredericton was said to be already claimed. Governor Carleton distinguished between the public obligation to the free blacks with military service, who were settled with their corps (there were only three such individuals), and responsibility to refugees "who had joined the British to escape slavery. He believed that technically the government owed the latter nothing further, but in New Brunswick, as in Nova Scotia, they had received town lots, chiefly at St. John, and enjoyed the privileges of British citizenship except "they have not been admitted to vote in Elections for . . . the General Assembly."[35]

In 1785 the New Brunswick governor backed a plan to encourage the blacks to farm. They were to form companies to which a tract, sufficient for 50 acres for each family, would be granted. If a family proved industrious, it could have more land. One such company was headed by Richard Corankapone, who was to become an outstanding citizen of the Sierra Leone colony. Corankapone and thirty-five other heads of families had been granted small lots at the new town of Carleton but couldn't make a living on them. On their behalf, Corankapone petitioned for 1,750 acres of "back land" near Glazier's Manor, King's County. "Your Petitioner hopes that those that know him think he sincerely desires that the Blacks, shou'd lead Industrious, honest Lives and instead of being a Burthen, shou'd be an Advantage to the Community," Corankapone stated.[36]

According to the governor, three such companies were organized, and 50-acre farms for 111 families were laid out on Nerepis Creek, at Milkish Creek and at Quaco, the last place allotting them shoreline which was usually reserved for whites. He said that only 5 families took up farming, and the lands, including some which Peters later claimed were unreasonably remote, were taken over by whites. Blacks had little option but to work as servants and laborers in St. John, where the city charter of 1785 excluded them from becoming freemen and only freemen could be licensed in a trade, to sell goods or fish commercially. "Good and decent and honest" "people of colour" might be granted special licenses; one case of such a license has been found.[37]

Peters' life in New Brunswick is almost undocumented. He worked as a millwright and there, as elsewhere, showed a lively concern for his fellows. Cases of reenslavement, such had been seen at Shelburne, were witnessed by him at St. John. In one case, two blacks were first jailed and then transported to the West Indies. They had joined the British forces at Savannah and gone with them to Charleston, where they had accepted an offer of work in the West Indies. After seven years, having received neither pay nor clothing, they left, unwilling to "consent to be Slaves." They made their way to New Brunswick; possibly they worked as seamen and jumped ship there. But they were traced, and through the offices of their "pretended master" they were imprisoned at Fredericton and at eleven one night put on board a schooner bound for the West Indies. Peters petitioned Governor Carleton, Justice James Putnam and Mayor Ludlow of Fredericton, but all appeals were ignored. Peters claimed to have been present on another occasion when sixteen men and women, whom he named, were likewise taken away. In a statement (which he gave to Granville Sharp) Peters said, "I follow them to water side where several of the slave holders followed me with Pistolls and Cutlasses—in order to murder me; but by the assistance of Providence got clare of them all."[38]

Peters fired a final shot at the resettlement program in 1790, when he personally delivered two petitions to the British government in London. Of this development, with its historic consequences for Sierra Leone, more will be told later. Here it is enough to say that in one of his memorials Peters described the predicament of the blacks in the maritime provinces in this vein:

> . . . notwithstanding they have made repeated Applications to all Person in that Country who they conceived likely to put them in Possession of their due Allotments, the said Pioneers with their Wives and Children amounting together in the whole

to the Number of 102 People now remain at Annapolis Royal have not yet obtained their Allotments of Land except one single Acre each for a Town Lot and tho' a further Proportion of 20 Acres each Private man (viz: about a 5th part of the Allowance of Land that is due to them) was actually laid out and located for them agreeable to the Governor's Order it was afterwards taken from them on Pretence that it had been included in some former Grant and they have never yet obtained other Lands in Lieu thereof and remain destitute and helpless.

. . . there is also a Number of free Black Refugees consisting of about 100 Families or more at New Brunswick in a like unprovided and destitute Condition for tho' some of them have had a Part of their Allowance of Land offered to them it is so far distant from their Town Lots (being 16 or 18 Miles back) as to be entirely useless to them and indeed worthless in itself from its remote Situation.[39]

Nova Scotia authorities did not concede that there had been any mishandling in the settlement of the black loyalists. "Every attention" had been paid them; lands were granted "wherever they chose to settle," and if Peters had not "hastily quitted" the Annapolis area, he would "have had his full share."[40] As the years passed, the blacks' discontent commonly was attributed, not to red tape and reluctant officialdom, but to the harsh climate. Wentworth, for one, resented such slurs on the Nova Scotia winters. Blacks, even those fresh from "the hottest Coasts of Africa," did well in northern winters if (an important if, of course) "they are well fed, warmly cloathed, and comfortably lodged." Their distress in Nova Scotia was wrongly imputed to "the only Cause which had really been friendly to them, *viz.* the Climate; in which they were still healthy, although poor, and almost naked." Wentworth had never heard a single black complain of the Nova Scotia weather however much they criticized other things. Alexander Howe, the Annapolis loyalist, agreed. Nine months of the year the Nova Scotia climate was as comfortable as Jamaica's, he opined. In the other three, "warm Houses and large Fires" made it very tolerable.[41]

The climate was an issue with the Maroons. They longed for the tropics. Maroons could never "thrive where the Pine apple does not."[42]

Whites on both sides of the Atlantic in succeeding generations have liked to think that the loyal blacks, too, were driven out of Nova Scotia and New Brunswick in 1792 by dreams of the steamy sunshine of Africa. The blacks themselves seldom mentioned the cold. It was well down on their list of grievances, which always led off with the failure to get land as freemen.

NOTES

1. Wentworth to Portland, October 29, 1796, CO 217/67.
2. Peters and Still to Parr, August 24, 1784, PANS 359/65; Richardson, Goding and French to Parr, October 7, 1786, PANS Land Grants, Petitions, Manchester Free Negroes, 1786; *ibid.*, Pompey Younge, 1785; Spray, *The Blacks in New Brunswick*, Appendix IV; "History of the Colony of Sierra Leone," Clarkson Papers, BL Add MSS. 41,263, f. 183 ff., apparently written by Thomas Clarkson with John Clarkson's aid.
3. Ells, "Claring the Decks for the Loyalists," pp. 54, 55.
4. Carleton to Parr, October 30, 1783, PRO 30/55/85; Carleton to North, November 8, 1783, PRO 30/55/86.
5. Carlton to Fox, October 21, 1783, PRO 30/55/84.
6. Gilroy, *Loyalists and Land Settlement*, p. 77.
7. These generalizations are based on evidence for peninsular Nova Scotia. The main source is Gilroy.
8. List of the Proprietors of PRESTON with the Proportion of Land Granted to Each, December 14, 1784, PANS 370/1-8; Survey of Town Lots, PANS 370/23, 25, 26, 27, 28; List of the Proprietors of a Tract of Land, Granted to Patrick Byrnn and others, March 23, 1786, PANS 370/11.
9. It is presumed for convenience that adult males would usually be heads of households. Clements and Shelburne summaries are from Gilroy. Two 50-acre grants were acquired by Demps Sullivan before he left for Sierra Leone. See Chapter 12.
10. Andrew Hill Clark, *Acadia: The Geography of Early Nova Scotia to 1760*, pp. 34, 54, 24; Rawlyk, "The Guysborough Negroes: A Study in Isolation," p. 25.
11. Return of Negroes and Their Families Mustered in Annapolis County, 1784, PANS 376; Muster Book of Birch Town, 1784, PAC, MG, 9 B 9-14, vol. 1; Ells, "Settling the Loyalists in Nova Scotia," pp. 107, 108.
12. Greaves, *The Negro in Canada*, p. 24; Carleton to Fox, October 21, 1783, PRO 30/55/84; Carleton to Fox, September 29, 1783, PRO 30/55/82.
13. Bourinot, *Builders of Nova Scotia*, p. 105: "State of Nova Scotia in 1783-84, from Col. Morse's Report."
14. Clairmont and Magill, *Nova Scotian Blacks*, p. 11; Petition of Annapolis

County Loyalists, May, 1786, CO 217/58; Macdonald, "Memoir of Governor John Parr," pp. 64, 54.

15. *Winslow Papers*, p. 443; MacNutt, *New Brunswick, a History: 1784-1867*, pp. 82-84; MacNutt, *The Atlantic Provinces*, p. 158. Italics added.

16. Esther C. Wright, *The Loyalists of New Brunswick*, p. 106.

17. Inglis to Archbishop of Canterbury, November 20, 1788, Letters of Bishop Charles Inglis, vol. 1, PANS; Inglis to Hawkesbury, December 4, 1789, bound with British Library copy of Charles Inglis, *A Charge Delivered to the Clergy of the Diocese at the Primary Visitation Holden in . . . 1788*.

18. Sydney to Parr, October 5, 1784, PANS 33, in which Parr is told that all the immigrants on the *Sally* had position or pensions, were ex-soldiers or "Gentlemen of the first Consequence" and entitled to assistance; Parr to Sydney, September 1, 1784, CO 217/59; Sydney to Parr, October 5, 1784, *ibid.*, *Winslow Papers*, p. 233.

19. Wentworth to Portland, October 29, 1796, CO 217/67.

20. Howe to Quarrell, August 12, 1797, CO 217/68.

21. Wentworth to Portland, October 29 and August 13, 1796, CO 217/67.

22. Richardson, Goding and French to Parr, PANS Land Grants.

23. Book of Negroes, PRO 30/55/100, ff. 150-51.

24. Rawlyk, pp. 25-27, 29-32; Warrant Thos. Brownspriggs 1787, PANS Land Grants; Inglis to Morice, April 7, 1788, December 20, 1788, and October 16, 1789; SPG Journal, vol. 25, 79-80, 149.

25. Clairmont and Magill, p. 12.

26. PANS 370/1-8, 11-13, 15-16; Chamberlain to Hartshorne, December 26, 1791, Clarkson Papers, BL Add. MSS. 41,262A; Inglis to Morice, July 7, 1790, Letters of Bishop Inglis, vol. 1. At least two blacks bought land. William O'Neal (O'Niel) and Peter Jackson paid Simeon Perkins £10 for 30 acres at Dipper Creek in 1788. Jackson drowned a year later. *Diary of Simeon Perkins*, vol. 36, May 3, 1788, and December 12, 1789.

27. Raymond, "The Founding of Shelburne," p. 272; PANS 376/1-19, 23-26.

28. Peters and Still to Parr, PANS 359/65.

29. Fergusson, *A Documentary Study of the Establishment of the Negroes in Nova Scotia Between the War of 1812 and the Winning of Responsible Government*, p. 17; Enquiry into the Complaint of Thomas Peters a Black Man, CO 217/63, f. 165.

30. *Ibid.*, copy of Millidge to Parr, March, 1785.

31. *Ibid.*, f. 167.

32. *Ibid.*, copy of Parr to Millidge, April 9, 1785; copy of Harris to Millidge, July 26, 1785; Examination of Thos. Peters . . . at Digby, November 19, 1791.

33. Hamilton and Leonard to Parr, n.d., enclosed in Parr to Millidge, April 9, 1785, CO 217/63; copy of Millidge to Morris, May 18, 1789; Fergusson, pp. 18-21; Gilroy, pp. 26-29. There is no record of completed grants.

34. Enquiry into Complaint of Thomas Peters, f. 166; Parr to Carleton, February 3, 1784, CO 217/59.

35. T. Carleton to Dundas, December 31, 1791, CO 188/4. See also Raymond, "The Negro in New Brunswick." Peters' petition is printed as Appendix I in Spray.

36. T. Carleton to Dundas, December 31, 1791, CO 188/4; Petition of Richard Corankapoon Wheeler (wheeler must have been his occupation), January 6, 1785, New Brunswick Provincial Archives. His name is often spelled Crankapone or Crankepone.

37. T. Carleton to Dundas, December 31, 1791, CO 188/4; Spray, pp. 34.

38. Sharp to Beaufoy, March 24, 1791, Granville Sharp Canada Papers, Hardwicke Court. The documents, which Peters must have given Sharp late in 1790, bear only one date, 1789, for these incidents.

39. The Humble Memorial and Petition of Thomas Peters a free Negro, CO 217/63, f. 58; also FO 4/1, f. 421; printed in Fyfe, *Sierra Leone Inheritance*, pp. 118-19.

40. Bulkeley to Dundas, March 19, 1792, CO 217/63.

41. Wentworth to Portland, June 13, 1796, and October 29, 1796, CO 217/67.

42. Maroon Captains of Preston to George III, August, 1798, CO 217/70.

Chapter 7

"A LITTLE HEAVEN"

> . . . the work of the Lord prospered among us in a wonder-
> ful manner.
>
> —Boston King[1]

When David George was pleased with a religious meeting he had
conducted, he would say, "We had a little heaven." It was not just a
pleasant metaphor; in the warmth of a crowded log cabin, transported out
of a humdrum or poverty-stricken existence by the emotion and song of
the Christian faith, the black refugees from scattered parts of the seaboard states came as near to heaven—to security—as any had come
before. Here they completed the process begun in New York of forming
groups in which they were no longer separate persons, whose enterprise
had brought them out of slavery by a great variety of routes, but members
of recognizable bodies linked to Baptists, Wesleyan Methodists and
Countess of Huntingdon Methodists near and far.

Others began to see them as a people who were "always to act together
and even to consider as one family those who came from the same
Country or Province."[2] Although in Nova Scotian churches blacks had
virtually their only opportunity to meet whites on anything like an equal
footing and even on occasion to preach to them, they tended to worship
by themselves. Bishop Inglis admonished the settlers near Digby about
this proclivity. Noting that Joseph Leonard seldom attended the Anglican
church in the town and had presumed to baptize and administer sacra-
ments himself at his Sunday school in the black settlement, the bishop
commented: "They seem to want to be entirely independent and separate
from the whites and to have a church of their own. I reproved Leonard for
these irregularities, and admonished him to instruct the children, which

117

was his proper duty; to come to church and persuade all the Blacks to come."[3]

It might not have occurred to the bishop that there might be more consolation in a kitchen congregation than on side benches in the house of worship. In the Anglican building program of the late 1780s, a gallery "for negroes, poor people, and soldiers in garrison towns" was added where enough money was available.[4]

Religious meetings probably were a significant social outlet for all elements of pioneer Nova Scotian society, and nowhere was this more true than in the backwoods where most of the black settlers found themselves. Sects were similar to those in the United States. The Church of England was established by a 1758 act of the Assembly (but Dissenters did not need to pay church levies under a 1759 decree). Its clergy were recruited and supported by the Society for the Propagation of the Gospel, and its presence was strongest in the military posts and the capital, Halifax. To common people, it smacked of an arm of government. The governor always headed the SPG corresponding board that controlled provincial operations. St. Paul's Church in Halifax was the best church to be seen in, and the seats nearest the governor's pew were the most coveted by the socially or politically ambitious.[5]

New England immigrants had brought the Congregational Church. Presbyterianism was introduced by the Scots-Irish from New Hampshire and immigrants from Ulster and Scotland. The Methodists were chiefly settlers from Yorkshire. There were minor numbers of Baptists, Quakers and Dutch Reformed. Catholicism was confined to the surviving Acadians.

The years spent by the future Sierra Leone settlers in Nova Scotia coincided with a revival which undermined the fashionable and formal churches and created a democratic and hot-blooded frontier religion. The Great Awakening, which had quickened the religious pulse of New England in the 1740s, had its Nova Scotia counterpart during the mainland Revolution. The neutralized fourteenth colony may have found in religion a release for its own frustrated longing for free expression or criticism of the old order.[6]

The Nova Scotia awakening was sparked by Henry Alline, who came from Rhode Island as a boy in 1760. A Congregationalist by birth, he experienced trances and visions which culminated in a conversion in 1775. Alline attended school only until the age of eleven, was never ordained, but felt the "call" to preach and followed it ardently to the end of his short life. He left Nova Scotia in August, 1783, and died the following February in the United States, so few of the black settlers could have seen or heard him, but his stamp was on his converts and disciples. Alline's version of the ''aggressive American Christianity'' of New England split churchgoers into New Lights, or friends of the movement, and Old Lights, or opponents of it. The New Lights stressed individual conversion, a personal awakening to the Gospel which did not depend on one's education or the availability of a trained pastor. Once converted, the flesh—not the spirit—could sin; a believer who erred was still saved. Alline himself never left the Congregational Church, and although his zealous ministry gave particular impetus to the Baptists, he personally saw no need for the ceremony of baptism. Such forms and disciplines were unimportant. Faith was everything, and salvation depended on the ''union of the inner man'' with God. Although his theology was derided as crude, he was ''clear as the morning light'' to his followers on such major points.[7]

''In hundreds of backwoods homes a new devotion and a new morality were kindled. The old shells of formalism and spiritual lethargy were broken through, and men and women found liberation and self-fulfillment in sharing in the fellowship and the enthusiasm of a democratic church,'' a historian of the awakening has said.[8]

It was a religion tailor-made for lonely, classless frontier life. Most hamlets had no ordained minister. The farmer or the cobbler could exercise his call to preach. The laity could debate, read sermons and testify to personal spiritual experiences. When a gifted traveling preacher like Alline arrived, the emotionally charged meetings became the highlights of the year. These sermons were not tedious intellectual exercises, but thundering expositions of familiar Scriptures in metaphors drawn from the rude life shared by preacher and participant alike. They met in schoolrooms, kitchens, chapels or the open air, any day of the week, and for long hours. Emerging from them, the people were no longer isolated —they were the elect of God.[9] Alline reputedly always rode a splendid horse at a rapid canter ''pausing only to proclaim . . . trumpet-toned, the Gospel of the Grace ōf God,'' the ''John the Baptist'' of Nova Scotia.[10] Crowds sometimes followed the itinerant preachers from place to place, and during the Revolution the provincial government had worried lest all this power be channeled into politics. Alline was viewed with such suspicion by the ''poor, dark people'' (by which he meant unenlightened folk) that he was refused beds at inns.[11]

''New England supplys us with Ignorant Illiterate Preachers on this side, and Lady Huntingdon from the other side the Atlantic,'' complained Governor Parr, "some of them the poorest of Miscreants, yet it is surprising to see the Numbers of their followers, and the length of time they devote (in all Weathers) to hear them, to the great loss and detriment of themselves and families."[12]

William Black's Methodism had a similar attraction to frontiersmen, although he offered a slightly more orthodox discipline than the New Lights. The new forms of worship were deplored by traditionalists as "enthusiasm," by which they meant fanaticism.[13] Faith was often expressed by loud cries or agitated movement, physical manifestations which were distasteful to the formal churches. The Reverend Jacob Bailey, Anglican missionary at Annapolis, disapproved the "pious frenzy" of the Methodists and New Lights at meetings where:

> ignorant men, women & even children . . . [were] employed
> to pray & exhort, calling aloud, Lord Jesus come down &
> shake these dry bones. Groanings, screamings, roarings,
> tremblings, & faintings immediately ensue, with a falling
> down & rolling upon the floor, both sexes together. . . . A
> rage for dipping, or total immersion, prevails . . . which is
> frequently performed in a very indelicate manner, before vast
> collections of people.[14]

The Scottish traveler Patrick Campbell was walking through a New Brunswick town when he heard what he thought was a fight. His companion smilingly informed him that the sounds came from a house where "religious fanatics" assembled at all hours, vying with one another to "bawl out loudest" and so prove to be the most devout. "I was struck with amazement at the hideous noise," said Campbell. He was told he could enter if he did not laugh, and in the house he found about sixty people on their knees and in tears, praying and crying out, "O Lord! O Lord!" He left with his hair "almost standing on end at the horror of the scene."[15]

The black loyalists who were Christians when they came to Nova Scotia were Methodist, Baptist or Church of England. In Nova Scotia they became predominantly Baptist or Methodist strongly affected by the New Light trend. They were by no means excluded from the Anglican Church. The loyalist tide swept an estimated 1,500 blacks, most of them free, into the Halifax parish, according to the Reverend John Breynton. Early in 1785 they were joined by another 600 from St. Augustine, most of whom had "fled from Slavery in the Southern Colonies where no regard is paid to the Religion of this unhappy species. Urged by the sober & pious Blacks of this Place they daily crowd to me for Baptism & seem happy with their Prospect of Religion & Freedom,'' the rector reported. Their eagerness did not guarantee them a place in overcrowded St. Paul's Church, but those who got in made "a decent appearance,'' and several unnamed blacks read the Bible and instruction books to gatherings of others. Slave or free, they were buried and baptized at St. Paul's.[16]

But Anglicans were thin on the ground. They did not permit laymen to act as ministers or adopt the itinerant system. One of the rectors with a visible interest in the blacks was the Reverend Roger Viets at Digby. His black communicants in 1786 outnumbered his white ones by nearly two to one, thirty-one to seventeen. The ratio evened out in subsequent years, but the black membership in his church continued high. He had thirty white and twenty-five black communicants in the autumn of 1791, but a year later only five of the latter remained; the others had left for Sierra Leone.[17] Church of England rectors at Shelburne only occasionally traveled the three and a half miles to Birchtown, although when they did, they found the blacks "very attentive to, & desirous of, Divine ordinances.'' In the settlement's first year, the Reverend George Panton baptized eighty-one adults and forty-four infants and married forty-four couples from the black population. A Birchtown resident named Limerick, a "Preacher & an Exhorter'' with "an exceedingly good character,'' was proposed as a catechist and schoolmaster. The new settlement at Preston asked for a missionary to serve both black and white immigrants, but although it was only four miles from Halifax, the Anglicans appointed none until 1793. The Church of England rather easily became linked in the eyes of the poor and black with privilege, with discrimination (as when the church claim to land prevailed over that of Peters and the Black Pioneers) and with the "anti-republicanism'' shown by officeholders and influential loyalists.[18] Bishop Inglis refused to ordain Methodist missionaries (they had to go to the United States for that) and objected to their use of Anglican pulpits. "The Church of X(t) is by no means what these people seem to suppose it—it is not a tumultuous, disorderly, & unorganized multitude,'' the bishop said firmly.[19]

None of the blacks fulfilled the requirements for Anglican ordination, but the SPG did, as we know, employ three as teachers, Brownspriggs, Blucke and Leonard, only one of whom, Leonard, was to leave for Sierra Leone. But the dissenting churches provided openings for several. David George was the outstanding example of a layman "authorized'' to preach in the United States. Driven from Shelburne by the rioting mob in 1784, he took refuge in Birchtown but remained fewer than six months. He may have found it uncongenial there, with Blucke regarded by whites as the community leader and several Methodist preachers competing for attention. He baptized about twenty and preached on invitation in various houses before taking his family back to Shelburne before Christmas.

In his absence, his meetinghouse had been taken over by "a sort of tavern-keeper, who said, 'The old Negro wanted to make a heaven of this place, but I'll make a hell of it.' " George regained possession, and his flock returned. In a few years his growing reputation brought invitations to travel. He went to Liverpool again and to the Ragged Islands. The blacks at St. John asked him to make the 200-mile journey to them, and there he baptized four, in the presence of a large, racially mixed crowd. When a few inhabitants, however, complained that he was preaching without a license, George traveled 100 miles upriver to Fredericton and, resourceful as always, got in touch with Isaac Allen, a former officer of the New Jersey Volunteers with whom George had an acquaintance dating back to Charleston. Allen was now a supreme court judge and large landowner. He had no difficulty persuading the governor's secretary to issue the necessary credentials to George. St. John proved fertile ground for Baptists, and Peter Richards of Shelburne, a onetime slave freed by his master at the start of the war, was left behind to exhort there.[20] Later George dispatched Sampson Colbert, one of his first Shelburne converts and now a Baptist elder, to St. John to carry on the work. "He was a loving brother, and the Lord had endowed him with great gifts," according to George.

On another occasion George returned to St. John to baptize ten converts. This time he traveled from Shelburne to Halifax by water and then walked across country, stopping at Horton, where Alline had established the first New Light Baptist congregation. It was a large church now, and George spent a happy Sabbath. His arrival at St. John was almost triumphal: "some of the people who intended to be baptized were so full of joy that they ran out from waiting at table on their masters, with the knives and forks in their hands, to meet me at the water side." The "dipping" was a public event again. "Our going down into the water seemed to be a pleasing sight to the whole town, White people and Black," George recalled. He stayed two weeks, then was summoned to Fredericton, where three converts waited to be baptized. That ceremony, at noon on a Sunday, was attended by a great number and Governor Carleton "said he was sorry that he could not come down to see it; but he had a great deal of company that day." As a result of the governor's hospitality, one of his servants could not be baptized.

One of the last missionary trips George described was to Preston, where five people joined the Baptists upon his immersing them and administering the Lord's Supper. He left Hector Peters, now an elder, in charge at Preston. Upon his return to Shelburne, George's boat was blown off course. Before it reached port, his legs were severely frostbitten. His church members met him at the landing and carried him home. That winter they built a wooden sled to pull him to meetings, and by spring he could walk again.

David George's gifts can only be inferred from the skeleton account of what he did. Simeon Perkins of Liverpool, recording George's visit in 1786 to the local New Light meetinghouse, said, "He Speaks Very Loud, and the people of that meeting, I understand, like him Very well." When it was proposed that the Liverpool New Lights share the Congregational meetinghouse, it was specified that "If Black David, a Preacher at Shelburne, comes he is to have Liberty to Speak in the Hous, on an Evening, but not in the Stated times of Worship," thus maintaining the distinction between ordained and lay preachers. The Reverend Harris Harding, a New Light Baptist preacher, went to one of George's meetings at Shelburne and described it thus:

> . . . as soon as I came I found about twenty or thirty made White in the Blood of the Lamb—singing Hosannahs to the Son of David, several of them frequently was oblig'd to stop and rejoice, soon after David Began in prayer, but was so overcome with joy was likewise oblidg'd to stop, and turnd to me with many tears like Brooks running down his cheeks desiring me to call upon that worthy name that was like Ointment pour'd down upon the assembly—My soul was upon a Mount Zion, and I saw whosoever worked Righteousness accepted by him.[21]

In the annals of the Nova Scotia Baptist Church, David George rates high. He is second only to Alline in Bill's history. He is credited with forming seven churches, at Shelburne, Birchtown, Jones Harbor, Ragged Islands, St. John, Preston and Halifax. When he with most of his Shelburne congregation and followers from other localities left in 1792 for Sierra Leone, most of these churches broke up, but a nucleus of

converts remained at each. At Shelburne the Baptists were revived
several years later through the labor of Mr. and Mrs. Taylor, who had
been George's supporters and friends.[22]

The Methodists were a much larger body, and blacks made up a
substantial proportion of their numbers. In 1790, of 800 Methodist full
members, one-fourth were black. When William Black visited the 200
Methodists in the Shelburne area in 1784, he reported that only 20 were
white. Digby, too, had a predominantly black Methodist congregation.[23]

Birchtown's leading Methodist was Moses Wilkinson. In Sierra Leone
chronicles he is always described as very old, but his age was given upon
leaving New York in 1783 as thirty-six, at the time of the Birchtown 1784
muster as thirty-two and as a recruit for Sierra Leone in 1791 as fifty.
Accounts agree, however, that he was blind and lame. One wonders how
he managed his escape in Nansemond County, Virginia, but since the
owners's family lost a substantial number of slaves to the British,
Wilkinson may have been assisted by his brethren.[24] He became a
Christian before he reached Nova Scotia, where in 1787 he received a
government warrant for 40 acres.[25] On his visit in 1784, William Black
and eight friends went to Birchtown. He was overjoyed at its progress
over the first winter and found Wilkinson busy with his congregation.
Black wrote:

> It is truly wonderful to see what a work God hath been carrying
> on amongst these poor negroes. Upwards of sixty profess to
> have found the pearl of great price, within seven or eight
> months; and what is farther remarkable, the chief instrument
> whom God hath employed in this work is a poor negro, who
> can neither see, walk, nor stand. He is usually carried to the
> place of worship, where he sits and speaks, or kneels and prays
> with the people.

Black met nine of the fourteen Methodist classes then meeting in
Birchtown and found "many . . . are deeply experienced in the ways of
God."[26]

The first who "turned from the error of their ways" under Wilkinson's
preaching at Birchtown was Boston King's wife, Violet. In his descriptions of her (and in due course his) conversion, King provides a vivid
picture of this crucial experience, an essential happening to all who
wished to share the fellowship of the Methodists or Baptists then.[27]

Of Violet, he recalled:

. . . she was struck to the ground, and cried out for mercy: she continued in great distress for near two hours, when they sent for me. At first I was much displeased, and refused to go; but presently my mind relented, and I went to the house, and was struck with astonishment at the sight of her agony. In about six days after, the Lord spoke peace to her soul: she was filled with divine consolation, and walked in the light of GOD's countenance about nine months. But being unacquainted with the corruptions of her own heart, she again gave place to bad tempers, and fell into great darkness and distress . . . which confined her to bed a year and a half.

However, the Lord was pleased to sanctify her afflictions, and to deliver her from all her fears. He brought her out of the horrible pit, and set her soul at perfect liberty. . . .

As the first in Birchtown to be saved, and because she exhorted others to follow her example, she was, her husband said, "not a little opposed by some of our Black brethren." But she carried on patiently and meekly.[28]

King's conversion was also painful and prolonged. His consciousness of sin at times terrified him:

I thought I was not worthy to be among the people of GOD; nor even to dwell in my own house; but was fit only to reside among the beasts of the forest. This drove me out into the woods, when the snow lay upon the ground three or four feet deep, with a blanket and a fire-brand in my hand. I cut the boughs of the spruce tree and kindled a fire. In this lonely situation I frequently intreated the Lord for mercy. Sometimes I thought that I felt a change wrought in my mind . . . but I soon fell again thro' unbelief into distracting doubts and fears, and evil-reasonings. The devil persuaded me that I was the most miserable creature upon the face of the earth, and that I was predestinated to be damned before the foundations of the world. My anguish was so great, that when night appeared, I dreaded it as much as the grave.

Most of King's workmates had felt the "divine presence" and they held prayer meetings night and morning. On January 5, 1784:

as one of them was reading the Parable of the Sower, the word came with power to my heart. I stood up and desired him to explain the parable; and while he was shewing me the meaning of it, I was deeply convinced that I was one of the stony-ground hearers. . . . I was astonished that the Lord had borne with me so long. I was at the same time truly thankful that he gave me a desire to return to him. . . . The first Sunday in March, as I was going to the preaching, and was engaged in prayer and meditation, I thought I heard a voice saying to me, ''Peace be unto thee.'' I stopped, and looked round about, to see if any one was near me. But finding myself alone, I went forward a little way, when the same words were again powerfully applied to my heart, which removed the burden of misery from it; and while I sat under the sermon, I was more abundantly blessed. Yet in the afternoon, doubts and fears again arose. . . . Next morning, I resolved like Jacob, not to let the Lord go till he blessed me indeed. As soon as my wife went out, I locked the door, and determined not to rise from my knees until the Lord fully revealed his pardoning love. I continued in prayer about half an hour, when the Lord again spoke to my heart, ''Peace be unto thee.'' All my doubts and fears vanished away: I saw, by faith, heaven opened to my view . . . and my Soul was dissolved into love. . . . I could truly say, I was now become a new creature. All tormenting and slavish fear, and all the guilt and weight of sin were done away.

Boston King reveals not only his own, but the intense spiritual life of Birchtown that first winter. Escape, transportation to a strange land, the harsh struggle to live had created an atmosphere in which the blacks were extremely receptive to the idea of spiritual as well as physical freedom and rebirth. The teaching that everyone was capable of imbibing and interpreting the Christian Gospel was ideal for a community thrown upon its own resources of leadership.

Like his wife, King felt his new conviction weakening in a while, and in this crisis the trained leader he needed arrived in the person of the Reverend Freeborn Garrettson. He encouraged Violet King to ''hold fast her confidence.'' And when King himself heard his sermon on ''One thing I know, that, whereas I was blind, now I see'' (John 9:25), King's doubts vanished, and from then on he ''walked in the light.'' He began to exhort his ''ungodly neighbours'' and to speak at prayer meetings.

Garrettson was sent by the 1785 Baltimore conference of Methodists after an appeal by Black for help in the mission field of Nova Scotia and

New Brunswick. Dr. Thomas Coke regarded Garrettson, a veteran of nine years on the circuit, as ideal for the job. "He makes me quite ashamed," Dr. Coke confessed in his journal, "for he invariably arises at four in the morning . . . and now blushing I brought back my alarm to four o'clock."[29]

During his own conversion in Maryland in 1775, Garrettson had experienced the powerful thought that he "must let the oppressed go free," and he manumitted his own slaves at once, from then on paying them wages. "Till then," he said, "I had never suspected that the practice of slave-keeping was wrong." During the Revolution he refused to bear arms and grew increasingly disturbed by slavery. In North Carolina he provoked white hostility by urging emancipation and arranged occasions to preach to slaves. After a few weeks in Halifax, Garrettson had launched a tour in March, 1785, walking 300 miles in the still-snowbound country, preaching twenty times in two weeks to the "sheep so widely scattered." Not infrequently, he faced rowdy audiences. He spent eight weeks at Shelburne, where a white mob tried to knock down his pulpit and pelted him with rotten eggs and stones. But he was comforted by the black Methodists and organized sixty into a class, baptized nineteen and administered the Lord's Supper to forty. His congregation grew so rapidly that the Anglican Reverend William Walter let him use the church until the vestrymen objected.[30]

Another American Methodist missionary, the Reverend William Jessop, came to Shelburne in 1788 and at Birchtown "Had great liberty & enjoyed sweet peace in my soul." On his next visit he stayed a week with one of the families. "The house being smoky I found it disagreeable, but why should I complain? It was better lodging than my dear Master had." On the Sunday he preached to a large gathering at Boston King's house "from Ezekiel's vision of dry bones, & there was a shaking among the dry bones. Had a prayer meeting at night, after we had spent an hour or two in singing & praying most of the people went away, but some were loath to leave, before long the power of the Lord came down upon us & a general shout of thanksgiving ascended to heavens for the space of an hour."[31]

Superficial observers might think that the Methodists and New Lights sounded much the same, but the Methodists disapproved of Alline and his followers almost as much as Bishop Inglis did. William Black quoted Alline as saying that "a believer is like a nut, thrown into the mud, which may dirty the shell, but not the kernel," adding, "That is, we may get drunk, or commit adultery, without the smallest defilement, &c. O Lord, suffer not the enemy of souls to deceive them thus!"[32] Garrettson likewise criticized what for some reason he always called the Allenites. "Almost all of them preach in public," he reported. "I was conversing with one who seems to be a principal person among them. 'As for sin,' said she, 'it cannot hurt me: not even adultery, murder, swearing, drunkenness, nor any other sin, can break the union between me and Christ.' " The New Lights regarded the Methodists as "neither Christians, nor called to preach." If they did not "feel" a preacher, he was considered unconverted and therefore unfit.[33] This was the dreaded "antinomianism," which, like "enthusiasm," was so objectionable to the Established Church to which the Methodists still belonged, although there appear good grounds for believing that the Nova Scotia Methodism "had never really been inside the Church of England."[34]

John Marrant, the young man so sensationally converted by Whitefield, had a brother who migrated to Nova Scotia. John was invited to go there to minister, and after his ordination in England in the Countess of Huntingdon Connexion he sailed in August, 1785.[35] He attracted some forty adherents at Birchtown and proselytized among the Indians as well. He and Charles Bailey (who had worked for Simeon Perkins) were issued a warrant for the survey of 38 acres of land in Shelburne County in 1787.[36] Marrant visited Liverpool and spoke in both the New Light and the Congregational meetings. Simeon Perkins reported on April 1, 1787, "A Black man, Called Morant, preached last evening at the New Light meeting. I understand they do not Approve of him." (By "they" he could have meant the congregation or the Methodists in the town, for Garrettson and the Reverend James Oliver Cromwell were busy in the area.) Two days later Marrant preached "in ye Great Meeting House. . . . I heard him & Liked him well," said Perkins.[37] It was Garrettson's opinion, when he paid a return visit to Shelburne in 1786, that Marrant had "done much hurt in [the Wesleyan Methodist] society among the blacks at Burch town. . . . I believe that Satan sent him. Before he came there was a glorious work going on among these poor creatures, now (brother Cromwell not being able to attend) there is much confusion. The devil's darts are sometimes turned upon his own miserable head." The next year there was better news. Garrettson wrote to John Wesley, "Most of the coloured people whom Morant drew off have returned."[38]

In 1789 John Marrant left Birchtown for Boston, where among other work he was chaplain to the African Masons. He returned to England in 1790 and a year later was dead at thirty-five.[39]

The lack of education in many who presumed to teach or preach

Christianity scandalized traditionalists. But no one felt his ignorance more than Boston King. He exhorted, as he was compelled to do, but with sorrow for his shortcomings. He was particularly embarrassed in front of whites. William Black, however, thought him good enough to be put in charge of the Methodists at Preston, and he moved there from Birchtown. There were thirty-four in his congregation. After a year, when he seemed to be making no gains, he prayed for the conversion of a single sinner as a sign of his "call." Toward the end of that day's evening service "the divine presence seemed to descend upon the congregation: Some fell flat upon the ground, as if they were dead; and others cried aloud for mercy." His first convert came forward and testified. "All the Society were melted into tears of joy. . . . From this time the work of the Lord prospered among us in a wonderful manner."

One other black who would return to Africa is known to have preached in Nova Scotia. "A Black Man, Called *Ball,* preaches in the Evening at the School House," Perkins noted on December 6, 1791. "He is said to be a Methodist. I attended, and think he performed very well considering his Situation and Colour." Richard Ball, now thirty, and freed when his master was killed at Camden, supported his wife and four small children at Birchtown as a preacher and laborer.[40]

The illiteracy of the blacks in general was not a peculiar trait in those days. Half of all the people could not read, and many more were unable to write or do sums. The only familiar book was the Bible. There were few schools.[41] Two societies related to the Church of England, Dr. Bray's Associates and the SPG, between them supported five schools for blacks in Nova Scotia. The Associates began to finance the Birchtown school, with Stephen Blucke as teacher, in 1785. Blucke's reports and letters, in a handsome flowing script, usually brought encouraging news to the London headquarters of his thirty-six to forty-four scholars. The local inspectors were "all agreeably well pleased with the management & conduct of it—Mr. Bluke deserves every commendation."[42]

Governor Parr had suggested a school near Digby to be inspected by Colonel Joseph Barton, a "suffering Loyalist & zealous churchman." Barton "assembled the negroes to consult them" and they proposed Joseph Leonard for schoolmaster. He started classes in his home on November 8, 1784, and it was planned to build a school when weather permitted. A daughter of Leonard's taught sewing. The school went well. Philip Marchinton, passing through, reported that the people seemed very thankful for it, adding, "there is some very sensible Men amoungst them such as would do honour to a white Man to converse with them." Several times a year the Reverend Mr. Viets visited the "Negroe Town" to preach a suitable "plain, practical Sermon" and inspect the school. Visitors found the blacks exceedingly poor—worse off than the majority of the impoverished whites—and from time to time the sponsors sent boxes of trousers and petticoats, shoes, yards of cloth, buttons, thread and a garment or two to serve as patterns.[43]

Leonard's pupils were typical of the Bray schools. They ranged in age from five to seventeen. Some of the older ones were apprentices. Each school was supplied by the Associates with a child's First Book, Bibles, Testaments, psalters, tracts, Watts' hymns and works in which religion was made easy. The children studied reading, spelling and sewing.[44] The schools were not intended to make blacks the equals of whites. Writing and arithmetic were skimped since "these were considered unnecessary accomplishments in children who would subsequently be required to perform the meanest tasks." The schools' success was judged by whites in terms of the good behavior of the children, who might be servants or apprentices by the time they were twelve.[45] The Associates paid the teachers the highest rate in their pay scale, 12 shillings per pupil per year, because wages ran so high in Nova Scotia. There also was an allowance for fuel. Leonard's work seemed satisfactory to everyone but Bishop Inglis, who disliked the Sunday school Leonard organized for forty-eight adults. Inglis said that Leonard not only could not read, spell or write correctly, but also leaned toward "enthusiasm." When Leonard went with most of his constituency to Sierra Leone, the bishop was not sorry, and a white ex-loyalist officer, James Foreman, was recommended to succeed him, at the request of the parents of the remaining twenty-eight children.[46]

Hearing from their friends in the Digby area of the Bray-sponsored schools, a group of blacks in New Brunswick in 1790 called them to the attention of the governor. They named Thomas Peters to act for them, but Peters was by then, no doubt, viewed as a militant troublemaker, and the petition was rejected on the grounds that he could not speak for others. No school appears to have been opened there.[47]

Mrs. Catherine Abernathy, like Leonard, ran afoul—but temporarily—of the church. A "capable & serious free Negroe woman," she was put in charge of the school at Preston, but after several good reports, her salary was stopped in 1789 because "embracing some Strange religious tenets, she has become less pleasing to the other negroes. Better information, I hope, will set her right and enable her to be yet useful as a School Mistress," the cleric-inspector reported. Within two years the school was flourishing and Mrs. Abernathy was reading part of the church service on Sundays. When she went to Sierra Leone, she was recommended to the London body as "very capable of doing much good among her Countrymen" if they decided to extend their work to Africa. "She reads remarkably well."[48]

A Halifax school with children from five to nineteen, a few of whom were bound out, was taught in part of the Orphan House by a William Frumage, but in 1788 he made himself obnoxious by performing marriages without a license, and Limerick Isaac, a black, was put in charge. The school records show him a far less able penman than Frumage, yet he zealously ran the school from nine to noon and two to five each summer day and ten to two in the winter. Isaac had been at Digby earlier, and Colonel Barton there regarded him as an "artful Cuning fellow" who preached mischief to the settlers. He, like Mrs. Abernathy, rehabilitated himself, however, and when he left Nova Scotia for Sierra Leone, he was recommended as a potential Bray teacher there if "under constant Instruction."[49]

NOTES

1. Boston King Narrative, p. 213.
2. Howe to Quarrell, August 12, 1797, CO 217/68.
3. Journal of Bishop Charles Inglis, September 10, 1791, PANS.
4. Fingard, *The Anglican Design in Loyalist Nova Scotia*, pp. 78, 168-69. In Digby in 1792 well-off blacks were allowed to buy pews.
5. Brebner, *The Neutral Yankees of Nova Scotia*, pp. 188-90; Thomas, "The First Half-Century of the Work of the Society for the Propagation of the Gospel in Nova Scotia," p. 6; Thomas, "St. Paul's Church, Halifax, Revisited," pp. 22, 10; Eaton, *The Church of England in Nova Scotia*, pp. 53-54.
6. Armstrong, *The Great Awakening in Nova Scotia, 1776-1809*, pp. 20-21; Fingard, p. 114; *Diary of Simeon Perkins*, D. C. Harvey's Introduction, pp. xv, 1v.
7. Mackinnon, *Settlements and Churches in Nova Scotia, 1749-1776*, p. 98; Samuel Delbert Clark, *Church and Sect in Canada*, pp. 18-21; Mode, *The Frontier Spirit in American Christianity*, p. 42; Armstrong, pp. 8, 124, 100-1; Bill, *Fifty Years with the Baptist Ministers and Churches of the Maritime Provinces*, p. 13.
8. Armstrong, p. 87.
9. Mode, pp. 54, 153-54, 155, 157-58; Clark, pp. 36-37, 88-89.
10. Bill, p. 13.

11. MacNutt, *The Atlantic Provinces*, p. 86; Arbuthnot to Germaine, December 31, 1776, CO 217/53; Bill, p. 13.

12. Parr to Morice, April 23, 1787, USPG, C/Can/NS 1.

13. Carpenter, *Church and People, 1789-1889*, p. 28; Armstrong, pp. 75-76, 13; Persons, *American Minds, a History of Ideas*, p. 87.

14. Fingard, pp. 123-24.

15. Patrick Campbell, *Travels in the Interior Inhabited Parts of North America in the Years 1791 and 1792*, p. 255.

16. Breynton to Society, November 21, 1783, SPG Journal, vol. 23; Breynton, May 8, 1785, USPG, C/Can/NS 1; Dr. Bray's Associates Minute Books, vol. 3, February 5, 1787; Fingard, p. 41; SPG Journal, vol. 24, p. 24 and vol. 23, p. 281; Reginald V. Harris, *The Church of Saint Paul in Halifax, Nova Scotia, 1749-1949*, p. 64. Wentworth had twenty recently purchased slaves baptized in a mass ceremony on February 10, 1784, before shipping them to a cousin in Surinam. *Ibid.*, p. 65.

17. SPG Journal, vol. 24, p. 372; vol. 25, p. 405; vol. 26, p. 100.

18. SPG Journal, vol. 23, p. 379 and vol. 24, p. 66; Fingard, p. 51, 29; Walls, "A Christian Experiment: The Early Sierra Leone Colony," p. 115.

19. Harris, p. 93; Fingard, p. 122.

20. David George Narrative. His New Brunswick license, p. 481, dated July 17, 1791, gives permission to "instruct the Black people." Book of Negroes, PRO 30/55/100, ff. 33-34.

21. *Diary of Simeon Perkins*, vol. 36, June 18, 1786, and vol. 39, January 11, 1790; Kirk-Greene, "David George: The Nova Scotia Experience," p. 106, quoting Harding to Miss D'Wolf, August 20, 1791.

22. Bill presents Alline in Chapter I and David George in Chapter II; Clark, pp. 176, 50; Benedict, *A General History of the Baptist Denomination*, vol. 6, pp. 295-96.

23. Findlay and Holdsworth, *The History of the Wesleyan Methodist Missionary Society*, vol. 1, p. 297; MacLean, *William Black, the Apostle of Methodism*, p. 28; Thomas Jackson, *Lives of Early Methodist Preachers*, vol. 3, p. 157; Barclay, *Early American Methodism 1769-1844*, vol. 1, p. 173.

24. Book of Negroes, PRO 30/55/100, ff. 90-91. Willis and Miles Wilkinson appear as onetime owners of twenty-one persons evacuated by the British from New York. Muster Book of Birch Town, 1784, PAC MG 9, B 9-14, vol. 1; List of the Blacks in Birch Town, 1791, CO 217/63.

25. Muster Book of Birch Town, 1784; Gilroy, *Loyalists and Land Settlement*, p. 114.

26. Jackson, vol. 3, p. 157.

27. Boston King Narrative.

28. There are occasional hints of religious bickering in the black community. Walter, Anglican rector at Shelburne, claimed in 1788 to have settled

"a difference among their religious societies." SPG Journal, vol. 25, p. 163.

29. [Coke], *Extracts of the Journals of the Late Rev. Thomas Coke*, p. 45; Bangs, *The Life of the Rev. Freeborn Garrettson*, pp. 39-40, 104, 105.

30. *Ibid.*, pp. 141, 143; Baker, "Freeborn Garrettson and Nova Scotia," p. 18; Blakeley, "Boston King: A Negro Loyalist Who Sought Refuge in Nova Scotia," p. 352.

31. Journal of Rev. William Jessop, March 3, 1788, PANS.

32. Jackson, vol. 3, p. 147.

33. Bangs, p. 144; Armstrong, p. 13.

34. Walls, p. 115.

35. Marrant's brother must have gone directly to Nova Scotia from Charleston, for the Book of Negroes compiled in New York lists only Millia and two children of that name, PRO 30/55/100, ff. 52-53. She had been the property of John Marrant and escaped at the siege of Charleston.

36. Gilroy, p. 107.

37. *Diary of Simeon Perkins*, vol. 36, April 1 and 3, 1787.

38. Bangs, pp. 152, 158.

39. Kaplan, *The Black Presence in the Era of the American Revolution*, pp. 96-99; *The Countess of Huntingdon's New Magazine, 1851*, p. 275.

40. *Diary of Simeon Perkins*, vol. 30, December 6, 1791; Book of Negroes, PRO 30/55/100, ff. 33-34; List of the Blacks in Birch Town, 1791.

41. Mackinnon, p. 61; Brebner, p. 196.

42. Dr. Bray's Associates Minute Books, vol. 3, February 3, 1785; Williams to Lyttleton, July 10, 1789, and Reports 1789 to 1794 in Dr. Bray's Associates Canadian Papers, USPG.

43. Dr. Bray's Associates Canadian Papers, USPG: Breynton to Breynton, November 15, 1784; Barton to Breynton, January 25, 1785; Leonard's report, October 4, 1788; Marchinton to Brunton, April 2, 1785; Viets to Lyttleton, April 13, 1789, and Millidge to Lyttleton, October 13, 1788; Dr. Bray's Associates Minute Books, vol. 3, July 1, 1784, February 3, 1785, July 5, 1792.

44. Dr. Bray's Associates Canadian Papers, Leonard's report, October 4, 1788; Dr. Bray's Associates Minute Books, vol. 3, February 3, 1785.

45. Fingard, pp. 135-36.

46. Dr. Bray's Associates Minute Books, vol. 3, February 3, 1783, November 3, 1791, and Petition of Byng, Custus and Catchpoll, June 1, 1792; Inglis to Lyttleton, November 30, 1792, SPG *Abstracts of Proceedings*.

47. Spray, *The Blacks in New Brunswick*, p. 36 and Appendix 2. There were fifteen male signers, of whom at least four (Anthony Stevenson or Stevens, Nathaniel Ladd, Samuel Wright and Robert Stafford) emigrated to Sierra Leone.

48. Dr. Bray's Associates Canadian Papers, Weeks to Society, October 16,

1789; Dr. Bray's Associates Minute Books, vol. 3, September 1, December 1, 1791.

49. *Ibid.*, July 3, 1788; Halifax school report September, 1787, June 3, 1790; Dr. Bray's Associates Canadian Papers, Barton to Weeks, December 13, 1786; Dr. Bray's Associates Minute Books, vol. 3, December 1, 1791. Also on the schools see Winks, *Blacks in Canada*, pp. 57-59.

Chapter 8

THE LURE OF AFRICA

> . . . the Blacks of America will seek an abode in some region of independence where their own laws alone are to be regarded . . . where all are upon an equality; and where a man that Nature cloathed with a white skin, shall not, merely on that account, have the right of wielding a rod of iron.
>
> —WILLIAM THORNTON[1]

In 1787 Boston King found his mind drawn to "my poor brethren in Africa." In his words:

> we who had the happiness of being brought up in a christian land, where the Gospel is preached, were notwithstanding our great privileges, involved in gross darkness and wickedness; . . . what a wretched condition then must those poor creatures be in, who never heard the Name of GOD or of CHRIST; nor had any instruction afforded them with respect to a future judgment. As I had not the least prospect at that time of ever seeing Africa, I contented myself with pitying and praying for the poor benighted inhabitants of that country which gave birth to my forefathers.[2]

It is intriguing that King dated his conscious interest in an African mission to the year when the first African-American settlers left England for Sierra Leone. It is almost certain that he knew about them. The Reverend Samuel Hopkins' plan in 1773 for an African mission had foundered in the Revolution, and the first scheme to come to life was the Sierra Leone settlement. It was closely watched in the United States by free blacks in Newport and Philadelphia, now banded together in "Afri-

can societies," who debated group migration to their ancestral home-
land. For whites as well, in the last two decades of the eighteenth
century, colonization was a popular intellectual exercise, producing
theoretical plans which were put up and shot down in much revealing
discourse.[3]

Notable among the white proponents of this period was William
Thornton. He dreamed of an independent "nation" of African-
Americans in Africa. He saw the American blacks as a nation, sup-
pressed within a white society. Thornton was a friend of, and probably
inspired by, the originator of the Sierra Leone scheme, Henry Smeathman. Thornton's activities among the New England blacks probably
were known to the black loyalists in Nova Scotia through traveling
preachers or black seamen. From his acquaintance with blacks, Thornton
was convinced that if the Sierra Leone settlement were "perfectly independent," it would attract thousands of colonists from the United States.
It became a British colony, however, and it attracted only those who had
already chosen to remain British.

Thornton was a West Indian Quaker, educated in Britain and Paris,
who in 1785 at the age of twenty-four inherited half of a sugar plantation
on Tortola and 70 slaves. He died in 1828, still possessed of the half
interest and with 120 slaves. But from 1785 to 1789 he devoted himself to
finding ways and means of establishing an African colony. He was the
spokesman rather than the leader of the interested American blacks.[4]
There were many such who had been born in Africa or were still familiar
with African culture.[5] Influenced by his English connections, Thornton
no sooner became an owner of slaves than he wanted to manumit them,
but was dissuaded by his family, who feared the effect on their other
slaves. Thornton then resolved to go with the most qualified of his slaves
to Africa, where they could own land, run schools, churches and scientific societies, teach West Indian skills and oppose the slave trade. When
Thornton was in England, his friend Smeathman was seeking a backer
for an African colony, and later Thornton kept in touch through a
relative, Dr. John Coakley Lettsom, who had inherited the distinguished
Dr. Fothergill's practice. Lettsom had liberated his own slaves on
impulse but was a lukewarm, or possibly simply skeptical, abolitionist.[6]
Thornton's plan existed only on paper when the Sierra Leone experiment
began. The sailing of the small fleet in 1787 was reported in the Boston
press.[7] In Newport, Boston and Philadelphia, Thornton inquired among
blacks whether they would be interested in Sierra Leone. He spoke to
large meetings, called together by elders, which enthusiastically en-

dorsed the concept of African colonization.[8] Thornton reported to Dr. Lettsom that he found:

> many free negroes very desirous of reaching the coast of Guinea, to form a settlement there. Many of them have families, and are regular industrious men. . . . They desire the most particular information. . . . [At the news of Sierra Leone, they] enjoyed with me the good intention of the English, but are very desirous to know whether they are to be considered as a colony of England, or perfectly independent. If the latter, it will flourish, because many would embark; and if to be dependent on England, none here will engage; for they think that they could alone be happy where there is perfect confidence in their law givers, and where their own voices are to be heard. . . . The Blacks of America will seek an abode in some region of independence where their own laws are alone to be regarded.

Thornton thought they were right; "I hate the word colony," he added. [9]

The Union Society of Blacks sent Thornton the names of seventy members willing to settle in Africa and a dozen young men offered to go, at some risk, to procure fuller information on the terms for landholding in Sierra Leone. Lettsom was urged to transmit a detailed report which could be "made known, not to a few men, but a nation of Blacks." Thornton estimated that 2,000 would venture to Africa if Sierra Leone sounded right to them, for "they have no inducement here to gain high characters, nor to acquire learning, being excluded from all offices by their colour merely."[10]

Thornton consulted Samuel Hopkins, who qualified his approval only with the private opinion that Thornton was "too flighty" to head the operation, and James Madison, Samuel Adams and Brissot de Warville, all of whom thought well of it.[11] The young Quaker was willing to gamble his property, valued at more than £8,000, and his future prospects in medicine to go to Africa with the "rejected and despised part of mankind." In January, 1787, seventy-three "African Blacks" petitioned the Massachusetts legislature for assistance to enable them to return to "our native country." Led by a committee of twelve Masons, including the grand master, Prince Hall, they signed an eloquent statement of their longing to remove to a land where they could live among equals and be more comfortable, happy and useful. They intended to send a delegation to obtain land, to form a society guided by a constitution and to maintain a church with one or more ordained pastors. They needed money, provisions, farm tools and certain building materials to carry out this plan, which had so many advantages to their heathen brethren and the commerce of the United States.[12] Legislators appeared favorable to helping when a site was obtained, though some objected to seeking one outside the United States. It seemed sensible to await events at Sierra Leone before proceeding, and the delay in the end proved fatal to this generation of would-be black emigrants in New England. Thornton remained in the United States and maintained an interest in colonization (helping found the American Colonization Society), but he ceased to be a moving spirit.[13]

The first African-Americans, therefore, to experiment with African colonization were the hundreds of loyalists who found themselves in London after the Revolution. Most were discharged seamen. Some had been servants of returning British officers, and others had been attached to regiments that were demobilized in England. Except for a few, they were exceedingly poor, often reduced to begging. None had been provided with land or provisions, as were many of their counterparts in Nova Scotia and New Brunswick. The livelihoods of a tiny sample of them are described sketchily in the forty-seven claims which blacks made to the British government for wartime losses,[14] along with some 5,000 whites. Shadrack Furman, a Virginia slave who had supplied British troops with food and information and was left blind and crippled by the Americans who captured and flogged him, played a fiddle in the streets. In 1788 he was awarded a pension of £18 a year for his services, the most generous settlement for any of the black claimants. David King earned 2 shillings a day as a shoemaker. John Robinson, a cook on British warships, now kept a cookshop. George Peters worked at a gentleman's house for 18 pence a week, and Benjamin Whitecuff, the British spy who had narrowly escaped death by hanging, set himself up as a saddler and chair bottom maker on his £4-a-year pension and a small dowry from his English wife, Sarah.[15] Many got intermittent work on ships.

The commissioners, who sat in a fine house overlooking Lincoln's Inn Fields to examine the loyalist claims, believed that the government owed the loyal blacks little, and with monotonous regularity, their clumsy petitions were dismissed with the remark that "probably in fact (instead of being Sufferers by the War) most of them have gained their Liberty & therefore come with a very ill grace to ask for the bounty of Government."[16] As the commissioners told John Provey, who had served in the

Black Pioneers, he was "in a much better Country where he may with Industry get his Bread & where he can never more be a Slave." In his appeal, Provey described himself as "an entire Stranger in this Country illeterate and unacquainted with the Laws thereof." Peter Anderson, a Virginia woodcutter who had been press-ganged by one of Lord Dunmore's officers, taken prisoner by the Americans at Great Bridge and escaped to rejoin the British forces voluntarily, was utterly destitute. "I endeavour'd to get Work but cannot get Any I am Thirty Nine Years of Age & am ready & willing to serve His Britinack Majesty While I am Able But I am realy starvin about the Streets Having Nobody to give me A Morsel of bread & dare not go home to my Own Country again." His tale struck the commissioners as "incredible," but because Lord Dunmore vouched for it, Anderson was given £10.[17]

At least the black loyalists were regarded as freemen. Many others of their race in the underworld of the poor were runaways from West Indian or British masters, in constant risk of being retaken, for in spite of what many thought Lord Mansfield had ruled in 1772, slavery was still legal. The black community, which dated to the sixteenth century, had now swollen to 14,000 or more.[18] London was nearing a million population. The shock of the metropolis to the blacks from American farms and villages can scarcely be imagined. Even white loyalists were dismayed. Jonathan Boucher's wife, at her first sight of it, begged her husband to stop till the crowd passed by. Another exile said he felt like "an atom" there.[19] In the older quarters the muddy streets and decaying houses were filled with waves of newcomers as the poor of Ireland, Scotland and the English countryside streamed to the capital to find work. In one area the Irish lived three or four families to a room. Beggars and vagrants abounded. All the London poor were regarded as vicious and dishonest. If anything, there was more tolerance of the destitute blacks. They lived in scattered sections. There were concentrations around St. Giles in the Fields and the riverside parishes from the Tower and St. Katherine's eastward through Wapping. When the government began its daily dole for the intending émigrés, the widely separated distribution points were the Yorkshire Stingo at the western outskirts and the White Raven at Mile End on the east side of London.[20]

In Britain, interest in African colonization was nourished by two streams, the anti-slave-trade movement and a charity formed to relieve the special plight of the "black poor." The resulting Sierra Leone settlement traced its lineage to Dr. Fothergill and his theory that sugar cultivated in Africa could prove the supremacy of free African labor over slave. In 1771 he and two friends sent Henry Smeathman to West Africa on a collecting and exploring expedition. Smeathman was nearly thirty, but still unsettled in life. Born in the North Sea fishing port of Scarborough, Smeathman showed an early talent for reading and drawing and an endless curiosity about natural history. He was a private tutor when he heard of Dr. Fothergill's interest in sending a scientific explorer to Africa, and he won the commission. Fothergill told him of his vision and of his willingness to put £10,000 of his own money into it and raise the balance from Quaker friends. Smeathman later spoke of all this to William Thornton.[21]

Smeathman spent nearly four years in the vicinity of Sierra Leone. He collected the data for a treatise on termites, sent thousands of valuable specimens to England, cultivated a rice farm and studied African customs and agricultural methods and how they might be improved by European expertise. He married into the families of two local rulers, King Tom on the mainland and Cleveland, the African-English chief of the Banana Islands. Both wives had died when Smeathman left Africa for the West Indies, where he spent another four years studying tropical agriculture.[22] He returned to England afire with the thought of an African "commonwealth" where redeemed slaves would cultivate rice and cotton and unemployed English artisans might settle. But Fothergill had died in 1780. To escape his creditors and to look for French funds, Smeathman went to Paris in 1783. He showed his plan to Benjamin Franklin, who complimented him on it. He supported himself by lecturing on termites and teaching English. Back in London, Dr. Lettsom and George Cumberland were seeking support on his behalf from such eminent figures as Granville Sharp, Richard Price and Richard Oswald, the onetime slave merchant and peace negotiator, and from a newly formed Quaker committee to oppose the slave trade. Price agreed that the scheme would be a blow to the slave trade. Oswald did not respond. The Quakers approved but opposed the suggestion that the colonists be armed to defend themselves. Sharp took the proposal very seriously and, in a memorandum written in August, 1783, cited a number of deficiencies, specifically the plan's failure expressly to prohibit slavery, prevent monopoly of land, limit the powers of managers or provide a government based upon mutual responsibility.[23] Smeathman had a reputation of flitting "with the Best Heart and intention in the world" from one enthusiasm to another, but he espoused his African plan tenaciously. Paris, however, had plenty of money to invest in slave trading, but nothing for a venture which could prove "second to nothing else if inferior to that of the American Independence.'' He became fascinated, like all Paris, with Montgolfier's balloon experiments and deduced a method by which balloons could be directed at inconceivable speed. In high spirits, ''busy as a pig before a storm,'' he wrote in the spring of 1784, ''My African Fever is strong upon me. If my Balloon invention succeeds it will inevitably make my fortune, and I will undertake the African Plan.''[24] But he returned to England that autumn empty-handed.

In 1785, while angling for the backing of certain London merchants, at least one of whom was in the slave trade, Smeathman testified to a House of Commons committee against the establishment of a convict colony in the Sierra Leone neighborhood. Although soon he would argue in glowing terms for the settlement of the loyal blacks there, now he pictured Sierra Leone as deadly. He was speaking of the effect of its climate on white convicts, who would, he believed, succumb to the first bout of fever. He also must have had in mind the harm a convict colony might do to his own scheme and the mercantile interests he hoped to attract. When his black colonists went out, he intended to go with them, to stay with them, to ''lift the first axe . . . and set an example of labour and industry.'' Soon his creditors were after him again, and he had to hide out under an assumed name.[25] His time came in 1786, when he made contact, probably through the aegis of Granville Sharp, with Jonas Hanway's Committee for the Relief of the Black Poor.

Hanway was another extraordinary person, whose numerous charities grew out of his constant search for sensible solutions to the crime, misery and injustice that haunted the urban slum dwellers.[26] In 1786 he took up the cause of the black poor as chairman of a committee of businessmen. Sharp was not a member, but he worked closely with it. He knew blacks and their problems better than anyone else in the enterprise. Hanway was seventy-four and in the last year of his life. He had suffered a stroke, and he lived in almost constant pain from a bladder ailment. His ill health could easily account for some of the testiness with which he latterly dealt with these destitute, but not very deferential, people. The committee, however, developed a working relationship with the black community that was a tribute to Hanway's basic respect for individuals.

The committee raised money—well over £1,000—and distributed it on cash relief, clothes for men offered seafaring jobs, passages overseas, lyings-in and a small ''sickhouse'' in Warren Street. Smeathman came to them in February with his plan for ''removing a burthen from the Public for ever'' by taking some of the black poor to Africa to open a ''channel of trade and commerce'' with Britain. The idea was approved in May, and the committee quickly obtained from the government a promise of financial support amounting to £14 per person. From then on the government authorized Smeathman to pay potential emigrants sixpence a day, and they turned up at the Yorkshire Stingo and the White Raven public houses for their dole.[27] The African settlement scheme coincided with the government's efforts to find new locations, now that the American colonies were lost, for the convicts filling the country's jails. After the testimony of Smeathman and others, the idea of a penal colony in West Africa was shelved and Botany Bay in New South Wales, Australia, fixed upon. Nova Scotia had been thought of for destitute blacks, but that province wanted no more refugees.[28]

When Smeathman's plan was published, passage was offered at 5 guineas a head to "any person desirous of a permanent and comfortable establishment in a most pleasant, fertile climate." Each emigrant would receive clothing, provisions and tools and as much land as he or she could cultivate. A special handbill directed to the "BLACK POOR" was put out by the committee from Batson's Coffee House, Cornhill, stating:

> It having been very maturely and humanely considered, by what means a support might be given to the Blacks, who seek the protection of this government; it is found that no place is so fit and proper, as the Grain Coast of Africa; where the necessaries of life may be supplied, by the force of industry and moderate labour, and life rendered very comfortable. It has been meditated to send Blacks to Nova Scotia, but this plan is laid aside, as that country is unfit and improper for the said Blacks.
>
> The Committee for the Black Poor, accordingly, recommended Henry Smeathman, Esq. who is acquainted with this part of the coast of Africa, to take charge of all the said persons, who are desirous of going with him; and to give them all fit and proper encouragement, agreeable to the humanity of the British Government.

Applicants were directed to go to an "Office for free Africans, No. 14, Canon-street."[29]

While Smeathman busied himself with physical arrangements and recruitment, it fell to Granville Sharp to write a plan of government. Representatives of the blacks approved the result before embarkation. Several sought Sharp's advice before signing to go. Some said that they knew the Sierra Leone area, and they assured him that there was good, unoccupied woodland available there.[30] The utopian society Sharp proposed for the black settlers will be studied later. In the summer of 1786 the immediate task was to organize the departures. It began happily enough. Even before his memorial went to the Treasury, Smeathman had 130 signatures, and officials contemplated providing for around 200. There was reason to think more would respond, but even the most optimistic predictions would not have "relieved" London of more than a small fraction of its black poor, if that were the main object. The committee organized the intending settlers into companies of twelve, each headed by a corporal. The first eight corporals, or headmen, were selected by Hanway in early June. They were James Johnson, a farmer from New Jersey, age thirty-one, who came to England as a ship's steward; John William Ramsay, twenty-four, a domestic servant from New York, also a ship's steward; Aaron Brookes, twenty-five, a New Jersey farmer who had been a captain's cook in the navy; John Lemon, twenty-nine, born in Bengal, a hairdresser and cook and one of many lascars (East Indian seamen) interested in the scheme; John Cambridge, forty, an African-born netmaker and servant whom Sharp had rescued from a slave ship; John Williams, twenty-five, born in Charleston, a seaman; William Green, forty, born in Barbados, a domestic servant; and Charles Stoddard, twenty-eight, born in Africa, a cooper and later a ship's servant. Brookes and Green could read and write, and all the others, except Ramsay, could read. The corporals soon had 192 persons on their lists, while at the same time 156 men and 52 women were receiving the sixpenny dole. The number who might go remained fluid for months.[31]

As preparations advanced, the committee arranged for Mrs. Mary Harris and Mrs. Mary Latouch, white wives of black prospective colonists, to be trained at the London Lying-In Hospital as midwives and approved the distribution of a fourpenny abstract of Bishop Thomas Wilson's "Christian Directions and Instructions for Negroes." It recruited an ordained clergyman, Patrick Fraser. It recommended that all emigrants not yet baptized be christened before they embarked. Less charitably, the committee ran a newspaper advertisement notifying deserted masters or creditors that the emigrants might be viewed at the White Raven at a certain time.[32]

The blacks were adamant about certain things. They insisted on arms to hunt game and defend themselves. They even asked for cannon, but the navy demurred. Four hundred guns and a supply of ball and powder were ordered. The blacks requested constables' staves, stationery and two movable forges. They also asked for documents to protect them from slavers on the African coast. A "passport" was drafted at their direction. It was printed on parchment and delivered to each settler in a twopenny tin box. It carried the royal coat of arms and certified that the bearer was a loyal British subject, entitled to all "the Emoluments, Liberties & Priviledges appertaining to a *Freeman* of the Colony of Sierra Leone or The Land of Freedom situated on the Grain Coast of Africa." Impressive though it looked, it did not confer unambiguous citizenship.[33]

Suddenly, Smeathman died from a "putrid fever" on July 1, 1786. By now 400 men and women were committed to sail. On July 15 their corporals told the committee that the only man who could command the same confidence among them as Smeathman was his clerk, Joseph Irwin, who had never seen Africa.[34] Hanway, exhibiting hitherto concealed suspicions of Smeathman's idea of redeeming (that is, buying the freedom of) slaves to cultivate cotton and rice, charged that the dead leader had intended *"trafficking in Men."* There was no other qualified person to take them to Africa, and New Brunswick was now the committee's choice. Not many weeks earlier, it had been Hanway who harangued them to forget their own doubts about establishing a free settlement in a slave-trade area. They had appeared convinced. Now they were offered New Brunswick. Only sixty-seven agreed to go, and five of them later retracted. They were totally averse to such alternatives as the Bahamas and Gambia, proposed by shipping interests. Their spokesmen held fast to the Smeathman plan, quoting a native, now living in London, who had told them that the Africans at Sierra Leone were "fond of the English & would receive them joyfully."[35]

Wearied by the lengthy business, the committe agreed on August 4, 1786, to recommend finally to the Treasury that the blacks go to Sierra Leone. A contract with a shipping firm was arranged at £8.14.0 per person.[36]

A notion grew up in America that the first Sierra Leone settlers were sent from London against their will. There was indeed, at the end, strong pressure on those who had signified an interest and then withdrew. Their shore allowances were stopped, and they were threatened with prison if found begging. But the public controversy that developed between the blacks and their sponsors during their last months in England contributed more than anything else to the unhappy image which the project gained in some quarters abroad.

The majority of London blacks steered clear of it. The most willing ecruits were the black loyalists who were tempted by the offer of land. By October, 1786, there were 992 men, women (including at least 25 white wives) and children receiving government support on the presumption that most of them would leave the country. The new agent, Joseph Irwin, obtained 675 signatures, again including some English wives, and confidently predicted at least 750 would sail, so three ships and a naval convoy were ordered by the navy. Under the agreement with Irwin, the volunteers for "THE LAND OF FREEDOM," in return for the government charity already received, contracted to board ship before October 20 (a date which proved highly optimistic) and help with shipboard duties as directed. Irwin, financed through the committee, was to provide clothing and "GOOD PROVISIONS" for the voyage and an ensuing four months.[37]

Only 199 of these names reappeared on the final embarkation list six months later.[38] It is something of a numbers game to work out from the fragmentary record the comings and goings of the prospective settlers, but clearly many began to fear and even dislike the leadership of men such as Irwin and the clergyman Fraser and hesitated to go into a slaving center with them. In addition, Jonas Hanway died on September 5, 1786, and his successors, George Peters briefly and then Samuel Hoare, the Quaker banker, did not have his well-meaning reputation among the poor. Decisions became more often unilateral, and a note of coercion crept into the committee minutes. Suspicions of the real intentions of the white authorities deepened when convict ships began to load beside their own for Botany Bay.[39] There was confusion in many minds over who was being deported, who transported and who emigrating voluntarily. Garbled press reports lumped the African settlers with the felons. Africa was said to be the destination for the tough convicted "villains" from London, while the rural criminals would go to Botany Bay to farm.[40]

Forebodings among the blacks appeared to be confirmed when the *Public Advertiser* carried an anonymous report that the Sierra Leone settlement was to have a government like that at Senegal or Cape Coast, with a fort such as at Goreé. All three were slave-trading stations, established and governed by commercial companies with government subsidy and military protection. Nothing could have been further from the original Smeathman-Sharp design. The *Advertiser* revealed twelve days later that leaders of "the seven hundred poor Blacks who had signed an engagement to go to a Free Settlement on the coast of Africa submitted the new system, intended for their government in Ethiopia," to Lord George Gordon, the hero of the London mob.

Lord George advised them not to go, and "four hundred of them declined the embarkation, and came on shore again. Thus the Sierra Leone expedition is delayed for the present." The ships lay in the Thames, while everyone waited to see what the government might do to "dispel the fears of the blacks, quiet their apprehensions, and prevail upon them to fulfil their engagements, under the most solemn assurances, that government will in no instance break faith with them."[41]

The involvement of the charismatic Lord George has hitherto escaped attention. But it was logical that they turned to him, for he had come out against the transportation of convicts. He had visited Newgate Prison to talk with those awaiting banishment and published a petition from them which he probably wrote, appealing against this penalty.[42] Lord George in his brief naval career had visited Jamaica, where he had deplored the "bloody treatment of the Negroes" and resolved to help improve their lot. After the American war, which he opposed, he constantly objected to new taxes, and "Gordon and Liberty" was a slogan frequently heard and seen in the streets. If "few men loomed larger in the public eye during the last quarter of the eighteenth century, if only as a public nuisance!" what more natural than that his counsel was sought by the uneasy blacks?[43]

The unsigned newspaper article which explained their defection was obviously contributed by a sympathizer (possibly Lord George himself) and contained a few grains of truth and many flights of fancy. It spoke of "engineers, surveyors, ecclesiastics, schoolmasters, midwives, and surgeons" being employed and declared that the "poor Blacks prefer liberty with poverty, and nakedness instead of cloathing, rather than submit to the plan." The only persons who remained with the expedition were "decoy Blacks," paid "enormous salaries" to go. It charged that the cost to government already was £20,000. (The final tally was to be under £15,000.) The article attacked such features of the plan as a "system of fines and forfeitures, for the most trivial offences," tithing and a proposed penitentiary with all guns pointed inward "for the secure confinement of offenders and contumacious persons."[44]

The first two points could be inferred from Sharp's regulations. His rules certainly had puritanical overtones regarding pious behavior, orderly work and responsibility for civic service and they included a tax on pride and indolence.[45] But self-government was assured, and there was no blueprint for a fearsome prison. Sharp did furnish the lone engineer, John Gesau, with plans for public works, including defenses, but these do not seem to have survived.

A rebuttal to the public assault on the expedition came on January 1

1787, in another anonymous article (probably from the committee or Sharp) in the *Public Advertiser* which declared, in part:

> They must be enemies to public tranquillity, to the police, and also to the Blacks, who studiously endeavour to fill the minds of these poor people with apprehensions of slavery. . . . No Ministry would think of breaking public faith with any body of men, however poor and abject. . . . Faith is kept by a nation, not because the persons to whom it is pledged are considerable and powerful, but because it is dishonourable to a nation to break its faith. . . . The Blacks, therefore, can have no real cause to apprehend that Government only wants to trepan them to Africa, in order to make them slaves. . . . [They] may therefore embark with confidence: their liberty . . . will be protected by Government; and . . . they will quickly perceive how much more eligible it will be for them to go to a country, where they will have lands assigned to them for their support, and all implements of husbandry supplied to them by the bounty of the nation, than to remain in indigence and want, strolling, wretched spectacles of distress, through our streets; constantly exposed to the temptation of comitting felonies, for which they may be either hanged or transported to Africa, and left defenceless on the coast, where they will perish with hunger, be killed by their savage countrymen, or taken by them and sold as slaves; so that they may at length meet real slavery, in consequence of their ill-grounded apprehension of an imaginary one.''[46]

As the scheme's critic had pointed out, there was no law to compel the blacks to embark or to hold them on board. But a mere two days after the official reassurance, the city of London ordered a roundup of all blacks found begging, and twenty were reported already in jail to be sent ''to the new colony which is going to be established in Africa.'' Within a week a contributor gloated: ''Those apparently deplorable objects, the Blacks, are no longer seen in our streets.'' (Nor were, it might be added, whites masquerading as blacks, a fairly common practice because London citizens were more generous to poor blacks.[47]) Even earlier, when the *Atlantic* and *Belisarius* were ready for boarding the shore allowances had been stopped. Granville Sharp facilitated the departures of many in his usual practical way. He spent almost £800 on cash gifts, loans, small comforts and the redemption of pawned clothes and goods without which some would not go.[48]

Sheer discomfort on shipboard those bitter winter days must have encouraged a spirit of mutiny. The general embarkation was completed on November 22, 1786, the desertion of about 400 had followed in December, and while the attempt was made to replace them, the early boarders were confined for weeks on end. Cold, crowding, a steady diet of salted food and outbreaks of fever began to take a toll. Fifty were to die before the voyage began. When the people tried to make themselves comfortable, they were accused of wasting wood, candles and water. The daily rum ration was blamed for disobedience and quarreling.[49] From Gravesend, where the ships lay, six of the "poor deceived people" came up to London to implore Lord George Gordon to use his influence to stop their sailing until Parliament should resume. A *Morning Herald* report of January 2 charged: "Their poverty is made the pretence for their transportation, and the inferior orders of them decoyed on board the ships are already subjected to a treatment and controul, little short of the discipline of Guinea-men."

By January 8 the *Belisarius* and *Atlantic* were loaded and directed to Spithead off Portsmouth. The *Vernon* arrived at the rendezvous a month later. There Captain T. Boulden Thompson in the *Nautilus* sloop took charge of the flotilla. While the ships waited for a fair wind, a meticulous roll of the passengers was prepared by Gustavus Vassa (Olaudah Equiano), the commissary of supplies and the only black engaged in the organization of the venture. He listed 459. The 344 blacks included 290 men, 43 women and 11 children; the 115 whites, 31 men, 75 women and 9 children.[50]

Still another demoralizing delay was to come. The fair wind arrived on February 22, and the ships weighed anchor. But caught in the channel in a severe gale, the *Vernon* lost its fore topmast and had to limp into Tor Bay for repairs. The other two vessels waited at Plymouth Sound, where the *Nautilus* and the *Vernon* joined them on March 17.[51] The three weeks at Plymouth were marked by continuing controversy. The black leaders of the summer before either had quit, died or lost their influence. Vassa, a belated ally, became the chief spokesman. Enslaved in Africa as a child, Vassa had purchased his freedom with the help of a Philadelphia Quaker merchant and had become a traveled, experienced seaman, navigator and clerk. He had just returned from a voyage as a steward on an American ship when he was invited by the Committee for the Black Poor to become commissary. He had many reservations about the project, especially the lack of advance preparations for securing a site in a center of slaving, but these were overcome.[52] His duties included dealing with surplus stores, as 750 had been provided for and far fewer were going, and preventing the embarkation of anyone not on the committee list. Almost at once he became embroiled in disputes with Irwin. He charged the agent with misuse of funds and failure to provide proper quantities or quality of medicine, clothing and bedding. He also accused Irwin of allowing unauthorized passengers on board. In his desire to represent the suspicious, dispirited, restless, shipbound passengers, Vassa carried his criticisms to the top, to Captain Thompson, the navy office and to the committee chairman, Samuel Hoare. But Irwin succeeded in winning over Hoare, who persuaded the Treasury to fire Vassa. Even though Captain Thompson regarded Irwin as completely unfit for his job, even though the navy found Vassa "acted with great propriety" and was "very regular in his information," it was the black who went. Captain Thompson had described him as "turbulent & discontented" with a seditious spirit which might be fatal to the new settlement and dangerous to its white leadership.[53]

The controversy surrounding the expedition continued. A letter from Vassa to John Stewart (Ottobah Cugoano, another important figure in London's black community) appeared in the *Public Advertiser* on April 4. Written on the day of his discharge, it denounced Irwin, Fraser and the surgeon as "great villains." Vassa denied that he had treated the whites with arrogance and the blacks with civility, "for I am the greatest peace-maker that goes out." They were vilifying him because of his open criticism of the way supplies were mishandled. Many blacks had died for lack of things to which they were entitled. "I do not know how this undertaking will end," he said, "I wish I had never been involved in it. . . ." In the same newspaper, a letter from Abraham Elliott Griffith, another Sharp protégé, now on the *Belisarius* at Plymouth, was quoted, saying that the people on board were "very sickly, and die very fast indeed, for the doctors are very neglectful to the people, very much so."

Vassa's friend Stewart, in the same newspaper on April 6, referred to memorials sent up from Plymouth by the blacks which alleged they had been "dragged away from London and carried captives to Plymouth, where they have nothing but slavery before their eyes . . . under the command of persons who have charge of them." The contract based on Smeathman's plan "has not been fulfilled in their favour, but a Mr. Irwin has contrived to monopolize the benefit to himself . . . they fear the design of some . . . is only to get rid of them at all events . . . and what gives them the most dreadful presage of their fate is that the whitemen set over them have shewn them no humanity or good-will. . . . And that they had better swim to shore, if they can, to preserve their lives and liberties in Britain, than to hazard themselves at sea with such enemies to their welfare. . . ."

The rebuttal came on April 11, again in the *Public Advertiser,* from "X," who implied that Vassa had been fired for misconduct. X tried to smooth out the affair:

> The Blacks have never refused to proceed on the voyage, but the ships have been delayed at Plymouth by an accidental damage . . . [S]hould the expedition prove successful, it can only be owing to the over-care of the committee, who, to avoid the most distant idea of compulsion, did not even subject the Blacks to *any* government, except such as they might chuse for themselves.[54] And among such ill-informed people, this delicacy may have fatal consequences.

Another anonymous defender of the committee in the same newspaper on April 14 charged that Vassa told lies "as deeply black as his jetty face." It threatened that if his "*black* reports . . . continued, it is rather more than probable that most of the *dark* transactions of a *Black* will be brought to *light.*"

Vassa appealed for an inquiry so that he could vindicate himself. He put in a bill for expenses totaling £32.4.0 (which included 5 guineas for a British flag for the settlement) and whatever wages were thought due him. Without a hearing, he was awarded £50 in full. The navy had set aside £60 for "Allowance to the Black Commissary (not yet demanded)" a fortnight before Vassa filed his bill.[55]

Vassa was put on shore at Plymouth along with thirteen other blacks. Also sent ashore were fourteen whites, among them Irwin's son, John, and John's two sisters; the sexton, the purser of the *Belisarius* and his mate, six white women and two male passengers, one of them John Smeathman, nephew of the originator of the plan. Another twenty-three, including five whites (a brickmaker, bricklayer, weaver, surgeon and one woman), departed on their own volition. Fearful that some of the blacks would be left on their hands, Plymouth magistrates complained of men from the transports "strolling about,"[56] which suggests that their confinement aboard was not very strict.

The voyage to Sierra Leone began on April 9. From Tenerife, Chaplain Fraser reported with satisfaction that the purge had been "attended with the happiest effects."

> Instead of that general misunderstanding under which we groaned . . . we now enjoy all the sweets of peace, lenity, and almost uninterrupted harmony. The odious distinction of colours is no longer remembered. . . . The people are now regular in their attendance upon divine service on the Sundays, and on public prayers, through the week. Now they do not, as formerly, absent themselves purposely on such occasions, for no other reason whatever than that I am *white*.[57]

Captain Thompson's final embarkation list shows that 411 persons sailed from Plymouth. Sierra Leone chronicles usually relate that among them were 60 to 70 white women prostitutes collected as companions for unmarried blacks. This is based entirely on the story told to Anna Maria Falconbridge in 1791. She found among the surviving first settlers in Sierra Leone several white women, one of whom told her that more than 100 women, mostly streetwalkers, had been made drunk at Wapping, tricked onto the ships and married to blacks they had never seen before. From then until sailing day, they had been kept "amused and buoyed up by a prodigality of fair promises, and great expectations." Although she said others corroborated this report, Mrs. Falconbridge could scarcely believe it[58] and time has not made it more credible. Nothing can be found in the records. To carry out such a gambit, with or without the connivance of the eminently respectable committee, would have risked exposure in the rumor-mongering London press.[59] The women could not have been concealed. It is not likely they were the unauthorized passengers Vassa complained of, for Hoare had approved them, and he had also conferred personally with Prime Minister Pitt on the white passenger list.[60] It is unlikely, too, that they could have been kept involuntarily, for others came and went from the anchored ships, or that their rosy hopes could survive the sheer discomfort of months on board. They could hardly have been kept permanently drunk from, say, December to April on the going rum ration.

What may be overlooked is that interracial marriages were not uncommon then. Single men predominated in the black population, and if they were to enjoy female companionship, they had to find it in the white race whatever their preference. Both Vassa and Stewart married white women, as did several of the loyal blacks whose records are known. On the whole, blacks were popular among the whites with whom they lived and worked, and not just in the "lower orders." Lord Mansfield's home was enlivened by the pert Dido, who drank coffee and promenaded with his guests and was said to govern his whole family. But if among the women who joined the Sierra Leone expedition there were some who once had been prostitutes, it should not be surprising. London was reckoned to have 30,000 to 100,000 women of that description, although the figures may have unfairly included any woman living with a man without a marriage ceremony.[61]

The status of each passenger was indicated, moreover, in the embarkation list Gustavus Vassa drew up at Portsmouth in February, 1787. He named seventy-five white women, four of whom were wives and one a sister-in-law of whites who were also sailing, and seven of whom were "wanting to be married." The other sixty-three were married to black emigrants.[62] Between then and the April departure eighteen of the white women disappeared from the roll (some may have died) and eleven new names were added, although the race of nine is not given. With discharges and runaways accounted for, a maximum of fifty-nine white women—wives—could have sailed for Sierra Leone.

One other contemporary witness confirms their marital status. Dr Lettsom, who recruited the surgeons and collected seeds and plants for the realization of his old mentor's dream, referred to the white women as "intermarried with the ulack men." He implied that some marriages were recent, and it is natural that weddings should have taken place shortly before such a momentous embarkation. Possibly, the committee which wanted everyone properly baptized also wanted all liaisons legitimatized. Relaying gossip of the voyage, Dr. Lettsom said, "The white wives, having become familiar to the blacks, no longer inspired respect or love, and the husbands and wives were continually fighting During the voyage scarcely any white lady had more than one white eye the other being usually black by blows. Battles have been carried on even under the oratory of the chaplain."[63] This was not the chaplain's line in his report from Tenerife, however, and Captain Thompson said that the black passengers conducted themselves "remarkably well."[64]

Nothing is known of the individual backgrounds or skills of the majority of the black settler families. All eight headmen selected by Hanway went on board, but two were discharged. Thirteen of the black loyalist claimants signed the agreement with Irwin, but only five went from Plymouth: John Ashfield and his white wife, Mary; William Cooper, John Thompson, Prince William and Richard Weaver with his wife, Lucy, and daughter, Judeah.[65] Weaver, from Philadelphia, had applied unsuccessfully to go from London to Nova Scotia in 1783. He was to become the first governor at Sierra Leone. Of the white men who engaged to go, most were artisans. Smeathman had planned a multiracial commonwealth, but those whites who sailed were not committed to become settlers. They had bound themselves to remain only four months.[66]

Regrettably, the spirit of high adventure which seemed to permeate the enterprise in the early summer of 1786 had changed by April, 1787, to a sour welter of charges and countercharges. With the deaths of Smeathman and Hanway, the project had lost its visionaries. There was still Granville Sharp, but he had no official standing. The experiment fell into the hands of men with a more bureaucratic cast of mind, who, in their impatience to see it carried out, did not find the time or see the need to communicate fully with the colonists. John Stewart (Ottobah Cugoano), watching from the sidelines, was probably right: "they were to be hurried away at all events, come of them after what would."[67]

NOTES

1. Thornton to Lettsom, February 15, 1787, in Pettigrew, *Memoirs of the Life and Writings of the Late John Coakley Lettsom*, vol. 2, p. 511.
2. Boston King Narrative, p. 209.
3. Hopkins to Sharp, January 15, 1789, Sharp Papers, Hardwicke Court; printed in *Works of Samuel Hopkins*, vol. 1, p. 141, and Hoare, *Memoirs of Granville Sharp*, pp. 125-28; Hopkins, *Discourse upon the Slave-Trade*, Appendix p. 23; *Works of Samuel Hopkins*, vol. 2, pp. 610-12. For the early colonization movement, Jordan, *White over Black*, pp. 546-69; Fladeland, *Men and Brothers: Anglo-American Antislavery Cooperation*, pp. 81 ff.; Staudenraus, *The African Colonization Movement, 1816-1865*, Chapter I; Sherwood, "Early Negro Deportation Projects," pp. 484-508.
4. On Thornton, Abraham, *Lettsom. His Life, Times, Friends and Descendants*, pp. 378 ff.; Hunt, "William Thornton and Negro Colonization," pp. 36-61; Jenkins, *Tortola, a Quaker Experiment of Long Ago in the Tropics*, pp. 58-61, 89-90; Sherwood, p. 502; Staudenraus, p. 5.
5. Meier and Rudwick, *From Plantation to Ghetto*, pp. 2-3.
6. Lettsom to Martin, April 4, 1791, p. 40; Thornton to Lettsom, July 26, 1788, pp. 520-26; Thornton to Lettsom, November 15, 1788, pp. 531-34, all in Pettigrew, vol. 2. Lettsom to Cuming, October 20, 1787, *ibid.*, vol. 1, pp. 132-36.
7. Thornton to Lettsom, May 20, 1787, *ibid.*, vol. 2, pp. 516-20.

8. Hunt, p. 58.

9. *Works of Samuel Hopkins*, vol. 1, p. 139; Pettigrew, vol. 2, pp. 507, 508 510, 511, 515, 522.

10. *Ibid.*, pp. 510, 515, 521-24. Also see George E. Brooks Jr., "The Providence African Society's Sierra Leone Emigration Scheme, 1794-1795: Prologue to the African Colonization Movement," pp. 185-202.

11. *Works of Samuel Hopkins*, vol. 1, p. 139; Hunt, p. 52; Pettigrew, vol. 1, p 518.

12. Kaplan, *The Black Presence in the Era of the American Revolution*, pp. 186 188.

13. Thornton to Lettsom, May 20, 1787; Thornton to Lettsom, November 18 1786, pp. 497-506; Thornton to Lettsom, July 26, 1788, and Thornton to Lettsom, November 15, 1788 all in Pettigrew, vol. 2; Draper, *The Rediscover of Black Nationalism*, p. 14; Redkey, *Black Exodus. Black Nationalist and Back-to-Africa Movements, 1890-1910*, p. 17; Hunt, pp. 49, 59. Thornton was made commissioner of patents by President Jefferson, and designed the Philadelphia Library, the first Capitol and a house for George Washington.

14. Norton, "The Fate of Some Black Loyalists of the American Revolution," p 404.

15. AO 12/102, f. 156; AO 13/29; AO 12/19, f. 351; AO 12/99, f. 12; AO 12/102, f. 25; AO 12/19, ff. 148, 150; T 1/643, Lists of Black Poor who have embarked, February 27, 1787 (Vassa).

16. AO 12/99, f. 82.

17. AO 12/101, f. 155; AO 13/93; AO 13/24, f. 227.

18. Common estimates for the black population are 14,000 to 20,000. Norton's "minimum" of 1,200 in London ("The Fate of Some Black Loyalists," p. 406 n. 11) seems to assume that the Treasury lists relating to the Sierra Leone expedition recorded all blacks in London. For the "black poor," M. Dorothy George, *London Life in the XVIIIth Century*, pp. 134, 135, 138, 139, 329 Walvin, *Black and White. The Negro and English Society 1555-1945*, pp. 46 ff. Shyllon, *Black Slaves in Britian*, examines their legal status thoroughly.

19. Boucher, *Reminiscences of an American Loyalist*, p. 143; Nelson, *The American Tory*, p. 154.

20. George, pp. 109-11, 116, 135, 137; Wadstrom, *An Essay on Colonization, Particularly Applied to the Western Coast of Africa*, Part 2, p. 228.

21. [Fothergill], *The Works of John Fothergill, M.D.*, vol. 1, pp. xxxvii, liii; Corner and Booth, *Chain of Friendship. Selected Letters of Dr. John Fothergill of London, 1735-1780*, p. 411 n.; Pettigrew, vol. 2, pp. 253-59, 499, 521, 534; Richard Hingston Fox, *Dr. John Fothergill and His Friends*, p. 213. The cosponsors of Smeathman in Africa were Sir Joseph Banks and Dr. William Pitcairn. For his plan, see also Curtin, *Image of Africa*, pp. 95-99.

22. Pettigrew, vol. 2, p. 266; Fyfe, *A History of Sierra Leone*, p. 14; Wadstrom,

Part 2, pp. 201-4; Pettigrew, vol. 1, p. 135; Fox, p. 213; Corner and Booth, p. 409.

23. Smeathman to Cumberland, August 31 and October 10, 1783, and March 30, 1784; Price to Cumberland, September 11, 1783; Cumberland to Highman, October 14, 1783 and January 5, 1784, all in Cumberland Papers, BL Add. MSS. 36,494; Hoare, vol. 2, p. 11; Memorandum, August 1, 1783, Sharp Papers, Hardwicke Court; Pettigrew, vol. 2, pp. 268, 272, 274.

24. Elizabeth Smeathman to Cumberland, May 22, 1784; Smeathman to Cumberland, August 31, October 10, November 1, 1783, and March 30 and April 17, 1784, all in Cumberland Papers, BL Add. MSS. 36,494.

25. Pettigrew, vol. 2, p. 281; Smeathman to Treasury, May 17, 1786, T 1/631; HO 7/1, f. 32, 35, 37; Wadstrom, Part 2, pp. 197-98, 206.

26. For Hanway, Hutchins, *Jonas Hanway 1712-1786*; Jayne, *Jonas Hanway: Philanthropist, Politician, and Author*; Pugh, *Remarkable Occurrences in the Life of Jonas Hanway, Esq.* Pugh, Hanway's protégé and clerk, devoted a half page out of 252 to the black poor. One hopes he was not quoting Hanway when he described the object of the expedition as being to "prevent the unnatural connections between black persons and white; the disagreeable consequences of which make their appearance but too frequently in our streets" (pp. 210-11).

27. Smeathman to Treasury, May 17, 1786, T 1/631; Rose to Hanway, May 29, 1786, T 27/38; Steele to Hanway, June 7, 1786, T 27/38; Norton, pp. 407 ff.

28. HO 35/1, February 9, 1785, August 18, 1786; Curtin, pp. 89-95; T 1/630, f. 1000.

29. Smeathman, *Plan of a Settlement to Be Made Near Sierra Leone, on the Grain Coast of Africa*, esp. pp. 23-24.

30. T 1/631, f. 1284; Sharp to Sharp, July 7, 1786, Sharp Papers, Hardwicke Court; Karibi-Whyte, "The Reception of English Law in Sierra Leone: A Historical Treatment," p. 113.

31. Rose to Navy Commissioners, May 24, 1786, T 27/38; T 1/631, f. 1334; Hoare, vol. 1, p. 371; Little, *Negroes in Britain, a Study of Racial Relations in English Society*, p. 180; Black Poor Committee Minutes, June 7, 1786, T 1/632. About fifty East Indians (or lascars) applied to go to Africa, though some had lived in Britain up to twenty-four years after being stranded by East India Company ships. Black Poor Committee Minutes, August 4, 1786, T 1/634, George, p. 138; *Public Advertiser*, January 1, 1787.

32. Black Poor Committee Minutes, October 13, 1786, T 1/638; Lists Embarked, February 27, 1787 (Vassa); T 1/632, f. 1513; T 1/631, f. 1334; Black Poor Committee Minutes, October 13 and 28, 1786, T. 1/638; SPG *Abstracts of Proceedings*, pp. 28-29; Steele to Committee, January 20, 1787, T 27/38.

33. T 1/631, f. 1284; Navy to Committee, October 18, 1786, T 1/636; ADM 106/2347, November 20, 1786; T 1/638, f. 2798; T 1/636, f. 2430; Karibi-Whyte, pp. 111-12; Rose to Navy Commissioners, October 24, 1786, T. 27/38.

34. T 1/633, f. 1633; Sharp, *A Short Sketch of Temporary Regulations . . . for the Intended Settlement on the Grain Coast of Africa, Near Sierra Leone*, pp. 40-41; *Public Advertiser*, July 4, 1786, where Smeathman is identified as author of the "Humane Plan for the comfortable and free Settlement of Black Poor . . . and of many ingenious treatises not yet published."

35. T 1/632, June 7, 1786; Jayne, p. 134; Pugh, pp. 218-19; T 1/634, August 4, 1786; *ibid.*, f. 1964; T 1/633, f. 1707; Black Poor Committee Minutes, August 4, 1786, T 1/634; *ibid.*, f. 1973; T 1/638, f. 285; T 1/634, f. 1903.

36. T 1/634, August 4, 1786; Rose to Peters, August 8, 1786, and Steele to Navy, August 24, 1786, T 27/38.

37. An Alphabetical List of the Black People who have received the Bounty from Government, T 1/638; Black Poor Committee Minutes, *ibid.*, October 24, 1786; Memorandum of Agreement, *ibid.*, October 6, 1786.

38. List of the Black Poor embarked for Sierra Leone (Thompson), December 30, 1788, Parl. Papers, 1789, XXIV, pp. 8-11.

39. Sharp to Lettsom, October 13, 1788, Huntington Library; also printed in Hoare, vol. 2, pp. 86-95, and Pettigrew, vol. 2, pp. 236-48.

40. *Public Advertiser*, January 4, 12, 29, 1787.

41. *Ibid.*, December 6, 18, 22, 1786.

42. Colson, *The Strange History of Lord George Gordon*, pp. 164, 165; Hibbert, *King Mob, the Story of Lord George Gordon and the Riots of 1780*, pp. 161-63, 175.

43. Robert Watson, *The Life of Lord George Gordon*, pp. 4, 5, 40-60.

44. *Public Advertiser*, December 18, 1786, T 1/645, f. 968.

45. Lynd, *Intellectual Origins of American Radicalism*, pp. 47-48, says Sharp modeled his Sierra Leone regulations on the "nastily Puritanical" proposals of James Burgh in 1764 for a Dutch settlement in South America, which included morals inspectors and penalties for lies and swearing.

46. *Public Advertiser,* January 1, 1787.

47. *Ibid.*, December 18, 1786; January 3, 6, 1, 1787.

48. Black Poor Committee Minutes, October 24 and December 6, 1786, T 1/638; Treasury to Committee, December 4, 1786, T 27/38; Hoare, vol. 2, pp. 87, 104; *The Philanthropist*, vol. 3 (1813), p. 390; Sharp to Lettsom, October 13, 1788.

49. T27/38, January 26, 1787; Sharp to Lettsom, October 13, 1788.

50. Lists of Black Poor Embarked February 27, 1787 (Vassa); Stephens to Steele, January 8, 1787, T 1/641; Thompson to Stephens, January 18, February 9, 1787, ADM 1/2594; Capt. Thompson's Log, ADM 51/627.

51. *Ibid*; Thompson to Stephens, March 10, 1787, ADM 1/2594.

52. [Equiano], *The Interesting Narrative of the Life of Olaudah Equiano, or Gustavus Vassa, the African*, vol. 1; Armistead, *A Tribute for the Negro*, pp. 192-239; Walvin, pp. 89 ff.; Kaplan, 193-206. I have used "Vassa" here

because it was the name he signed. It was Vassa who in 1783 alerted Sharp to the notorious Zong case.

53. Thompson to Navy Office, March 21, 1787, T 1/643; Navy to Treasury, March 23, 1787, *ibid.*; Thompson to Stephens, April 2, 1787, ADM 1/2594; *Public Advertiser*, July 14, 1787.

54. This ignores Sharp's work on a plan of government, which, according to Sharp, was approved by the blacks in the summer of 1786.

55. Vassa Memorial to Treasury, May 12, 1787, T 1/646; Navy Office to Treasury, April 26, 1787, T 1/645.

56. Smeathman to Cumberland, July 26 and 29, 1785, Cumberland Papers, BL Add. MSS. 36,495; Lists of Black Poor Embarked February 27, 1787 (Vassa); Parl. Papers, 1789, XXIV, List of Black Poor Embarked for Sierra Leone; Admiralty to Steele, April 2, 1787, T 1/644.

57. *Public Advertiser*, July 2, 1787, extract from unsigned letter.

58. Falconbridge, *Narrative of Two Voyages to the River Sierra Leone During the Years 1791-1793*, pp. 64-66.

59. Fyfe, p. 17, also doubts the story; West, *Back to Africa: A History of Sierra Leone and Liberia*, pp. 24-26, concludes the women must be wives because of the sheer implausibility of the alternative.

60. Black Poor Committee Minutes, January 16, 1787, T 1/641.

61. Long, *Candid Reflections upon the Judgement Lately Awarded by the Court of King's Bench . . . On what is Commonly Called The Negroe-Cause*, pp. 48-49, illustrates the fury of a Jamaica planter at interracial marriage; Hecht, *Continental and Colonial Servants in Eighteenth Century England*, p. 47; Curtin, pp. 35-36; Walvin, pp. 52 ff.; Little, p. 195; [Hutchinson], *The Diary and Letters of His Excellency Thomas Hutchinson*, vol. 2, p. 276; Shyllon, pp. 14, 240; Ford K. Brown, *Fathers of the Victorians: The Age of Wilberforce*, p. 24; Thompson, *The Making of the English Working Class*, pp. 55-56.

62. Lists of Black Poor Embarked, February 27, 1787 (Vassa); Norton, p. 415, n. 28.

63. Lettsom to Cuming, October 20, 1787.

64. Thompson to Steele, April 22, 1787, T 1/647.

65. Norton's analysis finds seven claimants and three widows of claimants emigrated, but the additional names do not appear on the April (final) sailing list.

66. Thompson to Stephens, January 23, 1788, Parl. Papers, 1789, XXIV.

67. Cugoano, *Thoughts and Sentiments on the Evil and Wicked Traffic of the Slavery and Commerce of the Human Species*, p. 140.

Chapter 9

THE PROVINCE OF FREEDOM

> I King Tom . . . on behalf of and for the sole benefit of the
> free community of settlers their heirs and successors now
> lately arrived from England and under the protection of the
> British Government . . . do grant, and for ever quit claim
> to a certain district of land . . . to be theirs, their Heirs and
> successors for ever. . . .
>
> —TREATY OF 1787[1]

The peninsula of Sierra Leone, washed by sea breezes and served by
the finest natural harbor on the West African coast at the broad mouth of
the Sierra Leone River, was a beautiful site for a new utopia. Its pure and
plentiful freshwater had been known to explorers and traders since the
fifteenth century, and fruit, rice and salt could be procured there as well.
Everyone who came waxed lyrical over the gently sloping wooded shore
beyond which loomed a chain of green mountains which looked leonine
to the Portuguese who saw it first and gave it a name. Up the river on
Bance (or Bunce) Island stood a fortified slave-trading post, now owned
by Messrs. John and Alexander Anderson of London, nephews of
Richard Oswald, from which 1,318 slaves were shipped between 1785
and 1789.[2] A French factor occupied Gambia Island in another branch of
the river. The local Temne population was small, partly because the soil
could not support a large one. Many of the Africans spoke or understood
English and worked for the slave factories or in the camwood trade.

"Can it be readily conceived," Ottobah Cugoano wondered, "that
government would establish a free colony for [the black poor] . . . while
it supports its forts and garrisons, to ensnare merchandize, and to carry
others into captivity and slavery?"[3]

It was not the paradox it seemed, for by the time the settlers weighed
anchor at Plymouth on April 9, 1787, the government's responsibility,

except for paying the transportation bill, had ended. The Committee for the Relief of the Black Poor closed its books. The link to Britain was through one man, Granville Sharp. It was not a colony, but a free and self-governing settlement which was to rise at Sierra Leone, and appropriately it was named Granville Town in Sharp's honor. It lay in what he called the Province of Freedom. It lasted only thirty months, from the arrival of the three transports May 9, to its destruction in a quarrel between local Africans and American slave traders in December, 1789. It constituted, however, a significant beginning for what came to be the colony of Sierra Leone, important for the promises made, the hopes aroused on both sides of the Atlantic, the errors committed, the risks run and the threat it posed to the established commercial (that is, mainly, slaving) interests.

Even with a stop at Tenerife in the Canary Islands, where Captain Thompson purchased a bullock for each ship (and where the black passengers were not allowed ashore to stretch their legs), Cape Sierra Leone was sighted within a month. The little fleet anchored in Frenchman's Bay (soon renamed St. George's), and the newcomers experienced their first "tornado," a rainstorm with thunder and lightning, the same night. It was the eve of the rainy season, a poor time to arrive. The weather en route had been fine, but the blacks, weakened by prolonged confinement in ship's quarters, insufficient fresh food and irregular habits (Sharp blamed the rum), continued to die. Of the 411 who embarked, 377 went ashore.[4]

Richard Weaver wrote to Sharp:

> Honoured Sir,
>   I now inform you of our proceedings during the time of our arrival at Sierra Leone, which was on the 9th day of May 1787; and on the 14th day the land was paid for; and the next day all the people went on shore to cut a passage to get on the hill, to display the English colours. Then the body of people called a meeting, on purpose to choose their officers, whereby they choosed me to be their chief in command.[5]

The path cleared through the bush led to a "beautiful Eminence arising from the side of a higher mountain . . . having a fine brook of fresh water." The site was selected by Captain Thompson acting on directions from Sir George Young, who, when he had ascended the Sierra Leone mountains some years back, "never was so struck before with beautiful

Landscapes of Woods and Water'' and ''found the Air so cool, that he could have born his Great Coat with Pleasure.''[6]

Settlers and planners alike, equally inexperienced, probably had pictured a rapid start on clearing land, laying out the town and building houses. Garden seed would be planted, and the government provisions would keep them going until the first crop was harvested. The reality was far less tidy. As Weaver put it, ''we came too late to plant any rice, or any thing else, for the heavy rains washes all out of the ground.'' James Reid, who succeeded Weaver as governor when the latter fell sick after ''three months and three weeks,'' corroborated that account. ''We did not find arrival at our new settlement according to our wishes,'' he informed Sharp, ''for we arrived in the rainy season, and very sickly, so that our people died very fast, on account of our lying exposed to the weather, and no houses, only what tents we could make, and that was little or no help to us, for the rain was so heavy it beat the tents down.'' The navy had furnished them with 3,000 yards of old canvas to use for shelter until their huts could be built.[7]

A tract stretching some ten miles along the river and thought to be twenty miles deep was procured at a ''trifling expense'' (£59.1.5, to be exact) in muskets, powder and ball, lead and iron bars, laced hats, rum, tobacco, cloth and beads for the ''Free Community of Settlers,'' their heirs and successors. The agreement dated June 11 was made between King Tom and two lesser rulers, Chief Pa Bongee and Queen Yammalouba, and three whites representing the settlers, Captain Thompson, Agent Irwin and Chaplain Fraser.[8] The transaction was regarded as a purchase by the British and the American blacks. In Temne law, however, there was no provision for land sale, though it was customary to permit outsiders (usually traders) to occupy land in return for annual gifts. If well behaved, the ''stranger'' would be protected by his ''landlord.'' The traders were interested not in acquiring land, but only in a trading base. There was no precedent for a settlement of outsiders. The legality of the Sierra Leone title was to crop up repeatedly.

To construct a functioning society in this alien environment was the daunting task facing the survivors of the passage to Africa. They had some experiences in common but were not a homogeneous group. A framework of government was supplied by Sharp in his *Short Sketch of Temporary Regulations (Until Better Shall Be Proposed)*, which authorized complete freedom to rule themselves so long as they did not adopt any law contrary to Britain's common law. To understand his conception of this new society, Sharp himself must be examined a little.

He was perhaps unique among the philanthropists of his time in his obsession with individual rights. He distrusted standing armies and strong executive power. He fought impressment, authoritarian religion (to him, Roman Catholicism) and slavery; indeed, he was the sole member of the 1787 Committee of the Society for Effecting the Abolition of the Slave Trade who stood for abolition of slavery itself. He left his job in the ordnance department at the onset of the American Revolution rather than help expedite arms to a war he disapproved of. The question of racial inferiority or superiority was not relevant to him. He studiously satisfied himself that blacks descended from the same human stock as whites "and must therefore, of necessity, be esteemed as Brethren." He was convinced that divine retribution awaited any government that even tolerated slavery.[9] He poured into his Sierra Leone plan his deepest convictions. The work of the Hanway committee was not just an opportunity to help deal with London indigents, including many blacks who depended on him personally, but a heaven-sent chance to set up a community based on verities long ignored. Sharp entrusted to the untutored settlers a complicated vision which was not well understood by his peers. If it seemed odd to his associates or to historians later that he would so depend on a few hundred freed slaves to make his dream come true, it never seemed odd to Sharp. He treated the blacks as people as capable of responsible self-government as any others, though like an anxious parent, he showered them with advice, books, Bibles and tracts and became angry or hurt—though never totally disillusioned—if they ignored it all. The Sierra Leone settlement, his "poor little ill-thriven swarthy daughter," became the best loved of his "countless schemes of beneficence."[10]

Sharp's "constitution" provided for a system of "mutual Frank-pledge," which he believed was rooted in ancient Hebrew as well as Anglo-Saxon law. Households were divided into tens or tithings (in fact, Sharp accepted dozens, for Hanway already had organized the blacks into companies of twelve), each of which would elect a tithingman. Every hundred households would choose a hundreder. All males over sixteen could vote in the common council or parliament (which Sharp hinted might be called a palaver in African style and which also could be likened to a New England town meeting). Among other civic duties, householders served as militiamen. Labor, the most valuable article in any new settlement, was to be the medium of exchange, with paper currency backed by the value of a day's work. The town would run rather like an institution. A public bell would signal each item on the day's agenda. Work would begin after prayers at 6 A.M. and end at 4 P.M. with a two-hour siesta, eight hours a day instead of the twelve commonly worked in England. With six hours on Saturdays, it added up to a forty-six-hour week, very liberal for the times. Sundays and three other days each year (Christmas, Easter and "Frankpledge Day") were holidays. Sixty-two workdays were a tax in public labor for the government, the poor and sick. Refusal to work, whether from pride, wealth or laziness, would be taxed. Slavery was prohibited, but runaway slaves could be paid for and then work out their redemption price. Work began and ended with prayers (Sharp even provided suitable samples).[11]

This "glorious Patriarchal System of *Frankpledge*," Sharp assured Dr. Lettsom and through him William Thornton in America, would maintain such an effectual balance of power that "the Whole can Act *as one Man,* tho' *every separate Family* shall still enjoy its due Share of Power, as far as is *consistent* with the Rights and Sentiments of the Majority." Although Sharp himself sometimes spoke of the Province of Freedom as a colony, he told John Jay, president of the New York Society for the Promotion of the Manumission of Slaves, that it should be regarded as "perfectly free," since the settlers could make any laws not inconsistent with Britain's, hold their own courts and assemblies, elect their own leaders and maintain control of their militia. If they followed this code, "they would become the freest and the happiest people on earth; because the poor are effectually provided for, and their rights secured, the meanest cottager being allowed a due share of the land, besides a property and interest in the settlement."[12]

The people, whom he addressed as "Dear Friends," always had the last word. Urging them to avoid disputes with ships over anchorage and water supply fees, or recommending against letting some ill-behaved person back into the community, or asking them to take in newcomers on equal terms, Sharp would "earnestly recommend" or say, "I have no authority to interfere, but am only anxious that. . . ." He recognized the necessity for full information if they were to run their own lives and suggested copies be made for distribution of pertinent letters, contracts, lists of provisions and the like.[13]

It was a central principle that the land was the responsibility of the community as a whole and that a majority vote was required to dispose of it. Each person, regardless of sex, over sixteen was entitled to a one-acre town lot and an "outlot," or small farm. The plans were drawn with the idea that Smeathman would be the agent, and for his "extraordinary efforts," he would have been allowed every tenth lot. When he died,

Sharp suggested the settlers might want to reconsider this special treatment for the substitute agent. Possibly they were reluctant to give Irwin so much, and this may have been a cause of friction in England. Before sailing, Irwin pressed the committee for a decision and was given Smeathman's generous share without consultation with the people. Sharp attended the meeting where this was agreed. Sharp had included a provision that future white settlers—so long as they were Protestants—might join within the first year on the same terms as the first arrivals.[14]

To naval Captain Thompson, the result of all this in the settlers' hands was anarchy. Abraham Elliott Griffith, a London servant whose education had been paid for by Sharp, agreed; the people "could not be brought to any rule or regulation, they are so very obstinate in their tempers," he wrote Sharp.[15] Griffith left Granville Town to become scribe and interpreter for King Naimbana at Robana and married the Princess Clara.

Thompson became increasingly critical of the settlers, reporting a "licentious Spirit" and "obstinacy and laziness, which neither remonstrance, persuasion, or punishment have yet been able to subdue." He had two of them flogged for "insolence and misbehaviour." His censure gained warmth until he told a parliamentary committee in 1790 that "the major part of them were a worthless, lawless, vicious, drunken set of people, and it was with the utmost difficulty that I could persuade them to erect a covering for themselves from the inclemency of the weather . . . a few only of them . . . I think had a prospect of doing well."[16]

Drawing largely on a journal kept by a white crew member of the *Nautilus,* the colonization enthusiast C. B. Wadstrom also depicted the settlers as no good:

> Laziness, turbulence and licentiousness of every kind so entirely pervaded this wretched crew, that scarcely a man of them could be prevailed on to work steadily, in building the hut that was to shelter him, or even to assist in landing the provisions by which he was to be supported. The rains set in on the 28th of June, and the mortality became dreadful: yet the infatuated survivors persisted in their excesses.[17]

The historical record, unfortunately, is lopsided. The scattered evidence largely derives from the self-serving opinions of whites. Captain Thompson may have taken upon himself greater powers of direction than were accepted by the people, for his orders had been only to convoy the three transports and as a king's representative to negotiate with Africans for land. The physical situation alone was difficult enough to overwhelm and disorganize any group. From Weaver's account, the blacks acted immediately to implement their plan of government by electing him as chief or governor, but there is no sign that Thompson or other whites recognized this or later elections. When the rains abated, the settlers planted rice and corn and bartered spare clothing to get poultry (and sometimes rum). They hired Africans to help them build houses. They experimented with the soil "to be sensible what it will produce, and find the more we cultivate the better the land seems to turn out, in regard of the country roots and herbs. But our English seeds do not thrive . . . being too old."[18]

Among the harshest critics of the settlers were the slave traders, rightly fearful that a successful Province of Freedom would cause havoc in their lucrative trade. James Bowie, agent in charge at Bance Island, denounced the newcomers as a "very dangerous bad set of people" who regarded themselves as better than whites. They had "intermixed with the Natives and have by telling them a number of Falsehoods given them a great many bad Notions of White Men in general that has made them more saucy and troublesome than ever they were known before." He accused individuals of insulting the crews of visiting slave ships, of threatening to make "minced collops" of him for once ordering them off Bance Island, of stopping slave ships and demanding payment to let them continue up the river and of plundering the neighborhood Africans. Some of the chiefs later confirmed that Bowie promised them arms if they would prevent the initial landing of the settlers.

Continual abrasive contacts demonstrated the constant danger in which the free blacks lived and the sheer nerve and resilience with which they faced it. The most shocking episode occurred in 1788 after five Granville Town residents (Richard Bradley, John London, Robert Moore, Adam Sabb and Lewis Sterling) robbed the store at Bance. Found out by their then governor, John Lucas, they were arrested with the help of other settlers, including Charles Stoddard, their "chief justice." The five burglars were turned over to the Bance Island factor to stand trial. The robbery was described to a "jury" of seven slave factory representatives and slave ship captains and five settlers. The defendants readily admitted their guilt and on June 26, 1788, were sentenced to banishment as the mildest feasible punishment for the most daring crime to date. But Bowie sold the five men to a French slaver leaving for the West Indies. Alexander Anderson, his employer, justified the action to a parliamentary committee under the "law of necessity" since "no ship would have taken them on freight," and there was no other way to carry out the sentence of banishment.[19]

When Granville Sharp heard about this, he was horrified. He praised the settlers for behaving with the "utmost propriety" in giving up the guilty men for trial but charged that the "factors, on their part, shewed neither mercy nor prudence."[20]

Among other recorded incidents was the time that King Tom attempted discipline by seizing and selling two settlers to a French trader. A Liverpool captain refused to pay for three days' care and the burial of one of his seamen at Granville Town and held a settler in irons for three days as a show of strength. Several settlers in turn seized the captain and held him prisoner until he agreed to pay a fine. When he heard this news, Sharp said it proved "that they really maintained some reasonable form of government among them, as well as an efficient civil power to support it." Thomas Clarkson saw in the settlers' belligerence a "considerable check" to the slave merchants, and he believed that if they had been able to enforce their justice often enough, they would have seriously affected the trade. Tom's successor, King Jimmy, once captured a settler boy and sold him at Gambia Island. In retaliation, some of the settlers took up arms and seized a man from Jimmy's town, an act which divided the settlement, however. In the ensuing row, John Cambridge was somehow made a scapegoat, jailed and flogged. He took refuge at Robana and worked in Naimbana's trading operations. Four settlers carried off by a slave ship, John Banks, James Crane, Charles Chilcot and George Stephenson, somehow escaped sale in the West Indies and found their way to England, where Sharp supported them until they could get back to Granville Town.[21]

The Temne king, Naimbana, was at first a friendly neighbor and observer of the free settlement, despite rumors inspired by the traders that the newcomers would take away his land. He helped adjudicate disputes, a traditional duty of the landlord, and foresaw great benefits to his country from this infusion of American-European culture. He did not think much of their democracy; a single strong leader would be better. In letters to Sharp and on a visit by three of them to England, the settlers described Naimbana as a kindly father, a ruler who would "frequently sit down with them & discourse freely" and who had imbibed enough Christianity from them to want more knowledge of it and a Christian baptism. Griffith, the king's secretary, also tutored Naimbana's children, and the eldest son was later sent to England to be educated.[22]

Whatever reports reached Sharp of defections or dereliction of duty he was heartened by one fact: ". . . the People who remained in the Settlement have carefully adhered to their promise not to permit the iniquity of slave-dealing in the *Province* of *Freedom,* so that tho' they have not kept up strictly to the other Regulations which I proposed for them, yet in this most essential point they deserve commendation."[23] Some who left the settlement, however, did not show this loyalty to principle or any abhorrence of the system that had enslaved them or their forebears. Some found work as clerks, laborers and artisans at the slave factories or took up slaving themselves. The slave trade, indeed, offered the only well-rewarded employment in the region, given the settlers' lack of capital, but it was a great gamble. The French were paying such a high price for slaves that "the poor Africans were tempted to waylay & kidnap each other, in a much more notorious manner than ever before." Several deserters from the settlement were among those so trapped. When, in 1791, a slave insurrection occurred in the French colony of Santo Domingo, Sharp attributed the uprising "in a great degree" to his own stolen former constituents "as they were become hardened fellows by Service on board the English Men of War; & in the British Army in America."[24]

As for those who entered the business voluntarily, Sharp realized that they were driven more by poverty than wickedness. The slave traders offered high wages to enter their "detestible Service" and the lure was powerful because of the "extream poverty of the Settlers, who had nothing to enable them to purchase any *live Stock*, without which it was impossible for them to obtain sufficient subsistence."[25] He permitted himself a rare moment of fury, however, when Henry Demane defected to become a slave dealer on the Bulom Shore opposite Granville Town. Demane was one of several blacks whom Sharp had rescued from forcible return to the West Indies. Sharp warned Demane of the "horrors and remorse which must one day seize those authors and abettors of oppression who do not save themselves by a timely repentence."[26]

Realizing the weak position of the free settlement, Sharp advised the settlers, in the mild vein which was to be the official position from then on, not to provoke the slave traders and to "be courteous and kind to all strangers . . . even though you know them to be slave-dealers or slave-holders, provided they do not offend your laws during their stay. What is done beyond your boundaries you cannot help or prevent, except the offenders belong to your community; neither must you interfere with others in the least, except by kind and friendly warnings of God's

impending vengeance . . . and this only when you have any fair opportunities of mentioning the subject, without giving personal offence."[27]

In every important way, the black settlers of 1787 stood comparison
with the whites who accompanied them. The latter contributed little to
the strength of the community (not always intentionally, for sickness and
death were rife) and added greatly to the tension and ill will. Joseph Irwin
notified them almost immediately that he had no intention of staying. He
blamed their attitude, but Captain Thompson did not accept this; Irwin
was not "at all calculated to establish an infant colony."[28] Irwin died, in
any case, on July 11, 1787.

The clergyman proved almost equally useless. He could not get the
people to build him a house or a church and had to hold his services under
a tree. It may be that the settlers felt they had their hands full getting
themselves under cover, or it may have been some suspicion of Fraser's
role and ambitions. Within weeks, Fraser had repaired, for reason of
health, to Bance Island, where he administered to thirty Englishmen and
many slaves, few of whom understood his English. Fraser informed the
Society for the Propagation of the Gospel that most of the blacks did not
intend to remain either. This was confirmed nearly a year later, when
Richard Weaver wrote to Sharp that "the chief part" of the people had
gone. Fraser, ill with tuberculosis, returned to England in the spring of
1788.[29] He reported that only 130 settlers were then at Granville Town,
though Sharp believed 200 was nearer the mark. More than a year later
Sharp was trying to locate Fraser to get from him the register of marriages
for which Mrs. Lucas and other "ladies of the settlement" had appealed.[30]

Death removed many of the whites on whose skills the planners had
counted. Of the thirty-three white settlers (not counting wives of blacks)
who were selected to go, only twenty-two actually sailed. None was
inclined to stay at a place where "the Blacks shewed no Attention or
Deference." In September, 1787, only six were still alive. The fatalities
included one doctor, the engineer, both farmers, the gardener, the
tanner, two smiths, the baker, flax dresser, carpenter and tailor. All six
survivors, including the three remaining doctors, entered the slave trade.
Twenty-six white wives of black settlers were part of the tragic toll from
"Fevers, Fluxes, and Bilious Complaints."[31]

The blacks were sometimes torn by dissension. The governorship
shifted rapidly from Weaver to Reid to Lucas, and it did appear that
without a strong executive, major works were difficult, if not impossible,
of achievement.[32]

The initial setbacks at the Province of Freedom were not known abroad for many months. Meanwhile, there was keen excitement and interest within church groups and other anti-slave-trade sections of British, American and French society. Sharp received daily applications from both blacks and whites to join the settlement. Among the latter were Thomas Clarkson, whose prizewinning essay on the slave trade had catapulted him into the front rank of abolitionists, and his younger brother, John, a naval lieutenant, recommended as "a gentleman in every way qualified to render you very essential service, as a member of your *free community*, whenever he may arrive." Twelve Swedes of "rank, great learning, and abilities" looked upon the Province of Freedom as a base for exploring the African interior in a Swedenborgian search for the true church. They included C. B. Wadstrom, the colonization historian and propagandist, Adam Afzelius, Augustus Nordenskiold and James Strand. Also eager to go was Alexander Falconbridge, onetime surgeon on a slave ship and now Thomas Clarkson's sturdy aide.

Black volunteers included Peter Nassau from Mesurado (now Liberia), who was being educated in England, and William Johnson, a mulatto who had redeemed Nassau from slavery in the West Indies. Another was Henry Martin Burrows, a free black from Antigua whom Sharp had saved from transportation to Honduras with a writ of habeas corpus. Burrows had suffered frostbite on shipboard, and both legs had been amputated, but this did not seem to disqualify him.[33]

An enticing view of the new settlement had been published by 1789. It depicted small houses lined up under a waving British flag with fat cattle grazing on shore and a mountain stream tumbling into the Sierra Leone River. A slave ship lay at anchor, and across the bay, in King Tom's town, Africans were busy with their boats. A shallow cove where ships could be built or repaired was indicated, and the waters were said to be abounding in excellent fish.[34]

Before then, however, news of the distressing events had reached London. Sharp's reaction was to muster a relief expedition. He obtained £200 from the government and more than £150 from the elder Samuel Whitbread and spent £900 of his own to charter and outfit the brig *Myro,* which sailed on June 7, 1788. The quota for new settlers was set at fifty, but only thirty-three sailed. Sharp provided bread, spruce beer and live pigs to kill en route so that these passengers would not suffer from a salt-food diet or from rum. Captain John Taylor was given money to buy cattle, poultry, goats, sheep and swine at the Cape Verde Islands as breeding stock. Other supplies and seeds were also to be picked up there.

For the only passage for which he bore full responsibility, Sharp also provided a set of rules to train the emigrants for life at their new home. This time only, women were allowed to vote with men to elect trustees to handle the stores. Fines were to be levied (in labor or provisions) for drunkenness, swearing or "any affront, indecency, or improper behaviour, in the opinion of the majority of the assembly, toward any woman, whether married or single. . . ." On the *Myro* were two surgeons and John Irwin, son of the deceased agent.[35]

The relief expedition was a partial success. Although death claimed 13 of the new settlers, the arrival of supplies and 20 new inhabitants attracted back some of those who had scattered, restoring the population to about 200. Twelve of them signed a flowery thank-you letter in which they declared that "the name of GRANVILLE SHARP, our constant and generous friend, will be drawn forth by our more enlightened posterity, and distinguishingly marked in future times for gratitude and praise." King Tom had died. King Naimbana, the overlord, who had not been a party to the original pact, had now cooled toward the settlement and would allow it to continue only with a new treaty. Captain Taylor, though not in the navy, negotiated an agreement, once more securing the land to the settlers for another £85 worth of goods. This was signed on August 22, 1788, by Naimbana and King Jimmy, among other Temne leaders, while two blacks, Richard Weaver and Benjamin Elliott, and a new doctor represented the settlers. Captain Taylor had neglected to purchase breeding stock and persuaded the settlers to buy his trade goods, instead, with the money. It was an early commitment to commerce instead of agriculture. Even the unfriendly agent at Bance admitted the settlers had a talent for trading.[36]

Just a month after the *Myro* anchored, James Reid in his letter to Sharp suggested the means for establishing a commercial life based on credit, so that the settlers would not be forced to sell scanty property for necessities. It would help:

> if we had an agent or two out here with us, to carry on some sort of business in regard of trade, so that we could rely a little sometimes on them for a small assistance, till our crops were fit to dispose of, and then pay them. . . . Provisions are scarce to be got—no, not one mouthful sometimes—which oblige us to dispose of all our clothes, and other few necessaries . . . though, God knows, they are not much, for we are almost naked of every thing.[37]

Sharp had not been noticeably interested in turning his pastoral society into a trading center, though he might have read a recently published letter by Gustavus Vassa citing the potentially rich African market for British goods once the slave trade was driven out.[38] But this appeal for "Merchants or Factors" to take charge of the trade stimulated him to approach various "respectable merchants and gentlemen to form a *Company*" to trade with Africa. His prospectus credited the idea to the settlers. The new organization was called the St. George's Bay Company, and it held its first meeting on February 17, 1790. Except for Henry Thornton, none had been connected with the Committee for the Relief of the Black Poor. Among those present were Sharp and his two brothers, Samuel Whitbread and Joseph Hardcastle, while William Wilberforce was an absent member. The company bought the *Lapwing*, a small cutter suitable for coastal trading, for £186 at a customshouse sale. A request for a charter was addressed to the king.[39]

Only two months later came the crushing news of the destruction of Granville Town the preceding December. The news was late, according to Thomas Clarkson, because slave ship captains refused to carry the settlers' messages, and an unnamed inhabitant risked passage on a slaver to England by way of the West Indies to bring the disaster report. Sharp credited his information to the Anderson brothers, who had the news from Bance Island.[40]

The events were these:[41] An American slave ship had kidnapped certain subjects of King Jimmy. The next boat belonging to an American slave ship to be seen in the river was headed for Bance Island with rum when it was attacked by Jimmy's people. The rum was seized, three crewmen were killed, and a fourth escaped to Bance. The boat was sold to a French slave factory. After hearing earlier of the dangers facing the settlers, Sharp had appealed to Pitt for protection, and on November 17, 1789, Captain Henry Savage of the warship *Pomona* dropped anchor in St. George's Bay. Abraham Ashmore, the incumbent governor, asked him to mediate in the pending disputes with King Jimmy and Bowie of Bance Island. The trader was summoned on board, and Captain Savage accepted his opinion that the "New Settlers were the aggressors." Bowie also warned that if the British ignored Jimmy's vengeance on the Americans, the river trade would be unsafe. Savage signaled King Jimmy to come on board. He refused, and Savage sent a party of marines under Bowie's command, with settlers as guides, to Jimmy's town. By accident or in reaction to a hostile reception a pistol was fired and a thatch set alight. The town went up in flames. One version had it a midshipman was responsible. Naimbana later claimed to have the pistol Bowie had used to fire the town.[42] The party fought its way back to the *Pomona*. On the British side, a lieutenant, a sergeant and a settler were killed. For several days the ship remained in the bay with working groups put onshore to bury the dead, take on water, wood and fruit and repair equipment. They were frequently menaced by Jimmy's men. On three days, Captain Savage shelled the beach and protective bushes, and the Africans returned musket fire, badly wounding one seaman. On November 27, a settler was shot near the watering place. Before he sailed on December 3, Savage arranged with Naimbana to hold a palaver to settle the affairs. After these bloody events the outcome could not be a surprise. King Jimmy could not retaliate against a warship, but Granville Town was an easy mark. The settlers were given three days to get out, and the town was destroyed. Three years later Governor Clarkson agreed to pay 100 bars damages for family spoons and a gold cross taken from Jimmy's house by a marine from the *Pomona*, finally closing the incident.[43]

The disaster ended a brief period of progress in which the settlers had begun to till small farms, increase their flocks of poultry and develop a limited trade. Even Bowie conceded that ''for these last eight or Ten months any of them that have come here with their small Trade have behaved themselves very quietly.'' Captain Savage vouched for their ''good behaviour in the management of their little government, their trade, and their cultivation, which was just beginning to be in a promising state of improvement.'' In the aftermath, eighteen settlers went off as seamen. With the help of Bance Island boats, eighty-seven moved to Bobs Island, but Bowie was antagonistic to their staying so close since ''they are a set of people we do not like.'' Seventy settlers, including Ashmore, stuck together in spite of the traders' efforts to disperse them. They obtained land from Pa Boson, a chief several miles upriver from Bance, where about ten of them worked from time to time. Several more settlers found a refuge at Robana with Naimbana. Others scattered along the coast and as far away as England.[44]

That strong bonds had been established within Granville Town, for all its faults and bad reports, is illustrated in the unity of the surviving families. A sympathetic visitor, well over a year later, found their community ''very regular; and they have a kind of church where they say prayers every Sunday, and sing the psalms very well.'' They were overjoyed to hear, through him, from Granville Sharp and to know that they had not been forgotten in England.[45]

The calamity spurred Sharp to seek government aid to provide the

survivors with clothes, trade goods and naval protection, and in a series
of letters to the prime minister through the summer of 1790, he spelled
out the reasons why the government should care what happened to the
black emigrants. If the site were not repossessed, it might be sold to the
French since a proposal for a similar free settlement had been published
in Paris. Sierra Leone could be the basis of a thriving British trade. The
scattered settlers could still be reassembled, but:

> if they are neglected much longer, they must perish and fall
> into the snares of their enemies, the neighbouring *slave-
> dealers*, by whose machinations their misfortunes have been
> occasioned, and the advantage of opening a free and honest
> trade with . . . Africa . . . will be irrecoverably lost; because it
> is not probable that ever such an opportunity may offer again of
> having above one hundred people, inured to that climate and
> ready on the spot, to adopt and support the free laws of British
> Government.[46]

After the first communication, Pitt asked Sharp for details. Then came
silence. Nor was Sharp successful in getting others to intercede. The St.
George's Bay Company, with some 100 members, would do nothing
until Parliament passed an act of incorporation which would limit their
individual liability. The business view became increasingly dominant,
and instead of the free trade Sharp had proposed, the company now
sought a trading monopoly for thirty-one years. This produced vehement
opposition from the Company of Merchants Trading to Africa.[47] In late
August the St. George's Bay Company agreed to ship £150 worth of
clothing and provisions on the *Lapwing*. Sharp wrote to the settlers with
his customary frankness about his failure to help them in a substantial
way. Even the few articles now going out to them would not be given
away, the *Lapwing* captain could only dole them out in exchange for
African produce or labor. At the same time, an agent of the company—
Alexander Falconbridge—would negotiate with the Temne chiefs to
restore the town site; as it had been "purchased twice," this was only
common justice. Sharp's argument to the chiefs, which also summarized
the present aims of the settlement as seen in London, was that "the
intention of making that settlement was *really* with a view to promote the
improvement and welfare of the natives of Africa, as well as for your
good and ours;—it being thought the best mode of establishing an honest
and honourable trade in the natural productions of the soil in Africa, in
return for English manufactures, and instead of the bloody and wicked

trade in their brethren the Negro Slaves. . . ." Since he was helpless to do more than offer a veiled threat that if the chiefs were recalcitrant, the English king might retaliate, he called upon the Africans to remember his personal record as a *"friend to Blacks"* who "has some right to claim their particular friendship. . . ."[48]

But Sharp was not deceived by what had happened. His biographer commented, "The fond expectation of *'a perfect good'* . . . was now at an end. He had been unable to establish 'the happiest and the freest government on the earth.' " New hands were taking charge. When the *Lapwing* arrived, belatedly, in January, 1791, its cargo was discovered to consist, not of food and clothing, but of trade goods, chiefly black-smith's and farm tools, plus a "prodigious number" of children's halfpenny knives and scissors.[49]

NOTES

1. Cession of a Territory on the Banks of the River Sierra Leona, for the Accommodation of the Black Poor, June 11, 1787, Parl. Papers, 1789, XXIV, p. 12; Fyfe, *Sierra Leone Inheritance*, p. 112.
2. Parliament Papers, 1789, XXV, p. 260.
3. Cugoano, *Thoughts and Sentiments on the Evil and Wicked Traffic of the Slavery and Commerce of the Human Species*, p. 142.
4. Captain Thompson's Log, May 10, 1787, ADM 5/627; Thompson to Steele, April 22, 1787, T 1/647; Sierra Leone Company 1791 Report, p. 5; Sharp to Lettsom, October 13, 1788, printed in Hoare, *Memoirs of Granville Sharp*, vol. 2, pp. 86-96; Porter, *Creoledom, a Study of the Development of Freetown Society*, pp. 20-21; Sharp to Franklin, January 10, 1788, Granville Sharp Papers, New-York Historical Society.
5. Weaver to Sharp, August 23, 1788, in Hoare, vol. 2, pp. 96-97, and Fyfe, p. 114.
6. Sharp to Lettsom, October 13, 1788.
7. Weaver to Sharp, August 23, 1788; Reid to Sharp, September 1, 1788, in Hoare, vol. 2, pp. 97-99 and Fyfe, p. 115; ADM 106/2347, February 3, 1787. Although it is impossible to be certain, this could be the James Reid who first settled at Birchtown. A pilot, he may have gone to sea and ended up in England.
8. Sharp to Lettsom, October 13, 1788; see Note 1. Weaver's earlier date might be the time negotiations began. Reid's widow in 1817 turned over to the Sierra Leone governor "the Grant of for [sic] the original Settlement of the black Settlers and two letters thereon from Mr. Granville Sharpe." CO 270/14, July, 1817.
9. Sharp to Boyd, March 13, and to Lord Poulett, March 18, 1773, York

Minster Library; Memorandum, April 17, 1797, Thompson-Clarkson Collection, Friends Library, 1/255, quoted in Lascelles, *Granville Sharp and the Freedom of Slaves in England*, pp. 71-72; Hoare, vol. 2, p. 234; Curtin, *Image of Africa*, pp. 99-101. Lynd, *Intellectual Origins of American Radicalism*, p. 25, includes Sharp in the handful of Englishmen and women whose writing cleared the way for the American Revolution. Hoare is the standard work on Sharp. His obituary by Thomas Clarkson appeared in *The Philanthropist*, vol. 3 (1813), pp. 383-96.

10. Stephen, *Essays in Ecclesiastical Biography*, vol. 2, p. 317.

11. Sharp, *Short Sketch of Temporary Regulations*, pp. 5, 7, 14, 15, 17, 20, 21, 22, 23, 24, 30.

12. Sharp to Lettsom, October 13, 1788; Sharp to Jay, March 7, 1789, in Hoare, vol. 2, p. 119.

13. Three important letters are: Sharp to the Worthy Inhabitants of the Province of Freedom in the Mountains of Sierra Leone, May 16, 1788, in Wadstrom, *An Essay on Colonization*, part 2, pp. 338-40; Sharp to the Worthy Inhabitants of Granville Town in the Province of Freedom, Sierra Leone, November 11, 1789, in Hoare, vol. 2, pp. 131-35; and Sharp to the Worthy Passengers on the Myro Brig, May 20, 1788, *ibid.*, appendix 11.

14. Sharp, *Short Sketch of Temporary Regulations*, pp. 36, 40-41, 122-23; Black Poor Committee Minutes, January 19, 1787, T 1/641.

15. Thompson to Stephens, January 23, 1788, in Parl. Papers, 1789, XXIV, p. 7; Thompson testimony, Parl. Papers, 1790, XXX, p. 174; Fyfe, *A History of Sierra Leone*, p. 23; Hoare, vol. 2, pp. 95-96.

16. Thompson to Steele, April 22, 1787; Thompson to Stephens, May 26, 1787, and July 23, 1787, ADM 1/2594; Thompson Log, July 16, 1787, ADM 51/627; Fyfe, *History*, p. 20; Thompson testimony, p. 173.

17. Wadstrom, part 2, p. 221.

18. *Ibid.*; Thompson to Stephens, January 23, 1788; Thompson testimony, pp. 167-68; Reid to Sharp, September 1, 1788.

19. Bowie to Anderson, July 18, 1788, Parliamentary Papers, 1789, XXV, pp. 271 ff.; extract Bowie to Andersons, December 22, 1789, PRO 30/8/363; Alexander Anderson testimony, Parliamentary Papers, 1789, XXV, pp. 271-81, including Josiah Smith to Anderson, February 8, 1789.

20. Hoare, vol. 2, p. 123.

21. Reid to Sharp, September 1, 1788; Fyfe, *History*, pp. 24-25; Hoare, vol. 2, p. 122; Thomas Clarkson, "Some account of the new colony at Sierra Leona, on the coast of Africa," p. 161; Cambridge to Governor, April 30, 1792, CO 270/2; Sharp to Worthy Inhabitants, November 11, 1789.

22. Sierra Leone Company 1791 Report, pp. 16-19; Hoare, vol. 2, pp. 161-66; Sharp to brother, September 23, 1791, Sharp Papers, Hardwicke Court.

23. Sharp to Hopkins, July 25, 1789, Hardwicke Court.

24. Porter, p. 22; Weaver to Sharp, August 23, 1788; Sharp to brother, January 14, 1792, Hardwicke Court.

25. Sharp to niece Jemima, August 8, 1788, Hardwicke Court; Wadstrom, part 2, p. 223.

26. Sharp to Worthy Inhabitants, November 11, 1789.

27. *Ibid.*

28. Thompson to Stephens, July 23, 1787, Parl. Papers, 1789, XXIV, p. 6; Thompson testimony, p. 173.

29. *Ibid.*; Fraser to SPG, July 27, 1787, SPG *Journal*, vol. 25; Fraser to Morice, September 15, 1787, USPG, West Africa; Sharp to Lettsom, October 13, 1788.

30. Kuczynski, *Demographic Survey of the British Colonial Empire*, vol. 1, p. 45 n.; Memorial of Granville Sharp . . . and Others, in Hoare, vol. 2, p. 140; Sharp to Worthy Inhabitants, November 11, 1789. After a lengthy convalescence, Fraser was sent by the SPG to the Bahamas in 1792. SPG *Journal*, vol. 25, p. 449.

31. Thompson to Stephens, January 23, 1788; List of the Black Poor embarked for Sierra Leona (Thompson), Parliamentary Papers, 1789, XXIV, pp. 8-11; Thompson to Stephens, July 23, 1787.

32. Weaver to Sharp, August 23, 1788; Reid to Sharp, September 1, 1788; Porter, p. 23.

33. Sharp to brother, January 19, 1788, Hardwicke Court; Sharp to Worthy Inhabitants, May 16, 1788; Hoare, vol. 2, p. 104; vol. 1, p. 371.

34. Wadstrom and others, *Plan for a Free Community upon the Coast of Africa, Under the Protection of Great Britain; but Intirely Independent of all European Laws and Governments.* Wadstrom, Augustus Nordenskiold, Colborn Barrell and Johan Gottfried Simpson tried to drum up interest in a settlement at Cape Mesurado.

35. Fyfe, *History*, pp. 21-22; Hoare, vol. 2, appendix 11. Spruce beer was made by boiling unpeeled twigs with molasses and fermenting the cooled mixture with yeast. It was considered antiscorbutic.

36. Fyfe, *History*, p. 23; Kuczynski, pp. 46-47; Wadstrom, *Essay on Colonization*, part 2, p. 223; Sharp to Pitt, April 26, 1790, Hardwicke Court; Old Settlers to Sharp, n.d., Hoare, vol. 2, pp. 114-15. Three of the white newcomers deserted to the slave trade.

37. Reid to Sharp, September 1, 1788.

38. Letter from Gustavus Vassa, late Commissary for the African Settlement, to Lord Hawkesbury, March 13, 1788, Parl. Papers, 1789, XXVI.

39. Granville Sharp, *Free English Territory in Africa*, p. 10; Sharp to Worthy Inhabitants, November 11, 1789; Hoare, vol. 2, p. 139; Wadstrom, *Essay on Colonization*, part 2, pp. 224-25; Memorial of Granville Sharp, Hoare, vol. 2, p. 140.

40. Clarkson, p. 161; Sharp to Lettsom, September 27, 1790, in Hoare, vol. 2, pp. 150-51.

41. Based on Savage to Stephens, May 27, 1790, ADM 1/2488; Log of the *Pomona*, ADM 51/703; Sierra Leone Company 1791 Report, pp. 6-7; *Gentleman's Magazine*, vol. 61 (1791), p. 483; extract, Bowie to Andersons, December 22, 1789, and Tilly to Andersons, December 20, 1789, PRO 30/8/363.

42. Falconbridge to Sharp, April 18, 1791, PRO 30/8/310.

43. [John Clarkson], "Diary of Lieutenant J. Clarkson, R.N.," p. 62. West African barter was based on iron bars, roughly valued at two shillings sterling each.

44. Sierra Leone Company 1791 Report, p. 6; extract Bowie to Andersons, December 22, 1789; Sharp to Pitt, June 10, 1790, in Hoare, vol. 2, pp. 144-47; extract Tilly to Andersons, December 20, 1789; Sharp to settlers, September 27, 1790, in Hoare, vol. 2, pp. 151.

45. Kennedy to St. George's Bay Company, February 9, 1791, in Wadstrom, *An Essay on Colonization*, part 2, p. 225.

46. Sharp to Pitt, April 26, 1790, in Hoare, vol. 2, p. 143; Sharp to Pitt, June 10, 1790, *ibid.*, pp. 144-45.

47. Sharp to settlers, September 27, 1790; Hoare, vol. 2, p. 149; Sharp, *Free English Territory*, p. 10; Propositions for establishing a St. George's Bay Company, n.d., PRO 30/8/363; [Campbel], *Reasons Against Giving a Territorial Grant to a Company of Merchants, to Colonize and Cultivate the Peninsula of Sierra Leona, on the Coast of Africa*, pp. 4, 13, 14.

48. Sharp to settlers, September 27, 1790.

49. Hoare, vol. 2, p. 150; A. M. Falconbridge, *Narrative of Two Voyages to the River Sierra Leone*, p. 67.

Chapter 10

THE AMERICAN RESPONSE

> Africa is the land of black men, and to Africa they must
> and will come.
>
> —John Kizell[1]

The image of the Sierra Leone settlement which was projected to
North America was, in essence, Granville Sharp's demiparadise, a
self-governing community under the benevolent eye of the blacks' most
renowned white friend. The vicissitudes of the Province of Freedom also
were reported, frequently by hostile witnesses, but the early general
impression was that the experiment might well succeed. Sharp's correspondence with Hopkins, Jay and (indirectly) William Thornton guaranteed that hundreds of American blacks received the word. Discussion
centered on the prospect of blacks still in the United States joining those
who had returned to Africa from London. Copies of the regulations were
sent. Sharp believed that up to 1,200 could be accommodated with free
land. In addition, there were newspaper and magazine accounts and the
word-of-mouth reports of seamen and travelers.[2]

In Nova Scotia a dinner-table conversation overheard by a black
servant led to the remarkable embassy of Thomas Peters. The sequence
of events was described by Thomas Clarkson in an article written for the
American Museum and published in April, 1792. The story must have
been obtained from Peters himself, for John Clarkson, and undoubtedly
his brother as well, had long and affecting conversations with the spokesman for the Nova Scotian blacks. Clarkson did not date the anecdote, but
from a list of names which Peters turned over to Sharp, and which may be
the families he represented, the incident could have taken place during
1789. Peters was in London, at any rate, by November, 1790.[3]

As Thomas Clarkson told it, the black loyalists in Nova Scotia were
almost reduced to despair:

when one day, some company at dinner happened to be conversing on the projected scheme of the Sierra Leone colony,
and mentioned Mr. Grenville [sic] Sharp, a name revered
among the negroes, as the patron of the plan. A sensible black,
who waited at table, heard the accounts with eagerness, and
took the first opportunity of spreading them among his countrymen. The hope of relief animated them, and they resolved to
send over their agent, one Thomas Peters, a respectable,
intelligent African, to wait upon the [St. George's Bay] company, and learn if they might expect encouragement to go to
the new colony. . . . Never did ambassador from a sovereign
power prosecute with more zeal the object of his mission than
did Thomas Peters the cause of his distressed countrymen.[4]

Further proof that the Nova Scotia blacks knew of the African settlement appears in a letter from William Wilberforce: "These poor people
hearing a confused report of an intended settlement on the coast of
Africa, sent one of their number . . . to London to inquire into the truth of
it, and to request, if it should seem expedient to him, that government
would transport them thither. We took up the cause. . . ."[5] And more
than half a century later a visitor to Sierra Leone was told by one of the
Nova Scotia emigrants how they had sent a delegate to England to say
they were "desirous of becoming colonists in the new settlement which
they had heard was about to be formed here." A similar version appeared
in an early report of the Sierra Leone Company.[6]

It is worth dwelling on the point because, in after years, it was passed
off as fortuitous that Peters reached London just as Sharp's modest St.
George's Bay Company was undergoing its metamorphosis into the
Sierra Leone Company. The thesis of this entire study is that the black
Americans who went to Sierra Leone acted knowingly at every stage.

Peters was now about fifty-three years old, a man of proved pride and
bravery and the experienced representative for disaffected Black
Pioneers at both Annapolis and St. John. How he voyaged, we do not
know. It is possible that he worked his passage or that his constituents
raised the £17 fare. If the latter be true, it is my own conceit that he
traveled with William Augustus Bowles, the adopted Creek Indian, on
the *Lord Dorchester*, a merchant ship which reached Spithead on
October 28, 1790. Bowles, with two Cherokee and two Creek companions, had come to Canada to get the governor general's support for his
mission, and Governor Parr paid their passages to England to present

heir "talk" to the king. They were seeking a treaty to allow the Creek to trade in the British West Indies. Richly embroidered accounts of the Indian mission and the "chiefs'" infatuation with the Covent Garden Theatre appeared in the London press, which seems to have ignored Thomas Peters. But a contact between Bowles and Peters may be one reason why years later Bowles called at Sierra Leone.[7]

Peters caused a stir, however, among the anti-slave-trade leaders, many of whom were now engrossed in plans to rescue the Province of Freedom. He found his old commander, Captain George Martin, who provided him with a reference dated November 4, 1790, which attested to his having served in the war "faithfully and Honoustly and on Every Respect becoming the Character of a good and faithfull Subject." Then he waited upon General Sir Henry Clinton, who endorsed the certificate and recommended Peters to William Wyndham Grenville. There is an undocumented interlude in which Clinton may have tried to see the secretary. Clinton did speak personally to Wilberforce on behalf of Peters and his fellow old soldiers, supporting their "claim on the protection and good offices" of Great Britain. Peters had two petitions to present, one protesting the discrimination the blacks had suffered in Nova Scotia and the other seeking government assistance to go to Sierra Leone. On December 26, 1790, Clinton provided him with a letter of introduction to Grenville which said:

> I wish to present to you a memorial of certain poor blacks who are deserving the Protection of Govt. & who seem to be the only Loyalists that have been neglected; Indisposition prevented my calling again at your office. I am now obliged to go out of Town for a few days, perhaps you will suffer the poor Black who is the bearer of this to tell his own melancholy Tale. He is deputed by others in similar situation; I remember this man a very active Serjt. in a very usefull Corps.[8]

Peters handed in his petitions and the testimonials on the same day. From the circumstantial evidence in Granville Sharp's surviving papers, it seems that Peters on his own or through Wilberforce got in touch with Sharp very early in his stay. Sharp must have helped him frame both petitions. They are much more polished than Peters' Canadian memorials, and they fit neatly into the anti-slave-trade campaign, as well as the activities of the men seeking an act of incorporation for the company which was to manage the African settlement. Certainly the references to

English law and the tone of moral outrage at the existence of slavery in the Maritime Provinces are typical of Sharp, and some of the same phrases occur in a letter he wrote about the same time to a brother.

In the petition respecting his mission (a portion of which was quoted in Chapter 6) Peters requested, first, ''some Establishment where they may attain a competent Settlement for themselves and be enabled by their industrious Exertions to become useful Subjects to his Majesty'' and, secondly, the provision of the due allotments for those blacks who preferred to remain in Canada. Sierra Leone was not named, but when Governor Parr was notified officially, the plans for Sierra Leone were mentioned, and it was said that Peters, encouraged by the sponsors, had decided to go there.[9]

The second petition furnishes a vivid glimpse into the thinking of the disgruntled black loyalists. In it, Peters contended that racial prejudice was worse than the failure to provide land, because the ''public and avowed Toleration of Slavery . . . as if the happy Influence of his Majesty's free Government was incapable of being extended so far as America'' led to ''such a degrading and unjust Prejudice against People of Colour in general that even those that are acknowledged to be free Inhabitants and Settlers . . . are refused the common Rights and Privileges of the other Inhabitants, not being permitted to vote at any Election nor to serve on Juries.'' This had made it impossible for them to recover wages owed to them or to get legal protection against violence and personal attack.

> Several of them thro' this notorious Partiality . . . have already been reduced to Slavery without being able to obtain any Redress from the Kings Courts, and . . . one . . . thus reduced . . . did actually lose his Life by the Beating and Ill Treatment of his Master and another who fled from the like Cruelty was inhumanly shot and maimed by a Stranger allured thereto by the public Advertisement of a Reward . . . who ''delivered him up to his Master'' in that deplorable wounded State. . . .

In a ringing summation, the petition called for compensation or relief:

> as the poor friendless Slaves have no more Protection by the Laws of the Colony (as they are at present misunderstood) than the mere Cattel or brute Beasts . . . and . . . the oppressive

Cruelty and Brutality of their Bondage is particularly shocking irritating and obnoxious to . . . the free People of Colour who cannot conceive that it is really the Intention of the British Government to favour Injustice, or tolerate Slavery in Nova Scotia.[10]

There was to be a brisk response on the complaint about land. The outcry against slavery was buried in the files. Thomas Clarkson, however, used it in his *American Museum* article, blaming the harassment of the blacks in Nova Scotia on Southern white loyalists and some British officers who "made frequent and successful attempts to reduce again to slavery those negroes who had so honourably obtained their freedom."[11]

In addition to Sharp and the Clarkson brothers, Peters came to know Joseph Hardcastle, who was to be a director of the Sierra Leone Company, and Henry Beaufoy, MP. Sharp sent Peters to Beaufoy as part of his campaign to have the company's incorporation bill drafted with due regard to the settlers' rights. He assured Beaufoy that Peters was well recommended "& his Ideas of the Stipulations to be made with the Company for the Land . . . are worthy of Attention."[12] Peters also had a formal interview with the company directors, including Henry Thornton, the chairman. Much later John Clarkson said that Peters "had been spoil'd in England." He had certainly chosen a momentous time to come. The anti-slave-trade crusade was warming up again, with evidence for Parliament being collected by the hardworking covey of "white negroes" (Pitt's sarcastic description), including the Clarksons, who used Wilberforce's London home and the nearby office of the Committee for Effecting the Abolition of the Slave Trade in New Palace Yard.[13]

A "madness for the blacks, began in England about the year 1790," according to Cobbett. The cruelties of the slave trade were the "*fashionable* cant of the day," and indeed during Peters' London stay, Coachmakers Hall in Foster Lane, Cheapside, was often hired for debates which were regularly won by the abolition side. Real-life reports of atrocities from Africans lately arrived in England were popular.[14] The Sierra Leone enterprise was inseparably linked with the abolition crusade, sharing leadership, resources and enemies.

Within weeks of Peters' coming, the St. George's Bay Company dispatched Alexander Falconbridge to Africa to reestablish Granville Town. Falconbridge was a big blunt Bristol man who had been driven by necessity to sign on as a surgeon on four voyages to Africa aboard English slave ships. He had left the trade, despite promises of a ship of his own to command, out of a slow realization of its horror. He had volunteered to help Thomas Clarkson in the dark days when witnesses were hard to find, and he had published in 1788 a searing indictment of the slave traffic. With more haste than sensitivity, the company bought passages for him and his spirited bride, Anna Maria, on the *Duke o, Buccleuch*, a slave ship of the Andersons of Bance Island. Falconbridge, more strident—and with more reason—than most of the abolitionists, predictably quarreled with the captain en route. It was a bitter pill to him that his brother, sent along as his assistant, almost at once joined the Bance factory.[15]

Falconbridge carried a warm letter from Sharp to "the worthy British Settlers," in which he explained that his hopes for their future now lay in the "merchants and gentlemen of the first fortune and credit" who planned to conduct an *"honourable trade"* with Africa. The government intended to transfer the land purchased by treaty in 1787 and 1788 to the new company, which would in turn "grant free lots of land" to them. It was to hold a trading monopoly, however, and only those settlers who promised to deal exclusively with it would be eligible for land. He urged the settlers to resume their militia service and erect effective earthworks and other defenses so that the settlement would not fall again.[16]

However Sharp might try to cushion the blow, the fact was that the new company intended to take over not only the trade, as James Reid had more or less requested, but the government as well. The company would make all the laws and regulations until the inhabitants had "attained the necessary Knowledge to make positive Laws," to which the company would then "cheerfully acquiesce."[17] Sharp was more nervous about this development than he told his African friends. After Thornton introduced the bill for the new trading company early in 1791, Sharp engaged in last-ditch lobbying to guarantee legal protections for the past and future settlers. However benevolent the individual subscribers might be, Sharp warned Beaufoy, a reform-minded member, "as a Company of *Merchts and Traders*" they would "have very little feeling for the rights & just privileges of the Settlers." Parliament therefore should write certain safeguards into any charter. Sharp apparently had discussed them with Peters. In the order he jotted them down in the draft of his letter to Beaufoy, these were:

1. If the company price for settlers' produce was not enough, they

should be able to ship it to England at a reasonable charge for sale.

2. Prices set by the company should be limited to a fixed profit.
3. The land to be *"regranted"* should be "deemed in every respect
    . . . to be held free," and a common system of justice should apply
    to settlers, seamen and company employees.
4. All land not actually enclosed or occupied by the company should
    be common land for "grazing, Hunting, Fowling, Fishing, Cutting
    Timber . . . gathering Honey, Gums, Cotton, Indigo, Grasses,
    Oranges and all other spontaneous provisions."
5. A time limit should be put on the company's trading monopoly,
    after which trade should be *"perfectly free."*
6. Equal lots of land should be granted free, not only to the first
    settlers, but also to the "Nova Scotia Negroes & all other persons
    whom Government shall think proper to send." Children of settlers,
    at the time of marriage, should also receive grants, free.[18]

The bill was fought by London and Liverpool slave-trading interests, as well as by West Indian planters, and Parliament in the end did not grant a charter, which would have delegated power to govern, but only passed an incorporation act for the company, whose name was changed in the legislative process to the Sierra Leone Company. This enabled the company to take over the original land grant and buy additional land, with a casual disregard of the fact—only pointed out by the opposing slave-trading spokesmen—that the tract was assigned by both the 1787 and 1788 treaties to the black settlers and their heirs and successors forever. This quibble was brushed aside by the act's sponsors with expressions of astonishment that anyone could oppose such a splendid experiment in "civilization" and high-minded commerce. The company justification was that the Old Settlers had abdicated their title by leaving the spot. Sharp's safeguards were not included; they would more appropriately have appeared in a charter. A clause did prohibit the company, but not others using the harbor, from engaging in the slave trade. The provision for a trading monopoly was dropped under pressure and it was agreed to limit the life of the company to thirty-one years. The final vote, on May 30, was 87 to 9, and the company came into existence on July 1, 1791.[19]

The first 100 proprietors or investors included at least 57 merchants and several other men with financial interests. Although Sharp's name came first, it was the thirty-one-year-old banker Henry Thornton who became chairman of the thirteen-member court of directors, which was elected on July 13. Sharp, Wilberforce and Thomas Clarkson were directors. Other influential members of the court were Hardcastle, a cotton importer, Thomas Furley Forster, and Philip Sansom, Samuel Parker, George Wolff and Vickeris Taylor, all merchants.[20] Although most, perhaps all, of the original subscribers were opposed to the slave trade, the company was not paraded as philanthropic but as a good investment. Trade, development of tropical agriculture and the spread of Christianity were the goals, and the settlers instruments to such ends. The reconstructed Province of Freedom would be a closely regulated mercantile colony, run by an absentee all-white board in London. Sharp had not foreseen the almost complete loss of influence he would suffer. His disillusionment was revealed in a letter to William Thornton concerning the changed and "very disagreeable circumstances." He saw little inducement now for the free blacks of New England to emigrate, for the settlement was turning into a "colony" such as Americans might shun:

> . . . the community of settlers, though they are now restored to their actual possessions in the settlement, are no longer *proprietors of the whole district* as before, as the land has been granted . . . to the *Sierra Leone Company*; so that they can no longer enjoy the privileges of granting land by a free vote of their own Common Council, as before, nor the benefits of their former Agrarian Law, nor the choice of their own Governor and other officers, nor any other circumstances of *perfect freedom* proposed in the *Regulations*; all these privileges are now submitted to the appointment and controul of the Company, and no settler can trade independently of it.
>
> I am very sure that such restraints cannot accord with your ideas of perfect liberty and justice. But I could not prevent this humiliating change: the settlement must have remained desolate, if I had not thus far submitted to the opinions of the associated subscribers.[21]

A few weeks before the final action on the company bill, the House of Commons defeated the latest anti-slave-trade motion, introduced by Wilberforce as the climax to a four-year public campaign. Energies were now poured into the Sierra Leone Company. Thomas Peters was an observer to both the parliamentary battle and the inauguration of the company. If he had any doubts, they were not sufficient to cause him to

hange his mind about going to Africa and taking his like-minded friends
vith him. Arranging for the migration of the Nova Scotians was the first
rder of business after Falconbridge wrote that he had found fifty-six
ettlers living in what he described as an intolerable swamp above Bance
sland. They had insisted on returning to a site as near as possible to the
riginal Granville Town, which Falconbridge considered too close for
afety to King Jimmy's. In a five-day palaver arranged by King Naim-
ana, the agent was able to persuade the Africans to turn over the original
ract to the (then) St. George's Bay Company for £30. The new Gran-
ille Town was begun to the east at an abandoned Temne village where
here were several empty huts, and by April, 1791, the settlers were
vorking hard to complete their houses before the rains began. New tools
nd arms were distributed; fish, game, rice and poultry were plentiful.

Falconbridge was dismayed by the vulnerability of the settlement,
owever, and urged that it be fortified. He pleaded, "for Gods sake send
ne a Ship of force." Falconbridge blamed the animosity of the Temne
ntirely on "That lump of deformity the *Slave Trade*," which had so
lebauched them that they were "lost to honor & honesty."

Falconbridge found the settlers, who for nearly four years had been on
heir own, unruly, though still "warmly attached" to their English
ponsors. Some of them, convinced that their previous weak government
ad contributed to their rout, were eager now for a strong hand at the
elm to lead them and to "punish them according to their desserts some
f them being a very bad sett of people having commited depredations on
eople here," said John William Ramsay. He nominated Falconbridge,
'who treats them with the utmost kindness, and whom they esteem as a
ather." But some settlers later complained that Falconbridge treated
hem like slaves, left his dishonest Greek servant in charge, instead of
ne of them, and took away, on a flimsy pretext, the seine they needed to
ish.[22]

The interest of the Nova Scotian blacks in the settlement could hardly
ave come at a more opportune time. Thomas Peters' petition received
he attention of government as soon as the company bill was passed. On
August 6, 1791, Secretary of State Henry Dundas sent copies to Gover-
or Parr at Halifax and Governor Carleton at Fredericton. If its facts were
rue, said Dundas, the blacks "have certainly strong grounds for com-
laint." Parr was directed to start an inquiry, and both governors were to
ulfill any promises which proved to have been neglected regarding land
rants for those who wanted to stay. The government was prepared to

give the others free passage to Sierra Leone, and the governors were to dispatch "a discreet Officer" to various parts of the provinces where the blacks now lived to advertise the terms of settlement.[23]

John Clarkson's offer to act as the company's unpaid agent in Nova Scotia and, with Peters, to escort the blacks to Africa was gratefully accepted. Steeped in the cause, Clarkson was naturally susceptible to Peters' petitions and the "distressing accounts which he gave me of their sufferings." After at least ten months in Britain, Peters sailed for America ahead of Clarkson to lay the groundwork for their move. Clarkson prepared himself for the most consequential task which had yet faced him, conferring at length with directors and government officials. Lawrence Hartshorne, a Halifax merchant, was named to work with him. Clarkson was handed his instructions by the directors on August 12 along with the printed terms to be offered the Nova Scotians. He embarked at Gravesend on the *Ark* a week later, but because of adverse winds in the Channel, it was September 8 before his voyage truly began.[24]

Clarkson was only twenty-seven, half Peters' age, but his qualifications included more than the facts that he was Thomas Clarkson's brother and had been a member of Wilberforce's "Slave Committee" for the last three years. He had been sent into the royal navy at eleven, was commissioned a lieutenant while serving in the West Indies during the American Revolution and had investigated the French slave trade at Le Havre in 1788. In May, 1791, both he and Henry Thornton were elected to the Committee for Effecting the Abolition of the Slave Trade. In addition, this clergyman's son was a devout Christian, imbued with a keen sense of honor and justice, unusually free of racial prejudice, and a believer in frank and full communication. His sense of duty (perhaps his call to adventure?) overrode personal feelings. He was engaged to be married to Susanna Lee, the daughter of a Norfolk landowner, yet cheerfully deferred his plans in the interests of the Sierra Leone settlement, which he and Thomas had once contemplated joining.[25]

Wilberforce wrote to Evan Nepean, permanent undersecretary at the Colonial Office:

> The young man who is going out as agent is a young Man of
> very great merit & a thousand good qualities both professional
> & personal, amongst which, believe me, discretion is one . . .
> added to all this he is a person for whom I feel a very sincere
> Regard: on these various Grounds, allow me to request you

will furnish him with any Letters that may tend to procure him
abroad with a Reception as he deserves.[26]

The haste with which the new Sierra Leone Company dispatched its
business could be explained by the pressure to reinforce the Old Settlers
before it was too late and the need to compensate for the defeat of the
slave-trade abolition bill and keep up the momentum of the crusade. If it
ever were to succeed, the public must be aroused; the flame, in Wilberforce's metaphor, must be fanned. To offer a humane alternative to the
trade would be even more effective than the fashionable West Indian
sugar boycott. The directors were without colonial experience except for
Sharp, who was not trusted to be practical, and Charles Grant, a close
friend of Thornton's who had been twenty years with the East India
Company before returning to England the previous year. With hindsight,
Thornton himself admitted this lack, but he rationalized that "even if
we had studied the histories of other settlements, we should have remained ill-qualified for our work, for the circumstances were entirely
new."[27]

Thornton was a highly successful financier and experienced politician.
A certain worldly wisdom allowed him a saving detachment that John
Clarkson would never achieve. Thus Thornton could write reassuringly
to the agent in Nova Scotia:

> I should have shrunk from the task if I had been aware what it
> was to be Chairman of the S. Leone Company, but industry &
> application make amends in some measure for my other
> deficiencies. . . . You need therefore no more to be terrified by
> the weight of the undertaking than myself—These things are
> not so difficult with a little honesty, industry and common
> sense as they appear. . . . I will quote you by way of removing
> a little of your diffidence a passage from a Latin author which
> has rather relieved mine—and what used to be rather familiar
> in the mouth of Mr. Pitt when he first ventured to take the reins
> of Government "Nesus me fili: quam parva sapientia regitur
> mundus."[28]

The decision to send ambiguous terms of settlement to the Canadian
provincial governors and for circulation in the black communities proved
ultimately to be the first major mistake, and it could be blamed on the

general hurry. Under date of August 2, 1791, the directors signed a handbill which announced:

FREE SETTLEMENT
on the
COAST OF AFRICA

The Sierra Leone Company, willing to receive into their Colony such Free Blacks as are able to produce to their Agents, Lieutenant Clarkson, of His Majesty's Navy, and Mr. Lawrence Hartshorne, of Halifax, or either of them, satisfactory Testimonials of their Characters, (more particularly as to Honesty, Sobriety, and Industry) think it proper to notify, in an explicit manner, upon what Terms they will receive, at Sierra Leone, those who bring with them written Certificates of Approbation from either of the said Agents, which Certificates they are hereby respectively authorized to grant or withhold at Discretion.

It is therefore declared by the Company,

That every Free Black (upon producing such a Certificate) shall have a Grant of not less than TWENTY ACRES of LAND for himself, TEN for his Wife, and FIVE for every Child, upon such terms and subject to such charges and obligations, (with a view to the general prosperity of the Company,) as shall hereafter be settled by the Company, in respect to the Grants of Land to be made by them to all Settlers, whether *Black* or *White.*

That for all Stores, Provisions, &c. supplied from the Company's Warehouses, the Company shall receive an equitable compensation, according to fixed rules, extending to Blacks and Whites indiscriminately.

That the civil, military, personal, and commercial rights and duties of Blacks and Whites, shall be the same, and secured in the same manner.

And, for the full assurance of personal protection from slavery to all such Black Settlers, the Company have subjoined a Copy of a Clause contained in the Act of Parliament whereby they are incorporated, viz.

—"Provided also, and be it further enacted, that it
shall not be lawful for the said Company, either directly
or indirectly, by itself or themselves, or by the agents or
servants of the said Company, or otherwise whosoever,
to deal or traffic in the buying or selling Slaves, or in any
manner whatever to have, hold, appropriate, or employ
any person or persons in a state of slavery in the service of
the said Company."[29]

This piece of paper was to be much fought over in ensuing years,
chiefly because of the murky reference in the second paragraph to "such
terms and . . . charges . . . as shall hereafter be settled by the Company."

It was autumn before the directors got around to delineating the terms
and November before they were published for the benefit of intending
settlers from Britain. The revised terms never reached Nova Scotia
before the blacks sailed; John Clarkson found them with other letters
awaiting him at Sierra Leone.

Clarkson, after his extensive briefings, understood the August terms to
mean that the settlers would help defray the costs of education and public
welfare through some form of taxation. His brother, a director, said in his
American Museum article, written sometime during these months, that
the land would be held in fee simple—freehold—by the settlers and their
heirs forever. Granville Sharp, also a director, notified the Old Settlers
that their regranted land would be "free."[30]

Under the provisions dated November 3 and circulated as "Terms of
the Sierra Leone Company, to all such Settlers as shall sail from England,
within three months . . . to Sierra Leone," a quitrent was introduced. It
was to be reckoned from midsummer, 1792, to start at a shilling per acre
per year and to rise at intervals of three years, at the company's discretion, to a maximum of 4 percent of the produce. Artisans and workmen
employed by the company, by an agreement of November 7, might be
granted land on the same terms after a year, if they chose to settle.[31]

At a meeting of proprietors on October 19 the directors made their first
report, promising profits, which "may hereafter be reasonbly expected
to be very important," first, from the quitrents, secondly, from the
company's own plantations and, thirdly, from trade.[32] With complete
disregard, or ignorance, of colonial experience, the fledgling directors
had imposed a tax on land ten times higher to start with than anything
known in America. A quitrent, Thornton explained to John Clarkson in

the letter received in Africa, would be easier to collect than customs duties. He added:

> I trust the Blacks will not consider this a grievance especially as it will be very light at first & that they will consider themselves as hereby paying the necessary expence of government & return to the English Subscribers who have stood forth so liberally to serve them . . . 4 per cent . . . being the utmost rate of tax their lands can ever have to pay.[33]

Shares in the Sierra Leone Company were limited and quickly snapped up. Anyone who sought belatedly to buy had to wait for one of the 500 proprietors to resign and sell, as Thomas Clarkson learned when he tried to find a few shares for Josiah Wedgwood.[34] But the company's purpose, was not just speculative trade, but a sincere effort to introduce into Africa "long detained in Barbarism the Blessings of Industry and Civilization." This unique combination of business and benevolence was clear, at least, to the directors, who brought to their work an inspired dedication. Although several, later identified with the evangelical Clapham Sect, were to be engaged in numerous other good works, the Sierra Leone colony was their first important joint venture. The leadership was young: Thornton and Thomas Clarkson were thirty-one, and Wilberforce was only thirty-two. Granville Sharp was a patriarch at fifty-six. All four were bachelors, and Thornton's London house was their chief meeting place until offices were found in Lawrence Poutney Lane in the City. Thornton almost totally neglected his banking business for this enterprise, in which the "happiness of Thousands & Millions of our fellow creatures" seemed to depend upon the ability of this band of Englishmen to plan the "civilization & cultivation of Africa & above all for the propagation of Christianity there." Thomas Clarkson, never at a loss for the rotund phrase, referred to the project as "the Noblest Institution ever set on foot, an Institution which embraces no less than an Attempt to civilize and christianize a great Continent, to bring it out of Darkness, & to abolish the Trade in Men." And Joseph Hardcastle said, "shd. the great & good parent of the Universe patronize our plan, & smile upon this infant Colony, we shall be thankfull to him for allowing Us to be at all instrumental in so beneficial a Work."[35]

Next to the quitrent, the form of government was to have most impact on the black settlers. Here the decisions again became controversial. The directors were handicapped by their failure to obtain a charter. All they could do was contrive a set of rules. Until 1800 the company government lacked legitimacy, a fact which acted as a brake on policy. Not yet knowing the new settlers, and with little confidence in the old ones or in Sharp's democracy, the directors (or a majority of them) kept decision-making in their own hands and set up a weak administrative council of eight top employees. The superintendent had only an equal voice, but a casting vote. Council members also served as judges but had no power to inflict capital punishment. Settlers could serve on juries, and each jury must have at least half its members from the same race as the defendant. Hundreders and tithingmen were retained as peace officers.[36]

C. B. Wadstrom attributed the decision not to delegate power to the settlement to fears of the infiltration of proslavery people, who would seek to alter its course or ruin it. It was true that a large number of the recruits for staff came from the military services or the West Indian colonies. Great care was taken in accepting shareholders or choosing staff to avoid men who were not committed to abolition of the slave trade. According to Thornton, some attention was given to the council forms of government used in India and Virginia, but chiefly the decision resulted from problems of staffing.

The choice for superintendent fell on Captain Henry Hew Dalrymple, son of a Grenada planter, who had served with the army at Gorée. He had testified against the slave trade, giving eyewitness accounts of cruelty to slaves in the West Indies. Thornton vetted each candidate and had each stay at his house to look him over thoroughly, and other directors did the same, but they had known Dalrymple only a week or two before his appointment. Some of his ideas of defense and expenditure struck them as "wild." They did not like giving him arbitrary power. Before the end of 1791 Dalrymple's habit of "hastily & warmly" objecting to every step the directors took, and in particular his demand for 150 soldiers when the directors were agreed to a tenth as many, led to a resolution voicing their deep concern which was followed by his prompt resignation.[37]

The logical second choice was Falconbridge, who had arrived home in September with the son of King Naimbana. Falconbridge reported that he had collected sixty-four Old Settlers in all (thirty-nine black men, nineteen black and six white wives; no children were recorded) and that four acres had been cleared and planted. The king and at least some of the settlers hoped Falconbridge would be the governor, but the directors rewarded him only with a pay raise and a new appointment as chief commercial agent, a post for which he had no experience whatever. He took the job because he needed it, and hoped it might show him how to make money.[38] The directors were uneasy about his hot temper and free criticism. Thomas Clarkson met him at Falmouth shortly after he reached England. Falconbridge had gone out to Africa under the St. George's Bay Company, largely run by Sharp. He returned to find himself working for the radically different Sierra Leone Company. He learned now that John Clarkson had been sent to Nova Scotia to collect some hundreds of new colonists. Fresh from the tribulations of Granville Town, Falconbridge thought this was "a premature, hair-brained [sic], and ill digested scheme, to think of sending such a number of people all at once, to a rude, barbarous and unhealthy country." He did not like the appointment of Dalrymple either. It was a blow to his pride that he was skipped over, even though he was entrusted with the company's £150,000 (and growing) investment as commercial agent. A dozen other men were interviewed before Falconbridge sailed for Africa, carrying sealed instructions which asked John Clarkson to take the superintendency temporarily. It must have been galling to Falconbridge to have young Clarkson, who had never been to Africa, put in a position to give him orders.[39]

Among others appointed were three of the Swedes who had approached Sharp in 1787. James Strand was made secretary to the council, Adam Afzelius went as botanist, and Augustus Nordenskiold as a mineralogist. Charles Taylor, a doctor, was sent to Halifax to help Clarkson and travel with the blacks to Africa. The directors voted for freedom of religion and appointed as clergymen two first cousins, Nathaniel Gilbert, scion of an important Methodist family in Antigua, and Melvill Horne, another son of a West Indian. Gilbert was solid and temperate, and Horne livelier and more zealous, sure to "be the delight of the Methodistical part of the Blacks," in Thornton's opinion.

The council was to consist of, in order of rank, Clarkson; Falconbridge; James Cocks, a surveyor; Dr. John Bell, physician; John Wakerell, storekeeper; Richard Pepys, works engineer; James Watt, plantation manager; and Taylor. On the whole, Thornton was pleased with the caliber of these "servants," although acknowledging it was hard to judge in England how they would work out in Africa. Before they left, there were unpleasant rumors of Dr. Bell's being "in liquor" now and then and quarreling with the others.[40]

Public interest was intense. Supplies of printed reports were quickly exhausted. The press recorded the second general meeting on February 8, 1792, where it was announced that five vessels had left for Sierra Leone. In response to company advertisements of the previous autumn,

320 people in Britain, "partly negroes, partly Europeans," had signed up to go as settlers. But when John Clarkson wrote from Halifax in mid-November that at least 540 and possibly as many as 800 Nova Scotian blacks wished to sail, the well-pleased directors took steps to discourage white British volunteers, believing that few but "eccentric or distressed persons" were likely to apply at this early stage. None could work in the sun, and few would have the means to hire hardy blacks. The blacks of London were "far from regular and industrious," compared with the uncorrupted black loyalists in Nova Scotia and New Brunswick. Several of Granville Sharp's "pensioners" were thus rejected for what seemed to him flimsy reasons. The voyagers from Britain, sent off in time to reach Sierra Leone ahead of the fleet from Canada, included, finally, eighty-five employees, counting workmen, sixteen soldiers and only eighteen settlers. They were charged to obey a historic regulation, an early, if not the first, fair employment act. The directors declared that every trace of prejudice or "invidious distinctions" must be "carefully eradicated." To this end, the company was to employ "so far as you are able, black and white men indiscriminately, and when you discern in any of the former, talents which might render them useful in any way, to endeavour to call these talents into action and afford them all possible means of cultivation and encouragement."

The place they were going was given by the directors the new and evocative name of Freetown.[41]

NOTES

1. Foote, *Africa and the American Flag*, p. 111.
2. Sharp to Hopkins, July 25, 1789, in Hoare, *Memoirs of Granville Sharp*, vol. 2, p. 130; Jordan, *White over Black*, pp. 550, 551.
3. Thomas Clarkson, "Some account of the new colony at Sierra Leona," pp. 229-31; [John Clarkson], *Clarkson's Mission to America 1791-1792*, p. 38; Granville Sharp Canada Papers, Hardwicke Court; Martin's certificate, November 4, 1790, and Clinton to Grenville, December 26, 1790, both FO 4/1, ff. 416, 418. Peters' arrival in London usually is dated 1791, sometimes as late as July of that year.
4. Thomas Clarkson, p. 230.
5. Wilberforce to Wyville, December, 1791, in Robert Isaac Wilberforce and Samuel Wilberforce, *The Life of William Wilberforce*, vol. 1, p. 323.
6. [Melville], *A Residence at Sierra Leone*, p. 234; Sierra Leone Company 1794 Report, p. 3.
7. Parr to Grenville, September 20, 1790, and Bowles' petition to Parr, CO

217/62; *Public Advertiser*, October 30, November 1, 2, 17, 20, 22, 1790; *Morning Chronicle*, October 28-30, 1790; *Gazeteer & New Daily Advertiser*, November 9, 17, 18, 19, 20, 1790; Zachary Macaulay Journal (to Selina Mills), May 28, 1798, Huntington Library.

8. Martin's certificate, November 4, 1790; *Life of Wilberforce*, vol. 1, p. 323; Clinton to Grenville, December 26, 1790; Humble Petition of Thomas Peters, a Negro, ff. 419-20, and Humble Memorial and Petition of Thomas Peters, a free Negro of late a Serjeant in the Regiment of Guides and Pioneers, ff. 421-22, both FO 4/1. The latter also in CO 217/63, ff. 58-59 and printed in Fyfe, *Sierra Leone Inheritance*, pp. 118-19, and in *Clarkson's Mission*, pp. 31-32.

9. Sharp to Dean of Middleham, January 17, 1791, Sharp Papers, Hardwicke Court; Memorial of Peters, FO 4/1, f. 421; Dundas to Parr, August 6, 1791, CO 217/63.

10. Petition of Peters, FO 4/1, f. 419.

11. Thomas Clarkson, pp. 229-30.

12. Hardcastle to J. Clarkson, May 2, 1792, Clarkson Papers, BL Add. MSS. 41,262A; Sharp to Beaufoy, March 24, 1791, Hardwicke Court.

13. *The Philanthropist*, vol. 4 (1814), p. 101; Sharp Canada Papers, Hardwicke Court; J. Clarkson to Hartshorne, August 4, 1793, Clarkson Papers, BL Add. MSS. 41,263; *Life of Wilberforce*, vol. 1, p. 255; Minutes of Committee for Effecting the Abolition of the Slave Trade, Add. MSS. 21,256.

14. *Cobbett's Weekly Political Register*, vol. 69 (1830), pp. 812 ff.; *London Times*, May 5, 26, 1791.

15. Parliamentary Papers, 1791, XXIX, pp. 581, 632; Falconbridge, *Narrative of Two Voyages to the River Sierra Leone*, pp. 15-16; A. Falconbridge to Sharp, April 18, 1791, PRO 30/8/310.

16. Sharp to Worthy British Settlers, January 22, 1791, in Hoare, vol. 2, pp. 154-56. The company later repaid Sharp £1,850 he had spent on the settlement. Meacham, *Henry Thornton of Clapham 1760-1815*, p. 104.

17. Propositions for establishing a St. George's Bay Company, n.d., PRO 30/8/363.

18. Sharp to Beaufoy, March 23 and 24, 1791, Hardwicke Court; Sharp to Smith, May 30, 1791, PRO 30/8/310.

19. *Parliamentary History of England*, vol. 29, cols. 430-431; 651, 652, 653; Thornton to J. Clarkson, September 14, 1792, Clarkson Papers, BL Add. MSS. 41,262A; E.C. Martin, *The British West African Settlements 1750-1821*, p. 111; Penson, *The Colonial Agents of the British West Indies*, pp. 209-10; *Public Advertiser*, May 24 and 31, 1791; *Morning Chronicle*, May 31, 1791; Act Creating the Sierra Leone Company, 31 George III, cap. 55, Public Acts, vol. 52, pp. 1551-74. Company papers, including directors' minutes, do not seem to have survived.

20. [William Wilberforce], "Observations on Dr. Thorpe's Pamphlet," Wilberforce Papers.

21. Sharp to [W. Thornton], October 5, 1791, in Hoare, vol. 2, pp. 158-59.

22. Falconbridge, pp. 60, 62, 67; A. Falconbridge to Sharp, April 18, 1791; Ramsey to Sharp, March 22, 1791, PRO 30/8/310; Old Settlers of Granville Town, March 27, 1792, CO 270/2.

23. Dundas to Parr, August 6, 1791, CO 217/63; Dundas to Carleton, August 6, 1791, CO 218/4; Parr to Dundas, September 27, 1791, CO 217/63.

24. *Clarkson's Mission*, pp. 31, 32, 34-35, 36-37.

25. Thomas Clarkson, *The History of the Rise, Progress, and Accomplishment of the Abolition of the African Slave-Trade by the British Parliament*, pp. 12, 20; MS. Biography of John Clarkson (by Thomas), Huntington Library.

26. Wilberforce to Nepean, August 6, 1791, HO 42/19.

27. *Life of Wilberforce*, vol. 1, p. 334, quoted in Grieve, *The Great Accomplishment*, p. 257.

28. Thornton to J. Clarkson, December 30, 1791, Clarkson Papers, BL Add. MSS. 41,262A. The quotation, often rendered as "See how little wisdom it takes to govern the world," usually is attributed to Oxenstierna, the seventeenth-century Swedish chancellor.

29. Copies of "Free Settlement," CO 217/63, f. 60; PANS 419/1, and other collections including Hardwicke Court, where Sharp's copy is marked "Promise to American Negroes." Printed in Sierra Leone Company 1794 Report, pp. 4-6, and *Clarkson's Mission*, pp. 35-36.

30. *Clarkson's Mission*, pp. 55, 94; T. Clarkson, "Some account of the new colony," p. 162; Sharp to Worthy British Settlers, January 22, 1791.

31. Terms of the Sierra Leone Company, November 3, 1791, copies at Sierra Leone Collection, University of Illinois at Chicago Circle, and Hardwicke Court; printed in Wadstrom, *An Essay on Colonization*, part 2, p. 228; Articles of Agreement, November 7, 1791, copy at University of Illinois, Chicago Circle.

32. Fyfe, pp. 116-18; Sierra Leone Company 1791 Report, p. 53.

33. Thornton to J. Clarkson, December 30, 1791.

34. T. Clarkson to Wedgwood, August 25, 1791, in [Wedgwood], *Correspondence of Josiah Wedgwood 1781-1794*, pp. 167-69.

35. Evans, "An Early Constitution of Sierra Leone," p. 31, 77; Thornton to J. Clarkson, December 30, 1791; T. Clarkton to J. Clarkson, n.d. [1791], Clarkson Papers, BL Add. MSS. 41,262a, f. 63; Hardcastle to J. Clarkson, November 9, 1791, *ibid.*

36. Thornton to Nepean, August 3 and 4, 1791, and Thornton to Dundas, August 17 and 31, 1791, CO 267/9 Curtin, *Image of Africa*, pp. 108-9, 117-19. Regulations, printed in Evans, were adopted on November 12, 1791, according to CO 270/2, f. 73.

37. Wadstrom, part 2, pp. 229-30; Thornton to J. Clarkson, September 14, 1792, Clarkson Papers, BL Add. MSS. 41,262A; Thornton to J. Clarkson, December 30, 1791; Parliamentary Papers, 1790, XXX, pp. 291-325; "Observations on

Dr. Thorpe's Pamphlet'' [Wilberforce]. Dalrymple and several officer friends, including Philip Beaver, in November, 1791, undertook to colonize Bulama Island, north of Sierra Leone. Nearly 300 settlers sailed in April, 1792. Dalrymple soon abandoned the island. See Beaver, *African Memoranda*, and Note 37, Chapter 5.

38. Sierra Leone Company 1791 Report, pp. 7, 9; Ramsay to Sharp, March 22, 1791; Naimbana to Sharp, n.d., in Hoare, vol. 2, p. 164; Thornton to J. Clarkson, December 30, 1791; T. Clarkson to J. Clarkson, n.d. [1791]; A. M. Falconbridge, p. 168.

39. *Ibid.*, pp. 125, 138, 168; Thornton to J. Clarkson, December 30 and 28, 1791, Clarkson Papers, BL Add. MSS. 41,262A.

40. Wadstrom, part 2, pp. 299, 236; The *Times*, February 6, 1792; Howse, *Saints in Politics: "The Clapham Sect" and the Growth of Freedom*, p. 171; Thornton to J. Clarkson, December 30, 1791.

41. T. Clarkson to Wilkinson, January 23, 1792, Friends Library MSS. Thompson-Clarkson Collection, 3/55; *Cabinet*, February 10, 1792; *Times*, February 10, 1792; Thornton to J. Clarkson, December 30, 1791; J. Clarkson to Thornton, November 28, 1791; Sharp to brother, January 14, 1792, Hardwicke Court; Evans, pp. 60-61, 70.

Chapter 11

THE EXODUS

> It is too late for the greatest part of us to reap any benefit in this country.
> —A BLACK SETTLER IN NOVA SCOTIA, 1791[1]

The Old Testament delivery of the Israelites from slavery in Egypt became the favorite subject for sermons in the chapels of Freetown, where the returned African-Americans worshiped the Christian God. At the very time of quitting Nova Scotia, they seemed to sense the ancient symbolism of their act. The man whom they saw as Moses was not their own Thomas Peters but Lieutenant John Clarkson of the British navy.

"We Believe that it was the handy work of Almighty God—that you should be Our leader as Moses and Joshua was bringing the Children of Israel to the promise land," James Lestor, who lived then at Preston, remembered five years later.[2]

Clarkson himself was prepared to believe that Providence had directed him to them, and he came perilously close to likening the Sierra Leone Company to the Almighty when with a paraphrase of Exodus 3:7-8 he recalled how the situation of the blacks in Nova Scotia and New Brunswick "reached the ears of Englishmen, particularly of those famed for religion and virtue; and as if God had inspired them, they no sooner heard of your distress than they were determined to endeavour to relieve you, and stand forward as your friends; 'for they were assured of your sorrows,' and they were determined to do all in their power 'to deliver you out of the hands of your oppressors.' " He was the fortunate messenger.[3]

During the tedious voyage to Halifax, he had ruminated on his mission. He had volunteered under the influence of Peters' conversation and because the directors were having a difficult time finding an agent. Alone at sea, he had "leisure to perceive the magnitude of the undertaking, and

197

although I felt an equal desire to assist these unfortunate people, yet I almost shrunk from the responsibility I had imposed upon myself." He decided he would not solicit any black to go to Sierra Leone but would simply explain the alternatives before them, "for I considered them as men having the same feelings, as myself, and therefore I did not dare to sport with their destiny."[4]

There were good tactical reasons for not touting for emigrants. Clarkson had received from Wilberforce, an accomplished politician, pointed advice on how to avoid alienating the white provincials. Wilberforce was fond of Clarkson, whom he usually addressed in jocular fashion as "My dear Admiral," and he cautioned him, "You will have many Enemies, on the watch to take advantage of any little faux Pas." In a farewell letter Wilberforce threw out a number of hints: Do not talk about abolition of the slave trade except where you are *"sure of your Company."* Do not dwell on the bad treatment of the blacks. Keep a distance from Thomas Peters so as not to share any censure he may incur. Win the confidence of the governors. Move swiftly for fear they change their minds about cooperating. Make clear the company is not trying to spread discontent but merely to give the blacks an accurate picture of the Sierra Leone settlement, so they will not be deluded by exaggerated reports.[5]

The *Ark* anchored in Halifax Harbor on October 7, and Clarkson was struck with the beauty of the capital with its painted white and yellow houses neatly laid out on a steep hillside that rose from the shore to the Citadel. Within two hours he had delivered his letters to Governor Parr, who politely invited him to dinner. He found lodgings at a coffeehouse near the wharf and called on Lawrence Hartshorne, the New Jersey loyalist and respected Quaker businessman who had volunteered to work with him. They were to become effective partners and fast friends. From Hartshorne, Clarkson learned that Peters had arrived safely and had set off at once for New Brunswick.[6]

In the three months and one week of his stay Clarkson supervised an unprecedented operation of locating the blacks who wished to go to Africa, collecting them at Halifax and preparing a fleet of fifteen chartered vessels. Compared to the muddle made in London of the black poor embarkation in 1786 and 1787, Clarkson's achievement at Halifax looks like a masterpiece of efficiency. Clarkson showed a flair for business which astonished the experienced Hartshorne. The directors expected about 220 colonists, from what Peters had told them. In the event, more than five times as many—1,190 adventurers (as Clarkson saw them)—embarked. Peters and the company agents did not even reach many parts of the province nor did the governors make a great effort to spread the word. Peters said, "Our number would have been far greater had the Agents of Nova Scotia inform'd the People according to the Truth."[7]

The eager response at first nonplussed Clarkson and he repeatedly urged applicants to stop and think. He made a warm impression on the blacks and might thereby have won them, however inadvertently, to the idea of emigrating. But the minds of the majority seemed to have been made up before his arrival. Equally surprising to Clarkson was the strength of the white opposition to their going. Of this he was made aware at his cool first meeting with Parr, and it mounted with the success of his mission.

Clarkson began by circulating copies of the August 2, 1791, terms for "Free Settlement on the Coast of Africa." He set up an office with an open door where "if a free black intended to emigrate to get rid of any debt, he might be seen by his creditor. Here, if he had violated the laws of the country, and had escaped, he might be recognized." Objectors to the scheme could come there to argue their case. The room was usually thronged with blacks, businessmen and onlookers, including such notables as Bishop Inglis and Chief Justice Thomas Strange. As lists of intending emigrants were prepared, they were posted publicly.[8]

Nova Scotian officials had been given little time to prepare for the mission. The letter from Secretary Dundas enclosing a copy of Peters' land petition had reached Halifax on September 24, hardly a fortnight before Clarkson landed.

Dundas ordered an inquiry, and governors of both provinces were instructed to see that the blacks got their full proportions of land "& in a situation so advantageous as may make them some atonement for the injury they have suffered by this unaccountable delay." The Sierra Leone Company terms were to be advertised and as a third alternative, able-bodied men were to be offered army service in a separate corps in the West Indies at normal British pay scales and with a bounty of one guinea per man.[9]

Stung, Parr termed Peters' petition a misrepresentation, for:

> having consider'd the Degraded situation in which these People are beheld in general, by His Majesty's Subjects of a different Colour, I have at all times peculiarly attended to their Settlements; which I provided in such places & manner as I conceiv'd would be most satisfactory to them; as far as it was in my Power. . . . I think I may with safety, say, that these

People were put on Lands, & in a situation, then much
envied.[10]

The *Royal Gazette* of September 27, however, carried a long extract
from Dundas' letter. Alexander Howe of Annapolis was appointed to
investigate Peters' complaints. Job Bennet Clarke was made agent for
emigrants in the Annapolis area. Stephen Skinner was given a similar job
in Shelburne, the only two Nova Scotia areas covered outside Halifax.
Governor Carleton in New Brunswick appointed the Reverend Jonathan
Odell, provincial secretary, as overseer there.[11]

Clarke and Skinner were opposed to the blacks' leaving the country,
events showed, and there was opposition in New Brunswick to letting
Clarkson "beat up for Volunteers" there.[12] The reasons for the appointment of unfriendly agents and for Parr's vacillations became clearer
when Clarkson learned in late November that the governor had received,
along with the public letter from Secretary Dundas, a private letter from
Evan Nepean advising him to do everything he could to "throw cold
water" on the Sierra Leone plan. Clarkson does not appear to have seen a
damaging letter from Parr to Michael Wallace, the Halifax businessman
chosen to take charge of shipping and supplies, saying, "You need not be
over anxious in procuring or persuading the Blacks to remove. Government is not sanguine in this Business, tho they countenance it, but I am to
request you will keep this to yourself."[13]

Why the British government should have adopted a two-faced attitude
is not known, although it can be surmised that ministers felt that a mass
migration would be unpopular with would-be employers in the Maritimes, while a strengthening of the African settlement would be disliked
by the powerful slave-trade interests. Moderate support would presumably keep the abolitionists quiet, and the government was not interested
at this time in enlarging its own colonial responsibilities.

The politics of the thing were far from Clarkson's mind, however, as
he plunged into his work. Interviews, calls, business deals and writing
filled the days and half the nights. His first visit to a black community
came on his fifth day in Canada, when with Hartshorne and James
Putnam, the Halifax barrackmaster, he crossed the river and rode four
miles through the woods to Preston, where they "called at the huts of
several of the inhabitants and stated to them the offers of the Sierra Leone
Company." Clarkson thought, "Their situation seemed extremely bad
from the poorness of the soil."[14] Perhaps because they were the first he
met and those because of proximity, whom he would see the most, the

Preston blacks became Clarkson favorites. Putnam recommended them as a body: There were no better, more honest or sober workingmen. Clarkson decided to buy the poultry and garden produce for the Atlantic crossing from them. About 220 people from Preston alone determined to go to Sierra Leone, and 39 of the male heads of families who "hath lived neighbours in the township of Preston between six & seven years" petitioned Clarkson "to settle us altogether on our lands at Sierra Leone without being intermixed with strangers." Preston spokesmen volunteered to support the unmarried women among them, often widows, until they could support themselves in Africa. When he assigned the emigrants from Preston to sail in the *Eleanor*, Clarkson observed, "This vessel will contain the flower of the Black people." At another point he wrote that "the majority of the men are better than any people in the labouring line of life in England: I would match them for strong sense, quick apprehension, clear reasoning, gratitude, affection for their wives & children, and friendship and good-will toward their neighbours." [15]

Boston King, who was living near Preston at the time, does not appear in Clarkson's Nova Scotia journal. He supervised the Wesleyan society at Dartmouth and supported himself at an unspecified job with "a gentleman" who paid him two shillings a day plus food and lodging. It was his dream of an African mission, rather than active discontent, which caused him to decide to leave. He approved the company's intention "as far as possible in their power, to put a stop to the abominable slave-trade." When he told the agents that "it was not for the sake of the advantages I hoped to reap in Africa, which induced me to undertake the voyage, but from a desire that had long possessed my mind, of contributing to the best of my poor ability, in spreading the knowledge of Christianity in that country," they "encouraged me to persevere in it." The Methodist preachers with whom he worked were to see him off with the Rules of the Society, various useful books and their prayers. [16]

On October 22, 1791, Clarkson embarked with Charles Taylor, his newly arrived doctor, for Shelburne and Birchtown. [17] Their small schooner, *Dolphin*, put into Port L'Herbert (Port Hebert) for the night. Wind and tide held them there until the twenty-fourth, and Clarkson made the most of the interlude to study wilderness life. He learned that poverty knew no color line. In this "illimitable wood," the scattered and "wretched" inhabitants grew scanty crops of potatoes and corn on half-cleared land "overrun with large naked rocks of granite." In winter they hunted, and the wealthier ones kept a few sheep or a cow. Tramping around the vicinity, Clarkson found two black families, headed by

Thomas Shepherd and John Martin, to whom he described the government's offers. Mrs. Shepherd was ill, and later, at Shelburne, Taylor obtained medicines to send back to her and a white neighbor. Clarkson never forgot the two isolated black families, who symbolized all those whom no one would reach. Although he sent them word when a passage was available and money later, neither family managed to join the fleet for Sierra Leone. Both Shepherd and Martin were former slaves from Norfolk, Virginia, who had settled at Birchtown. Both were sawyers—husky men, Martin marked by a stutter—but when Clarkson ran into them, they were sharecropping and desperately poor. Shepherd may have felt too old to move; he was sixty-four. Martin made a pathetic effort to get to Halifax. He had missed the sailing from Shelburne, and leaving his pregnant wife and three children, he set off for Liverpool hoping to catch up. When his wife was offered a passage for Halifax, she refused, not knowing where her husband was. Many months later Clarkson learned that Martin had reached Halifax—probably on foot—shortly after the fleet sailed. Martin fell ill of grief, disappointment and poverty. The good Hartshorne took care of him through the winter and sent for his family. He built the Martins a log house on his farm near Dartmouth, but Martin ended up on crutches, crippled with rheumatism, unable to work, though not yet forty.[18]

Birchtown had lost no time in reacting to the publicity surrounding the government's various offers. Stephen Blucke wrote to Hartshorne on October 10 that in view of differing reports afloat, he wanted details on "provision and transportation . . . for the encouragement of Adventurers."[19] At Shelburne, David George was delegated to go to Halifax "as they were at a loss to know how to act from the various reports circulated by interested people." He was on the point of departure when Clarkson landed on October 25. George was now forty-eight years old and the father of six. He listed his occupation as a sawyer, although he owned 50 acres of farmland, as well as five town lots. He kept two churches.[20] He was almost the first person Clarkson met at Shelburne, and he became a prized adviser and "steady friend."

Clarkson took rooms at the Merchants Coffee House and again kept his office open to the public during his twelve days there. He soon realized that Stephen Skinner did not favor the project, but he accepted Skinner's advice to address a mass meeting at Birchtown. David George was sent ahead to arrange it. A few hours at Shelburne were enough to show Clarkson that whites in the area were bitterly opposed to black emigration, while the blacks were exceptionally enthusiastic. Here, as elsewhere, the opponents harped on two points, both aimed at frightening the blacks. First, they painted the dangers from the climate and hostile natives in Africa, and secondly, they pointed to the ambiguous conditions set by the Sierra Leone Company for settlers, specifically alleging that the company intended to exact a quitrent. This was before the directors in London had publicized their decision to do so, so it must have been floated as the rumor best calculated to turn people against the settlement scheme. Nova Scotians were deeply disturbed over the potentially damaging economic effects if Sierra Leone skimmed off the cream of the black labor force.

Clarkson could understand their fears that only the fittest might be taken, and he decided to apply the criteria set by the company in the general sense of good character. Only free blacks would be accepted, and those with a connection to British military forces in the Revolution. Everyone would have to be able, however, to support himself, ruling out the seriously disabled. Single or elderly women could go only if a relative accepted responsibility for them.[21]

Rumors intended to frighten off recruits were harder to cope with. The story that King Jimmy had "cut off" (that is, wiped out, with virtually all the inhabitants murdered) the 1787 settlers had come up first at the governor's table. The captain of a packet reported that on the day he had left Falmouth, a ship had arrived from the African coast with an account of the disaster.[22] It is probable that this was a muddled report of the events of late 1789, when Jimmy did drive out the settlers and burn the town, and that it was revived in 1791, when Falconbridge returned from reestablishing them. He had been at Falmouth, meeting Thomas Clarkson, at about the time this Nova Scotia packet would have been leaving. Slave-trade interests continually spread inaccurate reports aimed at discouraging the abolitionists.

Governor Parr had seized the opportunity offered by this report to criticize the colonization plan, and Clarkson, startled into discourtesy, interrupted him to say that the report must be wrong, for neither the government nor the company would have let him come if such danger existed. He would have been warned by word brought by this very packet. "The conversation dropped by the Governors pushing about the bottle—, a favourite Employ of his," Clarkson noted.[23]

Clarkson kept bumping into the "abominable" story of "the savages having murdered" the settlers. He also clashed with Parr over the use of "Guinea" instead of "Africa" in an advertisement in the *Gazette*. The connection to the Guinea (slave) trade and Guineamen (slave ships) "would be made a handle of by many to frighten the Nova Scotia blacks," he feared. Clarkson thought Parr promised to erase the word, but it appeared just the same in the *Royal Gazette* on October 25 and for the next three weeks.[24]

At Shelburne and at Halifax, copies of an excerpt from the 1789 *Abstract of Proceedings* of the Society for the Propagation of the Gospel were being circulated assiduously. It quoted the unhappy Reverend Patrick Fraser on his breakdown in health, the tragic early mortality of the settlement and his gloomy forecast that the whole enterprise would collapse.[25]

In Halifax, also, there was published a statement signed "Philanthropos" which attacked the plan as doomed by the frightful African climate. Clarkson learned that the author was the father of Clarke, the governor's agent at Annapolis. He reported to Henry Thornton that white citizens "are reading it to the Blacks in every part of the town." A body of contemptuous Preston people, however, brought him a copy to "make me sensible how much they despised it." He was sure that not half the blacks of Annapolis or New Brunswick would have a chance to hear of the Sierra Leone proposals because of Clarke's bias.[26] Adam Abernathy of Preston, husband of the teacher Catherine and grantee of a 50-acre farm, told the whites who urged him to stay, "I am not afraid of the shaking of the Bush till I see what is in it therefore I will try."[27]

"Notwithstanding all that has been said by *Philanthropos* and others," commented the editor of the *Weekly Chronicle* on November 19, 1791, "a very considerable proportion of the sooty Brotherhood seem determined to emigrate to the new-settled Colony at *Sierra Leona*." This, he believed, would raise the price of labor. Only the best would depart, leaving "the maimed, the halt, the blind and the *lazy* (no inconsiderable number)." He concluded, "For G-d's sake, Gentlemen of the Company, take them *indiscriminately*."[28]

The prospect of physical danger seemed to have almost no deterrent effect upon the blacks of Nova Scotia. But they worried openly about the rumors that a rent would be charged for the land in Africa. Quitrents had been suspended, as we know, for ten years on loyalist land grants, and so general was the hatred of them that they were never collected. Sharp-eyed opponents of the Sierra Leone Company seized upon the vague language of the published terms to assert that the word "charges" meant an annual rent "most probably at an exhorbitant [sic] rate." Clarkson answered that no rent was contemplated. He probably said it many times,

but the Birchtown mass meeting on October 26, 1791, was the occasion
of his major recorded declaration on the subject.[29]

That autumn day Clarkson, Skinner and a small party[30] mounted their
horses at 10:30 A.M. and rode to Birchtown in the rain. "Great numbers"
of blacks were assembled, and after waiting in vain for the sky to clear,
perhaps 300 or 400 squeezed into Moses Wilkinson's church. Men and
women pressed around Clarkson, inquiring anxiously for a "true statement" of the company terms. So that all could hear, he was persuaded to
climb into the pulpit, an awesome act to a religious man. With every eye
fixed upon him:

> the most awful sensations came immediately upon me. . . . It
> struck me forcibly that perhaps the future welfare and happi-
> ness nay the very lives of the individuals *then* before me might
> depend in a great measure upon the words which I should
> deliver, and I felt myself obliged to pause before I could speak;
> at length I rose up, and explained circumstantially the object,
> progress, and result, of the Embassy of Thomas Peters to
> England.

Clarkson reviewed each of the three government offers of redress. He
urged them to think seriously of all three and confer among themselves
about them. According to his journal, he said of the Sierra Leone plan:

> I desired them to weigh it well in their minds and not to suffer
> themselves to be led away on the one hand by exaggerated
> accounts of the fertility of the soil, and on the other by the
> representations of the badness of the climate—I cautioned
> them not to be influenced by the novelty of the thing and
> particularized the various difficulties which they might expect
> to experience in a newly established Colony, pointing out that
> if they were not determined to work and be industrious they
> would in all probability starve. . . . I explained to them such
> expressions in the Company's proposals as they did not com-
> prehend and informed them [in answer to a direct question, by
> one account] that what was meant by the term, "holding their
> lands subject to certain charges and obligations," *was by no
> means to be considered as an annual rent which idea had been
> industriously disseminated amongst them but as a kind of tax*

for charitable purposes such as for the maintenance their
poor, the care of the sick, and the education of their chil-
dren. . . . [Italics added.] Upon their arrival in Africa I promised to make it my business to see that their proper allotments
of land were given them and declared I would never leave them
till each individual assured me he was perfectly satisfied.

The scene that dismal October day in the rude Birchtown chapel must
have been riveting. The pale and slim young English officer looked into
the faces of hundreds of black men and women who must have made his
antislavery commitment come alive. They stood on the threshold of
fateful decisions. No one had addressed them before with such earnest-
ness and solicitude. Nor had anyone made them such public pledges or
exhibited such respect for their own ability to choose for themselves. In
later years they were able to describe the scene and quote Clarkson's
words exactly. He had urged them to hear him without interruption, but
as he spoke, applause frequently "burst forth." When he had finished,
"they assured me they were unanimous in the desire for embarking for
Africa . . . and as they had already made up their minds for quitting this
country, they would not be diverted from their resolution though disease
and even death were the consequence." In the following three days, he
and Skinner enrolled 150 men, 147 women and 217 children for Sierra
Leone.[31]
    The Birchtown promises became the focal point of a long-running
controversy between the company and its colonists. Nearly all historical
accounts have accused Clarkson of some degree of misrepresentation. At
best he is said to have been carried away by love and sympathy into
saying what the blacks wanted to hear. At worst he is charged with
barefaced lying.[32] But such explanations do not satisfy, because they
assume Clarkson knowingly violated his instructions and overruled his
superiors, actions totally out of character with his previous record.[33] At
the time of his American mission he was in complete harmony with the
company directors and proud to play a part in their work. It remained his
steadfast belief that he "never in any one instance did an act, that was not
authorized by the spirit of my Instructions."[34] Clarkson's reputation and
that of the Nova Scotia blacks became inseparable; to defend one is to
defend the other. Clarkson spoke from the August 2 terms and his oral
briefings, unaware that a quitrent was being even then decided on in
London. During his whole time in Nova Scotia he did not receive any

letters or instructions from the directors. He acted under the brief orders of August 12 signed by the company secretary, J. R. Williams, which concluded: "the Directors commit all other matters to your own immediate direction in which they profess to have fullest confidence."[35]

Clarkson's own explanations are generally overlooked. Mainly because of abolitionist politics, his views about the Sierra Leone enterprise were never made public until 1814, when, in an attempt to trace the causes of the colony's "failure," William Allen published a history in his *Philanthropist*. Internal evidence suggests that this unsigned three-part article was written by that veteran pamphleteer Thomas Clarkson, with the collaboration of John and copious use of the latter's journal and related papers.[36] From it, we learn that when the quitrent issue was hoisted like a red flag to halt what was beginning to look like an exodus, Clarkson, as befitted one ignorant of colonial affairs, consulted Hartshorne, who was American-born and had lived in Nova Scotia since 1783. As they saw it, lands were first promised the loyal blacks in Nova Scotia as a reward for wartime services. In Nova Scotia, quitrents were suspended on such grants, and the grants were free in the sense that recipients paid nothing for them or for the surveying and registration charges. Now the British government pledged that the blacks who chose to remain in Nova Scotia should receive "every Acre promised them" there, under such terms. An alternative was to go to the Sierra Leone colony. It must follow that the substitute offer was at least as good as, and certainly no worse than, the previous offer. Therefore, in speaking of charges, "the Directors could have no intention of charging a Rent upon the Land for then their offer would be no benefit to the free Blacks. . . . The Directors could mean only . . . some Tax for charitable purposes."

Clarkson sent Thornton copies of the Halifax papers in which opponents of the expedition alleged that rents would be charged at Sierra Leone. He also reported by letter that such stories were being read to the blacks. But he did not, at least in the surviving record, say in so many words that he had denied the rumor flatly.[37] He "naturally inferred" it would be clear in London that if a quitrent were intended, the blacks would not go. His newspapers did not reach England, however, until "some weeks" after the directors had approved the quitrent levy. To later arguments that he should have explained the issue more fully, he replied that since he had "never entertained the notion of a quit rent, so neither could he imagine that such was ever in the contemplation of the Directors." Above all, he believed he had been given discretionary power to act in any unforeseen circumstance and that he had not abused it. When in Sierra Leone, after seeing the new terms, he issued grants for land, he stubbornly stuck to the original vague wording, for this was what the settlers had committed themselves on, and by his code "it was too late to retract the construction which he had given." The company, equally stubbornly, refused to consider his interpretation or to back the judgment of their own agent on the spot. They blindly pursued the will-o'-the-wisp of profits through quitrents.

In the eyes of Stephen Skinner, the blacks were pathetically deluded. Skinner epitomized the upper-class loyalists who had had to rebuild their lives in Nova Scotia after the Revolution. In New Jersey, he had been provincial treasurer, member of the royal council and a judge. He was jailed and proscribed by the rebels, and his property, valued at nearly £24,000, confiscated or destroyed. Eventually, he was compensated for about a fifth of it. In 1777, he raised a company of 100 volunteers and reached the rank of major in the war. With a pension of £140, but with ten children to support, he set up in business at Shelburne and was elected to the assembly.[38] In 1791 he was sixty-six years old, and once again, his way of life was threatened. Shelburne's dreams had never materialized. Residents were drifting away. That year the businessmen were appealing to Whitehall to make Shelburne a free port in an attempt to revive the timber trade. The cod fishing had slumped; the peace treaty was so liberal that Americans were fishing off the Nova Scotian coast and curing their catches on its very shore, and the competition was ruinous.[39] Now the reservoir of cheap labor in Birchtown was in danger of drying up.

Another highly unpopular measure affected Shelburne indirectly. During 1791 the British government was arranging to move the Nova Scotian whale-fishing industry to the home port of Milford Haven. Nova Scotians had subsidized the postwar settlement of about twenty-five families of Nantucket whalers, and the imminent loss of this business was depressing.[40]

It was no secret that Skinner fought the Sierra Leone scheme. Clarkson heard that he had promised the blacks two years' provisions free if they would stay.[41] He worked with that part of the black population led by Stephen Blucke that did not want to emigrate. Blucke served under Skinner in the militia. Skinner helped (possibly inspired) Blucke to petition the government for money so that those remaining could each buy one cow and two sheep "to make us comfortable on our little farms." Blucke and forty-nine men and six women signed this document in Skinner's presence, and Skinner, returning to Halifax with Clarkson, delivered it personally to Governor Parr and later forwarded a copy to the Secretary of State. It prophesied "utter annihilation" for those so "infatuated" as to embrace the Sierra Leone offer.[42] Skinner said to Dundas, "That they as well as numbers of the White Inhabitants have suffered, is notorious, but not more than might be reasonably expected, from the hardships and disappointments natural to the settling all new Countries. . . ." These laborers and servants had been "flattered by imaginary prospects of happiness to leave a comfortable and decent maintenance."[43]

How different it looked to David George and his neighbors! In his memoir, George observed: "The White people . . . were very unwilling that we should go, though they had been very cruel to us, and treated many of us as bad as though we had been slaves. They attempted to persuade us that if we went away we should be made slaves again."[44]

To Clarkson he had explained that the leading white families objected to losing the blacks, "well knowing that people of their own color would never engage with them without being paid an equitable price for their labour." George was afraid for his life because he talked with Clarkson in private, and he warned the latter not to venture cross-country to Annapolis and Digby because he would be waylaid. But George was "resolutely bent on leaving this country, and had sold off all his property for the purpose."[45] Another man:

> most sensibly remarked . . . it would be unwise . . . to think of remaining . . . for said he "had we received our allotments of land upon our arrival . . . when we were allowed provisions for three years with implements of husbandry, as well as arms & amunition we might have cultivated our lots to advantage, and by the time our provisions were stopped the lands of industrious men would have . . . secured to them a comfortable support; on the contrary, . . . the greatest part of us have received small allotments in a soil so over run with rocks and swamps that vegetation, with our utmost care, is barely sufficient to keep us in existence; nay some of us have actually perished from hunger and the severity of the climate—
>
> "It is therefore too late for the greatest part of us to reap any benefit in this country . . . for myself and many of my companions have been obliged to give up our small lots . . . and cultivate the lands of a white man for half the produce, which occupies the whole of our time and we should certainly perish,

even if the best land were given us now before we could clear it
and receive the benefit of a crop.''[46]

Clarkson had seen, with Shepherd and Martin, that half the produce
was "little indeed! It has reduced them to such a state of indigence, that
in order to satisfy their landlord and maintain themselves they have been
obliged to sell their property, their clothing, and even their very beds—"
His judgment was: "They are in short in a state of slavery."[47]

He continued, however, to assure the blacks that if they wished to stay,
the governor would see that they got good land. One man made this biting
reply: "Massa governor no mind King he no mind You."[48]

An African-born settler with "indifferent" English, when asked if he
understood the propositions, responded, "Mr. Massa, me no hear, nor
no mind, me works like slave, cannot do worse Massa, in any part of the
world, therefore am determined to go with you Massa if you please. . . .
[M]e can work much and care not for climate; if me die, me die, had
rather die in me own country than this cold place." Clarkson noticed that
most of the people signing to go were not expecting so much to improve
their own condition but wished to see their children "upon a better &
more certain foundation."[49]

As Clarkson's relationship with the blacks deepened, he became the
best-informed man in the province about their situation, and it pleased
him to correct such residents as claimed the blacks were all happy and
comfortable. He tried to maintain a neutral public face, especially in
front of the blacks. It had taken him less than a fortnight, however, to
decide that they would be better off in Sierra Leone. When Governor Parr
obliged Skinner with an order cutting off further applications from
Shelburne, Clarkson declared to the governor and council that those who
went to Africa would, in the end, be happier. He insisted that it was
unfair and contrary to government intent to prevent anyone from deciding for himself about going. A hot argument must have ensued. At last
the governor consented to give the Shelburne blacks free choice so long
as vessels could be found to convey them to Halifax.[50]

Clarkson's direct intervention in a number of cases did not endear him
to some Nova Scotians. Blacks turned to him as an ombudsman, an
emissary of the king they had taken an oath to serve, as their new
commanding officer. An outrageous example concerned Lydia Jackson,
who was deserted by her husband and invited into the home of a Henry
Hedley of Manchester as a "companion to his wife." After a week he
demanded that she pay board or bind herself to him for seven years. She

could not pay and refused an indenture for more than one year. The paper was drawn up, the figure of 39 substituted for 1, and the illiterate woman "made her mark" on it. Hedley then sent her to work out "the year" with Dr. John Daniel Bolman at Lunenburg, who informed her of the deception. He had paid £20 for her indenture. According to Lydia, the doctor, a surgeon to a Hessian regiment in the Revolution, and his wife frequently beat her, and though she was pregnant, the doctor knocked her down and stamped on her. She filed a complaint, and the case got to court but was dismissed. As a punishment, Dr. Bolman sent her to work on his farm and threatened to sell her to the West Indies. After three years she escaped and made the hazardous journey to Halifax, where she presented a memorial to Governor Parr and Chief Justice Strange. No action followed, and she turned to the Sierra Leone Company agent. He found, on legal advice, that if she sued for her wages due, it would take so long she would miss the sailing for Sierra Leone, where she now wished to go. He counseled her to drop the case and leave Bolman "to his own reflections," which she did.[51]

Caesar Smith of Preston had lost his house and possessions in a fire. He agreed to a five-year indenture of his daughter, Phoebe, to William Hughes, an English shipwright in the naval yard. Now the Smiths wanted to go to Sierra Leone, and Phoebe still had three years to serve. Clarkson applied to Hughes and importuned Mrs. Hughes, as a mother, to release the girl but made not the least impression. The Caesar Smiths did sail for Sierra Leone, but there is no record of Phoebe. Clarkson gloomily predicted that if she stayed in Halifax without her parents, she would be sold at the end of the indenture. He ran into several cases in which whites had taken children, ostensibly out of kindness, only to demand payment for maintenance if parents sought their return.[52]

At Shelburne, Clarkson persuaded a father to steal his own child. The boy had been bound to a butcher of "most vile and abandoned character." The master decided to return to Boston and intended to take the boy along. Two justices of the peace "partly" agreed. The ship was about to sail when the father appealed to Clarkson, who advised him to kidnap the child and hide him until the ship had gone. Then Clarkson obtained legal advice, appeared openly with the boy before the justices and, when no one appeared for the master, enrolled the family (not named) for Sierra Leone.[53]

It was also at Shelburne that Clarkson tried to buy the freedom of a slave whose "noble and elevated sentiments" reduced Clarkson and the others in the crowded interview room to tears. John Cottress (or Coltress), weeping himself, begged Clarkson to take his wife and children, who were free, declaring that though the separation would be death to him, the step would make them happy. Clarkson appealed to his master, Greggs Farish, to release Cottress for a price. Somehow Cottress and other "property" were involved in legal proceedings for debt, and the intricacies of the law could not be unraveled. None of the family went. Farish later left Shelburne for Virginia.[54]

Clarkson's small pocket notebook reveals the skeletons of many other cases: "It is a common custom . . . to promise a Black so much pr day and in the eveg when his work is almost finished the white man quarrels with him & takes him to a justice of the Peace who gives an order to mlct him of his wages." And: "Many of the men have paid for the plan of their Lands . . . and have never seen their property." Or: "payed taxes for their Land and not considered as free holders."[55]

In New Brunswick the "spirit of emigration" also appeared. Thomas Peters found his people at St. John in "high spirits." Like Clarkson, he gave them time to consider before taking their names. The active antagonism of Jonathan Odell, who, according to Peters, did "everything in his power" to stop them from going, did not deflect all of them. Odell spread the rumor that the company would sell them in Africa and Peters would collect "so much per head for his trouble."[56] Governor Carleton insisted that "None of the Blacks" in New Brunswick had authorized Peters to speak for them, and they knew nothing of his mission to Britain until his return. Most of them had become servants at high wages and had no grounds of complaint, the governor thought. He reported sailing arrangements made, however, for seventy-two men, sixty-four women and eighty-six children.[57]

After attending the inquiry into his petition in Annapolis, Peters and his family with ninety-four others arrived in Halifax on the day of Parr's state funeral. The governor had taken ill and died of gout on November 25.[58] Richard Bulkeley, the president of the council, became acting lieutenant governor and assured Clarkson that the Sierra Leone plan would go forward. By then it had its own momentum.

Clarkson reported that Peters had carried out his responsibilities with great propriety. Peters had been knocked down by a white man at Digby but had not prosecuted him on learning the man was drunk. He gave Clarkson a grim report of events at New Brunswick, where the opposition, in addition to spreading false rumors, had forged indentures and work agreements to prevent blacks from leaving, had refused to pay debts or wages owing to them or had demanded to see their wartime "passes," which many had by now lost. "What a pity I could not visit Saint John to make these wretches men!" Clarkson fumed.

On December 9, 1791, came confirmation of these tales when four blacks arrived on foot from New Brunswick. They had been prevented from sailing from St. John with the others by fraudulent claims for debt. Once free, they had struck out around the Bay of Fundy, easily 340 miles, Clarkson calculated, through dense and snow-laden woods "never before visited by man." The four—Richard Corankapone, Sampson Heywood, Nathaniel Ladd and William Taylor—made it in fifteen days.[59]

NOTES

1. *Clarkson's Mission*, p. 59.
2. Leastor (Lestor, sometimes Leicester) to Clarkson, March 30, 1796, Clarkson Papers, BL Add. MSS. 41,263.
3. Clarkson's sermon of October 28, 1792, MS. Journal of John Clarkson, property of Air Marshal Sir Nigel Maynard, a descendant. I am deeply grateful to Sir Nigel for permission to use this manuscript. Clarkson's journal of 1791-1793 is the single most important documentary source on the move of the American blacks from Nova Scotia and their first year in Africa. It is in three manuscript volumes, vol. 1, "Mission to America," August 6, 1791, to March 18, 1792; vol. 2, "Mission to Africa," March 19, 1792, to August 4, 1792; and vol. 3 (or vol. 2 of "Mission to Africa") August 5, 1792, to February 11, 1793, with appendices. At least four copies were made. The Maynard copy is the only known complete one and has never previously been cited. *Clarkson's Mission*, referred to above, makes vol. 1 available with an excellent introduction and notes by C. B. Fergusson. Other MS. copies of that volume are held by the New-York Historical Society and Howard University. Copies of vol. 2 are held by the New-York Historical Society and the University of Illinois at Chicago Circle. Part of vol. 3 was printed in *Sierra Leone Studies*, o.s., vol. 8 (1927). Substantial extracts from vols. 2 and 3 were used in Bishop E. G. Ingham, *Sierra Leone After a Hundred Years.* The Sierra Leone Archives, Freetown, hold Clarkson's draft journal for August 6 to November 23, 1791, and a letter book running from July to November, 1792. In quoting the journal, the designations here are: *Clarkson's Mission*, Clarkson Journal (New York), *Clarkson Journal* (SIS) and Clarkson Journal (Maynard).
4. *Clarkson's Mission*, p. 38.
5. Wilberforce to Clarkson, August 8, 1791, Clarkson Papers, BL Add. MSS. 41,262A; Letter to William Wilberforce, n.d. (but after August 15, 1815), Clarkson Papers, BL Add. MSS. 41,263, ff. 155 ff.

6. *Dyott's Diary*, p. 30; *Clarkson's Mission*, p. 39; Letter to William Wilberforce; *The Philanthropist*, vol. 4 (1814), p. 103.

7. Hartshorne to Thornton, January 16, 1792, Sierra Leone Collection, University of Illinois at Chicago Circle. Clarkson always used the figure 1,190 for the emigrants, but 1,196 seem to have left Halifax and 1,131 landed in Africa. Sierra Leone Company 1794 Report, pp. 6, 7; *The Philanthropist*, vol. 5 (1815), p. 34; Peters to Dundas, n.d. [April, 1792], CO 267/9.

8. "Free Settlement on the Coast of Africa" handbill, PANS; *The Philanthropist*, vol. 4 (1814), p. 103.

9. Dundas to Parr, August 6, 1791, CO 217/63, enclosing copy of Peters' petition and Sierra Leone Company's terms.

10. Parr to Dundas, September 27, 1791, CO 217/63.

11. *Royal Gazette and Nova Scotia Advertiser*, September 27, 1791; *Clarkson's Mission*, pp. 23-24; Howe to Bulkeley, October 28, 1791, PANS 419.

12. *The Philanthropist*, vol. 4 (1814), p. 115; Skinner to Dundas, March 10, 1792, CO 217/63; Nepean to Thornton, August 4, 1791, CO 267/9.

13. Clarkson's notebook, f. 12, Clarkson Papers, BL Add. MSS. 41,262B; *Clarkson's Mission*, pp. 86, 91, and Intro., p. 24, quoting Parr to Wallace, October 21, 1791, from PANS 224/77.

14. *Clarkson's Mission*, p. 40.

15. *Ibid.*, pp. 46, 117-18, 81-82; Clarkson's notebook, f. 2.

16. Boston King Narrative, pp. 261 ff.

17. For Shelburne trip, *Clarkson's Mission*, pp. 48 ff., unless otherwise noted.

18. Book of Negroes, PRO 30/55/100, ff. 86-87; Muster Book of Birch Town, 1784, PAC MG 9, B 9-14, vol. 1; Hartshorne to Clarkson, July 24, 1792, Clarkson Papers, BL Add. MSS. 41,262A.

19. *Clarkson's Mission*, p. 40.

20. List of Blacks in Birch Town who gave in their names for Sierra Leone, November, 1791, CO 217/63, f. 361 ff.; David George Narrative, pp. 482 ff.

21. *Clarkson's Mission*, pp. 42, 46, 72, 93.

22. *Ibid.*, pp. 39, 44.

23. *Ibid.*, the last remark occurs in the draft journal, Sierra Leone Archives.

24. *Clarkson's Mission*, p. 47.

25. Extract printed in *Clarkson's Mission*, p. 52, from SPG *Abstract of Proceedings*, February 15, 1788-February 20, 1789, pp. 28-29. Fraser's first name is wrongly given as James. Houseal to Morice, November 21, 1791, USPG, C/Can/NS 1, f. 80.

26. *Clarkson's Mission*, pp. 65, 66, 69, 80; *The Philanthropist*, vol. 4 (1814), p. 115.

27. Clarkson's notebook, f. 21.

28. Quoted in *Clarkson's Mission*, notes, pp. 195-96.

29. *Ibid.*, p. 52; account of Birchtown meeting from *Clarkson's Mission*, pp.

53-56; Letter to William Wilberforce; *The Philanthropist*, vol. 4 (1814), pp. 105-7.

30. *Clarkson's Mission*, notes, p. 193.
31. List of Blacks in Birch Town, 1791.
32. West, *Back to Africa*, pp. 41-42; Winks, *The Blacks in Canada*, p. 68.
33. I am working on a biography of John Clarkson.
34. Letter to William Wilberforce.
35. *Clarkson's Mission*, pp. 34-35, 84.
36. In *The Philanthropist*, vol. 4 (1814), pp. 88-91, William Allen speculated on the colony's discontents and the obstacles to its success and announced the forthcoming "History of the Colony of Sierra Leone," which ran on pp. 97-116, 244-264 and in vol. 5, pp. 29-37 (1815). Thomas Clarkson was a director of the Sierra Leone Company and in a position to know everything about its deliberations at the time. It is in his style of painstaking documentation of a case, and it contains descriptive information on African productions and native life which were of great interest to him and which he used in many ways. A first-person account prepared by John Clarkson as the Letter to William Wilberforce, already cited, incorporated similar material. The reconstruction is based on these sources.
37. Writing Thornton, November 6, 1791, after the Birchtown meeting, Clarkson said he had scrupulously "kept an eye to the expenses likely to be thrown upon the Government, the honour and prosperity of the Company, and the general happiness of these oppressed people," *Clarkson's Mission*, p. 61.
38. AO 12/14, f. 31; AO 12/100, f. 112; AO 12/101, f. 221; AO 12/109, f. 270; PRO 30/55/77, f. 8621.
39. Principal Inhabitants of Shelburne to Grenville, June 16, 1791, CO 217/63.
40. Whale-fishery correspondence in CO 217/36, especially ff. 1, 3, 5, 126. Also see CO 217/63, ff. 260 ff. *Morning Chronicle*, November 27, December 2, 1791.
41. Clarkson's notebook, f. 15.
42. Copies of petitions to Parr, November 1, 1791, with a total of fifty-five names on the two, CO 217/63, f. 367, and CO 217/72, f. 86.
43. Skinner to Dundas, March 10, 1792, CO 217/63.
44. David George Narrative, p. 482.
45. *Clarkson's Mission*, pp. 51, 52, 60.
46. *Ibid.*, pp. 58-59.
47. *Ibid.*, p. 50; Clarkson's notebook, f. 8.
48. *Ibid.*, f. 9.
49. *Clarkson's Mission*, pp. 60, 56.
50. *Ibid.*, pp. 82, 31, 104, 43, 65.
51. *Ibid.*, pp. 89-90, notes, pp. 202-3.
52. *Ibid.*, pp. 103-4, notes, p. 206; Clarkson's notebook, ff. 15-16, 19.

53. *Clarkson's Mission*, pp. 53, 59.
54. *Ibid.*, pp. 56-57, 73, notes, p. 197.   Two Cottress children, Rebecca, nine, and John, six, were enrolled at Blucke's school in 1789 and 1790.   USPG, Dr. Bray's Associates Canadian Papers, State of the Birchtown School.
55. Clarkson's notebook, ff. 15, 21.
56. *Clarkson's Mission*, pp. 41, 91.
57. Carleton to Dundas, December 13, 1791, and March 2, 1792, CO 188/4.
58. *Clarkson's Mission*, pp. 88, 63.
59. *Ibid.*, pp. 87, 91, 92, 100, 102.

Chapter 12

THE RETURN TO AFRICA

> The day of Jubilee is come;
> Return ye ransomed sinners home.
> —A COUNTESS OF HUNTINGDON CONNEXION HYMN

At the wintry end of 1791 blacks from scattered hamlets of New Brunswick and Nova Scotia were making their way to Halifax for the ingathering of the emigrants. Simeon Perkins at Liverpool wrote in his diary for Monday, December 5: "Some rain & Dull weather this evening. A Brig comes into the River in the Evening, bound from Shelburne to Halifax, with 160 Black people on board, who are bound to the River Sire Loan, on the Coast of Africa, to Settle there." And the following day: "I understand by the Master of the Brign. that there is several Vessels more on their way to Halifax, with Black people, in all to the Number of 479."[1]

A white man, meeting a band of blacks on the road headed for the waiting ships at Shelburne, asked them where they were going. One of them was said to have replied, "Oh, massa, we be going to Sire Leone to be made majesties of." John Kizell later recalled that it was indeed their expectation that "every black and white should be equal and the blacks should be Magistrates as well as the white."[2]

A London newspaper heard from a correspondent in Shelburne that the "disposition of several negroes to quit this province" was spreading and causing "very great alarm."

> They are much greater in number than we had any reason to expect, and they are determined upon emigration. The place they mean to emigrate to, is the new settlement at Sierra Leone; they have fixed their minds inflexibly upon this place:

here, they say, they shall feel no cold; here they shall be among
their own brethren; here they shall kiss their dear Malagueta.

The correspondent added that although the blacks had never been treated
with the slightest cruelty, now, because of the Sierra Leone scheme,
"they have become negligent of their duty; they sing and dance, and
positively resolve to quit the colony. They say they shall not work so hard
in their dear Malagueta; I am apprehensive, however, they will work
harder."[3] (It is interesting that the blacks spoke of "Malagueta," a
reference to the melegueta pepper or "grains of paradise" which had
given the region where they were going the English name of Grain
Coast.)

Almost all of David George's Baptists were in the Shelburne flotilla,
"except a few of the sisters whose husbands were inclined to go back to
New York; and sister Lizze, a Quebec Indian, and brother Lewis, her
husband, who was an half Indian."[4] It was during the stopover that
Richard Ball preached two nights running to the Liverpool Methodists.[5]

The Methodists, largest of the sects, went in the greatest numbers. In
addition to Boston King and Richard Ball, their leaders included Henry
Beverhout, now about thirty-four, who was born free in St. Croix. He
had settled at Digby first, but though he had obtained a one-acre house lot
and had a warrant for a 50-acre farm, he had moved to St. John, New
Brunswick, very likely with Thomas Peters. America Talbot went from
St. John also. With the Digby Methodists went Mingo Jordan, now about
twenty-seven, who had deserted a master in Isle of Wight County,
Virginia, and who had been given a house lot and 50-acre farm. The
Birchtown-Shelburne contingent, whose departure dealt a blow to the
Methodist congregation as a whole from which it never recovered,
included Moses Wilkinson, John Gordon and Luke Jordan. Gordon,
born in Africa and a slave in Dorset County, Maryland, was about forty,
married, with two sons. He had not claimed the 40 acres allotted by
government but listed himself as a farmer. Jordan, about forty-six, had
been a slave in Nansemond County, Virginia. He and his wife, Patience,
had five girls, the eldest five. Jordan worked as a sailor, owned two
improved town lots and had 40 acres from the government. Cato Perkins
and William Ash led the Countess of Huntingdon Methodists. Perkins,
forty-five or so, was a former slave in Charleston. He and his wife had a
son of eight. He worked as a carpenter and had not bothered with the 40
acres granted by the government though he had bought and improved two

town lots. Ash was also from Charleston and about the same age. He and his wife, Mary, had a daughter, nine. Ash worked as a mason and had built houses on two town lots and cultivated three of the 40 acres allotted by the government.[6]

Teachers, too, pulled out, with the notable exception of Stephen Blucke. At Digby, Joseph Leonard, in spite of his 100-acre farm and other marks of preferment, led "much the greater part of the Blacks" back to Africa. At Preston, Mrs. Catherine Abernathy left her school to accompany her husband, Adam. Preston was deserted by nearly all its blacks, those not sailing for Africa settling afterward at the capital. The Halifax blacks, including schoolmaster Limerick Isaac, "almost to a Man entered into an association to go to Sierra Leone or have enlisted to serve as soldiers in the West Indies."[7]

The offer of military service, however, was poorly received in general. It was advertised in the *Royal Gazette* soon after Lieutenant Francis Miller arrived to begin active recruitment. He and Clarkson dined together and were together in Shelburne, where fourteen volunteers were enlisted.[8]

Clarkson reckoned that those who decided on Sierra Leone constituted *"almost the entire black population of six towns or villages."* By his estimate, nearly 600 came by sea or overland from the Birchtown-Shelburne area, 220 from Preston and vicinity, 180 from Annapolis-Digby and 200 from New Brunswick.[9] This was at least two-fifths of the blacks who had been evacuated from New York. Unlike most of the 1787 settlers, who went to Sierra Leone after a relatively short, unsettled stay in the metropolis, the Canadian blacks traveled as families and neighbors. The Birchtown roster of 155 signers (heads of families, six of them women) which was kept by Clarkson and Skinner provides at least a limited profile of that portion of the migration. From it we learn that 50 (31 percent) were African-born and that these persons ranged in age from twenty-two to eighty. Nine were in their twenties and five more than sixty. Richard Herbert, a laborer, was the eighty-year-old. He said he had no family or property. (He does not appear, sad to say, on other records of the settlement.) John Kizell, twenty-eight, actually came from the Sherbro River hinterland, the son and nephew of chiefs. He had been seized in an attack on his uncle's village when he was only twelve. He listed himself as a farmer, but as he had no property, he must have worked as a hired hand. He and Phillis had three children under six.[10]

Of the family heads born in the American hemisphere, 55 (35.7

percent) came from Virginia; 36 (23.3 percent) from the Carolinas, and 4 each from the West Indies and New Jersey, 3 from Pennsylvania and 7 each from Maryland and Massachusetts.

Nearly 72 percent (or 110) were between thirty and fifty years old; 11 percent (17) were under thirty and 16 percent (26) were past sixty. Nearly all were married, but many were childless. The families averaged, therefore, just over 1.5 children. Only 39 had more than two children. The largest family was David George's brood of six. (At embarkation he was listed with only four, and there is no explanation of the difference.[11]) In all there were 217 children under eighteen years.

As frontiersmen they had added to the skills they had brought with them to Nova Scotia. The vast majority now regarded themselves as farmers, even though few were farming at the time they enrolled in late 1791. Most were living, in frame houses or log cabins they had built, on town lots with a vegetable garden, working for wages. Most of the men could fish. Many women and children could spin. In addition to the farmers, there were twenty-one carpenters, twelve sawyers or timber cutters, five masons, three calkers, three coopers, three sailors, two tanners, two blacksmiths and one each of the trades of pilot, blockmaker, saddler, barber, tailor, shoemaker, weaver and baker. All owned some worn tools or implements to take along.[12] Sixty-seven reported having seen military service, and forty-nine had their own muskets. Two at least were unemployable: John Godfrey, a wounded cripple, and Moses Wilkinson, the blind pastor.

The largest landholder, apart from David George, was Demps Sullivan, once a slave in Elizabeth County, Virginia, who supported a wife and two daughters as a farmer of two 50-acre grants.[13] He had built a house on one. In addition to the town lot the government gave him, he had bought four other town lots and a house. The common government farm allotment was 40 acres, but in a number of cases these farms had not been seen or claimed. Some of the artisans had bought additional town property and built one or more houses.

One can understand Skinner's lament that at least two-thirds were "good settlers, and in a promising way to gain a decent subsistence by their labour." Unlucky Shelburne stood to lose "upwards of Five hundred good and efficient Citizens." The governor's agent at Annapolis, Job Bennet Clarke, described the emigrants there as "an industrious, sober people," adding, "the inhabitants parted with them with regret."[14]

Clarkson dissuaded several from going, if they seemed well off,[15] and hardened himself against the tears with which certain British and Hessian disbanded soldiers begged to go to Sierra Leone. The company agents were supposed to help emigrants dispose of their property, but one gets the impression most of them sold precipitately or simply walked away from it. George said he sold his Baptist meetinghouse and a half acre of land at Shelburne for £7. It was at Shelburne that a trick was tried to pick up lands from blacks cheaply. To frighten some into going, a rumor was put about that if Shelburne became a free port, their American ex-masters could come at will and reclaim them. Clarkson issued a handbill reassuring the blacks who wished to remain that they would be secure.[16]

People at Preston, worried about falling into debt, quizzed Clarkson on what aid would be forthcoming to help them establish themselves without borrowing. Clarkson's brother and Wilberforce had advised him to pay legitimate debts of those who might otherwise be unable to leave, but warned him to do it at the last minute so that this generosity was not exploited. He also had a fund of about £100 contributed by well-wishers to help special cases. At the eleventh hour he paid the debts of eight, totaling £50.0.10, of which £26.4.3 1/2 was owed by Thomas Peters, £13.17.11 by Nathaniel Snowball and £3.5.7 1/2 by William Ash. Some Shelburne people raised the money to pay creditors of their comrades.[17]

The unforeseen number of "adventurers" posed problems in chartering sufficient shipping. Governor Parr had advertised in November for 1,000 tons "To convey the BLACKS from hence to Sierra Leona on the Coast of Africa." The Whitehall directive specified a ratio of two tons of shipping space per adult and one and a half tons per child, the allowance to include baggage. It was generous for the times. The loyalist evacuation in general had provided no more than one and a half tons per passenger, and estimates for evacuating Charleston, for example, were based on one and a half tons per white and three-quarters of a ton per black. It was common to calculate one person per ton for conveying emigrants, and some ships squeezed in more.[18]

Clarkson's obsession with shipboard space and comfort is understandable in light of his work in the anti-slave-trade campaign. A third of his charges had come to America as slaves and remembered the horrors of the Middle Passage. Slave traders insisted there was no profit on less than two men per ton of shipping and preferred five per two tons or as much higher as they could go without unbearable mortality. With the slaves laid in irons on bare shelves belowdecks, lying on their sides, a ship with a capacity of 150 tons' cargo could transport 600 slaves. Thomas Clarkson had found ships allowing two and four square feet per slave.[19] Alexander Falconbridge, had testified:

> They had not so much room as a man has in his coffin . . . to go from one side of their rooms to the other. . . . I have always taken off my shoes, and notwithstanding I have trod with as much care as I possibly could to prevent pinching them, it has unavoidably happened that I did so; I have often had my feet bit and scratched by them, the marks of which I have now.

In bad weather Falconbridge would go below, shirtless, into an inconceivable heat and stench from the dysentery-ridden human cargo, treading on boards covered with blood and mucus, more like a slaughterhouse than anything he could think of for comparison.[20]

Michael Wallace served as commercial agent, but Clarkson retained a veto on arrangements. He refused any double-decked ship without five clear feet of space between decks. Twice he made owners cut new scuttles for ventilation and add the steerage, usually used by the crew, to the space for passengers. As the ships collected in the spacious harbor, he visited them daily to see that charcoal fires were kept burning to dry and air the sleeping spaces. The black fleet consisted of four ships, nine brigantines and two schooners. The official embarkation return showed 1,990 tons for 1,190 passengers, including 456 children, very close to the government requirement. All but the *Beaver*, a brig from London, were Halifax-owned. Transport alone cost the government £9,592.13.0, while food, clothing and interim lodging at Halifax topped £6,000 more.[21]

Clarkson fussed about expenses and fretted over every delay that added to the costs. His first reaction to the shipowners' charges was that they were "shameful & extravagant," but he soon learned there were few ships available there, compared to London; seamen's wages were half again as high, and provisions were more expensive. The owners, too, were not keen to give up their winter trading voyages for what was generally regarded as an unhealthy destination. Clarkson was reduced to verbal protests and to countermanding orders for extra comforts on the *Lucretia* brig on which he had hoisted his pennant the day after Christmas.[22]

Clarkson had believed it possible to be ready to leave in early December, but this proved optimistic. Nearly 1,200 blacks had to be housed and fed in the capital for about five weeks. Fortunately the weather was fine, as pleasant a winter as Old Inhabitants could remember.

As the people streamed into town, the agents took over empty barracks and warehouses. When the fleet of eleven vessels from Shelburne hove into view, for example:

> Mr. Hartshorne & myself busy running over to town to hire store houses for their reception, fortunately met with one which could easily contain 300 Souls—In *three hours* after we had everything taken out, the place properly swept, and two stoves fitted up, and by eight at night, when the rooms were sufficiently aired, I ordered . . . the people to come on Shore—At ten the people had got their supper, and laths were laid upon the floor to put their beds upon; a sentinel was placed also at the door to watch them during the night—[23]

The next Sunday Clarkson found "about a Sixth of the People very neat & clean, and the rest as neat as they could be." As more people arrived, some had to live aboard ships. Thomas Peters, David George and John Ball (of whom no more is known) were named to act as intermediaries, as the blacks had begun to appeal to Clarkson for each "trifling want." He complained, "It is impossible for me to walk the streets three yards without meeting some one who is in great distress, asking me to lend them money to give them a shirt, shift &c." He found himself "teased" into speaking crossly, which shamed him, for "God knows, their applications are from extreme misery and want—"[24]

The Halifax sojourn strengthened communal bonds, for the blacks were housed by groups in a Shelburne barracks, an Annapolis barracks and so on. In these bleak dormitories they cooked and ate, washed, sewed and mended clothes, held religious services, fell sick, gave birth and died. A census was taken, and instructions and advice were distributed. Goods were sorted and packed for the voyage. Clarkson had yielded to several requests to take pets along, and he let Stephen Fickland take both a dog and a puppy. He drew a line at pigs. Chickens, pots, beds, bedding and tools could be carried, but not tables or chairs. He arranged for carts to bring belongings from Preston so that the people did not have to tote things the five or six miles "upon our heads." Provident families tucked into their chests the seeds of pumpkins, squash, watermelons, purslain, sage, thyme, beans and cabbages, which proved a blessing later when the seeds sent from England did not sprout.[25] The emigrants were divided into ship's companies, and each elected captains, subject to Clarkson's approval.[26]

A Mrs. Fennel, probably the wife of Andrew, gave birth to twins on New Year's Day, 1792. But that good news was overshadowed by the death of Thomas Miles, thirty-six, a "hearty, Stout, industrious good man," who was accidentally suffocated by charcoal fumes. Charles Taylor's records show that he had forty-one patients and eight deaths during the time. Sarah Wilkinson, forty, died after a miscarriage on a vessel from Shelburne. Her husband, ex-Black Pioneer Charles Wilkinson, was also taking his mother, Rebecca, and two small daughters back to Africa, where he had been born. Most of the others died of the ill-defined "fever & cough." One of them was John Primus, whose widow Marian (Ann) and children, Elizabeth and Nancy, sailed for Sierra Leone in David George's company.[27] Knowing long voyages could, under the best circumstances, take a toll, Clarkson tried to get a second medical man for the voyage, but the Nova Scotia council did not feel able to spend that much. Clarkson, even before this, "with that goodness of heart which so strongly marks all his actions," as his friend Hartshorne put it, had turned the *Lucretia* into a hospital ship, assigning to it the elderly and sick so that they would be under his eye and Taylor's. Clarkson was not just being nice; he realized that if the commodore sailed on the hospital ship, it would convince the blacks "of my ardent and disinterested zeal, for the promotion of their happiness. The cause required that I should use every honourable means . . . to win their affection; knowing the great advantage it would give me in their future management." A medical inspection was carried out in Halifax to prevent the embarkation of anyone with a contagious disease. Pregnant wives were assigned to the *Morning Star,* with special accommodation. Seven or eight births were expected en route.[28]

The government did supply shifts, shirts, petticoats and jackets for people arriving "almost" or "entirely naked," to keep them from being "starved to death" (*i.e.,* frozen), and other linen garments were hoarded for distribution on shipboard when they met warm weather. The agents were lucky at an auction, obtaining 139 white shirts, 380 yards of gray linen for trousers, 41 bed ticks, 47 rugs and 48 blankets for the neediest.[29]

Clarkson worked out a "Weekly Bill of Fare," which called for identical daily breakfasts and suppers of cornmeal mush with molasses, midday dinners of pork and dried peas on Sunday, fish with potatoes and bread on Monday, beef and turnips with bread on Tuesday and Thursday and fish with potatoes and butter on Wednesday, Friday and Saturday. The portions were generous. Tea and wine were carried for the sick.[30]

On December 23 Clarkson received a request from Thomas Peters and David Edmonds:

> The humble petition of the Black people, humbly beg that if it is convenient to your Honour, as it is the last Christmas Day we shall ever see in America, that it may please your Honour to grant us, our day's allowance of Fresh Beef for a Christmas dinner, if it is agreeable to you, and the rest of the gentlemen, to whom it may concern.[31]

Their good conduct made it easy for Clarkson to accede. Their behavior, indeed, was a frequent subject for praise from Halifax citizens. There were "not less than 1200 people in the town and upwards of 5 weeks in the depth of winter not so much as the least disorder from any one of them." In later years Clarkson would boast that in the whole time there had been no *"robbery, theft, or riot on their part, or even of disturbance or drunkenness"* and that the president and council thanked him *"for their exemplary conduct."* [32]

One December Sunday, Clarkson visited the Sugar House Barracks and:

> found my friend David George preaching, and I never remembered to have heard the Psalms, sung so charmingly, in my life before; the generality of the Blacks who attended, seemed to feel more at singing, than they did at Prayers—I left them sooner than I wished, fearing that David George, if he had seen me might have been confused, but I have too good an opinion of him to think that the presence of any one, would in the least deter him from offering up his praises to his Creator—

George preached from house to house while in Halifax and gave his last sermon in Nova Scotia at Marchinton's meetinghouse.[33]

On a weeknight, making his rounds with Samuel Wickham, Hartshorne's friend and, like himself, an inactive naval lieutenant who was now his second in command, Clarkson found the Methodists at prayer:

> The Preacher Moses Wilkinson is blind: during this man's discourse, I felt frequently distressed for him, his feelings were so exquisite and he worked himself up to such a pitch that I was fearful, something would happen to him—The Congregation appeared very attentive & the discourse tended to glorify God, and to point out to men the sure & certain road to eternal happiness.

A conscientious Church of England clergyman, if sent to the settlement, might have a "wonderful effect" if he knew how to read prayers well, Clarkson told the directors. He thought the settlers themselves would be willing to pay such a cleric. Once Clarkson was asked to ordain a preacher, and when Hector Peters, Simon Colville, Robert Harrison, Richard Richards and Thomas Saunders designated themselves, "being free Ethiopians," as Baptist "Teachers or Preachers," Clarkson was asked to endorse the action.[34]

They trusted him "to perform the promises" made by the company, and he vowed that he would die to defend "the meanest of them," as if he would make up for the fact that "ever since Europe called herself enlightened" blacks had experienced "the greatest teachery, oppression, murder and everything that is base, and I cannot name an instance where a body of them . . . have ever had the promises made them performed in a conscientious way."[35]

Fearful that the captains and crews of these Halifax-registered ships "would not behave . . . with that kindness and attention they had promised (from the Black people being considered in this Province in no better light than beasts)," Clarkson obtained from each shipowner written instructions to each captain to make the blacks as comfortable as possible, to keep their vessels clean and to see that the crew did not treat "with ill language and disrespect" the passengers, "whom the King is endeavouring to render more happy by sending them to their native Shore." He had promised them at Birchtown that no white sailor would be allowed to raise a hand against them with impunity, nor would they need to work on board except as volunteers.[36]

With the new year, the last of the emigrants had reached Halifax. After a New Year's Eve party at the Halifax garrison that lasted until 2 A.M., Clarkson was awakened at eight by thirty exuberant blacks, each with his gun, who collected on his doorstep to fire a volley to wish him "many happy returns of the day." The formal commission empowering Clarkson to command the fleet to Africa was delivered from Council

*These are to certify that the Bearer hereof
Serjeant Thomas Peters of the Black Pioneer Corps
has served his majesty since the year 1776.
Sworn before Alderman Waddel of this City By
order of Sir Henry Clinton &c during which —
time he has served faithfully and honestly —
and in every respect becoming the Character of a
good and faithful subject of Great Britain
and has gained the good wishes of his officers and
Comrades*

Given at N. York this 26 day of Oct 1783

(Signed) Allan Stewart Lt. Col.

To all Commanders

*Commanding the
Black Pioneers —*

*N York 26 Oct —
1783*

Thomas Peters' certificate of service in the Black Pioneers from 1776 to 1783. Issued at the New York evacuation by Lieutenant Colonel Allan Stewart. *Public Record Office*

HEAD-QUARTERS,

NEW-YORK, APRIL 15, 1783.

ORDERS.

IT is the COMMANDER IN CHIEF's Orders, that the following Extract, from the Seventh Article, of the *Provisional Treaty,* between *Great Britain* and the *United States of America,* be STRICTLY attended to, and COMPLIED with, by all Persons whatsoever, under his Command,

"AND His Britannic Majesty shall, with all convenient Speed, and without
"causing any *Destruction,* or carrying away any *Negroes,* or other *Property,* of
"the American Inhabitants, withdraw all his Armies, Garrisons, and Fleets,
"from the said *United States,* and from every Post, Place, and Harbour,
"within the SAME, leaving in all Fortifications, the American *Artillery,* that
"may be therein; and shall also Order and Cause, all the *Archives, Records,*
"*Deeds,* and *Papers,* belonging to any of the said States, or their Citizens, which
"in the Course of the War may have fallen into the Hands of his Officers, to
"be forthwith restored and delivered to the proper States and Persons to whom
"they belong."

ALL Masters of Vessels are particularly cautioned, at their Peril, not to commit any Breach of the above Article.

The Seventh Article of the peace treaty as published in New York, April 15, 1783, in a proclamation of the precautions to be taken to prevent the departure of "any *Negroes,* or other *Property*" of Americans. The broadside caused consternation among the black loyalists waiting to be evacuated.

Public Record Office

Vessels Names and their Commander	Where Bound	Negroes Names	Age	Description	Claimants Names	Residence	Names of the Person in whose Possession they now are
		Cudet	38	Ordinary fellow			Atwood Eve
		Sarah	30	Stout Wench			Michael black
		Aaro Denton	40	Stout fellow			Cornel Gray &c Lyn
		Dolbeth	25	ditto			ditto
		Henry Francis	17	ditto			Gilles & Eve
		Peter Desmine	30	ditto			ditto
		Tony	20	Stout Wench			Cornel Gray &c Lyn
		Sam	1				ditto
		Nicholas	20	Stout fellow			ditto
		James Wilby	21	ditto			Joseph Shoemaker
		John Stephinson	35	ditto			ditto
4th November 1783 Commerce Richard Strong	Halifax	Bob Wheaton	19	Stout fellow			Drummer Reg. Dubois
		Isaac Nichols	12	fine Boy			ditto
		Aben Nichols	36	Ordinary Wench			Regiment Dubois
		Nathan Townsend	17	Likely Wench Wm			ditto
Pallas James Smith	ditto	Peter Braillain	17	Stout Lad			Dura. Reg. A &c Goverts
Duke of Richmond Robt. Davis	ditto	George Mintoes	25	Small fellow			St bed Lemings Gent.
		Peter Cockwell	15	Likely Lad			ditto
		Henry Rhodes	24	Ordinary fellow			ditto
		William	14	Likely Boy			Capt. Frank
		Peter Gray	18	ditto			Dept. of co. Grantham
		Anthony Innes	19	Ordinary Lad			ditto ditto
		Sally Gustier	24	ditto Wench			bd Leming
		John Hoggens	20	Likely fellow			Drum. Do.
		Susannah	21	Likely Wench			ditto
		Sally McWater oles	..	Infant			ditto
Molly G. Leggett	ditto	John	13	Ordinary fellow			Mr. Mater Hyman Geen.
Mary Mathew Peacock	Ostens	Sam	20	Likely fellow			Col. Gruen Reg. Prina Charles
Athena Thomas Jackson	ditto	Milly	20	ditto Wench			Capt. Mat Care First Serg.
		Mr. Walter	15	ditto Lad			Drummer Reg. Co. Ventura
		Polsey	24	ditto Wench			Wife to the above
		John Pack	22	ditto fellow			Drummer Do. Regiment
		Gilbert	16	ditto			Capt. Mr.
Joseph James Mitchell	Annapolis Royal	Thomas Petters	45	Ordinary fellow			Black Pioneers
		Murfh Steele	30	ditto			ditto
		Grace Wench	35	ditto			ditto
		John	18	ditto Lad			Capt. Angus McDonald
		Sally Petters	20	ditto Wench			Black Pioneers
		Clarry	12	Likely Child			ditto
		John	1/2	Infant			"
		John Salles	25	Stout fellow			Black Pioneers
		Nancy Perkins	19	Likely Wench			ditto
		Lucy	25	Stout Wench			Capt. McDonald
		Absham	2	Infant			ditto
		Peter Stewart	40	Ordinary Wench			Mr. A. D.

From Carleton's "Book of Negroes," the registration record of the blacks who embarked at the New York evacuation, 1783. Pages 131–32 record the departure from the American colonies of Thomas Peters (here "Petters"),

Property of Sina Adwater Esq
Free as pr Certificate from her last Owner Thomas of London
Formerly the Property of William Jenkin of Jerkin   left him   in   1776   G. M. C.
ditto   of James Ronaldson of Smithfield Virginia   ditto   in   1776   ditto
ditto   of Simon Halyard Neck River   ditto   ditto   in   1779   G. B. C.
ditto   of John Stanly of Newberg North Carolina   ditto   in   1778   G. M. C.
Property of Coronel Gray of Wett of Sale
ditto   ditto   ditto

Formerly Slave to Benjamin Gistel Pennsylvania
Says he was free at Bridges Island of Jamaica, lived with Lawyer Davis
Proved to be free from the Island of Jamaica

Formerly Slave to Thomas Whelen Norfolk Virginia   left him   in   1779   G. M. C.
ditto   to Ben. Nichols Rhode Island   ditto   in   1778   G. B. C.
ditto   to ditto   ditto   in   1778   ditto
Served his time with ditto, but says she was free   ditto
Formerly Slave to William Sands Charlestown South Carolina   ditto   in   1779
ditto   to Thomas Gale Micies Town New Jersey   ditto   in   1777   G. M. C.
ditto   to Mr. McBrady Charlestown South Carolina   ditto   in   1780
Says he was free and Serve his time to John Grigg Graves end Long Island
Formerly Slave to Mr. Jackson Charlestown South Carolina   ditto   in   1780   G. B. C.
ditto   to John Radcliff   ditto   ditto   ditto   in   1780   ditto
ditto   to Thomas Ely Bolee   ditto   ditto   ditto   in   1780   ditto
ditto   to John Curtis Eastern Shore Virginia   ditto   in   1780   ditto
ditto   to Dennis Higgins Santee River South Carolina   ditto   in   1779   ditto
ditto   to John Sanguine Johns Island Sr.   ditto   ditto   in   1780   ditto
Born within the British lines
Formerly Slave to William Emmons Charlestown So. Carolina   ditto   in   1780   G. M. C.
ditto   to Thomas Wiler Norfolk Virginia   ditto   in   1779   ditto
ditto   to Barney Brahman Charlestown South Carolina   ditto   in   1779   ditto
ditto   to William James John Island   ditto   ditto   ditto   in   1779   ditto
ditto   to John Godfrey Charlestown   ditto   ditto   ditto   in   1779   ditto
ditto   to Ben Cattle Ashley River   ditto   ditto   ditto   in   1779   ditto
ditto   to John Bagg Charlestown   ditto   ditto   ditto   in   1780
ditto   to William Campbell Wilmington North   ditto   ditto   in   1776   ditto
ditto   to Mulford Daniel   ditto   ditto   ditto   in   1776   ditto
ditto   to John Kindle Eastern shore Virginia   ditto   in   1777
ditto   to Henry Sumore Cape Fare North Carolina   ditto   in   1780
ditto   to Mr. Bellinge Ashepoo South   ditto   in   1779   G. B. C.
ditto   to ditto   ditto   ditto   ditto
Born within the lines
Formerly Slave to Mr. Sal tel Philadelphia   ditto   in   1779   G. M. C.
ditto   to Benjamin Webb Charlestown South Carolina   ditto   in   1780
Certified to be free by Mr. Walton Magistrate of Police
Born within the lines
Formerly Slave to Alexander Stuart Esq. her own in Newyork   ditto   in   1776   G. M. C.

twelfth from the bottom, with his wife, Sally, and their two children, eighth,
ninth and tenth from the bottom, and others of the Black Pioneers.

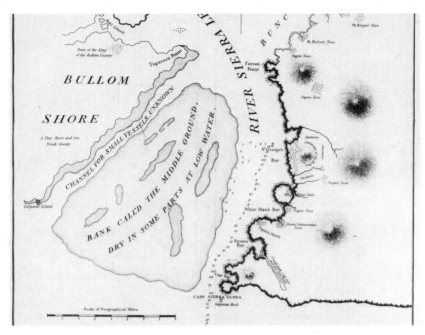

The "Settlement of the B. Poor" is indicated opposite St. George's Bay on this 1787 nautical survey of the Sierra Leone River. It was prepared by Captain Thompson of the *Nautilus,* who escorted the three ships carrying blacks from England. The site had been recommended by Captain George Young. Neighboring African villages and slave factories are located. *British Library Board*

Bance Island, the British slave factory in the river above Freetown. This sketch is by John Beckett in 1792. *From an original owned by a Clarkson descendant.* *Campbell Studio photograph*

General Sir Guy Carleton.
(Engraved by A. H. Ritchie.)
British Library Board

Granville Sharp. (Portrait by G. Dance,
engraved by Henry Meyer.)
British Library Board

Lieutenant John Clarkson, RN
*from a family miniature portrait
Stanley Travers Photograph*

Zachary Macaulay.
(Drawn by Slater in 1831.)
British Library Copyright

Shelburne in 1789. This wash drawing by Captain W. Booth of the Royal Engineers shows part of the town, with its simple clapboard and log houses under snowy roofs, and looks across the bay to the barracks on the opposite shore. Birchtown is to the right of the barracks but is not indicated.

Public Archives of Canada

The Province of Freedom. Looking north to the Bullom shore from the 1787 settlement on St. George's Hill where the British flag flies from a tree lopped of branches. This view of the "Free Black settlement" was first published in Britain in 1791. This copy is from the 1797 French edition of John Matthews' *Voyage a la Rivière de Sierra-Leone.* *British Library Board*

The black fleet at anchor in the Sierra Leone River, March 16, 1792. This pictorial record of the end of the voyage from Nova Scotia was drawn by John Beckett from information supplied by Governor Clarkson. The brig *Lucretia*, Clarkson's flagship, lies close in, opposite the three tents in center right. All the vessels are identified on the mount, which also carries the Sierra Leone Company's flag. The ship in the left foreground is an American vessel under way. Temporary tents occupy the ground cleared in the first week. Beckett "took" a series of views for Clarkson before his departure in December, 1792. On one occasion Beckett was sketching near the top of a mountain when his eye fell upon "a large Tiger." He withdrew slowly from the spot, then fled down one of the survey lines and arrived exhausted in Freetown. He fell ill with a high fever, and for a time Clarkson feared he would not recover. *Copy of original owned by a Clarkson descendant.* *Campbell Studio photograph*

Freetown, 1798. This picture of the black settlement was drawn by William Augustus Bowles, the Creek Indian leader who visited Sierra Leone in May, 1798. It became the frontispiece for Dr. Thomas Winterbottom's important work *An Account of the Native Africans in the Neighborhood of Sierra Leone,* published in 1803. On the hillside at the left is the Governor's House inside a stockade, removed from near the shore after the sack by the French in 1794.

British Library Board

421

To the Rt. Honble Lord Grenville one of his Majesty's principal Secretaries of State.

The humble Memorial and Petition of Thomas Peters a free Negro and late a Serjeant in the Regiment of Guides and Pioneers serving in North America under the Command of Genl. Sir Henry Clinton on Behalf of himself and others the Black Pioneers and loyal Black Refugees hereinafter described.

Sheweth

That your Memorialist and the said other Black Pioneers having served in North America as aforesaid for the Space of seven Years and upwards during the War afterwards went to Nova Scotia under the Promise of obtaining the usual Grant of Lands and Provision

That notwithstanding they have made repeated Applications to all Persons in that Country who they conceived likely to put them in Possession of their due Allotments, the said Pioneers with their Wives and Children amounting together in the whole to the Number of 102 People now remain at Annapolis Royal have not yet obtained their Allotments of Land, except one single Acre each for a Town Lot, and tho' a farther Proportion of 20 Acres each (viz.) about half the Allowance of Land

Thomas Peters' petition on behalf of the Black Pioneers for their due allotments of land in Nova Scotia or removal to another part of the empire. He and the others intended to go to Sierra Leone, but it is not specified.

Public Record Office

FREE SETTLEMENT

ON THE

COAST OF AFRICA.

THE SIERRA LEONE COMPANY, willing to receive into their Colony such Free Blacks as are able to produce to their Agents, Lieutenant CLARKSON, of His Majesty's Navy, and Mr. LAWRENCE HARTSHORNE, of *Halifax*, or either of them, satisfactory Testimonials of their Characters, (more particularly as to Honesty, Sobriety, and Industry) think it proper to notify, in an explicit manner, upon what Terms they will receive, at SIERRA LEONE, those who bring with them written Certificates of Approbation from either of the said Agents, which Certificates they are hereby respectively authorized to grant or withhold at Discretion.

It is therefore declared by the Company,

THAT every Free Black (upon producing such a Certificate) shall have a Grant of not less than TWENTY ACRES of LAND for himself, TEN for his Wife, and FIVE for every Child, upon such terms and subject to such charges and obligations, (with a view to the general prosperity of the Company,) as shall hereafter be settled by the Company, in respect to the Grants of Lands to be made by them to all Settlers, whether *Black* or *White*.

Terms of settlement in Sierra Leone taken to Nova Scotia by John Clarkson. The second paragraph promises grants "upon such terms and subject to such charges and obligations...as shall hereafter be settled by the Company." Granville Sharp wrote on the back of this copy, "Promise to American Negroes." *Granville Sharp papers, Hardwicke Court*

TERMS

OF THE

Sierra Leone Company,

TO ALL SUCH SETTLERS AS SHALL

SAIL FROM ENGLAND,

WITHIN THREE MONTHS FROM THE DATE HEREOF,

IN ORDER TO GO TO

SIERRA LEONE.

EVERY such Settler from Great Britain, producing a certificate under the Company's seal, which will be granted by the Directors in London, shall have a garden lot of one acre, within a convenient distance from a town, of which the situation shall be determined by the Council, on their arrival, and shall have in a neighbouring district *twenty acres of land* for himself, *ten* for his wife, and *five* for each child that he shall carry out. The usual reservation respecting mines and minerals will be made in favor of the Company.

Each Settler to have twenty acres of land for himself, ten for his wife, and five for every child.

Terms of settlement in Sierra Leone as published in London. November 3, 1791 (and received by John Clarkson in Africa in March, 1792). The second paragraph on page 1 spells out the quitrent levy. *Granville Sharp papers, Hardwicke Court*

Halifax 31 Decr. 1791.

Sierra Leone Company.

THE Bearer *Abraham Elli [Ficklin Tso]* having produced to us a fatisfactory Certificate of *his* Character as required by the Company we do hereby certify, that upon *his* Arrival at Sierra Leone *he* fhall receive, free of Expence, *twenty* Acres of Land, for *himfelf* and Family, confifting of *himfelf only* being the Proportion *he* is intitled to, agreeable to the printed Propofals of the Company.

John Clarkson } Agents for Sierra Leone
Law. Hartshorne } Company.

Land grant certificates such as this one were issued to all the black emigrants.
University of Illinois at Chicago Circle, Sierra Leone Collection

The earliest surviving document in which the black settlers seek a share in the government at Freetown. Dated June 26, 1792, it probably is in the handwriting of A. E. Griffiths, a 1787 settler. Most of the statement refers to the effort of Governor Clarkson to set wage scales at the time. The settlers' second point, page 1—"We are all willing to be govern by the laws of england in full but we do not Consent to gave it into your honer hands without haven aney of our own Culler in it—" is repeated and expanded on page 3: "Seventh We wish for pece if posable...but to gave all out of our hands we Cannot your honer know that we Can have law and ragerlations among our Self and be Consisent with the laws of england beCause we have Seen it in all the parts Whear eaver we have beng. Sir we do not mene to take the Law in our hands...but to have your honer approbation for we own you to be our had and govener."

University of Illinois at Chicago Circle, Sierra Leone Collection

Henry Thornton, chairman, Sierra Leone Company Court of Directors. (Engraved by T. Blood from the portrait by John Hoppner and published in 1815.) *Friends Library Photo*

Coins for Sierra Leone. To replace the long-standing African medium of iron bars, the Sierra Leone Company introduced coinage manufactured at Birmingham. The basic unit was the Spanish dollar, valued at five shillings English sterling. The obverse showed a crouching lion, and the reverse clasped black and white hands—the meeting of Europe and Africa. Silver "pieces" included the dollar, half dollar, twenty cents and ten cents, while the one-cent pieces were copper. The settlers' wages were to be paid in this specie. Also shown is the Sierra Leone Company seal, a full-rigged sailing ship. *British Library Board*

Sierra Leone Nov. 19. 1794

To John Clarkson Esq

A Most Respectable Friend to
Us the Setters in Sierra Leone —
In Your Being here We wance did call
it Free town but since Your Absince
We have A Reason to call it A town
of Slavery — — — —

Others mans tells — we do Long
to see you with our Longing Eyes — Our
Only Friend — John Clarkston Esq
it Realy will give us pleasure to see you
Or hear from Your Excellancy —

Your Well Wishes —
Luke Jordan   Moses Wilkerson preacher
Ino. Jordan   Isaac Anderson
Rubin Simmons   Stephen Peters —
America Tolbut Jas. Hutcherson —
A great many more   Sierra Leone
tho Paper wont afford

A group of settlers complain to their "Most Respectable Friend" Clarkson that in his absence, Freetown has become "A Town of Slavery."

Forty-nine men and women signed a petition, November 28, 1792, to the Sierra Leone Company urging the return of Clarkson as governor. In his last address to them from the pulpit Clarkson responded that it was 10 to 1 he would return. *University of Illinois at Chicago Circle, Sierra Leone Collection*

A "humbel petion" of the blacks assembled in Halifax requesting fresh beef for their last Christmas in America. *British Library Board*

The death in 1810 of David George is reported several years later to John Clarkson by Hector Peters. *British Library Board*

Nova Scotian women developed a distinctive style of dress, borrowing features from American and European fashion. It was noted by all visitors and one, F. B. Spilsbury, who was in Freetown in 1803, published this sketch. To him, "the fashion of the women's cloaths somewhat resembles the costume of a Welsh girl, and they are all exceedingly clean and neat." The women usually went barefoot, but rarely without jewelry and high crowned hats.

British Library Board

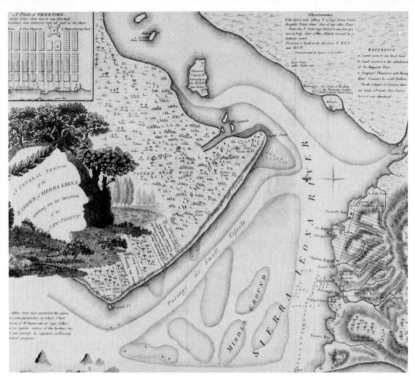

The Sierra Leone harbor in 1795, showing Freetown on the right. Granville Town is at the eastern boundary, near Signor Domingo's Town. Clarkson's Hospital on Savoy Point near Susan's Bay and Clarkson's Plantation across the river mouth on the Bullom shore are pointed out. Westward from Freetown toward the sea are King Jimmy's town and Pirate's Bay, where dissident settlers were to establish themselves. *British Library Board*

The colony grown up: Street scene in Freetown, sketched in 1847 by Loetitia Jervis Terry (and engraved by A. Laby and J. Needham). The houses of stone and clapboard with thatched or shingled roofs, the great harbor, the luxuriant trees, the spacious streets made visitors compare it to Washington, D.C. *British Library Board*

President Bulkeley on January 7. The charter agreements were signed, and Clarkson delivered his signals to the captains. They had filled their bumpers and drunk the commodore's health with three cheers and "not a little noise." On January 8 Clarkson made farewell calls on his many kind Halifax friends and slept on board the *Lucretia* for the first time. The next day the passengers for Sierra Leone embarked, in all 385 men, 349 women, 73 children from ten to sixteen years old, and 383 under age ten.[37] Clarkson and Michael Wallace spent January 10 rowing around the fleet, boarding each ship in turn. The passengers were mustered on deck, the roll was called, and Clarkson ceremoniously delivered to every household unit a printed certificate for the land to be given "upon their arrival in Africa." He and Hartshorne, assisted by the black captains, had worked several nights filling these out. They were dated December 31, 1791, and declared that the bearer would receive the appropriate number of acres "free of Expence" in accordance with the company's printed proposals.[38]

This climactic moment was followed by a reading of the rules for self-government on shipboard, which Clarkson and Hartshorne had drawn up. These recommended modest and decent behavior toward the ship's officers, personal cleanliness and attention to divine services. The reasons were given, too; for example, they were "not to make free with the Seamen, least they in turn should make free with you." If anyone so far forgot himself as to get drunk or fight, the chief black captain was to appoint five men to recommend a punishment, which would be reviewed by Clarkson before it was administered.[39]

Since the second week in December, Clarkson's health had begun to falter, and he was several times ill from fatigue and tension. The tour of the ships on January 10 lasted until eight at night, and Clarkson caught a violent cold from rowing about, standing in the frosty air on deck, then visiting the hot quarters below. The following day he was well enough, however, to receive from Bishop Inglis a copy of Bishop Wilson's collected sermons and from the provincial secretary a formal certification that everyone on board was free to depart.[40] At midnight he delivered the final instructions and sealed orders in case of separation to the captains and went to bed at one o'clock with a raging fever. The fleet should have sailed on January 12, but the harbor paperwork was not complete. Clarkson kept to his house in town, too ill to stir, and glad for a respite. Baffling winds held the ships on January 13. Almost apologetically, Clarkson recorded a frivolous sleigh ride with Hartshorne and some young ladies. He boarded the *Lucretia* at midnight and ordered everything made ready to sail in the morning. When, on January 14, the winds still blew against them, Clarkson was summoned to see the vice admiral, Sir Richard Hughes, who pointed out that it was costing the government £150 for each day's delay. Clarkson replied he had been ready to sail for a week and would seize the first chance. They parted amicably, and since he was already onshore, Clarkson borrowed Hartshorne's sleigh and horse and took the young ladies for another ride, supped with the Hartshornes, drank tea with George Deblois, a local merchant, and rushed back to his ship on receiving a false alarm that a shortage in the provisions had been discovered.

It was January 15, 1792, then, that the fleet got under way. At 9 A.M. a light wind sprang up from the west northwest, and Clarkson signaled to lift anchor. At eleven all the vessels were in motion, led by the *Felicity*, commanded by Wickham. While Captain Jonathan Coffin "stood off and on" in the *Lucretia*, Clarkson said good-bye to friends assembled on the wharf and scrawled a hasty note to Henry Thornton. He clambered back on board and, as the *Lucretia* slid away, "saluted the Admiral and the Town by lowering my Main Topgallant sail, as I passed it, which was returned by the waving of hats and handkerchiefs." His heart was full of gratitude to the town "where there is such universal hospitality shown to Strangers."

The message to Thornton said only: "I am now under sail with a fair wind and fine weather, having on board 1190 Souls, in fifteen ships, all in good spirits, properly equipped & I hope destined to be happy." Now he joined his fleet, six miles ahead and "running under an easy sail." The convoy passed Sambro Island lighthouse at the outer entrance to Halifax Harbor the following day.

No one has told us of these last moments among the blacks, but it could have been no less thrilling for them. More, indeed, for Clarkson's commitment was limited, while theirs was for life. Their fleet was unique in history. Nowhere else on the Atlantic was there another vessel laden with blacks who were also free.

The voyage of the *Lucretia* lasted fifty-two days. Some of the ships arrived in the Sierra Leone River before it. Clarkson was nervously pacing the deck at 8 A.M. on March 6, 1792, when he became (so he says) the first on his vessel to sight Cape Sierra Leone.[41]

What was it like, this journey out of Egypt?[42] For the first three weeks, the fleet was buffeted by storms, with strong gales and squalls of snow, hail or rain, according to the *Lucretia*'s log. The ships could not stay together, and soon only the *Venus, Eleanor, Felicity* and *Betsey* were in touch with the flagship. His bad cold, the bone weariness and anxiety with which Clarkson left Halifax developed into a fever with violent headaches, and on January 21 he quit the deck, leaving Wickham in general charge. Clarkson did not resume command for four weeks. The climax in his illness, and the turning point in the weather, came the night of January 29, when, in a rainstorm, a heavy sea broke over the deck. By then all the crew were sick, Captain Coffin and his mate alone on duty. Clarkson was unattended, and the storm would have killed him had not the captain come below to secure the porthole covers which had been smashed in by the wave. He found Clarkson, unconscious, his body "rolling from side to side, quite exhausted, covered with blood & water and very much bruised."

But from then on the fleet cruised in "light airs and fine weather." On February 18 Wickham helped carry Clarkson on deck on a mattress so that his cabin could be washed with vinegar and fumigated with tar and gunpowder.

Sixty-five of the settlers did die en route,[43] and two ship's captains, one of them Captain Coffin. At one time, Taylor found forty ill on the *Venus,* and eight died on her, the most on any ship. The first to die was the infant son of John Cockburn, a Black Pioneer veteran, the second day out, and Clarkson read the burial service for him.[44] Three men also died on the *Lucretia,* one of whom, Isaac Gratton, of Birchtown, had suffered a lung hemorrhage in Halifax before embarking. Clarkson reacted to all the deaths as if they were members of his family but particularly regretted it when Adam Abernathy, the indomitable Preston farmer, was taken. When he also heard that Peter Richards, one of the captains, and John Ball, a supervisor in Halifax, were gone, he was shocked into unconsciousness. He later reported, however, that the majority of the deaths on the passage were of persons "old and variously diseased at the time of their embarkation."[45] Clarkson's pain was matched by that of David George, for the Baptist leader lost three of his elders on the voyage— John Williams; Sampson Colbert, one of his first converts at Shelburne; and finally Peter Richards, who died as the fleet entered the Sierra Leone River and was buried on African soil.[46]

Boston King recalled that the storms they endured were the worst in the memory of old-time seafarers.[47] He said one (unnamed) man was washed overboard, leaving a wife and four children, "but what most affected me, was that he died as he had lived, without any appearance of religion." King's wife, Violet, was ill most of the way, and he fully expected her to die. He had a strong aversion to burial at sea and prayed that she be spared until they reached shore, and the Lord "restored her to perfect health." On the *Morning Star* there were three births.

Weather and sickness permitting, the Clarkson rules for the passengers' comfort were carried out. The decks were swept after each meal, bed boards stripped and cleaned each morning, decks and beams washed with vinegar heated with a red-hot iron so that the steaming liquid would penetrate every crevice and living space fumigated with heated tar. The black captains supervised the distribution of the casks of beef, pork and other provisions. Now and then the people were allowed to get their chests out of the hold and look them over on deck. A few days away from Freetown they were permitted to visit friends on other ships.

From early February on there were little diversions. A Dutch vessel bound for Surinam and a Danish ship headed for America were sighted. A Spanish ship at anchor, on the day Cape Barbas on the African coast was seen, was found to be fishing. The *Lucretia* traded salt beef for fresh fish, and the next day, February 21, they themselves fished. The only English vessel seen was on March 4, a Bristol slaver named *Mary* on the way to the Gold Coast, a chilling reminder of the normal traffic on the Atlantic.

On February 22, Clarkson took Taylor's medical advice to have an airing and had himself lowered over the side and rowed around the squadron. "Upon my going alongside each ship, the Black passengers had collected themselves upon deck with their Muskets, and fired three volleys, and afterwards gave three cheers, as they had entirely given up all hopes of my recovery, which was to them of the greatest consequence." He repeated the tour several times in ensuing days, happy to find them "all remarkably clean, and . . . recovering from their illness." One day he dined with Captain Richard Redman on the *Eleanor*, and "an old woman of 104 years of age who had requested me to take her, that she might lay her bones in her native country, begged to be brought on deck to shake hands and congratulate me upon my recovery." (She is reputed to have been Cato Perkins' mother. A few weeks later Clarkson introduced her to King Naimbana, who shook hands with her. This time, Clarkson said she was one hundred and eight; she was certainly very old.)[48]

Wickham was sent off on the *Felicity* to the Cape Verde Islands to buy livestock for the settlement. On March 4 Clarkson preached to the *Lucretia* contingent, complimenting them on their conduct on the passage. The next day he spoke in similar terms on each of the other ships near by:

All seemed in high spirits, and promised obedience and attention to the orders given them upon their landing—I was much
pleased with the happy and contented countenance of all of
them—Their expressions of respect and gratitude . . . were
most gratifying and affected me much. Most ardently do I hope
that the change they are about to make will ultimately turn out
to the advantage of them and posterity.

Remembering the rumor of native mayhem and being a stranger to the
coast, Clarkson on the night of March 6 sent the *Eleanor* ahead to make
soundings. At 2 A.M., upon a signal from her, he ordered the ships with
him to heave to. He went to bed until daylight and at six signaled the ships
to make sail. At eight he saw Cape Sierra Leone five leagues away. As
others made their own landfalls, "The passengers on board the different
ships gave three cheers and fired the vollies." Then to his "inexpressible
joy," Clarkson saw that the company's transports and some of the
vessels from Halifax lay in the river ahead.

The first of the black fleet—the *Parr, Brothers* and *Mary* (Captain
Maddocks)—had arrived on February 26. The others followed rapidly,
the *Beaver* on March 2, the *Mary* (Captain Bernard) March 3, the *Sierra
Leone* on March 4, and the *Venus, Somerset, Catherine, Betsey, Prince
William Henry* with the *Lucretia* and *Eleanor* on March 7.[49]

By March 8 fourteen ships had anchored, the *Morning Star* the last.
The *Felicity*, with the stock, came in the next day. The black captains,
"very neatly dressed," waited ceremoniously upon Clarkson and
"expressed the general joy of themselves & comrades at my safe arrival
with them at the Land of Promise which by the by from the river, exhibits
a most rich and beautiful prospect." The captains of the transports also
called and thanked Clarkson for the good behavior of the Nova Scotian
blacks, while the black captains expressed gratitude for the kindness of
the white captains. Harmony reigned.[50]

Except for the erection of a canvas house from England, nothing had
been done ashore to provide shelter for the new arrivals. Lieutenant
Wickham supervised the landing operation for the ailing Clarkson.
Ships' parties began to chop down the dense woods which had over-
grown the site since 1789. Freetown was to be built on the lap of the hill
now named for Henry Thornton. Tents were contrived out of sails and
spars from the company's vessels.

Thomas Peters, who in the largest sense had caused it all to happen,
reported the arrival to the British government. Clarkson's own offi-

cial notification of arrival was a humdrum account, but Peters said:

> We Your Lordship's Humble Servants, desire to return our
> Sincere Thanks to your Lordship, and to our gracious
> Sovereign, for the Faviours we have received in our removal,
> from Nova Scotia to Sierra Leone.
>   . . . we are intirely Satisfied, with the Place and Climate;
> and hope that our Fellow-sufferers, whose circumstances did
> not permit them to accompany us, may soon enjoy the same
> Blessing. . . .
>   The treatment we received on our Passage was very good;
> but our Provisions was ordinary; we was allowed Salt Fish four
> Days in a Week and one half of that was Spoilt, the Turnips
> also was no use to us, for the greater part of them was Spoilt.
> Nevertheless we are Satisfied if Government is not charged an
> extraordinary Price.
>   We also inform your Lordship, that the Natives are very
> agreeable with us, and we have a Gratefull Sense of His
> Majesty's goodness in removing us. We shall always en-
> deavour to form ourselves, according to His Religion, and
> Law's; and endeavour to instruct our Children in the Same.
>   Long may His Majesty and Royal Family live Blest with
> Peace and Prosperity here; and eternal Glory Hereafter. . . .[51]

Although Peters still regarded himself as the spokesman of his people,
the ascendancy of Clarkson in their hearts and the practical necessity of
leaving the details of organization in Halifax to the British agent and local
businessmen had shoved him into the background. Perhaps this mature
and war-toughened man had been responding to this slight when he had a
dispute with Clarkson which clouded their future relationship and possibly ended his chances of any future appointment. It had happened on
December 22, at a time when Clarkson was complaining almost daily of
fatigue and overwork. The two met to prepare the embarkation list for the
Venus. Without specifying what happened, Clarkson made a peevish
entry in his journal: "I was extremely mortified and distressed at the
behaviour of Peters this evening I can only attribute it to his ignorance—I
could not possibly enable him comprehend how necessary it was for
regularity and subordination on board the ships, he still persisted in his
obstinacy; he vexed me extremely and I went to bed, much indis-
posed."[52]

Recollections of the African homecoming were recorded by several others, at varying lengths of distance from the event. David George recalled a year or so afterward: "There was great joy to see the land. The high mountain, at some distance from Free-town . . . appeared like a cloud to us." To a girl, the experience was so scary and uncomfortable that a half century later she conveyed her uncertainties when she told an Englishwoman about it: The site was covered with rank "jungle," and the men clearing paths were cut by the knife-grass and prickly plants. Natives brought the newcomers cassava and groundnuts, but the Nova Scotians did not know how to cook them or how to ask directions in Temne. The women and children remained on shipboard until a tent was erected, where they stretched out "on the damp ground, with no other than a screen of canvas, in a wilderness exposed to wild beasts, and swarming with venomous reptiles and noxious insects. . . ."[53]

Anthony Elliott, a boy of fifteen at the time, who grew up to be a preacher, brought the exodus to a glorious conclusion in his memory:

> Pioneers . . . were despatched on shore to clear, or made road-way for their landing, which being done they all disembarked, and marched towards the thick forest, with the Holy Bible, and their preachers (all coloured men) before them, singing the hymn . . .
>
> > "Awake! and sing the song
> > of Moses and the Lamb,
> > Wake! every heart and every tongue
> > To praise the Saviour's name! . . .
> > [The day of Jubilee is come;
> > Return ye ransomed sinners home."]
>
> They proceeded immediately to worship Almighty God, thanking him for . . . bringing them in safety to the land of their forefathers. . . .[54]

David George preached the first Sunday, March 11, "a blessed time, under a sail." The canvas house was used for the first formal worship service of thanksgiving. All the officers and settlers, plus several curious Temne, attended. The Reverend Nathaniel Gilbert preached on the first verse of the 127th Psalm: "Except the Lord build the house, they labor in vain that build it: except the Lord keep the city, the watchman waketh but in vain."

Clarkson recalled:

We had all experienced great Mercies. The feeling and affecting way in which Mr. Gilbert read, the striking and novel
appearance of the scene before us, with the delightful manner
in which the Nova Scotians sang the appropriate Hymn The
year of Jubilee is come created such sensations as I have not
power to describe.[55]

Back in "the idle world of Halifax," there were titillating rumors that
the black fleet had met disaster: Six captains were reported dead, several
vessels were unable to find sufficient crew to return, and of the nearly
1,200 blacks, only 12 were still alive. When the fleet returned in May,
the truth proved different, though the deaths of three ship's captains were
mourned.[56] The *Morning Star* put into Liverpool, and Captain James
Fullerton told Simeon Perkins that "the Country is very fine, & the
Blacks very well Suited."[57] The affair left a bad taste, however. Peters
was not to be indulged in his hope that other blacks might follow.
Whitehall informed both provinces that there would be no more free
transport and any blacks lingering in Halifax in hope of it should be
induced "by every means in your power" to enlist in the "Black
Carolina Corps" in the West Indies.[58] Bishop Inglis deplored the loss of
both the whale fishery and the blacks as events which "wore the appearance of unkindness to this young Colony. . . ." Wentworth, returning to
Nova Scotia as lieutenant governor, noticed the shortage of labor and
vegetables, which the blacks used to bring to the Halifax market. He
wished the philanthropists who had helped the blacks to go had realized
that for an eighth the cost they could have made them all "perfectly
happy" in Nova Scotia.[59]

Speaking for the provincial government, Richard Bulkeley blamed the
emigration on laziness: The blacks had come from slavery, where they
were clothed and fed by a master, and faced with a cold climate and the
necessity of supporting themselves, they had "readily embraced the
Offer of going to a Warm Climate, with flattering hopes of a better
condition."[60] Something like this became the accepted version. The
loyal blacks had been a "curse" to the province, so good riddance. The
event slipped out of the pages of Nova Scotian history or received the
most slender treatment. One of the earliest Nova Scotian historians to
write of it in any detail called it a "deportation."[61]

At Shelburne the summer of 1792 was notable for "amazing Fires"
that ravaged the woods and fields and even destroyed houses, mills and
barns in the town and along the Birchtown road. Shelburne was saved,

after fifteen days of fire fighting, but presented a "Truly tradgigal Scene," according to Gideon White, a loyalist from Massachusetts:

> This last stroke has completely knock'd down this Settlement, the 800 Negros who were carried to Serea Leone was a serious loss but more so to me than any One—I had Eight Negro Families Tenants which had each a quantity of my Land and allowed me rent—each had his House &c. Those are all gone & the Houses destroyed. . . .[62]

NOTES

1. *Diary of Simeon Perkins*, vol. 39, p. 139.
2. T. Watson Smith, "The Loyalists at Shelburne," p. 77; Kizell to Commissioners of Enquiry, March, 1826, CO 267/92.
3. *Public Advertiser*, December 17, 1791.
4. David George's Narrative, p. 482.
5. *Diary of Simeon Perkins*, vol. 39, p. 139.
6. Book of Negroes, PRO 30/55/100, ff. 80-81, 76-77, 74-75, 94-95, 48-49, 41-42; Marion Gilroy, *Loyalists and Land Settlement*, pp. 8, 26, 16, 27, 110, 112, 107; A List of . . . People Who call Themselves Methodists, Sierra Leone Collection, University of Illinois, Chicago Circle; List of Blacks in Birch Town who gave in their names for Sierra Leone, November, 1791, CO 217/63.
7. Dr. Bray's Associates Canadian Papers, Rev. Weeks' Report, December 1, 1791, USPG.
8. *Royal Gazette and Nova Scotia Advertiser*, October 11 and 25, 1791; *Clarkson's Mission*, p. 64.
9. *The Philanthropist*, vol. 4 (1814), pp. 110-11.
10. For these generalizations: Blacks who gave in their names for Sierra Leone, 1791, and Muster Book of Birch Town, 1794, PAC, MG 9, B 9-14, vol. 1. Not all data are supplied for all entries. Armistead, *A Tribute for the Negro*, p. 348; African Institution 1812 Report, pp. 20-21.
11. *Clarkson's Mission*, p. 146.
12. *Ibid.*, p. 63.
13. Book of Negroes, PRO 30/55/100, ff. 94-95.
14. Skinner to Dundas, March 10, 1791, CO 217/63; *The Philanthropist*, vol. 4 (1814), p. 116.
15. *Clarkson's Mission*, pp. 85-86; Jacob Coffee, richest black in the province, was encouraged to stay, for example, p. 77.
16. David George Narrative, p. 482; *Clarkson's Mission*, pp. 61, 73, 57-58, 61, 62; copy of the handbill, University of Illinois, Chicago Circle.

17. *Clarkson's Mission*, pp. 47, 84, 151, 103; Wilberforce to Clarkson, August 8, 1791, Clarkson Papers, BL Add. MSS. 41,262A; Letter to William Wilberforce, Clarkson Papers, BL Add. MSS. 41,263, f. 171.

18. *Royal Gazette and Nova Scotia Advertiser*, November 15, 1791; CO 217/63, f. 56; Esther C. Wright, *The Loyalists of New Brunswick*, p. 72; Return of Loyalists at Charleston wishing to leave, August 13, 1782, PRO 30/55/97; Kraus, *The Atlantic Civilization: Eighteenth Century Origins*, p. 30.

19. Parliamentary Papers, 1789, XXIV, No. 633, Evidence on a bill to regulate transport of slaves; Coupland, *The British Anti-Slavery Movement*, p. 24.

20. Parliamentary Papers, 1790, XXIX, testimony March 8, 1790, pp. 589-90.

21. General Return of the Blacks Embark'd at Halifax for Sierra Leone, January 11, 1792, CO 217/63; Wallace to Bulkeley, May 13, 1793, CO 217/64; see Note 7, Chapter 11, on slight variations in embarkation figures; Return of tonnage chartered January 26, 1792, and Bulkeley to Dundas, February 6, 1792, in CO 217/63.

22. *Clarkson's Mission*, pp. 67, 79, 98; Wallace to Bulkeley, December 1, 1791, PANS 419/6; Wallace to Bulkeley, May 13, 1793, CO 217/64.

23. *Clarkson's Mission*, pp. 101-2.

24. *Ibid.*, pp. 104, 105, 118, 126.

25. *Ibid.*, p. 117; *The Philanthropist*, vol. 5 (1815), p. 251; Afzelius to Governor and Council, February 14, 1793, BL Add. MSS. 12, 131.

26. Letter to William Wilberforce, f. 169; *Clarkson's Mission*, p. 124; captains' list on back of Clarkson to Patterson, July 31, 1792, Clarkson Papers, BL Add. MSS. 41,262A.

27. Register of ill black people, Clarkson Papers, BL Add. MSS. 41,264.

28. *Clarkson's Mission*, pp. 119, 124; Hartshorne to Thornton, February 9, 1792, CO 217/63; Letter to William Wilberforce, f. 170.

29. *Clarkson's Mission*, pp. 108, 109, 115, 155, 159.

30. *Ibid.*, p. 141.

31. *Ibid.*, p. 115. Clarkson tidied up the spelling, original in Clarkson Papers, BL Add. MSS. 41,262A.

32. *Clarkson's Mission*, pp. 119, 134; *The Philanthropist*, vol. 4 (1814), p. 216.

33. *Clarkson's Mission*, p. 104; David George Narrative, p. 483.

34. Hartshorne to Thornton, February 9, 1792; *Clarkson's Mission*, pp. 108, 70-71, 94, 69, 95.

35. *Ibid.*, pp. 45, 45-46.

36. Folger to Bernard, *ibid.*, p. 157; p. 55.

37. *Ibid.*, pp. 123, 114; General Return of Blacks Embark'd at Halifax, f. 170.

38. *Clarkson's Mission*, p. 143; there are twelve certificates in the Clarkson Papers, BL Add. MSS. 41,262A, and another at University of Illinois, Chicago Circle.

39. *Clarkson's Mission*, pp. 144-45; Richards and others to Clarkson, January 12, 1792, University of Illinois, Chicago Circle.

40. *Clarkson's Mission*, pp. 107, 142; Wilson was also considered good reading matter for the 1787 settlers because he specialized in works for children. Final preparations and departure, *ibid.*, pp. 155-61.

41. The second voyage by black American settlers to Africa, and the only one ever organized by a black, was in the winter of 1815-16, when Captain Paul Cuffe of Massachusetts carried thirty-eight passengers in his brig *Traveller*. That voyage took fifty-six days, twenty of them marked by violent storms, and everyone but Cuffe was miserably seasick much of the time. See Sheldon H. Harris, *Paul Cuffe: Black America and the African Return*.

42. Account of voyage from *Clarkson's Mission*, pp. 161-69, except as noted; *The Philanthropist*, vol. 5 (1815), p. 244.

43. Sierra Leone Company 1794 Report, p. 7; Taylor reports sixty-four deaths, Clarkson Papers, BL Add. MSS. 41,264.

44. Cockburn (Colburn) was in David George's company on the *Lucretia*. The entry is confusing, but it appears that a son, Peter, died.

45. *The Philanthropist*, vol. 5 (1815), p. 245; Clarkson to Dundas, April 21, 1792, CO 267/9.

46. David George Narrative, p. 481.

47. Boston King Narrative, p. 262.

48. Ingham, *Sierra Leone After One Hundred Years*, p. 28; Clarkson Journal (New York), March 27, 1792; Butt-Thompson, *The First Generation of Sierra Leoneans*, p. 20; Butt-Thompson, *Sierra Leone in History and Tradition*, p. 100. Butt-Thompson's accuracy is open to question, but it is possible he rightly linked the old lady, who reputedly died at one hundred and ten, with Perkins. She is not, however, on the list of people leaving Birchtown. I. Gillen Campbell, a Nova Scotian descendant, told me in 1970 that Butt-Thompson got much of his material from Campbell's mother, who was born in 1865.

49. Clarkson Journal (New York), March 19, 1792.

50. *Clarkson's Mission*, p. 170; Letter to William Wilberforce, f. 178.

51. Clarkson to Dundas, April 21, 1792; Peters to Dundas [April, 1792], CO 267/9.

52. *Clarkson's Mission*, p. 115.

53. David George Narrative, p. 483; [Melville], *A Resident at Sierra Leone*, pp. 231-32.

54. Fyfe, *Sierra Leone Inheritance*, p. 120, quoting Elliott, *Lady Huntingdon's Connection in Sierra Leone*. J. B. was a son of Anthony Elliott. Fyfe locates the service on the site where St. George's Cathedral now stands in Freetown.

55. *Clarkson's Mission*, p. 171; Letter to William Wilberforce, f. 178.

56. Hartshorne to Clarkson, July 24, 1792, Clarkson Papers, BL Add. MSS. 41,262A; *Royal Gazette and Nova Scotia Advertiser*, May 29, 1792. A third captain died while the ships were still at Sierra Leone, *Clarkson's Mission*, p. 171.

57. *Diary of Simeon Perkins*, vol. 39, May 21, 1792.

58. Dundas to Bulkeley, January 15, 1792, CO 217/63; Dundas to Carleton, January 15, 1792, CO 188/4.

59. Inglis to Grenville, July 16, 1793, CO 217/64; Wentworth to Nepean, December 13, 1792, CO 217/64; Wentworth to King, September 14, 1792, CO 217/63.

60. Bulkeley to Dundas, February 3, 1792, CO 217/63.

61. Macdonald, "Memoir of Governor John Parr," p. 54; Archibald, "Story of the Deportation of Negroes from Nova Scotia to Sierra Leone," pp. 129-54. Raymond, "The Negro in New Brunswick," also speaks of the "deportation" of the blacks, p. 34. With the publication of Winks, *The Blacks in Canada*, the event was restored to its original significance in the history of the Maritimes.

62. Ells, *A Calendar of the White Collection of Manuscripts in the Public Archives of Nova Scotia*, pp. 46, 47.

Chapter 13

THE INFANT COLONY

> The infancy of a colony, like that of an individual, is a state of want and imbecility, from which it is impossible to predict either its future necessities or resources.
>
> —JOHN LEYDEN, 1799[1]

In each of his five official letters from Halifax, Clarkson had peppered Henry Thornton with ideas about the proper reception of the Nova Scotian blacks at Sierra Leone. He hoped they would find housing started or at least some wood cut for building. He brought with him, and handed to surveyor James Cocks on arrival, a survey plan obtained from Charles Morris, the experienced chief surveyor of Nova Scotia. He had dined with Philip Marchinton, the Halifax developer, whose advice was: "The sooner the people is put on their lands the better."[2]

Clarkson also had proffered thoughts on the form of rule the blacks would best accept. The governor must be strict in carrying out the company's orders but "in the most mild and pleasant manner to convince the people at large that the whole of his study is to promote their happiness." He had discovered they were hypersensitive to the manner in which they were treated by whites and that they attached great importance to the company's promise of nondiscrimination. Thus their governor:

> must always be on the watch to shock an unpleasant expression from any of the inferior officers, who from passion or partly from prejudice may wound their feelings; you may probably say that none will be appointed but those who detest slavery . . . but consider the education of many . . . and you will have reason to fear, for the people are taught to believe from me that they are to become men and that no distinction is to be made,

between them & the Whites—You must understand me. I
particularly allude to captains of your vessels, sailors, keepers
of the store-houses and inferior people, who would think no
harm in calling these people what I cannot mention on paper;
. . . if a bad example is set in the infancy of the Colony, I know
not what may be the consequence.[3]

But Freetown, like most colonies before it, was to start under the
weight of several handicaps, including ill-chosen personnel. Worse still,
control lay in London in an era of slow and uncertain communication. It
even began a trifle farcically. Thinking that he had spotted an old
comrade, the expected Governor Dalrymple, in one of the boats heading
toward his brig, Clarkson ordered a thirteen-gun salute. But on closer
examination, the boat bore a clutch of fancily dressed councillors with
the news that Clarkson himself was to be superintendent, first among
equals in the council of eight. Since the guns were primed, Clarkson
saluted the council, even though the briefest acquaintance—for all but
Falconbridge were strangers—demonstrated them to be a quarrelsome
lot. The joy at a safe arrival began to change to dread. Then Clarkson had
trouble working into harbor. The bowsprit of the *Lucretia* was knocked
off in a minor collision, so it was nearly midnight when the weak and
weary commodore took refuge on board the brig *Amy*, where Mr. and
Mrs. Falconbridge were quartered. After supper they talked about the
colony, "and I cannot say after everything I have heard that I was much
pleased," Clarkson noted.[4] In an office with no power but a casting vote,
he rightly saw little chance to deal with "what I see to be wrong." His
shattered health and his postponed wedding plans urged a return to
England. If things went badly here, he could not avoid the general
disgrace. But in the pile of letters that awaited him, various directors
importuned him to stay at least a few months. They had a confidence in
him "such as they cannot on a sudden place in any other man," Thornton
had written. Thomas Clarkson foresaw a rapid promotion in the navy if
his brother undertook the colonial leadership. "The eyes of England are
upon you & this Infant Colony. No Establishment has made such a Noise
as this in the Papers or been so generally admired."[5]

As well as such blandishments, Clarkson had an overriding concern
for the black settlers. No people on earth were more qualified to succeed,
if provided with "understanding" management, and that did not seem
likely to emerge from the men he had met, persons from "mean situations and the title of Councellor had turn'd their brain." He decided to

"accept the Government under its present objectionable form, and to remain with the poor Nova Scotians till the Colony is established or lost—"[6]

Consciously or otherwise, Clarkson already had made himself almost indispensable to the blacks. Mrs. Falconbridge, whose pungent accounts of the settlement shed an irreverent light on the company's official reports, believed that Clarkson's departure would have meant an "irreparable loss . . . being the only man calculated to govern the people who came with him, for by his winning manners, and mild, benign treatment, he has so gained [their] affections and attachment, that he can, by lifting up his finger (as he expresses it) do what he pleases with them." In spite of Falconbridge's bitter disappointment at being passed over for the superintendency, no blame was attached to Clarkson for the rebuke. On March 10, 1792, Falconbridge took the chair in the council for the sixth and last time, and Clarkson was sworn into office.[7] He had an unacknowledged rival, however, in Thomas Peters, who was not taken into account in the company-appointed all-white government.

Freetown was now a fairly large and completely novel community, made up of the 1,131 arrivals from Nova Scotia, the largest free migration of blacks in history; 119 whites who came from England in the first year, the largest ever migration of whites to West Africa; a handful of new black colonists from Britain; and the 60-odd survivors of Granville Town. Living with or near them were the seamen of company ships, crews of passing vessels, slave traders and local Africans, who from their villages along the shore came to trade fruits, vegetables and country lore for biscuit, beef, soap and spirits. The Africans were friendly, though one was skeptical: "These great guns, said she setting her foot upon one, you white men bring here to take my poor country." It was called the Camp by Africans.[8] It might well have reminded David George of Galphin's trading post in Georgia.

Wilberforce had an idea that it would be tactful to call the Nova Scotian blacks "Africans" instead of "Blacks or Negroes . . . as a means of removing the odium which every other name seems to carry with it,"[9] but once in Africa, the immigrants discovered that, like the American loyalists who streamed to Britain as the mother country after the Revolution, they were a different breed now: British North Americans of African ancestry. They were called, and called themselves, "the Nova Scotians." They spoke of the Britain most of them had never seen as "home."

A few of them were home literally, though most had ancestral roots in other parts of the coast. John Kizell had been taken from the Sherbro River country to the south. John Gordon, the Methodist leader, a Koranko, was born 130 miles inland and was sold from Bance Island when about fifteen. Four years after his return he was trading in Port Loko when he met the Mandinka man who had kidnapped and sold him. He thanked the man and gave him a present, saying, "Your thoughts were evil, but God meant it for good—I now know God and Christ."[10] Frank Peters, now thirty, who had deserted an owner at Monk's Corner, South Carolina, during the war, had been born in a village on the Sierra Leone peninsula. He and his wife, Nancy, had settled in Birchtown after the evacuation, and he had worked as a woodcutter. It was doubtless he who, upon landing in Africa, pointed to the spot where "a woman laid hold on him" and sold him to an American slaver fifteen years before. One day an elderly African exhibited "very peculiar emotions" on seeing his face. Finally, "she ran up to him and embraced him: she proved to be his own mother." Peters returned to his village, but several years later, accused of witchcraft, fled back to Freetown.[11] Martha Webb had been sold from this area when a youngster. A few years after her return she was to recognize a woman prisoner in a coffle of slaves at King Tom's town as her mother. The king allowed her to take her mother home for a visit and later, for a gift of wine, let her stay.[12]

The rainy season was barely a month away, and the Nova Scotians' first task was to build shelters. The canvas house was slept in by some of the company officials and in daytime served for "dining, preaching, praying, working, palavering, & Council Chamber." Temporary huts were erected in an African style with upright poles and thatched roofs. Saplings were driven into the ground, woven together and plastered with mud. The floors were beaten earth on a gravel foundation. The inside walls were hung with local matting.[13] Most of these "huts" were replaced by buildings of wooden boards on stone foundations in a "western" fashion.

A drawing of the black fleet at anchor was commissioned by Clarkson to commemorate the arrival. It was sketched by his secretary, John Beckett, and dated March 16, 1792, though actually made at the end of the year. In it, the fragile-looking sailing ships lie in St. George's Bay before beautifully wooded hills that roll toward a distant mountain. A broad swath has been cut on the rising ground leading up to Thornton Hill. On the knoll nearest the shore stand the rectangular canvas house and five large tents, made out of sails. Behind them on another rise are three more tents. The flag of the Sierra Leone Company, its arms featuring a sailing ship, an English merchant with his parcels and an African leaning on a huge ivory tusk, is flying. In a second view, dated November 10, Beckett depicted the astounding progress the colony had made in eight months despite extraordinary hardship. The waterfront has been cleared, and the original opening in the forest widened. Thirteen major framed buildings stand along the shore. The small rectangular settlers' homes are ranged on streets running at right angles from the water. Twelve streets named for the company directors were planned, but only six are shown. There are two "squares" or commons, in one of which stands a tower which housed the "great bell" that summoned everyone to work at sunrise. Allowing for Beckett's desire to present Clarkson with a flattering memento of his little realm, the November picture suggests a substantial and orderly settlement. The capital and much of the material had come from the company, but the labor, in temperatures that could shoot up to 114 degrees Fahrenheit at noon and often stood at 79 at dawn, was the Nova Scotians' own investment.[14]

The terrain was at least as hard to clear as the Nova Scotian wilderness. Trees, twelve-foot-high brush and sharp-edged grass covered it. But the settlers made the forest "resound with their axes." Richard Pepys, chief engineer and surveyor of works, praised the colonists' "industry and sobriety . . . a Company of Labourers, 70 or 80 men who had worked under him had drunk only three bottles of Rum per day diluted with water, though they had been left to help themselves."[15]

The first omen of the rainy season came about 3 A.M. on April 2, when a violent storm broke over the sleeping village. Lightning, torrents of rain, lashing wind and loud thunderclaps, repeated in the "deep roaring echoes of the Mountains, had an awful effect." The settlers were drenched, their huts were heavily damaged, and much of the new thatching was ruined. Alarmed, they insisted on spending full time on their houses, and the public buildings, on which they worked for wages, were delayed. It was ten days before the next downpour, after that the interludes between storms became shorter. The rains would continue until November, the heaviest falling from June to September.[16]

The councillors were pulling in all directions and quarreling openly. Their attitudes toward the blacks in some cases were exactly what Clarkson feared. Two weeks after the landing, he saw a councillor raise a fist as if to strike a Nova Scotian and privately upbraided him for it. "The feelings of the Nova Scotians are continually exposed to a degree of irritation, from an unfeeling way of addressing them; quite different to what I have accustomed them to, and from a want of Method in carrying on the business of the colony,'' he reported in his Journal. A few days later:

> Great dissatisfaction appears among the settlers, and many of them begin to be very troublesome. The bad example set them by the Europeans . . . the unfeeling manner in which they are often addressed, the promiscuous intercourse with so many dissatisfied sailors, and the old settlers, added to the many inconveniences . . . and the general sickness . . . may in a great degree account for the irritability of temper, and peevish disposition which it is painful for me to observe amongst them.[17]

When one of the carpenters accused Taylor of neglecting his critically sick wife, the doctor, now a councillor with judicial powers, had him locked up.

The bickering within the council affected the settlers less than the neglect of the medical men. Clarkson first laid eyes on his chief physician, Dr. Bell, when the latter returned from a visit to the Bance slave factory on March 12, "so drunk, as not to know who I was." He stayed drunk and the following day was in bed aboard the *Harpy* with a fever. That night, as the officers supped next door, he fell into "delirious ravings" and was found dead at ten. Taylor said that Bell had epilepsy.[18] Dr. Bell's conduct had so offended Clarkson that he was scandalized the next day when some councillors decided on an elaborate military funeral. He tried to argue them out of it on the ground that it would be bad for the blacks to see such a man honored, but his was the only negative voice. Flags were lowered to half-mast, and as the body was removed from ship to shore, guns were fired at one-minute intervals. Soldiers, with arms reversed, and the councillors dressed in the cockaded hats and epauletted uniforms the company had unhappily sanctioned accompanied the coffin to the burial spot. Clarkson went along for the sake of an appearance of harmony but was so weak that he had to be carried up the slope from the shore, and he soon turned back. When he was informed that a gunner had had his hand blown off while firing the salute, Clarkson was "seized with the most violent fainting fits and hysterics, which closed the mortifications of the day." The gunner, after an amputation, died the next morning.[19]

The surviving and less well-trained doctors were not much use when the colonists began to fall ill in large numbers. Taylor, for example, rambled off almost every day, bringing back observations about trees, wild beasts, anthills and oysters, samples of gums or dyes and moments of adventure to scribble into his journal. He developed a fondness for King Jimmy's town and sometimes stayed there overnight. One is tempted to think him lured by the African women whom he found "really handsome . . . I can see as much beauty in a Timmany negro, as I have formerly done in my own countrywomen." At his own first touch of illness Taylor asked to return home, and Clarkson had no wish to keep him. Another surgeon returned to England, and the third, J. W. Dunkin, said if his salary were not doubled, he would go, too.[20]

Some unexpected assistance came to the settlers when a young African woman sought protection from Signor Domingo, the African-Portuguese chief whose village lay upriver from Freetown. She said he intended to sell her. Clarkson had many such applications and tended to steer clear of internal African affairs if he could, but he agreed to speak to Domingo on her behalf. Meanwhile, she gained a reputation as a healer. A group of Nova Scotians asked Clarkson to buy her, pledging to repay him in money or labor. The appeal was signed by John Cuthbert, but Clarkson recognized the handwriting as that of Abraham Elliott Griffith, the Old Settler. Although Griffith had been hired by the council as an interpreter, Clarkson distrusted him and suspected he might pocket the money. He pointed out that the purchase would violate the company's terms.[21] But the peculiarity of their situation in slave-trade area was exposed when Clarkson himself agreed, as permitted by the regulations, to "redeem" a slave who had escaped from a French ship. He had been claimed by the first African to see him, under country law, and had fled into Freetown. There he found a relative, Abraham Smith, a cooper in his forties. Clarkson paid 150 bars, the people "promising to work it out."[22]

It proved to be one of the worst seasons of rain the West African coast had known. The doctors complained that they could not get around to see all the sick in their homes, but Clarkson could not persuade Captain Wilson of the *Harpy* to let him use this commodious ship for a hospital. Clarkson finally forced Wilson to accept the white patients on board.[23] What others suffered is glimpsed through Boston King's account of his wife, Violet, who on March 27 went to bed with the prevailing "putrid fever." She was unconscious and helpless for several days. "On Friday, while we were at prayer with her, the Lord mercifully manifested his love and power to her soul; she suddenly rose up, and said, 'I am well: I only wait for the coming of the Lord. Glory be to his Name, I am prepared to meet him, and that will be in a short time.' " On Sunday, surrounded by friends, she was still. But as they began to sing "Lo! he comes, with clouds descending, Once for favour'd sinners slain," she joined in "to the last verse, when she began to rejoice aloud, and expired in a rapture of love."[24] It was a deathbed that the English Evangelicals themselves might have envied.

By mid-April at least 700, by Mrs. Falconbridge's reckoning, were sick with "burning fevers . . . two hundred scarce able to crawl about, and . . . not more, if so many, able to nurse the sick or attend to domestic and Colonial concerns; five, six, and seven are dying daily, and buried with as little ceremony as so many dogs or cats." Clarkson had ordered no more coffins made, not even for himself should he die, to save the lumber for housebuilding. "It is quite customary of a morning," she went on, "to ask 'how many died last night?' " Her own sturdy constitution succumbed at last, and she suffered three weeks of "a violent fever, stoneblind four days, and expecting every moment to be my last. . . . I am yet a poor object, and being under the necessity of having my head shaved, tends to increase my ghastly figure. . . . It was very humbling and provoking."[25]

The first census on April 11 disclosed 112 deaths since the Nova Scotians had embarked, including 2 who died in the harbor and 38 who had perished onshore. There also had been 14 births. At the next muster, on September 22, the Nova Scotians numbered 995.[26] Even a better medical staff might have done little to cut the mortality. The "fever" was malaria, but no one knew it was caused by a mosquito-borne virus. It usually took the form of an "ague," marked by chills alternating with sweats. It sometimes developed into tuberculosis. Sunstroke, scurvy and rheumatism were also suffered. The remedies were few. Fever was usually treated with chinchona (Peruvian) bark, from which quinine was later derived. Strong drink was often regarded as a preventive, or cure, with sometimes fatal effect, and another favored medicine for various ills was opium or its derivative laudanum. All tropical places at the time were dangerous to newcomers. West Africa in general, but Sierra Leone in particular (because the mortality there was both high and publicized), gained notoriety as a "white man's grave" or "lovely charnel house."[27]

The settlers were particularly susceptible because of their lack of accommodation at the outset. Their huts were neither wind- nor water-tight, and few had bedsteads. Added to this were the "nauceous putrid stenches produced by stinking provision, scattered about the town." One disastrous result of an incompetent and divided government was the mishandling of supplies, which were often taken ashore, examined and tossed aside to rot or rust. The storekeeper and accountant did not come until May and careless untrained clerks were in charge. There was bad management in London, too. When a long-overdue cargo of foodstuffs arrived on the *Trusty* in May, it had been so badly packed as to be worthless. The store tent became unfit to work in. Clarkson railed at the "stench from rotten Cheese, rancid Butter, bad provisions, damaged pickled Tripe. Sacks of flour infested by insects and drenched with Molasses leaking from the Casks." He was convinced many died for lack of fresh foods. When "a fowl or a little Porter has been given, or a little Broth made for them, it has been surprising to see the effect." Most of the Nova Scotian men were "excellent sportsmen" and hunted and fished when well enough. Two shot an antelope whose hind quarter alone weighed thirty pounds, and they sometimes got a deer or wild pig.[28]

Their own health was hardly more important to the Nova Scotians than Clarkson's. For nearly four months he was enfeebled from his shipboard illness and plagued by loss of memory. On his arrival he could not walk without support. Strain or strong emotion, whether joy or anger, could throw him into "violent hysterics." Unnaturally for him, he was sometimes deeply depressed, and all his problems were aggravated by the waste and disorder to which he was a helpless witness.[29]

The settlers watched his shaky state with a compassion unmatched among his peers but still brought him all their troubles. He moved from the *Amy* to shore for convenience, but this only made him more vulnerable to their appeals. A few surviving written requests illustrate the range of problems. Luke Jordan, speaking for the *Brothers* company, apologized: ". . . I would Not Write to You because I know You are not As well as Aught to be but It is because We are In a Strange Country and we are Not well aquinted with the Rainey Season . . . but If it Should Come and we have know house what Should we do with Our Selvs." The men had cleared three temporary lots assigned for houses and gardens and had been given a fourth adjoining lot. But Cocks then had reassigned the fourth lot to the *Morning Star* company. Jordan's people did not want to be separated, and Clarkson determined that it was not necessary. He restored the fourth lot, reasoning, "People will not consider how often they have been deceived and how suspicious they are in consequence, & how necessary it is to be open and candid with them. These men had just reason to complain." They were "easily to be led but not to be driven, and from the spirit of their agreement ought not to be."

On the same day Clarkson had to deal with an African visitor who assaulted a sentry while drunk, a "horrible confusion" in the store tent, where food distribution had broken down, the arrival of the first African laborers introduced by Elliott Griffith, the unloading of rice from the company cutter, the calking of the *Harpy* and a friendly offer from Isaac DuBois, a newly arrived cotton planter, to do something else since farming seemed a distant vision. Clarkson put him in temporary charge of the store.

Susane Smith requested some soap: "I want . . . to wash my family Clos for we ar not fit to be Sean for dirt." Richard Dickson (Dixon) of Cato Perkins' company had found a young man willing to teach. An elaborate memorial from Andrew Moore on the day a daughter was born to his wife asked Clarkson "out of your Humanity and Gentle Goodness . . . to Give Orders that She and the Child have Some . . . Oat meal Molassis or Shugger a Little Wine and Spirits and some Nut mig" with, in a postscript, "one lb Candles for Light."[30]

Clarkson shunned the help of perhaps the one man qualified to be his deputy, Thomas Peters. When Peters seemed to challenge Clarkson's leadership, the latter saw it as an attempted coup. Others, including the generally reliable David George, believed Peters wanted only to be a deputy. The dispute, which went on from March through June, must rank as one of the most significant happenings of the first months in Africa.

It may well be that Peters, encouraged by his success in England, became ambitious for position and power in the settlement. The directors gave him none, no doubt unwilling to risk their investment in untrained hands. Wilberforce had cautioned Clarkson not to become too involved with him. Hartshorne had handed Clarkson a letter to be read at sea which warned him not to be "too much mortified if Peters should prove a different man than you have a right to expect, I am much afraid that the great attention paid to him in England, has raised his ideas of his own importance to too great a pitch for either his good or Your comfort." The spectacle of a council of white men, in effect eight different governors, most of whom were pretentious or incompetent, disgusted Peters. Some of them did not address the people as "Fellow Beings," and the epithet "black Rascals" was employed so much that the practice had to be publicly denounced. This was "almost enough to have given Birth to an Insurrection among a People, who had just emerged from Slavery, and who were therefore jealous of every action, nay of every Look, which came from white Men, who were put in authority over them," Clarkson conceded, and Peters played on their resentment. He was a proud man who so despised the council that he took no notice of them, according to James Strand, the secretary. Strand also suspected that Peters could not bear to see even Clarkson above him and tried continually to "inculcate on the minds of the Settlers his own importance among them as their only Deliverer, worthy & best qualified to be their Governor."[31]

Clarkson's record of the dispute begins on March 22, when Peters called on him with "many complaints; he was extremely violent and indiscreet in his conversation and seemed as if he were desirous of alarming and disheartening the people." Clarkson was angry. It may have been on this occasion that he gave Peters mortal affront by offering him a free passage back to America and vowing that he would never leave Freetown so long as Peters remained there. Soon afterward Clarkson met with some or all of the settlers and believed that he completely quieted their fears, but the effort exhausted him, and in his quarters aboard ship he underwent another bout of hysterics.[32]

On Easter Sunday, April 8, as Clarkson emerged from the canvas house where a service had been held, several letters were thrust at him. He put them into his pocket to read later. After dinner on the *Amy* he opened the first. It was from Tobias Hume and John Wilde and informed him that a faction intended to elect Peters governor. They wrote "with a trembling hand" for fear of reprisals. The people from Preston, they declared, had "no hand in the affair at all, but they mean to stand fast by your honor."[33] Quickly recovering from his shock, Clarkson buckled on his sword, ordered a boat and went ashore. He had Richard Pepys ring the bell. The people soon gathered, many "much agitated." Clarkson took up his stand under a large tree, fixed his eyes on Peters and, according to his journal, announced that "it is probable either one or other of us would be hanged upon that Tree before the Palaver was settled." In a private letter a year afterward he said that he only threatened to hang Peters if he could not clear himself of a charge of attempted usurpation. It was better to "hang three or four who might be the cause of future Misery . . . than to suffer the whole to experience Wretchedness," he said, but of course, he had no authority to hang anybody.

The meeting then became truly a palaver, with long-winded, heated argument from both sides. Clarkson contended that the colony would be ruined if Peters were made governor. It was illegal; only the company could select officers. He implied that the company would end its support. He talked of ingratitude, the sacrifice he and others had made to "pronmote their happiness" and the great sums the company had spent in the hope that they would be the instruments for spreading Christianity in Africa. He referred to the harm their bad conduct might do to blacks around the world.

The settlers told Clarkson that they had chosen Thomas Peters to speak for them since it was because of him that they had been able to leave Nova Scotia. On March 23, the day after Clarkson's unhappy session with Peters, 132 of them had signed a paper making him their go-between, and Peters was to have delivered this paper to Clarkson the previous night. Their intention was to "relieve the Governor from the fatigue of so many applications." They were alarmed and sorry that he had got so upset about it. Clarkson was hard pressed to persuade them they were in the wrong; by one account, he never did. Finally, they "gave way, and with the liveliest feelings of Gratitude and respect . . . promised all . . . I desired, begging of me with all the tenderness imaginable (some of them with tears), not to expose myself any longer to the Evening air, as they observed I was much fatigued."

The Easter Sunday uproar did not end there. A young woman whose husband had signed the Peters petition, seeing Clarkson march up the hill and hearing the bell rung, went into convulsions and died. As the meeting ended, fights broke out between Methodists (tending toward Peters) and Baptists. Peters' followers also turned on the men they suspected of warning Clarkson. Henry Beverhout, whom Clarkson recently had appointed parish clerk, "persisted in thinking it wrong for so many people to teaze the governor as they had done upon the most trifling occasions, and thought the plan proposed would have prevented it."

When Clarkson read the 132 names on the petition, he was inclined to agree that Peters did not have any real intention of ousting the government, an action which would never have been supported by many of the signers, one of whom was David George. He continued, however, privately to berate Peters as a man of "great penetration and cunning," a "rascal who had been working in the dark from the time he landed to get himself at the Head of the People, and if I had not acted by them as I did by taking care of their sick and indeed the whole of my Conduct . . . this Wretch would have driven all the Whites out of the Place and ruin'd himself and all his Brethren." He set unidentified persons to spy on Peters. He hardened in his resolve to demand stronger executive powers from the company.

At a general muster on April 11 everyone, including officials, signed an oath to observe the colonial government rules. On April 25 the *Felicity* sailed for London with the chaplain, Gilbert, who was to convey a detailed account of the settlement's predicament and an urgent appeal to alter the government to give the superintendent more power. Clarkson wrote his brother to be sure to support this proposal. "Your government," he told him, "is of the most absurd kind and calculated to make miserable those valuable people I brought with me from America."[34]

To Thornton, Clarkson said that the council form might work several years from now but at present it was disastrous: "Eight gentlemen, all invested with great power, each of them acting from himself, and none of them accountable to the other, form . . . a system of government, as pregnant with contradictions and inconsistencies as can be imagined." It perplexed the people. "Give me authority," he pleaded, "and if it does not come too late, I will pledge myself to remedy the whole." Without it, he would return to England. He refused to sign the dispatches from the council.[35]

The day after the *Felicity* sailed, Clarkson received from Laury White a complaint that Peters had stolen the effects of the deceased John Salter and disposed of them. White claimed the goods were bequeathed to him. Salter was a slave from Philadelphia who had joined the Black Pioneers in 1779 and had voyaged to Nova Scotia with Peters. He would have been about forty-four at the time of his death and left two children.

"Peters is certainly very restless and apparently dissatisfied & yet I cannot bring myself to believe that he has any hostile intentions; However as he has his Adherents I am cautious," Clarkson noted in his journal. A trial took place on May 1, with a jury of black captains who had continued to function as elected company leaders onshore. The lengthy arguments proved to the jury's satisfaction that Salter had on his deathbed given the keys of his chests to White. One Sunday, during church services, Peters went to the house, broke open the chest, took the contents with some hams brought from America, and about £20 in cash.[36] Peters' defense was that Salter owed him a commensurate sum, chiefly for helping ten years ago to recover his wife from slavery. The jury found Peters guilty, and its sharp reprimand had a reportedly "humbling effect." Clarkson delivered a long speech about the "enormity of the Crime and particularly when committed by a Man who ought to have set the Colony a better example." Then, as presiding magistrate, he passed a light sentence: Peters was to return the stolen property and pay the jurymen for losing a day's work. Peters gave up the property but appealed the verdict. Clarkson refused to act on the appeal.[37]

The struggle between the two men for the hearts and minds of the Nova Scotians now reached new intensity. Clarkson received daily reports from his informants. He saw Peters' hand in numbers of small incidents. He realized that underlying these symptoms of discontent was a strong sense of betrayal. The blacks had been told they would get their land upon arrival and that they would be treated equally in all things with whites. Neither had yet come true. Peters gave them "strange notions . . . as to their civil rights." According to reports reaching Clarkson, Peters claimed that it was he who had obtained the act incorporating the Sierra Leone Company and the company was not living up to its agreement with him. Beverhout was one of his important allies, but the other religious leaders counseled peace and saved the colony from "a blaze of rebellion."

During May, Clarkson held two full-scale meetings with the settlers at which wages, land grants and lesser matters were the subject of frank debate. He also met several times with the captains and scored further points on Sundays, when he stood in the pulpit of the makeshift church as a substitute for Gilbert. On the eve of a brief cruise, which pretty well restored his health, Clarkson met the captains, including Peters, for he had heard Peters intended to make himself "Speaker General" in his absence. He believed only two or three captains were on Peters' side now. The next day Peters asked permission "to speak a few words to [the settlers] to day for I do not mean to live in such confusion. . . . I wish to stand to the Company's agreement." Clarkson refused to do anything until he got back from the cruise, and he warned several captains to keep the peace *"as their very existence depended upon it."* [38] When he returned, Clarkson learned that Peters was attending nightly prayer meetings at preachers' houses. Clarkson began to go himself, without confiding in his fellow officers. After the service Peters would speak on the theme that the promises made to him in London were not being fulfilled. Then Clarkson would claim the floor and reply. He took pleasure in the number of "valuable thoughtful steady Men, who will hear reason and support me in promoting the Public Good." He congratulated himself on getting Peters "universally despised."

Clarkson exaggerated his powers of persuasion—as his successors were equally wont to do—taking signs of acquiescence at the face-to-face meetings for total agreement and submission. But he had a trump card that Peters could not match and none of his successors as governor ever held, and that was to threaten to abandon the settlers and return to England. At the first such hint they invariably "Begged him ardently not to desert them." The fear of his departure would always check the "licentiousness, of which under the name of liberty, part of them are very fond." Exposed to Clarkson's "pathetic manner," they "melted in gratitude & affection." He made "his own terms with them," said secretary Strand, "as they fear his going away."[39]

But like his successors, Clarkson did not appreciate the blacks' drive for liberty and self-government. On June 15, 1792, he was handed a proposal for the appointment of twelve men, including Peters and Elliott Griffith, to act as peace officers, to hear small disputes and keep order in the colony. The settlers were stepping into the vacuum created by the weak council government. Perhaps Griffith and the other Old Settlers who had joined the "Peters party" had explained the quondam government of Granville Town. Clarkson had read the company's regulation allowing limited settler participation, and he replied "To the Captains . . . and the Freeholders of Free Town" that "I very much approve such a mode" of bringing offenders to justice. He proposed a meeting, leaving it to them, as he always did, to fix the time and place so that it would be their fault if there were no crowd. The next night they gathered on the outskirts of the town. Clarkson agreed that they (*i.e.,* the males over twenty-one) might elect a "jury" with Peters and Griffith as foremen. However, he advised them to choose the black captains they had selected in Halifax, which would eliminate Griffith. After an election the winners' names should be submitted to him for approval. That night he noted that Peters "appears far from well." A week later Peters was too ill to attend a prayer meeting where Clarkson appeared. Beverhout's company sent a petition on June 25 arguing that the veto Clarkson retained would make them slaves. As the earliest surviving political statement of the colonists the petition follows, nearly in full. To understand it a little better, it is necessary to know that shortly before, Clarkson had suspended credit at the company store. It had been introduced during the sickly season and was now being abused, he said. Only those who cleared their accounts could buy on credit once more. And he had sought the settlers' agreement to a uniform wage of two shillings a day to put an end to the competition among councillors for laborers in their own departments. The petition was addressed "To His Excellency John Clarkson Governor & Commander in Chief of his Majesty's new Settlement of Sierra Leone & the Territories thereon depending," the latter presumably meaning Granville Town. It read:

> 1st. Sir the people of our Company consent to the Wages

that your Honour proposes, that is to work at 2ˢ/. [shillings] per day as long as we draw our provisions. 2ndly. We are all willing to be governed by the Laws of England in full, but we do not consent to give it to your honor without having any of our Color in it.

3rdly. there is none of us would wish for you to leave us here & go away, but your honor will be pleased to remember, what your honor told ye people in America at Shelburn that is whoever came to Sierra Leone that they should be free, & have laws & when there was any Trial, there should be Jury of both White & Black, and all should be equal so we take it that we have a right to chuse men that we think proper to act for us in a reasonable manner.

4thly. We are all willing to hold to your honors own words & to the hand Bill that we have got [*i.e.*, the terms of settlement] 5thly. Sir we think it very hard that your honour insists upon our paying for what we have taken up in the Store at this present for we expected to pay . . . in the produce of our Land according to the Sierra Leone Company in England required, & we are thankful to them for that good desire we have no reason to think but their intention is to make us happy, & we all give them thanks for their goodness & we pray that God will bless the Sierra Leone Company in England and prosper them in their undertakings whether we stand or fall.

6thly. We are all willing as yr. honor proposed, as to having Constables for keeping peace, all is very well, and we agree to that. 7thly. We would wish for peace if possible . . . but to give all out of our hands we cannot. Your honor knows that we can have rules and Regulations among ourselves &, we consent to the Laws of England because we have seen it in all parts we have been in. 8thly. We do not want any thing but what is fair honest just and right. Sir we don't mean to take the Law into our own hands for we own you to be our Governor & our Head, & we will be as good as our word to you in Halifax: We honour you for the many kindness that we recieved from you & we are willing to stand by your honor yet, for we know were well dealt by before we landed.

Sir your honor remember what was concluded upon at Halifax that we should assist you in public matters and we are willing to take the trouble off your honors hands by taking of small matters upon ourselves—This from your ffriends and well wishers in sincerity.

The Sierra Leone Company known by the
name of Beverhout.[40]

A second, similar letter reached Clarkson the following morning, June 26, along with the news that Thomas Peters had died in the night. In the hours of "Agitation and confusion," the letter had not been signed before delivery. Clarkson's own feelings can be conjectured as "mixed"—relief at the removal of his only rival, with some unspoken guilt for having engineered events that brought on the fatal illness or left Peters unable to resist it.

To Falconbridge, Sarah Peters sent a heart-rending appeal for the articles which would give her husband a funeral appropriate to his station:

> This is to beg the favor of you to let me have a Gallon of Wine One Gallon of Porter, & 1/2 Gallon of Rum 2 lbs. Candles 5 Yards of White Linen. My husband is dead and I am in great distress. I apply for the above things. my Children is all sick. My distress is not to be equalled. I remain aflicted Sarah Peters.

Clarkson, to whom it was referred, ordered the storekeeper to supply everything, and when a deputation, speaking "in behalf of the Colony," requested pine boards for a coffin, he broke his rule and granted them to convince "Peters friends that my opposition to him when alive did not proceed from any personal feelings or ill will towards him but from a sense of duty." As a further concession he gave permission for those wishing to attend the funeral to leave work.

It seems likely that little work was done that day in Freetown. Clarkson's journal is laconic, and others are silent on the event. "The people are tolerably quiet and Thos. Peters funeral went off without disturbance," the journal said. "There are many little rumours in the Colony for and against him which I take no notice of." Later he reported that "a great many" attended the rites. Peters, it would seem, had not been turned into a person "despised" as Clarkson had claimed.[41]

Exactly one month after his death the ghost of Thomas Peters was reported to have appeared. The ghost said that "he had no repose until he had confessed that he employed for his own use £100 which Genl. Clinton gave him in London for the poor pioneers in America on his return thither, with many other similar confessions. Peters was attended & tormented by half a dozen other Ghosts who reviled and ill-treated him." Clarkson found the ghost story useful "to quiet the minds of the people and therefore I let them enjoy it till . . . his person was forgotten." Then the governor preached a sermon denouncing superstition and calling on the people to demonstrate their gratitude and "perfect resignation" to God, who somehow again got identified with the Sierra Leone Company. He did, however, arrange a pension of £20 a year for Mrs. Peters, who, he said, had six or seven fatherless children, the eldest only eleven.[42]

Peters was the stuff of legends, and his death so early in the life of the colony was a personal tragedy. Whether from the start of his odyssey, Peters dreamed of a settlement in Africa with himself at its head, or whether he moved gradually toward the radical overthrow of the government from which he and all the other blacks were shut out, we cannot know. But Christopher Fyfe, the historian of Sierra Leone, is surely right in this epitaph:

> Without his astonishing faith and courage in crossing the Atlantic to see the wrongs done to his people righted, no Nova Scotian settler would ever have come to Sierra Leone. Without the Nova Scotians the Colony could not have survived its first misfortune. So in Thomas Peters we see, and should honour, one of its Founding Fathers.[43]

NOTES

1. Leyden, *A Historical & Philosophical Sketch of the Discoveries & Settlements of the Europeans in Northern & Western Africa*, p. 195.
2. *Clarkson's Mission*, pp. 79, 63, 125-26, notes 201; Clarkson to Hartshorne, August 4, 1793, Clarkson Papers, BL Add. MSS. 41,263.
3. *Clarkson's Mission*, pp. 93-94.
4. *Ibid.*, pp. 169-70.
5. *Ibid.*, pp. 180-81; Thornton to Clarkson, December 28 and 30, 1791; T. Clarkson to J. Clarkson, n.d. [January, 1792]; Wilberforce to Clarkson, December 28, 1791; Kingston to Clarkson, December 31, 1791, all Clarkson Papers, BL Add. MSS. 41,262A.

6. *Clarkson's Mission*, p. 181; Clarkson to Hartshorne, August 4, 1793.

7. Falconbridge, *Narrative of Two Voyages to the River Sierra Leone*, p. 139; Council minute, March 10, 1792, CO 270/2.

8. Kuczynski, *Demographic Survey of the British Colonial Empire*, vol. 1, p. 157; Journal of Dr. Taylor, March 9, 1792, Clarkson Papers, BL Add. MSS. 41,264; Clarkson Journal (New York), March 20, 1792; Fyfe, *A History of Sierra Leone*, p. 54; Sibthorpe, *The History of Sierra Leone*, p. 7.

9. Thornton to Clarkson, December 30, 1791.

10. Blacks in Birch Town who gave in their names for Sierra Leone, November, 1791, CO 217/63; Zachary Macaulay's Sierra Leone Journal, July 5 and 26, 1796, Huntington Library.

11. Book of Negroes, PRO 30/55/100, ff. 41-42; Sierra Leone Company 1794 Report, p. 108, where Peters is not identified by name; Macaulay Journal, February 25, 1799.

12. *Ibid.*, March 8, 1798.

13. Clarkson Journal (New York), March 24, 1792; *The Philanthropist*, vol. 4 (1814), p. 248; Sierra Leone Company 1794 Report, p. 8; *Adam Afzelius: Sierra Leone Journal 1795-1796*, p. 166 n.

14. I am indebted for photographs of these paintings to Lieutenant Commander A. J. Preston, a descendant of John Clarkson. Clarkson had a series of six views made by Beckett. Beckett, a godson of company director John Kingston, arrived in Freetown in September, 1792.

15. *The Philanthropist*, vol. 4 (1814), pp. 248-49; *Clarkson's Mission*, pp. 170, 171-72; Clarkson Journal (New York), March 21, 23, 24, 25, 1792; Ingham, *Sierra Leone After One Hundred Years*, pp. 21, 31.

16. Clarkson Journal (New York), April 2, 3, 15, 18, 1792; Winterbottom, *An Account of the Native Africans in the Neighbourhood of Sierra Leone*, vol. 1, p. 282. Dr. Winterbottom's meteorological table for 1793 shows a median temperature of 83° F. Rainfall measured over 86 inches.

17. Clarkson Journal (New York), March 21 and 27, 1792; Ingham, pp. 26-27.

18. *Clarkson's Mission*, p. 172; Taylor Journal, March 10 and 12, 1792.

19. *Clarkson's Mission*, p. 173; Falconbridge, pp. 135-36; Taylor Journal, March 14, 1792.

20. *Ibid.*, March 17 and 31, 1792; Clarkson Journal (New York), March 31, 1792; Clarkson to Thornton, April 25 and May 18, 1792, Clarkson Papers, BL Add. MSS. 41,262A; Council minute, March 30, 1792, CO 270/2.

21. Council minute, March 6, 1792, CO 270/2; Clarkson Journal (New York) May 29, June 27 and 29, 1792.

22. Clarkson Journal (Maynard), November 26, 1792.

23. Clarkson Journal (New York), July 1, 1792; Clarkson to DuBois, July 31, 1792, in Clarkson letter book, Sierra Leone Archives.

24. Boston King Narrative, p. 262.

25. Falconbridge, pp. 148, 154-55; Clarkson Journal (New York), July 26, 1792.

26. *Ibid.*, April 11, 1792; Clarkson Journal (SLS), p. 52; Taylor Journal, April 11, 1792.

27. For tropical illness, Curtin, *Image of Africa*, pp. 179-81; Kuczynski, pp. 15-16, 67-75; F. Harrison Rankin, *The White Man's Grave: a Visit to Sierra Leone in 1834*, pp. 163-69. Dr. Winterbottom made the first scientific study, concentrating on native-born Africans, see vol. 2, pp. 13-14, 16-17, 22, 32, 116, 121 for Nova Scotian references.

28. *Ibid.*, pp. 149, 162-63; Clarkson Journal (New York), May 25, April 5, 1792; Clarkson Journal (Maynard), p. 507: statement on climate and health; *Clarkson's Mission*, p. 46.

29. Clarkson to Hartshorne, August 4, 1793; *Clarkson's Mission*, p. 170; Clarkson Journal (New York), May 4, 1792.

30. Jordan to Clarkson, May 10, 1792, Sierra Leone Collection, University of Illinois, Chicago Circle; Clarkson Journal (New York), May 10, 1792; Smith to Clarkson, May 12, 1792; Dickson to Clarkson, May 15, 1792; Moore to Clarkson, August 24, 1792 (printed in Clarkson Journal [SIS], p. 33), all University of Illinois, Chicago Circle.

31. Clarkson Journal (New York), May 19, 1792; MS. History of the Colony of Sierra Leone, Clarkson Papers, BL Add. MSS. 41,263, n.d., in T. Clarkson's hand and addressed to J. Clarkson for correction, apparently a fragment of the history prepared by the brothers for *The Philanthropist*.

32. Clarkson Journal (New York), March 22, April 7, 1792; Clarkson to Hartshorne, August 4, 1793.

33. Clarkson Journal (New York), April 8, 1792. The account of the confrontation is from the journal; Ingham, pp. 39-43; Clarkson to Hartshorne, August 4, 1793; and *The Philanthropist*, vol. 4 (1814), pp. 252-53, in which Clarkson admits he was unable to persuade the people that they were wrong.

34. Clarkson Journal (New York), April 11, 1792; Ingham, pp. 44-45; Evans, p. 59 (oath supplied by directors); J. Clarkson to T. Clarkson, March 28, 1792, Thompson-Clarkson Collection, Friends Library, 3/209.

35. Clarkson Journal (New York), April 25, 1792; Ingham, pp. 53-58.

36. To replace the African medium of iron bars, the company introduced coinage based on the Spanish dollar, valued at about five shillings English sterling. There were units of dollar, half dollar, twenty cents and ten cents in silver, with one-cent pieces in copper. The obverse showed a crouching lion and the reverse clasped black and white hands. Settlers were paid in this specie and in paper currency as well. But the company's accounts and salaries paid employees continued to be in English sterling. Evans, "An Early Constitution of Sierra Leone," pp. 61-62; Claude George, *The Rise of British West Africa Comprising the Early History of the Colony of Sierra Leone*, p. 121.

37. Book of Negroes, PRO 30/55/100, ff. 131-32; Clarkson to Hartshorne,

August 4, 1793; Mr. James Strand's Journal of Occurrences, May 1, 1792, BL Add. MSS. 12,131. Both printed versions, in Ingham and *The Philanthropist*, left out Peters' trial, perhaps to preserve his reputation. Clarkson Journal (New York), May 1, 1792.

38. *Ibid.*, entries for May; Ingham, pp. 80, 83.
39. Clarkson Journal (New York), June 15, 1792; Clarkson to Hartshorne, August 4, 1793; Strand Journal, May 3, 7, 19, 1792.
40. Clarkson Journal (New York), June 16, 18, 25, 1792.
41. *Ibid.*, June 26 and 27, 1792; Clarkson to Hartshorne, August 4, 1793. Five others died the same day, and hundreds were ill.
42. Strand Journal, July 25, 1792; Clarkson to Hartshorne, August 4, 1793; Clarkson to Thornton, July 18, 1793, Clarkson Papers, BL Add. MSS. 41,263. I have found no other reference to money given Peters in London by Clinton, as in Strand's ghost story.
43. A classic case of mythmaking is Butt-Thompson, *King Peters of Sierra Leone*. For fact, see Fyfe, "Thomas Peters: History and Legend," pp. 4-13.

Chapter 14

COMING TO TERMS

> Upon the whole they are a good set of people; it would be
> difficult to find better subjects for Colonists.
>
> —JOHN CLARKSON[1]

The pressure for a voice in their own government survived Peters'
death, though no single person stepped into his shoes. It was frustrating
for the blacks to look on while the colonial offices—and the powers that
went with them—were handed about among the whites, more or less
regardless of qualifications, as this one fell ill or that one resigned or
another proved totally incompetent. The settlers were helpless to speed
up the distribution of the farmland, the issue of paramount concern to
them. But so, for some months, was Clarkson.

No one intended it to happen this way. Clarkson had arrived with one
plan from Nova Scotia, and the directors had sent two others, with
permission to alter them in view of the unexpectedly large number of
families. Each was first to get a town lot for a house and garden. Then
farms were to be laid out and again distributed by a lottery. If some
farms, because of the numbers, were too far away, then a second town
center might be built so that, as in the English village, the farmers would
live communally for safety and convenience but be only a short walk
from their fields. The directors specifically cautioned that the building of
Freetown should not occupy the settlers so long as to delay their getting
onto their land "within a few weeks." This was to be the first objective
of the colonial government.[2]

Clarkson intended to begin in March to run parallel lines from the river
toward the mountains, the width of a five-acre lot apart. Trees and shrubs
on these lines would then be cut to form "avenues." Parallel lines
intersecting at right angles would next be run and cleared. It might take
until September to clear the ground for planting, but meanwhile, the

260

settlers would know which were their farms and be able to look at them "with Pleasure *as their own.*" The settlers understood this arrangement, and many hoped that they would have at least a part of their farms tilled before the rains came, so that they would not have to depend entirely on the company's supplies. They had hardly been in Sierra Leone a month when the provision ration was cut because certain cargoes failed to arrive.[3]

Unfortunately, the responsibility for surveying and marking out allotments fell to James Cocks and Richard Pepys. The latter came highly recommended by the directors and was a competent surveyor, but as chief engineer he was also a councillor, which, said Clarkson, "had ruined him." He was a "stickler" for status symbols and would take no advice or direction. Good at planning, he was poor in execution. When he ordered pickaxes and hoes unloaded from a ship, there was no one onshore to receive them, and the settlers and Africans just helped themselves. When he took his recuperative cruise, Clarkson assigned Pepys to act for him, but this aroused fierce jealousy in the other officers, among whom Pepys was not popular. As for Cocks, amiable, inexperienced, immature and "too fond of Shew," he had taken a fancy to military display, for he captained the tiny band of company soldiers. When the lands would be surveyed, said Mrs. Falconbridge, "God only knows; the surveyor being a *Counsellor* and *Captain* . . . is of too much consequence to attend to the servile duty of surveying, notwithstanding he is paid for it." One day the officers (except Clarkson and Falconbridge) dined on board an American slave ship, and Cocks got very drunk. The ship's master dressed up his slave cook in Cocks' hat, coat and sword and had him perform the manual of arms with a mopstick for the amusement of the party. Even sober, Cocks had little interest in surveying, and he and Clarkson exchanged heated words more than once. Yet it was Cocks who moved in the council on May 12 that, to correct the confusion of so many bosses, all orders in future should go through Clarkson. The latter suspected Cocks was thinking of returning to England. The first precious weeks, therefore, were wasted. To add to the mounting antagonism between council and settlers over the land issue, both Cocks and Pepys were rough and thoughtless in their behavior toward the blacks.[4]

It was early May before the first garden lots were laid out, whereupon Cocks began to suffer attacks of illness. The settlers were increasingly alarmed at the standstill, but the wrangling went on until late June, when Cocks received permission to return to England and Pepys agreed to survey if he could add Cocks' title to his own to prevent Cocks' returning later in "triumph" to take credit for the work. Back in London, Cocks in fact did report that he had started surveying but had been advised by the council to delay![5]

June and July were the wettest months of the rainy season, when little could be done in the woods even with good men in charge. Yet it did not seem a sufficient excuse to the settlers, who by the end of July were "driven to such despair . . . as to appear many of them a different people. And were not Mr. C. here now, I should scarce think it safe to stay among them," James Strand noted in his journal.[6]

When it seemed that Pepys at last might get under way, he became embroiled in a fight between his wife and the large family of John White, the storekeeper, who wished to move onshore to a house next the Pepys' (it was Clarkson's house, shared with the Pepys). That "vile family," said Pepys, would give him and his ailing wife no rest. Clarkson tried to pacify them out of anxiety that Pepys would be too upset to survey. On July 31, his authority reinforced from London and hoping the worst of the weather was past, Clarkson shot off a series of directives to speed up various works, and chief among them was an order to Pepys to give up every pursuit that might interfere with the survey. On August 2 the clearing to run the survey lines began.[7]

The same pettiness, infighting and breakdown affected all other matters and contributed to the heavy climate of uncertainty that imprisoned the colony from March to August. Few issues were resolved in council, where Clarkson's influence was minimal. He spent more time with the settlers, trying to quiet their "murmurings."

On two points connected with the land, Clarkson exercised his own judgment in disregard of company instructions. The first was the imposition of the quitrent, due to begin in midsummer, 1792. He read about it for the first time in the mail which reached him at Sierra Leone. So far as the record shows, Clarkson did not mention this levy to the settlers. He had decided to stand by the position he had reached in Nova Scotia. There are inferences that he expected to discuss this and other issues in person in London with the directors in the reasonably near future. The second point concerned shore or water lots. Granville Sharp had learned from Thomas Peters how much the denial of access to water had meant to the black loyalists in Nova Scotia. The point was also raised with Clarkson there, and he had pledged that in Sierra Leone all lots wherever located would be drawn for in the same way. Again, nothing in his original instructions suggested otherwise. But the regulations opened at Sierra Leone clearly stated: "We desire that no land immediately adjoining the river shall be granted to settlers until further directions are received from us.''[8]

Clarkson tried to compromise, proposing that the company should reserve only the shoreland along the three capes or points where necessary public buildings, including defense works, could be accommodated. But the Nova Scotians objected heatedly. Isaac Anderson got so violent about it, when Clarkson and two other officers called at his house, that Clarkson walked out. What they were saying was that they had been excluded from the waterfront in America "by the white gentlemen occupying all the water lots, on which they built wharfs, and made such regulations which entirely prevented them from having any communication without payment; they were therefore unwilling to risk the like treatment again.''[9]

Clarkson saw the justice of this, and other company officers agreed with him, with the notable exception of Pepys. Clarkson pointed out privately that when and if the company ever required the waterfront, it could be bought "for the most trifling sum," far less than it cost to feed the colony each day that there was delay getting the people onto their farms. He directed John Wakerell, the accountant, to prepare a proclamation that no distinction would be made and that anyone who happened to draw a water lot would be free to build a wharf, warehouse or quay as he wished. It was posted on the door of the store. "This promise on my part satisfied the people," said Clarkson. "It also satisfied me, because I consider it but an act of common justice." Anderson, pleading that he was feverish at the time of his outburst, apologized "from my heart that there may not be any thing that may cause any more difference between us, & that we may all be good Citizens & good Governor.''[10]

Clarkson's policy sometimes only appeared to be mild. On another occasion when in an argument Robert Godshall attacked both Clarkson and Pepys "with violent and unbecoming language," Clarkson again walked away. But it was understood that an apology was required, and Godshall, like Anderson, made one. Had they not, Clarkson made clear, he would leave the colony. After Godshall's penitent note, Clarkson collected the captains and in Pepys' presence delivered one of his homilies about gratitude and the settlers' ''irrational'' fears of injustice.[11]

It was never easy, however, to satisfy the black settlers. And the day after his promise on the water lots, a memorial from Richard Corankapone, David George, Henry Beverhout and James Robinson "for the whole" demanded reassurance. Clarkson sent for the signers and gave them written copies of the promise. He wrote in his journal:

> The Company must abide by my instruction. Any regulations
> they may have adopted since my departure from England must
> give way to the general Spirit of my promises founded upon my
> Instructions & the understanding I had with the leaders of the
> Directors as to their Views & feelings towards the Nova
> Scotians if they wish to secure unanimity & Confidence among
> ye Settlers.[12]

Clarkson never met with the settlers that he did not feel obliged to
repeat the pledges on the land. The Easter Sunday confrontation with
Peters had not ended until he had promised that the lots would be laid out
as quickly as possible. During his ten months in the colony, Clarkson
recorded twenty-five other meetings with captains or groups of settlers,
and the apportionment of the land figured in virtually all. More than his
successors, and certainly more than the directors in London, Clarkson
understood what had gone wrong in Nova Scotia in the view of the loyal
blacks. It was summed up in a statement to him by an unidentified man:

> . . . we are all very thankful to the Sierra Leone Company . . .
> but you know Governor, the state you found us in in Nova
> Scotia & New Brunswick, & yet King George was good to us,
> God bless him and gave us many Articles to Comfort us and
> gave us promises of land . . . upon our arrival he also ordered
> us plenty of provisions to support us with, Arms & Ammuni-
> tion till we could get our Lands in a productive state but yet
> after being there for many Years we never received them, &
> when any of us . . . were able to get to the Seat of Government
> to deliver our Petitions . . . we were in general referred to an
> office where we were obliged to pay for a grant which we
> afterward found was laid down on paper only and in the midst
> of an immense forest. . . . we blame those who told lies to the
> king about us so that we now not having got our lands . . .
> makes us very uneasy in mind fearing we shall be liable to the
> same cruel treatment as we have before experienced from the
> same Cause.[13]

Unable to become yeoman farmers, the settlers of necessity became
wage laborers for the company. Again the councillors worked to cross-
purposes, each bidding against the other for the best workers by offering
higher wages. Clarkson believed that a shilling was a fair day's pay, but

bids of twice and even thrice as much were made in the various departments. After the council agreed in May that orders should funnel through him, Clarkson tried to enforce a general pay rate of two shillings a day, and fearful that to give the settlers free basic foodstuffs for three months and half rations for another three, if need be, might undermine their zeal to become self-supporting, he required them to pay two days' wages each week for the rations. The colonists were amenable, but when the food ran low in April, they protested the withholding. Clarkson did not give it up but promised to make up the deficiency when food became plentiful again. Work on the public buildings slowed, however, and at a lengthy public meeting on May 7 Clarkson tried to rally them, commiserating over their disappointments, but attempting to get them to see how much better off they would be when the wharves, officers' quarters, roads, schools and church were built. When he left them, they gave him three cheers, and the next morning the captains brought him a work plan they had developed during the night. Only four men had refused to go along with it. The captains "tenderly begged of me, not to trouble myself or fret about the behaviour of the people, that I need only to mention to one of them what I wanted to be done and they would see it executed." They were rewarded with $4 each. The plan was not described, but several were produced and discarded before the work force settled down to one in which they stayed together in ships' companies.[14]

The four whites in charge of working parties were usually Richard Pepys with thirty to seventy men on the survey; James Watt, temporarily diverted from developing the company plantation to putting up a hospital, prefabricated in London, on Savoy Point; Isaac DuBois, working on a warehouse on Susan's Bay (named for Clarkson's fiancée); and John White, the storekeeper. They were expected to keep tabs on the workers' families so that no one would suffer undue hardship through oversight. The Nova Scotians rapidly learned to use the only weapon they had, their labor or the withdrawal of it. They were thoroughly familiar, because of the councillors' carelessness in leaving papers around, with the regulations, especially those advising precautions to protect health, such as sufficient rest in the midday heat. They took advantage of the friction among the white officials. If Pepys pushed them too hard or failed to issue the beer ration, they would threaten to join the DuBois, Watt or White teams.[15]

In spite of the company's injunction about nondiscrimination in employment, only three blacks in the first year were put in "white-collar" jobs. Elliott Griffith, thought to be influential with King Naimbana, became the salaried chief interpreter, which also entitled him to a house in Freetown; Beverhout got the much lesser post of parish clerk; and Richard Dixon was made council messenger and part-time clerk at £25 a year. Griffith was the only settler admitted to any social equality, and that very rarely. He dined with the officers and captains of the Halifax ships at a kind of arrival celebration in March. Clarkson suspected him of dabbling in the slave trade, however, and grew to regard him as a troublemaker after he supported Peters' bid for leadership.[16] The census taken in April had listed "three or four" women capable of keeping a school, but illiteracy was a general handicap. Some of the adult craftsmen began to give up part of the noon rest period to learn to write and figure, so that they could keep their own accounts.[17] There were places for twenty men in the military, under a company plan to augment the force of eighteen English soldiers, who were often ill and generally thought useless. Cocks, while enjoying the rank of captain, tempted the Nova Scotians to enlist with promises of extra provisions and free rum. Some did, but after the first three months Clarkson put them back on the same footing as everyone else. By September only four of the original corps survived, and they were sent home at their own request. Having heard that the Africans were friendly, the company decided to do without troops, and after this the colony depended entirely on militia.[18]

Whatever the discontents or actions of the settlers in the first few months, the settlers' behavior was never reviled by Clarkson the way he denounced that of the white employees. "Pride, Arrogance self-sufficiency, Meanness, Drunkenness, Atheism and Idleness were dayly practiced," Clarkson confided to his Nova Scotian friend Hartshorne. He documented at least one charge by noting that the captain, mates, councillors and clerks living on board the *Harpy* managed to consume 144 dozen bottles of porter and 96 dozen of port wine in fewer than three months. In general, the whites set a bad example of grumbling, and "drunkenness—Pilfering the Cargoes—insulting the Natives—and debauching the Nova Scotian women were the most prevailing acts at the Commencement of this intended religious Colony."[19]

Clarkson was determined that justice at least be evenhanded, and just as the dispute with Peters was emerging into the open, he had a chance to demonstrate this. It was during the rush to get the settlers under shelter before the rains set in. The thatching grass was all cropped in the nearby meadows, and overcoming his scruples about Sabbath work, Clarkson directed the *Lapwing* cutter to go upstream for grass. Four of the seamen, all whites, refused the order to get under way, claiming that Sunday work violated the company rules. Clarkson doubted their piety. He was already annoyed at the unruly conduct of seamen, who were among the worst offenders in calling the settlers "black rascals" and using other offensive expressions. With the support of the council, he sent Captain Cocks and a party of soldiers to arrest the quartet. They were tried by the council early on Monday. One was acquitted, but the council voted ninety-five, sixty-seven and forty-six lashes respectively on the other three. Clarkson had authority to reduce the sentences, but he decided on a showy public execution of them. He ordered the Nova Scotian men to parade with their arms and summoned the captains and crews of all the ships in the harbor to watch.

For public flogger, he had appointed Simon Proof, thirty-three, a slave born in Virginia who was emancipated in the British army and joined the Sierra Leone venture from Birchtown. Before he began, Clarkson addressed the culprits publicly on their particular misdeeds and discoursed on the general bad behavior of seamen toward the Nova Scotians. To the latter he spoke of the need for cooperation. Then he signaled Proof to do his duty. The ringleader was biting on a bullet and did not appear to mind the first dozen strokes, but after the fourteenth he cried out, and Clarkson immediately ordered Proof to stop. The second and third men endured only a few lashes before also begging forgiveness. When the "bustle" had died down, Clarkson visited the seamen in the tent where they were confined. He gave them some "wholesome advice" and set them free. Then he had them row him out to the *Amy* on their way back to the *Lapwing*.[20]

With August, 1792, came such decided changes that Clarkson dated the true beginning of the colony from this time. With a brisk start on cutting the survey lines, spirits rose. Clarkson decided the time had come to incorporate the Old Settlers of Granville Town. They had mixed freely from the start on a personal basis, but Clarkson had been prejudiced against the 1787 survivors by Falconbridge's report of their "depravity." Shortly before the arrival of the Halifax fleet, Falconbridge had arrested Abraham Ashmore, sometime governor, for allegedly selling a fellow townsman, John Smith, but Ashmore had been released for lack of evidence. To protect his uncorrupted Nova Scotians, Clarkson banned the Old Settlers from Freetown. When the Old Settlers got into trouble with Signor Domingo, Clarkson refused to intervene in the ensuing palaver. In a letter to the council the Old Settlers pointed out that Domingo, a nominal Christian, had luckily behaved toward them as a good neighbor instead of wiping them out, but they protested being given

up by the Sierra Leone Company in "so careless a manner." What woul·
their friends at home think? "We have to beg Mr. Clarkson that if h
won't befriend us, not to do . . . anything that will injure us," the lette
concluded.[21]

Clarkson was ashamed; he ought to have considered their hardship
and defenselessness. The Old Settlers also gave a detailed rebuttal o
Falconbridge's accusations and criticized his handling of their resettle
ment. Clarkson decided to unite the two groups of American blacks, an·
on August 2 he sent a message to "the Freeholders of Granville Town"
that they were welcome if they obeyed the laws. Henry Beverhou·
Richard Corankapone, David George, James Jones, Joseph Berry an·
Daniel Profit delivered the letter and conducted the negotiation. The·
reported favorably, and Clarkson expressed his hope that "we ma·
begin, under the blessing of God, to date our happiness with that of you
posterity from this hour." On a visit in October he settled the disput
between Ashmore and Mrs. Smith by requiring, in the absence of proo
but the presence of strong suspicions, that Ashmore hereafter suppo·
Mrs. Smith. He also promised a new British flag to replace a worn-ou
one sent to them by Granville Sharp. The first patron of the settlemer
still heard from them. Lately they had complained that Freetown wa·
being built on land that belonged to them. They did not accept th·
company position that they had lost title by leaving it in 1789. Althoug
his advice was usually slighted, Sharp sent a meticulously thought-ou
and quintessentially Georgian plan for the one or more towns the colon
might support. He urged Clarkson to follow sound conservation practice
in felling trees and brush, and he added a characteristic admonition
"The first plant, however, to be protected must be RIGHTEOUS
NESS. . . ."[22]

Since mid-July Clarkson had been able to act with firmness an·
dispatch. He had received, on July 14, a resolution of the directors date
May 22 in which he was given unrestricted executive power, in respons·
to his request and Gilbert's personal testimony. It was a temporar
expedient, and on August 28 Clarkson received notice of the permaner
change in government which replaced the council of eight with a gove·
nor and council of two. To celebrate, Clarkson gave a dinner for th·
company officials and their wives at Harmony Hall, the new mess he ha
built for the unmarried staff. At church the following two Sunda·
Clarkson, still acting chaplain, read to packed congregations the direc
tors' letter declaring their intention to do "*full justice* to the free black
from Nova Scotia, giving them the enjoying of British rights, an·

ulfilling every expectation we have raised in them.'' The letter con-
nued:

> Having crossed the seas on the faith of our promises to them by
> Mr. Clarkson, . . . we are determined to cooperate with him
> in endeavouring to render their persons and their property safe,
> their industry productive, their character respectable, their
> condition in life more and more improvable and their future
> days happy.
>
> We consider them as the foundation of our Colony. To their
> courage and fidelity we must intrust its defence. We must in
> good measure trust to their industry for its growing wealth, and
> in our attempts to mend the morals of the surrounding nations,
> we trust a good deal to their good example. . . .

Many settlers commented approvingly on the directors' sentiments.
And Clarkson's added urgings to overcome their suspicion of white
people seemed well received.[23]

The surveying was halted abruptly in September because of disputes
with neighboring Africans. When the tract had been, as it were, ceded to
the settlers, the Africans had no idea that they would occupy more than a
coastal strip, as traders did. As the ''avenues'' or survey lines cut deeper
inland, they ran through villages and across planted fields or into sacred
bush. The existence of such forest villages was a surprise to the colonists.
In a palaver at Harmony Hall, presided over by King Naimbana, the
whole question of the title was raked up. In the end, Clarkson agreed with
King Jimmy to confirm their mutual boundary, fence one holy place and
skirt planted fields or villages. With Signor Domingo on the east and with
other river chiefs, it was agreed that the baseline would be put well
behind their towns and rice fields. Pepys and his men resumed hacking
out the lines. His ''avenues look beautiful as you pass them,'' Clarkson
observed.[24]

To stay within the new limits and in the interests of safety, Clarkson
decided on a single town. To keep the settlers within easy access, their
farms would have to be smaller, one-fifth the promised size, in fact.
Grants were prepared, stating that the holders of these allotments could
claim the balance in future, and ''with this arrangement they were all
satisfied, no one considering it as any breach of his promise,'' so far as
Clarkson knew. Mrs. Falconbridge compared the results of his negotiations unfavorably with the terms her husband had obtained and foresaw

trouble from the colonists and disgrace for their sponsors; there was no
room on the tract for them to have their full grants, and three-quarters of
the ground was rocky and hilly.[25]

By this time the settlers had held their first election, choosing an
unspecified number of "constables," who were sworn into office by
Clarkson on August 13, 1792. Based on Sharp's old frankpledge, the
process was formalized later, authorizing each ten families to elect a
tithingman or constable and every ten tithingmen to choose a hundreder
who would act on appeals.[26]

Freetown had also been strengthened by several white newcomers
DuBois, the American planter, who arrived in May, had proved able to
turn his hand to many things. He even nursed the sick during the worst of
the fever. About twenty-nine, he was the scion of a prosperous
slaveowning loyalist family in Wilmington, North Carolina, who had
been banished after the war. He had been a lieutenant in the New York
Volunteers and later spent some time in the Bahamas, where the family
had business connections, and in London, where he joined the Sierra
Leone Company. He was a hard taskmaster, but Clarkson thought the
Nova Scotians were "doatingly fond" of him.[27] Adam Afzelius, the
botanist, had disembarked with DuBois, and though the colony's straits
hindered his researches, his companionship, like that of the "very
amiable" young Dr. Thomas Winterbottom, who came in July, was
stimulating. Many settlers earned a bit extra collecting specimens for
Afzelius or helping in the botanical garden he created. He paid a
halfpenny for butterflies and sixpence for large bats. The eager new
chaplain, Melvill Horne, arrived in September with William Dawes, the
new first councillor. Zachary Macaulay, the second councillor, was to
follow in January, 1793.[28]

By November 13, 1792, the first small farms were ready for distribution by lot, and a day "dedicated to rejoicing" was arranged to celebrate,
as much as anything, sheer survival. Governor Clarkson and a large
party, including Dawes and sixty of the men who had worked on the
survey, climbed the highest hill overlooking the town. Clarkson named it
Directors' Hill; it is now Mount Aureol. As they wound their way to the
top, they paused for lunch at an "enchanting" spot where a brook spilled
over the rocks "in the most romantic manner." From the top they
scanned "the richest view imaginable, first, of the ocean; then of the
noble river, with the shipping riding at anchor below their feet; then of
the fine islands rising out of the bosom of the latter; and lastly, of the
adjacent country covered with the richest verdure as far as the eye could

arry." Clarkson and Dawes formally presented grants for "about 5 cres each" to forty families. A numbered list of allotments to Nova cotians from November, 1792, to March, 1793, shows that the first orty were drawn by eleven women and twenty-nine men. The forty dded up to 199 acres.[29]

A tent was erected, and dinner served. Clarkson offered a toast to 'The Sierra Leone Company and success to their virtuous exertions; and ay we the inhabitants of Free Town and Granville Town, be the istruments under providence of spreading the blessings of Christian nowledge through this unenlightened and unhappy country." As he oncluded, the "concourse of Nova Scotians" and others present gave 'three hearty cheers," the sixty survey workers raised their muskets and ired "three distinct vollies," and at this signal, the guns in the town elow saluted. Freetown residents cheered, and each company ship, olors flying, repeated the salute, "which had a beautiful effect . . . and have no doubt made an impression upon the whole neighbourhood," 'larkson reported. Numerous other toasts were drunk, to the officers, the habitants, Mrs. Pepys and the absent Miss Lee, Clarkson's betrothed, nd to "sweet hearts & wives, Wives & Sweet hearts."[30] There was still nother, his journal says shyly, "attended with rapturous cheering, ring, etc.," and it is not hard to guess that it hailed Governor Clarkson imself.

On October 28 Clarkson had announced from the pulpit that he was eturning to England at the end of the year. To the directors he had ecommended Wickham, as an old friend of the blacks, to succeed him. Vhen Dawes came, Clarkson was impressed with his ability and hard ork and within three days made up his mind to set a date for departing, aving Dawes in charge as acting governor. He embarked on a public lations campaign to "sell" Dawes to the skeptical Nova Scotians, who ound him "so stiff and serious, they do not like to ask him for any-ing—they say he may be a very good man, but he does not show it." 'larkson visited them in their homes to overcome their doubts and made awes the fount of rewards while he doled out the faultfinding. He then ok a three-week cruise in October to catch up on his paperwork. hough complaints about Dawes, "whose austere, reserved conduct (so verse to the sweet manners of the other)," still poured out from the ettlers, according to Mrs. Falconbridge, Clarkson was resolved to ave.[31]

His announcement followed an inspirational address based on a ser-on given him by Bishop Inglis in Halifax. The oration reflected his and the Nova Scotians' image of their joint adventure as the delivery of the Israelites into a "land flowing with milk and honey."[32] In his favorite guise as moral guardian, Clarkson expounded on liberty within the law, the responsibilities of Christians and the duty of everyone to accept his "ordained" rank in society:

> I do not hesitate to declare, that your general conduct . . . has made such an impression on my mind, that my future happiness in this world will be greatly affected by yours. I have observed in many of you a sincere wish to be partakers of a heavenly reward, and have with much pleasure retired from your religious meetings, enjoying my thoughts, that I had brought with me people possessed of such principles, to a country that has been so long in a state of barbarism.

By letting their light "shine before men," they would fulfill the great purpose of the Sierra Leone Company. He warned against idleness, "the root of all evil," against discontent over wages ("higher than any given in England") and of the danger that if the company did not approve their conduct, it would turn its money into other benevolent channels. He concluded with a plea for racial tolerance. After his benediction Clarkson volunteered to meet any delegation which might care to talk "on the subject of promises" so that he would not leave "till I have conscientiously performed every thing I may have promised, or given security that it shall be performed."

In the next few days Clarkson patiently adjusted complaints over the rocky soil or distance from friends of some of the first forty allotments, but he also, in an excess of concern over the drain on company funds, ended the provision allowance for the first forty families to be assigned land and put the rest of the colonists on half rations to conserve dwindling stocks. Petitions poured in. John Cuthbert and John Strong objected to the continued wage deductions under these circumstances. Twenty-eight men, including Boston King, appealed for restoration of the full ration for the workingmen or payment of their full wages so that they could buy food elsewhere.[33] They all were carpenters, earning at the time three shillings a day and paying four a week toward their food allotment. The governor saw reason in their plea but hesitated to put more cash in their hands, for many of the Nova Scotians had plunged into a lively trade for rum with passing ships or slave factories, and drunkenness was increasing. He preferred his old system of giving credit for undistributed food allowances. With this Dawes agreed. Before delivering the unwelcome news, Clarkson followed his usual practice of having a private word with the "leading and most serious men." They would prepare others to accept his position, and the colonists who were the most "illiterate and suspicious, and some amongst them ungovernable in their tempers" would not be drawn into an open clash with him. It was such diplomacy that made it possible for Clarkson to get the Nova Scotians to stomach one unpopular measure after another. He started at David George's prayer meeting, taking a few men aside to discuss the issue, and repeated the effort until he thought he had won over the "best part" of the colony. Certain events seemed to support his concern. The unsatisfied carpenters went on strike for a rum ration. (They returned to work a day later without it.) William Hooper was arrested for drunkenness and, when brought before Dawes, "insolently" insisted there was no law against it. (He was nevertheless fined 15 shillings.) Mrs. Abraham White came back from a trading trip to Bance Island with six jars of rum around the time that several barrels of meat and flour were reported stolen for use as trade goods.[34]

"When we first arrived here the Nova Scotians detested Liquor or at least only consumed a small quantity," Clarkson mourned. He was astonished that drunkenness should ever be a vice of this colony. There were only perhaps a dozen people, however, who got drunk and stirred up others, a very small proportion, considering "they have all spent the best part of their lives in Slavery and in the Army." And these were men who did not belong to any of the religious groups. He blamed himself for yielding to Pepys' request for rum for the hardworking survey parties. Requests from other working parties had followed, and it became a bad habit.[35]

The settlers' early leaning toward trade was partly for lack of farms to work and partly a natural reaction to living within full view of the profitable river commerce among Africans and between Africans and Europeans. The barter basis meant they could exchange anything unneeded or unwanted by themselves; no other capital was required for petty trading. The company's trade was almost totally neglected these first months. Clarkson was preoccupied, and Falconbridge, the commercial agent, crushed by his demotion, became a full-time drunkard. If Thomas Peters loomed as a tragic figure among the blacks, the tragedy among whites was Falconbridge. His story cannot be fully told here, and it did not directly affect the blacks. The directors, predisposed against him for some time, dismissed him in September, after which he drank as if to poison himself. It was a "mortal stab," said his wife. He died on December 19, by which time it came as "a happy release both to himself and those about him."[36]

Clarkson's fundamental objection to the settlers' engaging in much trade was that they would be involved with slaving. But two events encouraged them. The first was the arrival on August 7 of the *Calypso* packed with 153 dissident refugees from the failing Bulama colony and headed for England. It stayed in the Freetown harbor five weeks. The first choice for superintendent at Sierra Leone, Dalrymple, was on board, brokenhearted and ill. Clarkson took his friend into his own quarters. Most of the passengers were sick, and all needed medicine and food, which were furnished so far as supplies allowed. "I never beheld a more motley or miserable set," Clarkson noted. He dreaded the "unsettling" effect on the Nova Scotians of these "half-pay officers, decayed gentlemen, and dissolute adventurers." He fought off all requests for any of them to settle in Sierra Leone. The Nova Scotians, however, spotted a ready market with high prices. Clarkson soon banned the trade and closed the store for fear the unusual demand for goods would empty it, and when the settlers angrily objected, he gave them a tongue-lashing. For once they were not quick to repent, and when a man from the *Calypso* stole a settler's shoes, they refused to seek him out and arrest him. Only the stationing of the constables in every street prevented a riot.[37]

The second happening followed a petition to Clarkson to do something about the cost of fish. A settler named Robert Thornton had the only boat large enough to handle the seine net, which allowed him to dominate the market, and he was said to be charging too much. Clarkson directed the petitioners to fix a fair price in relation to wages. They decided twelve fish of a specified size should sell for a shilling, and Thornton signed an agreement to this effect. Further, Clarkson gave four Nova Scotians (Anthony Davis, James Jackson, America Talbot and John Strong) lumber to build a fishing boat. Soon everyone was "crazy for building boats," not only for fishing but for extended trade. The settlers, or many of them, proved very good at these commercial undertakings, but their "spirit of trade" was always regarded by the colonial officials and London directors as a sign of "laziness" and less useful than farming. Nevertheless, with a dozen boats engaged in fishing for market, the food supply greatly improved.[38]

Their resilience and adaptability were the saving characteristics of the black settlers, the qualities that allowed the majority to survive the ordeal of transplantation. Clarkson was deeply shocked when a census taken just before Christmas showed that 61 whites had died during the year and 166 Nova Scotians had perished. The latter figure doesn't square with his own report of September that there were 995 surviving Nova Scotians, a loss of 201. He later referred to 1,025 in the colony at the time of his departure, including births. The official company report stated that 57 whites and 203 Nova Scotians died the first year. Of the latter, 138 died in Africa. It was a toll of 17 percent of those who had left Halifax. The faulty knowledge about mortality was partly due to the fact that the blacks were buried by their own preachers, who did not always report vital statistics to the parish clerk.[39] But the confusion does not conceal the heavy loss. It was by any count the worst mortality of any period in the colony's history and the subject of wild rumors in London long before the anxious directors received a report from Clarkson. That it might have been worse, considering the lack of ready shelter on arrival and the early onset of the rains, did not much comfort the first governor.[40]

But the seasoned survivors at the end of 1792 were enjoying a moderate well-being. Houses had been made more weathertight, and gardens were flourishing with enough cabbages, pumpkins, beans and herbs to supply themselves and the officers' tables. Beef and pork, saved from the provision allowance, were hung in the rafters of many homes to smoke. In temporary allotments on the outskirts of town they grew sweet potatoes, cassava, peanuts, rice, corn and yams. Bananas, pawpaws, pineapples and oranges were plentiful. Pigs and poultry were multiplying, and the deer and boar brought in by hunters were welcome additions to the diet. The American settlers were never weaned away from the foods they had grown up with, which now had to be imported, such as wheat flour, tea, oatmeal, sugar, barley, butter, cheese and molasses.[41]

One of the Bulama colonists, Joshua Montefiore, who came independently to Freetown in November, 1792, provided a heartening picture:

> It is impossible to conceive the chearfulness with which they go to their daily labour at five o'clock in the morning, and continue till the afternoon, when each attends his domestic concerns, and cultivates his garden. In the evening they adjourn to some meeting, of which they have many, and sing Psalms with the greatest devotion until late at night. It is a pleasing sight on a Sunday to see them go to church, attired in their gayest apparel with content and happiness imprinted on their countenances.[42]

There was a growing market here, Clarkson advised the directors, for European foods and tools and for clothing as they had "a fondness for dress, and a great wish to be neat in their persons." It would be better to send cloth than garments, for few of the latter fitted properly, and they would also want needles, thread, pins, shoes, boots and umbrellas.[43]

Relations on the whole were good with the African neighbors. After one palaver with Signor Domingo which had attracted crowds into the town, Clarkson staged a display of cannon fire which brought shouts of astonishment and impressed the visitors with the colony's strength "without giving them offence." The performance was repeated by popular request.[44]

Most of newcomers had trouble getting used to the animal life. Several of the pet dogs brought from Nova Scotia were killed or mauled by leopards. David George scared one away from his pet, but it carried off another in its flight. Arthur Bowler frightened a leopard away from his sleeping wife and daughter. Large snakes were less bothersome than lizards and insects, especially ants, which struck terror when they stormed the houses. They followed the rainy season, and according to Mrs. Falconbridge:

> swarm over every thing . . . crickets, cockroaches, spiders, etc., are driven out of their crevices and jump about . . . in a distressing situation amongst their enemies. The large black ants conquer every living animal and devour it unless it escapes by flight. . . . when the settlers see that their course is directed through their houses, they have recourse to fire or scalding water, with which they attack them as they are pouring along the ground like a rivulet.[45]

Cuffey and Judith Preston saw their house and all they owned go up in flames when they tried to burn out the ants. A subscription was taken up for them. Mosquitoes were less fierce than in America, but there was a night chorus that could drown out the drums from King Jimmy's town. Night fell swiftly, "foretold by a concert of crickets, lizards, &c which continue their stridulous notes through the night," said Dr. Winterbottom. Sometimes there would be a lull "after which the vocal band proceed with redoubled ardour. Upon the falling of a few drops of rain, the concert is instantly joined by the deep bass of the frogs, and may be heard above half a mile from the shore." One species of cricket had the piercing sound of a saw being sharpened and tormented sick persons trying to sleep.[46]

Clarkson's announced departure created some alarm, but it was generally supposed he would return. Mrs. Falconbridge said he expected to be gone five or six months. A group of forty-nine men and women signed a petition to the Sierra Leone Company to send him back. It read:

> . . . we the Black pepol that Came from Novascotia to this place under our agent John Clarkson and from the time he met with us in novascotia he ever did behave to us as a gentilmon in everey resept, he provided every thing for our parshige as wors in his pour to make us comfortable, till we arrived at Sierraleon and his behaveour heath benge with Such a regard to us, his advice his Concil his patience his love in general to us all both men and wemen and Children and thearfour to the gentilmon of the Sierleon Companey in England we . . . wold desier to render thanks . . . that it heth pleased almighty god to put it into the heart to think . . . on us when we war in destress and . . . as our govener is a goin to take his leave of us . . . we wold Bee under Stud . . . that our ardent desier is that the Same John Clarkeson Shold returnen Back to bee our goverener our had Comander in Chef . . . and we will oBay him as our governer and will hold to the laws of England as far as lys in our pour. . . .[47]

To this "most gratifying" request, Clarkson responded in a farewell address on December 16.

> I am cautious of making promises, because when I make a promise, I do it with an intent to perform it, and I should be miserable if I could not comply with it conscientiously. I therefore cannot promise you to come back, but I will go so far as to say, that I think the chances are ten to one that I shall; for I do not know any employment in this world that would be more pleasing to myself and I hope to my Creator, than my best attempt to establish this Colony. . . . I really cannot at this moment see any employment of such magnitude and importance as that of my coming to this place again to be your friend and adviser. . . .[48]

The church was thronged, and the crowd overflowed under an awning outside for his appearance that day. It was a stern speech, calling for improved civic conduct and obedience to those in office, coupled with a warning that they jeopardized all support from Britain if they were defiant. He reminded them for the hundredth time that the "happiness of every Black man throughout the world" depended upon their success. If they would accept the leadership given them, "your children may stand as fair a chance of being considered as men, and of having a share in the government of Nations equal to that of the Whites." Some of his criticisms were so harsh that men walked out. "Many, very many felt greatly affected." Eli Ackim sent a note of approval. He hoped the governor would not "frown on all" for the bad behavior of a few, "as for my part I love the, and fear the, and am sorry to part from the; I hope from the bottom of my heart, that God will bles you for ever, for you goodness to ous all."[49]

The benedictory prayer with which Clarkson concluded that day still circulates in Sierra Leone, and copies of it sell particularly well in any period of crisis. "No European has ever won the love of the people of Sierra Leone as Governor Clarkson did," says Christopher Fyfe.[50]

When he started to visit each family, calling at houses street by street, to say good-bye and put in a word for Dawes as acting governor, Clarkson found he could not complete his rounds, being reduced so often to tears by the "expressions of Gratitude, Affection and respect."

Their first Christmas in Africa was celebrated by the colonists with the liveliness they used to spend on it in Nova Scotia. On Christmas Eve the night air was rent with gunfire and "general rejoicing." On Christmas Day the men continued to fire rounds, and "the People assembled together in parties with Drums & Fifes, and called upon all the officers, wishing them a merry Christmas and a happy new year." At daybreak Joseph Leonard, the schoolmaster, led the children through the town, stopping at various houses to sing hymns. At church Clarkson administered the sacrament to "a great number."

He boarded the *Felicity*, commanded by his friend Wickham, on December 28 after having received a parade of women contributing things from their larders for his comfort on the six-week voyage. He was richer by six dozen chickens, 600 eggs and countless yams, onions, fruits and even pigs. The officers came on board to take their leave on December 29, and the ship weighed anchor in midafternoon. The battery on shore fired a fifteen-gun salute, and "all the Officers and People . . . waved their hats and handkerchiefs, and gave three hearty cheers."

Clarkson had only a short while to enjoy his sendoff before he saw a gun on the *Amy* explode, killing a crewman. At his order, the *Felicity* did not return the salute but slipped quietly downriver.[51]

He had left without seeing the settlers on their farms. His aim had been to have each family in possession by Christmas, but the surveying was not finished. He had elicited from Richard Pepys, however, a promise that the last farms would be allotted within two weeks from his going.[52]

NOTES

1. Character of the Settlers, [February, 1793], Clarkson Journal, (Maynard), f. 499.
2. Evans, "An Early Constitution of Sierra Leone," p. 69.
3. History of the Colony of Sierra Leone, Clarkson Papers, BL Add. MSS. 41, 263, f. 183.
4. T. Clarkson to J. Clarkson [January, 1792], Clarkson Papers, BL Add. MSS. 41,262A; Clarkson Journal (New York), July 28 and 2, April 25, May 4, June 1 and 6, 1792; Falconbridge, *Narrative of Two Voyages to the River Sierra Leone*, pp. 139, 146-47; Council minute, May 12, 1792, CO 270/2; Clarkson Journal (New York), May 4, 7, 10, 1792.
5. Clarkson Journal (New York), June 1, 14, 17, 19, 1792; Council minutes, June 13, May 21, June 25, 1792, CO 270/2; Clarkson Journal (New York), June 26, 1792; Thornton to Clarkson, September 14, 1792, Clarkson Papers, BL Add. MSS. 41,262A.
6. Strand Journal, July 28, 1792, BL Add. MSS. 12, 131.
7. Clarkson Journal (New York), July 28-August 2, 1792; Letter book, Sierra Leone Archives, July 31, 1792.
8. Evans, p. 54; Thornton to Clarkson, December 30, 1791, Clarkson Papers, BL Add. MSS. 41,262A; *The Philanthropist*, vol. 4 (1814), p. 259; Evans, p. 70.
9. Clarkson Journal (New York), July 30 and 31, 1792; Ingham, *Sierra Leone After One Hundred Years*, p. 100.
10. Clarkson Journal (New York), August 1, July 30 and 31, 1792; Ingham, p. 101.
11. Clarkson Journal (New York), June 28-29, 1792.
12. *Ibid.*, August 1, July 30, 1792.
13. *Ibid.*, June 26, 1792.
14. *Ibid.*, March 20, April 27, May 1, 7, 8, 1792; Ingham, pp. 67-72; Council minutes, March 30, May 12, 1792, CO 270/2; Clarkson to Hartshorne, August 4, 1793, Clarkson Papers, BL Add. MSS. 41,263; Clarkson Journal (New York), May 18-20, 1792.

15. *Ibid.*, July 17, June 26, 1792; Ingham, p. 99; Evans, pp. 64, 68; Clarkson Journal (SLS), p. 18.

16. Council minute, March 6, 1792, CO 270/2; Clarkson Journal (New York), May 21, 1792; Clarkson Journal (SLS), p. 51; Taylor Journal, March 10, 1792, Clarkson Papers, Add. MSS. 41,264; Clarkson Journal (New York), many observations on Griffith, including April 17 and 18, June 16, 20, 22, 1792.

17. Clarkson Journal (Maynard), p. 501.

18. Evans, p. 71; Clarkson Journal (New York), May 31, 1792; Clarkson Journal (SLS), pp. 14, 47; T. Clarkson to J. Clarkson, July 17, 1792, Clarkson Papers, BL Add. MSS. 41,262A; Thornton to Clarkson, September 14, 1792.

19. Clarkson to Hartshorne, August 4, 1793 (continuing September, n.d.), Clarkson Papers, BL Add. MSS. 41,263.

20. Council minute, April 16, 1792, CO 270/2; Clarkson Journal (New York), April 15, 16, 1792; Blacks in Birch Town who gave in their names for Sierra Leone, November, 1791, CO 217/63.

21. Clarkson Journal (New York), March 30, 1792; Ingham, p. 35; Council minutes, February 17 and 21, 1792, CO 270/2; Clarkson Journal (New York), April 25, March 30, 1792; Ingham, p. 58.

22. Clarkson Journal (New York), March 30, 1792; Ingham, p. 35; Council minute, April 30, 1792; Clarkson Journal (New York), April 25, August 2, 1792; Ingham, p. 102-3. Clarkson Journal (New York), August 4, 1792; Ingham, pp. 103-4; Clarkson Journal (SLS), pp. 72-73; Sharp to Clarkson, July 24, 1972, Clarkson Papers, BL Add. MSS. 41,262A; Sharp's plan, Sierra Leone Collection, University of Illinois, Chicago Circle.

23. Clarkson Journal (New York), July 14, 1792; Clarkson Journal (SLS), pp. 26, 36, 35, 46.

24. *Ibid.*, pp. 56-57, 60-65, 100.

25. Fyfe, *A History of Sierra Leone*, p. 47; *The Philanthropist*, vol. 4 (1814), p. 261; Falconbridge, p. 173.

26. Clarkson Journal (SLS), p. 9; Council minutes, December 12 and 31, 1792, CO 270/2.

27. AO 13/118, packet D III; AO 12/101, f. 66; DeMond, *The Loyalists in North Carolina During the Revolution*, pp. 99, 113, 179, 252; Parliamentary Papers, 1803-1804, V, Report of Committee on Petition of Isaac DuBois; Clarkson Journal (Maynard), December 27, 1792; Clarkson to Hartshorne, September n.d., 1793.

28. Clarkson Journal (New York), May 6, July 13 and 14, 1792; Clarkson Journal (SLS), p. 42; Lindroth, "Adam Afzelius: A Swedish Botanist in Sierra Leone, 1792-96," p. 205.

29. Clarkson Journal (SLS), pp. 101-2; *The Philanthropist*, vol. 4 (1814), p. 260; Montagu, *Ordinances of the Settlement of Sierra Leone*, vol. 4, First Nova Scotian Allotments.

30. Toasts given at a dinner on the mountain, Clarkson Papers, BL Add. MSS. 41,262A. Miss Lee's name is in bold letters.

31. Clarkson Journal (New York), June 29, 1792; Clarkson Journal (SLS), pp. 44, 48, 45, 73; Falconbridge, p. 178.

32. Clarkson Journal (Maynard), ff. 587-617, full text of October 28 sermon, erroneously cited in Ingham, pp. 160-63 as Clarkson's last in Sierra Leone.

33. Clarkson Journal (SLS), pp. 102-3, 105-6; John Duncomb (Duncan) and others to Clarkson, November 19, 1792, University of Illinois, Chicago Circle.

34. Clarkson Journal (SLS), pp. 107-8; 110-11; 111-13.

35. Clarkson Journal (Maynard), November 27, December 8, 1792.

36. Falconbridge, pp. 167-68; Clarkson Journal (Maynard), December 19, 1792.

37. Clarkson Journal (SLS), pp. 3-10; Letter book, August 10. Some of the blacks in the Bulama colonization scheme were also loyalists. One was Philip Beaver's servant, James Watson, a former South Carolina slave, who stayed with him to the end in 1793 and then settled at Sierra Leone. Beaver, *African Memoranda*, pp. 205, 436; WO 1/352, 1802 census; Book of Negroes, PRO 30/55/100, ff. 21-22.

38. Clarkson Journal (SLS), pp. 34, 49, 88-89, 98; Letter book, September 17, 1792.

39. Clarkson Journal (Maynard), December 21, 1792; Ingham, p. 152; Clarkson Journal (SLS), p. 52; Clarkson Journal (Maynard), February 11, 1793; Sierra Leone Company 1794 Report, pp. 49-50; Clarkson Journal (SLS), p. 55.

40. Gilbert to Clarkson, July 13, 1792; Thornton to Clarkson, July 23, August 17, September 14, 1792, all Clarkson Papers, BL Add. MSS. 41,262A. Curtin, *Image of Africa*, Appendix, pp. 483-84, finds it is not untypical for a first-year colony.

41. Clarkson Journal (SLS), p. 51; Falconbridge, pp. 161, 162-63; Clarkson Journal (Maynard), December 14, 1792; Clarkson Journal (SIS), p. 59.

42. Montefiore, *An Authentic Account of the late Expedition to Bulam, on the Coast of Africa: with a Description of the Present Settlement of Sierra Leone*, pp. 47-48.

43. Clarkson Journal (Maynard), ff. 522-23.

44. *Ibid.*, November 27, December 3, 1792. The palaver was partly concerned with the case of James Harford, an Old Settler, charged with taking liberties with one of Signor Domingo's wives. Clarkson persuaded the chief not to shoot Harford. Clarkson Journal (SLS), p. 100.

45. Clarkson Journal (New York), March 20 and 21, May 24, 1792; Falconbridge, pp. 161, 162; Clarkson Journal, (SLS), p. 90; *The Philanthropist*, vol. 4 (1814), p. 259.

46. Clarkson Journal (Maynard), December 8 and 12, 1792; Winterbottom, *An*

Account of the Native Africans, vol. 1, p. 30, 30 n.; Clarkson Journal (New York), April 5, 1792; Falconbridge, p. 162.

47. Clarkson Journal (Maynard), November 28, 1792. There were two such petitions. Original of one quoted, University of Illinois, Chicago Circle.
48. Clarkson Journal (Maynard), December 16, 1792; sermon text appended.
49. *Ibid.*, December 16, 1792; Ingham, pp. 149-50.
50. The prayer is in Clarkson Journal (Maynard) appendix; Ingham, pp. 164-67. Fyfe. "Thomas Peters: History and Legend," p. 10.
51. Clarkson Journal (Maynard), December 25, 28, 29, 1792; Clarkson to Hartshorne, September n.d., 1793; "A List of People who gave me Eggs at my Departure" and "Hector Peters Received the Eggs from Deferent People—for Mr. Clarkson," both in Clarkson Papers, BL Add. MSS. 41,262A, f. 218, 219.
52. Clarkson Journal (SIS), pp. 82-83; Falconbridge, p. 187.

Chapter 15

THE PURSUIT OF PROMISES

> . . . we have not the Education which White Men have yet
> we have feeling the same as other Human Beings and
> would wish . . . to make our Children free and
> happy. . . .
> —SETTLERS AT THE NEW COLONY OF SIERRA LEONE[1]

ON New Year's Day, 1793, Mrs. Falconbridge wrote, "Two days ago
Mr. Clarkson sailed; his departure operated more powerfully and generally upon people's feelings, than all the deaths we have had in the
Colony." The people were plunged into a series of unsettling events
which soon erased the effect of his admonition to trust the officers of the
Sierra Leone Company. Richard Pepys had promised that the allotment
of land would be completed within two weeks. But all surveying work
stopped, and Pepys began to build a fort where once there had been a
simple palisaded area for refuge in case of attack. The new and grandiose
plan was much resented, for it diverted labor from the survey. Isaac
DuBois insisted that a storehouse was more valuable than twenty forts,
but acting governor Dawes and Pepys were "fort mad." DuBois had
Clarkson's written instructions to proceed with the officers' quarters, a
wharf and a storehouse. Abruptly, he was stripped of these responsibilities and told to concentrate on a company farm, the job for which he
was originally employed. Pepys took charge of all public works.[2]

The colonists grew edgy. They clamored for ammunition when drumming and gunfire were heard from King Jimmy's town. When Dawes
tried to include twenty feet from William Grant's lot inside the new
security fence, a crowd gathered and a spokesman declared that if one
inch were taken, they would pull the fence down. They "cried out loudly
for their Town & country lotts," DuBois related to Clarkson in a journal
he was keeping for the absent governor. Dawes threatened to leave them

if they did not behave, and to the old Clarkson bogey they now responded "with one voice, that you may do as soon as you please. *God Almighty will take care of us.*"

"Go! go! go!" Mrs. Falconbridge (now Mrs. DuBois) heard them shout. "We do not want you here, we cannot get a worse after you."[3]

Word spread that the farm surveys would not be finished for a year, and Pepys began to talk of returning to England on leave. The endless tinkering with plans and grants, which was to continue for years, now set in. The people were called together on February 6, 1793, to hear of a new plan for the town. They were to give up their old lots in exchange for new. One important effect of the new plan was to overturn Clarkson's ruling and exclude the colonists from the waterfront. A "great palaver" ensued. Told that the new lots were 500 feet from shore, the settlers retorted that Governor Clarkson had pledged that all would have equal chance to draw a water lot. Only if the lots began from the water's edge would they move. Clarkson had "told them they would be treated as free men & as well as white men—they believed Mr. Clarkson, they said, to be an honourable man & they were sure he would never have left them without performing his promises to them had he not been assured by the Gentlemen he left behind they should all be complyed with." They claimed the rights of free British subjects, and they raised the issue which was never far from their thoughts—the unobtained farms.

At this obstinacy, Pepys made the shocking charge that Clarkson had been drunk when he addressed them in Birchtown and that he had no authority for anything he promised. The absent governor, said Pepys, "seldom knew or thought of what he said."[4]

"Here they groaned and murmured, but said 'they believed Mr. Clarkson to be a man of honor. . . .' " The following day, the "blacks seem vastly alarmed and uneasy, nothing else is spoken of," Mrs. DuBois wrote. They decided to send two representatives to London to find out from the directors themselves what the promises meant. They were temporarily without their champion, and the only white man who knew exactly what their agreement was with the Sierra Leone Company. They chose Isaac Anderson and Cato Perkins as delegates and collected donations to pay their expenses, but it was June before the two men could sail.[5]

Meanwhile, some of the colonists prepared an alternative town plan and presented it to Dawes, but it was ignored. John Gray, commercial agent, thought the people so dissatisfied that if they could not win the argument "they will go and take Possession of Land where they like." If the people were cruelly deprived of their farms for a year, he wrote to Clarkson, it would be the ruin of the colony.

> We *want you much*, not only as heretofore to preserve Harmony, and by your Company and Conversation to enliven the scene . . . but also to do away disgust & discontent from the minds of the People—for they are Grumbling now more than ever I remember them to have done before—However you will not wonder at it when you are inform'd that *nothing at all* has been done towards laying out the Lots and putting the People in possession of their Lands since you left us. . . . instead . . . Mr. P. is . . . amusing himself . . . about building a fort on Thornton Hill.[6]

As early as February, acting governor Dawes, Zachary Macaulay and Pepys were acting in the conviction that Clarkson would never return, although his friends confidently expected him back. The orders he had left behind were laughed at. Slandering him seemed to be a calculated policy to wean the settlers away from their personal loyalty, but it served only to alienate them from their new governors. Factions developed also among the company officials, with the mischief-maker, Pepys, playing a leading part in widening rifts. He attached himself to Dawes, who had not known him long, and Macaulay, who had arrived in mid-January, and rapidly enlarged his influence.[7] DuBois was an old antagonist of his: Their tiresome quarrels over protocol or precedence had often distracted Clarkson, but he had appreciated the many skills and willing spirit of the American loyalist. In Clarkson's time, many had regarded Pepys as a hypocrite and a schemer, but his reputation stood high with the directors in London.

Clarkson himself reached London in February, 1793, a more mature figure, from all that had happened since August, 1791, and totally committed to the welfare of the settlers. He intended to render the full accounts which such problems as sickness, personal frailty and simple incompetence among the staff had prevented him from sending before; to seek pay raises for the abler employees; and, though it is indicated only by inference, to discuss his decisions on the terms of land settlement. Some of his points had already been raised rather hotly in letters to Thornton. The chairman, who felt equally hard driven, had resented the reflections on the directors' integrity contained in the governor's criticisms. Thornton's self-justifying responses to Clarkson's passionate presentations had not greatly advanced their understanding of each other. Furthermore, the directors had been seriously disturbed at some reports of heavy mortality at Sierra Leone from slave-trade sources when they were trying to keep an optimistic picture of their African experiment before the public.[8]

Thus when the enthusiastic governor burst upon the court of directors at Sierra Leone House, he was listened to warily. But his immediate offer to continue as governor was accepted, and he was given three months' leave. A frame for a house, to his own design, was ordered built to be sent out to Sierra Leone. Then for two unhappy months he tarried in London with nothing to do. No public notice was taken of him. Apparently he had caused deep offense with a shower of advice and criticism at his initial meetings with the directors. In particular, he deplored an embargo on shipping, because of the conflict with France, which was holding up provisions. He thought the directors "supine" for not exerting their influence on government to procure a naval convoy as the slave traders were doing.[9]

He was to say later that he found the directors niggardly, timid and careless. They were too tied to "nonsensical forms." He was affronted at their treatment of his friend Wickham, who for all his services was offered a £20 gratuity and command of the little *Felicity*, both of which Clarkson said, "I should have been ashamed to have offered him." When Clarkson remonstrated, he was told that one director had heard Wickham swear, "which they considered as such a Crime that they could not in conscience take him by the Hand." This prompted Clarkson for his part, for the first time in his life, to curse "illiberality and all such ignorant childish, methodistical notions."

Thornton and his closest associates were Evangelicals, and their choice of employees was often determined as much by an applicant's pious professions as his proved abilities. This weakness already had caught the eye of Mrs. Falconbridge. Before Clarkson left the colony, he had asked the company officials what advice they wanted him to offer in London. He had not asked Mrs. Falconbridge, but she recorded in her scathing book what she would have said had he paid her that courtesy:

> Let the Directors shake off a parcel of hypocritical puritans, they have about them, who, under the cloak of religion, are sucking out the very vitals of the Company; let them employ men conversant in trade, acquainted with the coast of Africa, and whose *religious tenets have never been noticed*; under this

description they will find persons of sound morals, fit to be intrusted, but they will ever be subject to imposition, while they employ a pack of canting parasites, who have just cunning enough to deceive them.[10]

She was probably getting in a poke at William Dawes, whose religiosity had raised even Clarkson's eyebrows. Dawes had arrived on the *York*, which had an earnest Methodist as captain and also carried the new chaplain, Melvill Horne. A ritual of morning and evening prayers was followed. Clarkson visited the ships at all hours, and as he later described it, "I was never so much surprized in my Life as I was one morning in going aboard the York. . . . [T]he Bell began to toll and a hymn Book was put into my hand when instantly everyone on board were down upon their knees." Clarkson was conscious that every delay in unloading meant demurrage might have to be paid, but since the *York*'s captain was "one of the Groupe" (meaning of the Evangelical bent), the directors probably would not object to this delay. Two small mutinies occurred on the *York*, and Clarkson learned that the sailors habitually embezzled from the cargo. He concluded that the constant application of prayer was having little effect in stopping their "violent oaths or in keeping them honest."

Dawes had come to the colony praised by Wilberforce as "an avowed friend of Religion & good order." One night Clarkson had supper in the cabin where Dawes also slept and was disconcerted when Dawes turned in early, "kneeling down before us all to say his prayers."[11] Clarkson's earthy Christianity, which relied on hard work, good cheer and "happiness here as well as forgiveness hereafter," touched no chord in Thornton, around whom the Clapham Sect grew, and Clarkson soon saw that except for some lingering fear that the colony would fail without him, they would not send him back as governor. Then came reassuring letters from Freetown, where Dawes and Macaulay had forged a partnership.[12]

"The one was at a loss for language to express his admiration of the other, and the official accounts were more Favourable than the private," Clarkson soon learned. In the two councillors the directors had found "men of their particular ways of thinking in religious matters." Macaulay had written that Clarkson's regime (which he had never experienced) contrasted poorly with Dawes' "steadiness, firmness." The settlers had been getting "harangues, consultation &c upon almost all occasions but now they are more happy and feel the difference of a man who will be determined in making them do their duty than of one

who was always accustomed to persuade them." (The years only added
to Macaulay's admiration for Dawes, "one of the excellent of the Earth.
With great sweetness of disposition, & self command, he possesses the
most unbending principles . . . a noble mind. . . ."[13]) Clarkson, who
was shown Macaulay's letter to Thornton, was surprised at the young
man's audacity in passing judgment on the colony's first year and set
Macaulay down as a man of "illiberality" who approved of arbitrary
power.[14] For his part, Dawes felt positively "*ashamed*" to find himself
superior in rank to a person of Macaulay's "uncommon abilities."

Clarkson had received different news from Freetown. He had been
told that the surveying had stopped, that he had been accused of making
the Nova Scotians drunken promises and that DuBois in frustration had
asked and been granted a leave of absence. On the day Clarkson left
London for Norfolk to be married, Thornton informed him that he need
not return to Africa. On a point of honor, Clarkson refused to resign, in
exchange for some handsome recognition. So he was dismissed.[15] But
the African colony had too many enemies for him to make public his
anger. He volunteered to do all that he could to reconcile the settlers to
the change of government.

His first letter was to Richard Corankapone. He reported on the
missions entrusted to him (getting watches repaired, arranging the purchase of a spinning wheel, tailor's tools, Luke Jordan's seine and hooks,
Mary Perth's spectacles, and Joseph Brown's loom, as well as trying to
trace, for Corankapone, John Cuthbert and others the British officers
they had known in America), but the bulk of the letter was an appeal to
support their new governor. He defended himself, however, against the
slurs of Pepys, and the whole of the message reinforced the settlers in
their understanding of their rights. Clarkson told them, untruthfully, that
the directors had not sent him back because he had married. The letter
serves here as a sample of many letters the former governor addressed
over the years to Sierra Leone:[16]

> Dear Crankepone, I have received your Letter . . . and am
> sorry to hear you have not got your Lands, but suppose . . . a
> variety of circumstances . . . has prevented Mr. Dawes from
> paying that attention to the disposal of them as he otherwise
> might have done.
>   I am sorry to have received accounts stating that Mr. Pepys
> has been telling the Nova Scotians, that I had no right to
> promise them what I did, & that he has been making free with

my name in an ungrateful and I may say wicked manner . . .
you may inform the People I brought with me from Nova
Scotia that the promises I made to them were in consequence of
authority given to me by the Sierra Leone Company . . . and
. . . the . . . Company will do everything in their power to
perform them conscientiously. I have no doubt that Mr. Dawes
will use his utmost endeavours to compleat my promises as
soon as possible agreeable to the orders I left with him . . . but
you must all consider his situation and not be riotous, but make
every allowance for the beginning of a new Colony—I assure
you the intentions of the S.L. Company are truly Honourable
. . . but you must give them time . . . the happiness of your-
selves your wives and children and in short almost every Black
Man throughout the World may depend upon your honest
industrious & peaceable conduct. I assure you I will always
support your rights as Men and will recommend you for not
suffering any people to take them from you but you must be
obedient to the laws or else the Colony will be at an end . . . it
becomes you to protect the property of the Company at the
hazard of your lives for they have run a great risk in advancing
large sums of money to enable you to change your situation
from slavery and oppression to freedom and happiness.

Clarkson urged them to support the company by buying from and
selling to the store so that all would prosper together, and they then would
be able "to educate your Children so that many of you may live to see
them possess'd of as much learning and as good abilities as any of the
White people . . . then the black race will begin to flourish and be
considered as respectable people in society prejudice against them will
wear away . . . and God will be glorified by innumerable beings who are
at present unacquainted with his goodness. . . . "
He commended Dawes and Macaulay but advised "the whole Colony
to be upon their guard" with Pepys. If any Nova Scotian had lost his copy
of the printed terms under which they came, he should apply at the
secretary's office for the extra copies Clarkson had left behind. He
ended: "I must now bid you farewell and that you and the whole Colony
may be happy in this world and to all Eternity is the sincere prayer of your
and their sincere & affectionate friend. John Clarkson."
To a largely illiterate people, Clarkson's accurately remembered
words were far more binding than any amount of printed paper, and the

settlers never accepted the company's position that Clarkson had misrepresented its terms. "Altho the promises that you Undertook by Authority and was Disappointed, we know that the fault laid to the S. Leone Company," John Cooper once wrote him. They sometimes addressed Clarkson as a "fellow Sufferer."[17]

Little of Clarkson's reports to the directors[18] found their way into the company's first published report, after the colony was reestablished, which appeared in 1794. Thornton was the author of this and all the subsequent reports, and the most prolific source he worked from was Zachary Macaulay. From the two of them, the historical image of the Sierra Leone settlement has mainly derived.

Though few settlers ever met him, Thornton was arguably the most important influence on their lives.[19] A complex man, he was among the wealthiest of the company directors and, with an investment of £2,900, the largest individual shareholder. Born at Clapham, a straggling village outside London, he had followed his father and grandfather into business, becoming an eminent banker and authority on paper credit. From 1782 until his death in 1815 he was a Member of Parliament for Southwark. His cousin and closest friend was Wilberforce. In 1792 Thornton bought a lovely Queen Anne house, called Battersea Rise, on Clapham Common. He enlarged it substantially, adding a library designed by William Pitt which opened into the garden. Thornton and Wilberforce shared the house until Thornton married in 1796, whereupon Wilberforce moved into a house built by Thornton nearby and also married. In the serene oval library the destinies of the Sierra Leone settlers were largely determined. The younger James Stephen remembered meetings of "earnest and famous men in Henry Thornton's high vaulted library," where "the ills of the world, and especially those of distant colonial societies, were discussed not by the victims but by diagnosticians. However poignantly reformers may feel the pain suffered by others, their position will still be miles apart from that of the actual victims of injustice."[20]

Thornton kept such strict rein on his emotions that he often seemed an icy figure. He was in poor health most of his life and could hardly sleep without opium. He devoted more than two-thirds of his income before marriage and a third afterward to the numerous causes he believed in, giving most generously to those which promoted his Evangelical views. The Sierra Leone colony was one of his first absorptions and his major contribution to the anti-slave-trade campaign. The Evangelicals were less humanitarians than religious reformers, and the slave trade was seen as one great obstacle to their mission abroad. Thornton never doubted that God ordained our stations in life. He would never comprehend upward aspirations. "How beautiful is the order of society . . . when every person adorns the station in which GOD has placed him; when the inferior pays willing honour to the superior; and when the superior is diligently occupied in the duties of his trust," he wrote in his *Family Commentary*, which went into thirty-one editions. In his soul-searching diary, Thornton berated himself for an "overbearing spirit," love of praise, being too "stiff and particular."[21]

The Evangelicals' concern for society contained what today seems an extraordinary streak of callousness, for they were in a practical sense indifferent to the comfort, happiness and progress of their fellow humans on earth. They saw everyone, as they saw themselves, as potential instruments of God. The Clapham Sect seems from afar like a collection of affluent, highly able men, mostly neighbors, contentedly married with large families. They lived in fine modern houses, enjoyed good food and the society of fundamentally like-minded friends. They seem dedicated, safe and smug. How could they imagine hardship? But did hardship in this life matter? Mrs. Marianne Thornton, Henry's "most affectionate and interesting wife," once described a christening service at which a beautifully clothed Clapham baby and its relations contrasted starkly with a thin and ragged child of parents so poor and hungry-looking that Wilberforce likened them to savages. Mrs. Thornton wept as she handed the poor mother a few shillings. "However I recollected that . . . it is only for a few fleeting days that the difference really exists—May they both be heirs of Salvation!" That afternoon about twenty children of the Thornton circle ate strawberries under a tulip tree while the local rector gave their parents an uplifting lecture on duty.[22]

Wilberforce's talents could dazzle, Zachary Macaulay once pointed out, but Thornton "carried away the Palm" for sound judgment "and the extreme considerateness and painful scrutiny" with which he approached everything. In performing self-denying duties—the major test of Evangelicals—Thornton came first again. Macaulay deeply admired the way Thornton always weighed the best course "so as to raise no false hopes, & to produce no future unhappiness."[23]

The colonists could examine for themselves the characters of William Dawes, their new governor, and Macaulay, the first councillor. Dawes now is the dimmer figure, for his later career was comparatively obscure and his family papers were destroyed.[24] But over the years and despite an inauspicious start, he proved a reasonable governor for his time. He was born in 1762, the eldest son of the clerk of works at the Portsmouth navy yard. He became a marine lieutenant and, like Clarkson, served during the American Revolution. In 1787 he volunteered to go with the first convicts to the new penal colony at Botany Bay. An engineer and artillery officer, he had sufficient scientific training to undertake exploration, surveying, mapmaking, anthropology, botany and his favorite hobby, astronomy. Among his associates he was known for learning, kindness and a Methodist faith. He was dismissed in late 1791 after a quarrel with the New South Wales governor. But he had developed a lifelong interest in missionary work. He carried home a letter of introduction from a Methodist clergyman to the Reverend John Newton which brought him into the Sierra Leone Company's orbit.

The first impression of him at Freetown was that he was stiff and somewhat severe. There is no evidence that he had the slightest sense of humor. Mrs. Falconbridge attributed his unbending air to Botany Bay, which she thought an inappropriate training ground for a place such as Freetown, "whose *basis is Liberty and Equality*, and whose Police is dependant [*sic*] . . . on the whimsical disposition of an ignorant populace, which can only be advantageously tempered by placidness and moderation."[25] Among Dawes' first acts was to institute morning and evening public prayers, signaled by the great bell. DuBois, Gray and Afzelius were the only officials who failed to attend, and they were branded "Deists & Atheists." Unscrupulous settlers used the ceremony as an excuse for arriving late at work, but it was "a *religious* Colony at last."[26]

Dawes was in and out of the colony's life for nearly two decades, but he never had the hold on the Sierra Leone Company of Macaulay, who served it in Africa from 1793 to 1799 and in London until it was dissolved. As its servant Macaulay once told the settlers, he was unaffected by their approbation or their censure. "I shall act . . . with a single eye to my employers' view," he said.[27] Macaulay was in effect a creation of the Clapham Sect, and like a true convert, he worked with matchless zeal. He was the perfect civil servant, carrying out policy rather than initiating it, an assiduous keeper of records and collector of information. He became the encyclopedia of the antislavery movement. "Let us look it out in Macaulay," Wilberforce would say when stumped.[28]

It was unfortunate (possibly disastrous) for the blacks of Sierra Leone that Macaulay's first major assignment for the Clapham Sect was to become a councillor there at the age of twenty-four and governor soon afterward. He had acquired the Evangelical interest in "pagan" or "savage" Africans and the mission of "civilizing" them, but he had little interest in or sympathy for the settlers from America who already knew about Christianity but who, in his opinion, got it all wrong. One of thirteen children of a Scottish clergyman, Macaulay was sent to Jamaica at sixteen, in 1784, to find a job. He became bookkeeper and later overseer on a sugar plantation. At first he was "revolted" by the misery of the slaves but had to "get rid of my squeamishness" and succeeded "beyond my expectations." After a year he told a correspondent, "You would hardly know your friend . . . were you to view me in a field of canes, amidst perhaps a hundred of the sable race, cursing and bawling, while the noise of the whip resounding on their shoulders, and the cries of the poor wretches, would make you imagine that some unlucky accident had carried you to the doleful shades." Toward the end, to his later horror, he was happy there.[29]

This intelligent and ambitious young man came to the attention of Thornton and Wilberforce through his brother-in-law Thomas Babington, one of the Clapham Sect. According to Wilberforce, Thornton "sent for him . . . that he might occupy some respectable station in the new colony," and for some time after his return he was "domesticated with Mr. H. Thornton who thought so highly of him as to propose that he should be appointed governor of Sierra Leone, as he soon was. . . ."[30] Macaulay chiefly made his home with the Babingtons at Rothley Temple, where Wilberforce was a frequent guest. Young Macaulay upon arrival was "boorish" and conceited, and Babington took on the job of improving him. Babington thought him "selected by the Lord . . . as his instrument" in Sierra Leone.[31] It is possible that Dawes and Macaulay acted with certainty that Clarkson would not be back because Macaulay was privy to Thornton's plans.

Macaulay had an unprepossessing appearance (he had congenital blindness in one eye) and a reputation for seriousness and lack of imagination which even admirers described as "chilling." Thornton introduced him to Clarkson as:

> solid, well informed, very resolute, clearheaded & sensible— strong in body—used to the West India climate & used to its fevers—well read & well instructed both in Sierra Leone matters & in all manner of colonization subjects—He is also extremely zealous in the cause, a friend to the abolition of the slave trade . . . he is diligent, fond of research & a man . . . of considerable general knowledge—I believe too he has much

more feeling & tenderness than he seems to have. . . . He has I believe also a high respect for religion—thinks reasons & argues upon it—likes to read religious books, admires religious people & goes out well understanding that the point to be labored is to make the Colony a religious Colony—I am even persuaded that he feels he is doing a duty to God in going out. . . .[32]

The unlikely choice of a former penal colony officer and a former plantation overseer to run the free black settlement did not escape the notice of slave-trade quarters. Macaulay arrived on January 15, 1793, on a Bance Island cutter which he and the Reverend Nathaniel Gilbert had boarded after the *Sierra Leone Packet* stopped at Gambia for cattle.[33]

The perfect faith of the directors in Macaulay and their confidence in Dawes made the Anderson-Perkins mission to London in 1793 a lost cause. But it demonstrated the settlers' determination to secure their rights. At the news that Clarkson had been replaced by Dawes, those who were preparing the London petition added "the most earnest solicitation for Mr. Clarkson to be sent out again." Others decided to leave Freetown, and still others tried to drive out the new governor with insults. Frank (Francis) Patrick, called Dawes a "White Rascal," refused to obey orders and actually threatened the governor. An anonymous letter cited the fate of Louis XVI and suggested a like one for Dawes, if the food supply did not improve.[34]

Anderson and Perkins obtained passages on the company's *Amy* in June. Pepys and Afzelius, both on leave, were also aboard. DuBois had been granted leave, but since the *Amy* was overcrowded, he and Anna Maria took passages on a slave ship via the West Indies and did not reach Plymouth until October, nearly two months after the arrival of the spokesmen from Freetown. The black delegates had their first view of England at Portsmouth, where they disembarked on August 16, 1793. The company agent there gave them two guineas to be repaid out of funds raised by their "fellow sufferers." They set out for London, found their way to Thornton and presented their petition.

The best description of their English experience, ostensibly in their own words, appears in Mrs. DuBois' book, where she devotes a chapter to the sins of the Sierra Leone Company. It must be read in the knowledge that she was embittered by her own humiliating treatment over money due her as Falconbridge's widow. Further, DuBois had his own grudge against the company and was an open partisan of the settlers. Yet her valuable report amplifies the official version and coincides in main points with documents Clarkson saved. Among the latter is a copy of the petition sent to him. It had been signed by thirty-one hundreders, tithing-men and preachers, but the names are missing from Clarkson's copy.[35]

Their chief grievances were:

1. After ten months the surveying was still not finished. They could have done the survey themselves in two months.

2. The soil was poor and rocky on many farms laid out so far.

3. They were forced to trade only at the company store; the paper money in which their wages were paid was not accepted elsewhere.

4. The store charged "extortionate" prices, which kept them in debt or unable to save. They were promised in Nova Scotia only a 10 percent markup on goods sold to them, but they were paying 50 to 100 percent. (Macaulay believed DuBois showed them an invoice on which imported goods were listed without the costs of freight, insurance and the like and had contrasted those prices with what they were paying.)[36]

5. Governor Dawes watered the rum—30 gallons of water to a puncheon—and raised the price by a shilling a gallon. (Mrs. DuBois said this was from religious motives.[37])

6. The only jobs were with the company, putting them "at the mercy of the People you send here." Employment was refused convicted offenders, who were also barred from buying at the only store.

7. Dawes exercised favoritism "and seems to wish to rule us just as bad as if we were all Slaves which we cannot bear."

The petitioners appeared to feel that the directors did not understand what was going on. The language was respectful, as from partners in an enterprise.

> The Promises made us by your Agents . . . were . . . far better than we ever had before from White People and No man can help saying but Mr. Clarkson behaved as kind and tender to us as if he was our Father. . . . Health and Life . . . is very uncertain and tho we have not the Education which White Men have yet we have feeling the same as other Human Beings and would wish to do every thing we can for to make our Children free and happy after us but as we feel ourselves much put upon & distressed by your Council here we are afraid . . . we shall be unhappy while we live and our Children may be in bondage

after us. But . . . as we hear you are amongst the best People in England . . . we think we may . . . tell all our Grievances to you in sure hopes that God will incline your hearts to listen to us. . . .

"Some of the White Gentlemen here" had told them Clarkson had no authority for his promises; was this true? Their choice would be that Clarkson return, "for he knows us better than any Gentleman & he would see every thing he Promised us Performed and so clear up his own Character." (The directors, at least Thornton, believed DuBois drafted the petition; both DuBois and his wife read it in Freetown and may have helped polish it up there or in England.[38])

To the delegates, Thornton at first appeared kind and compassionate. A few days later, after receiving letters from Africa, he called their complaints "frivolous and ill grounded." In three weeks, their money exhausted, Anderson and Perkins applied to Thornton and director Samuel Parker. They understood Parker to say he would give them money if they mortgaged or sold the land they were due to get. Thornton directed them to servants' jobs, where "we wrought for near a month, without hearing the most distant hint of an answer to our Petition." Neither man had ranked among the colony's "disorderly dangerous" or just "doubtful" people at the end of Clarkson's tenure,[39] but the London mission radicalized them both.

They wanted to see John Clarkson, then at Wisbech in Cambridgeshire, and repeatedly asked for his address. Clarkson knew they were coming; Thornton in September had written a friendly letter with word of the mission. Perhaps he meant to caution the former governor not to interfere. Thornton said that the delegates "pleaded a number of vague promises of yours," and he hoped that the recent arrival at Freetown of the *Harpy* with a cargo of flour would have silenced the complainers. He told Clarkson the lots were all laid out and "the new Town rising fast." The letter took a week to reach Clarkson, who was away in Norfolk, and he replied at once. He said the directors would be wise to pay attention to the settlers' requests. "Kindness to the *Deputies* and a conduct convincing on the part of the Directors that their intentions are truly just . . . will make a great impression . . . and send them Home satisfied—" Privately, he feared the complaint would be dismissed because it was written by the blacks "in a very simple way."[40]

Anderson and Perkins got in touch with Mr. and Mrs. DuBois after the couple reached England in October, and DuBois carried a letter to

Clarkson from them. Clarkson asked for and received a copy of their petition. He commented: "The justice of your petition strikes me forcibly, and altho you may have misunderstood me in one or two instances, yet upon the whole you appear right—" He proposed that he join them for a conference with the directors. Thornton did not answer his request, so Clarkson sent a letter to the delegates to deliver. It flatly reiterated: "the promises I made them were from the Directors of the Sierra Leone Company, and that they have as great a right to the performances of them as they have to dispose of their own property."[41]

The directors "did not seem well pleased." Anderson and Perkins were told to board the *Amy* and return to Sierra Leone. They would get their answer after they embarked. "We thought it very strange . . . and therefore objected, saying we wished . . . to consider, the answer before we left this country." They were told to put any further statements in writing. The directors' version was that upon hearing the resolution regarding their return, the delegates made a vehement and disrespectful reply.[42] It is probable that DuBois and his wife helped write the subsequent correspondence in which the grievances are put in a much more peremptory way. They expressed their confidence in the king ("God bless him") and asked that in future he appoint their governor or let them have a voice in the selection. They rejected any thought of interfering in the company's management of its property in Africa but declared, "We *will not* be governed by your present Agents in Africa." Speaking of their treatment in London, they said:

> We did not come upon a childish errand, but to represent the grievances and sufferings of a thousand souls. We expected to have had some attention paid to our complaints, but the manner you have treated us, has been just the same as if we were *Slaves*, come to tell our masters, of the cruelties and severe behaviour of an *Overseer*.

This diatribe brought a curt note from Thornton requesting particulars of the unkept promises. Their reply, a rehash of the printed terms distributed in Nova Scotia plus a new complaint about the absence of British justice, was ignored. The directors learned that they were in touch with DuBois, who was dismissed. In Thornton's public account the petition was made to seem spurious from the start, based on "misinformation" owing to hardship caused by the temporary shortage of provisions and encouraged by designing persons. The proprietors were assured that Anderson and Perkins sailed home in early 1794 "perfectly well disposed." But the delegates themselves wrote to Clarkson that they were sent back "like Fools." C. B. Wadstrom, about to publish his *Essay on Colonization*, vainly urged that the Nova Scotians' claims be investigated by a commission half of whose members should be named by the proprietors and half by the settlers.[43]

The mission was not without some side benefits. Perkins was "put . . . to Colledge till he leaves the country," possibly Trevecka College, Wales, run by the Countess of Huntingdon Connexion, and he apparently tried to get a missionary sent to Freetown. He spent a good deal of time with the Reverend Thomas Haweis, the late countess' adviser on missions and a founder of the London Missionary Society. In Freetown the governor and council agreed in principle to give up the retail monopoly and make credit available so that some settlers could set up shop. But the blacks did not leap at the chance, and it was more than a year before the first retailers were licensed: John Cuthbert, Martha Hazeley, Robert Keeling, Mary Perth, James Reid and Sophia Small.[44]

It might be possible to see the settlers' complaints about high prices, watered rum and favoritism as typical of disgruntled refugees,[45] but they were not refugees. The grievances of these voluntary colonists had to do with deeper problems of settlement, land allocation, earning opportunities and, above all, a share in government and administration of justice. These were the issues that would constantly reappear.

Although the settlers tried other direct appeals to London, they must have realized there was no forum for them there, for they concentrated on wresting from the surrogates as much power as possible. Even before Anderson and Perkins returned virtually empty-handed, hostility and suspicion against the rulers had deepened to the point that, when the storeship *York* caught fire in November, 1793, no one would help put out the blaze. There were rumors that the governor's ill-gotten gains or gunpowder were on board. The ships burned for two days, and £4,000 worth of African exports, most of the trade goods, large amounts of rum, beef and pork, plus the colonial accounts painstakingly prepared by Macaulay, went up in smoke at a loss to the company of more than £15,000. Macaulay heard some "rejoicing in the Calamity as a just judgement of Heaven on their Oppressors," and a few tried to loot the hulk. The "more respectable," however, volunteered to guard it. A week later, fires mysteriously destroyed the houses of those who had gloated over the loss.[46]

In the way of participation in government, 1793 brought some success. There is no record of a new election; the men elected in the autumn of 1792 must have held over. Two hundreders were made marshals at £20 a year, John Cuthbert for Freetown and James Reid in Granville Town. They had authority to summon juries, arrest offenders, execute writs, collect fees and fines ordered by the court, supervise the jail and command the tithingmen. Simon Proof was made jailer at £10 a year.[47]

Nothing in the regulations implied a legislature, but the settlers, with the governors' cooperation, began to develop one. Their first proposed law was to prevent hogs, sheep and goats from roaming the town, and it was approved by Governor Dawes. From then on, Dawes and later Macaulay encouraged their initiatives to some extent and used the tithingmen and hundreders as a channel for communication. Other laws that the settlers produced fixed price ceilings on fresh meat and bread, directed one-third of the meat supply be distributed to the sick and poor and set penalties for disorderly conduct, selling liquor without a license and using bad language (because of a glut of lawsuits for slander and use of such epithets as "whore, thief, robber"). A law on adultery was advanced by Macaulay after he obtained the "hearty acquiescence" of the settlers' representatives. Under it, guilty men were fined, and women logged and jailed.

Their most significant act came in 1795, fixing a road tax, the first tax to be collected from the colonists and payable by six days-a-year work. In 1796 another settler-inspired act prohibited strangers from obtaining land without written permission of the governor and council and imposed a residency requirement of a year and a day before such new citizens could vote or serve on juries.[48]

The hundreders and tithingmen chose surveyors of streets and roads, subject to approval of the governor and council. Their first choices were Myles Dixon, Peter Francis, James Jones and James Reid. Peter Francis even got a divorce through them. The Virginia-born carpenter, now in his forties, had come to Sierra Leone from Birchtown without his wife, Chloe, who had run off with someone else. After three years he appealed to the court for a divorce. No existing law covered the case, and Macaulay feared to introduce a divorce statute which might be abused. He advised Francis to "petition the legislature for a Bill of divorce," as British citizens appealed to Parliament. The hundreders and tithingmen examined witnesses and granted the petition.[49]

Macaulay's use of the word "legislature" in 1796 seemed to sanction an institution which the elected constables or peace officers had improvised. Macaulay even drew up rules for their deliberations. Under these, they met quarterly, and monthly meetings were held by hundreders with their tithingmen. A majority vote was binding, and a clerk was paid at the rate of a shilling a year from each family. Macaulay at one point informed the representatives that they "alone" had the power to impose taxes and disburse public funds, subject to his consent, for such work as mounting cannon on Falconbridge Point. He offered them a £50 loan to start a public treasury. This and similar suggestions raised numerous questions. Some skeptical Nova Scotians saw a trick to shift financial burdens onto them for the public works. They were given responsibility for organizing the militia and providing their own arms with the ammunition paid for out of the treasury.[50] While Macaulay was governor, he drafted a written constitution, on which Thornton and Sharp advised. It borrowed features from both the United States and Britain. It called for a bicameral legislature with six senators and a house of commons with thirty members. One-third of the seats would be filled each December. Bills passed here would be ratified by the governor and council. Each branch had a right to amend or "negative" bills along the way. Macaulay believed few vetoes would be needed because any bill the poorly educated settlers passed would be defective and require alterations. Among features of the proposed constitution were equal protection under law and freedom of conscience, but only Christians could vote. Other qualifications for voting were payment of twenty cents a year in direct tax. Ownership of an acre of land or town lot seemed also to be a rule. There was no sex qualification, and until 1797 women voted as heads of households in the elections for hundreders and tithingmen. All children, not just the eldest son, could inherit, widows automatically received a third of personal property and a life interest in real estate, limits were put on imprisonment for debt, and search and arrest warrants had to specify grounds based on at least one credible witness. Slave dealing was punishable by loss of civil rights forever, whipping, confiscation of goods and hard labor.[51]

In the 1796 election the number of hundreders was increased to six and that of tithingmen reduced to thirty, as if for the new legislature, but the election results so irked Macaulay that he shelved the constitution. The winners had campaigned against white participation. The burning issue was Macaulay's introduction of a quitrent, the running controversy that will be examined later. Men he regarded as extremists scored heavily "in general the most ignorant hard headed & perverse of our colonists." When fifteen of them, before being sworn in, approached him with questions and doubts about the proposed constitution, he gave them short shrift, and ridiculed their language in recording the incident:

Their spokesmen came forward . . . "Sorry to trouble your honour, but the peoples minds are all *flustrated*. They hears so much talk about the new *Consecution* they does not know what to think; they came to us but we cant make neither head nor tail of it." . . . I told them . . . to give the people the advice wh. I now gave them viz. to go home & mind their business.

On inauguration day, January 3, 1797, they insisted that the oath be read by a black instead of by John Gray:

but to their utter perplexity there was not one found among the new set who could read it distinctly. Gray did not fail to point out to them the inconvenience [of] having no Whites among them. They seemed convinced of it. They are however a very wayward people. . . . [W]ere I or Gray to point out a remedy, a plot wd. be immediately suspected.[52]

With Freetown in an exceptionally quiet period, Macaulay decided to ignore the new body completely. Nothing he proposed would be approved by "such a set of wrong heads," and "My silence & disregard of them will soon reduce them to insignificance. . . ." He regretted postponing the constitution, but was sure the people's representatives did not have the capacity to handle it anyhow.[53] Before the 1797 election, women lost the vote, reducing the number of tithingmen to twenty-five. This retrogression resulted from Thornton's second thoughts on the proposed constitution. The reduction was protested, but not on sexist grounds.[54]

The hundreders and tithingmen kept functioning, perhaps unaware that Macaulay had sent them to Coventry, and early in 1798 they revived the idea of a parliamentary government. Thomas Cooper and Isaac Streeter handed the governor and council a resolution which separated them into two houses with a joint committee to deal with the executive. The committee was composed of James Carr (white), Luke Jordan, Stephen Peters, James Reid, Streeter and Ishmael York. Macaulay subsequently vetoed a committee proposal that members of this early Sierra Leone "legislature" be exempt from the road tax (which caused Isaac Anderson and Stephen Peters to wonder aloud, and not for the first time, why his one voice counted for more than thirty of theirs). The settlers cited precedents for this which they claimed to know from the colonial Carolinas, Virginia, New York and Nova Scotia. Macaulay briskly refuted them from his British constitutional texts.[55]

The administration of justice gave the blacks another arena. This was not, as it claimed to be, "British justice," for the company had no royal warrant, but British precedent and law were followed to the extent of the knowledge and ability of the amateur jurists. Trial by jury was authorized, with at least half the jurors of the same race as the defendant. In practice the juries were nearly all-black. Company officials, all white, sat as justices of the peace and judges. The Nova Scotians took their jury duty seriously and needed an hour to settle a verdict in even a small case. Only one case of women serving is known. In a sensational trial for child murder in 1807, a jury of women was sworn to determine whether the defendant had borne a child.[56]

The quarterly court sessions attracted such crowds that the governors often used the occasion for announcements or harangues. Both Nova Scotians and Old Settlers, unable to attain complete self-rule, expressed themselves freely through the courts and became such a litigious lot that the council early on instituted a fifteen-shilling fine on losers, hoping to discourage frivolous suits. In 1795 the hundreders and tithingmen proposed, and the governor and council consented to, a measure to relieve the quarter sessions by allowing petty offenders to be put under citizen arrest and tried before any justice and four tithingmen sitting as a court. They could penalize by fines, the stocks or whipping. There was no appeal from these sentences.[57]

The irregularity of the courts might have been overlooked if it were not for the factor of race. At few, if any, other places in the world were blacks sitting in judgment or carrying out sentences on whites. There had been the public flogging of three mutinous white seamen in Clarkson's time and a year later three English sailors from a company-chartered ship had been convicted for wantonly killing a settler's duck. Mrs. DuBois, for all her sympathy for the settlers, was convinced the whole affair was illegal and she was outraged that blacks were meting out punishment to whites. The seamen, she wrote, were tried:

> not by their Peers, but by *Judge* McAuley, and a *Jury of twelve blacks*, who, without any evidence or defence from the prisoners, found them guilty. . . . [T]he *self-created Judge* then sentenced one of them to receive thirty-nine lashes by the common whipper, fined the other two in a sum of money each, and ordered them to be confined in irons, on board the York,

till their fines were paid. . . . [P]oor Jack was dreadfully mortified at being whipped by a black man. . . .

The ship's master appealed to Captain Newcomb of the frigate *Orpheus*. The latter brusquely demanded of Dawes and Macaulay "by what authority they tried White Men, the subjects of Great Britain, by a *Jury of Blacks*; it was so novel a circumstance, that it struck him with astonishment." Macaulay cited the incorporation act, but the captain, after studying it, declared "your Court is a mere usurpation, and a mockery of all law and justice." He ordered the prisoners released, and they were.[58]

The "*sham* Court" did well enough for the settlers' little quarrels, Mrs. DuBois believed, and they fully accepted its authority.[59] Indeed, the settlers were remarkably law-abiding considering how many activities—swearing, for instance—were illegal. One of the most serious early cases was that of James Lestor, tried for robbing the store of more than £30 in copper money. He pleaded guilty, and Macaulay and Dr. Winterbottom, the judges, pronounced a sentence of 100 lashes on four separate weeks, a month's jail and twelve months' hard labor on the storeship. Lestor had a record of thieving and was noted for "insolence, turbulence and opposition to government."[60] Marital discord probably furnished the most business for the courts. Once Macaulay was roused at dinner on Thornton Hill by "cries of murder." Picking up his telescope, he spotted a man beating his wife. He sent the marshal to bring them in. He told the still-defiant pair he did not object to wife beating if it wasn't noisy. Adultery was frequently charged. In one case a wife sued her husband and his mistress. Both were found guilty. The man was fined £4 and ordered to pay his wife separate maintenance of three shillings a week. The mistress was penalized by twenty-five lashes. The wife was granted a divorce. (Sharp had insisted that the local courts be able to judge divorce and adultery cases; he regarded the requirement of an act of parliament for divorce as a corrupt practice.[61])

However fragmentary, the historical record does provide a picture of a steadily evolving community at Freetown. It requires no stretch of the imagination to see it as a stirring and educational period for the loyal blacks. The conflicts were just as important in their development as the more frequent calms. Most of the inhabitants did not petition the government or go to court. Virtually all the time laws were obeyed, warrants served, court sentences carried out, militia duty was performed and road tax paid. They could look back to America and see their advance in civil rights. Blacks did not get the vote in Nova Scotia until 1837 and did not serve on juries until 1839, rights which came with emancipation a generation later and after desperate struggle in the United States. The African-American settlers were proving an enterprising and hardy set of colonists.[62]

NOTES

1. Petition of grievances, October 30, 1793, Clarkson Papers, BL Add. MSS. 41,263.

2. Falconbridge, *Narrative of Two Voyages to the River Sierra Leone*, pp. 188, 190. She heard it would cost £20,000 to build the fort. Gray to Clarkson, February 15, 1793, Clarkson Papers, BL Add. MSS. 41,263; Council minute, January 7, 1793, CO 270/2; DuBois Journal, January 3 and 13, 1793, Add. MSS. 41,263; Clarkson Journal (SLS), pp. 85-87; Council minutes, February 5 and 6, May 13, 1793, CO 270/2.

3. DuBois Journal, January 13 and 16, 1793. Grant was forty-one, from Virginia and had been a carpenter at Birchtown: Blacks at Birch Town who gave in their names for Sierra Leone, November, 1791, CO 217/63; DuBois Journal, January 25, 1793; Falconbridge, pp. 203-4. On December 27, 1792, Clarkson, after consulting Chaplain Horne, signed a marriage license for Mrs. Falconbridge and DuBois. He was surprised but sympathetic, for Falconbridge's treatment of Anna Maria had been "notorious." He asked the couple to wait a month, but they married eleven days later. Clarkson Journal (Maynard), December 27, 1792.

4. DuBois Journal, February 6 and 7, 1793; Falconbridge, pp. 205-6. By some accounts, acting governor Dawes was also present. J. G. [John Gray] to Dunkin, February 11, 1793, Clarkson Papers, BL Add. MSS. 41,263; Gray to Clarkson, February 15, 1793.

5. Falconbridge, pp. 206, 207, 211, 216.

6. J. G. to Dunkin, February 11, 1793; Gray to Clarkson, February 15, 1793.

7. DuBois to Clarkson, May 1, 1793, Clarkson Papers, BL Add. MSS. 41,263.

8. Clarkson-Thornton correspondence in Clarkson Papers, BL Add. MSS. 41,262A. Whenever dispatches arrived from Sierra Leone, notices were sent the press. Under the heading "Sierra Leone House," they put the best light on whatever news there was, *e.g.*, the *Times* July 11, December 4, 1792.

9. Account of Clarkson's dismissal mainly from Clarkson to Hartshorne, September, n.d., 1793; Clarkson to DuBois, July 1, 1793; Clarkson to Watt, July 30, 1793, and Clarkson to Gray, July 30, 1793, all Clarkson Papers, BL Add. MSS. 41,263. My search has not produced a "company side" to the incident.

10. Falconbridge, p. 186; Adam Afzelius noticed that loud professions of faith were a sure means of advancement: *Adam Afzelius: Sierra Leone Journal,* May 8, 1796.

11. Clarkson to Hartshorne, September n.d., 1793; Wilberforce to Clarkson, July 12, 1792, Clarkson Papers, BL Add. MSS. 41,262A.

12. Clarkson to Gray, July 30, 1793; letters from Freetown described by Clarkson to Hartshorne, September n.d., 1793.

13. Macaulay to Mills, April n.d., 1796, Huntington Library. The Macaulay Papers held by the Huntington Library are the most important single source of information for the 1793-99 period. In addition to a large correspondence and voluminous official dispatches, Macaulay wrote a running journal directed to Thornton. After his engagement to Selina Mills, he kept another simultaneously to send to her. Extracts from his journals and correspondence appear in his granddaughter's biography: Viscountess Knutsford (Margaret Jean Trevelyan Holland), *Life and Letters of Zachary Macaulay.*

14. Clarkson to DuBois, July 1, 1793.

15. J. Clarkson to T. Clarkson, May 5, 1793, Clarkson Papers, Add. MSS. 41,263.

16. Clarkson to Crankepone, July 27, 1793, Clarkson Papers, BL Add. MSS. 41,263.

17. Cooper to Clarkson, January 14, 1796, Clarkson Papers, BL Add. MSS. 41,263.

18. Clarkson Journal (Maynard) appendices.

19. For Thornton, Meacham, *Henry Thornton of Clapham, 1760-1815* and *Dictionary of National Biography;* also Colquhoun, *William Wilberforce: His Friends and His Times,* p. 272; Stephen, *Essays in Ecclesiastical Biography,* vol. 2, "The Clapham Sect," pp. 292, 295, 296; Clapham Antiquarian Society, *Clapham and the Clapham Sect,* p. 109; Forster, *Marianne Thornton, 1797-1887, a Domestic Biography,* p. 23; Ford K. Brown, *Fathers of the Victorians,* esp. pp. 387-80, 385. Wadstrom, *An Essay on Colonization,* subscribers' list, part 2, p. 352.

20. Quoted in Knaplund, *James Stephen and the British Colonial System, 1813-1847,* p. 14.

21. Meacham, p. 141. The *Commentary* was published posthumously. Thornton Diary, January 16 and 28, April 14, May 13, 1795.

22. Henry Thornton Diary, July 1, 1810; Thornton to More, June 5, 1801, both in Thornton Papers, Wigan Public Libraries.

23. Macaulay Journal (to Selina Mills), June 10, 1798.

24. B. Dawes to Grenville, July 18, 1789, CO 201/4; for Dawes, A. Currer-Jones, *William Dawes, R.M., 1762 to 1836,* by his great-granddaughter. He died in Antigua, where he was Church Missionary Society agent and founded a school for blacks.

25. Falconbridge, pp. 178-79.
26. J. G. to Durkin, February 11, 1793.
27. Council minute, March 7, 1795, CO 270/3.
28. Trevelyan, *The Life and Letters of Lord Macaulay*, p. 47; Charles Booth Zachary Macaulay, p. 105, where Booth sees him as a "Permanent Under Secretary for the Anti-Slavery Department."
29. Knutsford, pp. 7-8. Macaulay's stay in the West Indies is variously given from four to ten years. He testified that he was six years "in the Planting Business." Parliamentary Papers, 1803-4, V, p. 56.
30. Wilberforce to (unnamed), November 28, 1882, in R. I. and S. Wilberforce eds., *The Correspondence of William Wilberforce*, vol. 2, p. 509.
31. Thornton to Clarkson, July 12, 1792, Clarkson Papers, BL Add. MSS 41,262A; Babington to Macaulay, April 9, 1793, Huntington Library, Meacham, p. 47; R. Coupland, *The British Anti-Slavery Movement*, pp 77-78; R. Coupland, *Wilberforce, a Narrative*, p. 278.
32. Knutsford, pp. 1-2; Colquhoun, pp. 235-36; Coupland, *British Anti Slavery*, p. 78; Thornton to Clarkson, November 20, 1792, Clarkson Papers BL Add. MSS. 41,262A.
33. E. C. Martin, *The British West African Settlements*, p. 119; DuBois Journal January 15, 1793.
34. Falconbridge, p. 225; Macaulay Journal, November 16, 1793.
35. Falconbridge, pp. 228, 233, 255, 254; Petition of Grievances, October 30 1793; extracts of petition, Falconbridge, pp. 211-25.
36. Council minutes, October 29, 1793, April 1, 1794, CO 270/2. Company regulations set a maxiumum markup of 10 percent over the invoice price for th first few cargoes. This was raised to 25 percent in October, 1793, because th French war had increased costs of shipping, insurance and so on. Th November 3, 1791, printed terms set a profit margin of about 10 percent.
37. Falconbridge, p. 213 n.
38. Macaulay to Thornton, June 24, 1793, Huntington Library, implicate DuBois and says some settlers wanted portions deleted. Also, the settlers ha failed to follow regulations by not handing the petition in to the council.
39. Falconbridge, p. 255; Character of the Settlers by DuBois, confirmed b Clarkson, n.d., Sierra Leone Collection, University of Illinois, Chicago Circle.
40. Thornton to Clarkson, September 16, 1793; Clarkson to Thornton, Sep tember 24, 1793; Clarkson to Hartshorne, September n.d., 1793, all Clarkson Papers, BL Add. MSS. 41,263.
41. Perkins and Anderson to Clarkson, October 26, 1793; Clarkson to Perkin and Anderson, November 3, 1793, and same to same, November 11, 1793, al Clarkson Papers, BL Add. MSS. 41,263; Falconbridge, p. 258.
42. *Ibid.*, p. 259-60; Sierra Leone Company 1794 Report, pp. 31-32.
43. Falconbridge, pp. 260-70; Sierra Leone Company 1794 Report, p. 32 n., and for "official" version of episode, pp. 23-32; Anderson and Perkins to Clark

son, November 9, 1793, Clarkson Papers, BL Add. MSS. 41,263; Wadstrom, part 2, pp. 265-66.

44. Perkins and Anderson to Clarkson, October 30, 1793, Clarkson Papers, BL Add. MSS. 41,263; Wood, *Thomas Haweis, 1734-1820*, p. 190; Hair, "Sierra Leone and Bulama," p. 28. Hair suggests Perkins introduced DuBois, then interested in joining the Bulama colony (for news of its failure had not yet come), to Haweis. DuBois may have been intending to encourage dissident Nova Scotians to move to Bulama. Haweis learned that the company regarded DuBois as "too active respecting the blacks." DuBois also was suing them for compensation. Chaplain Horne wrote Haweis that Perkins was "of an unhappy temper, seditious in the Colony, and not loving to his people." Council minutes, October 29, 1793, CO 270/2; December 13, 1794, CO 270/3; Macaulay Journal, November 23, 1793.

45. West, *Back to Africa*, p. 47.

46. Sierra Leone Company 1794 Report, p. 28; Macaulay Journal, November 30, December 6, 1793.

47. Council minutes, April 1, May 27, 1793, CO 270/2.

48. *Ibid.*, June 4, August 3, 1793 and May 1, 1794; Council minutes, June 9, 1795, August 13, 1794; October 10, 1795, CO 270/3; July 8, 1796, CO 270/4.

49. Council minute, March 13, 1794, CO 270/4; Macaulay Journal, November 19, 1796; Council minute, November 19, 1796, CO 270/4; Blacks who gave in their names for Sierra Leone, November, 1791.

50. Council minutes, March 7, April 11, 1795, CO 270/3; Macaulay Journal, May 10, November 19, 1796.

51. Macaulay Journal (Mills), November 30, 1796, in which he outlined thirty-five provisions of the proposed constitution, of which no final copy seems to survive; Macaulay Journal, June 7, 1797; Sharp to Macaulay, February 14, 1797, New-York Historical Society.

52. Macaulay Journal, December 15 and 19, 1796; January 3, 1797.

53. *Ibid.*, December 21, 1796.

54. Macaulay to Directors, "Remarks on Sierra Leone," June 7, 1797, Huntington Library; Macaulay Journal, December 16, 1797.

55. Council minutes, January 29, February 3, 1798, CO 270/4; Macaulay Journal, March 6, 1798.

56. Knutsford, p. 45; Ann Edmonds Morgan case, Council minute, April 3, 1809, CO 270/11, and elsewhere, as in T. P. Thompson Papers, University of Hull. The women jurors were named in the *African Herald*, May 27, 1809, in CO 267/25.

57. Council minutes, March 1, 1793, CO 270/2; October 12, 1795, CO 270/3; Macaulay Journal, May 24, 1796.

58. Falconbridge, pp. 222-23.

59. *Ibid.*, p. 224.

60. Macaulay Journal, July 4, 6, 7, August 9, 1793.

61. *Ibid.*, July 6, 1793, and July 14, 1796; Sharp to Thornton, November 29, 1794, Sharp Papers, Hardwicke Court.

62. See for example, Macaulay to Directors, "Remarks on Sierra Leone;" Greaves, *The Negro in Canada*, p. 28; Hoare, *Memoirs of Granville Sharp*, vol. 2, pp. 279-81; Martin, pp. 143-44.

Chapter 16

BREAKING POINTS

> We wance did call it Free town but . . . we have a Reason
> to call it a town of Slavery.
> —MOSES WILKINSON TO JOHN CLARKSON[1]

The ills to which all young colonies are heir were exacerbated at Sierra
Leone, first, by the all-pervasive slave trade, secondly, by the Franco-
British war, which began in 1793, and, thirdly, by a peculiar determination of the Sierra Leone Company directors to impose a quitrent of
extraordinary severity.

Freetown was a tiny island in the sea of slaving operations, and
successive governors' efforts to *get along* with the powerful trade,
without *giving in* on abolitionist principles led to ambiguous behavior
which aroused indignation in many settlers and played its part in widening the gulf between them and their government. "Our present governor
allows the Slave Traders to come here & abuse us," complained Isaac
Anderson and Luke Jordan.[2] And several times settlers released their
resentment on the visitors or abetted the escape or concealment of
runaway slaves.

Zachary Macaulay ruminated, "We live in Africa, where, if we mean
to live & to do good, we must suppress our emotions." This accorded
with the 1791 regulations, in which the directors had advised:

> We wish you . . . not to surrender up any persons who are
> claimed merely as being slaves and . . . not to permit any one
> to continue to be a slave on our district; but your own prudence
> must dictate . . . the time and the mode of asserting these
> principles in perfect consistency with the safety of the
> Colony.[3]

Thornton told Clarkson, "Whether you will have strength to maintain the principle of universal Freedom or whether you must awhile connive & temporize, I think depends on circumstances.'' Clarkson, Dawes and Macaulay were able to divorce the white traders—whom they saw on the whole as congenial men—from their work, which they abhorred. (They could deal with the slave-trading African chiefs because they hoped in time to win them to an equally lucrative commerce in African exports.) Slave ship crews, however, were blamed for most of the immorality and misconduct in the colony. Relations were especially close with Bance Island. English newspapers were exchanged, social calls paid, ships of one carried passengers and dispatches of the other, company ships were repaired at Bance, company doctors treated the Bance sick, and in the face of French privateering threats, intelligence was shared and joint defense planned. The white expatriates at both outposts made life more tolerable for each other in numerous ways, and the black artisans often found paid work at Bance.

''These little civilities and attentions are necessary in a country where you stand in need of mutual assistance,'' Clarkson explained. And when he left the colony, he wrote warmly, ''I have uniformly experienced the kindest and most flattering attention from the Inhabitants of Bance Island . . . and I may safely say the same of the gentlemen at every Factory I have visited.''[4]

On March 1 each year, when the company's white staff dined together to celebrate the colony's founding, slave ship captains were sometimes invited without any apparent sense of incongruity. Macaulay thought he was a good influence on the Bance factor Tilley, who avoided swearing and obscenities when Macaulay visited him and attended church when he stayed at Freetown. Tilley was much offended one time when Governor Dawes sailed past Bance without calling.[5] The good relations presumably assisted the governors in one of their manifold duties which was to collect information on the slave trade to fuel the abolition campaign.

Clarkson's dislike of the settlers' trading proclivities was partly a fear that they might be attracted into the slave trade (as a few were) but even more that they were themselves salable should they wander too far or give offense and be seized. Only one black colonist was convicted of selling a slave in the early period, Old Settler John Cambridge. After Granville Town was razed by King Jimmy in 1789, Cambridge lived some years with King Naimbana at Robana, where he engaged successfully in the ''country trade.'' Soon after the Nova Scotians' arrival he petitioned to rejoin the colony, but a few months later he was charged with selling a man to a Dutch sloop. A jury found him guilty of violating the act of incorporation. Colony regulations prohibited capital punishment, and if this offense carried that penalty (the legal position is extremely obscure in the record), that is the reason why Cambridge was sent to England for sentence. It was a first offense, and Clarkson was inclined to leniency except that the case had created a sensation and the people "were clamorous for punishment as an example to others." Cambridge probably sailed on the *Duke of Savoy* on August 24, 1792, but no record seems to exist of what happened to him in Britain. A few days later a Dutch sloop with eighty slaves on board, probably the same ship that bought the man from Cambridge, was captured by Africans, run aground and pillaged. All but one of the crew were killed or wounded. Later the colony heard that the French factor at Gambia was arming 300 men to retaliate. Such was the climate of violence along the Sierra Leone River.[6]

Freetown was a magnet for escaped slaves and runaway seamen. Thornton had advised Clarkson that an agreement should be made with African neighbors to give up criminals, slave or free, "but if the slave is not a criminal, he has such a clear natural right to protection & freedom that I own I wish much we may find ourselves able to give him full protection."[7] Clarkson, in one recorded case—Abraham Smith's relative—had agreed to the redemption (critics might call it purchase) of a runaway slave.

Different governors interpreted the rules differently, and the blacks, always described as "ignorant" (meaning uneducated), might be excused for not being able to follow the twists and turns in their reasonings. On July 31, 1793, a group of settlers entreated Governor Dawes to protect five slave seamen who had escaped from a schooner which had delivered rum from one Horrocks, an English trader at the Isles de Los.[8] Macaulay was then running the company's trade and embarrassed by their action. He told the seamen to go back to "their duty." The ship's captain complained that the settlers were hiding the men onshore. The hundreders were summoned to explain. They "pleaded their having acted in strict conformity with a proclamation issued by Mr. Clarkson . . . purporting that the moment a man set his foot on the Coy.'s District, he became from that moment free." Clarkson was acting in line with African customary law and company policy. Dawes and Macaulay pulled out their copies of Blackstone and various unspecified parliamentary acts to persuade the hundreders that "British subjects had a Right to buy & to hold slaves" and that the latter were regarded "in the sacred & inviolate light of property."

When he justified this interpretation to the directors, Macaulay also cited the Sierra Leone Company Act which forbade anyone to be ill-treated or enslaved at Freetown, adding that in the Horrocks case "the Master who is deprived of his property, is the man who is ill treated." Macaulay claimed that the colony had no power to emancipate them: "Slavery already sanctioned by a superior power, cannot be reversed by us, and I should imagine that our power only extended to prevent actual violence, or the actual traffic in Slaves . . . or one who holds Slaves from being resident." In sum: "We had no more power to detain a Slave, than we had to detain a bale of goods."

The legalistic arguments failed to convince his Freetown audience. The hundreders agreed in principle that the captain should not be prevented from trying to recover his crew. He did try, but "The Settlers had furnished them with arms, and they expressed their determination to die before they would return." Dawes and Macaulay apologized to Horrocks by letter. In court a few days later, before the usual crowd, Macaulay "expatiated on . . . the desertion of Horrocks' slaves, and shewed them the illegality & impolicy of encouraging such desertions." Chaplain Horne preached on the duty of servants under the yoke, alluding to the "late transactions with respect to Slaves" as inconsistent with policy, justice and Christianity. Horrocks sent his partner, Jackson, to Freetown to get the men back. The runaways denied that they had been inveigled onshore; they had deserted because they understood Horrocks was leaving his failing factory and intended to trick them onto an American slave ship. Jackson proposed that the company pay 500 guineas' compensation, but Dawes and Macaulay would not accept liability. They felt sure that if Horrocks appealed to London, the only charge they would face would be failure to use force to return the five men. The settlers, and the runaways, "won," and Macaulay gloomily predicted that the colony would lose the goodwill of the coast. But the blacks knew what country law allowed. Within a month Horrocks was dead, and nearly all his slaves had deserted because the proprietors had started selling them off.[9]

This event was read about with some dismay in London when Macaulay's journal arrived. Opposite his assertion that the company would abandon the colony if the settlers persisted in harboring escaped slaves, someone wrote a firm "no."[10] Eventually Macaulay was convinced, not by the settlers but by an "intelligent native" (Robin Rufoy), that African law made it possible to carry out the company's intentions safely. Under it, an escaped slave became the property of the headmen in whose town he took sanctuary and could be retrieved only if the headmen were willing to give him up for a price. Defensively, Macaulay said that the law had been "most industriously concealed from us hitherto. . . . Bance Island people and other slave factors had employed all their arts to make us believe that no such law exists." When a man threatened with slavery later escaped from Signor Domingo's town, Macaulay gave him a job on the trading vessel *Naimbana* to pay off a small redemption advanced by the company.[11]

The Horrocks case was not made part of the official council record, but charges brought later that year by Richard Corankapone, a tithingman, against one of the company's ship captains, were. Corankapone accused Captain William Davis of buying two boys and keeping them in Freetown. A council inquiry found Davis guilty, and he was discharged. The boys, from what is now Liberia, were taken under Governor Dawes' wing, declared free and named Samuel Garvin and Isaac Watts.[12]

Like the 1787 settlers, the Nova Scotians were pugnacious where slave traders were concerned. They would exchange provisions for rum with them and work as carpenters at Bance but saw no reason to be polite. In 1794 a Captain Grierson of the slave ship *Thomas* was "insulted" by a settler "mob," and acting governor Macaulay (Dawes was on home leave) decided to punish the leaders of the fray. Inexorably, this brought on one of the confrontations which characterized Macaulay's style of rule. It was the worst so far.

According to the official version,[13] Robert Keeling, chief porter on the wharf, on June 13 incited a crowd to threaten Grierson while Scipio Channel "attempted to knock out said Capt. Griersons brains with a hammer." No motive was hinted here, but in a letter to John Clarkson, Luke Jordan and Isaac Anderson said that the captain "began to threaten some of the people working at the wharf—saying in what manner he would use them if he had them in the West Indies. And some of the people told him if he came here to abuse them they would not allow it."[14] Grierson complained to the council, which on June 16 agreed he had been injured. Keeling and Channel, far from denying their actions, defended them. Both were fired for disorderly conduct since it was deemed essential that "strangers should be protected from violence."

The next day Joseph Leonard, the teacher, and Myles Dixon presented a "Warm remonstrance" from the the hundreders and tithingmen, who threatened to resign. Macaulay castigated their protest as "highly reprehensible. . . . [N]o one, within the Colony, has a right to censure the Governor and Council or to interfere with them" in their right to hire and fire. Nor could elected representatives resign.

By June 20 the settlement was in uproar. A delegation—Channel, Samuel Goodwin, Simon Johnson, Lewis Kirby, Matthew Sinclair and Joseph Tybee—called on Macaulay, demanded an explanation and, not satisfied, verbally abused him "and even threatened my life." Corankapone, now the marshal, was beaten up by Kirby and Johnson and procured a warrant for their arrest. When he tried to serve it, a "mob" obstructed him. The hundreders and tithingmen refused to help. The ringleaders, reinforced by a few other settlers, "approached to the Gate of the Governor's yard bidding defiance to all law and authority and threatening instant destruction to whoever should oppose them."

Jordan and Anderson believed Macaulay reacted to the day's events badly since the initial violence was an "accident," but Macaulay "would not pay any attention to us." Although they were elected peace officers, he "does not respect us as such." Because the directors in 1793 had given Perkins and Anderson so little satisfaction, "the gentleman here thinks proper to use [us] in a very improper manner." They added, "We are sorry to think that we left America to come here and be used in that manner."[15]

Company employees were summoned to the governor's house and armed, and David George was sent to collect the "well affected" settlers to help repel an attack from the insurgents. Masters of all the ships in the harbor were notified to be ready to come ashore with their crews on a signal. During the night three leading troublemakers were arrested by a detachment under Richard Pepys, but the commotion did not subside. Government supporters were attacked, and the release of the prisoners was demanded. The company's office was plundered, and among other things Macaulay's current journal destroyed.[16]

Sunday, June 22, dawned calmly, and Macaulay and James Watt, a councillor pro tem, drew up a long address to the inhabitants. Copies were sent to the church, the meetinghouses and the hundreders. It appealed to the people as "Rational creatures . . . Fathers and Mothers but above all as . . . Christians" to uphold the law. The majority, by refusing to act against the rioters, had allowed the disorder to go on. They would be to blame if blood were shed or the government overthrown. Economic sanctions were brought to bear. The public works were halted, and the store was closed. No "rioter" would be employed "on any account or pretence whatever.'' All dissatisfied persons would be transported to Halifax free of charge.

The spirit of protest died, and the hundreders and tithingmen agreed to serve warrants for those dissidents still at large. Rewards of £20 each were offered for Goodwin, Kirby and Tybee. Macaulay bought the brig *Venus* (which he wanted anyhow for trade) from a slave trader in the Rio Nunez to make the voyage to Halifax, but no one wanted to return to America.[17]

Wednesday, June 25, 1794, was proclaimed a day of prayer, and Macaulay appealed for unity:

> As Friends to your dearest interests as Men who in remaining in an unhealthy climate, and among a murmuring People have it at heart to promote your welfare, and that of these your little ones, we would now exhort you to peace with God and with each other . . . to give again to each other and to give to us, the hand and the heart of Christian fellowship & to join together in building up God's Temple in this place . . . that when your head and ours are laid low in the dust, Freetown may exhibit a race of Men devoted to God, and acting in all things to his praise and glory.

The colonial government's seeming overreaction might be blamed on uneasiness about insurrection generated among ruling classes everywhere by the French Revolution and memories of the earlier slave uprising of Santo Domingo. Macaulay treated the ringleaders as rebels meriting more severe penalties than he could dispense. Scipio Channel turned state's witness. On July 1 he and Kirby and Ralph Henry were sent on the *Ocean* to London for trial. Goodwin, Johnson, Tybee, James Jackson and John Manuel were put on the *Amy* on August 4. The witnesses sent along included Myles Dixon, John Kizell, the elder and younger James Robinsons, Matthew Sinclair, Abraham Smith and Timothy Withers. Company regulations made no provision to send witnesses for the defense.[18]

At the August court session one man was fined and three women were ordered flogged for their parts in the trouble. Stephen Peters, who had heard Channel plot to kill Macaulay but had not warned the acting governor, was fired. Peters and Moses Wilkinson later tried to blame the uprising on provocative activities of two new teacher-missionaries

(Jones and Garvin), which gave Macaulay a chance to denounce the Methodists for immorality, encouraging dissent and resisting the law. They were "a rotten society."[19]

How the so-called rioters were dealt with in England has so far proved impossible to trace. Both ships were at Plymouth by September 23, 1794, and the directors adopted resolutions concerning the men two days later. These resolutions reached Sierra Leone on December 7, after the colony had been captured and almost destroyed by the French. Macaulay warned that if any of the men were acquitted and sent back, the whites there would feel "very unsafe" and probably leave.[20] Sentences of banishment may have been imposed. When Granville Sharp appealed to Henry Thornton to arrange subsistence allowances for their families in Freetown, he urged that they be allowed to go home, but he realized the directors were "extremely intimidated with the apprehension of a further insurrection." The witnesses who had come to convict them, he pointed out, were also appealing for their return to Freetown now. The founder of the Province of Freedom said:

> It is magnanimous to forgive injuries; and I should never fear any bad consequences from the performance of this first of Christian duties, under reasonable caution to prevent mischief, but I should have real apprehension from persisting in a refusal to pardon in the present case. Governor Dawes's kind interference . . . to obtain their pardon from the Company on due promise of submission, and leave to return as soon as their release can be obtained, will remove all difficulties and dangers.[21]

The advice was unheeded. John Clarkson also questioned whatever it was the directors did. In December, 1796, he wrote to Thornton about a request to him to help Lewis Kirby, whom, with James Jackson, "I consider to have been treated in a very unjust way." Clarkson enclosed a letter which reported, "Poor Kirby seems now to be driven to despair he is almost hungerd to death. . . . he has been given up by the benevolent Society, and the woman where he lodges must be paid, and to me he appears to be in the very Jaws of destruction." Jackson was reported to have gone to sea.[22]

The following spring Macaulay was petitioned by several tithingmen to let Kirby and Jackson return. He agreed if six householders would put up bond for them. Walking to the Thompson's Bay farm one day, he met

Tybee, an ax in his hand. Macaulay, surprised, put his finger on the trigger of his spring bayonet, but Tybee humbly begged to be readmitted, and Macaulay told him to see him at Thornton Hill. [23]

The younger Robinson came back to Freetown with a few pieces of gingerroot, out of which he got a flourishing crop. The witnesses asked for and collected pay for 204 lost working days, less ninepence-a-day maintenance while in England and the allowances given their families at home. Dawes, in England on leave, had been considering resigning, but the "tumult" revived his zeal for the colony. Macaulay was suffering intermittent bouts of fever, and Dawes' mature presence, the directors agreed, was sorely needed. [24]

Two months after the June "riot" came the French attack, in late September, 1794, and it cost more in terms of worsened communal relations than it did in capital losses. The colony had done everything it could to avoid attention in the war, signing a neutrality pact with Renaud, the French trader at Gambia Island, and concluding a conditional agreement to buy him out when he wanted to quit the trade. An invitation from the English at Bance to help wipe out Gambia was declined. A wary watch was kept on French maritime activities because it was rumored that the African leaders would take advantage of a French attack to pounce on the settlement themselves. [25] Basically, however, the colony was confident that the French would be under orders to leave them alone. This was a false sense of security. Although the French Convention had shown a friendly interest and a committee had requested a list of ships so that they could be exempted from molestation, the Sierra Leone directors had responded only after asking permission of the British government. Thomas Clarkson believed so strongly that the company should act independently, since Freetown was "unconnected with national quarrels," that unable to carry the majority, he resigned his directorship. Perhaps because of the anti-Jacobin climate, the directors failed to send an emissary to Paris to plead for the colony. A majority believed the matter "too delicate" and feared to jeopardize possible succor from the British government if they were in touch with the enemy. [26]

The French were encouraged to ransack Freetown and were piloted into its harbor by two American slave ship captains with deep grudges over runaway slaves and abuse from the settlers. "I shall glut myself with revenge," one had sworn after a stoning. When the seven strange vessels were reported heading toward Sierra Leone, there was no alarm. It seemed too large for a French force. In the bustle of equipping Gray and Watt to journey to Timbuktu, the fleet was forgotten. During evening prayers on Saturday night Macaulay heard a signal for coming to anchor.[27] On Sunday, September 28, the ships moved in easily on a fair wind, flying English colors and rigged in the English fashion. Hoping it really was a friendly squadron and deciding, if it were not, that resistance was futile, Macaulay and his colleagues watched from the balcony of his house on a knoll while a crowd of settlers gathered on the waterfront. Then Macaulay discerned a man on a frigate "with great care pointing a gun into my piazza." The governor's party beat a brisk retreat as shots whistled past. Macaulay ordered the Sierra Leone flag lowered and a white tablecloth hung on the veranda, but the French continued to pour shells into the town. A doctor, Lowe, hailed the ships to point to the truce flag. Back came a demand to raise the flag of liberty. Lowe replied that they didn't have one. After an hour and a half, by David George's reckoning, the firing stopped, and the seamen landed.[28]

At the governor's house no one was hurt, but on the shore a child of seven was cut in two, held in the arms of a woman who escaped unscathed. Another woman had a leg blown off, and a man lost a foot. One or two others were wounded. It was God's mercy, said George, that there were not more casualties in the "multitudes" at the waterside. "Whites and Blacks were obliged to run back into the mountains." Later some settlers accused Macaulay of surrendering too easily, but he rightly reckoned the colony's 24 guns, on rotted carriages, and a dozen barrels of gunpowder were no match for 130 twelve-pound cannon and 1,500 men. Highly fortified Bance Island surrendered to a smaller force. Some of the settlers, however, would have preferred a fight.[29]

The sailors were undisciplined and greedy. "Never did I behold a more ragged, lawless set of rascals: well might they be called Sans Culottes before they came; but upon their return they looked more like Dutchmen," observed Lowe. They pulled on suit over suit, shirt over shirt and hat upon hat. Men who swarmed ashore in rags reappeared in gowns and petticoats or with yards of cloth wrapped around them. George was stripped with the rest, left without a "second shirt to my back. My wife and children were almost naked." The commodore, Citizen Arnaud, had no control over the pillage. To all pleas to spare the colony for humanitarian reasons, his only reply was, *"Citoyen, cela peut bien être, mais encore vous êtes anglais."* Macaulay then begged them to spare the blacks, who were "not Englishmen," and the commodore seemed to acquiesce. Although normally the settlers would resent being dubbed not British subjects, some of them in this crisis were telling the

French that they were Americans, therefore allies.[30] They may have known that the National Convention had abolished slavery.

The French occupied Freetown from September 28 to October 13, 1794, and in the fortnight stole, smashed or killed almost everything of value. They set fire to every company building and burned ten settlers' houses "by mistake." Eight vessels were burned, and the two others stolen. Shops like those run by Mary Perth and Sophia Small were looted of goods they had bought on credit, such as glassware and rum. The new printing press was lost, records were destroyed, telescopes and weather instruments smashed. All the coin was stolen. The town library was sacked, and any volume resembling a Bible "torn in pieces and trampled on." Medicines were seized. Twelve hundred hogs were killed, and most of the poultry. Wounded dogs and cats were left to die in the streets. A breed of asses just introduced was wiped out. The botanist Afzelius lost the manuscript of his life's work, and his largest to date collection of specimens was despoiled, the live animals and birds killed and thrown away or eaten. He was shocked how the French "amused themselves with abusing, stripping & beating our people." He saw settlers stoop to robbing one another. There had been many dogged attempts to raise English apples in Africa. After the French withdrew, only one tree was left, in the orchard of John Spears, a settler who brought it with him from England in 1792. It bore several fruits this unhappy season, and the one apple which ripened was presented to Macaulay on October 27 and preserved in spirits.[31]

During the occupation, officers and settlers were kind and helpful to one another. Macaulay, who was fluent in French, first stayed aboard the French flagship in the hope of influencing events, then moved to a settler's house in Granville Town. Mary Perth shepherded the African children who lived and were schooled under Macaulay's roof to Pa Demba's town for safety. Macaulay visited them there, and Mrs. Perth prepared tea and a bed for him. "As there were a good many Settlers there," recounted Macaulay, "we had the pleasure of joining together at night in the worship of God." Most of the black families fled to the woods, to their farms or African villages roundabout. The men went into Freetown by day and rejoined their families at night. The French did not venture far outside the town for fear of reprisals.

It was the last straw when, on October 10, the well-laden *Harpy* returning from England sailed into harbor unaware and was seized. John Cuthbert, a passenger, was robbed: "they even took the hat off my head." It took him a day and a half to find his wife and children. Describing the calamity to Baptist friends in England, he asked for a hymnal and psalmbook in large print, for "the French have got my spectacles." Luckily, he had not carried with him the £200 donated by British friends for a new Baptist meetinghouse. The nails and ironwork he had brought for it were stolen.[32]

The chief casualty among the whites was Richard Pepys. At the first shot, he appeared to lose his wits, and hearing that the settlers had set a price on his head, he fled into the woods with his wife and son, refusing all offers of shelter. Settlers gave the family food and finally got them over to the Bulom Shore, where Pepys died of exposure on October 6. The company in its 1795 report lauded Pepys for "extraordinary exertions" in laying out the land.

By sharing such flour, biscuit, rice, oatmeal, beef and brandy as the French had been persuaded to leave along with the settlers' homegrown fruits and vegetables, the colonial population carried on when the French sailed. Macaulay rented the best of the settlers' houses for himself and other officers. He was "much better pleased with their conduct than I had yet been." They were "universally kind & even affectionate." He reported to his employers that the men had managed to save quantities of goods from destruction by spiriting them away: "They had stript off & removed the lining of many of the houses & the frame of the old Hospital was almost entirely saved. They had also saved 2 or 3 of the Company's Boats & a great quantity of Ironmongery."[33]

But the good feeling was shattered on October 14, when Macaulay summoned the hundreders and tithingmen and demanded the return of all the salvaged material, for which he would pay 20 percent of value. Wretched and guilt-ridden at the huge loss (£40,000 plus buildings) to the company, he harped on the colonists' duty to the directors, and he warned that anyone who held back anything would get no further employment, medical care or schooling for their children. "I told them . . . they were in justice bound to restore the Company's property now, as much as if they had assisted in rescuing their Neighbours' furniture from Fire. . . . They afterwards wrangled a good deal among themselves about it and some of them were loud & vehement in their protestations." An elaborate oath was drawn up which had to be attested before the "favors" of jobs, schooling or medical attention would be available. The schoolmasters were ordered to admit no children and the physicians to attend no family where the signed certificate could not be produced.[34]

Many of the blacks, with reason to be proud of their conduct under stress, were furious. They had salvaged property which otherwise would have been irretrievably lost; it was not theft to keep it. The French had "restored us some things, and some we got out of the water and on the beach some we saved from the fire," said Eli Ackim, never a radical before. When the French left:

> we divided our spoil with the distressed European Civilians, that they might have subsistence as well as ourselves and also we returned many things to the Govenor. The Govenor then called us thieves and many Children were not allowed to go to School on that same account, and this kept a dispute on both sides, as we could not consider ourselves thieves, as the French had given us things, which we begged them for, telling them that we was Americans from North America.

As for a new oath: "We was British subjects eighteen & twenty years before we came here, and after our arrival hear we all took the Oath of Allegiance to our King and Country, we therefore refused to comply," Ackim explained. A broad arrow—the mark of government property—was put on the houses of those who refused.[35]

Moses Wilkinson and fellow Methodists (all "Malcontents" in Macaulay's book) wrote to Clarkson: "We wance did call it Free town but since your Absence—we have a Reason to call it a town of Slavery." God had seen the "tyranny" they suffered and sent the French as a "Message of his power to attack the Barbarous Task Masters." Of the salvage, the "Enemy have pity our Case and Bestowed a little few Necessary upon us," which the governor now claimed they had taken. "Consider if any man see A place is to be Destroyed by fire and Run the Risk of his life to save of that Ruin . . . do you not think the protector of those articles have a just Right to this property." Had Macaulay approached them "in a fare Manner . . . God only knows we would give it up with all Respect—but in Stead . . . he came . . . to tell us if We did not give them up we should . . . be Blotted Out of the Company's Book." As usual, they sought Clarkson's return; "We do Raly look to see you with our Longing Eyes—Our Only Friend. . . ."[36]

Some lumber, a few nails and tools were handed over, but the total did not amount to a tenth or twentieth part of the missing material. No more than 120 signed the oath, about a third of the household heads. Some months later the number had risen to nearly half. From among these "staunch friends of order," Macaulay hired carpenters and laborers to build a storehouse on the old foundations with space on a second floor for a church to seat 500. A house and storehouse were planned for Clarkson's Plantation (the mile-square tract rented in 1792) on the Bulom Shore as a refuge for the white staff in case of future attack. Moving the government there with a "select few" colonists to form a model community, leaving contentious Freetown to run itself, was even considered. About 150 children of dutiful colonists, half the normal enrollment, resumed their studies, while other families combined to employ their own teacher. "This they are well able to do," fumed their acting governor, "from the quantity of lumber &c . . . which they have in the most bare faced manner applied to their own use."[37]

In the sour aftermath of the occupation, with most of the people ill and destitute, wild rumors spread that Macaulay had surrendered to save the property with no thought of the settlers, that he had urged the French to take them all away, that the storehouse was full of goods meant for but kept from them and that the council would try to wrest the salvaged property from them by force. Isaac Anderson, who in 1793 had been assured the governor did nothing except at their order, now wrote the directors to ask whether they had told Macaulay to give them up to the French. A letter was sent the directors stating their claim to the salvaged property. The hardiest notion was that because the council records had been destroyed—that is, the "Law Book"—there was no law running in the colony now. In the ill-humored atmosphere, Macaulay advised the whites to keep aloof. The restraints were "very thin indeed." The people were "angry & are ready to fly in one's face."[38]

How much hardship was caused by the denial of medical care is impossible to tell. Nathanial Snowball registered one complaint. After nearly six months the council relented to allow nonconforming families to be treated if they paid for the medicine, at five times the cost price. Many got into the habit of doing without and died of ailments that should not have been fatal. In a strange aftermath, Snowball, his wife, Violet, and a daughter all fell dangerously ill in 1802 while staying with his son and namesake. Snowball refused to take any medicine or let it be administered to the others. All three died. Anzel Zizer and Henry Morrison were denied the agricultural prizes they had won because they would not sign an oath.[39]

To the faithful, many things seem providential. Sampson Heywood was convinced that it was God's vengeance when nothing went right for him after he refused to return his salvaged property. Similar cases were a subject of gossip. One man, who boasted of taking enough to "live like a Gentleman for seven years," died in seven months of consumption. This belief in divine retribution pleased Macaulay.[40]

The nonsigners of the oath were also deprived of the vote. At the February, 1795, election, they amounted to seventy families, and seven tithings were left vacant. Macaulay was at this time proceeding with the general object of developing a legislature based on a constitution and provided the elected representatives with rules. He hoped that from this small beginning a "future house of Commons might arise and give Laws to Africa." His speech to the newly elected men, interrupted occasionally by dissidents, is a classic illustration of Macaulay's liberal intentions betrayed by the manner of a born-and-bred autocrat. He derided the colonists' ideas of rights to land, to the waterfront, to jobs, schools, medical care or credit. As always, they were told that they had misunderstood Clarkson's promises. In everything but the full allotment of land, the company had fulfilled its part of the bargain. When they claimed they were not treated equally with whites, they confused privileges of office with civil rights. Whites lived better because they could afford it. They were paid more because they deserved it. "Write as well, figure as well, Act as well, think as well as they do & you shall have a preference. I have anxiously sought among you for men to fill offices, nor is there at this moment an office in the Colony filled by a white which a Black could fill."[41]

Ishmael York, a thirty-nine-year-old onetime Carolina slave and Nova Scotia farmer[42] who was now a tithingman and increasingly a spokesman for the antigovernment faction, chided Macaulay for playing favorites instead of, as a "Father," regarding all his "Children" equally. He made the apparently ingenuous observation that kindness would promote peace and mercy would make friends of all. Macaulay retorted:

> If by kindness you mean personal Civility, if by kindness you mean hearty wishes & earnest endeavours to promote your happiness, I find no room to accuse myself of unkindness. Whom have I abused? Whom have I treated among you with harshness & severity—to whom have I returned railing for railing? . . . But if by kindness you mean giving away the Company's property, without any measure but your own fancied notions of your deservings you must excuse me. I am content to be looked on as unkind & cruel.

Governor Dawes had returned in the spring of 1795 and Macaulay had sailed for England and a well-earned year's leave when the issue of the salvaged/stolen property was brought up again, this time by the diehard outcasts, mainly Methodists, who claimed to be unfairly reported to the directors as "people of a ranglesome nature." They asserted that after the French capture it had been necessary to wait to hear from the directors whether the settlement was to go on and, if so, under what laws. They proposed, since they were not represented by tithingmen, that Jonathan Glasgow, Luke Jordan and Nathaniel Snowball be their spokesmen since many of them individually had "a very hasty temper knowing not how to discourse to their superiors officers." But the governor and council were interested in nothing but capitulation to the conditions to which by now a majority of the colonists had bowed. The dissidents in reply once more poured out their inchoate grievances and their contrasting view of the recent events and insisted that they would take their case if need be to Parliament. The adamant tone again shows how insistent some were on maintaining their position and testing the boundaries of their recently won freedom.

> . . . if the Governar or his Counsil wanted to have any Clames upon the people for any property they should not so quick surrender to the Enemy—for there was People ready to protect the Colony . . . throw our own kindness which we was not under any obligation to do" many officers had been provided with the necessities of life but afterwards they showed no kindness in return. Unjust terms could not be accepted now for "we have long ago been Empressed upon with Tyranny . . . which we are determined not any longer to be so, but to Enjoy the privileges of Freedom—which if our Request can not be complyed by Government as we would not wish to make any strife—we will lay all of our grevances to the Court of Directors if not Parliament must act its part—for we yet do not know upon what footing we are upon wheather to be made Slaves or to only go by the Name of Freedom.[43]

They had to wait until Macaulay's return in March, 1796, for their reply from London. He summoned the hundreders and leaders of the "disaffected party" to hear an answer prepared by the one director they might heed, Granville Sharp. The letter is not recorded, but Macaulay noted in his journal that he had emphasized the parts where "Mr. Sharp animadverts with great severity on the heinousness of the Petitioners' conduct.'' Glasgow, Jordan and Snowball, according to Macaulay, "hung down their heads and appeared much ashamed."[44]

Since the Dawes administration in 1793 had claimed the entire waterfront for the company, it had proved impossible to move one cluster of blacks from their sites on Brothers Street (named for the ship on which they came to Africa but better known to the company's men as Discontented Row) near Susan's Bay. Macaulay apparently returned from London with a directive to take the issue to court. The company proceeded to sue Jordan and Snowball and their associates, and the case came to trial before a jury with Macaulay, now the governor (since Dawes had returned to England), and John Gray, a councillor, sitting as judges.[45] Witnesses claimed that they had heard Clarkson tell the men they could remain on these lots.[46]

The company submitted a mass of written documents and oral testimony supporting its claim. The case went to the jury, which next day sought clarification of certain points. Macaulay heard that eleven jurymen had agreed on a verdict for the company but the holdout had conferred with the defendants. He declared a mistrial. After the new hearing the jury again deliberated at length but at midnight presented Macaulay with a verdict for Snowball and Jordan. It was, Macaulay said, the only "unjust decision I had ever known a Sierra Leone Jury to come to." Later four of the jurors signed depositions that they understood the verdict to be that Jordan and Snowball could keep the land if a signed statement were obtained from Clarkson that he had promised it to them. Macaulay did not, however, contest the verdict. Anything touching land grants was explosive and ranged the majority of settlers against the company, not just the militant hard core.

Jordan and Snowball wrote Clarkson that the land "which we understood you gave us we have had difficulty to hold. . . . There have been two tryals concerning it & in the last the jury gave it in our favour but as yet the matter is not quite settled."[47]

The same year, 1796, marked the first time that the quitrent disagreement, the most profound of all the controversies, came into the open. Clarkson had not imposed the tax because it violated the agreement he had reached with the blacks in Nova Scotia, but succeeding governors understood little of the issue, certainly not the depth of American colonial resistance to it. To them it was simply a tax, the revenue from which was to go to investors in London, to whom, they loyally believed, the settlers were much obliged. Looking no farther back than the settlement terms printed in November, 1791, which included the quitrent, they (or at least Macaulay) may have really believed that the Nova Scotians emigrated knowing they would be liable to it.[48]

The directors apparently dreamed of 250,000 acres of farmland yielding a shilling an acre or £12,500-a-year direct revenue, plus the profits of the export of surplus produce. (So far only 2,560 acres had been allotted to 500 men and women, and the quitrent revenue could not have exceeded £128 a year.) The quitrent was fifty times as high as the suspended quitrent in Nova Scotia and New Brunswick and ten times as high as anything ever imposed in the North American colonies, but the settlers only argued that it was five or six times as much as any they had heard of in America. Also, the directors intended to raise the levy steadily to 4 percent of the harvest.[49] But the exact amount of the quitrent probably made less difference to the blacks than the principle of the tax, which seemed to make them tenants of their land. The company's stubborn insistence on a quitrent can be attributed to an attempt to uphold the principle of its right to tax as it wished. But it must be remembered what a departure this represented from the original Province of Freedom, where, as the Old Settlers could testify, the land belonged to the people and they alone had power to grant it by their own free vote.[50]

From 1796 on the pattern of unrest in Freetown follows the alternate application and reduction of pressure to collect the quitrent. The first public mention of it was May 6, 1793, when Governor Dawes spoke of it to "some" of the people. It wasn't among the grievances taken to London that year, so clearly it had not sunk in. Many settlers believed that they first heard of it on March 7, 1795, when Macaulay addressed the newly elected hundreders and tithingmen. This should not have been so because in late 1793, after a number of complaints about the poor farmland on the peninsula, Dawes arranged with the African chiefs to lease another tract near Clarkson's Plantation on the Bulom Shore, where up to twenty families could be accommodated on level and, they hoped, more fertile soil. The published terms of settlement included a quitrent of a bushel of rice per year per acre or its money equivalent. No one sought a grant. Even when all the conditions except the quitrent were dropped, no one would move there. According to Mrs. DuBois, but undocumented elsewhere, another two-man delegation arrived in London in August, 1794, to object to the Bulom Shore tax. By her reckoning, the bushel of rice would mean a rent of more than 10 shillings per acre. Even at Cox-George's estimate of 4 to 5 shillings an acre, depending on the fluctuating price of rice, it was an extraordinary level for such a tax.[51]

When Macaulay returned from the bracing air of Clapham in March, 1796 (to, incidentally, an enthusiastic welcome which astonished and touched him), he brought a determination to start collecting the quitrent. In council, he fixed the shilling per acre—which he constantly referred to as a "trifling" sum—to begin from January 1, 1797. Also from that January, the settlers were to begin paying 7 1/2 percent interest on old debts, presumably including quitrent arrears, a crippling blow. The rate was higher than the English usury law allowed.[52] These actions guaranteed that the quitrent would be the central issue in the rancorous year-end election. (There was also an issue of religious freedom, which will be looked at later.)

Governor Macaulay, also in 1796, decided to issue new grants or titles for the allotments. Many residents had lost theirs through the French sack of their homes. In redrafting them, he added the quitrent with a proviso that it would stop at a shilling an acre, which he thought would quiet apprehensions. This was the second such mandatory exchange of titles and was greeted with deep distrust. Out of 300 prepared, fewer than half were called for. Snowball denounced the new grant as "a Chain . . . to bind him a slave for ever."[53]

Not content with these actions, the governor embarked on a policy of selling land to whites. The original instructions barred them, but the directors in a move to stave off salary increases ruled in 1796 that white employees might own land. Property would also entitle them to vote, previously the exclusive privilege of blacks. Macaulay further intended to make sure that all whites were eligible by extending the franchise to those earning £40 a year.[54] John Gray became the first white property owner. He told the council in January, 1796, that he wished to "constitute myself a citizen of Africa by purchasing *an Acre* of Land." His and other grants to whites were issued on December 1, and the white landholders were included in the voters' list for the December 13 election.[55]

The blacks believed that year that if they elected only blacks, these representatives would be able to abolish the quitrent. This was the root of the antiwhite campaign waged by Ishmael York and Stephen Peters, who did not want whites ever to have the vote. Their argument, as interpreted by Macaulay, was that "Whites formerly deprived us of our just rights & trampled upon us. Now it is in our power it is but right we should secure ourselves against their encroachments and even if that should not be necessary yet it is but right we should retaliate." The governor commented, "There was something so unique in making a *White* face a civil disqualification that really provoked me to laughter." Macaulay directed the marshal to see that no one interfered with the white voters and invited York and Peters to see him so that he could point out their "extreme folly," but "They were so much abashed . . . that they did not chuse to come." He ridiculed their efforts to others and believed the campaign died away. After one argument with the pair, Macaulay had uttered the weary judgment:

> I wish no further punishment to those who extol vox populi as vox Dei, than to have to encounter for twelve months the wayward humours, the perverse disputings, the absurd reasonings, the unaccountable prejudices, the everlasting jealousies, the presumptuous self-conceit, the gross ignorance & insatiable Demands of our Settlers.

In spite of his exertions, no white stood for office in the election, and the "extremists" scored heavily. Only six members survived from the old body. Macaulay had argued without avail that the blacks should elect whites for their "superior intelligence . . . in explaining things . . . or in drawing up resolutions." When the news got out that all the hundreders and tithingmen were again black, "some 30 or 40 of the Settlers got together & gave three cheers." After the election the governor and council withdrew York's liquor license on charges of bribing voters with drinks and overpricing the rum sold to Africans.[56]

Macaulay prepared thumbnail descriptions of the victors in the 1796 election. The hundreders:

> *Ishmael York*—a noisy factious fellow, exceeding griping & selfish, which makes him of little weight. An elder of Lady Huntingdon's Sect, and a great talker about religion, but sadly unprincipled.
> *Stephen Peters*—equally devoid of principle but more decorous . . . & more artful. . . . His influence is considerable among the Methodists, he being one of their great thundering Orators. He is plausible & specious among ignorant people from a kind of affected gravity, but he is one of the most perverse. . . .
> *John Cuthbert*—least exceptionable . . . because he means well, but he is weak and irresolute and too conceited . . . (wh. indeed is a general fault). . . .
> *Nathaniel Snowball*—This man may truly be called a pestilent

fellow. . . . He is factious, noisy, busy, bold & blind. His influence is considerable with a certain class . . . but it is diminishing daily. . . .

Isaac Anderson—He is as disaffected as ever.

George Carrol—A Man of much the same Stamp but more hot & passionate & more ignorant.

Of the tithingmen, ten were dependable "at least at present" but timid and easily swayed. Twelve were "dubious" or "unquestionably bad." The other eight were scarcely better.[57]

The first quitrent installment was due on July 1, 1797, and when the notice was published, the hundreders and tithingmen and all the church groups debated what to do. The Baptists, under David George, a consistent government supporter, agreed to pay. Lady Huntingdon's society left it to the individual conscience, but the leaders said they did not intend to pay. The far more numerous Methodists said anyone who paid the rent would be expelled. George Carrol and Isaac Streeter, a tithingman, addressed the council in no uncertain terms:

We are to inform you that we have left Lands to come here in expectation to receive Lands in the same condition as we received them in Nova Scotia, But we find it to the contrary of that, for . . . the Company says the Land is theirs. Sir if we had been told that, we never would come here . . . for before we will pay the shilling pr Acre we will reply [apply] to Government for lands or to the Kings of the Country. Sir we are astonished why the Company could not tell us after three years we was to pay a shilling pr acre. . . . if the Lands is not ours without paying a Shilling pr Acre, the Lands will never be ours, no not at all. . . .[58]

They asked the governor to explain, and he scheduled an address for August 22. On the day before the town was in a commotion. "The people had flocked in from the Country. Meetings & Cabals were holdg in every Street. Every individual had in his countenance the marks of an anxious mind. . . . There reigned at the same time an unusual stillness. All seemed to be transacted in a kind of whisper. . . ." The hundreders and tithingmen told people not to attend the meeting, and only 150—half the household heads—came. To them Macaulay delivered some 10,000 words of advice, then had 100 copies of the speech printed and circulated.[59] It was closely argued, with many well-taken points, and was listened to in silence. At the end Macaulay saw that a few were "rather enraged." Macaulay's statements about how much they owed the company (no one ever mentioned the reverse debt) and their need for its protection to survive were not unusual. But he asserted erroneously that none of them had received a grant of land in Nova Scotia and also insisted that they came to Africa knowing the quitrent would be levied, again untrue.[60] In an unfortunately worded passage, he denounced the people for failing to trust and respect him and the council and for listening:

> to every prating, malicious, designing tale-bearer; to every selfish and base deceiver, who . . . would abuse or revile your Governors and misrepresent their conduct. You have often been made to see the folly of acting thus, and yet you still return like the sow, to flounder in the same dirty puddle.

He refused to answer any questions. When he had gone, Isaac Anderson produced a copy of Mrs. DuBois' *Narrative of Two Voyages to the River Sierra Leone* and had certain passages relating to his mission in 1793 read aloud. Stephen Peters delivered a tirade against the governor (so Macaulay heard), and when Thomas Cooper, an African born in England and the black most respected by the whites, got up to speak, he was drowned out. The meeting ended in tumult. Cooper went around the town explaining the governor's position to individuals, and Macaulay talked with several in private as well. Then he met the hundreders and, opening Anderson's "favourite book," attempted to dispose of all the arguments of the 1793 mission to London. Macaulay reported that his audience was convinced of his viewpoint, but they asked and received permission to send another petition to the directors.[61]

Instead of working on it, however, the activists, dominated by the Methodists, campaigned to get those settlers who had accepted the new grants to return them, claiming that the land was theirs by treaty with the African chiefs and the company was trying to trick them to extort money. They set up a "court" outside town to "try" those who refused to collaborate, threatening to burn the houses of or flog recalcitrants, according to Macaulay. He was certain that some intended to try to overthrow the government, and he set a guard on the powder magazine and organized the whites and fifty reliable Nova Scotians to defend Thornton Hill. He publicly threatened to hang anyone who burned the house of a government supporter, and privately he was determined to hang two or three ringleaders, whether or not it was legal.

Neither the militant settlers nor Macaulay's government were strong enough at this point to force a violent showdown. The government did not collect the quitrent, and the crisis blew over. "A face of loyalty was spread over the place."[62]

It was true that some of the settlers were determined on self-rule. Snowball was the leader of this mainly Methodist faction, which in 1795 had obtained a tract of land on Pirate's or Cockle Bay, halfway between Freetown and Cape Sierra Leone, from Prince George, Jimmy Queen and other headmen "forever." Their number rose to about seventy families. By early 1796 they were clearing a site for a town, with plans to move out of Freetown during the dry season. Snowball was elected governor with Luke Jordan and Jonathan Glasgow as a council. Macaulay could do little but warn them of the risk they were running among slave traders. He suspected they had persuaded a trader named Durant to set up a factory where they could buy at less than Freetown prices. They built houses along the bay and a meetinghouse. America Talbot was their preacher.[63]

Macaulay blamed the breakaway on Snowball's incorrigible ambition, but all the explanations sent to Clarkson were related to supposed "oppression," specifically the quitrent. His correspondents urged Clarkson to come back. "As you have took that Great undertaking As Mosis & Joshua did—be with us Unto the End," pleaded James Hutchinson and Moses Murray,[64] so though they were anti-white-rule, they were not anti-all-whites.

Boston King was not of the group and indeed did not figure in any of the settlement's disputes, having been in England from 1794 to late 1796, but he predicted that half the families would leave Freetown because of the quitrent. Others were moving onto their country farms to live away from the town, and a "noble crop" was making it possible for a great number to become independent.

Clarkson was alarmed at this development. He wrote King that the Nova Scotians "ought never to separate themselves, but live in harmony . . as the only sure means of protection from the Natives as well as the Europeans." They should remember what happened to the Old Settlers before they went "wandering about amongst the Natives." He exhorted:

You have all of you a serious task to perform, and when you

consider that the situation of millions of your own Colour may
be greatly benefited by your good example, you should be
circumspect . . . & not quarrell with each other or with your
Rulers, but put up with little Inconveniences to insure the
future happiness of your posterity. . . . consider where there
are so many, it is impossible to please the whole—

King showed this letter to as many people "as I was dere to," and
many, he thought, did not leave Freetown because of it. In 1799
however, there were still eleven families at Pirate's Bay.[65]

NOTES

1. Wilkinson and others to Clarkson, November 19, 1794, Clarkson Papers, BL
   Add. MSS. 41,263.
2. Wilberforce to (unnamed), November 28, 1827, in R. I. and S. Wilberforce,
   Correspondence of William Wilberforce, p. 509; for cases of trouble with
   slavers, April 9, 1794, CO 270/2; December 11, 1794, CO 270/3; Knutsford,
   Life and Letters of Zachary Macaulay, pp. 133-34; Anderson and Jordan to
   Clarkson, June 28, 1794, Clarkson Papers, BL Add. MSS. 41,263.
3. Macaulay Journal, Huntington Library, June 18, 1793; Evans, "An Early
   Constitution of Sierra Leone," pp. 60, 37-38.
4. Thornton to Clarkson, December 30, 1791, Clarkson Papers, BL Add. MSS
   41,262A; Clarkson Journal (SLS), p. 8; Clarkson Journal (Maynard)
   December 21, 1792.
5. Macaulay Journal, March 1, 1797; May 25, June 5, April 21, 1796; Knutsford, pp. 137, 140.
6. *The Philanthropist*, vol. 4 (1814), p. 26; Council minute, April 30, 1792, CO
   270/2; Clarkson Journal (SLS), pp. 9, 10, 11, 16-17; Ingham, *Sierra Leone
   After One Hundred Years*, pp. 105-7. Search of London court records for the
   Cambridge case so far has been fruitless, and no company records seem to have
   survived. Clarkson Journal (SLS), pp. 35, 93; Strand Journal, September 2,
   1792, BL Add. MSS. 12,131.
7. Thornton to Clarkson, December 30, 1791, Clarkson Papers, BL Add. MSS
   41,262A.
8. For Horrocks' slaves case, Macaulay Journal, July 31, August 3, 1793, and
   Knutsford, p. 43, except as noted.
9. Macaulay Journal, September 8, 20, 1793; Knutsford, pp. 45, 47, 52.
10. Knutsford, pp. 43 n., 44 n.; Evans, pp. 37-38.
11. Knutsford, p. 51; Macaulay Journal, September 18, November 15 and 14,
    1793.

12. Council minute, November 4, 1793, CO 270/2; Macaulay Journal, November 2, 3, 8, 1793.

13. Council minutes, June 16-August 1, 1794, CO 270/2, except as noted.

14. Jordan and Anderson to Clarkson, June 28, 1794, Clarkson Papers, BL Add. MSS. 41,263.

15. *Ibid.*

16. Knutsford, p. 60.

17. Clarkson also offered return passages. Told that the people were unhappy and wished to go back to America, he asked if it were true, and "They *all* laughed at the idea." Clarkson Journal (New York), May 3, 1792; Ingham, p. 63.

18. Evans, p. 53.

19. Macaulay Journal, August 20 (no names given), July 23, 1794.

20. Macaulay to Directors, November 15, 1794, Huntington Library; Council minute, December 7, 1794, CO 270/3. There seems to be no record of the cases being tried in London courts.

21. Sharp to Thornton, November 26, 1794, in Hoare, *Memoirs of Granville Sharp*, vol. 2, pp. 179-80. Dawes was in England on leave.

22. Clarkson to Thornton, December 11, 1796, Clarkson Papers, BL Add. MSS. 41,263, enclosing Ellison to Clarkson, December 9, 1796.

23. Macaulay Journal, April 12, 1797, August 26, 1796. It can be supposed he let Tybee stay.

24. *Adam Afzelius: Sierra Leone Journal*, February 11, 1796; Council minutes, March 27, April 3, 1795; Sierra Leone Company 1794 Report, p. 27.

25. Macaulay Journal, June 19, August 18, 20, June 29, 1793.

26. *Baptist Annual Register for 1794-1797*, p. 217; Wadstrom, *Essay on Colonization*, part 2, p. 289 n., pp. 288-95; Thornton Diary, June 3, 1795, Wigan Public Libraries; Phillips to (unnamed), February 8, 1793, Friends Library Thompson-Clarkson MSS. 2/35; Letter of Mr. Stone with questions from the French Convention, December 19, 1792, CO 267/5.

27. Macaulay Journal, August 18, 1794; Knutsford, p. 62. Account of French attack from Macaulay Journal, September 28-October 13, 1794, of which a large part is printed in Knutsford, pp. 64-77, and Sierra Leone Company 1795 Report, except as noted. A full account by Afzelius to the Swedish ambassador, printed in Wadstrom, part 2, pp. 279-84.

28. Lowe to Lettsom, November 1, 1794, in Pettigrew, *Memoirs of the Life and Writings of the Late John Coakley Lettsom*, pp. 248-49; Knutsford, p. 64; George to Rippon, November 12, 1794, in Sierra Leone Company 1795 Report, Philadelphia edition, p. 23, and *Baptist Annual Register for 1794-1797*, pp. 215-16.

29. Macaulay to Directors, November 15, 1794; Lowe to Lettsom, November 1, 1794, p. 252; George to Rippon, November 12, 1794; (victims not named); Macaulay Journal, November 25, 1794; Wilkinson and others to Clarkson,

November 19, 1793, and Leaster to Clarkson, March 30, 1796, both Clarkson Papers, BL Add. MSS. 41,263.

30. Lowe to Lettsom, November 1, 1794, p. 249; Sierra Leone Company 1795 Report, pp. 7-8, George to Rippon, November 12, 1794; Ackim to Commissioners of Enquiry, CO 267/92.

31. Afzelius to Banks, November 13, 1794, Banks Papers, BL Add. MSS. 33,979; Council minutes, March 30 and 31, 1795, CO 270/3; Sierra Leone Company 1801 Report, p. 29; Afzelius to Smith, November 19, 1794, Smith MSS. vol. 1, Linnaean Society; Account of the Public Gardens before the arrival of the French and after, November 27, 1794, BL Add. MSS. 12,131. Macaulay reported a settler named Leman (possibly Old Settler John Lemon) freed from jail by the French and kitted out in a fancy suit meant for an African chief.

32. Macaulay Journal, November 15, 1794; Sierra Leone Company 1795 Report, Philadelphia edition, pp. 23-24; *Baptist Annual Register for 1794 1797*, pp. 216, 255. English Baptists sent George and Cuthbert books and five chests of clothes. The elder Samuel Whitbread gave £20 for shirts and shifts and all those who received these garments signed a letter of thanks which reached London a few hours after Whitbread's death. *Missionary Magazine* vol. 1 (1796), p. 171. Later it was said the raiders were privateers sponsored by French slaving interests to attack English factories (which lost £400,000 by French actions). Witnesses thought they belonged to the French navy, and Abbé Grégoire, after a study of records of the commandant of the squadron, concluded the attack was a mistake, based on an assumption that Freetown was an ordinary English mercantile base. Wadstrom, Part 2, p. 290; Knutsford, p. 82. Gregoire, *An Enquiry Concerning the Intellectual and Moral Faculties, and Literature of NEGROES*, p. 151.

33. Macaulay Journal, November 26, 1794; Knutsford, p. 83.

34. Macaulay Journal, October 14, 1794; Knutsford, p. 78; Council minute October 14, 1794, CO 270/3; Sierra Leone Company 1795 Report, p. 25; The *Times*, March 2, 1795; Council minute, October 20, 1794; CO 270/3 Macaulay Journal, October 17, 1794.

35. Ackim to Commissioners of Enquiry, CO 267/92.

36. Wilkinson and others to Clarkson, November 19, 1794; Macaulay Journal November 26, 1794.

37. *Ibid.*, October 17, 1794; Governor and council to Thornton, March 11, 1795 CO 268/5; Macaulay Journal, October 22, November 26, 1794; Macaulay to Directors, November 15, 1794; Clarkson Journal (Maynard), December 4, 10 1792.

38. Macaulay Journal, November 26, 1794; Knutsford, p. 83; Macaulay Journal, May 23, 1796; Governor and council to Thornton, March 11, 1795 Address to hundreders and tithingmen, March 7, 1795, CO 270/3; Macaulay

to Directors, November 15, 1794; Macaulay Journal, November 26, 1794.

39. Council minutes, April 3 and 7, 1795, CO 270/3; June 1, 1797, CO 270/4; July 31, 1802, CO 270/8; April 3, 1795, CO 270/3.

40. Macaulay Journal, August 22, 1796.

41. Council minutes, March 7, 1795, CO 270/3.

42. Blacks in Birch Town who gave in their names for Sierra Leone, November, 1791, CO 217/63.

43. Council minute, April 21, 1795, CO 270/3; Settlers to governor and council, April 28, 1795, CO 270/3.

44. Macaulay Journal, March 23, 1796; Council minute, March 22, 1796, CO 270/4.

45. Macaulay Journal, July 12 and 20, 1796.

46. Clarkson Journal (SLS), pp. 31-32, 35.

47. Jordan and Snowball to Clarkson, July 29, 1796, Clarkson Papers, BL Add. MSS. 41,263.

48. Address to settlers, August 21, 1797, CO 270/4.

49. Curtin, *Image of Africa*, p. 130; Ludlam to Governor and council, November 17, 1801, CO 270/6. The quitrent set, but never collected, in Nova Scotia was 2 shillings per 100 acres annually. The highest in the American colonies was 10 shillings per 100 acres (see Chapter 4).

50. Cox-George, "Direct Taxation in the Early History of Sierra Leone," pp. 20-35, especially p. 30; Montagu, *Ordinances of the Settlement of Sierra Leone*, vol. 4, First Nova Scotian Allotments.

51. Address to settlers, August 21, 1797; Council minutes, October 12 and 29, November 11, 1793, CO 270/2; June 3, 1794, CO 270/2; Falconbridge, *Narrative of Two Voyages to the River Sierra Leone*, p. 271 n.; Cox-George, p. 26.

52. Macaulay Journal, March 19, 1796; January 9, 1797; Council minutes, June 30, 1796, January 4, 1797, CO 270/4; Cox-George, p. 27.

53. Governor and council to Thornton, October 7, 1796, CO 268/5; Macaulay Journal, September 16, 1796.

54. Council minutes, April 1, 1794, CO 270/2; March 22, 1796, CO 270/4; Macaulay to Thornton, October 6, 1796.

55. Council minute, January 29, 1796, CO 270/3; Macaulay Journal, December 8, 1796. When the grants were formally registered, there were ten white landowners, Council minute, March 27, 1797, CO 270/4.

56. Macaulay Journal, December 15, 10, 22, 1796; Council minute, December 25, 1796, CO 270/4.

57. Macaulay Journal, December 21, 1796. All but Carrol were from Birchtown.

58. Macaulay Journal, August 5, 1797; Council minute, August 17, 1797, CO 270/4.

59. Macaulay Journal, August 21, 1797; Address to colonists, August 21, 1797 Council minute, August 22, 1797, CO 270/4; Macaulay Journal, August 19 and 22, 1797.

60. Provincial land records show grants and warrants registered to blacks. See Gilroy, *Loyalists and Land Settlement in Nova Scotia.*

61. Macaulay Journal, August 26, 1797. Macaulay speaks of DuBois as author an odd mistake. It was written ''to revenge himself on the Company by abusing them in England and by stirring up strife in Sierra Leone,'' he told the settlers.

62. Macaulay Journal, September 30, October 2, 1797; Knutsford, p. 175 Macaulay to Thornton, December 1, 1797; Knutsford, p. 176; Ludlam to governor and council, November 17, 1801.

63. Leaster to Clarkson, March 30, 1796; Macaulay Journal, April 8, 1797 Snowball and Hutchinson to Clarkson, May 24, 1796; King to Clarkson January 16, 1798, both Clarkson Papers, BL Add. MSS. 41,263; Macaulay Journal (Mills), November 12, 1798.

64. Hutchinson and Murray to Clarkson, May 24, 1796, Clarkson Papers, BL Add. MSS. 41,263.

65. King to Clarkson, June 1, 1797, January 16, 1796; Clarkson to King October 2, 1797, *ibid.*; Council minute, December 13, 1799, CO 270/4 notifying the Pirate's Bay breakaways that their Freetown lots would be confiscated.

Chapter 17

FULFILLING A PROPHECY

> Ethiopia shall soon stretch out her hands unto God.
> —PSALMS 68:31

The work of proselytizing native-born Africans—the great object of the Sierra Leone settlement's sponsors—was begun, not by salaried chaplains or British-sponsored missionaries, but by Boston King, the black loyalist carpenter. Like David George, Moses Wilkinson and Cato Perkins who brought whole congregations, and thus the dissenting Protestant faith, to tropical Africa, he is an almost forgotten figure. Of all the innovations the Nova Scotians introduced to their adopted Africa—distinctive speech, dress, foods, ideas of land tenure and government—the most striking in many ways was their religion. Whether it was Baptist, Wesleyan Methodist or Countess of Huntingdon by name, it was an amalgam of Christian Scripture and the rich and rowdy forms of worship developed on the North American frontier.

Under the peculiar conditions of Freetown, the churches (or meetinghouses, for the Anglican faith supported by the Sierra Leone Company held exclusive right to the appellation of church) became far more important than they had been even in Nova Scotia. They were wellsprings of social as well as spiritual life, and above all, they were political centers. Topical issues were debated in them nightly, and it was in this atmosphere that the foundations of their black nationalism were laid.[1]

Boston King began to satisfy his old hunger to carry Christianity to the Africans upon arrival in Sierra Leone. He took his turn preaching to the Methodists but also went on Sundays to preach at nearby towns, and to get more time for "conversing" with the Africans, he asked Governor Dawes to let him work at Clarkson's Plantation on the opposite Bulom Shore. The governor did better, and on August 3, 1793, he appointed King a missionary and schoolteacher at £60 a year. He was to devote any

337

spare time to cutting ship timbers for James Watt, the overseer, who treated King kindly and lent him six men to help build a house. At first, the Africans were reluctant to send their children to him. So in his inaugural sermon—delivered through Prince George as interpreter— King exhorted the parents:

> It is a good thing that God has made the White People and that he has inclined their hearts to bring us into this country, to teach you his ways . . . and if you will obey his commandments he will make you happy in this world, and in that which is to come. . . . He now gives you an opportunity of having your children instructed in the Christian Religion. But if you neglect to send them, you must be answerable to God for it.

The number of scholars rapidly rose from four to twenty, as "apt to learn as any children I have known." King taught them the alphabet, simple spelling and the Lord's Prayer. He was not sanguine about winning their parents from their "evil habits" without a visitation from the Lord. Macaulay, calling at the mission, thought he diagnosed part of the trouble. King, although zealous, had not sufficiently clear views of the Gospel to "unfold them" to those unacquainted with such abstruse subjects. "It is absurd for a man, such as King has done, to insist much on Faith in Jesus Christ without explaining beforehand, who Jesus Christ was, and what was the occasion of his advent."[2]

King knew his own inadequacies and leaped at the chance to sail to England with Governor Dawes in March, 1794, to train as a teacher. He stayed there, associating with various Methodists, including Dr. Thomas Coke, until the autumn of 1796, with much of his time spent at Kingswood school near Bristol.[3] However friendly his reception, King felt his own shortcomings so keenly that he determined never to preach in public among these "wise and judicious people." They finally overcame his modesty, and one Sunday he was particularly blessed and found it possible for the first time to love white people:

> I had suffered greatly from the cruelty and injustice of the Whites which induced me to look upon them, in general, as our enemies: And even after the Lord had manifested his forgiving mercy to me, I still felt at times an uneasy distrust and shyness towards them; but on that day the Lord removed all my prejudices; for which I bless his holy Name.[4]

In King's absence Lazarus Jones, brother of James, now the teacher at Granville Town, was given the Bulom missionary post. Macaulay rated Lazarus as "without an exception the most intelligent" of the Nova Scotians, and honest and humble as well.[5]

In late 1796 King returned to a colony in turmoil over the imposition of the quitrent and developments viewed by many as threats to religious freedom. On the death of James Jones, King became the Granville Town teacher. He earned Macaulay's praise for being "humble & teachable & willing to adopt any plan I suggest." When the school enrollment sank to twelve there, King was transferred to a Freetown school. He died about 1802 in the Sherbro, whether a trader or missionary there we do not know. But he was faithful to his dream of working among Africans.[6]

David George's missionary ambitions were probably aroused during his visit to England. He had told Governor Clarkson of his hope of meeting Baptist brethren in Britain, and he had applied directly to Henry Thornton as well. The latter authorized five guineas to be paid him for his expenses, and he sailed with Clarkson in December, 1792. From the time of their meeting on the wharf at Shelburne, Clarkson had found George a staunch supporter, and in Sierra Leone he had had "the firmness to preach against Thomas Peters' conduct, altho he was threatened with assassination for so doing."[7] Chaplain Melvill Horne gave George letters of introduction to several clergymen, including John Newton. The Freetown Baptists were left in the charge of the elders, Hector Peters, John Colbert and John Ramsay. The visit was a triumph for George. His life story was told to Dr. John Rippon, and the Reverend Samuel Pearce of Birmingham, an ardent promoter of missionary activity, became a correspondent of George's and, according to his biographer, never rested until the missionary society which he had helped found sent two men to the colony in 1795, Jacob Grigg and James Rodway. George was in England for six months and went home with new clothes and gifts totaling £150. When he was dictating his memoir, George told his English friends that Clarkson "was a very kind man to me and to every body; he is very free and good natured, and used to come to hear me preach, and would sometimes sit down at our private meetings; and he liked that I should call my last child by his name." But when they parted in England, after Clarkson had been fired by the company, the ex-governor detected a certain coolness which he attributed to directors' efforts to "wean away" George's affections. His suspicion was confirmed when from Sierra Leone Myles Dixon wrote that "Mr. George has spoke very much against you since he has come back," and Clarkson scribbled on the cover of the letter "David George's Ingratitude."[7] Macaulay reported to Thornton that George "talks highly of England and the great kindness he experienced. . . . The humility of English Gentlemen is his constant theme, and he tells the settlers in one of his whispers, that they have more pride than all the great & wise & rich men he met with in England."[8]

By contrast, King, who had been promised free passage by the company to and from England if he would work to support himself there, saw the promise broken. Because he went down the Thames to visit Clarkson and his wife at Purfleet, Thornton ordered the captain to charge King 15 guineas for his passage. Reporting this to Clarkson, King wrote, "but Sir I regardeth not because I know I shall be able to pay them and I do ashoure it will only serve To attch my love more to you because I knew it was only out of Spite."[9]

George's loyalty to the governor of the day was well known in the colony, and the more radical Methodists believed he was the carrier—and even inventor—of many tales "against those who differ from them in things which pertain to religion."[10]

The Sierra Leone Company and its agents gave lip service to the idea of using the blacks as instruments for evangelizing Africa, but they did little to make this happen, and after the first year or two, nothing at all. The English Baptists, however, because of their contact with David George, John Cuthbert and John Kizell, hoped to see the black preachers "remove themselves as Missionaries into some of the Villages of the natives, who have manifested a desire to be instructed in the manners and religion of the settlers" as soon as their places could be filled by others in Freetown. The Baptists were vigilant about religious liberty in the colony, publicly announcing that it would be a great blunder and a blow to missionary effort to let any sect "usurp authority by *establishing* itself" in Sierra Leone.[11] The Sierra Leone Baptists were "a *handful of corn upon the top of a mountain.*" The prophecy that "Ethiopia shall soon stretch out her hands unto God" seemed ready for fulfillment. "Who can tell but that you, and all the godly settlers with you, may be come to *Africa* for such a time as this; and that by the *little leaven* at *Sierra Leone*, the whole continent shall in some future period be leavened!"[12]

In 1795 George intended to go with Thomas London, a Nova Scotian born in Africa as interpreter, to preach inland, but the plan was blocked by an intertribal war. London, age forty-one when he migrated from Birchtown to Sierra Leone, was a cooper who had served in the engineers after his escape from slavery in Charleston. He left the colony to set up his own trading post at Wongapung, where he could also teach or preach. Henry Beverhout was to live and preach there for a time, and London entertained exploring visitors from Freetown with chicken and palm-oil dinners.[13]

Mingo Jordan gave missionary service, in a way, when he was appointed teacher of the special class of African children sent into Freetown for schooling. Among four settlers who struck out on their own to grow rice on a large scale on the Rokel River was one who could read and who was asked by African neighbors to instruct them. A Rokel headman, Smart, impressed with the Freetown schools, arranged with a Methodist preacher to come to his town.[14]

Many churchgoing Nova Scotians saw themselves as evangelists, to judge from a fragment of a Baptist sermon (very likely David George's) which was reported to England by the company's chaplain. The text was from Exodus 14:13, and the preacher "made a pretty comparison between the state of the Israelites and his hearers, in the following words, or nearly so:

> we all mind since it was so with us; we was in slavery not many years ago! Some maybe worse oppressed dan oders, but we was all under de yoke; and what den? God saw our afflictions, and heard our cry, and showed his salvation, in delivering us, and bringing us over de mighty waters to dis place. Now, stand still and see de salvation of God. God make his salvation go from dis city, tro' dis heaten land; and as Moses and de children of Israel sung a song when dey were delivered, and had seen de salvation of God, so I hope to see de heatens about us going tro' de streets of dis city, singing hallelujahs and doxologies to God. I hope to see it. Now, it is said, dey soon forgot his works, dey murmur 'gainst God, and his servant Moses. Take care, my friends, and do not like dem; stand still, &c see what God is still doing for our nation, putting into de hearts of his people, to come from far distant nation, to come over de mighty waters, and great deep, to bring de salvation of God to dis nation, to Africans. . . .[15]

Cato Perkins was unsuccessful in obtaining a Huntingdon mission in 1793 and 1794, but the Reverend Thomas Haweis saw the opportunity in Sierra Leone. The parent Anglican Church, however, would not ordain the available candidates. Haweis said, "I hope the Lord will yet open our way into Africa. Never did the access seem more promising. If a zealous able minister or two were then assisted by the serious blacks, some impression might be made on the natives."[16]

Melvill Horne joined the company, not just to serve as its chaplain in Freetown, but to establish a mission at Robana, Naimbana's town. He delivered a single sermon to a mixed audience of Africans, settlers and "gentlemen of the colony" at Signor Domingo's town in early 1793 and gave up all hope of a missionary career because, to his bitter regret, "I saw I could not carry my point." His sermon, to which the Africans reportedly listened with round eyes, was printed in England as "The *only* Discourse which has been delivered to the Natives in the Western parts of Africa" and was entitled "We Preach Christ Crucified." Each sentence had to be relayed through an interpreter.[17] He spent the rest of his fourteen months in Sierra Leone writing an emotional appeal to Christians to become missionaries. It was credited with helping establish in 1795 the London Missionary Society and successors.[18] His dream was greeted on the scene with some skepticism by fellow officers, who were invited to contribute 5 to 10 guineas each toward it. The idea of converting *"Grown up Natives"* seemed "foolish, and . . . fruitless" to John Gray. Not only did Horne not speak a word of Temne, but "as King Jimmy says, 'this Country People no like dry Palavers.' "[19]

Macaulay sensibly concluded in 1797, after disillusioning trials with Methodist laymen sent by Dr. Coke, that until missionaries developed the "gift of tongues," little could be done, and he proposed stationing candidates along the coast to learn local languages, customs, laws and religions before they tried to penetrate the interior. But there was little enough encouragement for missions. However eager the Africans were to acquire reading and writing skills to deal with foreign traders, they were satisfied with their traditional spiritual life, and John McCormack, the Irish merchant who spent most of his adult life in Sierra Leone, was to say in 1830, "I do not think there is an instance of one native, turning Christian."[20]

The first missionaries sent to Sierra Leone were Jacob Grigg and James Rodway. Grigg, from Cornwall, was a student at the Baptist Academy in Bristol when he applied to the Particular Baptist Society for Propagating the Gospel Amongst the Heathen for a post. Rodway was a new minister at Burton-upon-Trent and offered to go with Grigg. Both carried letters of recommendation to George, Cuthbert and Kizell. Rodway wrote home of his new friends, "as to their outward hue they are black—by grace they are comely, and brethren in Christ." George reassured the English sponsors that the missionaries appeared "two most excellent young men." The Freetown Baptists held prayer meetings on the first Tuesday of each month "for the success of the Gospel in all the churches, and *for its spread throughout the whole earth*," with a special day of fasting and prayer for the missionaries.

Rodway was continually ill, however, and after a relatively inactive eight months, he returned to England. Grigg went to Port Loko on January 5, 1796, with John Kizell, who was to set up a company factory there. Grigg disliked the combination of Christianity with commerce, particularly since a slave factor in the town consistently undersold Kizell, whose higher prices were set by the company and resented by the customers. Their being together, Grigg pointed out, "made the natives suspect the goods were *mine*," and he could make no progress in his mission. He returned to Freetown to learn Temne, teach[21] and preach in first the Baptist and later the Methodist meetinghouses.

Macaulay himself was probably the most persevering missionary of those first years. He worked with the African children sent to the settlement for education now, as for generations they had been sent to Europe. At first, the children were put in a class (under Mingo Jordan), and then Macaulay brought them into his household, in care of Mrs. Perth, so that he could protect them from contaminating town influences. All the men whom the company chose to govern Sierra Leone were Christians, but religion seemed to obsess Macaulay. Especially during his second tour of duty in Africa, after his betrothal to Selina Mills, the protégée of Hannah More, he absorbed himself in the schools and the religious instruction of the colony. He had learned from Mrs. More how to run Sunday schools, and he now introduced them into Sierra Leone. Macaulay was never happier than when with his "little family" of some twenty-five boys and girls. With servants, and their children, his household numbered around forty.[22]

He had returned to Sierra Leone with John Clarke, a Scots Presbyterian, the most vigorous chaplain the company had recruited thus far.[23] Macaulay set up a Sunday school for about 200 settler children, meeting at 5 P.M. The chaplain served as catechist and Bible study teacher. Schoolteachers were required to attend with their classes. (Rather than attend, John Garvin, a Methodist and company-employed teacher, resigned and took up preaching.) Some of the parents looked on, but Macaulay dared not encourage more of them to come for fear of alarming "the self-created preachers" who were holding their own services. A separate Sunday school for the African children and houseboys was held afterward. Macaulay loved to return from a day's exertions to a "hearty welcome from my children," and he could boast, "The most absolute peace reigns in my family. . . . We really eat our bread in quietness, and my will is generally the law to all within our pales." To leave his African family became Macaulay's sole regret when it was time to go back to England for good.[24]

His Sunday schools relied on rewards instead of punishments. Children who under the traditional schoolmasters' "system of terror" were thought "dull, stupid & intractable" now performed well. Twice a year there was a prize giving. In June, pupils with model behavior received hats (if boys) and handkerchiefs (if girls). On New Year's Day the top three boys and three girls were given complete outfits, and fifty other children had lesser awards. All the children would then march from the church to Thornton Hill to dine on stewed beef with yams and rice pudding under a marquee. Clarke would preach, and the children sing. Like their elders, the Nova Scotian children sang beautifully. Of one church service, Macaulay wrote, "no sooner had our Children raised their voices and joined in full Choir, than an effect was produced . . . like that of Electricity. The involuntary tear started into the Eye of almost every one. . . ."[25]

One of the Sunday school's brightest boys died after being attacked by a shark. Macaulay comforted the bereaved parents with a recital of the boy's achievements at Sunday school. All the schoolchildren and most of the adult population attended the boy's funeral. Such rites often drew hundreds, marching, singing, to the burial ground.[26]

The settlers' religious vitality was remarked from the first. Most of them conducted family prayers night and morning, as well as attended their chapels. When Clarkson left, he mentioned, in addition to the established church, "4 or 5 meeting houses" with George, Wilkinson, Joseph Brown and Mingo Jordan as preachers. Mrs. Falconbridge counted seven, each with one or more preacher, who alternated at the all-night prayer meetings. "I never met with, heard, or read of, any set of people observing the same appearance of godliness, for I do not remember, since they first landed here, my ever awaking . . . without hearing preachings. . . ." At another time it was said there were eleven meetings and twenty-two preachers. They habitually "repair to their respective places of worship in a neat and orderly manner," Clarkson had said. Joseph Leonard and his two daughters, Flora and Phoebe, who also taught school, used to lead "a long train of well dressed and healthy children" to the Anglican service. On a Sunday there was some service somewhere at almost every hour "as in London," and groups met in homes "to hold conversations on Religious subjects both on Sundays and other days."[27]

There were frequent intervals when the Anglican church had no incumbent and the governor then became chaplain. The longest such period was Clarkson's stint from April to September, 1792. It was already a tradition among the blacks to find political leaders among their preachers, and Clarkson's chaplaincy strengthened his bonds with the Nova Scotians. His major addresses were sermons delivered from the pulpit. He came down in history, as viewed in Sierra Leone, as a "philosopher-saint." Clarkson became very proud of his "Sunday flock." Dr. Winterbottom, upon arrival, was much impressed with the "solemn and orderly" behavior of the worshipers. Macaulay did not like to substitute for the chaplain. To act as intermediary "with the throne of Grace" was too solemn an undertaking. Both men read sermons by others, Bishop Wilson's for Clarkson and, often, Henry Thornton's compositions for Macaulay.[28]

One of Freetown's lasting claims to fame was its strict Sabbath observance, inaugurated by mutual agreement between Clarkson and the settlers. He proposed in May, 1792, the establishment of Sunday schools and the prohibition of Sunday trading. The people added that "they had often with grief observed the practice of fishing on Sunday," and Clarkson promised to try to stop that. Sunday, May 13, 1792, became "the first Sabbath instituted in that part of Africa according to the custom of . . . the Protestant persuasion."[29]

Some settlers were too puritanical even for Clarkson. In the initial period of hardship and depression, he had tried to encourage music and dancing "with a view of drawing away melancholy . . . which in this Country is just as fatal as poison," only to have Henry Beverhout reproach him for "downright impiety." Clarkson dismissed him as a "well meaning man but being uneducated, Bigotry has got possession of his mind." On one memorable church outing, a party from Freetown, including Chaplain Horne, Dawes, Clarkson and a number of Nova Scotians, went by boat to Granville Town for an afternoon service. "In the evening," Clarkson recounted, "we returned by moonlight, the weather calm and serene, all the company in the boats joining in singing hymns and praises to God for the mercies bestowed upon us, and for the blessings likely to arise to the poor pagan inhabitants of this unhappy country."[30]

The gentlemanly Thomas Cooper set to music for the Anglican church Alexander Pope's ode "The Dying Christian to His Soul."

Horne began his ministry with an effort to restrain the fervor of the black preachers. He was effective: His Sunday sermon was "like a pitch pipe" that kept the Methodists in tune throughout the week, Macaulay observed. And James Strand thought that after Horne's inaugural sermon, the "prayers of the Settlers . . . instead of being indecent & arrogant vociferation sometimes endangering the suffocation of the black preacher . . . are now uttered with a lower humble & devout voice." Perhaps because of his obligation to the preachers for supporting him many times, Clarkson did not join "the fashion to cry down these different sects, and the Black Preachers for their ignorance, extravagant notions, and apparently ridiculous way of expressing their thoughts."[31] Another observer wrote:

> They have such a flow of spirits in prayer that I am sometimes afraid they will hurt themselves. . . . their joy or sorrow is naturally excessive. In celebrating the divine praises, all stand on their feet; the men sing at one time, the women at another, then all unite together. Their tunes have a great variety of music in them, and they are sung so well, that I do not remember to have ever heard such melody. In prayer, every one kneels; many utter the word *Amen* to most of the petitions, while others are using different expressions. This was disagreeable to me at first, but it is not so now.

He had heard no doctrinal sermon from any of them, which was just as well, since they worked all day and had no time for study. "But they seem to speak their own sentiments as they occur with ease and freedom."[32]

Macaulay was told of a Methodist revival meeting at Granville Town, where "the wildest extravagances had been committed. . . . People falling down as if dead and remaining in a trance for some time. Others bellowing with all their might, pretended that the Devil overpowered by the preachers of the word but unwilling to leave them was wrestling with their spirits." Rodway thought that the Methodist preachers sometimes competed to see who "shall bawl the loudest." He took down some of their expressions: "May thy word be quick & powerful, sharper than a two edged sword, to cut sin from joint to joint and from marrow to

marrow." And when praying for the unconverted, "Lord take them &
shake them over the belly of hell, but do not let them drop in."[33]

An eleven-year-old girl, describing her conversion under "Daddy
Moses" Wilkinson, said she went to him under *"conviction of sin,"* and
when she prayed as he directed, the spirit of God came to her and forgave
her everything. Wilkinson's ways with converts—the "indecorum" of
the girls, the "affected tones in which they delivered their stories," the
"unscriptural remarks & advices of Moses"—shocked Clarke. The
people said there were 1,000 spirits in heaven converted by Wilkinson's
ministry. The most sensational convert was Elliott Griffith. After "loud
and vehement declarations" in the Granville Town streets and round-the-
clock prayers by Methodist preachers, "god was pleased to reveal
himself to him." Macaulay was probably not the only one who suspected
Griffith's straitened circumstances might have helped him see the light;
the Africans of Robana were bringing palavers for debt against him, and
he wished to regain the protection of the colony.[34]

One settler believed that the Lord had told him that a certain plant was
a "chocolate plant." It was not remotely like one, said Macaulay,
venturing to "tell him that the Spirit who spoke to him was a lying
spirit." While her husband was in England, the second Mrs. Boston
King became convinced she was haunted by the ghost of a dead man. She
wanted the chaplain to exorcise it. It was logical that spiritual experiences would have weight with this generation, few of whom could read
the Bible for guidance. It had been the same with whites of their station in
Nova Scotia and the United States. Therefore, a sermon by Horne,
intended to expose the Methodists' "folly" in taking "dreams, visions
and the most ridiculous bodily sensations as incontestable proofs of their
acceptance with God" (a woman, for example, had spoken of the spirit
of God entering through her nose as a "warm stream"), produced a
strong reaction. Henry Beverhout denounced the chaplain and the company and compared Governor Dawes to Pharaoh, urging his listeners to
bear their sufferings like Israelites until God delivered them.[35]

Many of the dissenting settlers attended Anglican services as well as
their own, but after Macaulay took his adamant stand on the return of
company property "stolen" or "salvaged" in the French occupation,
Wilkinson's followers began a boycott which lasted several years. The
governor asserted that "those . . . who have fattened on robbery & spoil
are the longest & loudest & most punctual in their prayers." He suspected that Methodist women prostituted their daughters to visitors. It

was a favorite theme of his that religious zeal and moral rectitude did not go hand in hand in Sierra Leone. Even David George, whose Baptists rarely suffered opprobrium in Macaulay's records, encouraged drinking after he opened an alehouse to help support his large family. Rebuked by Macaulay, George gave up the license.[36] No sect was more preoccupied with religious duties than the Huntingdons. Their daily ritual began with a 5 A.M. prayer service (3 A.M. on the anniversary of their coming to Africa and on Good Friday), and each night there was a sermon. Sunday had not a moment free from prayers, meetings, services and Sunday school. It ended with visits to the sick. There were quarterly communions and once or twice a year a "love feast" at which people shared bread, water, songs and prayers. Many Huntingdonians in Macaulay's eye were "very disorderly" and guilty of "rank antinomianism" in private. He claimed that three-fourths of the preachers were only nominal Christians or of bad moral character.[37] Ignorance was their excuse, Horne believed.

> The conjugal union is little understood or regarded and a woman who has preserved a character for chastity . . . is hardly to be found. The young people are licentious, but this is easily accounted for by those who understand the manner of life common among slaves in America and our Islands. . . . The mercenariness of the people, their exorbitant demands and expectations, and the rooted hatred for the whites which is perpetually recurring, are the most unpleasant things I know of.

But he was optimistic that eventually a "black colony will be formed on that coast, which for opulence, religion and laws may be a model for Africa."[38]

Enough has been said of the settlers' churches to show how fundamental they were to their lives. They were the only institutions of their own creation, and they guarded them jealously. Only a man as self-righteous as Macaulay would therefore have been surprised at their violent reaction to the "crusade" he and Clarke launched in 1796. It was well intended—to improve the quality and discipline of worship by guidance and example—but it led to a near insurrection among the blacks. In this they were joined (some would say led) by two whites, the missionary Grigg and the schoolteacher Garvin.

Grigg brought to the colony a much more liberal, even radical outlook than any previous European had done. He was steeped in English nonconformity and a sympathizer with the American and French revolutions. Amid false alarms of another French attack earlier that year, he had delivered a pacifist sermon from the Methodist pulpit (the loyal David George had banned him from the Baptist) and urged the settlers not to work on the fortifications. Stiv Jakobsson points out that in this Grigg may have echoed the settlers' pro-French views, but he also represented the antiwar feeling among British Baptists during the American conflict and the joy with which many nonconformists greeted the French rebellion as a new age with greater liberty for dissenters. In contrast, Evangelicals like Macaulay disliked "French levelling and republicanism." Furthermore, Grigg sided with the settlers over the quitrent, citing American arguments about taxation without representation, and he favored there being more than one political party—a ·"strange . . . dogma" to Macaulay, who had no time for pluralism.

Garvin was a man of lesser abilities and a "firebrand." He had applied unsuccessfully to the Baptists to be made a missionary, then found that the Methodists would support him as a preacher once he had resigned his company post.[39]

The reasons for what Macaulay described as their campaign against Clarke and the Established Church again partly lie, as Jakobsson has seen, outside Sierra Leone, for an uncommon degree of religious freedom already prevailed in the colony. But British Baptists, influenced by the separation of church and state in America, were fighting for equal rights through the abolition of the Corporation and Test acts.[40]

In Clarke, the colony had acquired a cheerful and tireless man. On Sundays he would end a day of preaching and teaching "scarce able to speak." He had to change his sweat-soaked jacket, trousers and shirt after each sermon, even though the church was still half finished and open to the breeze. Macaulay thought it was Clarke's strong Scots accent and penchant for minutely detailed argument that muted his impact, but Adam Afzelius, the outsider, interestingly enough believed Clarke to be too "fanatic or bigoted" to succeed among the heathen or even Christians of a different belief.[41] Clarke had been given a warm welcome. His first sermon on March 20, 1796, with nearly everyone in attendance at the governor's request, had brought such comments as "What a dear man you have brought us." A few days later Clarke spoke at George's Baptist meeting, and Macaulay reported, "The old man is quite delighted with him." George arranged his own services at an earlier hour so his parishioners could attend Clarke's sermons on Sundays.[42] In April, Clarke began, with the consent of the preachers, to visit settlers in their homes and, denying that he was attempting to become their pastor, to talk of their Christian duties, the instruction of their children and kindred subjects. Heartened by early success, he proposed that the preachers do as David George had done and alter their hours of worship so that more people could come to hear him. This raised the hackles of the Methodists. Some received his calls coolly, and when he asked them their names or family particulars, they said, "We are Methodists . . . we will not change our religion for anything you can say to us." One couple, told that he wanted to "persuade them to come to Christ," replied, "Sir we don't want you. We are in Christ already and have been for these 22 years. . . . if you were not lazy, you would go among the natives." They showed him two books by Wesley which "we abide by." Could they read them? he asked. "We can't read it is true, but *our souls* can read them."

Undaunted, Clarke capped his eager advances with morning and evening sermons on May 22, 1796, on Luke 14:23: "And the lord said unto the servant, Go out into the highways and hedges, and compel them to come in, that my house may be filled." He was careful to say that persuasion was the only compulsion meant.[43]

The colony seethed with rumors that the government intended to close the meetinghouses because Clarke was said to regard the black preachers as ignorant blasphemers. An angry meeting was held with fourteen of them which nearly ended in blows. It was not, one would have thought, the ideal time to meddle further. Yet on July 5, 1796, Macaulay promulgated a new law taking marriage out of the hands of the preachers. This time David George, who had previously defended Clarke publicly, led the denunciations. Macaulay's act was not even as liberal as the current British law. He had used *Blackstone's Commentaries* but did not have a copy of the 1781 act which gave non-Anglican preachers the right to perform marriages for members in their churches. Eighteen months later he admitted to Thornton that his law might well be amended. As proclaimed, it directed that all banns must be published on three successive Sundays in the Church of England, with ceremonies performed by a person "in holy orders" or by the governor or his appointee. The hundreders and tithingmen had seen and approved the measure by a "large majority," although some preachers among them "were very tenacious of what they imagined was a religious right" and debated it several hours. They may have recalled that in their time in Nova Scotia the government had put marriages under the control of the Anglicans, but the law was widely flouted. Macaulay was impelled to introduce the law, it seems, because of two cases of bigamy and some instances of marriages dissolved by the couples themselves.[44]

Mild David George told Clarke they would never submit to such a law; it would be resisted "even to blood." He had no trouble alerting the Methodists, the seedbed of sedition in Macaulay's opinion. They were the largest organized body in the colony, and they had in Isaac Anderson, Henry Beverhout, Luke Jordan, Stephen Peters and Nathaniel Snowball leaders who were talented and eloquent. For perhaps the first time, the Methodists gathered in a single body on the following Sunday for what was advertised as their last free meeting. As Macaulay heard it, some preachers declared that the governor was going to force the people to his church, silence the preachers and "make Calvinists and Presbyterians" of all. The general answer was: "We will die first." George went to Macaulay in a last-ditch effort to avert trouble, and the Baptists, on his advice, ceased open opposition. But the Methodists sent a letter over the names of 128 men representing "The Independent Methodist Church of Freetown." They were sorry, they said, to act in such a way as to confirm his already poor opinion of their loyalty:

> But when we see our religious rights struck at, all regard for our own Characters is lost. . . . We consider this new Law as an encroachment on our religious rights, and as such we not only Mean to be inattentive to it, but influence the minds of all . . . against it. . . . we are dissenting, and . . . as such we consider ourselves a perfect Church having no need of assistance of any other Church, much less of any wordly power to appoint or perform religious Cerimonies for us, our ministers we consider as much in Holy orders as if they had been sent out by the Presbytery in the Kirk of Scotland. . . . Our meeting House sanctified by the presence of the Almighty we count as fit for any religious purpose as the House you call the Church. We cannot persuade ourselves that Politics and religion have any connection and therefore think it not right for the Governor of the One to be Middling with the other.[45]

Macaulay took his case—that marriage was a civil contract—to the next public gathering, which happened to be a court session. This was one viewpoint in contemporary Britain, but "to Grigg and the lay preachers the marriage ceremony was and was meant to be a religious act.'' Macaulay denounced the Methodists' letter as an act of rebellion. Later, he said, ''numbers'' of the signers protested that they had not understood its full import. Garvin was charged with inspiring the letter and forging the names of Friday Snipe and Stephen Peters to it. Robert Keeling said that his name was used without his consent. Macaulay had the marshal seize all of Garvin's papers in hope of finding the original draft, but nothing was discovered. If indeed ''numbers'' changed their minds, it must have been because they, like Keeling, were dismayed to find that Macaulay considered their protest seditious. Keeling said, ''I have much cause to bless God & the Company, for the goodness done me in bringing me to this place, and I consider myself by duty & gratitude bound to obey the Laws . . . & to live peaceably under this government where I enjoy peace & quietness.''

Although he believed that the protesters acted from ignorance rather than evil intent, Macaulay thought harsh measures were required when a religious body was ''erected into a kind of Jacobin Club,'' with every measure put before the hundreders and tithingmen debated by ''the Junto of preachers.''[46] With the settlers split again into factions, with Clarke once more welcome in the meetinghouses, he could have claimed a victory and forborne to press the issue. But in Britain, the Baptist and Methodist friends of the settlers heard accounts sent by Grigg and Garvin with deepening concern. Macaulay found himself forced to justify his conduct, and this may have caused his implacable anger against the missionary and the teacher. His object was now to get rid of them. Macaulay spent hours, even as the quitrent issue was simmering, building a case against Grigg. He felt a little compassion when Grigg fell ill and his spirit was ''Broken,'' but he dispatched a long complaint to the Baptist missionary society just the same and requested it to recall Grigg. If David George ever suspected the fears of the British Baptists for him, he would be astonished, grumbled the governor.[47]

He told the Baptists that even Grigg admitted now that there had been no real danger to the sects, because a dozen Europeans could not force a thousand ''Africans'' to accept any unpopular measure. Grigg's ''sneers'' at the unfinished Anglican church, his ''insinuations'' that taxes would lead to slavery and his ''holding up to admiration the doctrine of King killing'' were passed over ''because tho they tend to shake our little tottering state to its very base, they cause no alarm to you.'' But Grigg lacked ''moral rectitude'' and must be recalled. Macaulay's journal suggests he suspected insanity in Grigg.[48]

Macaulay was even more upset over a letter which Garvin had sent to the former chaplain Horne, which said, "Mr. M. Storms & rages, like a disappointed tyrant." When he received a copy from Horne in early 1797, Macaulay called a meeting of preachers, with Garvin present, and won the blacks to his side with a three-and-a-half-hour speech. Garvin, however, remained "insolent," and to discredit him completely, Macaulay ordered a public inquiry. It was only a few weeks after the antiwhite election, and he may also have wished to show where the power still lay. Grigg had been the intellectual leader in this dispute, but he had been sent by the British Baptists, and if he were tried, it would confirm their fears of what was happening in Sierra Leone. It might also have ruined the cause of future missions. Garvin was only an ex-employee, a layman supported by his Methodist followers. Macaulay charged him with being an enemy to the company, disturber of the peace, gross slanderer and liar and a danger to the colony's well-being. Garvin pleaded guilty only in part. The "jury" for this show trial consisted of twelve company officers. Macaulay acted as prosecutor, and after wringing corroborating statements out of several settlers and obtaining a verdict of guilty on all counts, he put on his judge's hat to pronounce the sentence of banishment. Garvin had called no witnesses and offered no defense, except to claim that he had acted always as a Methodist.[49]

Macaulay gave Garvin a little money and Grigg "many good advices," and the failed challengers embarked for the United States. A year later Macaulay was still blaming the Methodists' mutinous spirit on the "leaven" introduced by Grigg and Garvin, although it seems clear that since it existed both before and after their interventions, the pair had moved only on an undercurrent. In December, 1798, Garvin wrote to the Methodist preachers from Virginia, where he was teaching, to cherish "the very superior blessings they enjoy at Sierra Leone to what any blacks in America enjoy." That was the month when Clarke, worn out with his service, died. The Methodists, Macaulay noted wryly, "extolled him to the very skies" as "their Father, their best friend." Grigg joined the Emancipating Baptists, who favored complete emancipation as soon as possible, and worked with David Barrow in Virginia and later in Kentucky.[50]

A month after Grigg and Garvin departed, Macaulay invited David George to walk to his mountain farm, established at the directors' request as a healthful retreat and an example of husbandry. The governor wanted to correct the antinomianism of his hardiest supporter. He had been looking for a chance for a "full & free" conversation ever since he had berated the preacher for allowing his son to bring home a girl after their banns were published only once. Macaulay, "with a Bible in my hand," had proved that George had broken three commandments, and the "poor old Man burst into tears!" The conversation this day lasted from noon to midnight. The governor brought up the Baptists' various "delusions," their drinking, neglect of children's instruction, unchastity. He chided George for preaching that "every little sin" meant no loss of interest in Christ for "once in Xt, *always* in Xt. and whom he loves, he loves to the end." Macaulay smothered George's explanations with Scripture until the black man said Macaulay had indeed opened his eyes and he was very thankful. As always, however, Macaulay was dubious whether his "converts" would last, for the antinomian idea was "a most seducing one," requiring no exertion and no "crucifying of lust." For the settlers who did not come to hear the chaplain, it was a choice between the "conscience searing tenets" of the Baptists or Huntingdonians and the "enthusiastic hairbrained unmeaning rhapsodies of our mad Wesleans." "Rivers of water run down Davids eyes because men kept not Gods law," Macaulay mourned to Selina Mills, "I can say that my heart is deeply affected with the sight of people all around me, perishing for lack of knowledge, & arrogantly calling themselves . . . Xtns."[51]

In their correspondence Macaulay and his fiancée frequently exchanged confessions about their faults. On his birthday, May 2, 1797, Macaulay mused on his conduct toward Grigg, Garvin and the others who had angered him. He admitted his hasty temper, love of praise, sensitivity to opposition. He had been slow to pray for them and had heard of their sickness with an indifference "not far removed from malevolence."

"I have laboured much to correct the unkindness of my look & manner," he said, "but I find this difficult." A year later he drew up a set of forty-five resolutions for self-improvement, and No. 15 was "to cultivate a temper of more benignity towards the Settlers, and . . . attend more to the outward expressions of love and kindness."[52]

Mary Perth was another who failed to live up to Macaulay's high expectations. Her husband, Caesar, a carpenter at Birchtown, where their daughter, Susan, was born in 1783, had come with her to Sierra Leone, and seven acres of land were registered in his name. His death had been memorable. Surrounded by weeping friends, he had told them, "Your sorrow is my joy." Clarke later based a sermon about dying saints on Mrs. Perth's account of it. She would have been about fifty-two on reaching Africa, and she established herself as a shopkeeper. At least part of Macaulay's time there, she managed his household and looked after his African family. She also at some time kept an ordinary, or boarding-house, for company staff and took care of their laundry. She owned a house on Water Street, and when a northern climate was recommended for her ailing daughter, she was able to send £150 to Thornton to invest so that their visit to England would be comfortably financed. She was popular with the officers. Dr. Winterbottom wrote from England to "Tell my dear Mary that her cloth pleased very much," and sent his love "to Mary & all my dear Patients."[53]

Clarke was so delighted with her and her sound Methodism that he immortalized her in the *Evangelical Magazine*, where his dispatch, entitled "Singular Piety in a Female African," appeared in 1796. Clarke thought she was then about seventy, but if earlier records are correct, she was in her late fifties. She was a woman "the like of whom I never talked with; she is more like one come down out of heaven to earth, than like one who is only preparing for glory." In the presence of this "militant saint," he blushed and "find I know nothing—freely give vent to my tears . . . hours pass away like minutes." She was his best assistant, next to his Bible. She spoke with childlike simplicity, yet "celestial subliminity." "I need not tell you she is a black," he added. "This I can assure you is no hindrance to our Christian fellowship. I am as happy in her company, and in that of some others, as ever I was in that of any Christian of my own colour."

She was a favorite with Macaulay, too, and through him became known to Hannah More's circle. One day Mrs. Perth entered his room as he was tying a miniature of Miss Mills on a ribbon to wear under his neckcloth. She was delighted and told the governor, "I shall yet see her before I die." She sent presents to the More household—African cloth, a canister of homegrown coffee, some "preserved sweetmeats." Macaulay apologized for the latter, noting the shortage of sugar in the colony. "I am afraid they are not well done, indeed I *see* they are not, but then they are Sierra Leone sweetmeats." Hannah More replied, "We shall be delighted to see a specimen of Mrs. Perth's confectionary talents, after having been used to consider her for her *intellectual accomplishments*, and her talents for religious instruction. Pray remember us kindly to her, and tell her we desire her prayers for our schools."[54]

But her prosperity and her fame "unhinged" her, Macaulay reported sorrowfully (and in immense detail). She became temperamental, arrogant and even, despite her age, a prey to "evils of a certain description.'' She allegedly overcharged her customers, and though it was proved that she was not directly responsible, she was fined $60 for carelessness. The money was paid into the colony's welfare fund.

Macaulay, who used to think of Mrs. Perth "arrived as she is now near the close of what I justly deemed a well spent life, as a fine settg sun about to set but rise again with renewed splendor,'' now discovered she was treating the African children harshly and took them out of her hands but prudently allowed her to go on managing the household. He lectured her until "Her tears began to flow, and she either felt or affected to feel a deep contrition.'' Clarke was convinced of it, and Macaulay prayed she would feel true repentance. She must have done, because when he left Sierra Leone for good on April 4, 1799, he took with him twenty-five of his black pupils and Mrs. Perth and her daughter to look after them. Macaulay, who had dreaded losing the children, "whom God . . . had placed under my care,'' was taking them to Clapham to a special school. Mrs. Perth helped with it and the children until her return to Freetown on December 16, 1801. One of the pupils, Elizabeth Gould, came back with her and made her home with Mrs. Perth, who appears to have lost her own daughter. Later she provided meals for the Church Missionary Society clergy, who began their connection with the colony in 1804, and she was married to an unnamed bridegroom on February 13, 1806, according to their reports. By 1813 she had died.[55]

Macaulay severed his personal connection with the Nova Scotians when he returned to England; there are no letters from them in his archive. He retired from his tumultuous governorship to the relative peace of Birchin Lane as secretary of the company. His departure from the colony and his reception in England are a study in contrasts with John Clarkson's. No recorded tears were shed on his leaving, nor did he leave a farewell address or message. In England, Thornton had written in high anticipation to Hannah More, "he will make his triumphal entry into this Island with a train of twenty or thirty little black boys & girls at his heels, the Trophies which he brings with him from Africa.''[56]

NOTES

1. Hair, "Christianity at Freetown from 1792 as a Field for Research,'' pp. 128, 131, 132. It is not intended to duplicate here the studies of settler churches by Fyfe—"The West African Methodists in the Nineteenth Century,'' pp. 22-28; "The Countess of Huntingdon's Connexion in Nineteenth Century Sierra

Leone," pp. 53-61; "The Baptist Churches in Sierra Leone," pp. 55-60—and Walls, "The Nova Scotian Settlers and Their Religion," pp. 19-31.

2. Boston King Narrative, p. 263; Council minute, August 3, 1793, CO 270/2; Macaulay Journal, August 3, 6, September 28, 1793 (all Macaulay papers cited from the Huntington Library).

3. Boston King Narrative, pp. 264, 256. The memoir was written at Kingswood School and dated June 4, 1796. M. Dorothy George, *England in Transition: Life and Work in the Eighteenth Century*, p. 65.

4. Boston King Narrative, p. 264.

5. Council minute, April 1, 1794, CO 270/2; Macaulay Journal, April 4, 1797.

6. Council minute, March 29, 1797, CO 270/4; Macaulay Journal (Mills), April 2, 1797; Council minute, November 10, 1797, CO 270/4.

7. Clarkson to Hartshorne, September n.d., 1793, Clarkson Papers, BL Add. MSS. 41,263.

8. David George Narrative, pp. 483, 484; Carey, *Samuel Pearce, M.A., the Baptist Brainerd*, pp. 26, 179; Clarkson to Gray, July 30, 1793 and Clarkson to Hartshorne, September n.d., 1793, both Clarkson Papers, BL Add. MSS. 41,263; Dixon to Clarkson, October 14, 1793, Sierra Leone Collection, University of Illinois, Chicago Circle; Macaulay Journal, August 11, 1793. George's son, John, inherited some town property from his father (who died in 1810) and became a boatbuilder. Council minute, January 5, 1813, CO 270/13.

9. King to Clarkson, January 16, 1798, Clarkson Papers, BL Add. MSS. 41,263.

10. Jordan and Snowball to Clarkson, July 29, 1796, *ibid.*

11. MS. Accounts of the Particular Baptist Society for Propagating the Gospel Amongst the Heathen, f. 32, quoting Cambridge *Intelligencer*, November 16, 1793.

12. *Periodical Accounts Relative to the Baptist Missionary Society*, vol. 1, p. 102, Baptist Society . . . to the baptized Church of Christ at Sierra Leone, under Brother David George, September 16, 1795.

13. *Baptist Annual Register for 1794-1797*, p. 256; Book of Negroes, PRO 30/55/100, ff. 45-46; Blacks at Birch Town who gave in their names for Sierra Leone, November, 1791, CO 217/63; *Adam Afzelius: Sierra Leone Journal*, January 22, March 18, April 3, 1796.

14. Macaulay Journal, September 18, 1793; Council minutes, September 19, August 23, September 21, 1793, CO 270/2.

15. *Missionary Magazine for 1796*, vol. 1, p. 77, with the heavy italicizing dropped for readability.

16. Wood, "Sierra Leone and Bulama: A Fragment of Missionary History," pp. 18-19.

17. *Baptist Annual Register for 1794-1797*, Horne's sermon, pp. 249-55.

18. Horne, *Letters on Missions: Addressed to the Protestant Ministers of the*

British Churches, pp. v, viii, ix; Macaulay Journal, August 29, 1793; Groves, *The Planting of Christianity in Africa*, p. 199; Jakobsson, *Am I Not a Man and a Brother?*, p. 76.

19. Gray to Clarkson, February 15, 1793, Clarkson Papers, BL Add. MSS. 41,263.

20. Macaulay Journal, August 2, 1797; McCormack testimony, CO 267/92.

21. The first Methodist missionary, George Warren, came in 1811 after appeals from Joseph Brown's Methodists, again on the initiative of the settlers. *Periodical Accounts*, vol. 5, pp. 1, 103, 241-45, 247, 256; Accounts of the Particular Baptist Society, April 7, June 11, 1795, ff. 45, 47; Jakobsson, pp. 84-85.

22. In 1788 it was said that there were usually about fifty African children (some of whose fathers were British traders) in school at Liverpool, as well as others at Bristol and London. Liverpool delegates' letter, Parliamentary Papers, 1789, XXVI, part 1, no. 4; Macaulay Journal, July 16, 1798.

23. *Evangelical Magazine for 1796*, vol. 4, pp. 163-64; Jakobsson, pp. 93-94; Walls, pp. 27-28.

24. Macaulay Journal, May 2, March 27, May 1, September 28, October 16, 8, 13, December 11, 1796; Macaulay Journal (Mills), February 4, June 11, November 7, 1798; Knutsford, *Life and Letters of Zachary Macaulay*, pp. 180, 194-95; Macaulay to Mills, March 25, 1797.

25. Macaulay Journal, May 15, 1796; *Missionary Magazine*, vol. 1, p. 30; Macaulay Journal (Mills), June 11, 1798, January 1, 1799; Macaulay Journal, March 20, 1796.

26. Macaulay Journal, June 11, 1796; Macaulay Journal (Mills), March 23, 1797.

27. Clarkson Journal (Maynard), ff. 501, 600; Falconbridge, *Narrative of Two Voyages to the River Sierra Leone*, p. 201; *Missionary Magazine*, vol. 2, p. 93.

28. Alhadi, *The Re-emancipation of the Colony of Sierra Leone*, p. 10; Clarkson Journal (New York), May 6, 13, 1792; Ingham, *Sierra Leone After One Hundred Years*, p. 70; Clarkson Journal (New York), July 15, 1792; Clarkson Journal (SLS), p. 23; Macaulay Journal (Mills), May 25, 1798.

29. Clarkson Journal (New York), May 7, 1792; Ingham, pp. 66-72; *The Philanthropist*, vol. 4 (1814), p. 254.

30. Clarkson Journal (New York), May 21, 1792; Clarkson Journal (SLS), p. 96; Ingham, pp. 139-40.

31. Armistead, *A Tribute for the Negro*, p. 478; Macaulay to Thornton, December 20, 1797; Strand Journal, September 9, 1797 (wrongly marked August), BL Add. MSS. 12,131; Clarkson Journal (Maynard), November 27, 1792.

32. *Evangelical Magazine for 1796*, vol. 4, p. 420, Letter from a Gentleman [James Wilson] at Freetown, April 22, 1796.

33. Macaulay Journal, October 3, 1793, June 26, 1796; Knutsford, p.

143. Women also preached, and Paul Cuffe in 1811 said "Milia Baxter" (Amilia Buxton) had held services in her home for many years. Spilsbury, *Account of a Voyage to the Western Coast of Africa . . . in 1805*, p. 38; Sheldon H. Harris, "An American's Impressions of Sierra Leone in 1811," p. 38.

34. Macaulay Journal, July 7, May 20, 1796; Macaulay to Thornton, May 30, 1798; Macaulay Journal, October 13, 1793; *Adam Afzelius: Sierra Leone Journal*, June 5, 1795. Griffith had returned to Robana, got rid of his wife, Clara, taken several mistresses, and gone into debt. He died in jail in 1802. Council minute, January 1, 1803, CO 270/8.

35. Macaulay Journal, August 24, December 22, 1796, September 15 and 17, 1793. Beverhout later was fired as a teacher and parish clerk when accused of taking liberties with schoolgirls. Thomas Jones became clerk. Council minute, June 14, 1794, CO 270/2. Beverhout lived and preached for a time at Factory Island and Wongapung. *Adam Afzelius: Sierra Leone Journal*, April 3, 1796.

36. Macaulay Journal, November 26, 1794; Macaulay Journal and letter to Directors, October 6, 1796. George also had a job as a messenger in the company secretary's office. Council minutes, January 1, 1796, CO 270/3 and January 18, 1797, CO 270/4.

37. Elliott, *Lady Huntingdon's Connexion in Sierra Leone*, pp. 20-24; Macaulay Journal, November 23, 1796; Macaulay to Thornton, December 20, 1797.

38. Horne to Haweis, January 28, 1794, in Hair, "Sierra Leone and Bulama." Walls, p. 29, notes how religion welded the settlers together.

39. Jakobsson, pp. 88-91; Macaulay to [Baptists], July 29, 1796; Garvin to Horne, May 16, 1796, in Proceedings of Enquiry, February 22, 1797, CO 270/4.

40. Jakobsson, p. 95; Richard W. Davis, *Dissent in Politics, 1780-1830*, p. 29; Walls, pp. 27-28.

41. *Missionary Magazine*, vol. 1, pp. 79-80, 82; Macaulay to Directors, n.d. [1796]; *Adam Afzelius: Sierra Leone Journal*, May 8, 1796.

42. Macaulay Journal, March 20 and 23, 1796; *Baptist Annual Register for 1794-1797*, p. 409, extract of letter from David George, April 19, 1796.

43. Macaulay Journal, April 23, June 7, May 22, 1796.

44. *Ibid.*, May 30, 1796; Council minute, July 8, 1796, CO 270/4; Jakobsson, p. 97; Macaulay to Thornton, December 20, 1797; Macaulay Journal, July 4, 5, 7, 1796; Bumsted, "Church and State in Maritime Canada, 1749-1807," p. 56; Reverend Jacob Bailey, *The Frontier Missionary*, p. 209; Armstrong, *The Great Awakening in Nova Scotia*, pp. 19-20; MacNutt, *The Atlantic Provinces*, pp. 106-7.

45. Macaulay Journal, July 5, 1796; Knutsford, p. 144; Macaulay to Thornton, December 20, 1797; Knutsford, p. 144, 145; Governor and council to Thornton, July 30, 1796, CO 268/5.

46. Macaulay Journal, July 14, 1796; Knutsford, p. 147; Jakobsson, p. 96;

Council minute, July 18, 1796; Macaulay Journal, July 21, 1796; Proceedings of court of Enquiry, February 22, 1797, CO 270/4. The African-born Keeling later left his wife, Amy, and four children to live on the Rokel River, WO 1/352, 1802 census.

47. Macaulay Journal, July 26, 27, 30, August 8, 1796; Macaulay to [Baptists], July 29, 1796; Macaulay to Thornton, December 20, 1797; Macaulay Journal (Mills), October 5, 1796.

48. Macaulay to [Baptists], July 29, 1796; Macaulay Journal, November 30, September 12, 1796.

49. Garvin to Horne, May 16, 1796, in Proceedings of court of Enquiry, February 22, 1797, CO 270/4, quoted in Macaulay Journal (Mills), January 22, 1797; Macaulay to Thornton, February 13, 1797; Macaulay Journal (Mills), February 13, 18, March 8, 25, 1797; Knutsford, p. 162; Jakobsson, pp. 98-99; Proceedings of court of Enquiry, February 22, 1797; Macaulay Journal (Mills), February 22, 1797; Council minute, February 25, 1797, CO 270/4.

50. Macaulay Journal (Mills), March 16, 1797; Macaulay to Mills, December 1, 1797; Macaulay Journal (Mills), December 23 and 7, 1798; Woodson, *The History of the Negro Church*, pp. 33, 35; Benedict, *A General History of the Baptist Denomination in America*, vol. 2, p. 247; Hartzell, "Jacob Grigg— Missionary and Minister." Grigg died in Virginia in 1835 or 1836.

51. Macaulay Journal, April 29, 1796; Macaulay Journal (Mills), February 17, April 25, 1797.

52. *Ibid.*, May 2, 1797; July 1, 1798.

53. Muster Book of Birch Town, 1784, PAC, MG 9 B 9-14, vol. 1; Montagu, *Ordinances of the Settlement of Sierra Leone*, vol. 4, First Nova Scotian Allotments; *Evangelical Magazine for 1796*, vol. 4, p. 452; Council minutes, December 13, 1794, March 30, 1795, CO 270/3; Macaulay Journal, February 22, 1797; Philip, *The Life, Times and Missionary Enterprises of the Rev. John Campbell*, pp. 176-77; Dawes to Clarkson, December 9, 1796, Clarkson Papers, BL Add. MSS. 41,263; *The Philanthropist*, vol. 5 (1815), p. 251; Macaulay to Mills, June 8, 1797; Winterbottom to Macaulay, June 23, 1796.

54. *Evangelical Magazine for 1796*, vol. 4, pp. 460-64; Macaulay to Mills, February 4, June 8, 1797; Roberts, *Letters of Hannah More to Zachary Macaulay*, p. 16.

55. Macaulay to Thornton, May 30, 1798; Macaulay to Mills, May 23, July 2, 1798; Council minute, November 10, 1797, CO 270/4; Council minute, December 16, 1801, CO 270/6; WO 1/352; 1802 census; Renner to CMS, October 15, 1896, and Renner Journal, February 13, 1806, CMS CA1/E-1; *The Philanthropist*, vol. 5 (1815), p. 251.

56. Thornton to More, October 26, 1798, Thornton Papers, Wigan Public Libraries.

Chapter 18
THE NEW SOCIETY

> I think that colony different from all others . . . and if it is
> hesitated to bring forward the black population, it cannot
> succeed.
>
> —JOHN McCORMACK[1]

The early, essentially political struggles of the African-American
settlers had profound effects on the economic and social structure of their
emerging community. It might seem a frontier village to European or
American visitors, yet with its 1,200 residents and some 300 African
transient workers, it was the largest port on Africa's west coast. As mud
huts and canvas houses gave way to stone and timber edifices, the
immigrants laid the foundations of a society which would be known in the
next century as Creole, neither African nor Anglo-American, but drawing on all three sources for its ingredients.

Considering how thoroughly the French had destroyed the principal
buildings in the autumn of 1794, the physical recovery was remarkable.
Before the French sack, the major buildings had stood along Water
Street, parallel with the shore. As seen by an English slave ship captain
not long before, they included a "neat and compact" governor's house; a
"commodious" courthouse, which had verandas all around "in the West
Indian Stile"; a simple church large enough to seat 1,000 on benches,
topped with a cupola and bell; good houses and offices for the white
officials; and "two tollerable Hospitals." The settlers' huts were the
"meanest" he had found in Africa, but other visitors rated them far
superior to homes of Africans in general. For defense, there were six
howitzers at the governor's house, a dozen cannon at the central "Plat-
form and Flagstaff" and nine cannon at the landing place.[2]

Two years later, when Dr. Winterbottom departed, the town had been
rebuilt, and handsomely to his affectionate eye.[3] The new governor's

house, a fine single-story wooden building surrounded by an airy veranda, was situated further inland on Thornton Hill (where the statehouse now stands). When palisaded (later walled), it became Fort Thornton. Below it lay some 400 houses on an 80-acre expanse, lining nine streets stretching from the river toward the mountains and intersected by three broad avenues running parallel to the shore. Each street was 80 feet wide, except for Water Street, which was double that width. The spacious scale of the town, with its impression of "salubrity and prosperity," excited a later visitor to compare Freetown to Washington, D.C.[4] The streets were "paved" in Bermuda grass, cropped by wandering cattle, sheep or goats. Many of the residents' wattled huts were supplanted by clapboard houses, generally measuring 30 by 15 feet and divided into rooms. Often they were raised a few feet off the ground on stone piers. Windows were shuttered, not yet glazed. American-style wooden shingles had replaced many an African thatch. There were still no chimneys. The cooking fires burned in the yards or detached outbuildings. Each house was half hidden in fruit trees and coconut palms and had its own kitchen garden and poultry yard on a 48-by-76-foot lot.[5] From the governor's porch, a homesick Winterbottom recalled:

> the eye . . . dwells with pleasure upon the surrounding picturesque scenery. . . . The cheerful tints imparted by a vast profusion of shrubs are finely contrasted by the sombre shade of venerable trees. . . . Over the town is seen St. George's Bay, enlivened by the appearance of ships, or the frequent passing of boats and canoes. . . . On the right hand is seen the river flowing majestically together with several of its islands, and the whole extent of the Bullom shore . . . the land richly clothed with wood, and edged with a fine white sandy beach. On the left hand are the mountains, forest crowned . . . running with a gentle declivity towards the Cape. The back ground is closed by immense forests, which rise like an amphitheatre, and occasionally have their summits veiled in fleecy clouds.

After the French destruction the homeless whites had moved into settlers' houses, and it became a practice to rent staff accommodation. This income helped the settlers build better, and more, houses. Frequently the ground floors served for offices or shops. The houses in time were whitewashed with shutters and doors painted bright colors. Imported furniture, crockery, and utensils gradually accumulated to augment the articles brought from Nova Scotia or made on the spot. The greatest hazard was fire. Thatched roofs were easily ignited. In the worst such disaster in the 1790s, twenty-two houses and a Baptist chapel were destroyed in half an hour.[6]

The shore was the heart of the town. Communication and transportation were almost entirely waterborne, although it was common to walk to Granville Town or the nearer African villages. There were no wheeled vehicles and few mules or horses to draw any. Loads on land were carried on the head. At the waterfront, visited daily by about 200 Africans arriving by canoe, fishermen, traders and boatbuilders congregated. There were three commercial wharves. Each arriving vessel drew a throng of men seeking jobs unloading cargo and women going aboard to pick up laundry. Both sexes engaged in barter with the visiting crews.

The British sponsors foresaw a community of yeoman farmers who would grow enough food to maintain themselves and provide a surplus for export. The soil beneath the lush vegetation was believed to be as fertile as that of the West Indian plantations. Although in an early report, the company admitted to "disappointment of the most serious kind" in the land around Freetown, it continued to urge the settlers to farm and to move farther inland, where the soil was marginally better. For years the colonists were reproached for not making a success of farming, and this "failure" was attributed to "inherent indolence . . . and not to the barrenness of the country," which was in fact submarginal and comparable to the mountainous areas of Britain.[7] Most of the peninsula had a red lateritic soil, gravelly, light and somewhat acid. It was easily penetrated by rainfall, which, in Eli Ackim's words, washed "the strength out of the earth." But Afzelius thought some advantage could be taken of every acre. The steep mountainsides should be left forested, to produce timber for ship- and housebuilding. The hilltops and slopes had deep enough soil for cotton, vines, vegetables, fruit, even tea. The lower ground, especially near the water, would support cassava, yams, other vegetables, ginger, pepper and rice.[8] Properly motivated and equipped, many settlers might have succeeded to some degree as farmers. But they were neither. Not all of them had farmed or worked as field laborers before; a considerable number had followed other trades. Most, if not all, were capable of scratching out a subsistence, however, and they all had come expecting to take up land and farm. They did not share the evangelical mystique that manual labor, especially on the land, was a good in itself and the test of civilization. Having known little but hard labor, they were not likely to idealize it. For American blacks, above all, agricultural labor was inseparably linked with slavery, unless the land they cultivated was their own beyond a doubt. This security of title was never permitted them in Sierra Leone. Even those with a vocation for farming were discouraged by the interminable and not wholly explicable delay in allotments, the reduction in acreages forced by circumstances, the imposition of a high quitrent, which the company remained power-less to collect but refused to abandon in principle, and repeated tinkering with the language of the grants by successive governors. The Sierra Leone Company's misguided land policy was finally criticized publicly in the report of an 1826 parliamentary inquiry, but by then the surviving Nova Scotians were identified with other ways of life, chiefly commerce and building, a rational accommodation to their situation however much the company directors might decry their alleged predilection for work requiring "less bodily exertion" than agricultural toil.[9]

A number of families did indeed take up country allotments, but the total acreage under cultivation was not large, and basic foodstuffs still had to be imported. After the French attack about fifty new farms were begun, but the small movement inland was arrested by the open hostility of the surrounding Temne at the turn of the century. The underlying uneasiness—even cynicism—could not be overcome by such induce-ments as the annual agricultural prizes, to which a loyalty oath was attached. In farming, as in other lines, the settlers were always handi-capped by a lack of capital, and rather than invest their earnings in farms which could be forfeited if certain company conditions were not met, they were likely to put them into town property or trading goods. The company refused to see a connection between the quitrent levy and the disinterest in farming. The governors reported that it was the settlers' "desire of Gain concurred with their fickle, unsteady & naturally indo-lent tempers" which turned them to trade. Only one, Ludlam, conceded that for men with nothing but their own labor, "to save up a capital . . . is a long and tedious process."[10]

Their poverty made nonsense of the pretensions of Macaulay and other whites to set them an example in farming. When Macaulay in 1796 bought a farm three miles from town, he bargained with Isaac James and Andrew Moore, neighbors, to build his house. He kept one adult settler and two "native boys" at the place. Even with plenty of help, his ambitions for crops were not realized, his only recorded crops being some fine cabbages and twenty pounds of "pretty good" sugar made from his own canes. There were twenty to thirty mountain farms doing fairly well, but he categorized the settlers as too lazy to climb the hill—where farming would make them rich—preferring to live miserably down below. They wanted a quick yield—an easy enough ambition for a salaried official, able to await a return on investment, to deride.[11]

John Gray, James Carr and five other company employees established small farms near Freetown, buying or leasing the land from settlers, but remaining on the company payroll. Gray and Carr built houses on the riverside and walked out of an evening to check on the progress of their hired hands. Gray also took on a small coffee farm in the mountains. The company's large-scale plantations did not develop. Clarkson's Plantation on the Bulom Shore, though it had better soil, did not realize a profit. Macaulay reduced it to four acres, planted with coffee, plantain, cinnamon and mangoes, and put Lazarus Jones in charge, assisted by four or five Africans. The company had reserved some good land for its own use on Thompson's Bay, and DuBois began a cotton plantation there, but it lapsed after his departure. When some settlers began to move in on the place, the company reasserted its claim, ordered a house built, hired twelve Africans and made John Cuthbert overseer at £60 a year. Plantain, yams, cotton, Indian corn and coffee were planted for what seemed a "trifling expense."[12] It was impossible for a "poor cultivator possessed of no means beyond the manual labor of his own family"[13] to emulate such operations.

Andrew Moore was an exception. A former slave near Augusta, Georgia, now about thirty-six years old, he had farmed in Nova Scotia and in Sierra Leone took up land near modern-day Leicester. There, on February 5, 1796, he discovered that "there is Coffee growing wild in the mountains." This was exactly the sort of cash crop much desired by the company, and plants from the Caribbean had been introduced in the belief that it was not an indigenous plant. Moore had been cutting and burning brush that day when he recognized some coffee beans on the ground. A search quickly located the tree nearby. Moore brought the beans to Governor Dawes, who, in some excitement, summoned Afzelius and others to see the "treasure."

A party headed by the governor and guided by Moore trekked the three miles to the site the following morning. Afzelius' diary gives us some of the pleasure of that historic day. They set off at six o'clock, at a brisk pace which slowed as the ascent grew steeper.

> About half the way . . . we crossed a brook with fine cool and
> chrystalline water, which attempted us to sit down on the side
> of its sweet murmur and take our first breakfast consisting

of bread and water . . . mixed with some wine. . . . we . . .
arrived to the famous tree about 8 o'clock. . . . We set directly
about to search for some seeds and we were lucky enough to
find a little quantity each of us. . . . But we were not able to
discover more than only one tree. . . . The ground was high
mountanous dry gravelly or rather stony and seemingly very
poor. . . .

They walked on to Moore's farm, then another mile to look at Isaac
James' farm before turning back to:

a charming brook, where the water ran slow and limpid, being
besides of the most exquisite taste and refreshing coolness
which induced us to sit down and take our second breakfast,
consisting of water and bread, on an enchanting place . . .
where the piercing sun could not reach us, the soil was deap
and rich, and the air resounding of the different voices of
warbling birds, and the noise of groveling beasts. . . . On both
side of this brook the . . . rich black mould, was digged up . . .
by wild Hogs, of which Andrew Moore told us there was a
great quantity; He also informed us, that he had seen there
great flocks of . . . Birds large as a Turkey, but not able to fly,
only . . . running away with a wonderful swiftness.[14]

Rested, the explorers headed downhill to Freetown, now bathed in a
"scorching sun," and arrived at Thornton Hill in time for dinner. After
the meal Afzelius headed for his own house with the coffee beans but was
repeatedly stopped and surrounded by curious colonists, who "would
see the new discovered Coffee, and whom I was obliged to shew the
differences of this tree from others, that they should be able to seak for it
in the woods." Afzelius described it as a small tree, twenty feet high and
thirteen inches in circumference, with smooth gray bark and narrow
pointed leaves. The governor awarded $10 to Moore for his discovery
and offered $2 for each additional tree found. In a week Moore had
located another. Corankapone, too, was successful, and within a few
days a dozen trees had been spotted. On March 1, there were enough
beans for a tasting. Governor Dawes ordered some boiled after dinner.
He, Afzelius, Dr. Winterbottom and John Witchell each had a cup, "and
we all agreed that it was by no means inferior to our usual Coffee brought
out from England." Witchell said it was better, even though drunk

without milk. Dawes "sent also a full coup of it to the kitchen to be tasted of the people there, but I did not hear their resolution about it," Afzelius wrote. He marveled that "we four . . . should be the first who ever tasted the real Coffee beans in their wild state at least I am pretty sure, that nobody tasted this Coffee before." Macaulay considered the flavor of the Sierra Leone product at least as good as the West Indian.[15]

Coffee for a time became the chief export. But marketing was one of the obstacles that the settler-growers never overcame. John Kizell recalled that he and others tried to cultivate sugarcane, cotton, pepper and ginger to sell to the company store, but Gray, the commercial agent who succeeded Macaulay as governor, suddenly stopped taking their produce. He allowed credit only to those who wanted goods to trade with the Africans outside the colony, presumably in an attempt to boost the export business of the company, whose investors were getting impatient for returns. (Such a decision does not appear in the council minutes.) Kizell also claimed that James Wilson, who ran the communal sugar mill, would take the settlers' crop but at an extremely low price—two or threepence for "as much as a man can carry"—which provided no incentive. Kizell quoted Wilson as saying that if sugar were manufactured in Sierra Leone, it would spoil the West Indian trade. (Wilson lost interest in the sugar mill and went into trade. Both he and Gray later turned to slaving.) When Governor Ludlam made one of the periodic efforts to revive interest in agriculture toward the end of the century, "the people was disappointed and taken in so very often that they paid no much heed," according to Kizell.[16]

About half the heads of families in 1798 were supporting themselves to some extent from farming, but thirty years after their arrival in Africa no householder classified as Nova Scotian was living on a farm or chiefly dependent on it. Only one, George Carrol, considered himself a farmer, but he drew his main income from work as a stonemason and a considerable amount of town property. His son was not interested in the coffee plantation (by now 3,000 trees, producing over three hundredweight annually), and it lay neglected. There were at this time 62 craftsmen, 29 traders, 8 fishermen, 6 clerks and 3 river pilots among the 109 Nova Scotian male heads of families for whom occupations were cited.[17]

One outsider whose interest took some concrete form to open up markets for the settlers, and this nearly twenty years after they came, was Paul Cuffe, the black American merchant, who saw at once the commercial prospects of Freetown. He told William Allen:

> Their young men are too fond of leaving the colony and become seamen for other people. I have thought if commerce could be introduced . . . it might have this good tendency of keeping the young men at home, and in some future day they become thus qualified to carry on commerce, I see no reason why they may not become a nation to be numbered among the historians' nations of the world.

It was clear to Cuffe that a handful of whites ran things at Freetown and that the settlers could not be said to be equal. "But I believe much lieth at their door. When they become capable of self government, much of this evil will be overcome." With Kizell and nearly thirty other leading Nova Scotian and Maroon men, he set up a Friendly Society—a marketing cooperative—to break the white stranglehold. The society sent some £1,000 worth of goods to England, where Thomas Clarkson joined Allen and others in sponsoring a supporting body to buy a ship which would bring the settlers' camwood, ivory, palm oil and coffee to England.[18]

Many of the settlers' initiatives went unexploited for lack of means. Warwick Francis manufactured an excellent dye from the native indigo but lacked the capital to produce it for export. Kizell and Job Allen grew and cured tobacco but were given no encouragement to process it on a commercial scale. Mrs. Fanny Logan successfully made soap from the ashes of dried banana stems and leaves.[19]

Annual prizes were offered for cattle rearing, as well as growing foodstuffs or export crops, but the records say little of success with anything but the ubiquitous pigs and goats. An ox given by King Naimbana at the time of Clarkson's leave-taking was the only one of note until July, 1795, when Richard Corankapone's "famous Ox" was slaughtered. Among those who dined on it was Afzelius, who pronounced it the "fattest and tenderest in fact the best beef I have seen and tasted in Africa, except that of King Naimbanna's Ox." The company employed a herdsman (at one time Abraham Hazeley held the post), and one of his problems was to defend the beasts against African rustlers. The stealing became extremely bold in 1799. A fine cow belonging to John Cuthbert disappeared, and after Eli Ackim also lost one, some of the settlers took their guns, marched into King Tom's territory west of Freetown and seized suspects. The next day Tom retaliated by capturing three settlers. Both sets of prisoners were released without harm. A palaver was brought. No indemnification was obtained for Ackim's cow because the settlers had taken the law into their own hands, but Cuthbert won $50 compensation.[20]

While the botanist Afzelius lived among them, a number of the Nova Scotians took a keen interest in horticultural experiments. Among them John Spears was outstanding. After his apple orchard was ruined by the French, he resumed farming near Granville Town, where he once gave Afzelius a good dinner and a tour of his plantings: an acre of ginger, ten apple trees and a fine garden of cabbages, beans, and "sallat" greens. He had named a native bulb with a nutty taste "Sierra Leone walnut."[21]

Commercial enterprises brought into prominence two colonists, Thomas Cooper and Kizell. Cooper, born in England of African parents, came to Sierra Leone as a settler on the ship which brought Macaulay in 1793. Very soon he was appointed to run a company retail shop. A man of some education and considerable presence, he won respect from both the whites and the black settlers and was often able to mediate between them. His shopkeeping monopoly drew some criticism, and the settlers were invited to open competing shops, with goods advanced on credit, but were slow to respond. Though they bought goods at the company store at retail prices and then resold them, the settlers were wary about taking goods in large quantities, perhaps from their old fear of debt, plus a general ignorance of accounting procedures. The first six retailers were therefore not licensed until December, 1794. Cooper did not continue, having become a schoolmaster at £80 a year, twice the salary paid the other black male teachers. He was chosen in 1795 to run the company's first factory in the Rio Pongo area, where it was hoped to open contact with Fula caravans from the north. He was paid £100 a year plus a commission of 1 percent on ivory, rice, wax, gold and cattle.[22]

Cooper at times employed other settlers, such as young Sam Perry, who "writes a distinct hand," and Charles Bias, a carpenter who helped build the store, warehouse and wharf. Thomas Cox, a white company store assistant, became Cooper's clerk. Cooper sold his Freetown house for $360 to the company for an apothecary's residence and shop but continued to farm part time and to serve as a hundreder until the antiwhite election in 1796, when, presumably, he was regarded as too much a company man. He was returned to office in 1797. While at Freeport he married Elizabeth, a daughter of David Edmonds. He was always addressed as Mr. Cooper. Under the change of government brought by the grant of a royal charter in 1800, Cooper became the first black to be named an alderman, and his death from pleurisy in 1801 shocked both the colony and the directors. He was extolled in the company's next report as a man who "raised [the Nova Scotians] by the dignity of his mind, to a level with Europeans."[23]

For John Kizell, with a Sherbro background, trading came naturally. He had learned to read and write in Nova Scotia, and he became active in the Baptist church. When he was sent to England as a witness for the 1794 riot prosecutions, he made useful friends and returned to Sierra Leone in March, 1795, with an unspecified "venture . . . which he sold extremely well." Although he farmed, having drawn one of the larger allotments (nine acres), he also ran a liquor store, and he served as a tithingman.[24] With an eye on the more distant coastal trade, Kizell with Richard Corankapone and Abraham Smith in 1795 built the largest craft constructed at Freetown, capable of carrying twelve tons of cargo. To finish it, they borrowed £5 from the council, secured by Corankapone's combined salaries as marshal and inspector of farms. *The Three Friends* was launched in January, 1796. It was probably their boat that returned from the Sherbro with five tons of rice that spring, and on another reported occasion nine bullocks were unloaded. By the following year "many" settlers had boats which would carry two to eight tons of rice, camwood or stock.[25]

For a time Kizell represented the company as a factor at Port Loko. He invested in three houses and a lot in Freetown. He was the only Nova Scotian employed on diplomatic missions, first with Governor Ludlam, in 1805, negotiating with the Sherbro chiefs to allow the British to trade from York Island, and in 1810 representing Governor Columbine on a mission to explain the British abolition of the slave trade. His letters to Columbine are filled with acute anthropological, geological and commercial observations. He obtained land for a small town on the north shore of Sherbro Island at Camplar, where he established a trading post and a church in which he preached in Sherbro. This became his home in later life.[26]

The trading of even the most active settlers was overshadowed by their white competitors. Originally, the company had denied any employee the right to trade on the side, but in 1797, in the steady retrenchment which followed the losses of 1794, the rule was rescinded. Trading rights would reduce demands for higher pay. They were not, of course, to deal in slaves, compete with the company or make profits above 7 1/2 percent. James Carr promptly resigned from the council and obtained from it a credit of $3,000 to start up in business. Michael Macmillan, Alexander Smith and James Wilson followed, each receiving a credit of

$1,500. Even one of the recently arrived missionaries wanted to get into trade on the pretense that it would bring him closer to the Africans. The "love of gain" cooled the religious fervor of many of his colleagues, to Macaulay's distress.[27]

At first, Macaulay encouraged the trend, hoping that the new traders would allow the company to drop business but leave it in "respectable" hands. He had always found barter "tedious and embarrassing." But it did not work out that way. John Gray, as commercial agent, reported in 1799 that instead of selling to the company, the white traders were bartering with the slave traders. Their excuse was the shortage of goods in the company store owing to a failure of a series of ships to arrive. The white merchants also strenuously and successfully objected to the imposition of customs duties by threatening to pull out of the settlement. In succeeding years the export trade was dominated by a handful of white businessmen, including, after 1807, Macaulay himself, operating with a nephew as Macaulay and Babington.[28]

A number of settlers turned to the slave trade, some of them to "throw off the Company's yoke" and develop influence with the Africans. Macaulay once referred to five having done so, two in the Rio Nunez and three in the Rio Pongo areas. A number of whites also found it irresistible, about fifteen in all, including Gray, who served as governor, the major licensed traders and at least three men who came to Africa as doctors.[29]

After the French laid Freetown to waste, acting governor Macaulay had cut the company's costs by refusing to employ any settler who harbored what was deemed to be stolen property and also by hiring men by the job instead of keeping workers on the payroll all the time. John Cuthbert and Corankapone, for example, were given a contract to unload salt and crockery from a chartered ship at a rate of two shillings a ton. This narrowing of employment locally diverted many into trade or scattered them to work at distant places, including slave factories. Antrim Lawrence, an armorer, and his wife were among those who went, but Lawrence took the precaution of getting formal permission from Macaulay to work in the Rio Nunez so that they would retain their claim to their Freetown property. Lawrence died, and his wife, upon her return, found that the house and lot had been turned over to a company employee. Although she and her second husband, Lazarus Jones, repeatedly brought suits, they were never successful in reestablishing title.[30]

For any Nova Scotian who could read, teaching was a well-paid occupation in the early years. The curriculum was generally limited to (for boys) reading, writing, arithmetic and church hymns and (for girls) reading, needlework and church hymns.[31] For women, teaching was the only salaried job open. At least nine Nova Scotian women taught at some time and were paid around £24 a year, compared to £40 for the nine men recorded as having taught. Mary Perth had done well in business, but the wealthiest woman shopkeeper was Sophia Small. She also kept a tavern and invested heavily in Freetown and Granville Town property.[32] Most of the women worked for wages as laundresses, seamstresses, midwives, nurses or housekeepers for company staff.

Only rarely do contemporary journals and reports lift a curtain on the sexual relationships between the blacks and whites of Freetown, but despite the strictures of Henry Thornton that anyone guilty of immoral conduct should be discharged (since no "professional talents . . . can atone for a licentious life & compensate the mischief which examples of this kind cannot fail to produce—I allude particularly to the taking black or indeed white women into keeping . . ."), relationships were established and recognized. There were two distinct castes, white and black, and Macaulay, for example, counted as "ladies" or "worthy of esteem" only the very few white women who accompanied their husbands or fathers to the colony. Blacks never dined at the governor's table unless they were African chiefs. It was far from the community of equals promised in the original terms of settlement, but the two groups did mingle perhaps more comfortably than at any later colonial period. Certainly the blacks could speak plainly to their white rulers, who overlooked considerable provocation. Most of the whites were young men, temporarily removed from family ties. An undetermined number kept mistress-housekeepers. At the death or departure of the men it was customary to give the women a life interest in their property, which passed to their children.[33]

James Carr, the accountant, onetime tithingman and later prosperous merchant and slave trader, profited nicely from his attachment to his Nova Scotian mistress, Elizabeth (Betsy) Walker, the widow of William Walker. On the town lot she had inherited from her husband, Carr erected buildings worth £1,000. She ran his slave factory in his absence, and a visitor found her house in excellent order and the slaves "at liberty and in perfect obedience, looking up to her as their protector and friend." At her death her late husband's heirs contested Carr's right to her "considerable quantity" of money, clothes and furniture.[34]

Sophia Small's daughter, Jane, whose father was white, brought her husband, George Nicol, an English carpenter, a handsome dowry which established him as a leading businessman. He and his wife not only had Mrs. Small's house, but built on a Water Street property an establishment worth £3,500, the most valuable in town, and had two vacant lots and some odd buildings as well.[35] A later immigrant, John McCormack, who opened a timber export business and founded a Baptist Church of God before retiring to his native Ireland a half century later, married a daughter of John Cuthbert. He attributed his steady good health at this "white man's grave" to his partiality for the local diet based on rice, palm oil, fish and fruit.[36]

The early Church Missionary Society representatives also married Nova Scotian women. The Reverend Melchoir Renner was particularly happy in his union with Elizabeth Richards, who taught about sixty girls at the Rio Pongo mission which occupied John Gray's slave factory after the latter's death. She was guide, adviser and interpreter for Renner to the Susu. She was "neat, clean & plain in her dress, like the English fair sex," he told his sponsors. A visitor related that "tho' she is a black woman, she is more pleasing and conversable than many white women are, and manages her family much better." Renner said of their marriage: "The Lord has joined black and white together in love, peace & harmony."[37] From time to time, Mrs. Renner would send her regards through her husband "To all those who have not much aversion to coloured people," but after some time as a missionary teacher, she dared to write directly to Secretary Josiah Pratt herself, sending a length of country cloth to his wife. "I am not only happy in having a good husband in Mr. Renner," she said, "but feel myself very happy to be in a way where I can serve God and the cause of Christ." Childless herself, she went on: "I like children. . . . It goes now in the fourth year that I am . . . in the Society's service, in a busy and large family, but I am not yet tired of it, and if God upholds my feeble constitution I like to stir about and to sit with my girls and do for them much as I can." Mrs. Pratt responded with an English shawl as a token of her regard.[38]

Many Nova Scotian women appear to have been highly independent souls, and not least of such was Mrs. Renner. It came to her attention that each married missionary received a £25 allowance for his wife, and nothing her husband or his associates could tell her "in a most gentle manner" would convince her that this was not her "salary." Since the money she had brought to the marriage had been spent on the mission work, it was finally agreed that in fairness she should have the £25 a year for herself. Out of it, Betsy Renner acquired a lot in Freetown, upon which a house soon began to rise.[39]

The Reverend Gustavus Nylander in his turn married a twenty-one-year-old schoolteacher, Phillis Hazeley, daughter of Abraham. She had been taken to England by Governor Dawes in 1794 and educated. Back home she opened her own school. Renner, who performed the ceremony, thought them a "smart couple." After only eight months, to her husband's great grief, she died. His second wife was Ann Beverhout, another Nova Scotian teacher. A third missionary, Charles Wenzel, widowed when his English wife died in childbirth, married Ann's sister, Fanny.[40]

Not all relationships were so conventional, however. At some point—but surely after Macaulay's day—the custom arose for Nova Scotian widows to give an annual picnic dinner to the white officials. What Nylander criticized in 1812 may have applied to some of the whites' behavior at an earlier period:

> The Europeans in the Colony live cheap with their women; because those poor creatures think it a great honour to be in a white man's house as ——— and then they do every thing in the house for mere food and cloathing, and oftentimes accept of a good portion horse-whipping besides; and when the European returns to Europe he leaves perhaps a couple of little Mullattos without support . . . running about in the Colony, & perhaps begging with their mothers. . . . There are about 20 Mulatto children here . . . born since I am in the Colony and a great many older ones. It seems to be rather a disgrace for a European to marry a black person. And on the other hand it is almost a shame if a European does not get children by a black person in an unlawful manner.

The first Crown governor, tempestuous young T. Perronet Thompson, probably the bitterest critic the Nova Scotians ever inspired, also delivered such judgments. He was scandalized by liaisons of some holdover Sierra Leone Company officers who, among their lesser sins, gave "*fêtes champêtres* to their mulatto housekeepers."[41]

Outward aspects of the unique Freetown culture either fascinated or irritated observers. After 1800 Freetown was a melting pot in which the American blacks were one of many, though a very influential, ingredient. But they imposed upon the community a "Western" style of life. They guaranteed that the lingua franca was basically English. It was often imperfectly learned and not identical with that spoken by whites, for it had its African as well as American influences. It was to evolve further, with additions from other Europeans living on the coast and Maroon and Liberated African settlers into a language now called Krio. "I never heard such gibberish . . . it takes half an hour to make out what they mean to say, and yet they are quite indignant if you imply that they cannot speak our language," wrote an irritated Mary Church in the early nineteenth century. "I believe the English make them worse . . . by imitating them . . . the people say if I do not, the Africans will never understand me." But she attacked the problem in the time-honored British way when among foreigners: "I hope that by repeating my words a great many times, they will manage to do so." In the same spirit of practicality, the Nova Scotians kept their American acquired names. They entrenched potatoes, wheat flour and tea in the diet, along with other imports, and introduced numbers of American or English dishes, such as a banana pie which Afzelius didn't like. Their semi-European life-style was sometimes criticized because it cost more and led to demands for high wages.[42]

The prestige they attached to education impressed visitors favorably. Their children were more eager to learn than were those of the working-class population in Britain, and school achievements were much talked about. Some sent their children to England to school at their own expense. The wife of a British judge discovered that her young servants would leave her table uncleared to read or write and "your only chance of a clean glass . . . is to say . . . 'Now until these be properly done, I shall give you neither paper, pens, nor ink.' "[43]

It was difficult to supply white schoolteachers. The school at Clapham, to which Macaulay brought his African family, began as an experiment in bringing Africans to England to be trained for missionary work rather than sending out Europeans to an unhealthy climate.[44] The idea belonged to John Campbell, director of the Edinburgh Missionary Society. It was approved by Thornton and Wilberforce, but because of the difficulty they foresaw in raising money during the Franco-British war, the proposal rested until Campbell's friend Robert Haldane offered more than £6,000. Campbell invited Macaulay to bring about thirty children home with him. Campbell heard nothing more until Macaulay reached England. Campbell visited the youngsters at Clapham, where they, "jet black cheerful and happy," were one of the village sights. Because of a smallpox scare, they did not go to Edinburgh and instead were put into St. Pancras Hospital for inoculation. While they were convalescent, they were whisked out of Campbell's hands by the

Clapham Sect, which organized its own Society for the Education of Africans and quickly raised funds, Thornton putting down the first £300. Macaulay supervised the school run by a resident schoolmaster and his wife under the careful eye of John Venn, rector of Clapham. Among the pupils, it appears from various records, were James Wise and the sons of Abraham Hazeley, David Edmonds, Sophia Small and John Kizell, all Nova Scotian children. Wise came home and was appointed government printer, and Hazeley became an assistant. Other second-generation settlers were given job training at Freetown. James Edmonds went into the apothecary shop, William Pitcher was apprenticed to the master of works, and Scipio Lucas was put under the shipwright. Joshua Cuthbert was placed in the dispensary, and Nathaniel Snowball, Jr., became master of the *Dawes*, trading in the Rio Nunez with a crew of Africans.[45]

Something else which distinguished the Nova Scotian settlers was their "American" breezy informality, which set the teeth of British visitors on edge. The Nova Scotians were very fond of shaking hands. James Wilson, who came out with Clarke in 1796, recalled walking up from the shore and shaking forty hands in six paces. "They are open and free, and their regard and love for white people is almost childish," the newcomer reported. "If I look any of them in the face, I am almost sure of a courtesy or bow, if not a shake by the hand, which they reckon a great compliment. They talk pretty good English and are very dressy after the English stile."[46]

Mrs. Melville, who lived in Freetown in early Victorian days, had a young "settler woman" recommended to her as a seamstress.

> [She] volunteered her services by walking, or rather *swinging*, her portly figure unannounced into the drawing-room; and, holding out her hand to be shaken, said, with a movement meant to be a low curtsy, "I am the sewing-girl marm!" She was followed at a respectful distance by her attendant, and arrayed in a gaudy-patterned gown, with high head-dress, gold earrings, and coral necklace, fanning herself all the while with a handkerchief redolent of musk, so as to display the numerous silver rings which glittered on her large hand.[47]

Mary Church had a similar experience with an elderly woman candidate for a servant's post:

She seemed not to consider herself at all inferior, for she walked across the room and took possession of the sofa with the greatest composure in the world, and insisted on shaking hands with me. Gradations of society, said I to myself, certainly do not seem very well understood here . . . but I . . . do not see any reason for shaking hands with an African servant more than an English one.[48]

An arriving Englishman was intrigued when:

A black pilot, of very American externals, boarded us. . . . It was novel to find a black treating a white man with aristocratic independence. In due time, however, his dignity condescended to unbend itself "a few," as he would have expressed it; but never so far as to allow us to forget that he was a free black man of Freetown. . . .

He was to find that blacks there often exhibited "an ungrateful arrogance under the plea that the white man is but a casual intruder in the land of the African."[49]

Everyone commented on the Nova Scotian dress, a Western contrast with that of the other blacks of the area, even though they usually went barefoot in African fashion. Mrs. Church's caller, for example, was wearing "a muslin gown and apron . . . a coloured handkerchief tied round her head, and over that, a man's shaped blue beaver hat—in one hand an umbrella, and the other tossing about her pocket handkerchief."[50]

Mrs. Melville said that a typical Nova Scotian wore a scarlet moreen petticoat, yellow silk shawl, light cotton print gown, high-crowned black beaver hat and snowy headdress. The young women wore their hair "either clipped and disposed in fantastic shapes like some antique yew-tree of a Dutch garden, or else twisted into short stiff plaits." Veils, necklaces and parasols were much in evidence. Well-off men wore European suits composed of jacket, waistcoat and trousers made in wool, white duck or thin blue cotton. Sundays brought out the best. An Englishman told of a communicant headed for the Lady Huntingdon chapel who "tripped along with the air of a queen; her best earrings gleaming in the sun, her naked feet trampling the burning dust [with] . . . her white pocket-handkerchief and Bible." At the Anglican service, "you would judge them dressed for the playhouse, had we any such places here. The men are dressed in ginghams, nankeens, &c. and the women in the same, or muslins with turbans on their heads; and many of each sex wear straw, or beaver hats." In the Anglican church, blacks and whites sat on the same benches. White visitors did not often attend the nonconformist services partly because they were so packed that it was uncomfortably hot.[51]

There were surprisingly few instances in which the returned Africans adopted or reverted to African customs. Twice settlers arranged trials by ordeal to prove guilt in alleged robberies, but Macaulay and Dawes acted vigorously, and with the support of the majority of colonists, to stamp out practices which they believed would bring ridicule on the settlement. On the whole, from the reestablishment of the colony to 1801 relationships with the African neighbors were amicable. It was a sure sign of friendship when the settlers and the Africans deloused one another. A red water trial at a nearby village would draw the colonists and whites alike as fascinated onlookers of the exotic rite. Hannah Dick, a popular figure among the townspeople with whom she traded, invited a number of them, including Mrs. Perth, to her own ordeal at Pa Demba's town. She drank twenty-four calabashes of the bitter brew before vomiting up the kola nut which proved her innocence.[52]

Adventure, adversity and a multitude of experiences created such a powerful sense of separate identity among the black settlers that some of their descendants more than 160 years later objected to independence from the British Crown out of fear that they would be dominated by the far greater numbers of "upcountry" Africans.

Progress of the Sierra Leone settlement continued to be watched throughout the Atlantic world. In Newport the Reverend Samuel Hopkins heard in 1793 that Freetown "goes on with success and agreeable prospects" and that the settlers "are all contented and pleased and healthy,—appear sober and pious. . . ." There were "upright, benevolent" men from England in charge of them who were "very friendly to the blacks, treating them upon an equality with themselves." The secretary of an African society in Providence arrived in Freetown in January, 1795. He was James Mackenzie, who represented a number of free black families wishing to leave America. Macaulay was much impressed by his education and the news that the immigrants would pay their own way, seeking only land and the citizenship denied them in the United States. He envisioned a dozen Thomas Coopers able to make an important contribution to colonial life. Mackenzie was offered land on the

Bulom shore for twelve families, and Macaulay asked Hopkins for character references because of past difficulties arising from ''the injudicious admission of persons of doubtful character'' with ''fallacious notions of civil rights . . . extreme vehemence of temper . . . low, confused imperfect ideas of moral rectitude.'' It was to be hoped that the ''Poison of the age of Reason'' had not pervaded the black class; the arrival of even one such unbeliever might be ''an evil beyond all calculation.''[53]

Mackenzie returned to Africa with two other men, but without the character references Macaulay demanded. He sailed on to Gorée, sold his goods for three or four slaves and returned with them to America. One of his companions, Frazer, a tailor, was allowed to stay at Freetown and work, but not admitted as a settler.[54]

NOTES

1. McCormack to Select Committee, July 13, 1830, Parliamentary Papers, 1830, X.
2. Kup, ''Freetown in 1794,'' pp. 161-64; Sierra Leone Company 1794 Report, pp. 68-70; Winterbottom, *An Account of the Native Africans in the Neighbourhood of Sierra Leone*, vol. 1, p. 276.
3. Winterbottom, vol. 1, pp. 275-79.
4. Report from Select Committee on the West Coast of Africa (Robert Madden), Parliamentary Papers, 1842, XII, p. 244.
5. Spilsbury, *Account of a Voyage to the Western Coast of Africa*, pp. 37-38; Poole, *Life, Scenery, and Customs in Sierra Leone and the Gambia*, vol. 1, pp. 235-36.
6. [Melville], *A Residence at Sierra Leone*, p. 4; Church, *Sierra Leone: or, the Liberated Africans*, p. 44; Macaulay Journal, April 5, 1798 (all Macaulay papers from Huntington Library); Council minute, April 5, 1798, CO 270/4.
7. Sierra Leone Company 1804 Report, pp. 7-8; Curtin, *Image of Africa*, pp. 60-61; Sierra Leone Company 1794 Report, p. 19; McGarva, ''Sierra Leone,'' p. 537.
8. F. J. Martin and H. C. Doyne, *Soil Survey of Sierra Leone*, pp. 7-9, 25-28; Ackim to Commissioners of Inquiry, CO 267/92; Afzelius to Clarkson, December 29, 1792, Clarkson Papers, BL Add. MSS. 12,131.
9. Curtin, p. 62; Report of Commissioners of Inquiry, Parliamentary Papers, 1826-7, VII, p. 10, also CO 267/91; *The Philanthropist*, vol. 5 (1815), pp. 244-45; African Institution 1815 Special Report, pp. 18, 19.
10. Sierra Leone Company 1796 Report, p. 10; Governor and council to directors, June 5, 1798, CO 268/5; Ludlam to Macaulay, May 12, 1808, CO 267/24.

11. Macaulay Journal, April 29, 1796; *Adam Afzelius: Sierra Leone Journal*, April 29, 1796; Macaulay Journal, December 12, 1796; Macaulay Journal (Mills), July 26, November 16, 1798; Macaulay Journal, June 5, 1798; Macaulay to Thornton, June 7, 1797.

12. Macaulay Journal, April 27, 1796; Macaulay to Thornton, June 7, 1797; Council minutes, December 31, 1794, May 19, 1796, CO 270/3.

13. K. Macaulay to Commissioners of Inquiry, CO 267/92.

14. Book of Negroes, PRO 30/55/100, ff. 66-67; Fyfe, *A History of Sierra Leone*, p. 62; *Adam Afzelius: Sierra Leone Journal*, February 13, 15, March 1, 1796. The bird is identified as a dodo.

15. *Ibid.*, February 6, 1796; Botanical Description of a New Species of Coffee, February 10, 1796, BL Add. MSS. 12,131; *Adam Afzelius: Sierra Leone Journal*, February 13, 15, March 1, 1796; Council minute, February 6, 1796, CO 270/3; Macaulay Journal, November 24, 1796.

16. Governor and council to Hallowell Inquiry, June 12, 1803, WO 1/352; Kizell to Commissioners of Inquiry, CO 267/92; Council minutes, January 23, April 25, 1801, CO 270/5; September 15, 1801, CO 270/6.

17. Sierra Leone Company 1804 Report, p. 8; Report of Commissioners of Inquiry, pp. 71-72, Parliamentary Papers, 1826-7, VII, also CO 267/91.

18. Sheldon H. Harris, *Paul Cuffe*, pp. 237-39, 242, 255; Sheldon H. Harris, "An American's Impressions of Sierra Leone in 1811," p. 39. *The Philanthropist*, vol. 5 (1815), pp. 247-50.

19. Gabbidon and Savage to Commissioners of Inquiry, CO 267/92; *Adam Afzelius: Sierra Leone Journal*, May 23, 1795.

20. *Ibid.*, July 30, 1795; Council minutes, October 1, 1795, CO 270/3; March 23, 1798, and June 24, 1799, CO 270/4.

21. *Adam Afzelius: Sierra Leone Journal*, May 9, 1796.

22. WO 1/352, f. 172; Macaulay Journal, November 23, 1793; Council minute, October 29, 1793; Macaulay to Thornton, June 7, 1797; Council minutes, April 3, May 26, 1795; CO 270/3; Fyfe, pp. 66-67; Council minutes, March 31, September 1, 1795, CO 270/3; Sierra Leone Company 1796 Report, p. 8; Council minutes, July 8, November 18, 1796, February 6, 1797, CO 270/4. For more on Freeport and company relations with traders, Mouser, "Trade, Coasters, and Conflict in the Rio Pongo from 1790 to 1808," pp. 45-64.

23. Council minutes, February 3, 1796, CO 270/3; March 25, October 27, June 7, July 8, 1796, CO 270/4; Macaulay to Mills, January 5, 1799; Sierra Leone Company 1801 Report, pp. 39-40.

24. At least two accounts of Kizell's enslavement exist, African Institution 1812 Report, pp. 20-21, 145, and Macaulay Journal, August 27, 1796, and February 16, 1798, in which he is said to have been born in Dahomey. *Baptist Annual Register for 1794-1797*, p. 255; *The Philanthropist*, vol. 4 (1814), p. 245; Council minutes, December 15, 1796, CO 270/4; May 5, 1795, CO 270/3.

25. Council minute, November 5, 1795, CO 270/3; *Adam Afzelius: Sierra*

Leone Journal, January 16, 1796; Macaulay Journal, May 16, November 3, 1796; Macaulay to Thornton, June 7, 1797.

26. Governor and council to Thornton, February 6, 1796, CO 268/5; *The Philanthropist*, vol. 3 (1813), pp. 251, 253, 255; extracts of Kizell to Columbine, African Institution 1812 Report, pp. 113-53; Fyfe, pp. 96, 132; Ashmun, *Memoir of the Life and Character of the Rev. Samuel Bacon, A.M.*, p. 258. An attempt of the American Colonization Society to settle there failed, and Liberia was chosen.

27. Council minutes, December 8 and 18, 1797, CO 270/4; Governor and council to Thornton, January 22, 1798, CO 268/5; Council minutes, January 5, July 28, 1798, CO 270/4; Macaulay Journal (Mills), April 24, May 23, 1798.

28. Macaulay to Thornton, June 7, 1797; Council minutes, March 1, 1799, CO 270/4; April 25, 1801, CO 270/5. Of six ships sent out in 1798 and 1799, four were captured by the French, and a fifth was wrecked. Goods valued at £13,000 were seized by the French in 1800. Fyfe, 71, 72; Sierra Leone Company 1801 Report, pp. 29-31.

29. Macaulay to Mills, December 1, 1797; Macaulay Journal, August 8, 1797; Parliamentary Papers, 1803-4, V, p. 126; Macaulay Journal, April 8, 1797, and November 18, 1796.

30. Council minutes, November 18 and 19, 1794, CO 270/3; Memorandum of Lazarus Jones, June 8, 1826, CO 267/92.

31. Kup, p. 164.

32. Council minute, January 16, 1813, CO 270/13.

33. Thornton to Clarkson, December 30, 1791, Clarkson Papers, BL Add. MSS. 41,262A; Macaulay Journal (Mills), December 30, 1797, July 2, 1798; cases of Rachel Trion and Maria Conner, January 5, 1813, and March 25, 1812, CO 270/13, for example.

34. Spilsbury, p. 23; *The Philanthropist*, vol. 5 (1815), p. 256; Council minutes, October 31, November 24, December 5, 1812, CO 270/13.

35. *The Philanthropist*, vol. 5 (1813), pp. 251, 252, 253, 256, 261; Fyfe, p. 103; Council minute, January 16, 1813, CO 270/13.

36. Curtin, p. 278; Marke, *Origin of Wesleyan Methodism in Sierra Leone*, p. 10; Fyfe, pp. 125, 218, 286; Easmon, "A Nova Scotian Family" pp. 57, 60; McCormack to Select Committee, July 13, 1830, Parliamentary Papers, 1830, X, p. 461.

37. Hole, *The Early History of the Church Missionary Society for Africa and the East*, p. 133; Renner to Pratt, December 24, 1810, February 14, 1812, Church Missionary Society (CMS) CA1/E-2; Renner to Pratt, June 8, 1812, CA1/E-3.

38. Renner to Pratt, July 13, 1811; Mrs. Renner to Pratt, February 12, 1812, both CMS CA1/E-2; Mrs. Pratt to Mrs. Renner, October 13, 1812, CA1/E-3.

39. Renner to Pratt, June 8, 1812, December 31, 1813, CMS CA1/E-3.

40. Renner to Pratt, March 13, 1810; Nylander to Pratt, April 11, December 7,

1810; September 2, 1811, all CMS CA1/E-2; Wenzel to Pratt, October 31, 1812, CA1/E-3; Fyfe, p. 103.

41. Melville, p. 239; Nylander to Pratt, February 28, 1812, CMS CA1/E-2; Thompson to Castlereagh, October 2, 1809, Thompson Papers, Hull University, 1/23.

42. Porter, *Creoledom*, pp. 11, 34; Fyfe, p. 378; Church, pp. 11-12; F. Harrison Rankin, *The White Man's Grave*, pp. 98-99; Council minute, February 23, 1803, CO 270/9; *Adam Afzelius: Sierra Leone Journal*, May 23, 1795; Governor and council to Castlereagh, October 31, 1808, Thompson Papers, 1/23.

43. Melville, pp. 253, 239, 255; Parliamentary Papers, 1826-7, VII, p. 336.

44. Philip, *The Life, Times and Missionary Enterprises of the Rev. John Campbell*, pp. 166-77; Knutsford, *Life and Letters of Zachary Macaulay*, pp. 201, 221, 223, 224-25.

45. Sierra Leone Company 1801 Report, p. 19; 1808 Report, p. 10; WO 1/352, 1802 census; Fyfe, p. 100; Council minutes, October 1 and 8, 1796; December 20, September 14, 1798, CO 270/4; October 24, 1808, CO 270/11.

46. *Missionary Magazine for 1796*, vol. 1, pp. 108-9; *Evangelical Magazine for 1796*, vol. 4, pp. 420-21.

47. Melville, pp. 22-23.

48. Church, p. 8.

49. Rankin, pp. 4-5, 49.

50. Church, p. 8; Melville, pp. 245, 244, 242, 21-22; Rankin, pp. 61-62; *Missionary Magazine*, p. 109; *Evangelical Magazine*, p. 421; Claude George, *The Rise of British West Africa*, p. 433; Rankin, p. 262.

51. Council minute, February 19, 1795, CO 270/3; Macaulay Journal, February 16 and 20, 1798; *Adam Afzelius: Sierra Leone Journal*, January 10, February 2, 1796.

52. *Works of Samuel Hopkins*, vol. 1, pp. 148-49, 150-51; Governor and council to Thornton, January 31, March 8, 1795, and Macaulay and Watt to Hopkins, March 19, 1795, CO 268/5; Council minute, January 26, 1795, CO 270/3; Sierra Leone Company 1796 Report, p. 13. Also, George E. Brooks, Jr., "The Providence African Society's Sierra Leone Emigration Scheme, 1794-1795," pp. 183-202.

53. Macaulay Journal, July 29, 1797. James Frazer is "the Taylor" in the 1802 census, WO 1/352.

Chapter 19

THE LAW OF THE SETTLERS

> The poor people I brought with me from America begin to
> feel the sweets of a free government, and I am convinced
> they would follow the example of France, should they be
> disturbed in their endeavours to maintain their newly-
> acquired freedom.
>
> —JOHN CLARKSON TO LAFAYETTE, 1792

> Perhaps the greatest significance of the American Revolu-
> tion was the precedent it set.
>
> —WALLACE BROWN[1]

In an age of revolution it was almost inevitable that the steady pres-
sures for self-determination exerted by the loyal blacks of Freetown
should reach a climax in a rebellion. It came in 1800. It lasted scarcely as
many days as the American Revolution had occupied years. Its object
was to overthrow the rule of white men. It failed. Afterward the settlers
lost their limited right to elect representatives. Strengthened by a charter
and backed by military force, the company was able to protect its
commercial and evangelical beachhead on the African continent. The
reactions of the company directors to the settlers' aggression were
equally a part of the age of revolution, a reflection of the anti-Jacobin
mood which permeated the British ruling class with a horror of the
"mob." It was a dark age for reform, and it affected, among other good
works, the campaign for the abolition of the slave trade.[2]

The immediate sequence of events leading to the break began in 1798,
the quietest year so far in terms of settler-company relations, in spite of
Governor Macaulay's forebodings. He was waiting, with admirable
patience, the arrival of a successor. At the end of 1797 he had sent
gloomy reports which spoke of a "mutinous spirit" abroad in the colony.

After the quarrel over religious liberty and a near insurrection against the quitrent, he saw the settlers growing in "enthusiasm" and "blind attachment" to partisan politics. "The silly people thought their preachers must know best. . . . they began . . . to say the Coy. had no right to the Land . . . from [the natives] alone they would hold it. They would not acknowledge the Coys. title to allot." To him, as to his superiors, their chances seemed slim for remaining free and "civilized" without continuing and firm British control. Alone, they would be "fair game" for the surrounding "barbarians."[3]

Nevertheless, the election in December, 1797, had gone reasonably well. With women excluded from voting for the first time, the settlers had elected twenty-four tithingmen, including two whites. Only one tithing did not elect.[4]

Those of the 1796 antiwhite faction who were defeated were loath to give up power. The election of the two whites was also protested briefly. At the swearing-in on January 22, 1798, Macaulay became so annoyed at their "idle" questions and general impertinence that although suffering a feverish swollen throat, he spoke at length, later ruefully admitting that all he accomplished was to make his own condition worse.[5]

A last attempt to go over the head of the governor came when three colonists—Isaac Anderson, Stephen Peters and Ishmael York—carried a petition to Captain Ball of the frigate *Daedalus*, a naval officer and therefore the king's senior representative on the coast. Ball was an old Botany Bay colleague of Dawes' and a welcome guest. The settlers asked him for clarification of their status. Were they still subjects of the king? Were they rightfully assessed for defenses, roads and poor relief? Would he arbitrate their dispute over the quitrent which they were "shamefully Calld upon to pay"? According to Macaulay, the people so far had been asked for no more than a week's work on the fortifications, were minimal contributors to the poor and had assumed responsibility for the roads voluntarily. The quitrent was not negotiable. Ball was told that "if fair methods wd. not procure redress . . . they did not know what unpleasant things might follow." The captain brought their petition directly to the governor.[6] For some time events seemed to show that it was an empty threat.

Although Macaulay does not seem to have revived the idea of a constitution, the hundreders and tithingmen formed themselves into two chambers with a committee serving as a channel to the council. After some sparring over Macaulay's veto of a resolution that would exempt the elected officials from the road tax, there was no dispute worthy of record during the year.[7] For several weeks a reassuring harmony was produced by the rumors of another attack by the French. The colonists helped strengthen the defenses and transport valuables and records upriver for safety. Company staff and settlers smoothly shared militia duty until word came on May 21 that the enemy fleet had sailed for Europe.[8] Some excitement was created by stirrings among the Africans as well. King Tom early in the year had broken off a palaver over the disputed land on the western boundary and denounced Macaulay as a bad man who spoiled the country by lowering the price of rice. But he did stop the dancing and drumming on Sundays, sounds of which had drifted across St. George's Bay to disturb church services. Later that year it was rumored that there was an African plot to kill Macaulay during a palaver and seize Fort Thornton. The colonists who had no guns were allowed to buy them.[9]

Twenty-three-year-old Thomas Ludlam arrived in April to join the government. Macaulay was at first reluctant to leave affairs in his inexperienced hands. Ludlam was to serve three terms as a company governor. The son of a mathematician, he had been apprenticed to a printer. In contrast with Macaulay, he was not physically strong, and in viewpoint he was undoctrinaire with "mild and conciliatory manners." He lacked Macaulay's cultural arrogance. After a brief acquaintance, Macaulay predicted that he would make a "comfortable and useful associate." He passed the test on religion, although he seemed a bit too open-minded. When the veteran employee John Gray returned from home leave in October, Macaulay began to count the weeks until his own departure.[10]

The placid interval was suddenly broken by a renewed demand for payment of the quitrent. Gray had brought from London orders to enforce the hated levy. The edict was thought to have been made palatable by a decision that the revenues would be applied to colonial needs and not sent back to London as heretofore intended. Believing passions were sufficiently cool to attempt it, the governor and council announced the quitrent demand and offered new grants incorporating the terms. Settlers were to apply for them before December 15. Hardly a dozen responded, though as before they remained in occupation.[11] "From this period," Ludlam later wrote, "the colony had no peace till the time of the insurrection: almost every friend of the Government among the Hundredors & Tythingmen was thrown out at the ensuing election; and the boldness, turbulence and power of the factious leaders continued thro' the whole of the year 1799 rapidly increasing."[12]

The quitrent was the one issue guaranteed to produce a majority against the government, and Macaulay, for all his early derision of Clarkson's policy of "harangue" and persuasion and his theory that a hard line would succeed, was unable to collect anything before his departure in April, 1799. During his last weeks he kept loaded guns in his bedroom and a light burning through the night. Gray succeeded him as governor, and seven months later Ludlam took over.[13]

Ludlam's capacity for conciliation immediately came into play, and he acted forthrightly on both the quitrent and the vindictive education policy to check the rising rebelliousness. Macaulay's decision of November, 1794, to exclude from the company's schools children of parents who would not take a loyalty oath and return property claimed by the company, had struck a blow at a cherished institution. Only about half the children qualified to attend. In the spring of 1797 the council had, on review, admitted children on payment of $1 per quarter in advance. But the situation still did not return to normal. In budgeting for 1799, the directors slashed the education item by half, allowing £150, or enough for only fifty boys and thirty girls. Macaulay decided again to use a political test, and only children of parents who agreed to pay the quitrent were to be enrolled. The rest would have to pay the cash advance if they wished to attend. So low was the response that a few months later the ban on children of recalcitrant parents was "tacitly relinquished." Meanwhile, a group of opposition parents invited a man named Nicholson, left ashore because of illness by a South Sea whaler, to set up a competing school, which attracted seventy children. When Nicholson died, none of these pupils applied for the company classes. Indifference to education was so unlike the settlers that Ludlam knew it had to stem from the deep-rooted opposition to the quitrent. One of his first acts as governor, therefore, was to drop all conditions for school enrollment, reopen three schools in town and one in the country for "all children whatever" and pray for contributions from friends in Britain to meet the bills. However reasonable it might seem that friends of the company should be favored and enemies punished, the appearance of partiality had prevented the company from doing any good at all, Ludlam concluded. He wished, but did not dare, to exclude girls from the writing and arithmetic classes and save a little money that way. But fearing that the parents would withdraw all their children if such a restriction were adopted, the girls were admitted as before.[14]

Ludlam let the quitrent die. None had been paid in 1799, and at the end of the year the office of collector was dropped as part of the continuing budget reductions. Faced with convincing evidence that it was unworkable, the council recorded fatalistically, "As it is impossible to collect the quit-rents, the office of Collector sinks of itself. . . . If the Quit rents are to be collected, it must be by other authority than the Company's."[15]

Although the tax would be resuscitated, it was for now a victory for the colonists and should, in earlier times, have been sufficient to cut the ground from under the radical leaders. Ninety percent of the people opposed the quitrent "with steadiness and vigour"; it was "the great, the constant, the successful argument by which the people were persuaded that they were abused, oppressed & enslaved." But the momentum toward rebellion was now virtually irresistible, and a new issue took its place—the allegedly unfair administration of justice. Such an issue could be troublesome but, like other sources of dispute, was never enough for the majority of people to take up arms. What stands out in examination of the record, even though it is compiled almost entirely by the white rulers, is the settlers' steady intent to build a viable community. There was always a moderate majority in favor of law and order.

The judicial system was not a new issue. Its legality had been questioned because of the company's lack of a charter, but to the blacks the real question was its built-in white bias. Although they served on juries, the judges were always company officials who could also act as prosecutors. The hundreders and tithingmen resolved early in 1799 "that it would be right and Jest for to have two Justices of the Peace of the black People and one Judge for we Due thank that it Will due a grat Deail of good." Macaulay ruled that although this might be fair, it was not practical since no settler was sufficiently versed in English law. He could not see that injustice could possibly arise so long as a jury of settlers determined guilt before a judge sentenced.[16] There had been hints that even in Nova Scotia the settlers pictured a future in which some of them would be magistrates. Now, unsatisfied, they determined to appeal "home," because "we Due not think our Selves Dun Jestises to in the Colenney Not by no Meains." As for their ignorance, with the help of company officers, settler-judges "may Due Very well for we unlarnt People." The governor and council agreed to transmit the appeal to London and asked for particulars of cases which the settlers alleged had been unfairly handled.

Three months later, without waiting for the directors' reply, the colonists selected Mingo Jordan as a judge and John Cuthbert and Isaac Anderson as justices of the peace and sent their names to Governor Gray.[17] While the colonial government temporized, the hundreders and tithingmen moved on another controversial front, to decide just who was a citizen. By one resolution, foreigners (whites) who came to Freetown would be required to pay whatever tax the hundreders and tithingmen might set and have no vote or voice in legislation unless the black colonists so willed. In reply the governor and council pointed out that the whites whom the settlers wished to exclude were the "most active, enterprizing and intelligent" members of the community. The settler-sponsored law of 1796 which required a year's residence before voting was cited as curb enough on newcomers. They rejected the view that the black settlers alone were the legitimate landholders.[18]

With Macaulay's arrival in London and appointment as secretary for the company, the directors applied in July, 1799, to Parliament for the royal charter so long denied. At the same time they were negotiating to supervise the move of more than 500 unhappily exiled Jamaican Maroons from Nova Scotia to West Africa. It was the directors' opinion that the weak government dictated by the limited powers of the incorpo-ration act had brought the colony more than once to the verge of civil war and lowered its prestige in the eyes of surrounding Africans. An incident of the sort deplored by the directors occurred in February, 1800. The captain of a Liverpool slave ship refused to pay the customary anchorage fee to King Tom. The governor was forced by a group of settlers to make the captain pay a "ransom," which the company later refunded. There would be no more talk of a constitution or democratic elections for such subjects. Wilberforce denounced them as:

> thorough Jacobins as if they had been trained & educated in Paris. Nothg. but the greatest firmness of wisdom & temper in our governors could for 9 years have prevented their ruining the colony & rendering themselves miserable—They have lately become more unmanageable than ever & the sound part among them who . . . have hitherto kept the disaffected in awe, are become less equal to the Task, by their combin-ing with the Natives, to take the Governt. into their own hands.

The application for a charter was approved in July, 1800. A request for a military force of fifty men from the garrison at Gorée was granted.[19]

The directors' rejection of the demand for black judges reached Sierra Leone on November 4, 1799, but Ludlam delayed informing the hun-dreders and tithingmen, possibly hoping that augmented power would reach him before he had to deal with their predictable anger. He finally faced them on December 5 and explained that under British law only the king or his representatives could appoint judges at home or abroad. Isaac Anderson, once more a hundreder, and tithingmen James Robinson and Nathaniel Wansey announced their determination to go ahead anyhow, but they were not immediately backed by others. The 1799 election proceeded—the last ever for these offices—and the new body was sworn in on February 11, 1800. There were few new faces on it.[20]

Less than a month later a bill of particulars against the colonial government was submitted by several tithingmen headed by their chairman, Wansey, to prove "we cannot get justice from the White people." It cited two instances in which Ishmael York was prevented from pursuing charges or obtaining redress. It accused the company store of refusing to accept their paper money and refusing to take their bids at auctions of damaged goods. It exhibited resentment at public rebukes of individuals and declared that such grievances had not arisen in the days of Governor Clarkson and Dawes.[21]

In April a resolution appointing James Robinson and John Cuthbert to be, respectively, judge and justice of the peace was handed to the governor and council. At this point an armed brig, the *Nancy*, sent by the company for defense against either African or internal aggression, arrived in the harbor. (The *Nancy* carried Major Peregrine Francis Thorne, whom the directors wished to establish as a planter. He was granted the 225 acres of the former Clarkson's Plantation on the Bulom shore. He rapidly withdrew from the scheme, deciding the Africans were too difficult to deal with.[22] Ludlam augmented the ranks of peace officers by adding six reliable settlers—Job Allen, George Clark, Warwick Francis, Henry Lawrence, Anthony Wilkins and Thomas Wilson. On May 20, 1800, an address drafted by Ludlam but delivered by Richard Bright, for Ludlam was ill with the bowel complaint that dogged him all that year, gave the settlers their first official knowledge that the company was daily awaiting a charter and additional power. The audience was a mere twenty-seven people.

Ludlam's statement had concentrated on the demands for black judges and a request for an appeals court. It was possible, he argued, for uneducated settlers as jurors to arrive at a verdict based on the evidence presented in court, but to apply the appropriate penalties as judges required knowledge of law and ability to read. He saw no evidence that white judges had been prejudiced, and he charged that those who sought to replace them wanted mere personal advancement. The company had once considered naming two or more justices from among the settlers, he disclosed, but under the coming charter, it would be the king's prerogative. If they then refused to obey, they would be tried for high treason. This sanction would apply to all, including "those who say they are *Africans* and therefore being in their *own* country are not bound to obey the King and laws of England."[23]

It was a clear signal to the activists that their move should not long be postponed. They set out to depose the whole white-run government. One idea, which the company took seriously enough to publish, was to put all the whites into an open boat without sails, oars or compass and set them adrift.[24]

Whether the settlers were told about the company's involvement in the transportation of the Maroons is not established, but it might not have aroused uneasiness even if known, for the original plan was to settle them in a separate colony. Both Gray and Ludlam had been cool to overtures from the government to take in the Maroons. They explained to Nova Scotia's Governor Wentworth:

> We have had much trouble with our present Settlers on the score of either real or pretended promises which they have continued to allege were made to them previous to their leaving Halifax. . . . tho' since they have been here every thing has been done for them that either Men or money could effect to make them comfortable and satisfied, and to ensure them all the privileges & blessings of Free men. . . . Tho' they have been excused the payment of their Quit Rents. . . . tho' the Compy. have been at a vast annual expence in providing them with European schoolmasters, Chaplains, Physicians and Surgeons. . . . Tho' they have had every indulgence . . . in regard to the payment of their old debts . . . they are still not satisfied. . . .[25]

At the insistence of the Maroons and those who supported their request for reestablishment in a tropical climate, the British government had turned naturally to the Sierra Leone Company with its experience of colonization and its reputation for frugality. And the directors had been willing to undertake the job at the government's expense in return for the charter and military aid. The directors were weary of sole responsibility for a settlement which was fulfilling none of their expectations. A former company man, George Ross, was hired as agent, with strict instructions that the Maroons were not to be consulted on the terms of their settlement in Africa. They were to be allowed no guns. The land grants were to be substantially the same as for the loyalists, except that a quitrent was stipulated and a number of conditions regarding cultivation were attached. Freetown officials attempted to find a site for them in the Banana Islands and, when that failed, on the river but at some distance from the older colony. The Maroons refused to sign the terms but were understood to have accepted them orally.[26]

In late summer of 1800 the settlers began to meet to discuss grievances and strategy. At times 150, almost half the heads of families, participated. All the hundreders favored rebellion, and about half the tithingmen. As the spirit hardened, progovernment elected representatives were replaced by more militant leaders. Isaac Anderson emerged as head of the rebel alliance, John Cuthbert as its chief judicial officer and Zimrie Armstrong as its secretary.[27] On September 3 the dissidents, gathered at Cato Perkins' meetinghouse, drew up a code of laws "just before God and Man." It dismissed the governor and council from all responsibility except the Sierra Leone Company's trade and gave administrative power to the hundreders and tithingmen. It was signed by three hundreders— Anderson, James Robinson and Anzel Zizer—and by Wansey as chairman of the tithingmen. The document concluded: "all that come from Nova Scotia shall be under this law or quit the place." Any supporter of the company government would be fined £20.[28]

The new "laws" had to do with bread-and-butter problems. If anyone refused to sell goods to a settler and then carried them out of the colony to trade, he could be fined £20 or banished. Price ceilings were set for palm oil, salted beef and pork, rice, rum, soap, cheese, sugar, salt and butter. Fines were set for keeping a "bad house," for trespass, stealing, drawing a weapon, threatening, lying "or scandalizing without a proof," breaking the Sabbath, adultery or killing (stray) animals. It was also against the law for children to misbehave; they could be fined or "severely corrected" by parents. No summons or warrant could be issued without reference to the hundreders and tithingmen. No company debt could be collected until the same bodies confirmed that the claim was just. (The resistance to paying old debts at the store arose from the suspicion that, especially at first, the inept clerks had intentionally or otherwise fiddled the accounts and that they were charged simply to make the books balance.)[29] The company was required to take the settlers' produce in exchange for goods, which were to be duty-free.

A week later, on September 10, a notice was posted on Abraham

Smith's house that "the law of the Sirra Leona Setler" was to come into effect on September 25, when Anderson, Robinson and Zizer would take over. Councillor Bright saw the notice and argued Smith into taking it down. Another meeting was held at Perkins' chapel, where Ishmael York (according to Ludlam) charged that the governor meant to dismiss the hundreders and tithingmen. On September 25, 1800, the code was nailed to Smith's window shutter, and all hope of averting a conflict ended. Few saw it that night, but it drew crowds the following morning. Gray and James Wilson copied it down and read it aloud. Hearing it, some settlers reportedly were indignant at the usurpation of power.

The "daring overt act of sedition" compelled the governor to act. Supporters were called to Thornton Hill and armed. Robinson and Wansey were summoned to explain their conduct. Both made excuses. At 7 P.M., informed that the four signers of the code and others were at Ezekiel Campbell's house and were calling in their country partisans, Governor Ludlam sent an armed party under Marshal Corankapone with warrants for their arrest. The constables arrived just as the meeting was breaking up. Robinson was walking away when Corankapone called on him to surrender. Robinson refused and struck the marshal a hard blow on the cheek with his stick (or pelloon, a club used to thresh rice). The marshal in turn clubbed Robinson, who surrendered. Two or three impetuous constables rushed the house, shouting to those inside to yield. Wansey knocked out David Edmonds with his stick, and seeing the constable unconscious, his companions opened fire. Edward Willoughby and Daniel Carey were wounded, and Wansey was stabbed with a bayonet but escaped. The marshal's party returned to the governor's house with Robinson and Zizer, who had offered no resistance. Among the wounded loyalists, in addition to Corankapone and Edmonds, were Jesse George, Henry Lawrence, Joseph Ramsay and Thomas Richards. This, at least, is what the official record said took place. John Kizell told it differently, years later. He said that the people attending the meeting "had no arms whatsoever" when "the governor's party came and fired on [them]. . . . The men rund out of the house . . . took fence sticks and began to knock the governors people down and wounded many . . . with their sticks, and clubs."

This was corroborated, in the main, by Eli Ackim's memory that the conference was surprised when "a party of soldiers marched to the spot, forced an entrance . . . and fired upon them. Indignation became vehement: the party which refused to deliver up their grants rapidly increased; the flame spread."[30]

On September 27 Anderson and about fifty followers—the "bulk of the young men," said Ackim—collected at the bridge on the road to Granville Town. At Thornton Hill were a dozen whites, about thirty settlers and about forty African seamen from the company's trading fleet. The risk of defeat if battle was joined was keenly felt. There were too many neutrals and some fear that nearby Temne would join in the fray. Ludlam proposed arbitration by the first naval captain to arrive. Rewards of $100 each were announced for Anderson and Wansey and $50 each for Carey, Charles Elliot and Frank Patrick on charges of treason. Robinson and Zizer, already in custody, signed an appeal to Anderson to "lay down your arms . . . for mercy's sake come in . . . let us fulfil our promises and hear the Governor's answer." Anderson's answers to every communication were, in the governor's view, insolent.

On Sunday, September 28, Anderson announced that he would attack Thornton Hill. He demanded release of the prisoners and the women and children. Ludlam refused. "I must do my duty to the English Government," he said, "and bring to justice all who rebel against it."

Detachments of rebels were said to have taken a gun and some powder from the governor's farm. Powder, shot and $100 were stolen at Thomas Wilson's; mats and hides from Corankapone's; liquor, sugar, tea and clothing from the farms of Gray and Carr. Ludlam warned that looters would be treated as traitors. By September 30 the governor's force, confined in Fort Thornton, was becoming impatient to attack before King Tom became involved. He, as landlord, was offering to settle the conflict if the colonists could not do it themselves by the weekend. But about ten o'clock, "Behold! a most unexpected intervention of providence completely changed the face of affairs." The *Asia*, a naval transport carrying the 500 Maroons from Halifax, was sighted offshore and anchored in the evening. On board also were 45 British troops of the Twenty-fourth Regiment on their way home on sick leave and commanded by Lieutenants Lionel Smith and H. D. Tolley.

On October 1 the Maroon chiefs, led by elderly General Montague James, were called to Thornton Hill, where their terms of settlement were reviewed and agreed. When Ludlam pointed out that "the rebellion then raging in the heart of the Colony" would delay the allocation of their land, the chiefs made "an unanimous & hearty offer" to take the field, glad, as Thornton was to jest to Hannah More, "to *stretch their legs* a little."[31] Thus reinforced, the governor sent a warning to the rebels that further resistance was futile. He promised that if the wounded loyalists recovered, no rebel would be executed. The two army officers and the officer commanding the *Asia*, Lieutenant John Sheriff, set a deadline of 10 P.M. for surrender. The rebels' reply, seeking time for consultation, was regarded as frivolous.

An attack was planned for shortly after midnight on October 2. A detachment of Maroons under Alexander Macaulay (Zachary's sea captain brother) and Lieutenant Sheriff was to travel in boats from the *Asia* to Thompson's Bay to land in the rebels' rear. It was to be guided by Charles Jenkins and Thomas Wilson. A second force under Lieutenant Smith was to march from Thornton Hill directly to the bridge. A third, led by George Ross, was to cut the rebels off from the haven of the hills. The insurgents' position was poorly chosen for defense, as if they had anticipated no attack or felt sure they could retreat into the woods if necessary. The last two detachments came ashore for arms during a violent thunderstorm, and their start was delayed until morning. At daybreak the first detachment attacked alone. The rebels were completely routed after a skirmish. Most escaped. Two (unnamed) were killed. On October 3 the rebels were invited to talks, and some responded. They were cautioned that the Maroons were accustomed to give no quarter, and as if to prove their fierce reputation, a Maroon searching party fired on two fleeing African laborers at the governor's farm, killing one and severely wounding the other. Everyone was warned to stay indoors or, if accosted by a search party, on no account to run. After a week thirty-one prisoners had been taken. Rewards were posted for the fourteen rebels still at large.

Speedy trials were decided upon because of the expense and insecurity of long detention. The charter of justice, though it had received the king's assent in July, had not yet been delivered, so the governor was still without the power to carry out capital punishment. The device of a military tribunal composed of Smith, Tolley and Sheriff was therefore adopted.[32] Official records provide the names of fifty-five active participants in the rebellion. In the weeks following the uprising, two were hanged and thirty-three banished, facing 300 lashes if caught at Freetown. Under civil proceedings, all the offenses possibly would not have warranted such severe penalties, but the governor and council were convinced that the colony must get rid of these men. The charges read against James Robinson, a sample of those filed against others, were: hostility to the colonial government and the company's interests, violation of oath as a hundreder, framing with others a code of laws which annulled the authority of the governor and council and entering a powerful combination which by various overt acts resulted in "open & unprovoked rebellion." Robinson, now in his late sixties, was banished for life to Gorée. His defense was that he had wanted only to "promote the good of the Colony in all his actions and designs."

On October 12, 1800, a printed copy of the new charter arrived, and a true copy with the royal commissions for governor and council followed. On November 6 the charter was ceremoniously carried ashore by John Watts, commander of a British sloop of war, *Osprey*, and solemnly delivered to Governor Ludlam "under a royal salute of Cannon."[33]

Francis Patrick and James Harford had been bound over by the military tribunal for trial at the first quarter sessions of the new government, and to their cases were added those of the rebel chief, Isaac Anderson, John Stober and Joseph Waring, who had been turned in by King Firama after the tribunal ended. Cases of high treason were still outside a local court's jurisdiction, and rather than face the complications and costs of removing the trials to Britain, Anderson and Patrick were charged with "capital felonies." Anderson was hanged, therefore, for sending an anonymous and threatening letter to the governor. Patrick went to the gallows for stealing a gun.[34] Stober was banished to the Bulom shore for ten years and Harford for five, a sentence later commuted to hard labor in the colony. A banishment sentence on Stephen Williams was similarly commuted. Waring's indictment was dismissed.[35]

Ishmael York, who lost an arm in the fighting, was banished to the Rio Nunez, where he could trade for a living since his days of manual labor were over. Sentenced for life to exile and hard labor at the Gorée penal colony were, in addition to Robinson, John Cuthbert, Robert Morris, Henry Morrison and Natus Plantus (Planter). Twenty-four others were banished to the Bulom shore. These were Thomas Bird, Thomas Cato, Joseph and Samuel Elliot, Andrew Fennel, Richard Ferguson, Francis Gordon, Micaiah Isaacs, John Lee, Mingo Leslie, George Lewis, Henry Richardson, York Shepherd, Matthew Sinclair, Abraham Smith, John Smith, Anthony Stephens, Antony Waring, Samuel White, Isaac Williams, John Williams, Ansel Zizer and two men whose names conjured up the remembrance of the American war and loyalist flight—Henry Washington, ex-slave of the father of American independence, and British Freedom. All the convicted rebels forfeited their property, and their farms, with houses and crops, were distributed to the Maroons, who were settled, not in a separate colony, but at Granville Town.[36]

Services of progovernment settlers were praised in the company's 1801 report. Particular recognition went to Corankapone, "an old and faithful servant. . . . To whose intimate knowledge of the individual

settlers both loyal and seditious, we have been uniformly indebted . .
and who exerted his usual courage and fidelity on this occasion.'' Isaa
James, Charles Jenkins, Andrew Moore, William Mungo (a onetime
servant in Granville Sharp's family), George Ogram (an Old Settler
Peter Scott and Thomas Wilson were cited for services as guides in t
face of ''great danger, as it was continually in the power of the rebels, l
lurking in the bush and long grass, to pick off any one whom they chose
single out with little hazard to themselves.'' David Edmonds was con
mended for faithful service. Maroons and settler guides shared rewar
totaling $400 (it came to $2.70 each) for the capture of several rebels.

Peace came to the settlement. Loyal colonists were content with th
results, and those who were still ''disaffected'' were respectful. Since
number of rebels remained at large, however, farms were neglected, an
people living on the outskirts were reluctant to remain. Many of th
insurgents had been farmers, among them the ill-fated Isaac Anderson
who only two years before had proudly sent a barrel of his own rice
John Clarkson so that he could partake first of the fruits.[38]

On a visit the following spring to Clarkson's Plantation, Ludlam foun
exiled rebels building houses and clearing the land. Samuel Elliot an
Henry Washington were their chosen leaders. Some had split off to liv
under a local chief's protection. One, Micaiah Isaacs, had died
dysentery. The rice that had been stored there for the expected arrival
the Maroons had been distributed to them and was nearly eaten up.
number were employed cutting timber in the hope of selling it
Freetown.[39]

Always a reluctant governor, unwell and troubled deeply by th
uprising, and its aftermath, Ludlam had resigned even before the reb
trials were completed. The directors had persuaded Dawes to go bac
and he arrived on January 6, 1801. His first undertaking was to build
blockhouse and barracks for the troops from Gorée and to improve th
gun emplacements.[40] Various government changes dictated by the ne
charter were speedily put into effect, and the year 1801, not 1789 c
1791, became the real end of Sharp's Province of Freedom as th
old-style elected representation was swept away. Since 1792, sevent
five Nova Scotian and Old Settler men had served as hundreders an
tithingmen, and they had exerted considerable influence on the nature c
government. The new charter was modeled on the East India Compar
except for the retention of trial by jury in civil actions. If Sierra Leones
became even more famous for going to court, perhaps this was becaus
litigation was the chief remaining avenue for expression. The governm

nd council continued as the executive branch and appointed a mayor and
hree aldermen for Freetown and a court of commissioners for small
ebts.[41] Many blacks were to serve as commissioners. Company officers
nd the growing number of independent white businessmen filled the
ther offices. Until now the company had been forced to rule by consent.
Jow its directives were backed by military strength.

It was fortuitous that the Maroons and troops arrived exactly when
hey did, but the odds were against the revolt in any case. The rebellion
eveloped from a lengthy struggle for rights within a framework of
British law into a total rejection of white rule, an extreme position which
vas not generally supported. It would have been impossible for a rebel
overnment to govern long. The attempt, however, was the first in West
Africa to overturn white supremacy, "a first step towards 'negritude' and
lack 'African' nationalism."[42] And it is still not certain what the
utcome would have been had the conflict centered on the quitrent.
Adam Jones, whom Governor Ludlam regarded as "the most respect-
ble" of the hundreders in office at the time, but a determined critic of the
overnment over the quitrent issue, parted company with the leadership
vhen, with the quitrent battle apparently won, it made the issue of judges
he key. In addition, Jones and some others opposed the proposed price
ixing. These were secondary objectives and many were not prepared to
o to extreme lengths to win them. The rebellion had been led in the end
y the less able men.[43]

Yet in the memories of some settlers the rebellion was directly con-
ected with the quitrent. John Kizell recollected that plans to enforce it
ad caused the settlers to "set in council among themselves, to appoint a
nan to command us, and Justices."[44] Eli Ackim was equally positive
bout the cause and the event when he related it to visiting F. Harrison
Rankin. He was quoted as saying, "When the threatened land-tax was
nnounced, they [hundreders and tithingmen] assembled to consider
vhether it were best to accept these renewed grants and pay the impost,
r to abide by the original agreement." This was the subject under
iscussion when the arresting party arrived. Mrs. Melville, too, was told
y her informant, an Old Settler woman, that the rebellion occurred
'owing to a small quit-rent having been levied upon the little farms, on
vhich, under so many disadvantages, they had laboured for seven
ears."[45]

Few lessons were learned from the bloodshed and violence, and
lack-white relations continued to fester because of the failure to treat the
nisunderstanding about land distribution and land titles. Ludlam alone

was willing to let the quitrent sink into oblivion. A year after th
rebellion, from a seat in the council, he made a masterly plea fo
eliminating or at least modifying the divisive issue. It was a brave attac
on a sacred cow, and one wonders with what emotions Macaulay an
Thornton read the council minutes which contained it. Nothing happene
until the 1826 parliamentary inquiry, when, in effect, the commissioner
found the settlers' land-related grievances justified. Not coincidentally
this seems to be the only one of numerous early inquiries into Sierr
Leone affairs which took testimony from blacks. Commissioners Jame
Rowan and Henry Wellington took cognizance of the "original cause"
of trouble between settlers and company, "not only because the seed
were thereby sown of a discontent which time has not entirely eradicated
but because the question of right and justice which it involves, does no
appear ever to have been decided, at least to their satisfaction." Th
settlers were promised land *"free of all expense"* and afterward found
"burthened with an annual quit rent, in breach, as they conceived, of tha
assurance upon the faith of which they had been induced to emigrate."
There was room here for misconception "on the part even of person
more enlightened than the Nova Scotian blacks could then have been."
And they agreed that:

> whatever the intentions of the Company . . . sound policy at
> least would have been best consulted by a fulfilment of the
> terms, in their most liberal and comprehensive acceptation.
> The plan pursued appears to have been highly instrumental in
> exciting that spirit of discontent, with which the Nova Scotians
> have so frequently been charged; and their resistance to the
> claim as an infringement of the terms upon which they had
> been induced to become colonists, has frequently led to acts of
> insubordination.[46]

Ludlam's letter to the governor and council in 1801, although
seemed to achieve nothing, contributes to an understanding of the set
tlers' position. He wrote after another futile effort had been made, unde
Governor Dawes, to collect the quitrent and tamper with the grants, thi
time to incorporate a clause against slavery and the slave trade. Now th
Maroons, as well as the Nova Scotians, opposed it, and once more th
attempt was abandoned.[47] Ludlam had listened to the colonists. The
believed that a single failure to pay the rent, through neglect, delay o
misfortune, would cause the land to be forfeited. Most widows and al

orphans could lose their property under it. It was a tax in perpetuity. It was far too high in relation to the value of the land; in twenty years the quitrent would pay for the land, yet it went on forever. Ludlam recognized that the printed terms offered in Nova Scotia had not mentioned the quitrent and that the company's authorized agent, Clarkson, "perhaps the most popular governor in the colony," had specifically assured them it was "unjust & ought not to be imposed."

Ludlam had taken the trouble to find out whether their fears of the tax's effects were justified, and he found that they were. It was not a foolish fancy that their children could be deprived of their inheritance. Ludlam happened to be the guardian of the eldest son and heir of Henry Lawrence. He had learned that if he could not sell the land for the boy, it would be financially best to surrender it, rather than to pay a shilling an acre for it until the lad came of age, for the same money and the interest it might earn could purchase an equal amount of land if and when the boy wanted it.

By Ludlam's reckoning, even the company gained little—a revenue of £100 to £200 a year out of which a collector must be paid £15 or £20, a slim return on a quarter-million-pound investment. More of a realist than he might be given credit for, Ludlam said that the quitrent ought to be abolished, but he proposed only that it be lowered and imposed in a manner to reward loyal settlers and cause as little hardship on widows and orphans as possible.[48]

The Sierra Leonean economist N. A. Cox-George has described the quitrent as a classic example of the "role that . . . little administrative devices can play . . . on the course of economic development and . . . race relations." It caused a mass movement away from the land, the migration (and expulsion) of the better farmers and a legacy of suspicion and insecurity which was handed down for generations—a fear that white people would dispossess the blacks of their land. In 1803, as a reward for loyal service in the Temne hostilities, it was dropped without fanfare by Governor Day and his council, composed of Ludlam and Dawes. But it was revived—at a lower rate, it is true—in 1812 under the Crown government and not abolished until 1832. By contrast, the road tax, set at six days' labor annually or its money equivalent, which the settlers themselves had instituted and which in financial terms was at least as high as the quitrent, lasted until 1872, with substantial benefits to the communications and economy of the colony.[49]

The crushing of the 1800 rebellion and the arrival of a second, vigorous population group put an end to the Sierra Leone settlement as a

community of black Americans returned to Africa. It was to become a
conventional link in the chain of British Empire, distinguished chiefly for
its increasingly polyglot residents, whose one common bond was their
color. It would be another 160 years to independence. The Nova Scotians
were disheartened. Many of the best farmers were exiled, and many
young men went off to sea or new homes in other African nations. The
last serious threats to the security of the colony under company rule, were
the attacks in 1801 and 1802 by King Tom and other Temne chiefs. In
both, the Nova Scotians rallied alongside company employees and the
recently arrived troops and fought valiantly for their homes, families and
freedom. The hostilities may have been encouraged by fugitive rebels,
but they arose from the unresolved dispute over the settlement's legality
of occupation, which was activated by the arrival of reinforcements and
the strengthening of fortifications. The first assult was a dawn attack on
Thornton Hill on November 18, 1801, with Nathaniel Wansey and
Daniel Carey in the lead. Governor Dawes, wounded in the first on-
slaught, organized a bayonet charge, led by John Gordon and Old Settler
George Clark, which drove off the assailants. There were heavy losses on
both sides. Among the settlers killed were two who had arrived in 1787
John Battis and Constable George Ogram; the gardener Tarleton Flem-
ing; John and Joseph Ramsay; and Thomas Saunders. Hector McLean
was only wounded, but his wife was carried off and believed killed
Norfolk Scarborough lost his wife and was wounded himself. A daughter
of Mingo Jordan was killed, and his wife and another child were
wounded. But no loss was more keenly felt than that of Richard Coran
kapone, a court commissioner and undersheriff under the new charter
government. He had rushed to the governor's house at the alarm, "but
his solicitude for the safety of those who remained in the town caused him
to return thither. He received his first wound on his way back to the Fort
Still pressing forward with unabated Spirit, he received a second, and a
third which terminated a Life distinguished for years by the most important services," Henry Thornton reported to the War Office. In all, there
were eighteen fatalities and thirty-eight wounded.[50]

Farms were pillaged, crops burned and vessels sunk. Granville Town
was evacuated, with the Maroons crowding into Freetown, already
swollen by the influx from the countryside. Soon detachments from the
colony systematically drove the Temne out of the district, burning their
villages from Freetown to Cape Sierra Leone. At the British government's behest, the colonists also took over deserted Gambia Island.[5]
After a short-lived truce came a second surprise daybreak attack by King

Tom and 400 followers on April 11, 1802. The colony was better prepared, and the battle lasted only twenty minutes. Among the settlers who died were Norfolk Scarborough, Prince Salter and the wife of Peter Scott. Later that year a party of whites and Nova Scotians negotiated the return of the rebels who had taken asylum among the Mandinka. Wansey, Carey and Sampson Heywood were brought back to Freetown in irons. Their fate is not recorded. Sebe (Saby) Barnett, one of the others sought, fell into debt and was sold into slavery by his African creditors.[52]

Desultory warfare with the nearby Africans continued until mid-1807, when the land west of Freetown was formally ceded. This was also the year when the Sierra Leone Company arranged to hand over its African colony to the British government, after receiving an annual subsidy since the Maroon involvement. The rebellion seemed to have put an end to whatever lingering interest the directors and proprietors had in the settlement. During the later years the administration simply marked time. Negotiations (but no consultation with the colonists) began at least as early as 1803,[53] and a brief act of Parliament, almost entirely concerned with matters of property, dissolved the company and effected the transfer as of January 1, 1808.[54] It was Thomas Ludlam who found himself the last company governor. His final instructions contained a brief paragraph of farewell addressed to the colonists. He was asked to tell them "the satisfaction we have felt in contemplating their encreasing good order, under trying circumstances, for several years past; and to assure them, that although we cease to govern them, we shall not cease to do whatever may be in our power to promote their happiness."

NOTES

1. Clarkson to Lafayette, July 2, 1792, Clarkson Journal (New York); Ingham, *Sierra Leone After One Hundred Years*, p. 93. Clarkson sent the letter by way of Thornton, who did not forward it when he learned Lafayette was in prison. Wallace Brown, *The Good Americans*, p. ix.
2. Kraus, *The Atlantic Civilization*, pp. 157, 259, and Carpenter, *Church and People*, among others, make the point.
3. Macaulay to Thornton to Mills, December 1, 1797 (Macaulay papers cited from Huntington Library).
4. Council minute, December 28, 1797, CO 270/4; Macaulay Journal, January 17, February 20, 1798. James Carr was one white elected; the other is not identified.

5. Macaulay Journal (Mills), January 22, 1798; Macaulay Journal, January 22, February 16, 1798.

6. Council minute, January 16, 1798, CO 270/4; Macaulay Journal, January 1, 2, 15, 1798; Knutsford, *Life and Letters of Zachary Macaulay*, pp. 184, 188; Macaulay Journal (Mills), January 16, 1798.

7. Macaulay Journal, January 29, 1798; Council minutes, January 29, February 3, 1798, CO 270/4.

8. Council minutes, April 23, May 21, 1798, CO 270/4; Macaulay Journal, April 23, 24, 26, 27, 29; May 7, 12, 1798; Macaulay to Mills, May 5, 1798.

9. Council minute, January 6, 1798, CO 270/4; Macaulay Journal, March 25, 1798; Council minute, August 8, 1798, CO 270/4; Macaulay Journal (Mills), June 21, August 5, 1798.

10. Council minute, April 20, 1798, CO 270/4; Macaulay to Mills, May 5, 1798; *Dictionary of National Biography*; Fyfe, *A History of Sierra Leone*, p. 76; Hole, *Early History of the Church Missionary Society*, p. 137; Council minute, October 22, 1798, CO 270/4.

11. Council minutes, November 15, December 18, 1798, CO 270/4.

12. Ludlam to governor and council in minute of November 17, 1801, CO 270/6.

13. Macaulay Journal (Mills), January 27, 1799; Council minutes, April 4, November 4, 1799, CO 270/4.

14. Council minutes, April 29, 1797; December 29, 1798; January 16, November 4, December 30 and 31, 1799, all CO 270/4.

15. *Ibid.*, December 30, 1799.

16. Council minute, February 18, 1799, CO 270/4.

17. *Ibid.*, March 4, June 4, 1799.

18. *Ibid.*, September 10, 1799.

19. Sierra Leone Company 1804 Report, pp. 7, 12; 1801 Report, pp. 10-11; Wilberforce to Dundas, April 1, 1800, Melville Papers, BL Add. MSS. 41,085; Sierra Leone Company 1801 Report, pp. 8-9.

20. Council minutes, November 4, December 16, 1799, CO 270/4; January 25, February 11, 1800, CO 270/5.

21. *Ibid.*, March 4, 1800.

22. *Ibid.*, April 16, May 1, 8, 1800.

23. *Ibid.*, May 10, 1800; January 4, 1801; May 20, 1800; Sierra Leone Company 1801 Report, pp. 3, 6.

24. Sierra Leone Company 1801 Report, p. 11.

25. Gray and Ludlam to Wentworth, June 24, 1799, CO 217/70. For Maroon background and stay in Nova Scotia, Winks, *The Blacks in Canada*, pp. 78-94; Dallas, *The History of the Maroons*, vol. 1 and to p. 172 in vol. 2. Their pleas to go to a tropical climate in CO 217/70 and 218/27.

26. Portland to Wentworth, October 8, 1799, CO 218/27; Sierra Leone Company 1801 Report, pp. 55-57; Instructions to governor and council, March 22,

1799, and Portland to Thornton, March 5, 1799, CO 217/70; Council minute, October 1, 1800, CO 270/5.

27. Rebellion, unless otherwise noted, from Sierra Leone Company 1801 Report, pp. 12-21; Council minutes, September 25-October 2, 1800; Narrative of rebellion and appendix to narrative, all CO 270/5.

28. Code of laws printed in Fyfe, *Sierra Leone I-heritance*, pp. 124-26.

29. Ludlam to governor and council in minute of November 17, 1801, CO 270/6.

30. Kizell and Ackim to commissioners of inquiry, CO 267/92.

31. Thornton to More, February 16, 1801, Thornton Papers, Wigan Public Libraries.

32. Council minute, December 24, 1800, CO 270/5.

33. *Ibid.*, November 6, 1800.

34. The company reported three were hanged; the third was not named.

35. Council minute, December 31, 1800, CO 270/5.

36. *Ibid.*, January 23, 1801; December 27, 1800, March 31, 1801.

37. Sierra Leone Company 1801 Report, p. 19; Council minutes, March 1, June 27, 1801, CO 270/5; June 27, 1801, CO 270/6. Lieutenant Smith (like the other officers) was promoted on the strength of this action and began a distinguished career which included governorships at Barbados and Jamaica. His mother was the novelist Charlotte Smith. Thornton to Mrs. More: "If he has met with any beauteous African at Sierra Leone, I suppose his mother will publish a new novel." February 16, 1801, Thornton Papers, Wigan Public Libraries.

38. Sierra Leone Company 1801 Report, p. 18; Council minute, August 5, 1801, CO 270/6; Ackim to commissioners of inquiry, CO 267/92; Anderson to Clarkson, January 21, 1798, Clarkson Papers, BL Add. MSS. 41,263.

39. Council minute, April 7, 1801, CO 270/5. Some convicted rebels returned to Freetown years later under a general amnesty. See, for example, Bird, Cato, Samuel White and Abraham Smith cases among others in CO 270/13, 14.

40. Council minutes, January 6, 14, March, 1801, CO 270/5.

41. Sierra Leone Company 1801 Report, pp. 9, 12-13, 42-47; Charter in Newbury, *British Policy Towards West Africa*, pp. 470-74. First appointments, council minute, November 8, 1800, CO 270/5.

42. Hair, review of Fyfe, *A History of Sierra Leone, Sierra Leone Studies*, pp. 285-86.

43. Ludlam to governor and council, November 17, 1801, is the source, unless noted, of discussion of his position.

44. Kizell to Commissioners of inquiry, CO 267/92.

45. F. Harrison Rankin, *White Man's Grave*, p. 91; [Mrs. Melville], *A Residence at Sierra Leone*, p. 236.

46. Parliamentary Papers, 1826-7, VII, Report of Commissioners of Inquiry on the State of Sierra Leone, p. 10.

47. Council minutes, January 27, April 4, 10, 28, 1801, CO 270/5; June 2, 1801 CO 270/6.

48. Council minute, January 6, 1802, CO 270/7.

49. Cox-George, "Direct Taxation in the Early History of Sierra Leone," pp. 20, 31, 33, 34; Council minutes, April 18, 1803, CO 270/9; June 1, 1812, CO 270/13.

50. Thornton to Sullivan, February 13, 1802, WO 1/352. Also on the war, see Council minutes, November 18, 1801, CO 270/6; January 27, April 11 September 27, November 3, December 8 and 9, 1801, all CO 270/8; Sierra Leone Company 1804 Report, pp. 11, 40-41; Claude George, *Rise of British West Africa*, pp. 54-63; Melville, pp. 236-38; census, July 31, 1802, WO 1/352.

51. Mrs. H. Thornton to P. More, February 10, 1802, Thornton Papers, Wigan Public Libraries; Thornton to Hobart, February 26, 1802, February 21, 1803 WO 1/352; Council minute, November 20, 1801, CO 270/6; Thornton to Hobart, February 21, 1803, WO 1/352.

52. Council minute, July 25, 1816, CO 270/14.

53. Sierra Leone Company 1804 Report, p. 44.

54. Parliamentary Papers, 1806-7, I, pp. 57-59; Sierra Leone Company 1808 Report, pp. 4-7. Company's petition and transfer act both in Newbury.

Epilogue

By coincidence, the rebellion of the black loyalists at Sierra Leone occurred in the same year as "Gabriel's Insurrection," the "most sophisticated and ambitious slave conspiracy" in American history.[1] For both groups of blacks the Revolution of 1776 was unfinished. Those in Africa were free but did not have their land, the prerequisite for independence as they saw it. Those in Virginia were still slaves. Both incidents were political manifestations directed to solving grievances by replacing white governments. In both cases, conditions at the time were better than they had been before the Revolution, but both places were on the brink of developments which would result in harsher controls.[2] For blacks everywhere, as for whites, the Revolution had heightened expectations.

The American antecedents of the Sierra Leone settlers were frequently mentioned as a source of their belligerence and resistance to authority, but no one put the point more bluntly than chauvinistic young Governor Thompson, who took over from Ludlam in 1808. He hated the Nova Scotians. He loathed their pretensions to social equality. He resented them because, in reaction to his wholesale denunciations of the previous regime, they entered a kind of alliance with the agents of the Sierra Leone Company who had remained behind to wind up its business or go into commerce on their own. To Thompson, the Nova Scotians and Old Settlers combined represented "every thing that is vile in the American & all that is contemptible in the European. The most absurd enthusiasm is their religion & wild notions of liberty are their politics." Whenever they "insulted & abused a European trader, or defied their own Government," they started by saying, " 'This is Free-Town.' " The very name was "perverted to purposes of Insubordination & Rebellion." He retaliated by changing it to George Town. He gave the numbered streets the names of British military leaders, and he abolished the money called dollars and cents.

Thompson's massive dispatches to Lord Castlereagh bristled with vituperative remarks about the "negro Sans Culottes" with their "half comprehended notions of American independence," of the "runaway slaves . . . full of every species of ignorant enthusiasm and republican frenzy."[3] He was quickly recalled, not because of anything he had done or said about the settlers but because he accused the Sierra Leone Company of trafficking in slaves and the new apprenticeship system of being nothing but a euphemism for reenslavement of those Africans liberated from the slave ships by the navy after Britain abolished the slave trade. Back home, a wall of silence and inaction greeted his attempt to destroy the reputation of a company which had been metamorphosed into the African Institution, to oversee enforcement of the abolition act.

The Americanism of the first generation of Sierra Leone settlers also militated strongly against any expansion of their numbers from the United States. In no part of America did the idea of resettlement of blacks receive such fascinated attention as in Virginia, and in the last decade of the eighteenth century it grew into a virtual "campaign" to get rid of them.[4] The interest sprang from a combination of factors, including the slaves' undutiful turn to the British during the war, the sheer increase in their numbers, the fear of slave conspiracies, the cultivated horror of miscegenation and the growth of a small and disliked class of free blacks. The American Constitution had sustained slavery, but there had been enough discussion of emancipation to cause some people actively to seek ways of preventing the growth of a mixed society. Most of these theoretical colonizationists preferred a Western settlement to the costly and complicated task of transporting freed slaves to Africa.[5]

Thomas Jefferson ably represented the mixture of economic self-interest, simple prejudice and pseudo-scientific thinking that pervaded the various proposals. He never wavered in his own certainty that blacks were inferior and a multiracial society was out of the question, and he never found an emancipation or colonization plan he could support. At one time he dismissed all emancipation talk as "an English hobby."[6]

In the aftermath of Gabriel's "rebellion," President Jefferson inquired in 1802 through the American ambassador in London, Rufus King, whether it would be possible to send more blacks to Sierra Leone. It was not. The company was thinking of giving up the colony, and "in no event should they be willing to receive more of these people from the United States, as it was exactly that portion of settlers which . . . by their idleness and turbulence, had kept the settlement in constant danger of dissolution."[7]

Inquiries from American blacks continued into the nineteenth century, however, and a few drifted into Freetown "on their own bottoms." In 1816, on his own initiative and at his own expense, Paul Cuffe brought seven families to join the colony.[8]

There were always two Freetowns, one belonging to the Sierra Leone Company and one to the settlers, image and reality. Only the first "failed." It was never what the directors thought it was, and it sank under a plethora of expectations. They turned their governors into harassed bookkeepers to keep information flowing back which would be published under tidy headings of "trade," "cultivation" and "civilization," but all the data failed to reveal much about the settlers' day-to-day lives or the unique community which was striking root on the banks of the Sierra Leone. Thomas Clarkson, after intensive academic study of the slave trade, one day on the deck of a ship in the Thames took into his hands a length of African cloth. He then saw Africa and was deeply moved.[9] He collected a trunk full of such samples to help others see its reality. When the directors were confronted by sample settlers, their reality as representatives was questioned.

In terms of the settlers' personal dreams, the Sierra Leone experiment triumphed. Their pluck and work enabled the colony to survive.[10] The new life was full of hardship and discouragement but immensely more challenging, creative, exciting and influential than any they could have led in the United States, Canada or Britain in that time. It would be good to think this may have been in Henry Thornton's mind when he said, "Even tho' the colony should fail to be durably and beneficially established, a variety of happy consequences may incidently result from the attempt, and . . . tho' I have lost £2000 or £3000 . . . I am on the whole a gainer."[11]

These black Americans had asserted the humanity of blacks in an Atlantic world just awakening to their race and its rights. They had pushed back the horizons of their liberty measurably. Later arrivals would swamp them in numbers and, with fresh energy and fewer illusions, outstrip them economically. A visitor who half a century after their arrival talked with a number of the original settlers remarked: "I have . . . seen few persons whom you can more highly gratify by showing anything like an interest in their history."[12]

NOTES

1. Mullin, *Flight and Rebellion*, pp. 136, 140-63.

2. The cotton gin was to harden the institution of slavery in the South. The introduction of charter government was to strengthen authority in Sierra Leone.

3. Thompson to Castlereagh, November 2, 1808, Thompson Papers, Hull University 1/23; Thompson to Castlereagh, February 17, 1809, CO 267/25; L. G. Johnson, *General T. Perronet Thompson, 1783-1869*, p. 49; Council minute, November 11, 1808, CO 270/10; Thompson to Castlereagh, November 2, 1808; Thompson to Castlereagh in council minute, February 8, 1809, CO 270/10.

4. Jordan, *White over Black*, p. 542.

5. Sherwood, "Early Negro Deportation Projects," p. 486; Locke, *Anti-Slavery in America*, p. 192; Drimmer, *Black History*, pp. 98, 100-1; Frederic Bancroft, *The Colonization of American Negroes, 1801-1865*, pp. 153-54.

6. Tinkoom, "Caviar Along the Potomac. Sir Augustus John Foster's 'Notes on the United States,' 1804-1812," pp. 101-3. Morgan, "Slavery and Freedom: The American Paradox," brings out Jefferson's fear of all landless poor.

7. *The Writings of Thomas Jefferson*, vol. 9, pp. 303-4; Archibald Alexander, *A History of Colonization on the Western Coast of Africa*, pp. 73-74.

8. Council minutes, November 16, 1815; April 10, 1813; February 26, 1816, CO 270/4; January 15, 1813, CO 270/13; African Institution 1817 Report, pp. 40-41.

9. Griggs, *Thomas Clarkson*, p. 31.

10. Peterson, *Province of Freedom: a History of Sierra Leone 1787-1870*, pp. 36-37, 44.

11. Quoted in Meacham, *Henry Thornton of Clapham*, p. 119; Hair, "Henry Thornton and the Sierra Leone Settlement."

12. [Melville], *A Residence at Sierra Leone*, p. 244.

Bibliography

PRINCIPAL MANUSCRIPT SOURCES:

Individual documents have been identified in the relevant notes. This summary provides the location and general contents of the various collections used.

Baptist Missionary Society, London
> Accounts of the Particular Baptist Society for Propagating the Gospel Amongst the Heathen, 1792-1799.

British Library, London (BL)
> Additional Manuscripts (Add. MSS.):
>> 12,131. Various documents relating to Sierra Leone 1792-1798.
>> 21,254-21,256. Minute Books of the Committee of the Society for Effecting the Abolition of the Slave Trade, 1787-1819.
>> 33,978-33,979. Sir Joseph Banks Correspondence, 1765-1821.
>> 35,621. Hardwicke Papers.
>> 36,494-36,495. Cumberland Papers.
>> 41,085. Melville Papers.
>> 41,262-41,267. Correspondence and Papers of Thomas and John Clarkson.
>> 46,119. Correspondence of Sir T. Thompson.

British Museum Botany Library, London
> Sir Joseph Banks Correspondence (Transcripts)

Church Missionary Society, London (CMS)
> Papers of the West Africa (Sierra Leone) Mission, 1803-1914.
>> Early Correspondence.

Friends Library, London
> Thompson-Clarkson Collection, covering persons cited in Thomas
>> Clarkson's *History of the . . . Abolition of the African Slave-Trade.*

Henry E. Huntington Library and Art Gallery, San Marino, California
> Thomas Clarkson Papers, 1787-1846.
> Zachary Macaulay Papers, 1793-1799.

Linnaean Society, London
> Smith Manuscripts, vol. 1: Scientific Correspondence of Sir James Edward Smith.

Methodist Missionary Society, London
    North America, Box No. 1, 1791-1818.
    Sierra Leone Box, 1812-1834.
New Bedford Free Public Library, New Bedford, Massachusetts
    Paul Cuffe Collection
New-York Historical Society, New York
    John Clarkson Journals, 1791-1792, 2 volumes (see Note 3, Chapter II).
    Granville Sharp Papers
New York Public Library, New York
    William Smith, Historical Memoirs of the Province of New York, vol. 7,
        1780-1783.
Public Archives of Canada, Ottawa (PAC)
    Port Roseway Records, MG 9, B 9-14, vol. 1
Public Archives of Nova Scotia, Halifax (PANS)
    John Clarkson Journal, 1791-1792, 1 volume (see Note 3, Chapter II).
    Journal of Bishop Charles Inglis, 1791-1799.
    Letters of Bishop Charles Inglis, vols. 1 and 2, 1775-1791.
    Journal of Reverend William Jessop, 1788.
    Official and other manuscript documents in volumes as cited in notes.
Public Record Office, London (PRO)
    Official British government records (with class and piece numbers cited in
        Notes) from these departments:
        Admiralty (ADM).
        Audit Office (AO).
        Colonial Office (CO).
        Foreign Office (FO).
        Home Office (HO).
        Treasury (T).
        War Office (WO).
    Manuscript collections:
        Carleton Papers (PRO 30/55). Records of British Army Headquarters in
            America, 1775-1783.
        Chatham Papers (PRO 30/8).
        Cornwallis Papers (PRO 30/11).
Sierra Leone Archives, University of Sierra Leone, Freetown
    Letter Book of Governor Clarkson, 1792.
    Draft Journal of Governor Clarkson
Syracuse University Library, Syracuse, New York
    Thomas Clarkson letters in Gerrit Smith Papers.
United Society for the Propagation of the Gospel, London (USPG)
    Dr. Bray's Associates Canadian Papers, Nova Scotia and New Brunswick,
        1784-1836.
    Bray Associates Minute Books, vol. 3, 1768-1808.

SPG Journal, vols. 23-26, 1782-1792.
SPG *Reports*, Abstracts of Proceedings, 1783-1789.
Canadian Papers, (C/Can/N.S. 1), 1722-1790.
West African Papers (C/AFW - 1), 1753-1849.
University of Hull Library, Hull
    Thomas Perronet Thompson Papers, Section 1.
University of Illinois at Chicago Circle Library, Chicago, Illinois
    Sierra Leone Collection: Documents of John Clarkson and the Sierra Leone
        Company, 1791-1793.
University of Michigan, William L. Clements Library, Ann Arbor, Michigan
    Clinton Papers: Lists of Names of Negroes Belonging to Capt. Martin's Co.
    Shelburne Papers: Memorandum on the Right of Englishmen Under the 7th
        Article of the Treaty to Withdraw Negroes from the States. 87: 389.
    Wray Papers: Muster Rolls of the Civil Branch . . . of Artillery, Charleston,
        So. Carolina, 1781-1783.
Wigan Public Libraries, Wigan
    Thornton Diary and Letters, 1777-1815.
York Minster Library, York
    Granville Sharp Letter Book, 1768-1793.
In private collections:
    Granville Sharp Papers, property of Miss Olive Lloyd-Baker, Hardwicke
        Court, Gloucestershire
    William Wilberforce Papers, property of C. E. Wrangham, Rosemary House,
        Catterick, North Yorkshire
Also consulted at the British Library:
    Parliamentary Papers, volumes as cited in notes.
    The Parliamentary History of England (debates), as cited.

BOOKS AND ARTICLES:

ABBOTT, WILBUR C. *New York in the American Revolution.* New York: Scribner's,
    1929.
ABRAHAM, JAMES JOHNSTON. *Lettsom. His Life, Times, Friends and Descendants.*
    London: William Heinemann Medical Books Ltd., 1933.
ADAMS, CHARLES FRANCIS. *Familiar Letters of John Adams and His Wife Abigail
    Adams During the Revolution.* New York: Hurd and Houghton, 1876.
[ADAMS, JOHN]. *The Works of John Adams, Second President of the United States,*

with a Life of the Author, ed. Charles Francis Adams. Boston: Little Brown, 1850-1856. 10 vols.

AFRICAN INSTITUTION. *Report of the Directors*. London: 1807 to 1815 incl.

————. *Special Report of the Directors*. London: Ellerton & Henderson, 1815.

African Pilot, Being a Collection of New and Accurate Charts, on a Large Scale, of the Coasts, Islands, and Harbours of Africa, The. London: Robert Laurie & James Whittle, 1799.

Adam Afzelius: Sierra Leone Journal, 1795-1796, ed., Alexander Peter Kup. Uppsala: Almqvist & Wiksells Boktryckeri Artiebolag, 1967.

AJAYI, J. F. A., and MICHAEL CROWDER, eds. *History of West Africa*, vol. 2. Longman Group Ltd., 1974.

AKINS, THOMAS BEAMISH. "History of Halifax City." *Nova Scotia Historical Society Collections*, vol. 8 (1895), pp. 3-272.

ALEXANDER, ARCHIBALD. *A History of Colonization on the Western Coast of Africa*. Philadelphia: William S. Martien, 1846.

ALEXANDER, JAMES EDWARD. *Narrative of a Voyage of Observation Among the Colonies of Western Africa, in the Flag-ship Thalia; and of a Campaign in Kaffir-Land, on the Staff of the Commander-in-Chief in 1835*. London: Henry Colburn, 1837. 2 vols.

ALHADI, AHMED. *The Re-emancipation of the Colony of Sierra Leone*. Freetown: Michael Maurice Printing Works, 1956.

————. *American Archives*. (5th series, vol. 1 and 2, Washington: M. st. Clair Clark and Peter Force, 1848, 1851).

ANBUREY, THOMAS. *Travels Through the Interior Parts of America*. London: William Lane, 1789. 2 vols.

APTHEKER, HERBERT, ed. *A Documentary History of the Negro People in the United States*. New York: Citadel Press, 1951.

————. *American Negro Slave Revolts*. New York: Columbia University Press, 1944.

————. *The Negro in the American Revolution*. New York: International Publishers, 1940.

————. "The Quakers and Negro Slavery." *Journal of Negro History*, vol. 25 (1940), pp. 331-62.

ARCHIBALD, ADAMS G. "Story of Deportation of Negroes from Nova Scotia to Sierra Leone." *Nova Scotia Historical Society Collections*, vol. 7 (1891), pp. 129-54.

————. "Life of Sir John Wentworth, Governor of Nova Scotia, 1792-1808." *Nova Scotia Historical Society Collections*, vol. 20 (1921), pp. 43-109.

ARMISTEAD, WILSON. *A Tribute for the Negro*. Manchester: William Irwin, 1848.

ARMSTRONG, MAURICE WHITMAN. *The Great Awakening in Nova Scotia 1776-1809*. Hartford: American Society of Church History, 1948.

[ASBURY, FRANCIS]. *The Journal and Letters of Francis Asbury*, ed. Elmer T. Clarke. London: Epworth Press, 1958. 3 vols.

ASHMUN, JEHUDI. *Memoir of the Life and Character of the Rev. Samuel Bacon, A. M.* Washington: Jacob Gideon, 1822.

ASIEGBU, JOHNSON U. J. *Slavery and the Politics of Liberation, 1787-1861, a Study of Liberated African Emigration and British Anti-Slavery Policy.* London: Longmans, 1969.

AUSTEN, RALPH A., and WOODRUFF D. SMITH. "Images of Africa and British Slave-Trade Abolition: The Transition to an Imperialist Ideology, 1787-1807." *African Historical Studies*, vol. 2 (1969), pp. 69-83.

"Authentic Account of Sierra Leone, with Reasons for Not Abandoning It," *Anti-Slavery Monthly Reporter*, vol. 3 (1830), pp. 157-88.

BAILYN, BERNARD. *The Ideological Origins of the American Revolution.* Cambridge: Harvard University Press, 1967.

BAKER, FRANK. "Freeborn Garrettson and Nova Scotia." *Wesley Historical Society Proceedings*, vol. 32 (1959), pp. 18-20.

———. *Methodism and the Love-Feast.* London: Epworth Press, 1957.

BAKER, WILLIAM. "William Wilberforce on the Idea of Negro Inferiority." *Journal of the History of Ideas*, vol. 31 (1970), pp. 433-40.

BALLEINE, G. R. *A History of the Evangelical Party in the Church of England.* London: Church Book Room Press, 1951; first published 1908.

BANCROFT, FREDERIC. *The Colonization of American Negroes, 1801-1865.* Three essays completed in 1917 in Jacob E. Cooke, *Frederic Bancroft, Historian.* Norman: University of Oklahoma Press, 1957.

BANCROFT, GEORGE. *History of the United States of America from the Discovery of the Continent.* Author's last revision. New York: D. Appleton & Co., 1885. 6 vols.

BANGS, NATHAN. *The Life of the Rev. Freeborn Garrettson, Compiled from His Printed & Manuscript Journals & Other Authentic Documents*, 5th edition. New York: Carlton & Lanahan, 1832.

BANTON, MICHAEL. *The Coloured Quarter: Negro Immigrants in an English City.* London: Jonathan Cape, 1955.

Baptist Annual Register, ed., John Rippon. London: 1793, 1797.

BARCK, OSCAR THEODORE, JR. *New York City During the War for Independence, with Special Reference to the Period of British Occupation.* New York: Columbia University Press, 1931.

BARCLAY, WADE CRAWFORD. *Early American Methodism, 1769-1844*, Vol. 1, *Missionary Motivation and Expansion.* New York: Methodist Church Board of Missions, 1949.

BARTLET, WILLIAM S., ed. *The Frontier Missionary: A Memoir of the Life of the Rev. Jacob Bailey, A.M., Missionary at Pownalborough, Maine; Cornwallis and Annapolis, N.S.* Boston: Ide & Dutton, 1853.

BARTRAM, WILLIAM. *Travels Through North & South Carolina, Georgia, East & West Florida, the Cherokee Country, the Extensive Territories of the Mus-*

cogulges, or Creek Confederacy, and the Country of the Chactaws; Containing an Account of the Soil and Natural Productions of Those Regions, together With Observations on the Manners of the Indians. Philadelphia: James & Johnson, 1791.

BASSETT, JOHN SPENCER. "Slavery and Servitude in the Colony of North Carolina." *Johns Hopkins University Studies in Historical and Political Science*, 14th series, vols. 4-5 (1896), pp. 11-86.

———. "Slavery in the State of North Carolina." *Johns Hopkins University Studies in History and Political Science*, 17th series, vols. 7-8 (1899), pp. 7-111.

"Battle of the Great Bridge, The." *The Virginia Historical Register and Literary Companion*, vol. 6 (1853), pp. 1-6.

BEAVER, PHILIP. *African Memoranda: Relative to an Attempt to Establish a British Settlement on the Island of Bulama, on the Western Coast of Africa, in the Year 1792. With a Brief Notice of the Neighbouring Tribes, Soil Productions, &c and Some Observations on the Facility of Colonizing That Part of Africa, with a View to Cultivation; and the Introduction of Letters and Religion to Its Inhabitants: but More Particularly as the Means of Gradually Abolishing African Slavery.* London: C. & R. Baldwin, 1805.

BELL, WINTHROP PICKARD. *The "Foreign Protestants" and the Settlement of Nova Scotia.* Toronto: University of Toronto Press, 1961.

———. "A Hessian Conscript's Account of Life in Garrison at Halifax at the Time of the American Revolution." *Nova Scotia Historical Society Collections*, vol. 27 (1947), pp. 125-46.

BELLOT, LELAND J. "Evangelicals & the Defense of Slavery in Britain's Old Colonial Empire." *Journal of Southern History*, vol. 37 (1971), pp. 19-40.

BEMIS, SAMUEL FLAGG. *A Diplomatic History of the United States*, 4th edition. New York: Holt, Rinehart, 1955.

———. *The Diplomacy of the American Revolution.* Edinburgh: Oliver & Boyd, 1957.

———. *Jay's Treaty, A Study in Commerce and Diplomacy*, revised edition. New Haven: Yale University Press, 1962; first published 1923.

BENEDICT, DAVID. *A General History of the Baptist Denomination in America, and Other Parts of the World.* Boston: Lincoln & Edmunds, 1813. 2 vols.

BENEZET, ANTHONY. *A Caution to Great Britain and Her Colonies in a Short Representation of the Calamitous State of the Enslaved Negroes in the British Dominions.* London: James Phillips, 1784.

———. *Some Historical Account of Guinea, Its Situation, Produce, and the General Disposition of Its Inhabitants, with an Inquiry into the Rise and Progress of the Slave Trade, Its Nature, and Lamentable Effects.* London: J. Phillips, 1788.

BERKELEY, FRANCIS L., JR. *Dunmore's Proclamation of Emancipation.* Charlottesville: Tracy W. McGregor Library, University of Virginia, 1941.

BILL, INGRAHAM E. *Fifty Years with the Baptist Ministers and Churches of the Maritime Provinces of Canada.* St. John: Barnes & Co., 1880.

BINDER, FREDERICK M. *The Color Problem in Early National America as Viewed by John Adams, Jefferson and Jackson.* The Hague: Mouton, 1968.

BLAKELEY, PHYLLIS R. "Boston King, a Negro Loyalist Who Sought Refuge in Nova Scotia." *Dalhousie Review*, vol. 48 (1968), pp. 348-56.

[BLAND, THEODORICK, JR.]. *The Bland Papers: Being a Selection from the Manuscripts of Col. Theodorick Bland Jr.* ed. Charles Campbell. Petersburg: E. & J. C. Ruffin, 1840. 2 vols.

BOND, BEVERLEY W., JR. *The Quit-Rent System in the American Colonies.* New Haven: Yale University Press, 1919.

BOORSTIN, DANIEL J. *The Americans: the Colonial Experience.* London: Weidenfeld & Nicolson, 1958.

BOOTH, CHARLES. *Zachary Macaulay: His Part in the Movement for the Abolition of the Slave Trade and of Slavery, an Appreciation.* London: Longmans & Co., 1934.

[BOUCHER, JONATHAN]. *Reminiscences of an American Loyalist 1738-1789*, ed. Jonathan Bouchier. Boston: Houghton Mifflin, 1925.

BOURINOT, SIR JOHN G. *Builders of Nova Scotia.* Toronto: Copp-Clark Co. Ltd., 1900.

BRACKETT, JEFFREY R. "The Status of the Slave, 1775-1789," in J. Franklin Jameson, ed. *The Constitutional History of the United States in the Formative Period 1775-1789.* Boston: Houghton Mifflin, 1889.

BRADLEY, A. G. *Lord Dorchester.* London: Oxford University Press, 1926.

BRAND, OSCAR. *Songs of '76: a Folksinger's History of the Revolution.* New York: M. Evans & Co., 1972.

BREBNER, JOHN BARTLETT. *The Neutral Yankees of Nova Scotia: a Marginal Colony During the Revolutionary Years.* New York: Columbia University Press, 1937.

———. *New England's Outpost.* New York: Columbia University Press, 1927.

BRIDGE, HORATIO. *Journal of an African Cruiser.* reprint with Introduction by Donald H. Simpson. London: Dawsons, 1968; first published 1845.

BRISSOT DE WARVILLE, JACQUES PIERRE. *New Travels in the United States of America: Including the Commerce of America with Europe; Particularly with France and Great Britain*, 2d ed. London: J. S. Jordan, 794. 2 vols.

BROOKES, GEORGE S. *Friend Anthony Benezet.* Philadelphia: University of Pennsylvania Press, 1937.

BROOKES, GEORGE S., JR. "A View of Sierra Leone ca. 1815," *Sierra Leone Studies*, n.s., vol. 13 (1960), pp. 24-31.

BROOKS, GEORGE E., JR. "The Providence African Society's Sierra Leone Emigration Scheme, 1794-1795: Prologue to the African Colonization Movement." *International Journal of African Historical Studies*, vol. 7 (1974), pp. 183-202.

BROOKS, WALTER H. "The Evolution of the Negro Baptist Church." *Journal of Negro History*, vol. 1 (1922), pp. 11-22.

BROWN, FORD K. *Fathers of the Victorians: The Age of Wilberforce*. Cambridge: Cambridge University Press, 1961.

BROWN, ROBERT E., and B. KATHERINE BROWN. *Virginia 1705-1786: Democracy or Aristocracy?* East Lansing: Michigan State University Press, 1964.

BROWN, WALLACE. *The Good Americans: The Loyalists in the American Revolution*. New York: William Morrow & Co., Inc., 1969.

———. *The King's Friends: The Composition and Motives of the American Loyalist Claimants*. Providence: Brown University Press, 1965.

———. "The Loyalists and the American Revolution." *History Today*, vol. 12 (1962), pp. 149-57.

———. "Negroes and the American Revolution." *History Today*, vol. 14 (1964), pp. 556-63.

BRUNS, ROGER. "Anthony Benezet's Assertion of Negro Equality." *Journal of Negro History*, vol. 56 (1971), pp. 230-38.

BUMSTED, J. M. "Church and State in Maritime Canada, 1749-1807." *Canadian Historical Association Report, 1967*, pp. 41-58.

BURNABY, ANDREW, *Travels Through the Middle Settlements in North-America in the Years 1759 and 1760, with Observations upon the State of the Colonies*. Reprint of 2nd edition, 1775. Ithaca: Cornell University Press, 1960.

BURNETT, EDMUND C., ed. *Letters of Members of the Continental Congress*, vol. 7. Washington, D.C.: Carnegie Institution, 1934.

BURT, A. L. "Guy Carleton, Lord Dorchester: An Estimate." *Canadian Historical Association Report, 1935*, pp. 76-87.

———. *The United States, Great Britain and British North America from the Revolution to the Establishment of Peace After the War of 1812*. New Haven: Yale University Press, 1940.

BUTT-THOMPSON, F. W. *The First Generation of Sierra Leoneans*. Freetown: Government Printer, 1952.

———. *King Peters of Sierra Leone*. London: Religious Tract Society, n.d. Catalogued by the Royal Commonwealth Society as a novel.

———. *Sierra Leone in History and Tradition*. London: H. F. & G. Witherby, 1926.

BUXTON, THOMAS FOWELL. *The African Slave Trade and Its Remedy*. London: John Murray, 1840.

CALHOON, ROBERT M. "Loyalist Studies at the Advent of the Loyalist Papers Project." *The New England Quarterly*, vol. 46 (1973), pp. 284-93.

CALLAHAN, NORTH. *Flight from the Republic: The Tories of the American Revolution*. Indianapolis: Bobbs-Merrill Co., 1967.

[CAMPBEL]. *Reasons Against Giving a Territorial Grant to a Company of Mer-*

chants, *to Colonize and Cultivate the Peninsula of Sierra Leona, on the Coast of Africa.* London: 1791.

CAMPBELL, G. G. *History of Nova Scotia.* Toronto: Ryerson Press, 1948.

CAMPBELL, PATRICK. *Travels in the Interior Inhabited Parts of North America in the Years 1791 and 1792,* ed. H. H. Langton. Toronto: Champlain Society, 1937.

CARPENTER, S. C. *Church and People 1789-1889: A History of the Church of England from William Wilberforce to "Lux Mundi."* London: SPCK, 1933.

[CARTER, LANDON]. *The Diary of Col. Landon Carter of Sabine Hall, 1752-1778,* ed. Jack P. Greene. Charlottesville: University Press of Virginia, 1965. 2 vols.

CHANNING, EDWARD. *A History of the United States,* Vol. 3, *The American Revolution 1761-1789.* New York: Macmillan, 1912.

CHASTELLUX, MARQUIS FRANCOIS JEAN DE. *Travels in North America, in the Years 1780, 1781, and 1782.* London: G. G. J. and J. Robinson, 1787. 2 vols. Also, Howard C. Rice Jr., ed. Chapel Hill: University of North Carolina Press, 1963. 2 vols.

CHURCH, MARY. *Sierra Leone; or, the Liberated Africans, in a Series of Letters from a Young Lady to Her Sister.* London: Longman & Co., 1835.

CLAIRMONT, DONALD H., and DENNIS W. MAGILL. *Nova Scotian Blacks: An Historical and Structural Overview.* Halifax: Institute of Public Affairs, Dalhousie University, 1970.

CLAPHAM ANTIQUARIAN SOCIETY. *Clapham and the Clapham Sect.* London: By the Society, 1927.

CLARK, ANDREW HILL. *Acadia: The Geography of Early Nova Scotia to 1760.* Madison: University of Wisconsin Press, 1968.

CLARK, SAMUEL DELBERT. *Church and Sect in Canada.* Toronto: University of Toronto Press, 1965; first published in 1948.

CLARKE, W. R. E. *The Morning Star of Africa, or Tales the Cotton Tree Could Tell of Freetown, Sierra Leone.* London: Macmillan & Co., Ltd., 1960.

———. *Some Folk Tales of Sierra Leone.* London: Macmillan & Co., 1963.

[CLARKSON, JOHN]. "Diary of Lieutenant J. Clarkson, R.N." *Sierra Leone Studies,* vol. 8 (1927), pp. 1-114.

———. *Clarkson's Mission to America, 1791-1792,* ed. Charles Bruce Fergusson. Halifax: Public Archives of Nova Scotia, 1971.

CLARKSON, THOMAS. *The History of the Rise, Progress, and Accomplishment of the Abolition of the African Slave-Trade by the British Parliament.* London: Longman, Hurst, 1808. 2 vols.

———. "Some account of the new colony at Sierra Leone, on the coast of Africa." *The American Museum; or, Universal Magazine,* vol. 11 (1792), pp. 160-62, 229-31.

CLIVE, JOHN. *Macaulay: The Shaping of the Historian.* New York: Alfred A. Knopf, 1973.

[COKE, THOMAS]. *Extracts of the Journals of the late Rev. Thomas Coke comprising Several Visits to North-America and the West-Indies; His Tour Through a Part of Ireland, and His Nearly Finished Voyage to Bombay, in the East-Indies; to which is Prefixed a Life of the Doctor.* Dublin: R. Napper, 1816.

COLEMAN, KENNETH. *The American Revolution in Georgia 1763-1789.* Athens: University of Georgia Press, 1958.

COLQUHOUN, JOHN CAMPBELL. *William Wilberforce: His Friends and His Times.* London: Longmans, 1867.

COLSON, PERCY. *The Strange History of Lord George Gordon.* London: Robert Hale, 1937.

———. *Their Ruling Passions.* London: Hutchinson & Co., 1949.

COMMAGER, HENRY STEELE, ed. *Documents of American History.* New York: F. S. Crofts, 1938.

———, and Richard B. Morris, eds. *The Spirit of 'Seventy-Six. The Story of the American Revolution as Told by Participants.* New York: Harper & Row, 1967.

CORKRAN, DAVID H. *The Creek Frontier 1540-1783.* Norman: University of Oklahoma Press, 1967.

CORNER, BETSY C., and CHRISTOPHER C. BOOTH, eds. *Chain of Friendship. Selected Letters of Dr. John Fothergill of London, 1735-1780.* Cambridge: Belknap Press of Harvard University Press, 1971.

CORRY, JOSEPH. *Observations upon the Windward Coast of Africa, the Religion, Character, Custom &c. of the Natives; with a System upon Which They May Be Civilized, and a Knowledge Attained of the Interior of this Extraordinary Quarter of the Globe; and upon the Natural & Commercial Resources of the Country.* London: James Asperne, 1807.

COUPLAND, REGINALD. *The British Anti-Slavery Movement.* London: Thornton Butterworth, Ltd., 1933.

———. *Wilberforce, a Narrative.* Oxford: Clarendon Press, 1923.

COX-GEORGE, N. A. "Direct Taxation in the Early History of Sierra Leone." *Sierra Leone Studies*, n.s., vol. 5 (1955), pp. 20-35.

———. *Finance and Development in West Africa: The Sierra Leone Experience.* London: Dennis Dobson, 1961.

CRARY, CATHERINE S., ed. *The Price of Loyalty: Tory Writings from the Revolutionary Era.* New York: McGraw Hill Book Co., 1973.

CREVECOEUR, ST. JOHN DE. *Sketches of Eighteenth Century America: More Letters from an American Farmer*, eds. Henri L. Bourdin, Ralph H. Gabriel and Stanley T. Williams. New Haven: Yale University Press, 1925.

CROOKS, J. J. *A Short History of Sierra Leone.* Dublin: Nation Printing & Publishing Co., 1900.

CUGOANO, OTTOBAH. *Thoughts and Sentiments on the Evil and Wicked Traffic of the Slavery and Commerce of the Human Species, Humbly Submitted to the Inhabitants of Great-Britain.* London: T. Becket, 1787.

CURRER-JONES, A. *William Dawes, R.M., 1762 to 1836. A Sketch of His Life, Work and Explorations (1787) in the First Expedition to New South Wales: also as Governor of Sierra Leone, and in Antigua, West Indies.* Torquay: W. H. Smith & Sons. Ltd., 1930.

CURTIN, PHILIP D. *The Image of Africa: British Ideas and Action, 1780-1850.* Madison: University of Wisconsin Press, 1964.

DALLAS, R. C. *The History of the Maroons, from their Origin to the Establishment of their Chief Tribe at Sierra Leone: including the Expedition to Cuba . . . and the State of the Island of Jamaica, etc.* Facsimile of 1803 edition. London: Frank Cass, 1968. 2 vols.

DAVIS, DAVID BRION. *The Problem of Slavery in Western Culture.* Ithaca: Cornell University Press, 1967.

DAVIS, RICHARD W. *Dissent in Politics 1780-1830: The Political Life of William Smith, M.P.* London: Epworth Press, 1971.

DAY, THOMAS. "A Fragment of a Letter on the Slavery of the Negroes," in Thomas Day and John Bicknell, *The Dying Negro, a Poem.* London: John Stockdale, 1793.

DE MOND, ROBERT O. *The Loyalists in North Carolina During the Revolution.* Durham: Duke University Press, 1940.

DONNAN, ELIZABETH. *Documents Illustrative of the History of the Slave Trade to America.* Washington: Carnegie Institution, 1930-1935. 4 vols.

DRAKE, THOMAS E. *Quakers and Slavery in America.* New Haven: Yale University Press, 1950.

DUBOIS, W. E. BURGHARDT. *The Gift of Black Folk: the Negroes in the Making of America.* Boston: Stratford Co., 1924.

———. *The Suppression of the African Slave-Trade to the United States of America 1638-1870.* New York: Schocken Books, 1969; first published 1896.

[DYOTT, WILLIAM]. *Dyott's Diary 1781-1845. A Selection from the Journal of William Dyott, Sometime General in the British Army and Aide-De-Camp to His Majesty King George III* ed., Reginald W. Jeffery. London: Archibald Constable, 1907. 2 vols.

EASMON, M. C. F. "A Nova Scotian Family," in *Eminent Sierra Leoneans in the Nineteenth Century.* Freetown: Sierra Leone Society, n.d.

EATON, ARTHUR WENTWORTH H. *The Church of England in Nova Scotia and the Tory Clergy of the Revolution,* 2d ed. New York: Thomas Whittaker, 1892.

ECKENRODE, HAMILTON JAMES. *The Revolution in Virginia.* Boston: Houghton Mifflin, 1916.

EDWARDS, J. PLIMSOLL. "The Shelburne That Was and Is Not," *Dalhousie Review,* vol. 2 (1922), pp. 179-97.

———. "Vicissitudes of a Loyalist City," *Dalhousie Review,* vol. 2 (1922), pp. 313-28.

EGERTON, HUGH EDWARD, ed. *The Royal Commission on the Losses and Services of American Loyalists 1783 to 1785, Being the Notes of Mr. Daniel Parker Coke, M.P.*. Reprint from 1915 edition. New York: Burt Franklin, 1971.

EINSTEIN, LEWIS. *Divided Loyalties: Americans in England During the War of Independence.* London: Cobden-Sanderson, 1933.

ELKINS, STANLEY M. *Slavery, a Problem in American Institutional and Intellectual Life,* 2d ed. Chicago: University of Chicago Press, 1968.

ELLIOT, JOHN, ed. *A Complete Collection of the Medical and Philosophical Works of John Fothergill . . . with an Account of His Life.* London: John Walker, 1781.

ELLIOTT, J. B. *Lady Huntingdon's Connexion in Sierra Leone: A Narrative of Its History and Present State.* London: Society for the Spread of the Gospel at Home & Abroad, 1851.

ELLIOTT-BINNS, L. E. *The Early Evangelicals: A Religious and Social Study.* London: Lutterworth Press, 1953.

ELLS, MARGARET. *A Calendar of the White Collection of Manuscripts in the Public Archives of Nova Scotia.* Halifax: Public Archives of Nova Scotia, 1940.

———. "Clearing the Decks for the Loyalists." *Canadian Historical Association Report, 1933,* pp. 43-58.

———. "Settling the Loyalists in Nova Scotia." *Canadian Historical Association Report, 1934,* pp. 105-9.

[EQUIANO, OLAUDAH]. *The Interesting Narrative of the Life of Olaudah Equiano, or Gustavus Vassa, the African,* ed., Paul Edwards. London: Dawsons of Pall Mall, 1969; first published 1789.

EVANS, L. E. C. "An Early Constitution of Sierra Leone." *Sierra Leone Studies,* vol. 18 (1932), pp. 26-77.

FAIRFAX, FERDINANDO. "Plan for Liberating the Negroes Within the United States," *The American Museum, or Universal Magazine,* vol. 8 (1790), pp. 285-87.

FALCONBRIDGE, A. M. *Narrative of Two Voyages to the River Sierra Leone During the Years 1791-1793, with a Succinct Account of the Distresses and Proceedings of that Settlement; a Description of the Manners, Diversions, Arts, Commerce, Cultivation, Custom, Punishments &c and Every Interesting Particular Relating to the Sierra Leone Company. Also the Present State of the Slave Trade in the West Indies, and the Improbability of Its Total Abolition.* Facsimile of 2nd edition 1802. London: Frank Cass, 1967.

FALCONBRIDGE, ALEXANDER. *An Account of the Slave Trade on the Coast of Africa.* London: J. Phillips, 1788.

FERGUSSON, CHARLES BRUCE. *A Documentary Study of the Establishment of the Negroes in Nova Scotia Between the War of 1812 and the Winning of Responsible Government.* Halifax: Public Archives of Nova Scotia, 1948.

FINDLAY, G. G., and W. W. HOLDSWORTH. *The History of the Wesleyan Methodist Missionary Society.* London: Epworth Press, 1921-1924. 5 vols.

FINGARD, JUDITH. *The Anglican Design in Loyalist Nova Scotia 1783-1816.* London: SPCK, 1972.

FISHEL, LESLIE H., JR., and BENJAMIN QUARLES, eds. *The Black American, a Documentary History.* New York: William Morrow & Co., Inc., 1970.

FISHER, SYDNEY GEORGE. *The Struggle for American Independence.* Philadelphia: Lippincott, 1908.

————. *The True History of the American Revolution.* Philadelphia: Lippincott, 1903.

FITCHETT, E. HORACE. "The Traditions of the Free Negro in Charleston, South Carolina." *Journal of Negro History,* vol. 25 (1940), pp. 139-52.

FITCH-JONES, B. W. "Fort Thornton." *Sierra Leone Studies,* vol. 15 (1929), pp. 16-28.

FLADELAND, BETTY. *Men and Brothers: Anglo-American Antislavery Cooperation.* Urbana: University of Illinois Press, 1972.

FLEMMING, HORACE A. "Halifax Currency." *Nova Scotia Historical Society Collections,* vol. 20 (1921), pp. 111-37.

FLEXNER, JAMES THOMAS. *George Washington in the American Revolution 1775-1783.* Boston: Little, Brown, & Co., 1967.

FOOTE, ANDREW H. *Africa and the American Flag.* London: Dawsons of Pall Mall, 1970, reprint of 1854 edition.

FORSTER, E. M. *Marianne Thornton 1797-1887, a Domestic Biography.* London: Edward Arnold, 1956.

[FOTHERGILL, JOHN]. *The Works of John Fothergill, M.D.,* ed., John Coakley Lettsom. London: Charles Dilly, 1783. 2 vols.

FOX, RICHARD HINGSTON. *Dr. John Fothergill and His Friends: Chapters in 18th Century Life.* London: Macmillan, 1919.

FOX, WILLIAM. *A Brief History of the Wesleyan Missions on the Western Coast of Africa: Including Biographical Sketches of All the Missionaries Who Have Died in That Important Field of Labour, with Some Account of the European Settlements, and of the Slave Trade.* London: Privately printed, 1851.

FRANCKLYN, GILBERT. *Observations, Occasioned by the Attempts Made in England to Effect the Abolition of the Slave Trade.* London: Logographic Press, 1789.

FRANKLIN, JOHN HOPE. *From Slavery to Freedom: A History of Negro Americans,* 3d ed. New York: Vintage Books, 1969.

FREEHLING, WILLIAM W. "The Founding Fathers and Slavery." *The American Historical Review,* vol. 77 (1972), pp. 81-93.

FREEMAN, DOUGLAS SOUTHALL. *George Washington, a Biography,* Vol. 5 *Victory with the Help of France.* London: Eyre & Spottiswoode, 1952.

FYFE, CHRISTOPHER. "The Baptist Churches in Sierra Leone." *Sierra Leone Bulletin of Religion,* vol. 5 (1963), pp. 55-60.

————. "The Countess of Huntingdon's Connexion in Nineteenth Century Sierra Leone." *Sierra Leone Bulletin of Religion*, vol. 4 (1962), pp. 53-61.

————, and ELDRED JONES, eds. *Freetown, a Symposium*. Freetown: Sierra Leone University Press, 1968.

————. *A History of Sierra Leone*. London: Oxford University Press, 1962.

————. *Sierra Leone Inheritance*. London: Oxford University Press, 1964.

————. "Thomas Peters: History and Legend," *Sierra Leone Studies*, n.s., vol. 1 (1953), pp. 4-13.

————. "The West African Methodists in the Nineteenth Century," *Sierra Leone Bulletin of Religion*, vol. 3 (1961), pp. 22-28.

General Baptist Repository, Adam Taylor, ed. vol. 1, London: J. Skirven, 1802. Supplement: "An Account of the Jamaica Baptists with Memoirs of Mr. George Liele," pp. 229-40.

GEORGE, CAROL V. R. *Segregated Sabbaths: Richard Allen and the Emergence of Independent Black Churches 1760-1840*. New York: Oxford University Press, 1973.

GEORGE, CLAUDE. *The Rise of British West Africa Comprising the Early History of the Colony of Sierra Leone, the Gambia, Lagos, Gold Coast, etc. with a Brief Account of Climate, the Growth of Education, Commerce and Religion and a Comprehensive History of the Bananas and Bance Islands and Sketches of the Constitution*. Reprint of 1904 edition. London: Frank Cass & Co., 1968.

[GEORGE, DAVID]. "An Account of the Life of Mr. DAVID GEORGE, from Sierra Leone in Africa; Given by Himself in a Conversation with Brother Rippon of London, and Brother Pearce of Birmingham," in John Rippon, ed. *The Baptist Annual Register for 1790-1793*, pp. 473-84.

GEORGE, M. DOROTHY. *England in Transition: Life and Work in the Eighteenth Century*. London: Penguin, 1953.

————. *London Life in the XVIIIth Century*. London: Kegan Paul, Trench, Trubner & Co., Ltd., 1925.

GEWEHR, WESLEY M. *The Great Awakening in Virginia, 1740-1790*. Durham: Duke University Press, 1930.

GILROY, MARION. *Loyalists and Land Settlement in Nova Scotia*. Halifax: Public Archives of Nova Scotia, 1937.

GORDON, WILLIAM. *The History of the Rise, Progress, and Establishment, of the United States of America: Including an Account of the Late War; and of the Thirteen Colonies from Their Origin to That Period*. London: Privately printed, 1788. 4 vols.

GRANT, JOHN. *An Account of Some Recent Transactions in the Colony of Sierra Leone; with a Few Observations on the State of the African Coast*. London: J. J. Stockdale, 1810.

GRANT, JOHN N. "Black Immigrants into Nova Scotia, 1776-1815." *Journal of Negro History*, vol. 58 (1973), pp. 253-70.

GREAVES, IDA C. *The Negro in Canada*. Montreal: McGill University Press, 1930.

GREENE, EVARTS B., and VIRGINIA D. HARRINGTON. *American Population Before the Federal Census of 1790*. New York: Columbia University Press, 1932.

GREENE, LORENZO JOHNSTON. *The Negro in Colonial New England 1620-1776*. New York: Columbia University Press, 1942.

———. "Some Observations on the Black Regiment of Rhode Island in the American Revolution." *Journal of Negro History*, vol. 27 (1952), pp. 142-73.

GREGOIRE, COUNT HENRI BAPTISTE. *An Enquiry Concerning the Intellectural and Moral Faculties, and Literature of NEGROES; Followed with an Account of the Life and Works of Fifteen Negroes & Mulattoes Distinguished in Science, Literature and the Arts*, trans., D. B. Warden. Brooklyn: Thomas Kirk, 1810.

GRIEVE, AVERIL MACKENZIE. *The Great Accomplishment*. London: Geoffrey Bles, 1953.

GRIGGS, EARL LESLIE. *Thomas Clarkson, the Friend of Slaves*. London: George Allen & Unwin, Ltd., 1936.

GROVES, C. P. *The Planting of Christianity in Africa*. London: Lutterworth Press, 1948-1958. 4 vols.

HADAWAY, WILLIAM S. "Negroes in the Revolutionary War." *Westchester County Historical Society Quarterly Bulletin*, vol. 6 (1930), pp. 8-12.

HAIR, P. E. H. "Africanism: the Freetown Contribution." *Journal of Modern African Studies*, vol. 5 (1967), pp. 521-39.

———. "Christianity at Freetown from 1792 as a Field for Research," in *Urbanization in African Social Change*. Edinburgh: Centre of African Studies, 1963.

———. "Freetown Christianity and Africa." *Sierra Leone Bulletin of Religion*, vol. 6 (1964), pp. 13-21.

———. "Henry Thornton and the Sierra Leone Settlement." *Sierra Leone Bulletin of Religion*, vol. 10 (1968), pp. 6-10.

———. Review of Christopher Fyfe, *A History of Sierra Leone*. *Sierra Leone Studies*, n.s., vol. 17 (1963), pp. 281-96.

———. "Sierra Leone and Bulama 1792-4: Further Notes." *Sierra Leone Bulletin of Religion*, vol. 6 (1964), pp. 26-31.

HALIBURTON, GORDON. "The Nova Scotian Settlers of 1792." *Sierra Leone Studies*, n.s., vol. 9 (1957), pp. 16-25.

HALLOWELL, A. IRVING. "American Indians, White and Black: The Phenomenon of Transculturalization." *Current Anthropology*, vol. 4 (1963), pp. 519-31.

[HAMILTON, ALEXANDER]. *The Papers of Alexander Hamilton*, ed., Harold C. Syrett, Vol. 3, *1782-1786*. New York: Columbia University Press, 1962.

———. *The Works of Alexander Hamilton; Comprising His Correspondence and His Political and Official Writings, Exclusive of the Federalist, Civil and Military*, ed., John C. Hamilton, vol. 1. New York: Charles C. Francis, Ltd., 1851.

HANNAY, JAMES. *History of New Brunswick*. St. John: John A. Bowes, 1909.

HARRELL, ISAAC SAMUEL. *Loyalism in Virginia: Chapters in the Economic History of the Revolution.* Durham: Duke University Press, 1926.

HARRIS, REGINALD V. *Charles Inglis, Missionary, Loyalist, Bishop (1734-1816).* Toronto: General Board of Religious Education, 1937.

————. *The Church of Saint Paul in Halifax, Nova Scotia: 1749-1949.* Toronto: Ryerson Press, 1949.

HARRIS, SHELDON H. "An American's Impressions of Sierra Leone in 1811." *Journal of Negro History,* vol. 47 (1962), pp. 35-41.

————. *Paul Cuffe: Black America and the African Return.* New York: Simon and Schuster, 1972.

HARTGROVE, W. B. "The Negro Soldier in the American Revolution." *Journal of Negro History,* vol. 1 (1916), pp. 110-31.

HARTZELL, HOWARD GRIMSHAW. "Jacob Grigg—Missionary and Minister." *The Chronicle: A Baptist Historical Quarterly,* vol. 6 (1943), pp. 83-90, 130-43.

HECHT, JOSEPH JEAN. *Continental and Colonial Servants in Eighteenth Century England.* Northampton: Smith College Press, 1954.

HEPBURN, JOHN. *The American Defence of the Christian Golden Rule, or an Essay to Prove the Unlawfulness of Making Slaves of Men.* [New Jersey]: n.p., 1715.

HERSKOVITS, MELVILLE J. *The Myth of the Negro Past.* Boston: Beacon Press, 1967; first published 1941.

HEWATT, ALEXANDER. *An Historical Account of the Rise and Progress of the Colonies of South Carolina and Georgia.* Reprint of 1779 edition. Spartanburg: Reprint Co., 1962. 2 vols.

HIBBERT, CHRISTOPHER. *King Mob: the Story of Lord George Gordon and the Riots of 1780.* London: Longmans, Green & Co., 1958.

HIGGINBOTHAM, DON. *The War of American Independence: Military Attitudes, Policies, and Practice, 1763-1789.* London: Collier-Macmillan, 1971.

HILDRETH, RICHARD. *The History of the United States of America, from the Discovery of the Continent to the Organization of Government Under the Federal Constitution.* New York: Harper & Bros., 1849. 3 vols.

HOARE, PRINCE. *Memoirs of Granville Sharp, Esq., Composed from His Own Manuscripts, and Other Authentic Documents in the Possession of His Family and of the Africa Institution,* 2d ed. London: Henry Colburn, 1828.

HODGE, FREDERICK WEBB. *Handbook of American Indians.* Washington: Government Printing Office, 1910. 2 vols.

HOFSTADTER, RICHARD. *America at 1750, a Social Portrait.* London: Jonathan Cape, 1972.

HOLE, REV. CHARLES. *The Early History of the Church Missionary Society for Africa and the East to the End of A.D. 1814.* London: Church Missionary Society, 1896.

[HOLLINGSWORTH, S.] *The Present State of Nova Scotia: With a Brief Account of Canada, and the British Islands on the Coast of North America,* 2d ed. Edinburgh: Wm. Creech, 1787.

HOLMAN, JAMES. *A Voyage Round the World, Including Travels in Africa, Asia, Australasia, America, etc. etc. from MDCCCXXVII to MDCCCXXXII.* London: Smith, Elder, 1834.

HOLMES, EDWARD A. "George Liele: Negro Slavery's Prophet of Deliverance." *Foundations*, vol. 9 (1966), pp. 333-45.

HOOKER, RICHARD J., ed. *The Carolina Backcountry on the Eve of the Revolution: The Journal and Other Writings of Charles Woodmason, Anglican Itinerant.* Chapel Hill: University of North Carolina Press, 1953.

HOPKINS, SAMUEL. *A Discourse Upon the Slave-Trade, and the Slavery of the Africans. Delivered in the Baptist Meeting-House at Providence, Before the Providence Society for Abolishing the Slave-Trade etc.* Providence: J. Carter, 1793.

————. *The Works of Samuel Hopkins, D.D., First Pastor of the Church in Great Barrington, Mass., Afterwards Pastor of the First Congregational Church in Newport, R.I., with a Memoir of His Life and Character.* ed., Edwards A. Park. Boston: Doctrinal Tract & Book Society, 1852. 3 vols.

HORNE, MELVILL. *Letters on Missions Addressed to the Protestant Ministers of the British Churches.* London: Thames Ditton, 1824.

HOWE, JOSEPH E. "Quit Rents in New Brunswick." *Canadian Historical Association Report, 1928*, pp. 55-72.

HOWSE, ERNEST MARSHALL. *Saints in Politics: The "Clapham Sect" and the Growth of Freedom.* London: George Allen & Unwin, 1952.

HUNT, GAILLARD. "William Thornton and Negro Colonization." *American Antiquarian Society Proceedings*, n.s., vol. 30 (1920), pp. 32-61.

HUTCHINS, JOHN H. *Jonas Hanway 1712-1786.* London: SPCK, 1940.

[HUTCHINSON, THOMAS]. *The Diary and Letters of His Excellency Thomas Hutchinson*, ed., Peter Orlando Hutchinson. London: Sampson Low, 1883-1886. 2 vols.

INGLIS, CHARLES. *A Charge Delivered to the Clergy of the Diocese of Nova Scotia, at the Primary Visitation Holden in the Town of Halifax in the Month of June 1788.* Halifax: Anthony Henry, 1789.

JACK, ISAAC ALLEN. "The Loyalists and Slavery in New Brunswick." *Royal Society of Canada Transactions*, vol. 4 (1898), pp. 137-85.

JACKSON, LUTHER P. "Virginia Negro Soldiers and Seamen in the American Revolution." *Journal of Negro History*, vol. 27 (1942), pp. 247-87.

JACKSON, THOMAS, ed. *The Lives of Early Methodist Preachers Chiefly Written by Themselves.* London: John Mason, 1837. 3 vols.

JAKOBSSON, STIV. *Am I Not a Man and a Brother? British Missions and the Abolition of the Slave Trade and Slavery in West Africa and the West Indies 1786-1838.* Gleerup: Lund, 1972.

JAMES, C. L. R. *The Black Jacobins: Toussaint L'ouverture and the San Domingo Revolution.* London: Secker & Warburg, 1938.

JAMESON, J. FRANKLIN. *The American Revolution Considered as a Social Movement.* Princeton: Princeton University Press, 1926.

JARVIS, W. M. "Royal Commission and Instructions to Governor Thomas Carleton, August 1784." *New Brunswick Historical Society Collections*, vol. 2 (1905), pp. 391-438.

[JAY, JOHN]. *The Correspondence and Public Papers of John Jay*, ed., Henry P. Johnston. New York: Putnam, 1890-1893. 4 vols.

———. *On the Peace Negotiations of 1782-83, as Illustrated by the Secret Correspondence of France and England.* New York: Knickerbocker Press, 1888.

JAYNE, R. EVERETT. *Jonas Hanway: Philanthropist, Politician, and Author 1712-1786.* London: Epworth Press, 1929.

JEFFERSON, THOMAS. *Note on the State of Virginia*, ed., William Peden. Chapel Hill: University of North Carolina Press, 1955.

———. *The Writings of Thomas Jefferson*, ed., Paul Leicester Ford. New York: Putnam's, 1893-1899. 10 vols.

JENKINS, CHARLES F. *Tortola: A Quaker Experiment of Long Ago in the Tropics.* London: Friends Bookshop, 1923.

JENSEN, MERRILL. "The American People and the American Revolution." *Journal of American History*, vol. 57 (1970), pp. 5-35.

JOHNSON, L. G. *General T. Perronet Thompson 1783-1869. His Military, Literary and Political Campaigns.* London: George Allen & Unwin Ltd., 1957.

JOHNSON, RT. REV. T. S. *The Story of a Mission: The Sierra Leone Church, First Daughter of C. M. S.* London: SPCK, 1953.

JONES, THOMAS. *History of New York During the Revolutionary War and of the Leading Events in the Other Colonies at That Period*, ed., Edward Floyd De Lancey. Reprint of 1879 edition. New York: Arno Press, 1968.

JORDAN, WINTHROP D. *White over Black: American Attitudes Toward the Negro 1550-1812.* Baltimore: Penguin, 1969.

KAPLAN, SIDNEY. *The Black Presence in the Era of the American Revolution 1770-1800.* Washington: New York Graphic Society and Smithsonian Institution Press, 1973.

KARIBI-WHYTE, A. G. "The Reception of English Law in Sierra Leone: A Historical Treatment." *Sierra Leone Studies*, n.s., vol. 19 (1966), pp. 109-18.

KEITH, GEORGE. "An Exhortation & Caution to *Friends* Concerning Buying or Keeping of Negroes," printed as "The First Printed Protest Against Slavery in America." *Pennsylvania Magazine of History and Biography*, vol. 13 (1889), pp. 265-70.

KENNAN, R. H. "Street and Place Names in and Around Freetown." *Sierra Leone Studies*, vol. 9 (1927), pp. 9-34.

KENNEY, WILLIAM HOWLAND, III. "George Whitefield, Dissenter Priest of the Great Awakening, 1739-1741." *William and Mary Quarterly*, vol. 26 (1969), pp. 75-93.

KERR, W. B. "The Merchants of Nova Scotia and the American Revolution." *Canadian Historical Review*, vol. 13 (1932), pp. 20-36.

KING, BOSTON. "Memoirs of the Life of BOSTON KING, a Black Preacher," *The Methodist Magazine for the Year 1798*, vol. 21 (1798), pp. 105-10, 157-61, 209-13, 261-65.

KIRK-GREENE, ANTHONY. "David George: The Nova Scotian Experience." *Sierra Leone Studies*, n.s., vol. 14 (1960), pp. 93-120.

KLINGBERG, FRANK J. *The Anti-Slavery Movement in England, a Study in English Humanitarianism*. New Haven: Yale University Press, 1926.

———. *An Appraisal of the Negro in Colonial South Carolina, a Study in Americanization*. Washington: Associated Publishers, 1941.

KNAPLUND, PAUL. *James Stephen and the British Colonial System 1813-1847*. Madison: University of Wisconsin Press, 1953.

KNUTSFORD, VISCOUNTESS [MARGARET JEAN TREVELYAN HOLLAND]. *Life and Letters of Zachary Macaulay*. London: Edward Arnold, 1900.

KRAUS, MICHAEL. *The Atlantic Civilization: Eighteenth-Century Origins*. New York: Russell & Russell, 1961.

KUCZYNSKI, R. R. *Demographic Survey of the British Colonial Empire*, Vol. 1, *West Africa*. London: Oxford University Press, 1948.

KUP, ALEXANDER PETER. "Freetown in 1794." *Sierra Leone Studies*, n.s., vol. 11 (1958), pp. 161-64.

———. "Freetown's Early Days: View of a Portuguese in 1820." *West African Review*, vol. 33 (1962), pp. 58-59.

———. "John Clarkson and the Sierra Leone Company." *International Journal of African Historical Studies*, vol. 2 (1972), pp. 203-20.

LAMB, R. *An Original and Authentic Journal of Occurrences During the Late American War from Its Commencement to the Year 1783*. Dublin: Wilkinson & Courtney, 1809.

LASCELLES, E. C. P. *Granville Sharp and the Freedom of Slaves in England*. London: Oxford University Press, 1928.

[LAURENS, HENRY]. "A Narrative of the Capture of Henry Laurens, of His Confinement in the Tower of London, &c 1780, 1781, 1782." *South Carolina Historical Society Collections*, vol. 1 (1857), pp. 18-83.

LEDER, LAWRENCE H., ed. *The Colonial Legacy*, Vol. 1, *Loyalist Historians,* and Vol. 2, *Some 18th Century Commentators*. New York: Harper Torchbooks, 1971.

LEE, HENRY. *The Campaign of 1781 in the Carolinas; with Remarks Historical and Critical on Johnson's Life of Greene*. Philadelphia: E. Littell, 1824.

———. *Memoirs of the War in the Southern Department of the United States*, ed., H. Lee. Washington: Peter Force, 1827.

"Letters and Documents Relating to Slavery in Massachusetts." *Massachusetts Historical Society Collections*, 5th series, vol. 3 (1877), pp. 373-437.

[LEYDEN, JOHN]. *A Historical & Philosophical Sketch of the Discoveries & Settle ments of the Europeans in Northern & Western Africa, at the Close of th Eighteenth Century.* Edinburgh: J. Moir, 1799.

LINDROTH, STEN. "Adam Afzelius: A Swedish Botonist in Sierra Leone, 1792-96," trans. Michael Banton. *Sierra Leone Studies*, n.s., vol. 4 (1955), pp. 194-207.

LINDSAY, ARNETT G. "Diplomatic Relations Between the United States and Grea Britain Bearing on the Return of Negro Slaves, 1788-1828." *Journal of Negr History*, vol. 5 (1920), pp. 391-419.

LITTLE, K. L. *Negroes in Britain, a Study of Racial Relations in English Society* London: Kegan Paul, 1948.

LIVERMORE, GEORGE. *An Historical Research Respecting the Opinions of th Founders of the Republic on Negroes as Slaves, as Citizens, and as Soldiers* Boston: John Wilson & Son, 1862.

LOCKE, MARY STOUGHTON. *Anti-Slavery in America from the Introduction c African Slaves to the Prohibition of the Slave Trade (1619-1808).* Boston: Gin & Co., 1901.

LOGAN, GWENDOLYN EVANS. "The Slave in Connecticut During the America Revolution." *Connecticut Historical Society Bulletin*, vol. 30 (1965), pp 73-80.

[LONG, EDWARD]. *Candid Reflections upon the Judgement Lately Awarded by th Court of King's Bench, in Westminster-Hall, on What Is Commonly Called th Negroe-Cause.* London: T. Lowndes, 1772.

LONGLEY, R. S. "The Coming of the New England Planters to the Annapoli Valley." *Nova Scotia Historical Society Collections*, vol. 33 (1961), pp 81-101.

LUBKA, NANCY. "Ferment in Nova Scotia." *Queen's Quarterly*, vol. 76 (1969), pp 213-28.

LUCAN, TALABI AISIE. *Our Sierra Leone, a History for Sierra Leone Primar Schools.* London: Longmans, 1965.

LYDEKKER, J. W. *The Life and Letters of Charles Inglis.* London: SPCK, 1936

LYND, STAUGHTON. *Class Conflict, Slavery, and the United States Constitution* Indianapolis: Bobbs-Merrill, 1967.

————. *Intellectual Origins of American Radicalism.* London: Faber & Faber 1969.

————. "Slavery and the Founding Fathers," in Melvin Drimmer, ed., *Blac History, a Reappraisal.* New York: Doubleday & Co., 1968.

MACDONALD, JAMES S. "Memoir of Governor John Parr." *Nova Scotia Historica Society Collections*, vol. 14 (1910), pp. 41-78.

MACDOWELL, DOROTHY K. "George Galphin: Nabob of the Backwoods." *Sout Carolina History Illustrated* (1970), pp. 51-56.

MACEACHEREN, ELAINE. "Emancipation of Slavery in Massachusetts: A Re

Examination 1770-1790.'' *Journal of Negro History*, vol. 55 (1970), pp. 289-306.

MACKINNON, IAN F. *Settlements and Churches in Nova Scotia 1749-1776*. Montreal: Walker Press, 1930.

MACLEAN, JOHN. *William Black, the Apostle of Methodism in the Maritime Provinces of Canada*. Halifax: Methodist Book Room, 1907.

MACNUTT, W. S. *The Atlantic Provinces: the Emergence of Colonial Society 1712-1857*. London: Oxford University Press, 1965.

———. *New Brunswick, a History 1784-1867*. Toronto: Macmillan of Canada, 1963.

MADISON, JAMES]. *The Papers of James Madison*, eds., William T. Hutchinson and William M. E. Rachal, vol. 7. Chicago: University of Chicago Press, 1962.

MAIN, JACKSON T. ''The One Hundred.'' *William and Mary Quarterly*, vol. 11 (1954), pp. 354-84.

Manual of the Corporation of the City of New York. ''Papers Relating to the Evacuation of New York, in the Year 1783,'' pp. 772-844. New York: Common Council, 1871.

MARKE, REV. CHARLES. *Origin of Wesleyan Methodism in Sierra Leone and History of Its Missions*. London: Kelly, 1913.

MARRANT, JOHN]. *A Narrative of the Lord's Wonderful Dealings with John Marrant, a Black (Now Going to Preach the Gospel in Nova-Scotia) Born in New-York, in North-America*, ed., Rev. [W.] Aldridge. 2d ed. London: Gilbert & Plummer, 1785.

MARSDEN, JOSHUA. *The Narrative of a Mission to Nova Scotia, New Brunswick, and the Somers Islands; with a Tour to Lake Ontario, to which Is Added The Mission, an Original Poem, with Copious Notes. Also, a Brief Account of Missionary Societies, and Much Interesting Information on Missions in General*. Plymouth-Dock: J. Johns, 1816.

MARTIN, E. C. *The British West African Settlements 1750-1821*. London: Longmans, 1927.

MARTIN, F. J., and H. C. DOYNE. *Soil Survey of Sierra Leone*. Freetown: Government Printer, 1932.

[MASON, GEORGE]. *The Papers of George Mason 1725-1792*, ed., Robert A. Rutland. Chapel Hill: University of North Carolina Press, 1970. 3 vols.

MATHEWS, HAZEL C. *The Mark of Honour*. Toronto: University of Toronto Press, 1965.

MATTHEWS, JOHN. *A Voyage to the River Sierra-Leone. Containing an Account of the Trade and Productions of the Country and of the Civil and Religious Customs and Manners of the People . . . with an Additional Letter on the African Slave Trade*. Facsimile of 1788 edition. London: Frank Cass & Co., 1966.

MAYS, BENJAMIN ELIJAH and JOSEPH WILLIAM NICHOLSON. *The Negro's Church.* Reprint of 1933 edition. New York: Arno Press, 1969.

MAZYCK, WALTER H. *George Washington and the Negro.* Washington: Associated Publishers, 1932.

McCOLLEY, ROBERT. *Slavery and Jeffersonian Virginia.* Urbana: University of Illinois Press, 1964.

McCRADY, EDWARD. *The History of South Carolina in the Revolution 1780-1783.* New York: Macmillan, 1902.

McGARVA, W. B. "Sierra Leone." *Chartered Surveyor,* vol. 93 (1961), pp. 535-38, 595-601.

McLEOD, R. R. "Historical Sketch of the Town of Shelburne, Nova Scotia." *Acadiensis,* vol. 8 (1908), pp. 35-52.

McMANUS, EDGAR J. *A History of Negro Slavery in New York.* Syracuse: Syracuse University Press, 1966.

MEACHAM, STANDISH. *Henry Thornton of Clapham 1760-1815.* Cambridge: Harvard University Press, 1964.

MEHLINGER, LOUIS R. "The Attitude of the Free Negro Toward African Colonization." *Journal of Negro History,* vol. 1 (1916), pp. 276-301.

MEIER, AUGUST, and ELLIOTT M. RUDWICK. *From Plantation to Ghetto, an Interpretive History of American Negroes.* New York: Hill & Wang, 1969.

MELLON, MATTHEW T. *Early American Views on Negro Slavery from the Letters and Papers of the Founders of the Republic.* Boston: Meador Publishing Co., 1934.

[MELVILLE, MRS.] *A Residence at Sierra Leona, Described from a Journal Kept on the Spot, and from Letters Written to Friends at Home,* ed., Mrs. C. E. S. Norton. London: John Murray, 1849.

Memoir of Captain Paul Cuffee, a Man of Colour: to Which is Subjoined The Epistle of the Society of Sierra Leone, in Africa, &c. York: C. Peacock, 1811.

MILLER, JOHN CHESTER. *Origins of the American Revolution.* Stanford: Stanford University Press, 1959.

MILLER, HUNTER, ed. *Treaties and Other International Acts of the United States of America,* Vol. 3, *1819-1835.* Washington: Government Printing Office, 1933.

Missionary Magazine, The, vol. 1 (1796); vol. 2 (1797).

MODE, PETER G. *The Frontier Spirit in American Christianity.* New York: Macmillan, 1923.

MOHL, RAYMOND A. *Poverty in New York 1783-1825.* New York: Oxford University Press, 1971.

MONTAGU, ALGERNON. *Ordinances of the Settlement of Sierra Leone, Passed in the Years 1868 and 1869; Royal Charters; Treaties with the Native Chiefs, Commissions &c.,* vol. 4. London: HMSO, 1870.

MONTEFIORE, J. *An Authentic Account of the Late Expedition to Bulam, on the*

Coast of Africa; with a Description of the Present Settlement of Sierra Leone, and the Adjacent Country. London: J. Johnson, 1794.

Monthly Review; or, Literary Journal, The, vol. 73 (1785).

MOORE, FRANK. *Diary of the American Revolution.* New York: Charles T. Evans, 1863. 2 vols.

———. *Songs and Ballads of the American Revolution.* New York: D. Appleton, 1856.

MOORE, GEORGE H. *Historical Notes on the Employment of Negroes in the American Army of the Revolution.* New York: Charles T. Evans, 1862.

———. *Notes on the History of Slavery in Massachusetts.* New York: D. Appleton, 1866.

MORGAN, EDMUND S. "Slavery and Freedom: The American Paradox," *The Journal of American History,* vol. 59 (1972), pp. 5-29.

MORRIS, RICHARD B. *The American Revolution Reconsidered.* New York: Harper Torchbooks, 1967.

———. *Government and Labor in Early America.* New York: Columbia University Press, 1946.

MORTON, LOUIS. *Robert Carter of Nomini Hall, a Virginia Tobacco Planter of the 18th Century.* Williamsburg: Colonial Williamsburg, Inc. 1941.

MOUSER, BRUCE L. "Trade, Coasters, and Conflict in the Rio Pongo From 1790 to 1808." *Journal of African History,* vol. 14 (1973), pp. 45-64.

MULLANE, GEORGE. "Old Inns and Coffee Houses of Halifax." *Nova Scotia Historical Society Collections,* vol. 22 (1933), pp. 1-23.

MULLIN, GERALD W. *Flight and Rebellion: Slave Resistance in Eighteenth-Century Virginia.* New York: Oxford University Press, 1972.

MURDOCH, BEAMISH. *A History of Nova-Scotia, or Acadie.* Halifax: James Barnes, 1865-1867. 3 vols.

NADELHAFT, JEROME. "The Somersett Case and Slavery: Myth, Reality, and Repercussions." *Journal of Negro History,* vol. 51 (1966), pp. 193-208.

NELL, WILLIAM C. *Services of Colored Americans, in the Wars of 1776 and 1812.* Boston: Prentiss & Sawyer, 1851.

NELSON, WILLIAM H. *The American Tory.* Oxford: Clarendon Press, 1961.

———. "Last Hopes of the American Loyalists." *Canadian Historical Review,* vol. 32 (1951), pp. 24-42.

NEWBURY, C. W., ed. *British Policy Towards West Africa: Select Documents 1786-1874.* Oxford: Clarendon Press, 1965.

New York City During the American Revolution, Being a Collection of Original Papers . . . from the Manuscripts in the Possession of the Mercantile Library Association of New York City. New York: Privately printed, 1861.

NORTON, MARY BETH. *The British-Americans: The Loyalist Exiles in England 1774-1789.* Boston: Little, Brown & Co., 1972.

————. "The Fate of Some Black Loyalists of the American Revolution." *Journal of Negro History*, vol. 58 (1973), pp. 402-26.

O'BRIEN, WILLIAM. "Did the Jennison Case Outlaw Slavery in Massachusetts?" *William and Mary Quarterly, or Repository of Ancient and Modern Fugitive Pieces, Prose and Poetical*, vol. 17 (1960), pp. 219-41.

"Old New York and Trinity Church." *New-York Historical Society Collections*, (1871), pp. 147-408 .

OTHELLO. "Essays on Negro Slavery." *The American Museum*, vol. 4 (1788), pp. 412-15, 509-12. Reprinted *Journal of Negro History* as "What the Negro Was Thinking During the Eighteenth Century," vol. 1 (1916), pp. 49-60.

OTTLEY, ROI. *Black Odyssey, The Story of the Negro in America*. London: John Murray, 1949.

[PAINE, THOMAS]. *The Writings of Thomas Paine*, ed., Moncure Daniel Conway, vol. 1. New York: AMS Press Inc., 1967.

PASCOE, CHARLES F. *Two Hundred Years of the S.P.G.: an Historical Account of the Society for the Propagation of the Gospel in Foreign Parts 1701-1900*. London: SPG, 1901. 2 vols.

PEASE, WILLIAM H., and JANE H. PEASE. *Black Utopia: Negro Communal Experiments in America*. Madison: State Historical Society of Wisconsin, 1964.

PENNINGTON, EDGAR LEGARE. *Thomas Bray's Associates and Their Work Among the Negroes*. Worcester: American Antiquarian Society, 1939.

PENSON, LILLIAN M. *The Colonial Agents of the British West Indies, a Study in Colonial Administration, Mainly in the Eighteenth Century*. London: University of London Press Ltd., 1924.

————. "The London West Indian Interest in the Eighteenth Century," in Rosalind Mitchison, ed., *Essays in 18th Century History from the English Historical Review*. London: Longmans, Green, 1966.

PERKINS, CHARLOTTE ISABELLA. *The Romance of Old Annapolis*. Annapolis: Privately printed, 1934.

[PERKINS, SIMEON]. *The Diary of Simeon Perkins*, ed. C. Bruce Fergusson, vols. 36 and 39. Toronto: The Chaplain Society, 1958.

PERSONS, STOW. *American Minds, a History of Ideas*. New York: Holt, Rinehart, 1958.

PETERSON, JOHN. *Province of Freedom: A History of Sierra Leone 1787-1870*. London: Faber & Faber, 1969.

PETTIGREW, THOMAS JOSEPH. *Memoirs of the Life and Writings of the Late John Coakley Lettsom with a Selection from His Correspondence*. London: Nichols, Son & Bentley for Longman, Hurst, 1817. 3 vols.

Philanthropist, The, vol. 3, 4, and 5, London: 1813, 1814, 1815. Especially, "History of the Colony of Sierra Leone," vol. 4 (1814), pp. 88-91, 97ff, 244-64; vol. 5 (1815), pp. 29-37. "Colony of Sierra Leone; with engraved

Plans of Freetown, and of the Allotments in that Colony,'' vol. 5 (1815), pp. 251-61.

PHILIP, ROBERT. *The Life, Times, and Missionary Enterprises of the Rev. John Campbell.* London: John Snow, 1841.

POOLE, THOMAS EYRE. *Life, Scenery and Customs in Sierra Leone and the Gambia.* London: Richard Bentley, 1850. 2 vols.

PORTER, ARTHUR T. *Creoledom, a Study of the Development of Freetown Society.* London: Oxford University Press, 1963.

PRICE, RICHARD. *Observations on the Nature of Civil Liberty, the Principles of Government, and the Justice and Policy of the War with America.* London: T. Cadell, 1776.

"Proceedings of a Board of General Officers of the British Army at New York, 1781." *New-York Historical Society Collections,* vol. 49 (1916), pp. 1-258.

PUGH, JOHN. *Remarkable Occurrences in the Life of Jonas Hanway, Esq. Comprehending . . . a Short History of the Rise and Progress of the Charitable and Political Institutions Founded or Supported by Him; Several Anecdotes, and an Attempt to Delineate His Character.* London: J. Davis, 1787.

QUARLES, BENJAMIN. "Lord Dunmore as Liberator." *William and Mary Quarterly,* vol. 15 (1958), pp. 494-507.
———. *The Negro in the American Revolution.* Chapel Hill: University of North Carolina Press, 1961.
———. *The Negro in the Making of America.* New York: Collier Books, Macmillan Co., 1964.
———. "The Negro Response: Evacuation with the British," in Melvin Drimmer, ed., *Black History, a Reappraisal.* New York: Doubleday & Co., 1968.

RADDALL, THOMAS H. *Halifax, Warden of the North.* Toronto: McClelland & Stewart, 1948.

RAMSAY, DAVID. *The History of the American Revolution.* Philadelphia: R. Aitken & Son, 1789. 2 vols.
———. *The History of the Revolution of South-Carolina, from a British Province to an Independent State.* Trenton: Isaac Collins, 1785. 2 vols.

RANKIN, F. HARRISON. *The White Man's Grave: a Visit to Sierra Leone in 1834.* London: Richard Bentley, 1836. 2 vols.

RANKIN, HUGH F., ed. *The American Revolution.* London: Secker & Warburg, 1964.

RAWLYK, G. A. "The Guysborough Negroes, a Study in Isolation." *Dalhousie Review,* vol. 48 (1968), pp. 24-36.

RAYMOND, W. O., ed. "Benjamin Marston of Marblehead, Loyalist, His Trials and Tribulations During the American Revolution." *New Brunswick Historical Society Collections,* vol. 3 (1907), pp. 79-112.
———. "The Founding of Shelburne: Benjamin Marston at Halifax, Shelburne and

Miramachi." *New Brunswick Historical Society Collections*, vol. 3 (1909), pp. 204-77.

———, ed. *Kingston and the Loyalists of the "Spring Fleet" of A.D. 1783, with Reminiscences of Early Days in Connecticut: A Narrative by Walter Bates, to Which Is Appended a Diary Written by Sarah Frost on the Voyage to St. John, N.B., with the Loyalists of 1783*. St. John: Barnes & Co., 1889.

———. "Loyalists in Arms 1775-1783." *New Brunswick Historical Society Collections*, vol. 2 (1904), pp. 189-223, 224-72.

———. "Loyalist Transport Ships, 1783." *New Brunswick Historical Society Collections*, vol. 2 (1904), pp. 273-79.

———. "The Negro in New Brunswick." *Neith*, vol. 1 (1903), pp. 27-34.

———, ed. "A Sketch of the Province of Nova Scotia and Chiefly of Such Parts as Are Settled 1783." *New Brunswick Historical Society Collections*, vol. 2 (1904), pp. 142-62.

———, ed. *The Winslow Papers*. St. John: New Brunswick Historical Society, 1901.

REDKEY, EDWIN S. *Black Exodus: Black Nationalist and Back-to-Africa Movements, 1890-1910*. New Haven: Yale University Press, 1969.

RICE, DAVID. *Slavery Inconsistent with Justice and Good Policy*. New York: Samuel Wood, Rebellion Record, 1812.

RIDDELL, W. R. "Slavery in the Maritime Provinces." *Journal of Negro History*, vol. 5 (1920), pp. 359-75.

RIFE, CLARENCE W. "Edward Winslow, Junior: Loyalist Pioneer in the Maritime Provinces." *Canadian Historical Association Report, 1928*, pp. 101-12.

ROBERTS, ARTHUR, ed. *Letters of Hannah More to Zachary Macaulay, Esq. Containing Notices of Lord Macaulay's Youth*. London: James Nisbet & Co., 1860.

ROBERTS, WILLIAM. *Memoirs of the Life and Correspondence of Mrs. Hannah More*, 2d ed. London: Thames Ditton, 1834.

ROSSITER, CLINTON. *Seedtime of the Republic: The Origin of the American Tradition of Political Liberty*. New York: Harcourt, Brace, 1953.

[RUSH, BENJAMIN]. *The Autobiography of Benjamin Rush: His "Travels Through Life" Together with His Commonplace Book for 1789-1813*, ed., George W. Corner. Princeton: Princeton University Press, 1948.

———. *Letters of Benjamin Rush*, ed., L. H. Butterfield. Princeton: Princeton University Press, 1951. 2 vols.

RUSSELL, PETER. "The Siege of Charleston; Journal of Captain Peter Russell, December 25, 1779 to May 2, 1780." *American Historical Review*, vol. 4 (1899), pp. 478-501.

SABINE, LORENZO. *The American Loyalists, or Biographical Sketches of Adherents to the British Crown in the War of the Revolution*. Boston: Charles C. Little & James Brown, 1847.

SANCHO, IGNATIUS. *Letters of the Late Ignatius Sancho, an African, to which are Prefixed Memoirs of His Life by Joseph Jekyll, Esq. M.P.* Reprint of 1803 edition. London: Dawsons of Pall Mall, 1968.

SCHAW, JANET. *Journal of a Lady of Quality; Being the Narrative of a Journey from Scotland to the West Indies, North Carolina, and Portugal, in the Years 1774 to 1776*, eds., Evangeline Walker Andrews and Charles McLean Andrews. New Haven: Yale University Press, 1921.

SCHLESINGER, ARTHUR M. *The Birth of the Nation, a Portrait of the American People on the Eve of Independence.* London: Hamish Hamilton, 1969.

SHARP, GRANVILLE. *A Declaration of the People's Natural Right to a Share in the Legislature; Which Is the Fundamental Principle of the British Constitution of State.* London: B. White, 1774.

[———]. *Free English Territory in Africa.* London: n.p., (1790).

———. *A Short Sketch of Temporary Regulations (Until Better Shall Be Proposed) for the Intended Settlement on the Grain Coast of Africa, Near Sierra Leona*, 2d ed. London: H. Baldwin, 1786.

SHEPPERSON, GEORGE. "Notes on Negro American Influences on the Emergence of African Nationalism." *Journal of African History*, vol. 1 (1960), pp. 299-312.

SHERWOOD, HENRY N. "Early Negro Deportation Projects." *Mississippi Valley Historical Review*, vol. 2 (1916), pp. 484-508.

———. "Paul Cuffe." *Journal of Negro History*, vol. 8 (1923), pp. 153-229.

SHYLLON, F. O. *Black Slaves in Britain.* London: Oxford University Press, 1974.

SIBTHORPE, A. B. C. *The History of Sierra Leone*, 4th ed. London: Frank Cass & Co., 1970; first published 1868.

SIEBERT, WILBUR H. "The Dispersion of the American Tories." *Mississippi Valley Historical Review*, vol. 1 (1914), pp. 185-97.

———. *The Flight of American Loyalists to the British Isles.* Columbus: F. J. Heer Printing Co., 1911.

———. "General Washington and the Loyalists." *American Antiquarian Society Proceedings*, n.s., vol. 43 (1933), pp. 34-48.

———. "The Legacy of the American Revolution to the British West Indies and Bahamas: A Chapter Out of the History of the American Loyalists." *Ohio State University Bulletin*, vol. 17 (1913), pp. 1-50.

———. *Loyalists in East Florida 1774-1785.* Deland: Florida State Historical Society, 1929. 2 vols.

Siege of Charleston by the British Fleet and Army Under the Command of Admiral Arbuthnot and Sir Henry Clinton, Which Terminated with the Surrender of That Place on the 12th of May, 1780, The, ed., Benjamin Franklin Hough. Albany: J. Munsell, 1867.

SIERRA LEONE COMPANY. *Substance of the Report of the Court of Directors Delivered to the General Court of Proprietors.* London: James Phillips or W. Phillips, 1791, 1794, 1795 (2), 1796, 1801, 1804, 1808. Philadelphia: Thos. Dobson, 1795. Titles vary slightly.

SMEATHMAN, HENRY. *Plan of a Settlement to be Made Near Sierra Leona, on the Grain Coast of Africa Intended More Particularly for the Service and Happy Establishment of Blacks and People of Colour, to Be Shipped as Freemen Under the Direction of the Committee for Relieving the Black Poor, and Under the Protection of the British Government.* London: T. Stockdale, 1786.

SMITH, PAUL H. "The American Loyalists: Notes on Their Organization and Numerical Strength." *William and Mary Quarterly*, vol. 27 (1970), pp. 259-77.

———. *Loyalists and Redcoats, a Study in British Revolutionary Policy.* Chapel Hill: University of North Carolina Press, 1964.

———. "Sir Guy Carleton, Peace Negotiations, and the Evacuation of New York." *Canadian Historical Review*, vol. 50 (1969), pp. 245-64.

SMITH, T. WATSON. "The Loyalists at Shelburne." *Nova Scotia Historical Society Collections*, vol. 6 (1888), pp. 53-89.

———. "The Slave in Canada." *Nova Scotia Historical Society Collections*, vol. 10 (1899), pp. 1-146.

[SMITH, WILLIAM]. *The Diary and Selected Papers of Chief Justice William Smith*, ed. L.F.S. Upton, Toronto: Champlain Society, 1963. 2 vols.

SPARKS, JARED. *The Diplomatic Correspondence of the American Revolution.* Boston: N. Hale & Gray & Bowen, 1829-1830. 12 vols.

SPILSBURY, F. B. *Account of a Voyage to the Western Coast of Africa; Performed by His Majesty's Sloop Favourite, in the Year 1805.* London: Richard Phillips, 1807.

SPRING, DAVID. "The Clapham Sect: Some Social and Political Aspects." *Victorian Studies*, vol. 5 (1961), pp. 35-48.

SPRAY, W. A. *The Blacks in New Brunswick.* Fredericton: Brunswick Press, 1972.

STEDMAN, CHARLES. *The History of the Origin, Progress, and Termination of the American War.* London: Privately printed, 1794. 2 vols.

STAUDENRAUS, PHILIP J. *The African Colonization Movement 1816-1865.* New York: Columbia University Press, 1961.

STEPHEN, SIR JAMES. *Essays in Ecclesiastical Biography.* London: Longman, Brown, Green & Longmans, 1849. 2 vols.

[STILES, EZRA]. *The Literary Diary of Ezra Stiles, D.D., LL.D., President of Yale College*, Vol. 1, *1769-1776*, ed., Franklin Bowditch Dexter. New York: Charles Scribner's Sons, 1901.

SWAN, JAMES. *A Dissuasion to Great-Britain and the Colonies from the Slave-Trade to Africa, Shewing the Injustice Thereof, &c.* Boston: J. Greenleaf, 1773.

SWANTON, JOHN R. *Social Organization and Social Usages of the Indians of the Creek Confederacy.* Bureau of American Ethnology Report 42, Washington: Government Printing Office, 1928.

SWEET, WILLIAM WARREN. *Revivalism in America, Its Origin, Growth and Decline.* New York: Scribner's, 1945.

——. *Religion on the American Frontier.* Chicago: H. Holt & Co., 1931-1946. 4 vols.

SYRETT, DAVID. *Shipping and the American War 1775-1783, a Study of British Transport Organization.* London: Athlone Press, University of London, 1970.

TAPPERT, THEODORE G., and JOHN W. DOBERSTEIN, eds. *The Notebook of a Colonial Clergyman.* Philadelphia: Muhlenberg Press, 1959.

TARLETON, LT. COL. [BANASTRE]. *A History of the Campaigns of 1780 and 1781, in the Southern Province of North America.* London: T. Cadell, 1787.

THOMAS, C. E. "The First Half-Century of the Work of the Society for the Propagation of the Gospel in Nova Scotia." *Nova Scotia Historical Society Collections,* vol. 34 (1963), pp. 1-31.

——. "St. Paul's Church, Halifax, Revisited." *Nova Scotia Historical Society Collections,* vol. 33 (1961), pp. 21-55.

THOMPSON, E. P., *The Making of the English Working Class.* London: Victor Gollancz Ltd., 1965.

THORNTON, HENRY. *An Enquiry Into the Nature and Effects of the Paper Credit of Great Britain (1802),* ed., F. A. v. Hayek. London: George Allen & Unwin, Ltd., 1939.

THORNTON, WILLIAM. *Political Economy: Founded in Justice and Humanity.* Washington: Samuel Harrison Smith, 1804.

TINKCOM, MARGARET BAILEY. "Caviar Along the Potomac. Sir Augustus John Foster's 'Notes on the United States,' 1804-1812." *William and Mary Quarterly,* vol. 8 (1951), pp. 68-107.

TOWNER, LAWRENCE W. " 'A Fondness for Freedom': Servant Protest in Puritan Society." *William and Mary Quarterly,* vol. 19 (1962), pp. 201-19.

——. "The Sewall-Saffin Dialogue on Slavery." *William and Mary Quarterly,* vol. 21 (1964), pp. 40-52.

TREVELYAN, GEORGE OTTO. *The Life and Letters of Lord Macaulay.* London: Longmans Green, 1889.

TUCKER, ST. GEORGE. *A Dissertation on Slavery: with a Proposal for the Gradual Abolition of It in the State of Virginia.* Philadelphia: [Mathew Carey], 1796.

[——, and DR. JEREMY BELKNAP]. "Queries Respecting the Slavery and Emancipation of Negroes in Massachusetts, Proposed by the Hon. Judge Tucker of Virginia, and Answered by the Rev. Dr. Belknap." *Massachusetts Historical Society Collections,* 1st series, vol. 4 (1795), pp. 191-211.

UHLENDORF, BERNARD A., ed. *Revolution in America: Confidential Letters and Journals 1776-1784 of Adjutant General Major Baurmeister of the Hessian Forces.* New Brunswick: Rutgers University Press, 1957.

——, ed. *The Siege of Charleston, with an Account of the Province of South Carolina: Diaries and Letters of Hessian Officers from the von Jungkenn*

Papers in the William L. Clements Library. Ann Arbor: University of Michigan Press, 1938.

VAN TYNE, CLAUDE HALSTEAD. *The Loyalists in the American Revolution*. New York: Macmillan, 1902.

[VON CLOSEN, BARON LUDWIG]. *The Revolutionary Journal of Baron Ludwig Von Closen, 1780-1783*, ed., Evelyn M. Acomb. Chapel Hill: University of North Carolina Press, 1958.

WADSTROM, C. B. *An Essay on Colonization, Particularly Applied to the Western Coast of Africa, with Some Free Thoughts on Cultivation and Commerce; Also Brief Descriptions of the Colonies Already Formed or Attempted, in Africa, Including Those of Sierra Leone and Bulama*. London: Privately printed, 1794.

———. *Observations on the Slave Trade, and a Description of Some Part of the Coast of Guinea During a Voyage, Made in 1787, and 1788, in Company with Doctor A. Sparrman and Captain Arrehenius*. London: James Phillips, 1789.

———, and others. *Plan for a Free Community Upon the Coast of Africa, Under the Protection of Great Britain; but Intirely Independent of All European Laws and Governments*. London: R. Hindmarsh, 1789.

WAINWRIGHT, REV. KENNEDY B. "A Comparative Study in Nova Scotian Rural Economy 1788-1872, Based on Recently Discovered Books of Account of Old Firms in Kings County, Nova Scotia." *Nova Scotia Historical Society Collections*, vol. 30 (1954), pp. 78-119.

WALLACE, DAVID DUNCAN. *The Life of Henry Laurens with a Sketch of the Life of Lieutenant Colonel John Laurens*. New York: Putnam's, 1915.

WALLS, A. F. "A Christian Experiment: the Early Sierra Leone Colony," in G. J. Cuming, ed. *The Mission of the Church and the Propagation of the Faith*. Cambridge: Cambridge University Press, 1970.

———. "The Nova Scotian Settlers and Their Religion." *Sierra Leone Bulletin of Religion*, vol. 1 (1959), pp. 19-31.

WALVIN, JAMES. *Black and White: the Negro and English Society 1555-1945*. London: Allen Lane, the Penguin Press, 1973.

———. *The Black Presence: A Documentary History of the Negro in England, 1555-1860*. London: Orbach & Chambers, 1971.

WARREN, MRS. MERCY OTIS. *History of the Rise, Progress and Termination of the American Revolution, Interspersed with Biographical, Political and Moral Observations*. Boston: Manning & Loring, 1805. 3 vols.

[WASHINGTON, GEORGE]. *The Diaries of George Washington 1748-1799*, ed., John C. Fitzpatrick. Boston: Houghton Mifflin, 1925. 4 vols.

———. *The Writings of George Washington from the Original Manuscript Sources. 1745-1799*, ed., John C. Fitzpatrick. Washington: Government Printing Office, 1931-1944. 39 vols.

WASHINGTON, JOSEPH R., JR. *Black Religion, the Negro and Christianity in the United States.* Boston: Beacon Press, 1966.

WATSON, JOHN F. *Annals of Philadelphia, Being a Collection of Memoirs, Anecdotes, & Incidents of the City and Its Inhabitants from the Days of the Pilgrim Founders.* Appendix: "Olden Time Researches and Reminiscences of New York City." Philadelphia: E. L. Carey and A. Hart, 1830.

WATSON, REV. JOHN L. "The Marston Family of Salem, Mass." *New England Historical and Genealogical Register and Antiquarian Journal,* vol. 27 (1873), pp. 390-403.

WATSON, ROBERT. *The Life of Lord George Gordon, with a Philosophical Review of His Political Conduct.* London: H. D. Symonds & D. I. Eaton, 1795.

[WEDGWOOD, JOSIAH]. *Correspondence of Josiah Wedgwood 1781-1794,* ed., Lady Katherine Eufemia Farrer. London: Privately printed, 1906.

[WESLEY, JOHN]. *The Letters of the Rev. John Wesley, A.M.,* ed., John Telford, vol. 7. London: Epworth Press, 1931.

WEST, RICHARD. *Back to Africa, a History of Sierra Leone and Liberia.* London: Jonathan Cape, 1970.

WHARTON, FRANCIS, ed. *The Revolutionary Diplomatic Correspondence of the United States,* vol. 5. Washington: Government Printing Office, 1889.

[WHITEFIELD, GEORGE]. *George Whitefield's Journals with His "Short Account" and "Further Account."* London: n.p., 1905.

WILBERFORCE, ROBERT ISAAC, and SAMUEL WILBERFORCE. *The Life of William Wilberforce,* 2d ed. London: John Murray, 1839. 5 vols.

[WILBERFORCE, WILLIAM]. *The Correspondence of William Wilberforce,* eds., Robert Isaac Wilberforce and Samuel Wilberforce. London: John Murray, 1840. 2 vols.

WILLCOX, WILLIAM B., ed. *The American Rebellion. Sir Henry Clinton's Narrative of His Campaigns, 1775-1782.* New Haven: Yale University Press, 1954.

WILLIAMS, ERIC. *Capitalism and Slavery.* Chapel Hill: University of North Carolina Press, 1944.

———. "The Golden Age of the Slave System in Britain." *Journal of Negro History,* vol. 25 (1940), pp. 60-106.

WILLIAMS, GEORGE W. *History of the Negro Race in America from 1619 to 1890. Negroes as Slaves, as Soldiers, and as Citizens.* New York: Putnam, 1883. 2 vols.

WILLIAMS, HELEN MARIA. "Memoirs of the Life of Charles Berns Wadstrom." *The Monthly Magazine,* vol. 7 (1799), pp. 462-65.

"Williamsburg—the Old Colonial Capital." *William and Mary Quarterly,* vol. 16 (1907), pp. 1-65.

WILMOT, JOHN EARDLEY. *Historical View of the Commission for Enquiring Into the Losses, Services, and Claims of the American Loyalists . . .* London: J. Nichols, 1815.

WILSON, JOSEPH T. *The Black Phalanx, a History of the Negro Soldiers of the United States in the Wars of 1775-1812, 1861-'65*. Hartford: American Publishing Co., 1888.

WINKS, ROBIN W. *The Blacks in Canada, a History*. New Haven: Yale University Press, 1971.

WINTERBOTTOM, THOMAS. *An Account of the Native Africans in the Neighbourhood of Sierra Leone to which is Added an Account of the Present State of Medicine Among Them*, 2d ed. London: Frank Cass & Co. Ltd., 1969; first published 1803.

WOOD, A. SKEVINGTON. "Sierra Leone and Bulama: A Fragment of Missionary History." *Sierra Leone Bulletin of Religion*, vol. 3 (1961), pp. 16-22.

———. *Thomas Haweis 1734-1820*. London: SPCK, 1957.

WOODSON, CARTER G. *The History of the Negro Church*. Washington: Associated Publishers, 1921.

WRIGHT, E. J. "Granville Town," *Sierra Leone Studies*, n.s., vol. 12 (1959), pp. 188-95.

———. "Remarks on the Early Monetary Position in Sierra Leone with a Description of the Coinage Adopted." *Sierra Leone Studies*, n.s., vol. 3 (1954), pp. 136-46.

WRIGHT, ESTHER C. *The Loyalists of New Brunswick*. Fredericton: Privately printed, 1955.

WRONG, GEORGE M. *Canada and the American Revolution: The Disruption of the First British Empire*. New York: Macmillan, 1935.

YOSHPE, HARRY BELLER. *The Disposition of the Loyalist Estates in the Southern District of the State of New York*. New York: Columbia University Press, 1939.

YOUNG, A. H. "Dr. Charles Inglis in New York, 1766-1783." *Canadian Historical Association Report, 1932*, pp. 87-96.

ZILVERSMIT, ARTHUR. "Quok Walker, Mumbet, and the Abolition of Slavery in Massachusetts." *William and Mary Quarterly*, vol. 25 (1968), pp. 614-24.

Index